OYSTER SHORE

E 11 KPB

RUTH SABERTON

To all the key workers across the globe who kept us going. To the doctors, nurses, teachers, healthcare workers, scientists, virologists. To everyone who worked so tirelessly to keep the wheels on the wagon. Thank you.

This book is for you.

NOTE FROM THE AUTHOR

Dear Reader,

A series of lockdowns in the United Kingdom from 2020-21 meant I rarely travelled beyond the corner of Cornwall I'm lucky enough to call home. During this time, like so many of us, I was apart from friends and family and people I loved were lost and unwell. This was unsettling and also frightening at times. Seeking solace I spent a lot of time walking along the banks of the Fowey, watching the river flow and the reflections of trees and clouds trembling in the water. There's something timeless about a riverbank and I found comfort in this. How many other people had wandered these footpaths? Rested in the shade of the trees? Glimpsed the sapphire dart of a kingfisher? Who else had written about these places? And what stories were waiting to be told?

On my walks I explored the world of the river. When the tide turned and the sand was exposed I would tug on my wellies and walk along the shore. Further along the riverbank, tucked inside a wooded meander, I came across an abandoned house. Totally concealed from the lane and invisible from the small town across the river, it was a secret and magical place shielded by tangles of brambles and specimen plants gone rogue. The winding drive was cracked, the house wore an ivy shawl and the small boathouse slipped further into the river with each turning tide. When the water peeled away the ribs of old boats rose from the sand and the shore was covered in oyster shells. It felt as though I had stepped into another world and a story whispered to me in the magical way stories do.

For the next ten months *Oyster Shore* became my escape (and my obsession!) as the story and characters took shape. I lost myself in writing and when I walked along the riverbank I was always surprised not to see the places and people I was spending so much time with. The book evolved and grew and my patient editor and readers waited for it far longer than I ever anticipated – but these have been extraordinary times and this is a novel which helped me through them.

I really hope you enjoy the world of *Oyster Shore.*

x Ruth x

GLOSSARY

A note on names

Fowey = Foy
Lo-**wenn**a
Pendennys = Pen-**denn**is
Pen**drag**on
Tre-**bil**cock
Tre-**hunn**ist
Trelyon = Tre-**li**on
Tre-**vell**an
Tre-**wen**
Vyvyan = **Viv**ian

PROLOGUE

1963

London

Gerald

Each night, during the dreadful hours before daylight came, Gerald returned to Oyster Shore. Transported to the no man's land between waking and sleeping, he wandered the familiar tideline where dreams were dashed on the shore and hearts picked over by cruel-beaked seabirds. There he saw Madalyn again, a slender figure in white, following the ragged shell line with a pail swinging from one hand as she stooped to pick up precious pieces of flotsam. Although her face was turned from him, Gerald knew her green eyes were bright with excitement and her cheeks dusted with sand as she pushed away the unruly curls which refused to be bullied into place by pins.

How he longed to beg her forgiveness! In his dream Gerald stretched out his hand – but his grasp always fell short, the air slipped through his fingers, and Madalyn remained out of reach, pail swinging and skirts trailing in the sand. Engrossed in picking up bright nuggets of sea glass and holding them to the light, she gazed right through him. Then the tide turned and she was gone, lost to him once more.

His face wet with tears, Gerald would turn for the boathouse and spot Ned sitting on the riverbank with a pen held loosely in his hand and a notebook splayed on his knees. He longed to tell Ned he was sorry, that since then not a day had passed when he hadn't wished he could turn back time to undo the mistakes he'd made and be a better friend. He knew his eternal soul was stained with guilt; a drunken decision born of jealousy had been the defining moment of his life and the fork in the road that led to his own hell.

"For what shall it profit a man if he shall gain the whole world but lose his soul?" he muttered, his hands clawing the blanket and his eyes wide open. "I have lost my soul! My soul!"

The nurse who sat with him each night had become used to such laments and these incoherent monologues. Brother Snowe always cried out in his sleep and sobbed. At first she had pitied him for he was so frail and shrunken-looking, often weeping in that raking and despairing manner old folk did, but once she'd gleaned a little sense from his ramblings her pity trickled away. If she hadn't needed the pay so badly, she thought, she might have handed in her notice altogether. She tried to ignore her patient's ramblings now, but some things could not be unheard.

When she had been interviewed for the position the Abbot had told her that Brother Snowe was quite mad, and had been for many years. He was dying, and the morphine affected his mind. He didn't always know what he was saying or even where he was. He wandered the land of his childhood and she might hear words only intended for a confessor – so, like a priest, she must carry this man's secrets to her grave. Brother Snowe was the seminary's greatest benefactor, and her discretion was paramount. Was she prepared to carry such a burden? Was she willing to sign legal documents which bound her to silence?

She had said she was. She would have said anything to secure the position, for her husband was sick and she needed the money. Besides, she couldn't imagine what this poor old boy might have to say that could be so bad. A few screams wouldn't frighten her, she'd insisted, for she'd worked in asylums. She was made of sterner stuff.

But once hired, the nurse soon discovered that her new patient was very different to the troubled souls she'd tended in the past. They had certainly been muddled and pitiful, and some even dangerous, but when Mr Snowe cried out into the blackness and pleaded with people she couldn't see but who were as real to him as though they were perching on the edge of his bed, she was chilled to the marrow. The fervour in his eyes was religious in its zeal, and his conviction was absolute. The more her patient's mind unravelled, the more the nurse suspected the reason for his religious vigour was very dark indeed. Sometimes she even crossed herself. She didn't wish ill on him, but surely the old boy couldn't last much longer?

The sands of Gerald Snowe's life were running out. He was growing weaker by the day, the nurse reminded herself, but his words would stay with her just as whatever crimes he had committed would always remain with him. She straightened his counterpane and returned to her knitting, longing for dawn to chase away the darkness and herald the end of her shift.

As his nurse knitted the old man wandered through the past. He saw a book, pages blank with promise, and knew that time had rewound itself in this liminal place between life and death. Here a man was offered all the richness of his life's choices for a second time, and he could make amends if he could only be heard! Surely *somebody* would listen?

"Madalyn!" he cried. "Come back! I didn't mean it!"

Abruptly, he was on the riverbank once again, but the girl he sought was not to be found. Above his dark head patches of sky shone through dense leaves, and the glimpses of light were so bright that patterns danced across his vision and haunted him even when he closed his eyes. The brackish water had retreated, to reveal a muted treasure-chest of pink rocks, emerald weed and gleaming channels of mud. The young man on the pontoon began to write, his pen capturing the submerged relics of a lost maritime world. Gulls and egrets strutted over his page just as they worked the tideline with timeless intensity, plucking out stranded sea creatures from secret hiding places as their webbed feet followed tracks known only to seabirds. They picked their way through the ribbons of dark weed hurled higher upriver by summer storms, balanced *en pointe* like ballerinas atop green tressed boulders as graceful foils to the orange-footed gulls; and Ned scribbled it all down in his notebook.

The scene was captured for ever, just as Gerald knew that his fate – indeed the fate of all three of them – was sealed yet again. Why could he never change this dream when it seemed to offer him a new path? Why must it always be the same no matter what he did? Hadn't he tried hard enough? Hadn't he given Bess everything? Why hadn't she allowed him to atone? Why wasn't he granted peace?

"Holy Mary, mother of God, pray for us sinners," he cried out. "Now and at the hour of our death!"

Somebody was beside him, a woman with frosted hair and a starched cap. Matron? Nanny? Mama? But not Madalyn.

"You're not Madalyn!" he cried, lashing out with his clawed hand. Despairing tears slid down his sunken cheeks, wetting his thin hair and trickling into the pillow. "Where is she? Is she in the river? What have you done with her?"

"Shh, Brother Snowe. It's just a dream," the woman said. But Gerald no longer saw her, for the focus had shifted and he was in the boathouse once more, hidden amongst the shadows and watching two little boys hide their secret treasures. The scene was set, the players were in place, and the curtain was poised to rise. All was still to unfold, and he wept to know he couldn't change events no matter how hard he tried. Only those who came after could do that, if only he could make them understand.

"Help me!" he begged. "Please, help me. I must go back and tell them! I must stop Madalyn."

But Gerald couldn't return to his past self; the people we used to be are marooned in time and cast away on the shores of memory. Their course cannot be changed any more than the tide can be ordered not to rise with the silvered moon. As the rocks are covered and the water soothes the ribs of rotting hulls and nibbles the riverbanks, so time feasts on what used to be, altering it indelibly until all we once knew becomes both familiar and foreign, like a once-loved tune played in a minor key.

Yet in the place between life and death there is redemption, and when Gerald saw three children playing on the riverbank he knew that if he could make amends all might yet be well. As he straddled life and death he understood that the past and the present and the future run side by side, and sometimes the veil is thin. Somebody might glimpse through it. Perhaps it would be the girl with violet eyes and the spaniel that he saw in his dreams? Or the man with pale curls, whose face was so familiar and yet unknown? In the hinterland of death Gerald could cross time, and now he saw them both, these people of the future, as clearly as he saw those from his past. Did they see him? Would they be his salvation?

There was an older woman, too, whose memory swam like his, and she sometimes visited him with a young woman. They both promised they were sending someone to him, but Gerald could never catch who this might be or when they might arrive. Maybe the women had never said it at all and this was no more than another false hope. Then he would never be able to make amends and he would die unforgiven.

"Madalyn," he wailed. "Oh Madalyn!"

The nurse leaned forward. "Who's Madeline, my love? Was she your wife?"

He swatted her away angrily. Was this harpy hiding Madalyn from him? "Where's Madalyn? What have you done with her? Is she still in the river?" he demanded.

Why could he never change this dream? Why was it always the same no matter what he did? Hadn't he given Bess everything, the key to it all? Why hadn't she allowed him to atone? He'd been but a boy, a stupid, selfish boy. He hadn't understood what he had set in motion. He'd been a different person then. A stranger to the self he had become.

"It all ended as it began," he whispered, struggling to sit up, his voice as thin as the cord which tethered him to life. "On Oyster Shore. That's where all this began and where it will end. On Oyster Shore."

"Oyster Shore?" The nurse had no idea what he was talking about. "Where's that, my love? Is it a holiday resort?"

But her patient did not reply. His head fell forward to slump onto his bony chest, and when she touched his throat the nurse knew he'd taken the answer with him. She crossed herself and closed his eyes, feeling no sadness, only relief that she would no longer have to hear the confessions of his tortured soul. Wherever he had gone, wherever this Oyster Shore might be, her patient wouldn't be returning to speak of his past crimes or plead with invisible onlookers for forgiveness. He would never call out again, because the sands in his hourglass had run out.

Gerald Snowe, once one of the wealthiest men in England, was gone – and with him his tangled web of guilt, regret and long-kept secrets.

1

THE PRESENT

Cornwall

Lowenna

The sign hanging from the gate hides behind tangles of ivy, a lichened whisper of a half-forgotten name.

Oyster Shore.

I glimpse a listing gate slumping behind waist-high grasses, and cow parsley foaming into the lane like breaking surf. The letting agent was right: you'd never know there was a house here. It's perfect for me, because a place to be forgotten and a place to forget is exactly what I need. I've already driven past this overgrown entrance twice, and if my attention hadn't been snatched this time by the promise of water through the leaves I would be sailing by it on my third pass. Finding this place has been through luck rather than map-reading.

"You have reached your destination!" bellows the satnav, jolting me from these thoughts. "Re-routeing!"

Ordered to attention, I stand on my brakes while clinging to the wheel – I haven't made it this far to veer into a hedge at the eleventh hour – and send a bottle of Evian tumbling into the footwell. Breakspear, dozing on the back seat, barks reproachfully.

"Sorry, Breaky!" I say, delving for the bottle. I've gone too far past the gate to reverse, which I find impossible in these unforgiving narrow lanes, so I decide I'll carry on to look for a turning space. "Not much longer now. We'll soon be having a lovely walk."

If cocker spaniels could speak I suspect Breakspear would say, "Yeah, right," in the same weary tone my niece Ellie adopts when adults say something she considers lame. If dogs had iPhones Breaky would probably be messaging his friends to moan about his mad human dragging him away from pavements and his beloved patch of garden with all his carefully buried bones. Seven hours in a car, even with several lengthy stops for exercise along the way, is practically a case for the RSPCA, he'd complain, and in the exact tone of voice Ellie used when her parents had booked a family holiday in Cornwall.

"No mobile signal. Crap wifi," she'd wailed. "Have you any idea what that's going to be *like*?"

"Heaven. Maybe we should take things a step further and leave all our devices at home? Have a digital detox as well as a holiday?" her mother, my big sister Marina, had threatened.

Ellie had paled. Glued to her phone, she needed social media like the rest of us need oxygen.

As a lead resus officer in a busy London hospital, Marina has bigger problems to contend with than teenagers moaning because they can't access TikTok from their holiday cottage. Ellie, who knew better than to push her luck, shut up like a clam. Besides, she secretly loved every salt-soaked minute of their Cornish holidays, just as Marina and I once had. Growing up in London, we lived for our summers at our grandparents' cottage just a pebble's toss from Readymoney Cove. The wooden floors were strewn with sand as we'd wandered back and forth to the beach, our hair bleached by salt and sunshine and our faces as freckled as the eggs we'd collected from Granny May's chickens.

As I drove westwards this morning I felt my heart grow lighter with every mile that slipped beneath the bonnet. When I crossed the Tamar Bridge a huge weight lifted off me, plummeting into the depths, sinking to the muddied riverbed, and leaving me lighter than I had felt for a long time. The life I'd sleepwalked into was behind me, and I was back in Cornwall. I was free to be Lowenna Scott once more, because my Cornish name and my Cornish roots anchored me to this magical county. I was home.

As a young child, going down to Cornwall to visit Granny May and hearing her tales of her Cornish childhood, I'd fallen in love with the idea of living in a place where your family was as much a part of landscape as the crying gulls and crash of breaking waves. In London, though, nobody knew the Scott family. We were anonymous in our Harrow semi in an unremarkable street lined with cars and dusty plane trees, and if we'd vanished overnight I doubt our neighbours would have noticed. My mother liked this; she said there was nothing worse than everyone knowing your business, but Granny May always disagreed. She was proud that there had been Penwurthies living in Trevellan since God was a boy. Their blood ran in my veins, she told me, and their names were carved on the harbourside war memorial. Why, it was a sign of just how much she'd loved Grandpa Bill that she'd allowed herself to be uprooted the whole twenty miles to Fowey!

"Didn't you go back and visit?" Marina had once asked.

"Bless you, love, of course I did, but it wasn't my home any more, was it? My home was here with Grandad, and I had your mum to keep me busy."

"You could go back and live in Trevellan now Mum's grown up. She won't mind as long as she can stay at home," I'd pointed out. My mum was really old, at least thirty, and she didn't need Granny May to look after her any more. In fact, the more I'd thought about it the more I realised our mother didn't need Granny at all. Mummy rarely stayed more than a couple of days when she dropped us off with our grandparents, and it was always Daddy who picked us up because he liked digging on the beach, staying in the dolls' house cottage and eating the delicious pasties Mummy said were fattening.

My grandmother had laughed a lot at my suggestion. It was as though I'd made a joke, even though I didn't think I'd said anything funny at all.

"You're right there, Lowenna my bird! I often think the stork dropped the wrong one off with us. She's a townie through and through, your mum."

Marina and I nodded (although we suspected the stork wasn't real). Mummy liked shops and busy streets and restaurants. Daddy liked the countryside, but as he always did what Mummy wanted we lived in the town. I'd supposed that doing what someone else wanted rather than what made you happy was how you showed you loved them: Granny May had left the place she loved for Grandad, and Daddy had stayed in London for Mum. I'd internalised this lesson which, as it turned out, was not a good thing.

"Would you like to go back to Trevellan one day?" Marina asked.

There was always a wistful look on Granny May's face when she recalled her childhood home. She wove tales of haunted moors, and recalled legends of smugglers stealing through the narrow streets. My favourite tale was the haunting story of a local girl who'd drowned a long, long time ago and whose loss Granny May said was still felt when the sea mists rolled in. We'd clamour to know who she was and where she had drowned, but Granny May didn't know any more of the story. Maybe she hadn't drowned at all and the piskies had stolen her? Or perhaps she walked through a tear in time's fabric and couldn't return? Cornwall was full of such places, Granny warned: standing stones, old crosses and shifting tides – all these could whisk the unwary somewhere far, far away. Was this true or was it just another of her tales? It was hard to tell when you slept beneath beams made from the timbers of wrecked ships and the sea whispered below your bedroom window. True or not, these tales made Marina and me shiver, and we'd loved Granny's stories.

"Maybe I'll retire to Trevellan when I'm very old? Older than I am *now*, that is, before you say a word!" Granny May would say. "But Fowey's my home now and Grandad wouldn't want to leave here for all the tea in China. Besides, there aren't any of my family left in Trevellan nowadays. I'm the last of the Penwurthies. The family box and your old granny are all that's left of them."

As well as being the keeper of stories, Granny May possessed a collection of family belongings which she kept safe inside a wooden box. On wet days when the whole world dripped she would let us look inside at her treasures and we would make up her own games and stories about the contents.

"Mind how you go with it," she'd warn each time. "My mother kept this box safe all her life, and before she died she made me promise I'd look after it."

"Why?" we'd ask and Granny would shrug.

"Blowed if I know. It was hidden under the stairs, but she'd go spare if anyone moved it or dared try to look inside. Ma could give a sharp slap when she needed to!"

"Is it worth a lot of money?" Marina asked, hoping for treasure.

"Aren't you your mother's daughter! Sorry, bird, but it's only of sentimental value," Granny said. "All I can really remember about it is that a man delivered it to our cottage when I was very small. I answered the door because Ma was feeding the baby —"

"Was that baby your brother who died in the war?" I asked.

We knew the story of the brave uncle who'd died flying a Spitfire. Great-uncle Eddie was a hero, and if he had lived there would have been more Penwurthies; and Granny always said, too, that if Eddie had lived her father might have not been quite as unhappy; Marrick Penwurthy's black moods had been famous in the village and everyone had been afraid of him.

"That's right, Wenna, God rest him. Anyway, our caller was a smartly dressed man, a gentleman as we'd have said back then, and I'd never seen one of *those* on our doorstep before. He had an ebony cane with a silver top, which he leaned on heavily, and his dark hair was slashed with grey, but he wasn't old. No older than my Pa, probably. It was his eyes I noticed, because they were so very sad. I was only a dot of a thing, but I thought he must be the saddest man in the whole world."

"What did he want?" Keen on the Famous Five and Secret Seven, I'd loved the mystery element of the tale. If only I could solve it!

"He said he was looking for my father and called Pa by his name as though he knew him well. I was surprised at that because Pa was just a fisherman. How would he know a gentleman? Of course, I shouldn't have opened the door to a stranger," she added swiftly, "but it was different back then. We all knew everyone, and the village had a bobby at the police house."

"Who was he?" Marina asked.

"Lord only knows," shrugged Granny May. "Nobody ever told me, and in those days children were seen and not heard."

Marina and I took the hint and stopped asking questions. Granny May continued with the story. Her gaze was distant as though she was seven again and back in her childhood home.

"My pa was at sea and Ma tried to slam the door when she saw the visitor. She was furious, but he pleaded with her to take in a box he'd brought, and said something about it making our fortune. Ma was hissing like a cat and wouldn't give him house room. She had a fierce temper on her, my mum. Nobody ever crossed Elizabeth Penwurthy!"

"She sounds just like me," Marina remarked, tossing her curly dark hair. "Mum says I have a temper!"

"A bad temper is *not* something to be proud of," Granny scolded, but my sister didn't believe her and neither did I. I was in awe of Marina's temper and would have liked a fraction of it for myself. Even as a child I was always too quick to placate others and too swift to put aside what I wanted in order to keep the peace.

"Anyway, Ma sent the man packing and I never saw him again," Granny concluded. "She shoved the box under the stairs and that's where it stayed. Eddie and I peeked in sometimes, and when Ma caught us nosing we felt the back of her hand."

"What did your dad say? Was he angry too?" I wondered. Great-grandfather Marrick was a shadowy figure, part war hero and part bogeyman.

"I don't think she dared tell my father about the visitor. Pa hated talking about the past, and Ma must have learned how to avoid setting him off on the rampage. His moods were dreadful. We all tiptoed around him," said Granny May. "He was a very angry man."

Marina frowned. "Why was he so angry?"

"Oh, love, that's a hard question to answer. It was the war that changed him, or so I was told. He saw some dreadful things and he never got over them. Mum lost her brother in the trenches and she said my poor dad saw him killed. They'd been best friends since school. Can you imagine what that was like for him? The First World War was awful."

We couldn't. Although we knew about poppies, sold in school with sharp pins to poke through your jumper, the First World War was so long ago. It was strange to think Granny May's father had fought in it. To my sister and me it was a storybook event rather than something real.

"After the war ended lots of the men who went back home were in a dreadful way. Some had lost arms or legs. Others were badly injured or burnt. That was almost better because at least everyone could see what was wrong – but others, like my father, were hurt in their minds. Shellshock they called it back then, and my poor old dad had it pretty bad. When he had a funny turn we all hid. I expect Mum was scared that mentioning the visitor, or passing on the box, would set him off."

"But you told us it was meant to make your fortune!" I said.

"I probably dreamed that bit, Lowenna," Granny smiled. "Children have vivid imaginations – as you know!"

I loved writing stories and spent hours scribbling in exercise books but nothing I'd ever invented was as exciting as Granny's stories. She was imaginative and could hold us for hours. Looking back I often think she should have been an author.

"Maybe's a treasure map hidden in there?" Marina had been hopeful, but Granny rolled her eyes.

"Nothing so useful. Just some drawings and old photos. Mum put some of her own bits and bobs in there too over the years, photographs and buttons and the like, just like you two will, I expect. Although it's our family box now, it won't mean much at all one day. I expect when I'm gone your mum will chuck it out."

"We won't let her," promised Marina.

"Well, good luck with that," said Granny May.

"Who *was* the man?" I asked.

Granny May ruffled my hair. "No idea, my love. I only saw him that once, and for a few minutes. I think he must have been an officer who'd been in France with Pa because, as I said, he was what we called a toff. That's an old-fashioned word for a posh person. As for making our fortune, there was definitely no treasure map. Heaven knows we could have done with a few bob. We had hardly any money once Pa stopped fishing."

This was always the part in the story where Granny would tell us moralistic tales of shoes with holes, darned clothes and no television. These tales were designed to make Marina and me grateful for Clarks shoes and British Home Stores, but invariably caused us to tune out since her stories bore absolutely no relation to our world of *Neighbours* and *Tammy Girl*. We preferred the fortune story by far, and the box had become our treasure-chest. Marina and I would empty the contents onto the hearthrug and pore over our booty. We especially loved the collection of washed sea glass kept in a small black velvet bag and squabbled over the blue and green wave-smoothed nuggets. To us these were precious stones, and we would hold them up to the light and arrange them in order of size on the rug.

There was one special item which truly seemed treasure to us, and this was an enamelled ornamental hair comb in the shape of a blue bird with a glowing red eye, bright sapphire plumage and cruel golden claws. Even in its chipped state, and missing several teeth, whichever of us managed to pin her hair up with it felt like a princess and oversaw that day's games. Often this role fell to Marina, with me as her willing handmaiden.

Other favourite treasures were postcards and pictures. One was of a mansion which we thought looked like a castle, and another of an elegant white house with two little boys and a girl posed stiffly on the terrace. One of the boys wore a sailor suit and a scowl, and the other looked like a ragamuffin, at least according to Granny, who tutted at his bare feet. The little girl was beautifully turned out in a white dress and white hat, which I imagined she longed to rip off and stamp on. I liked to picture the trio running away shrieking and laughing once the shutter had clicked and they were free to play. Marina and I made up names for them and played detailed games, taking it in turns to pretend to be the little girl, who we called Princess Clementine, for no better reason than because Grandad Bill liked clementine marmalade. We christened the two boys Henry and Joe; these lads got into all kinds of trouble and were always rescued by Clementine, the brains of the operation.

"Who are they?" we always asked, but Granny May said she had no idea. Friends of her mother's perhaps? Elizabeth Penwurthy would have been a little girl at the turn of the century, the period which seemed to fit their clothes, but there were no names written on the back of the picture, only faint pencil scribbles that looked like lines of verse. There was no record of who might have taken the photo, and Granny May didn't recognise the house.

"It might be the St Wyllow River near Trevellan," she suggested. "I know, though, the stately home in the postcard is Vyvyan Court. Lots of us Penwurthies were in service there, including my mother at one point. It's been empty for years; the family who owned it died out, and when the American soldiers went home after the war it was left empty."

When my sister and I tired of Princess Clementine and her minions we played with a set of marbles from the box or invented stories about the handsome man in uniform who Granny said was her scary father when he was still young and smiley.

"Pa was one of the lucky ones, because he came back," she explained. "But so many of his friends didn't. They were only boys when they enlisted, and they wouldn't have had a clue what they were in for. None of Pa's brothers came home, and that broke my grandmother's heart. They said she died of grief."

This was a sad story, but it belonged to the history books and didn't hold our attention any more than the dog-eared paperback book covered in scrawled numbers and smelling of damp. We much preferred the old sketch book with its yellowed pages, each filled with drawings of a handsome young man, and endless sketches of a wooded riverbank. The young man had thick pale hair and often had his shirt sleeves rolled up as he bent over a book or gazed into the distance. One sketch showed him sitting on a pontoon with a pen held loosely in his hand and a notebook balanced on his knees. Another depicted him bare-chested and sprawled across a bed. Looping handwriting at the bottom of this drawing declared *N. OS. 1914.*

Was this his name, N? Or was it the artist's signature? We'd asked Granny May, but she hadn't known this either, nor could she tell us who the artist was, although she did frown and tut at the bed sketch.

"Some things are lost in time, which may be just as well!" she said firmly, shutting the sketch book and placing it back in the box. "These must have meant something once, but I can't imagine what, and I have no idea who that bold young man was! I think the river in the drawings could be a higher stretch of the Penhayes Estuary. Remember when we went to Trevellan, girls? We crossed the river by car ferry and had a pub lunch."

That day is still a happy memory of sunshine, crab sandwiches and hot plastic seats sticking to bare legs. We only visited Trevellan once, though, because Granny May died when I was ten and Grandpa Bill, who'd doted on her, hadn't lived much longer. Their cottage was sold, and our sunny Cornish summers were consigned to the land of childhood past.

The years rolled by, but Cornwall remained a magical place in my imagination and one which held my heart as I devoured every Poldark and du Maurier novel I could get my hands on. Whenever possible I would snatch a weekend in Fowey to revisit childhood haunts, but London is a long drive from Cornwall and if I yearned for salted air, torn sky and sweeping beaches, I did my best to ignore these longings and told myself it was time to focus on my relationship and my career. Asserting my desires had become alien to my nature.

Today, though, as I crawl along the high-banked lane in search of a turning place, I believe with all my heart that my Cornish roots have drawn me here. Trevellan, the village where my forebears lived for generations, is only three miles from Oyster Shore, and the landscape of my grandmother's stories is all around me. Although uprooting my entire life to live in a place I haven't seen makes no sense on paper it makes perfect sense to my heart. It is quiet and healing here. It is safe. I can rest, and I can write again. Coming to Cornwall is the right thing to do. I feel certain of this.

"Beep! Beep!"

A sturdy Landrover Defender is coming head-on towards me. As it's built like a tank, and with enough dents to suggest it's had more than a few close encounters with drystone walls and gates, I don't fancy my chances if I don't get out the way quickly.

"At the first available opportunity perform a U-turn," repeats the satnav as I frantically attempt to steer my car and dive for the Evian, which is still rolling about, in danger of bursting. This is as hard as it sounds, and my car slaloms until I'm able to grab the runaway bottle. Heart racing, I return my full attention to driving and not a moment too soon since the Defender shows no signs of slowing. The driver, hidden behind a pair of wrap-around mirrored shades, appears intent on driving straight at me. I'll be squashed flat before I've even arrived. Not quite the new start I'm hoping for.

"At the first available opportunity perform a U-turn!"

"Yes! Yes! I know!" I say, grinding gears. "I need a turning place! Any thoughts?"

Sunken lanes are pretty but very steep, and there isn't anywhere I can turn or even pull in since there's a ditch on one side and a stone wall on the other. I've already gone along this road twice so I know it opens up in about half a mile and there's a clearing where I can swing around, and although there's a caravan parked there, surrounded by beautiful wooden sculptures, nobody has comes out to tell me off for turning there, which is a relief.

The Defender's headlights flash. Is this a friendly signal, signifying he's going to pull into the edge so I can creep by? Or is it an aggressive local code for *out of my way you stupid emmet?* This thought makes my hackles rise. I've got as much right to drive down this lane as he has. No more being bossed about. I'm through with all that.

"This is it, Breaky," I say. "Like Russell Crowe at the start of Gladiator, I will hold! At my signal unleash hell!"

Actually, on second thoughts, maybe not. That Defender looks very solid, and my little car is made of tin foil. Maybe I ought to reverse. Is that what he's asking? Cornish lanes, I'm quickly learning, are governed by a rather lethal game of chicken where whoever holds their nerve for the longest forces the other party to reverse. It's easy to spot the locals, though, because they go back to a passing place at dizzying speeds. So far today I've been given the finger by a puce-faced man in a Jag, a merry wave by a tractor driver and a pitying look by an old lady who swiftly backed up half a mile while I ground my gears in panic.

Emmets, I imagined them saying pityingly. *Townies can't reverse.* Well, let them navigate the Hangar Lane gyratory system in rush hour! Or how about the one-way feeder system into Heathrow Terminal Three? That tangle of roads and feeder lanes makes London cabbies blanch, but I can do it blindfold.

Beep! Beep! Flash! Flash!

Four-lane carriageways, jet-lagged ex-partners and low-flying aeroplanes vanish. I'm back in the lane with Defender man closing in on me by the second. I grab the gear stick and do my best to find reverse. The gears grind, and abandoning any hope of preserving my paintwork I reverse into a gateway in the walls.

The Defender draws alongside and the driver winds down the window. Pushing his shades into thick blond hair, he leans out and beams at me.

"G'day! You lost?" The broad Australian accent, more *Neighbours* than *Poldark,* takes me by surprise.

"I've seen you drive past a couple of times. Trevellan's the other way if you want the village," he adds when I don't reply.

"I'm fine. Just looking for a place to turn around," I say, recovering from the shock of bumping into Bradley Cooper's better-looking twin. "But thanks anyway."

"Easier said than done around here, hey? There's a turning place just round the corner by my van. You can spin around?" The grin widens. "Again?"

So much for not being spotted.

"Sorry about that," I say. "I didn't know anyone was home."

He waves a tanned hand. "No worries. I'm used to it. You'd be surprised how many people miss the turning for Trevellan and end up out here. I'm always giving directions to the village or, if they're in a flash car, sending them up to Vyvyan Court."

"Are you suggesting my car isn't flash?" I say, deadpan.

"British humour, right?"

We study my old car. Nobody could accuse a twelve-year old Peugeot 207 of being flash.

"A guess," I admit. "Anyway, I'm not lost. I overshot my turning."

I consider telling him I'm going to be living in the old boathouse on Oyster Shore but Breakspear interrupts with a volley of impatient barks.

"Are we holding you up, mate?" the driver asks as Breakspear thumps his tail delightedly, straining against his car harness and frantic to say hello. So much for guarding me from strangers when I'm all alone in my new house. I'd be better off with the snarling satnav, which is still issuing curt orders from the dashboard.

"At the first available opportunity, turn around!"

"Jeez! She doesn't take any shit! Better do what she asks," Defender man chuckles. Afternoon sunshine lights his eyes, startlingly green against tanned skin peppered with golden stubble. Faint white stars beam outwards from the corners of his eyes and dive into his thick hair. "I'll squeeze by. There should be enough room."

"*Should*?" I say nervously – but it's too late to worry because the Defender is creeping forwards and there's only a few inches between its mud-splattered flanks and my car's glossy black paint. I hold my breath and even suck in my stomach in sympathy, exhaling with relief when our cars are clear of each other. In my wing mirror I see him give a cheery thumbs up before accelerating away. I continue down the lane, feeling relieved to have escaped disaster. From now on I'll work on improving my backing-up technique – or perhaps walk everywhere. It could be easier.

I spin my car around by the caravan, noting the tubs of bushy herbs placed on the steps and the small vegetable patch dug alongside. I take a little more interest in the sculptures too, now I've met their creator. No crude chainsaw toadstools here, but a selection of delicate carvings of woodland creatures, abstract shapes and even a powerful rearing horse. An artist, then? Or an Aussie traveller, stopping for the summer and picking up some casual work – although he seems a little mature to be a backpacker. I'd have said he was just a bit older than me. Early forties, perhaps? Not that it's any of my business. I haven't come here to socialise. Quite the opposite.

Once back at Oyster Shore's turning all I can distinguish of the drive is a choppy sea of concrete waves where tree-roots have erupted, furred with emerald moss and edged with receding pools of bluebells. Somewhere deep within the rhododendrons and azaleas the old house sleeps, and I'll see it properly for the very first time soon, the crumbling white walls and shuttered windows becoming a reality rather than blurred images from an out-of-date website.

No wonder this property has been so hard to let. These deep ruts and potholes will render access impossible for any vehicle other than a four-wheel drive. David's Mercedes convertible won't stand a chance, even if he does decide to follow me. If I loop the rusty gate-chain around the gatepost behind me and hide my car inside, nobody will guess Oyster Shore is now inhabited.

This is perfect. Excitement dusts my skin with shivers, for this place is everything I'd hoped for and so much more. It's a romantic setting, the drive melting into dark trees echoing the mysterious Cornwall of du Maurier novels, and the bright splashes of water conjuring endless Enid Blyton summers.

I drive in and the car judders along the drive. Once around the bend, out of sight of the road, I pull the car onto the verge, kill the engine and exhale. Lowenna Scott has reached her destination.

Hopping out, I stretch my arms skywards and rotate my stiff neck. It's so good to feel the salt breeze against my cheeks and hear birdsong. I think I can even hear the whisper of waves breaking on the beach, so the sea can't be very far away. This is perfect!

"Okay, Breakspear," I say, opening the back door. "Ready to explore our new home?"

2

THE PRESENT

Cornwall

Lowenna

I stumbled across Oyster Shore by accident, or perhaps I ought to say an accident of Fate, since the instant the webpage appeared on my laptop screen I knew this was where I was meant to be. It was the very place I needed. Maybe it's more than a place? A state of mind?

As a freelance writer I spend a lot of time online, allegedly researching possible projects or ghost writing for more successful authors, but in reality scrolling through Facebook/Twitter/Instagram while cobbling pitches together. Several weeks ago I was doing my best to concentrate on ideas for a new commission and ignoring the latest flurry of guilt-inducing messages from David. Uninclined to give up – par for the course, since David Blake never ever lets something go he believes is his – he's been pinging his emails into my inbox at an impressive rate. He's obviously determined to wear me down, but it won't work. Not this time.

Everything was different now. *Everything.* Most importantly, *I* was different now that I knew for certain I wasn't mad or paranoid or jealous or possessive or any of the other descriptions he'd flung my way in the past. It was as though I'd hopped through the looking-glass, but rather than the world being back to front it was now the right way around. Everything made sense. Everything was the right way up.

How easily life can pivot on a chance decision. So often it's not big world events which alter our lives so much as the mundane choices we scarcely acknowledge. In my case this was being too lazy to change the pre-set station on the bedside radio and sticking to Radio Four as David prepared for a breakfast meeting and I dashed around getting ready to leave his flat. If I hadn't been distracted by a fascinating piece on Mary Shelley, I wouldn't have been running late to drop Breakspear with the dog sitter. If I hadn't been late to do that, I wouldn't have missed my bus – and if I'd caught it I wouldn't have noticed I'd forgotten my phone until I was several miles away. It would have been far too late for me to have retraced my steps, frown at seeing the spare key left in the ajar front door and step inside. It would have been too late for me to have followed the trail of clothes strewn along the hallway. Too late to push the bedroom door open, and far too late to see the look of utter shock on David's face when he glanced in the mirror and met my reflected gaze.

All this from choosing to take a unit on Gothic Literature at uni because I'd fancied the lecturer! Imagine if he'd decided to specialise in linguistics instead? Or postmodernism? Then I'd probably have had no interest in the genesis of Mary Shelley's greatest work and would have flipped over to Capital for a few minutes, left David's flat on time and never known the truth. I wouldn't have ever found the anger to do what I should have done the very first time he ...

Anyway, that's all in the past. I guess my point is that maybe life's no more than a series of chances over which we have no true control. Who knows how many lovers never meet, how many children are unborn, how many great scientific discoveries are missed, because someone chooses to pause and tie a shoelace or take a trip to the bathroom? If you thought a little too much about all the roads untaken and the endless parallel universes of possibility, it could drive you crazy. Instead I choose to believe that Fate likes to give us a nudge in the right direction. How else would I find myself walking down this overgrown drive, only a few miles from the place known and loved by generations of my family?

Since that awful clichéd moment I've come to realise that my instincts are worth listening to. My intuition is valid. I'd tugged the ring from my finger and dropped it onto the floor, where it spun for a moment before rolling away, taking with it the life I'd almost tumbled into irretrievably. While David scrabbled for his bathrobe I turned and walked away, already knowing I'd never return, and the realisation was like gulping oxygen after having your head held underwater.

My heart ached, but it would heal. *I* would heal. I was free.

My mother thinks I'm crazy to 'let David go'. He's solvent, has a nice car (high on her list) and is successful. A thirty-eight-year-old single daughter is a huge worry to her, and she has tried hard to persuade me to change my mind.

"Don't you want to get married, Lowenna?" she'd say

sadly. "Don't you want children? A family? Time's not elastic, you know."

The answer to this is complex. *Yes* to all the above, but also a resounding *no* if it isn't with the right person. My own parents divorced when I was sixteen, and my father now lives in a remote farmhouse in the Pyrenees with his new wife. He's blissfully happy, at least as far as I can tell – but my parents must have truly believed they were in love once and would be together forever, otherwise they would have never married. So how do you ever know for certain? And what is love anyway? Maybe it's simply something authors peddle to sell books? Growing up, I'd always thought I'd recognise love in a deep-down, depths-of-your-soul kind of way. Cathy and Heathcliff didn't ponder their feelings, and neither did Romeo and Juliet. Surely it would be the same for me?

But as time has passed I never have found the fireworks I'd once hoped for. I can count the serious relationships I've had on one hand. There's my sweet university relationship with barrister Jon (who now lives in New York with his husband) and after him came English teacher Drew. I'm on good terms with them both and love them dearly as friends. But David Blake was the only man to sweep me off my feet. My new boss at Erasmus Publishing House, he was every inch the tall, dark and powerful hero. He was every Mills & Boon cliché made flesh. Christian Grey without the cable ties. Edward Cullen without the fangs. When David asked me out for dinner I was flattered, yet bemused: there was an entire office of shiny twenty-somethings with long racehorse legs and flowing blonde manes to choose from. Why me?

"What do they know about Yeats or Heaney?" David had asked, when I'd pointed this out. We'd been eating a late supper at a small trattoria just off Covent Garden, all wax-dribbled Chianti bottles with candles stuffed in the necks and air heavy with the scent of garlic and tomatoes, but when I looked up I caught him staring sourly at me mopping up the dregs of my carbonara with a big hunk of garlic bread. I'd suppressed an uneasy feeling about his obvious disapproval. I love food. Cooking it, shopping for it, eating it. Not the way to be a size zero, obviously, but by thirty-five I'd accepted I was more likely to visit Mars than to be skinny. And who wanted to go into space anyway?

"Absolutely nothing," I admitted. Most of the girls who interned at Erasmus Press, usually called Poppy or Binky or Sophia, were only there because Daddy had a contact and they fancied 'doing something in publishing' while husband-hunting. What they knew about literature could be fitted onto a postage stamp with room to spare for Beowulf. "But what's that got to do with it?"

David reached for my hand. "Everything. Don't you see, Lowenna? That's the whole point. You're different. You're refreshing. And you're bloody sexy. I can't keep my eyes off you."

This was heady stuff. I was certainly different, but I'd never seen this as a positive quality before. I'd tried using hair straighteners, bought minimiser bras to disguise my cleavage and even convinced myself for a while that skinny jeans and knee boots was a look I could pull off, but by the time David arrived on the scene I was, if not at peace exactly, resigned to crinkly hair and waiting for bootcut jeans to come back into fashion. It required a certain paradigm shift to see myself through his eyes, but once I'd adjusted I liked what I saw, and I liked David too. He was funny and clever and without a doubt utterly brilliant at his job. Since he'd been appointed, Erasmus had flourished, sales were through the roof, and we'd signed several big-name authors. On paper he was perfect, and caught in the full beam of his attention I truly thought I'd found the man I was looking for. Later, when he hurt me hugely, I realised that I'd ignored the warning signs. If I'm really honest with myself, though, it wasn't all his fault. We simply weren't right for each other. We never were and we never will be. I should have trusted my instincts and listened to what my heart was saying during that first meal. We should have ended then.

"He made a mistake, Lowenna," my mother said when I told her the engagement was off. "Don't be hasty."

I stared into the mirror. A swollen-eyed goblin with Rudolph's nose and limp hair looked back – but the goblin had a glint in her eye which looked a little like self-respect.

"He was with someone else, Mum. It's not like forgetting to put the bins out."

"Well, no. He shouldn't have done that, but men aren't like us, darling. They have moments of weakness. Look at your father."

My father had been remarried for almost two decades. His 'moment of weakness' had lasted longer than his marriage to my mother, but I chose not to point that out. Anyway, I didn't deserve a weak man or one who couldn't stay faithful. I deserved a man who loved me with every breath he took. Somebody who would stay by my side until we reached the winter of our lives. A man who would hold me when I wept and comfort me when I was sick, whose love shone in his eyes and who smiled at me when my eyes fluttered open in the morning, and who laughed with me until they closed again at night. A man whose foot would reach out for mine beneath the covers, who would hold my hand when we watched a movie, and love animals as much as I do. It was a dream – no more than an echo from cherished novels or fragments of films – but my heart told me there had to be more, and I was determined to hold out for it.

"It's over, Mum," was all I said before asking whether she still had Granny May's box. Was it tucked away somewhere? Could I have it?

"Honestly, Lowenna, I sometimes think you're not all there. Have you listened to a word I've been saying?" Mum sounded exasperated, but this was nothing new. "What's Granny's box got to do with anything?"

I wasn't sure, but it felt important. If Princess Clementine, the curly-haired young man drawn with such love, and the other treasures still existed, then I wanted to return them to Cornwall. Maybe I could work out what their significance was and uncover the identity of the sad stranger who had delivered the box. Knowing Mum wouldn't understand this at all, I plumped for a half-truth.

"I thought it might be nice to see if I could visit some of the places in the pictures."

"Honestly, Lowenna, I've no idea where that box went. There was a lot of clearing up to do when your grandfather died. Their cottage was stuffed with junk."

"Could you have a look for it? I'd hate to think it's lost. Don't forget, Granny said it would make our fortune," I said.

"I'll see what I can do. Eric can have a look in the attic – I've some bits for him to put up there – but don't get your hopes up; the box probably went to the tip with the rest of their stuff. And as for family fortunes, Mother talked a whole load of nonsense most of the time. Piskies, knockers, ghosts, smugglers and whatnot. I had to take her to task for scaring you two witless."

"We loved her stories," I protested, but my mother had

moved on from the past and was recounting the latest instalment in the saga of the neighbours' untidy garden. Normally when she described my stepfather trimming Mrs Avery's overgrown bush I sniggered like a fifteen-year-old, but this time I was quiet, simply relieved not to be given another lecture about David. By the time Mum rang off, I could only hope that Granny May's box wasn't forgotten.

Unlike Mum, who'd have David and me back together in a heartbeat, my sister wants to throttle him. No manner of grisly end is too dreadful for David as far as Marina's concerned, even though I've tried to explain that I don't hate him. David might not be my favourite person on the planet, I'd explained to her when visiting, but I don't wish him any harm. I just want him as far away from me as possible.

"You didn't love him, then," was her conclusion. "If Tony cheated on me I'd chop his knob off and beat him around the head with it."

My brother-in-law, quietly making coffee, winced. "Babe, really? Do you *have* to?"

"What?" Marina demanded, whirling around. She was chopping onions, and as she brandished the knife Tony stepped back in alarm. "You should be pleased to know just how much I love you."

Tony cowered behind the Nescafe jar. "Maybe show it by giving me a foot rub? Or sex?"

Marina lowered the knife. "I'm only saying what I'd do if you ever cheated because I *love* you so much. I would be *destroyed* and, trust me, a foot rub would not be on the list and neither would sex once I was finished." She tossed her black curls. "Unlike Lowenna, I'm a passionate woman. I feel things deeply. It's our Romany heritage."

With her wild hair, deep blue eyes and hot temper

Marina had always pounced on Granny May's stories about our family descending from a gypsy horse whisperer. But being small with crinkly toffee-coloured hair and an allergy to equines, I was something of a disappointment to the genetic pool.

"I *am* passionate. I'm just not bloodthirsty like you," I protested.

My sister snorted like one of the Peppa Pig cartoons my nephews were addicted to. "If you'd truly loved David you'd be *savage*. Trust me. You, little sis, have never been in love. One day it will creep up and bite you on the bum and then you'll realise I was right. If you loved David like I love Tony you'd want to *kill* him!"

I glanced at my brother-in-law to see what it was I was missing. Portly, balding, and fond of sportswear (even though his idea of exercise is lifting the Sky remote) Tony was an unlikely object of desire. But didn't they say beauty was in the eye of the beholder? Marina certainly adored him, and when he wasn't hiding behind the kitchen island he adored her too.

I've thought a lot about that conversation since, and reflected on my relationship. At times it was hard to recognise quite what I did feel beneath the disappointment and hurt. Working with David was going to be awkward now, so to solve the problem I'd gone freelance, which meant I'd avoid the office. I found it rather revealing to see just how little of my own life away from work had been knitted into David's, which said something about the nature of our relationship.

I'd never moved in with him, which lots of my friends found odd, but I'd always justified this because my rented flat in Hanwell had a garden that was perfect for Breakspear, who loved the nearby park as well. Sometimes David had stayed over, and sometimes I stayed with him in Hammersmith, but we never discussed moving in together, just as we'd never started to plan the wedding. He loved the inner city, and I loved my garden flat where I could watch trains speed over the Hanwell viaduct, my heart carried away with each one along the tracks of the Great Western Railway and over the long miles between London and Cornwall.

David and I weren't meant to last. We were not soulmates. We weren't even true friends. Maybe there's somebody perfect for me and maybe there isn't. Whatever the truth, I know I won't settle for less. I want a love that lasts a lifetime – and if the closest I come to finding it is my dog, then so be it.

So I have left the past behind. Oyster Shore, my new chapter, will be written and I can hardly wait for it to begin.

3

THE PRESENT

Cornwall

Lowenna

"This is your new home," I tell Breakspear, but he's too busy tugging on his lead to pay any attention to a word I have to say. I consider letting him off, but until this morning he was a city dog and I'm not convinced that with all this excitement his recall will be up to much. I know how he feels, because I'm tempted to run down the drive, hurtling into the unknown and whooping with glee. I slip my hand into my jacket pocket and close my fingers around the big brass key I'd collected earlier from the letting agent. I can hardly wait to slip it into the lock, turn it and step into my new home.

My new home. I can hardly believe it. I have a *new home*!

If life can swivel on the head of a pin I know the exact moment mine did exactly that. It was mid-morning and, with one edited manuscript completed and sent, I minimised my inbox and leaned back in my chair. My desk overlooked a small garden and if I cricked my neck I could glimpse the arches of the Hanwell viaduct beyond a slice of park as green as key lime pie. Watery sunshine dripped through ancient horse chestnuts and the pale blue sky was criss-crossed with vapour trails. Journeys, I'd thought wistfully, and new starts. There was a world of possibility beyond my window, and how I longed to be part of it.

I opened a new Word document. A fresh page has all the potential in the world but that morning I couldn't dredge up a single idea. I had a magazine editor waiting for an article, and the features department at *The Mail* were keen to commission several women's interest pieces. These projects would pay well, but the harder I tried to come up with something the tighter my mind knotted itself. What was women's interest anyway? Was there a male equivalent? I doubted it.

"Relationships? Marriage? Breakups? My own life?" I suggested to Breakspear, who thumped his tail approvingly. These were rich seams to mine, but – and maybe I was being old-fashioned here – I couldn't face the thought of dishing up choice morsels of my own life even for a healthy cheque and the possibility of more lucrative commissions. Some freelance writers are happy to tell all in a Jeremy Kyle-style word-vomit across newspaper and magazine pages, but I'm not one of them.

No. My cherished dream was to write a biography that would be original, academic and, I hoped, critically acclaimed. I had yet to settle on a subject or save the funds to block out the time required to focus on such a project, but having spent five years editing other people's efforts I knew I was up to the task. As soon as the muse visited me I would start, or so I told myself. If only she wasn't so elusive.

"You think I should choose Lassie, don't you?" I said to Breakspear. "I think somebody relatively unknown would be good. Somebody who's hiding in plain sight and who has a fantastic story. But who could that be?"

I always drew a blank at this point. To lure the muse, I opened up the file where an outline of an idea was sketched out. *Lost Literature of Cornwall* was the title, and I was very excited about my fledgling idea. The seed had been planted last summer when, on holiday with Marina and her family, I'd visited Rosecraddick Manor on a rainy day. This stately home in south-east Cornwall had once been the home of a First World War poet, Kit Rivers, and was the place where he had written the bulk of his early work. I'd spent hours in the Kernow Heritage Foundation's museum there, reading about his life before leaving the gift shop clutching a book of his poetry and nursing a headful of ideas. I'd read until the small hours, utterly captivated by the beauty of the verse, and as I lay in bed it had occurred to me that there must be a wealth of other Cornish poets and authors whose work had slipped through the cracks of time. For every du Maurier there must be several other talented writers whose work was out of print and waiting to be rediscovered. Magical second-hand bookshops would have battered tomes pushed to the back of shelves or propping open doors. Car boot sales were treasure troves of lost literature, too – all I had to do was search. Once I found the perfect subject I'd be up and running.

This was proving easier said than done. So far I'd drawn several blanks and stumbled down more blind alleys than I cared to admit. If I was to find a subject for my book it stood to reason that I needed to be in Cornwall not London. I closed the document and glanced out of the window just as an intercity whisked over the viaduct in a silver blur of engine and carriages. I wished I was on it. A young man's fancy might turn to thoughts of love in the spring, or according to Tennyson anyway, but this young woman was dreaming of cliffs, creeks and copper-coin sunsets.

And then I experienced another fork-in-the-road moment, for as I stared wistfully at the empty viaduct, longing to be on board a train watching the London terraces and narrow houses blur as I left the city, it occurred to me that I could be doing *exactly* that. There was nothing to anchor me in London. I was single. I was freelance. I rented my flat. With the wonders of the Internet at my fingertips I could work anywhere I wanted. I could *live* anywhere I wanted.

I could live in Cornwall.

I opened the web browser and flexed my fingers over the keyboard. Where would I want to go if I had the whole of Cornwall to choose from? Where could I make a new start? The answer was obvious. Where better to begin than the place where my family had once lived? A flurry of faded post-card images drifted through my memory. A wide river sparkling in the sunshine. Lurid orange ice lollies. Granny paddling in the shallows, legs white and shins measled. The old ferry clanking its way across the water to Penhayes. Sludge-grey crabs dangling from a line ...

Trevellan. *Google*, I thought as I typed, *do your worst!*

houses to rent Trevellan

Within seconds the screen was flooded with links to beautiful holiday cottages, all honeyed floorboards, denim-blue sofas and driftwood art, and rental rates that made my eyes water. Just one week at any of these properties would cost more than my rent for an entire month. Granted, most of the holiday homes were far better equipped than my full-time abode and came with stunning sea views as opposed to dustbins and parked cars, but I was still shocked at how much Cornwall had changed since the bucket-and-spade holidays of my childhood. It was all about fine dining and lifestyle these days, and it became very apparent very quickly that Trevellan was out of the question unless I had a lottery win. Undaunted, I widened my search area, added 'long-term rental', and perhaps it was Fate or just a strange coincidence, but within seconds of hitting Return I knew I'd found exactly what I was looking for.

Summer rental – The Boathouse, Oyster Shore, Trevellan

There was a grainy picture of a small building paddling in the shallows of a wooded creek. Lead-paned windows lent the exterior a slightly ecclesiastical appearance, and ivy clung to the terracotta brickwork, scaling the roof like a green cat burglar and veiling the coy porch.

I tingled from head to foot. Even the ends of my curly hair, clamped on the top of my head with a bulldog clip, tingled, because I *knew* this place. Although there was no logic to this surge of familiarity, I recognised the scene instantly.

This made no sense. Granny May hadn't taken us here, and it wasn't an area I'd explored during later holidays. Yet I still felt a punch of recognition. I knew waves would lap the shore day and night just as I knew that when the tide was high the pontoon would lift and swell, creaking like a ship in full sail and listing whenever the wind took hold. Like the glint of a mackerel's scales beneath the water, an image flickered through the years.

Faded pencil lines pressed into yellowed paper. A young

man sitting on a riverbank and gazing across the water, curls lifted by the wind and book held loosely in his hand. Were initials of the setting rather the author's name? OS for Oyster Shore? Was this place the setting for those sketches? The place where Princess Clementine had played with her friends all those years ago? The more I studied the image on the screen the more certain I was that this was the same spot. OS wasn't a name of a person but the name of a *place*.

OS. Oyster Shore.

Excited, I clicked on the booking link. When nothing happened, I tried the text. Still nothing. I clicked several more times but every link had expired and there didn't seem to be any helpful information. Refusing to be defeated, I decided to do things the old-fashioned way, and phoned the lettings company, where the answering agent was puzzled by my enquiry.

"Oyster Shore boathouse isn't rented out any more. That web page shouldn't still be live."

My stomach was a cold slither of disappointment. It couldn't end here. I had to rent that place. I *had* to. "Oh, that's such a shame. It looks perfect. Could you check for me just in case?"

She laughed. "It might look idyllic, but the reality's a little different. The last people who booked demanded their money back."

"Really? Why?"

"Mainly because they live in the twenty-first century! The boathouse hasn't been touched since the eighties. If you're interested in Trevellan and Penhayes, we've got some beautiful properties available."

But I wasn't interested in any other property; I was already picturing myself in the boathouse. I'd sit in the window and write, looking up now and then to lose my thoughts in the slow-moving water. I would walk Breakspear along the shore and collect shells and sea glass. It would be perfect. I tuned out while she continued to tell me how the private trust that owned the property had been told it wasn't good enough to be a holiday let, and how her company had the highest standards and won several industry awards.

What did I care about the décor or luxury hot tubs? All I cared about was renting the boathouse exactly as it was. I already knew this was where I'd write my book. It was where I was meant to be. I would camp there if necessary.

"Surely without being occupied the building will deteriorate even further?" I pointed out once the agent finished her hard sell.

"Yes, I guess so, but that's not strictly our problem. It's up to the owners to ensure a place is maintained. We only manage the bookings. There was a local man who keeps an eye on the property, but he just keeps it aired and clears the garden. It's such a waste. If it was up to standard I know we'd let it in an instant. The setting alone sells it."

"But it is still on your books? Technically?"

There was a pause. "Technically, yes, I suppose it is."

"So technically I could rent it?"

I probably sounded crazy. I'd certainly felt a little crazy. Even Breakspear was looking at me with a concerned expression.

"I imagine so, if the owner is agreeable," the agent said cautiously. "But I must warn you that the drive's practically impassable and the kitchen's very basic."

"The more inaccessible the better," I laughed, before explaining that I was a freelance writer in search of a quiet place to work with no distractions. "I could pay a reduced rent if it's in such a bad state. I'll even do some repairs myself and at my own expense. That would hopefully keep the boathouse from deteriorating further. I'd be doing the owner a favour."

She laughed. "The value's in the land, not the building. No doubt the site'll be redeveloped at some point."

"Perhaps I could speak to the owner?" I said. "I'm sure we could come to an agreement."

I was hoping the owner might be more receptive than their letting agent, but it turned out that Oyster Shore was owned by an investment trust and had no real purpose other than to gently increase in value as the years and tides turned and Cornish property became ever more desirable. The agent tried once again to persuade me to look at some other properties nearby (clearly under the impression that all writers have J. K. Rowling's budget) but eventually I was able to convince her I was serious about Oyster Shore, and she grudgingly went away to make some calls. This was when the Universe moved in my favour because she called me back half an hour later with the news that the trustees who dealt with the property were happy to rent the boathouse for a peppercorn rent in return for it being inhabited and maintained.

"We should have suggested a long-term rental ages ago," she said, no doubt thinking of all the missed commission. "They say the place is yours for as long as you want it."

Two weeks later here I am, picking my way down the rough drive towards the river and ready to see the boathouse for the first time. My flat has been re-let, my worldly goods are in storage at Mum's and my laptop is charged and ready for the muse to rock up. The sun's shining from a powder-blue sky, and warm air, rich with wild garlic, quivers with birdsong and the thrum of bees. I feel very, very lucky.

Breakspear strains against the lead, his tail a black blur of impatience as he longs to investigate the wealth of wonderful new smells and scurrying woodland creatures. I stop for a break, check my pocket for the key once again, then hoist my rucksack back onto my shoulders and carry on down the drive. This is it. This is where my new life begins.

The trees crowding the submerged drive are dense, pressing in on me in a way that feels almost curious and a little oppressive. It's darker in the woods and when the sun scoots behind a cloud I pause, oddly hesitant to continue, for without the sunlight's dancing patterns the yawning drive is laced with shadow and the mossy floor is dank and dismal. The entwined branches above become gnarled claws which could reach down at any moment, and even the birdsong seems to falter. Oyster Shore is its own kingdom, lost deep within a hidden world, and although my name might be on the boathouse lease, it feels as though I'm trespassing. A twig snaps behind me and I spin around, heart racing and filled with the sensation that I'm being watched by curious eyes.

The locals think it's unlucky. They talk about a curse. Nonsense, of course.

Recalling the letting agent's parting words as I left the office in Plymouth, I feel oddly unsettled. It was easy to dismiss this comment when I was in Plymouth, but not nearly as simple to laugh superstitions off now I'm all alone, miles from the bustle of a city. Then the cloud floats by, the sun comes out, and birdsong swells. Breakspear pulls on the lead and I shake my head, half-amused with myself and half-frustrated. I haven't even been away from the city for twenty-four hours and already I'm letting my imagination run wild.

Too many gothic novels, that's the problem, and from now on I'm banning myself from listening to spooky podcasts!

Breakspear bounds forward on the scent of something only he can detect. My shoulder wrenched, I stumble after him, tripping on ruts and slithering on moss. A creature scurries through the dense bracken to my left and Breakspear barks loudly. A deer? A rabbit? I can't see through the tangles of briars and ivy-cloaked trees, but I sense the hidden creatures watching us pass. But I scold myself for my earlier fears; I'm in the countryside now, and I'd better get used to sharing my new home with all kinds of wildlife.

Even so, I quicken my pace. And then the drive switchbacks and the white façade of Oyster House glimmers through the foliage just as I feel certain new adventures and ideas will emerge from my tangled thoughts. When I glimpse a sliver of sparkling water, excitement banishes all nerves and my heart thumps so loudly I can almost hear it. I may have grown up in the city, but during those years I spent hours staring out of my bedroom window over the inland rooftop sea and longing for a place far beyond my reach. I wrote stories about smugglers, and pressed my ear to the shells I'd collected from Readymoney Cove, hoping to catch the whisper of waves. I missed the cold kiss of the sea against my bare toes, and I longed to wade into rock pools where the mirrored world hung over my shoulder and my own white face trembled up at me. Perhaps it's an obsession? My DNA? Or even the Law of Attraction? Whatever the explanation, I've always known I'll live here one day.

I am home.

4

THE PRESENT

Cornwall

Lowenna

Oyster House, part of the great Vyvyan Estate in SE Cornwall, was built in the 1890s as a summer retreat for William Trelyon, 7th Viscount Vyvyan and one of the last merchant princes of Cornwall. Edward VII, a close friend of the Viscount, is rumoured to have stayed here and 'besported himself with young ladies' in the private pleasure boathouse located half a mile along the foreshore. As with many great estates, Vyvyan fell into decline after the First World War. Vyvyan Court is now an exclusive hotel. Oyster House was abandoned in the mid-1920s and the riverside pleasure gardens lost beneath under-growth. The boathouse is used as an occasional holiday rental. Oyster House remains in private ownership.

These are the only details I've found providing the back-ground to my new home; no more than a footnote in a pamphlet the local history society has put online. I've emailed the society, but there's been no response and all further digging has revealed very little information about this property – which I find rather intriguing in itself. This spot was once the summer retreat of the wealthy and privileged. The cream of Edwardian society visited it for boating and picnics. Even the King spent time here. Oyster Shore would have been a prestigious address, but over one hundred years later it's hard to imagine the elegant carriages and stately motor cars that bowled along this drive, ladies in white dresses and big hats sitting beside moustached gentlemen in goggles, and I feel sad the place has been allowed to fall into such a decline. Whatever happened here for such a breath-taking spot to be abandoned? Why did the owner walk away and never return? These are some of the first questions I'm determined to answer when I begin my research. There's a mystery here, and where there's a mystery there's usually a story. Maybe I'll abandon the biography idea and write a novel; I used to dream of doing that when I was a child, so why not realise my early literary ambitions?

Sunlight drips through the foliage, and more glimpses of the house are revealed through the trees as the drive winds riverwards. The fairytale setting has brooding undertones. A sleeping-beauty house buried in the wooded valley, laced in by brambles and belted tightly by a rocky shore, all unloved and abandoned. The air of melancholy is palpable when the sun hides behind a cloud. As the drive twists sharply to the left and plunges deeper into dense foliage I enter a prehistoric world where monstrous gunnera tubas are caged by bamboo as thick as a man's wrist and knotweed crawls along the ground. Strange palms claw upwards for the light, and vast ferns spout from cracked paving stones, alien specimen plants brought in from overseas by Victorian enthusiasts to flourish in the mild Cornish climate and claim the place as their own. They lend this section of the drive a sense of the primordial, and I tug Breakspear to heel just in case a predator is lurking or a giant Venus fly trap is poised to gobble him up. In its day the gardens here must have been magnificent – a Heligan in miniature, perhaps, or another Trebah.

From this point I can just make out the town of Penhayes across the river. It's so remote here and so silent that it seems impossible that bustling streets and noise are only a short boat ride away. On the shore oystercatchers work the water's edge, oblivious to anything except worms and shellfish and the rising tide, while the sky settles in molten metal veins in the exposed riverbed. There is the sense of being in another world and another time here, and my London life already feels like a dream as I continue to walk down the drive. When it turns again it's with such unexpected sharpness that I'm surprised to find myself so abruptly arriving at the house.

Reclining in a scooped-out woodland bowl, Oyster House is part of the landscape yet also set apart in its crumbling grandeur. Tethered by brambles and chained with ivy, it's trapped on a terraced apron where even more specimen plants have run amok. Himalayan balsam and Japanese knotweed claw the delicately laid paving, splintering balustrades and terrace in a sea of stony waves. The remains of the drive are covered by thin grass, like once-thick hair on a balding scalp, rendering this spot truly the end of the road. I fully understand what the letting agent meant when she said the boathouse was inaccessible by car. It looks as though I'll be doing a lot of walking.

Was this where Princess Clementine once stood with her

friends to have their picture taken? I wish I could remember in more detail what the house in the old photograph had looked like. Not much like this, for little remains of the elegant white façade, but this place feels familiar. The shutter clicked and froze three children in time, but to me it seems as though they left only minutes ago and if I can wait just a few moments more they'll reappear, childhood playmates laughing and shrieking as they run wild in the grounds.

I'd like to take a closer look at the house, but Breakspear pulls hard on the lead. He wants to continue to the beach, where the water flows like syrup and egrets pick their way along the shell line, so I unclip his harness and watch him bound ahead, barking joyfully at his freedom. There will be plenty of time to explore, I think, as I follow him – and I can't wait, because I'm mesmerised by this place and falling more and more in love with every footstep closer to the river. The untamed beauty, wild decay and sense of isolation are thrilling. It's a little like being cast away on a desert island.

Breakspear reaches the water's edge. He barks at a flock of seabirds and bounds towards them as they suddenly take flight, making me jump back over the wet sand and into a pile of storm-tossed bladderwrack. Outraged flies swarm upwards and, recoiling, I catch the back of my shoe on one of the many oyster shells which smother the beach and lend this place its name. Breakspear needs to watch out, for these won't be kind to soft paws. I touch one with a fingertip and wince at the razor-sharp bite.

While Breakspear digs up sand, I study the curve of shore which peels away from the water and melts into dense foliage. The low tide reveals ribs of boats, emerging gently from alluvium like dinosaur remains. Lumps of metal draped with green weed and bladderwrack are standing stones from a lost industrial past. An old winch rusts flake by flake, and half a mile across the grey sand a splintered pontoon comes to an abrupt end over the silt. Set at the far end of the pontoon is a low brick building which obviously commands sweeping views of the river and the wooded valley across the water. It's the boathouse, my new home, tucked into the meander of the bottle-green creek, and as if the place wants to give me a welcome a kingfisher darts along the bank, a vivid streak of sapphire against the emerald vegetation, and the sun turns water trickling through the narrow channels to pure gold.

Breakspear and I go back up to the high tide line and pick up a path which dives back into the trees and concludes at the far side of another wooded area where, quite incongruously, the ornate red brick boathouse has been erected. A fairytale construction with barley-sugar twists of chimneys and lead-paned windows framed by shutters with hearts cut out of the woodwork, it's the sort of dwelling Hansel and Gretel might have stumbled across in the woods or Goldilocks been tempted to force entry into. Even covered in ivy and with the diamond-paned windows dull with grime it's fit for a king, for the images online haven't done it justice.

"Some boathouse," I remark to Breakspear.

But my dog doesn't respond. He's given up barking at the gulls and is watching the beach instead, his dark eyes trained on the shore and his ears pricked. I follow his gaze and am surprised to see a girl wading through the shallows. I'm irrationally rather put out since I'd thought this was a private place. Although any one can walk along the foreshore at low tide, I hadn't thought this likely in such a remote spot.

I wave but she doesn't see me, intent upon something in the water and leaning forward to scoop it up. A shell? Or perhaps a nugget of sea glass? This must be a wonderful spot for beachcombing. Bracken-red hair pinned onto the crown of her head and her dress tucked up above her knees, a metal bucket swings loosely from one hand, and as I watch she drops something into it before straightening up. I smile and raise my hand again, but she doesn't acknowledge my greeting and my hand falls away. Locals aren't keen on incomers, I guess.

Breakspear whines and presses himself hard against my legs. I rest a hand on the dome of his head, surprised he's not tried to bound over and introduce himself. He's usually a very sociable soul. Beneath my fingertips he is tense.

"Hey, it's all fine," I promise, clipping on his lead and running his silky ears through my fingers. "You'll love it here, boy, I promise. We'll have lots of lovely walks. Maybe I'll even find us a boat!"

But Breakspear isn't interested in my crazy plans for boats or day trips. His attention fixed on the beachcomber, a low growl rumbles from his throat. Beneath my fingers I feel his hackles rise.

"Breaky! Shh!" I scold, but my dog continues to snarl. Is he being protective because I'm on my own? It's certainly out of character for such a friendly little spaniel.

"Stop it!" I order, but Breakspear's gaze is still fixed on the beach. Maybe I can call her over? If we say hello he might feel more settled. I squint against the glare of light on the water, shading my eyes with my hand, but the creek's empty. There's no sign of the beachcomber anywhere.

How odd. I'd only looked away for a moment. Perhaps she's rounded the headland? Or, and this is more likely, has clambered onto the bank and wandered into the woods? This is private land, but Oyster Shore's been empty for so long the locals probably think of it as theirs. She's probably annoyed I've muscled in on her place. Perhaps even now she's calling her friends and complaining? I sigh. The last thing I need is a bunch of disgruntled locals.

"Thanks for protecting me, Breaky," I say, patting him. "What would I do without you?"

Breakspear wags his tail and barks happily. His mood has passed and he's a ball of energy again, bounding ahead to my new front door along a path through the nettles. It's clearly been recently strimmed, so maybe this girl spends time here with her secret lover? Or perhaps she's a holidaymaker exploring? Or even a time traveller? My heart rises as ideas flood in with the tide. There are stories everywhere here. A novel is calling me!

The main part of the boathouse is set on stilts above the water so vessels can be stored in the space beneath and launched easily when the tide rises. A flight of steps leads to the porch, and I hesitate at the bottom. The unknown lies behind that door, and with it all my hopes and dreams. Once I turn the key and step inside these become reality. Will the boathouse be welcoming to me?

I swallow and turn the key, knowing as I look in that I'm being ridiculous. This little house is gorgeous. Once I've pulled the ivy from the windows and given the glass a good clean it'll be flooded with light and become the perfect hideaway to write in. David, if he even drove this far, would never risk his Italian shoes to walk here. This is the bolthole I'd dreamed of. It is my retreat.

The door swings open easily. The hinges must have been oiled recently, and the large open-plan room is surprisingly clean and tidy. There's a living area at the river end, and a kitchen at the rear complete with a cooker, scrubbed pine table and a museum-piece microwave. A fridge hums away to itself beneath a solid wood counter, and a clock with vegetables rather than numbers, ticks contentedly above an elderly range.

It's perfect – if you were to be marooned here in the eighties. The musty aroma mingled with the damp instantly whisks me back in time to my grandparents' cottage, and I already know that when I look closely at the curtains and the walls I'll see familiar speckles of black mould. Nothing that a good wash with bleach won't cure, as Granny May always said.

Breakspear shoots between my legs and tears about, sniffing at skirting boards and barking at whatever he imagines might lurk within them. I shrug off my rucksack and follow him around, admiring the intricately tiled floor, the dark rafters that arch above me, and the exposed brickwork set with elaborate patterns and continuing in a flourish above an enormous fireplace with a wood burner lost in its cavernous depths. There's no sign of any logs, though, and I recall the letting agent pointing out that this is the only way of heating the place. I hadn't given heating much thought, but now I'm here I can appreciate the difficulty involved in bringing firewood to the property. Nobody will deliver, though, so will I have to cut my own? On the positive side there's no shortage of trees.

"We'll have to buy a chainsaw," I say to Breakspear, and my dog shoots me a concerned look. He's right; it would be carnage, and I'd last moments before it all went very wrong. I'm lethal enough armed with the kitchen scissors. A fan heater, then, or electric blanket?

"Maybe log deliveries come by boat?" I wonder out loud. Breakspear can't shrug, but he looks as though he'd like to.

"Fine. I'll call the letting agent. She might have some suggestions, although I suspect what she'll want to say is *I told you so.*"

My dog snuffles around and I continue to explore. The more I see of the boathouse the happier I feel. The living area is simple but cosy and I picture myself curled up by the fire reading something from the bookcase in the corner, which is crammed with well-thumbed paperbacks. I love books with cracked spines and turned-down pages; they speak of enjoyment and love and avid reading, and I pull one out, sniffing it as though inhaling the bouquet of a fine wine: vintage du Maurier, *Frenchman's Creek*, published by Doubleday, pages age-brittled and print-smudged from eager page turning. I slide it back onto the shelf and make a note to reread it. What could be better than losing yourself in du Maurier, by a creek and in the county she made her own?

Under the big picture window is a small table topped with a crochet cloth and vase of dusty dried flowers. I earmark this as my writing spot and the only place I've found so far where I can get a bar of mobile signal for tethering to the Internet. Perfect! Even more perfect, in Breakspear's eyes anyway, is the big sofa, draped in motheaten throws. He instantly decides to curl up there, and grunts with happiness.

An armchair slouched at right angles to the sofa is turned towards the Methuselah of a cathode ray tube television perching on a listing drinks trolley. Complete with buttons on it for changing channel and a set of sliding colour adjustments, it's crowned with the kind of space-gun-style aerial my grandparents used to have. A fleeting memory of Granny holding theirs aloft and lowering it inch by painful inch while snowstorms raged across the screen and Grandad bellowed, “Left!” or, “Up a bit!” makes me smile. Some things about Cornwall haven’t changed so much after all.

The kitchen is basic, but as far as I’m concerned you can’t go wrong with a loaf of bread and Marmite, and since there’s a toaster I’ll be just fine. There’s a washing machine and lots of freestanding cupboards with shelves peppered in rodent droppings, and beneath the narrow window with its oblique view of the river is a big butler’s sink. A cast-iron potholder is suspended from one of the rafters, laden with an eclectic assortment of pans ranging from classic seventies orange Le Creuset to cheap and cheerful charity shop offerings. The plate rack above the draining board sports blue and white Cornish ware, and the scarlet mug tree bears the kind of soup cups I remember my parents collecting from the garage a lifetime ago. Seeing these feels like being greeted by old friends.

At the far end of the kitchen is a small door leading to a narrow passage. A windowless room contains a metal sink and a basic shower. A scullery, perhaps? Somewhere where servants would have prepared delicacies for the King to feed his mistress? Or would the royal food have been delivered from the main house and left discreetly outside? I’m imagining a stout man popping sugared plums between the lips of a corseted beauty while the servants scurry around preparing cold cuts and veal pie.

What a contradiction this place is. Such beautiful architecture and exquisite design, stitched together with scandalous history and tacked up over the years with lengths of plasterboard, MFI furniture and odds and ends from an assortment of tenants. I’m just another few lines in its story. Perhaps in another century somebody will stand here and wonder about me. What will I leave behind?

Another door opening from the passageway reveals a

winding staircase, beautifully carved from dark wood and leading to an attic bedroom. Breakspear bounds ahead and hurtles into a long room where a brass bedstead piled with quilts huddles beneath low eaves. The walls are papered in a flowery print I vaguely recognise as William Morris, and although a few sections are peeling and several damp patches crawl across the ceiling it retains a sense of faded elegance. A studwork wall thrown up at the far end divides off a small bathroom in eighties salmon pink, and to my delight I discover I can bathe overlooking the river, which feels very decadent. I evict a couple of sullen spiders before turning a tap to swill away the dust and dead flies which coat the bottom. There's a pause, followed by an ominous gurgle before a rust-coloured jet splutters into the tub. The cold tap continues to spurt all manner of material before finally running clear, but the hot tap refuses to play ball. If I want to wallow up here I'll need to check out the immersion or boil lots of kettles. The plug seems to be blocked too. Not wanting to flood the place, I turn the tap off.

Making a mental note to buy cleaning materials and a sink plunger, I abandon the bathroom and turn my attention to the grimy windows in the bedroom. I rub one with my sleeve before lifting the latch to push it open. It's shoved right back by a tangle of branches as oak and ash press against the glass and cast a murky green light across the room. The upstairs feels submerged and as though it's been dragged beneath the river deep into the world of tangled weeds and darkness, drowning out the light and closing over my head. Dragging me under and away ...

I shut the window and turn away, jolted by the image. What a horrible notion. Where on earth has that come from? Perhaps I'll cover the windows with silk scarves. I could make this whole room look like an eastern boudoir or the inside of an exotic tent. That could be fun and a lot less gloomy.

"This house needs some love and attention, doesn't it?" I ask Breakspear, who ignores me. Head on one side and ears pricked up, he's intent on something I can't see.

"What is it, Breaky? Is it mice?"

I tense and listen. When I hear it too my blood flows cold and slow, for footsteps are stomping across the floor below. I hear the thud of something heavy dropped, and the footsteps pause before crossing the floor once again. This is not my imagination or nerves. There's no mistaking the heavy thread of boots on hard tiles. I am alone no longer.

Someone else is here in the boathouse.

5

THE PRESENT

Cornwall

Lowenna

Breakspear shoots between my legs and dives down the stairs in a black blur leaving me alone in the doorway, torn between following him to face whoever's down there or diving under the duvet and praying the intruder goes away. There's a certain comfort in the *if I can't see him then he can't see me* school of thought. I'm suddenly acutely aware just how isolated Oyster Shore is. I'm all alone, miles from anywhere and without any mobile signal. I've seen the films. Scream masks. Blair witches. Mad axemen ...

On the riverbank, no one can hear you scream.

"G'day, little guy! What are you doing here?"

The voice, conversational and very loud in the silence, is unmistakeably Australian and familiar. The storm-surge of dread ebbs, and I descend the stairs as fast as I can without stumbling; and sure enough, framed in the kitchen doorway and gilded by the afternoon sunshine, is the Landrover driver I met earlier. White teeth flash in bronzed skin, and pale smile lines star those striking green eyes again as he beams at me.

"Hey, we meet again!" he says, patting Breakspear. "You may want to rethink your choice of guard dog! He's a beaut, but not really cut out for the job."

"What the hell are you doing in here?" I don't mean to snap but no matter how handsome this man is, or how much my dog seems to like him, he has absolutely no right to wander into the boathouse. He's taken ten years off my life.

His smile fades and he looks stricken. He's also older than I first thought, for now we are in close proximity I can see that his blond curls are frosted with silver and the laughter lines are carved deeply into his tanned skin.

"I'm so sorry I gave you a scare. The door wasn't locked."

I resist the urge to say this doesn't mean *just come on in* because for all I know it might mean exactly that in Cornwall. Or in Australia. For all I know people wander in and out of each other's houses all the time in Trevellan just like they did in nineteen-eighties Ramsay Street.

"I really should be asking what you're doing in here," he continues when I don't say anything. "Thing is, right, this place is private property."

I stare at him. "Why?"

"This is a private shore," he says patiently. "It's not open for visitors, so technically you're trespassing."

"I'm not," I say firmly. "And anyway, I could ask you the same. Are you trespassing? Or squatting?"

His lips twitch and I realise he's trying not to laugh. "Sorry to disappoint, but nothing so exciting. I do the maintenance here, but don't judge me on it, yeah? There's only so much one man can do. I was told to get the place aired, put some milk in the fridge and have the log store filled, so here I am. I'm expecting Scott. Is he your husband?"

Of course. This is the maintenance guy I was told about.

"That's me. Scott's my surname," I tell him. "I'm Lowenna Scott."

He slaps his palm against his forehead. "That'll teach me to not read my emails properly! Now I know where you were heading when I saw you earlier. I'd have given you a lift down if I'd known. I was on my way to get your logs."

"I enjoyed the walk," I say.

"Just as well. You'll be doing a lot of walking living here. Anyway, nice to meet you, Lowenna Scott. I'm Noah Wilson. Caretaker and gardener, among my many jobs."

He holds out his hand and as we shake. Noah's grasp is firm and his smile warm. "Am I forgiven?" he asks.

"If you have a sink plunger," I say. "The bath drain's blocked. And if you can fix the hot water all is forgiven."

He laughs. "I'm sure I can sort that. Least I can do to make up for scaring you."

Noah Wilson is familiar with the boathouse, and once he's located the plunger and cleared the drain, he gives me a brief tour and fills me in on practical details such as where the fuse box is, how to switch the immersion on and the best way to coax the wood burner into life.

"I know it's not that cold, but this place smells damp to me. The log burner's a good background heat and you'll appreciate it in the morning. I can light the range too if you like."

I glace at the cast-iron monstrosity squatting at the far

end of the kitchen. I last saw one of these in use when I was watching Downton Abbey.

"I'm happy to stick with the conventional oven, but the wood burner sounds like a good idea."

"No probs," says Noah. "I'll light it right now and make sure I bring more logs to keep it ticking over."

"You carry firewood all this way?"

Already dreading lugging my bags down, I'm impressed. No wonder Noah's arms are so well-muscled.

"I'm not that much of an iron man! I use the Landy to get up and down to Oyster Shore. It's about the only thing that can cope with what's left of the drive. I can bring your things down later if you like."

"That can't be in your maintenance remit, surely?"

"I've never known anyone rent the boathouse so my remit's open to interpretation. Anyway, it's the least I can do to make up for nearly driving you into a wall and then scaring you just now." Noah sits back on his haunches, arranging kindling and logs like a work of art, and chatting easily about the best way to arrange the logs. While I make coffee he works away and sprinkles instructions with warnings about northern winds making the flue smoke, the risks of chimney fires, and spring tides necessitating sandbags. There's far more to living here than I'd realised. No wonder the rent's cheap.

"Flooding's the reason for the tiled floor," he finishes. "Makes it easier to mop up."

"Are there lots of floods?"

"It can be wild here in the winter," he says as the fire catches. "You've definitely arrived at the best time."

"That must have been a bit of a shock for you, the winter."

He laughs. "Because I'm an Aussie? I should be in shorts

with a surfboard under my arm and chucking shrimps on a barbie?"

Noah Wilson laughs a lot. I find myself warming to him and smiling back.

"Do you wear your hat with corks on while doing all that?" I ask, and he laughs even harder.

"Sure! And we're all drinking tinnies, singing Waltzing Matilda and watching roos hop around."

"Really?"

"No, not really. Sorry to disappoint. How about you? Do you enjoy Morris dancing? Drinking tea? Cucumber sandwiches?"

"I have two left feet, I drink coffee and I hate cucumber. I think that makes me a total failure as a Brit," I confess. "To be honest, Noah, I don't know a great deal about Australia. Only the usual things like the opera house and the wildlife."

"Don't forget Kylie. She's practically our patron saint. You look a lot like her, actually."

I roll my eyes. Being five feet tall and a similar vintage I'm often compared to Kylie and never come out of it well.

"Australia's a great country and the weather's amazing," he's saying, having moved on from Kylie. "My first winter here was a shock. I thought I'd never see the sun again."

"We feel like that every year in England. Sometimes in the summer too."

"Yeah, I can understand that, but when the sun comes out here you're hard pushed to find anywhere better. Oyster Shore's a special place. It's a healing place. You'll love it, trust me."

Beyond the picture window slices of sky float in silvery ribbons and an egret picks at a pile of inky weed.

"It's beautiful," I say. "I can't quite believe my luck being able to live here."

"You might not say that when you're trying to carry your shopping down in a gale," Noah warns. "It's not exactly practical!"

"This was only a summer retreat, wasn't it?"

"Yep. Both this and Oyster House were summer getaways from Vyvyan Court. That's a hotel now. This place and the house are all that's left of the original estate, and I don't think they'll last much longer. The trust that owns it all has little interest in maintaining the place. I guess it's just an investment in the land."

I think of Oyster House weeping paint as the wedding-cake plasterwork is prised apart by ivy, iced chunks falling into the nettles to crumble into nothing. "It's a shame."

"Or maybe it's a blessing, because otherwise this would either be some millionaire's second home or carved up and developed into a rash of holiday homes. At least this way Nature can claim back what's hers. I guess none of us belong here for long anyways. We're only passing through."

As he says this a heron takes flight from the far bank, the silent beat of grey wings lifting it high above the tree-line and into infinity. Noah's right: there is a sense of timelessness here, a feeling that our existence is the briefest blink of an eye. I think of how the house on the riverbank that was once the setting for parties, the jewel in the crown of the wealthy landowners, is now quietly decaying, and the architectural *memento mori* makes me shiver.

"I wonder why the owners abandoned it all those years ago?" I say.

Noah spreads his hands and I'm shocked to find myself

checking for a ring. I look away hastily, hoping he hasn't noticed my eyes flicker to his left hand.

"No idea," says Noah. "My mum could have told you all about that. She was crazy about Cornish history. She did a bunch of work on Trevellan. Mum was definitely the brains of the Wilson family."

"My big sister's the brains in ours." I think of Marina with her nursing degree and the string of letters after her name, a woman who can bring someone back from the brink of death by choosing the right processes and procedures. Her skills put my scribbling into context. "She thinks I've dropped out."

His eyes meet mine. "And have you?"

I pick up a pen and fiddle with it, clicking the nib in and out. "For a while. I want to write a book, and this seems the perfect spot."

Noah raises his coffee mug. "Here's to dropping out."

We chink mugs.

"To dropping out," I say. "Sounds like that applies to you as well?"

"I prefer to say I'm having a gap year several decades too late. Better late than never, right?"

"Definitely better late than never," I agree.

"It's never too late," Noah says firmly. "Make the most of every second you have, Wenna."

Wenna. The old abbreviation of my name sounds different when spoken with his warm accent. It's rich, alien, new, and I like it. It feels as though this is my new identity. I am Wenna Scott who lives in a Cornish boathouse, drinks coffee with handsome neighbours and writes books. The writer part of me is dying to know why Noah Wilson exchanged Australia for Cornwall. He looks like the hero of a novel with his tanned skin, snug blue jeans and boyish smile.

But there's far more to him than good looks; there's a backstory here, and I wonder what it is.

"I sometimes think I've left writing a book far too late," I admit. "Maybe I've already missed my chance?"

Noah sets his mug down on the hearth. Flames leap in the wood burner and he leans across to push the doors shut, sealing dancing ribbons of scarlet and amber behind sooty glass.

"You're in the right place to write books. The other guy did, so why not you?"

I frown. "What other guy?"

"The author who lived here. Years ago. That was what made you go for the boathouse, right?"

"That's the first I've ever heard of it. Are you sure? Who was it? When?"

Noah looks a bit taken aback by my volley of questions. "Sorry, Wenna, I don't know any details, but there was definitely a book written here. I do some gardening for an elderly lady in the village and she mentioned it ages back. Did you really not know?"

I shake my head. "I had absolutely no idea. Nothing came up online."

Noah whistles. "Fate brought you here. That's what Treena, my woo-woo friend from the farm, would say."

"It's certainly a coincidence," I agree cautiously. I daren't get my hopes up because he might be wrong. The letting agent never mentioned anything about literary connections, which would surely be a major plus point for a holiday rental. It's possible Noah's elderly customer is muddled.

"You can ask Treena about it sometime. You're bound to see her wading along the shore. T's big on beachcombing and making things out of her finds."

I recall the girl I saw on the shore. "I think I saw her earlier."

"Really? I thought she and Gareth were heading to the Penhayes market. They're farmers, and their veggie boxes are doing really well. I left you one on the side with some of Treena's scones as a welcome gift."

"Thanks," I say, but my mind isn't on veg boxes or scones. All I can think about is the mystery author at Oyster Shore. I want to ask Noah more about this but he's busy telling me about growers' collectives and organic certificates now, and the moment's passed.

"I'll introduce you to G and T, as they're known," he says. "They're your nearest neighbours. Gareth's family, the Trehunnists, have farmed here for years. Another branch of the family are car dealers and absolutely loaded. They throw great parties."

I'm intending to be an utter hermit and I'm wondering how to explain this without sounding rude when the fire roars and flames shoot up the chimney. Noah leaps forward, fiddling with vents and dampers until the flames are tamed. It's a far cry from adjusting the boost on my flat's central heating.

"You'll get the hang of it. It's worth the effort," he promises.

"I don't doubt that it. It's warmer already," I say. The building also feels more welcoming as timber creaks and settles. It's as though the whole place is exhaling. Is it fanciful to think the boathouse is relieved to be inhabited again?

"So, any ideas who the writer was?" I ask once I've carried our empty mugs through to the kitchen and placed them in the chipped butler's sink. Noah, who has followed me to demonstrate where to switch on the hot water, shrugs apologetically.

"I honestly can't remember. Not a famous name, I'm afraid. They must be very obscure."

I'm thinking of my fledging book idea. The more obscure the author the better, as far as I'm concerned. Imagine if I'm able to breathe life back into their work and conjure them back into existence by preserving their words and thoughts. How incredible would that be?

"There was nothing online about a writer living here," I say carefully, not daring to allow myself to get my hopes up.

"Maybe they were only famous locally," Noah suggests.

"Is that what you heard?"

"I didn't hear much at all – it was just something said in passing. Whoever it was might have had a link to the Trelyons if they were writing in the boathouse, because the Trelyons owned this place and pretty much everything else. You'll find their name all over the place. I'd start there if I wanted to know more about Oyster Shore and a writer."

"Are you a historian?"

" 'fraid not. I'm just a guy from Oz moonlighting as a gardener."

"That's a long way to come to mow lawns."

"I'm in global demand for my exceptional mowing! Truth is I usually do my best to teach art to high school students. Gardening makes a refreshing change since plants don't flick paint or backchat."

I recall the exquisite carvings I'd spotted outside the caravan. Of course. Noah Wilson's an artist.

"I saw your carvings outside the caravan earlier. They're beautiful."

He looks pleased. "Hey, thanks! Although my great

granny was really the artist in our family, or so Mum found that when she got into Ancestry. It was a cool find, although I bet she'd secretly hoped to find a convict or two. That makes you royalty in Oz!"

"Should I bow?"

"You're good. Mum didn't get as far back as convicts, but her research did take her back to Cornwall in the early twentieth century. This is where her side of the family hail from, and she was desperate to find out more."

"And did she?"

A cloud passes over his face. "Mum passed away before she had the chance to finish. She wanted to see this part of the world so badly, but there was never the right time. I thought she was obsessed – especially when she made me promise I'd come here after she was gone. Oyster Shore was all she talked about at the end, and not a lot of it made sense. She had Alzheimer's, you see, Wenna. Jeez. It's the cruellest bloody thing. Her sharp mind and memories were totally rubbed away."

"I'm sorry," I say. "That must have been awful."

"Yeah, it was tough. The illness took hold so fast. It was like she aged several decades overnight, and she was so confused. There were still flashes of her now and then, but they became less and less, and then they stopped altogether. The day she thought I was a stranger wasn't great ..." He pauses and collects himself. "Anyway, she didn't last long after that, and it seemed as good a time as any to roll the dice. I made the trip to Cornwall for her and I've stayed on far longer than I ever intended. It probably sounds a little whack, but there's something about this place that feels familiar, as though I knew it already. Maybe it was the family roots calling to me?"

"Maybe it's ancestral memories? A sense of belonging to the land?" I offer, struck by hearing my own thoughts echoed by this near-stranger.

"My Aboriginal mates would definitely agree with that, and I think Mum would feel the same way too. She was adamant I should finish her research. There was a relative way back who sold her engagement ring to get to Oz, and Mum was really keen on that story – she called it our spin on the ten-pound poms – but I've not got round to doing any more work on it. I guess I prefer looking to the future."

I have the impression there's more to this narrative, but Noah falls silent, studying the riverbank with an intensity which carries him far beyond rising water and drifting swans. His mother's death must be recent because sadness lies beneath the sunshine of his smile like the melancholy hint of autumn in late summer mornings.

Noah turns back to me and I watch him swim through past pain to surface in the present.

"Mum was a history teacher, so this kind of thing was right up her street. She spent hours on it, and there's a bunch of information about this area in her notes. You can have a look if you like. There might be something about your mysterious writer. You never know."

"That would be brilliant. Thanks."

"No worries. I think you're better suited to sifting through it all than me. Teaching might be the family profession, but I'm happier with a sketchbook than a notebook."

"You take after your great-grandmother, then?"

"I'd love to think that was the case. Mum once said if she'd lived now she would have been well known."

"Would you like that? To be well known, I mean?" I ask, thinking about my own cherished dreams of academic and literary recognition. David was always talking about building author brands and making household names: the bigger the better as far as he was concerned. It's probably one of the reasons I'm drawn to writers who lived, worked and died in obscurity. I'll be their advocate now, and make sure their neglected voices are heard once again.

"No fear! It's enough for me just being here and enjoying what I do. I have a roof over my head, a few good friends, great surf not too far away, and awesome wildlife. I can forage for food and whittle some chainsaw animals and," he smiles, his teeth white against the tanned skin, "sometimes I even get to deliver logs to interesting new arrivals who make me coffee. It doesn't get much better than that."

I think of my ex with his new sports cars, designer clothes and insatiable drive for success. With him it's always the next book deal, the next author, the next acquisition, the next something else. What Noah Wilson cherishes would be beyond his comprehension.

"Just wait until you see the wildlife here, Wenna," Noah continues, his green eyes lit with enthusiasm. "There's a badger sett in the woods, deer that graze the banks and even otters upstream."

"I've never seen otters before."

"You'll see lots here," Noah promises. He glances across at the clock and whistles. "I'd better be getting on. I've got a few veg boxes to deliver for Treena. If you tell me when's good we can hook up to put your things in the Landy so I can drive them down. Is tomorrow too late?"

"Tomorrow's fine. I'll get a few bits for tonight."

It's already late afternoon. Long shadows yawn across sand already succumbing to the tide. The egrets have vanished, and although the sun is still above the riverbank it won't be long until it slips behind the far side of the valley.

"Do you want a lift up?" Noah asks.

"Thanks, but I think Breakspear could do with another walk."

We both glance at the spaniel, asleep by the wood burner with all four paws twitching in the grips of doggy dreams of rabbits and squirrels. It would be hard pushed to find a dog less inclined to move.

I laugh. "Okay. The truth is I need the exercise after all the snacking on my drive down. Breaky doesn't want to move."

"He's well at home," Noah says approvingly. "Animals always know when a place is good. At the risk of sounding like Treena, I've always thought the boathouse has a nice energy."

Breaky does seem settled, unlike his strange moment on the beach when he spotted the beachcomber. Maybe he was picking up on my nerves? I was tense from the drive and he's always been sensitive to my moods. Yes, that must be it.

Once Noah has departed, leaving his mobile number to arrange the bag swap, I stack the wood burner and wander through the boathouse, claiming possession. I'm tempted to make another coffee and curl up in the armchair with a book. My drive was tiring, and the river, fully on the flood now and creeping gently upstream, is hypnotic. I could sit by the window for hours hoping for another arrow of blue or the flicker of an otter. I wonder who else once stood in this spot watching the water flow by. Was it the mysterious writer Noah mentioned? Did he also think these ribboned channels look like bird's feet or struggle to describe so many shades of green?

I need to fetch my laptop because I *have* to start writing. I also have a burning desire to scoot about the Internet and see what information I can glean about this place. I'll drive to Trevellan, pick up some supplies and have a wander round the village. Maybe treat myself to a pub meal. After all, a new home, new friend, and a new book idea are all reasons to celebrate.

I reach for Breakspear's lead.

"Come on, boy," I say, feeling excited. "Let's explore!"

6

THE PRESENT

Cornwall

Lowenna

My grandmother's village is tiny. I parked outside the Londis, a time capsule of a shop selling everything from white sliced bread to fishing bait, and which closes in the afternoon. Abandoning hope of finding supplies or gleaning any information about the mystery author from helpful locals, Breakspear and I explore the narrow streets instead.

My first port of call is the cottage where Granny May grew up. I pause outside and imagine her as little girl in pinafore and pigtails helping her mother, scary Elizabeth Penwurthy, peg out washing or perhaps playing with her little brother. How had an entire family managed to live in such a tiny cottage? It was little more than two rooms. My niece and nephews all had their own bedrooms; I couldn't imagine they'd be impressed with topping and tailing like the generations of Penwurthies who'd lived and died in the narrow house with its bowed white walls and lichen-speckled roof. Cobble Cottage was where my granny had been born. It was where she had waved her brother off to war and where she'd woken up on the morning she left to marry Grandpa Bill. This cottage was where my family came from, and my heart ached at being a stranger.

Today the cottage is a holiday home, a sage-painted and Disneyfied take on a fisherman's dwelling. There are no signs of the outdoor privy or the mould-freckled walls Granny had remembered, and no evidence that the Penwurthies had lived there for generations. Still hoping to catch a glimpse of the world my Granny had known I turn into School Lane to retrace her journey to lessons, but the red brick Victorian school has also been transformed into a beautiful second home. Only carved letters declaring *Boys* and *Girls* above the doors at each end of the building hint of the days when scraped-kneed children shrieked in the playground, intent on games of hopscotch and tag, and stern schoolmasters rapped knuckles with rulers.

The schoolmaster's house is also a holiday let and, according to the sign on the blue front door, is managed by the same agency that cares for the boathouse. The same is also true of the Methodist church, the post office, the sweet shop and countless others. I retrace my steps feeling disheartened; it wasn't only the Penwurthies who'd left Trevellan, then, for everyone and everything has been displaced. Is there anyone left here Granny May might have known? Any old Trevellan families remaining?

I'd intended to explore the church, but St Nun's is perched above the village, clinging onto the side of the valley with grim determination, and my legs are already protesting from the climb from the boathouse to the car. It's a visit for another time, and instead I visit the harbourside war memorial where my great-uncle's name is carved alongside those of his contemporaries. Then there are the names of all the men who died in the First World War, friends of my great-grandfather, and far too many of them share surnames with those who fell three decades later. So much loss in such a tiny place must have broken the heart of the village. No wonder my great-grandfather suffered black moods and night terrors for the rest of his life.

The tide is coming in. Across the water Penhayes beach is a slim band of yellow, and the glassy sea is petrol-hued, reflecting the sky until it's hard to distinguish just where air melts into water. The world feels nebulous, and as I sit in the window seat of the Trelyon Arms, watching the car ferry shuttle across the river mouth, it strikes me that the infinity of crossings is straight from Homer; a never-ending journey destined to be repeated until the end of time, the clanking chain the backing track to life in the village, and the ferry its beating heart. Without it Trevellan would end in a watery nowhere; there would be no reason to visit and no reason for the place to exist at all.

Needing to pull my thoughts away from melancholy, I descend steep granite steps to a sickle of beach and throw Breakspear's ball until my arm aches and he's more sand than spaniel. The exercise and sea air make me hungry, and the scent of fried food wafting down from the pub make my mouth water. Fish and chips eaten overlooking the sea will be perfect, and the lure of the Trelyon Arms is impossible to resist and I'm still working my way through what looks like a battered whale accompanied by a tonne of chipped potatoes as the evening falls and the fishing boats return.

"Everything all right with that?" The landlord, hands full of empty glasses, pauses by my table and nods at my plate. "Fresh yesterday," he adds. "You won't get better, not even at Stein's. Davey Tuckey caught it." He points to a stocky man with an enormous beard who raises his glass at me.

"It's lovely," I say. My stomach feels fit to burst. Maybe I could ask for a doggy bag?

"Are you staying in the village?" The landlord deposits the glasses on the bar. "If you are, then come back on Friday for curry night. Folk come from Penhayes for our tikka masala."

Penhayes is only half a mile across the river. I recall Granny May's comments about Fowey being a foreign land in Cornish miles, and smile.

"If I'm not still digesting this lot, I'll definitely come back for a curry night. I'm not on holiday though; I've moved here. I'm Lowenna and this is Breakspear."

"Welcome to Trevellan, Lowenna! I'm Pete Symons. Moved here last year myself with the wife."

"Bleddy incomers," says fisherman Davey. "Least Lowenna has a Cornish name."

Pete grins. "Bleddy incomer *who owns the pub*."

Davey holds out his glass. "Might as well make the blooming emmet richer!"

"You'll soon see how welcoming it is here for new arrivals," remarks Pete as he pulls a pint.

"Actually, my family are from Trevellan." I feel the need to stake my right to be here. "My granny was a Penwurthy."

"Aye, that's a local name," agrees Davey. "My second cousin married a Penwurthy. That makes us related."

"Don't get too excited. Everyone's related in Cornwall," Pete warns me. "Isn't that right, Davey?"

Davey mumbles something into his beard. It doesn't sound complimentary

"Did you know Lowenna's folks, Miss Trewen?" says Landlord Pete, turning to the elderly woman who has put down her book to listen in. With a beak of a nose, piercing dark eyes and thick mane of white hair rising in a widow's peak, her alert manner brings to mind a bird of prey.

"There were lots of Penwurthies here back in the day. Strange to think they've all gone now." The elderly woman studies me intently, her sharp eyes narrowing. "You do have a look of them about you. They were small, and had unusual eyes like yours, dark blue. Curly hair too, I seem to recall, although the ones I knew were dark-haired. Which ones were your Penwurthies?"

"May Penwurthy was my grandmother. She lived here with her parents, Elizabeth and Marrick. Did you know her?"

"Not well. May was quite a lot older than me, but my father was crew on the Penwurthy fishing boat for a while. Their boy died in the Second World War, which left the boat with nobody to work it when your great-grandfather couldn't manage. I think it was sold about the same time the daughter married and moved away."

"That would have been my grandmother. She moved to Fowey when she married my grandfather. I'd love to find out more about my family. I'm staying at Oyster Shore. Do you know it?"

Pete dives in and scoops up my plate. "Oyster Shore? Never heard of it."

"That's because you're an incomer," Davey reminds him.

"Oyster Shore's on the Penhayes estuary. Lots of oysters there, see."

"Who owns them?" Pete asks, no doubt wondering if he can help himself and double the pub's profits.

Davey shrugs. "Dunno. The place used to belong to the big estate. There's a house down on the shore. Not in that, are you, maid? Place is a bleddy ruin."

"No. I'm renting the boathouse."

Davey's shaggy brows shoot towards his knitted hat. "Hell! Is that still standing? The place where the King used to take girls so he could—"

"Yes!" I say swiftly. "It's still there."

"Christ! Rather you than me. It's an unlucky place."

"Rubbish!" barks Miss Trewen. "You know better than to repeat silly stories, Davey Tuckey!"

"Sorry, Miss T, but it's what Mother always said."

"You know the place too, Selina?" Pete says.

She nods. "It was part of the Vyvyan Estate when I was a girl, but that's long broken up now."

Davey is tugging his beard as though this helps pull out the memories. "Ma told us to keep away. People had drowned there, she said, and it was unlucky."

"More likely she didn't want you getting into trouble with the Trelyons," says Miss Trewen tartly. "You always were one for trouble. I seem to recall you fell in the village pond on May Day."

While the other drinkers tease Davey about his schooldays, the older woman turns to me. "Don't let their daft talk worry you, my dear. Oyster Shore's a lovely spot and rich in history. I always admired the boathouse when I used to row by as a girl."

"I heard the last lot who rented that did a runner because it was so bad," says the barmaid, who's eavesdropping.

"I heard they saw a ghost," says another local.

"More like they ran up a big tab at the bar and didn't want to pay it," Pete scoffs. "And talking of bar tabs, yours needs settling, Owen Trebilcock! When are you intending to do that?"

"Dreckly," says Owen. He holds out his glass. "After one more? And one for the lads, on me. What do you say?"

"I say I must be mad," sighs the landlord, but he refills the glass anyway before fishing a stick of chalk out from a pot and scribbling a tally mark onto a beam where it joins at least twenty others.

"Treena Trehunnist says Oyster Shore is haunted," says the barmaid.

Owen Trebilcock snorts into his pint. Foam dots his beard.

"That one's away with the fairies. Poor bleddy Gareth. They'd have burned her at the stake in the old days, all that picking herbs and brewing spells. And she's made him go organic. They'll be bleddy vegans next, you watch."

There's a ripple of horror.

"Treena's an aromatherapist," protests the barmaid, but nobody's listening; they're all far too busy having a good gossip. Noah's beachcombing neighbour sounds more interesting by the minute.

Fisherman Davey turns to me. "You wouldn't get me staying there. Rent yourself a nice caravan with a sea view. My cousin owns the site at the top of the village, and since we're related he'll do you a deal."

Now I get it. Scare the incomer to the campsite. And to

think that for a moment I was almost sucked in by their tall tales.

The landlord winks at me. "I've never met such a superstitious bunch, what with piskies and knockers and sea monsters! You'll be scaring Lowenna away at this rate."

"I'm not scared," I say quickly. Far from it. I'm loving Oyster Shore with its air of mystery. I'm not put off in the slightest, and I can hardly wait to get back and make some notes.

"Mock all you like, Pete Symons, but one thing you learn at sea is not to tempt Fate or disrespect superstition," Davey says gravely. "My grandad always said somebody drowned there a long time ago. Maybe that's why it's unlucky."

Somewhere, submerged deep in childhood memories, I recall Granny May's tale of a drowned girl and weeping willows. Was it Oyster Shore she was describing all those years ago? Suddenly I don't feel quite so brave.

"People drown all the time in Cornwall," Landlord Pete scoffs. "It's a hazard of being surrounded by water."

"I heard a writer used to live there too. Is that right?" I ask Davey.

He lifts his hat and scratches his head. "I'm not one for books, maid. Maybe. Perhaps he cursed the place?"

Sensing a story, I lean forward. "Why would he do that?"

"I dunno. Writer's block? Bad reviews?"

"Trust me, all writers are cursed with those at some point," I say. "It *is* intriguing, though. There's got to be a reason nobody lives there any more."

"All the local kids stay well away. They don't make camps or play there," Owen Trebilcock adds. "Makes you wonder why."

"They can't be bothered to walk that far, and there's no

mobile signal, that's why. My kids thought they were hard done by if they had to walk home from school," says Pete. "There's no way they'd have trekked a mile or so down to a riverbank, not when they could have a sneaky fag in the bus shelter."

Owen reaches into his pocket and pulls put a packet of cigarettes. "Talking of, anyone coming outside for a smoke?"

"The only thing that surprises me is that nobody's already developed the place if it's prime waterfront," Pete says once the fishermen have departed into the beer garden. "It's only a matter of time, I suppose."

"I hope not. It's a beautiful spot and the wildlife's amazing. I saw a kingfisher earlier," I begin, but Pete's attention has turned to chalking up the next day's specials on a board and arguing with Selina Trewen about the position of the apostrophe in Ploughman's Lunch.

"How do I know how many bloody ploughmen?" he grumbles as he scrubs out the first attempt. "They haven't been in yet, have they?"

"Is the place you're staying in really falling down?" the barmaid asks me. "If it's bad, my mum does B and B."

"It's not falling down at all!" I say firmly. "It's just a bit dated, which is why it didn't let very easily. There's no wifi either."

"You're staying in a place without wifi? I'd literally die. What will you do, stuck there all on your own?"

"Walk up and down to my car mostly," I admit. "Anyway, I'm not on my own. I've got Breakspear and there's a maintenance guy who keeps an eye on the place and delivers logs."

"Oh! You must mean Noah Wilson! He can keep an eye on me any time! He's hot, for an older guy!" she giggles.

"Get in the queue, Julie Heller!"

Another girl, sitting at the far end of the bar working her way through a huge plate of pasta, glowers at us. Laden fork paused an inch from her mouth, she adds, "I saw him first."

I start to laugh, but when her eyes narrow I realise she isn't joking but is genuinely staking her claim. Yikes.

"All's fair in love and fit men, Fi," says Julie airily. "Although Lowenna's got the advantage since she lives nearest to his van."

Fi spears a forkful of pasta and shoots me an evil look.

"I'm just here to write," I say quickly so she can be in no doubt of my intentions. "Noah's virtue is safe from me."

"It's not from *me*," Julie sighs. "And it definitely isn't from Fi. She's been stalking him for months."

"I'm not stalking him. I just like walking up the lane where his van is," Fi huffs.

"You probably think we're all quite mad, Lowenna," Julie says, "and we probably are, but living in the arse end of nowhere we don't get out much. A fit new man is the most excitement we've had for decades. No wonder all the girls in Trevellan are fantasising about travelling Down Under!"

I brace myself for some awful Carry On-style quip, but luckily Julie's attention turns to serving her next customer and scary Fi is still chewing. Is Noah Wilson aware of the stir his presence causes? Something about his gentle manner and kind smile tells me he has no idea of the effect he has on women, and that if he had he wouldn't exploit it. Noah has the air of a man who is content with his own company.

While I've been eating and chatting twilight has crept in. The first stars freckle the sky. Reluctant to leave, I order a cappuccino, which Pete sets about making with great flamboyance and much frothing of milk and grinding of beans. By the time he's satisfied with the dusting of chocolate powder in the shape of a star several more customers have settled down for supper and the fishermen return, bringing with them the scent of night-time and tobacco.

"The Oyster House must be in a bad way nowadays." Miss Trewen joins me. The candlelight shadows her lined face and casts deep pools of shade beneath her eyes, rendering her timelessly ancient and wise.

"It's not great. It must have been so beautiful once."

"Oh, it was. It really was." She gestures to the seat opposite. "May I?"

"Please do."

She slides into the pew and pushes the cushions aside. "At my age it doesn't do to slump. You never know if you'll be able to get up again." She holds out her hand. "Selina Trewen. Cat lady and spinster of the parish."

"Lowenna Scott. Dog lady and also spinster of the parish," I reply as we shake and Selina arches a pencilled-on eyebrow.

"That will certainly ruffle a few feathers around here – especially if a certain Noah Wilson is involved."

"You know Noah?"

"I do indeed. He does my garden. It's too much for me these days – damn nuisance getting old – so Noah helps out, and very pleasant it is too having him about the place." She settles back into her seat and fixes me with a beady gaze. "So, Oyster Shore. I trust the tall tales haven't put you off."

"Not so far, although the fisherman seemed to know quite a few."

"Well, yes. Local legends and a few drinks are a potent combination. I used to teach Davey Tuckey, and he always had a powerful imagination – mostly regarding making up excuses as to why he wasn't in class when I knew full well he'd gone out to set some lobster pots."

"You were a teacher?"

"I'm *still* a teacher. I don't think one ever escapes from pedagogy. I taught at the village school from the sixties right until they closed it. Most people of a certain age in this village were in my classroom at some point. That's why they don't get away with anything and can all use apostrophes correctly! Unlike our new landlord!"

"I walked up to the old school earlier on. My granny went there."

"Yes, she would have done. Did you see the schoolhouse? It was my home for many happy years. It's a private dwelling now; some banker from Surrey owns it and visits once a year. That's progress, they say, but it makes me sad. Generations of schoolmasters lived there with their families back in the day when teaching was a respected profession ... but you don't want to listen to me rambling on about the good old days. You want to know about Gerald Snowe."

"Do I?"

"I assume so. I heard you asking Davey about a writer at Oyster Shore. You may as well have asked him about Henry the Eighth's foreign policy or how to split an atom."

I'm not sure quite what to say to this. I'm not sure I have a clue about Henry the Eighth's foreign policy either. Getting divorces and cutting off heads is about as far as my Tudor history extends, and atom-splitting isn't my forte.

Fortunately, Selina Trewen isn't expecting an answer. She is in full teaching mode and gearing up to deliver a lesson on local history. "Gerald Snowe is the name of the writer you're referring to. He lived at Vyvyan Court during the Great War and into the early nineteen-twenties."

"I thought the Trelyon family owned the property?"

"That's correct, but the estate was entailed, which meant it would be inherited by the nearest male in the line even if there was a direct female descendant. So in the early nineteen-hundreds the inheritance went to a very distant member of the family and one who was not keen to take up the reins of a country estate."

"Why not?" I ask, intrigued. For most people, inheriting a stately home would be a dream come true.

"I imagine because an estate like Vyvyan would be dreadfully costly to maintain. In those days it would have required an army of servants and gardeners to run it. That's why English aristocrats were all trying frantically to marry American heiresses."

"Like the Earl of Grantham in Downton Abbey."

"And the real-life Duke of Marlborough. These big estates were money pits. Anyway, the new Viscount Trelyon leased Vyvyan out and stayed in London. The Snowe family rented Vyvyan in the early nineteen-hundreds, back when my father was a boy. Pa used to play in the grounds with the village children, and sometimes the family's son, Gerald, would join in. Father said he was a sickly lad who couldn't keep up and they used to run away from him, all except for the schoolmaster's son, who had a kind heart. I think my father felt bad in later life about teasing Gerald. Children can be cruel, you know."

I picture a gaggle of Trevellan's youngsters tearing through the woods. Boys in hobnail boots and with scabbed knees and falling-down socks running through the trees while a pale lad in a sailor suit scurried to keep up. Were my Penwurthy great-grandparents among them? Did they know this Gerald Snowe? Did they tease him, or were they his friends?

"By the turn of the last century the direct Trelyon line had all but died out. Too much fast living and besporting will do that, you know." Selina Trewen sits a little straighter and pulls her shoulders back. "I myself seldom eat lunch, always go to bed by eleven and never drink alcohol. Indulgence does nobody any good."

I glance at my coffee. This is about as decadent as my life gets lately, and I'm certainly not about to besport with anyone, no matter what Julie and scary Fi might think. I'm guilty of slumping and I attempt to sit a little taller. Selina must have been a terrifying teacher.

"Who owns Vyvyan Court now?" I ask.

"Certainly not the Trelyons. It's part of a hotel chain."

"But you said it was entailed? How could it be sold?"

"The entail must have been broken at some point, probably in the twenties, which was when the estate was sold off piecemeal. The First World War caused all kinds of problems with the inheritance of these great estates. No young men left, you see, and nobody to maintain them. Things had to change. Progress, as I said earlier. None of us can turn back time. The past is a foreign country, as they say."

Sometimes that's a good thing – and it isn't nearly far enough away, I think, as I sip my coffee.

"Can you tell me anything more about Gerald Snowe? What did he write?"

"I'm rather ashamed to say I know very little about him. I believe he spent much of his childhood here, but he vanishes from history in the nineteen-twenties and I don't think he stayed here long once the Great War was over. For someone who set his greatest and only work in Cornwall he doesn't appear to be very attached to the place. He's not Trevellan's answer to du Maurier, if that's what you were hoping."

"I suppose I was."

"Then you're out of luck," Selina says briskly. "He must have been out of print for over a century. I do recall my father saying the book was very literary, and he rated it highly even though he didn't like Gerald very much." She pauses, her eyes clouding as she recalls a conversation with her long-gone father. "Oh dear, I can't remember why he disliked him. What a bother! Anyway, I expect Gerald lorded it over him. My father was a blacksmith's son, you see, and social order was something he was always very conscious of. He wouldn't have liked being reminded of his place: childhood feuds are seldom forgotten, especially in a small place like this. Pa did well, though. He got an education and went into law. He was a gentleman by the end of his life even if he'd never started off that way."

"So Gerald's book was good?" I nudge Selina gently back on topic.

"Sorry, my dear. I was reminiscing. Yes, the book was very good, according to Father. I think it was quite the talk of the village at the time, having a literary sensation in our midst. Isn't it sad to think it's forgotten now? I wonder why some authors stand the test of time and others fade away?"

If I hadn't worked in publishing I'd be wondering this too, but after years in the industry I know that good luck plays just as big a part in the success of a book as talent. David liked to tip the odds by calling in a favour with the right celebrity or journalist, which never seems quite fair.

"Can you remember what Gerald Snowe's book was called?"

Selina's brows draw together.

"Blast! I can't. Isn't old age an absolute bore? He fell out of fashion long before I was born. *At Oyster Shore*? *By Oyster*

Shore? It's definitely something like that, and the story was set there too. If you're interested in finding out some more it'd be worth a trip across the water to see Hamish Pendragon."

"*Hamish Pendragon*?"

"I don't imagine for one minute that's his real name," she chuckles, seeing my open mouth. "But he's a wonderful character, and a Cornish bard to boot. Hamish owns an absolute treasure trove of a book shop in Penhayes, and there's not much he doesn't know about this county and its literature. He'll have all your early edition du Mauriers and Quiller Couches, and he might be able to lay his hands on a Snowe. Even if he can't, he's bound to know something useful that'll help you."

"That's fantastic. Thank you." I can hardly wait to take a trip to Penhayes, now a blur of spilled light in the dark river and one which I hope contains all kinds of secrets about my new home and the mysterious Gerald Snowe.

"My pleasure," says Selina. "And don't let all those daft stories about ghosts and curses put you off. Most of those were spread by smugglers to stop people sticking their noses in. Creeks are handy for moving contraband – both then and now. I've always found Oyster Shore beautiful. There's a sense of the autumnal there that owes nothing to the seasons and everything to its isolation."

She's right. 'Autumnal' perfectly encapsulates the suite of emotions I would have chosen to identify with the riverbank. A timeless beauty tinged with sadness. Weeping willows and slow waters. Lonely gulls and empty sand. Tides that can never stay.

We talk a little about literature, but Selina is keen to be home in time for 'Book at Bedtime' on Radio Four, and my coffee is finished. Not wanting to cost Pete potential customers I pick up Breakspear's lead and leave with Selina. We part by the war memorial, where I promise to keep her up to speed with anything I might discover.

"I keep thinking there's something important that I've missed," she says. "It's dreadfully frustrating. Ah well, if I remember whatever it is I've forgotten I'll make sure to tell Noah. He can pass it on."

"Please don't tell scary Fi if you do that," I beg.

"Don't let her worry you. Fiona's got a heart of gold and her bark's worse than her bite. Her mother's just the same. They'll eat out of your hand if you buy your groceries in their shop. Anyway, can't stand here chatting all night. I'll miss my programme."

"Goodnight, and thanks again," I say, but Selina's already gone, swallowed up by the deep shadows which muster in the unlit street. I stare after her, but in the thick darkness it's as though she'd never existed. One of the first things I invest in will be a powerful torch. It's going to be pitch-black in the woods. I'm very glad I have my dog at my side and a slice of moon to guide me back to the car, for tall tales or not, the talk of ghosts and curses stays with me long after the lights of the village vanish from my rear-view mirror.

7

THE PRESENT

Cornwall

Lowenna

"Please don't worry, Mum. I'm fine. The river's idyllic."

I pull a face at Breakspear sitting by the door and looking fed up. It's a perfect morning for a walk, he says. Hurry up! He'll be lucky. My mother, convinced her youngest daughter is having a breakdown, won't be fobbed off so easily.

"Rivers are damp. The whole of Cornwall's damp," she sniffs. "It'll set off your asthma, Lowenna."

"It's not damp in the boathouse. There's a lovely wood burner and the place is toasty. Anyway, I haven't had an asthma attack since I was five."

I can't see Mum, but I know she's looking in the mirror and grimacing at her pained reflection.

"You're miles from anywhere, and without proper phone reception. What if something happens?"

"There *is* reception if I put the phone in the right spot. That's how I could see you'd been calling me."

I've learned that unless I prop my phone against the window, where it may or may not pick up a single capricious bar of signal, I'm definitely incommunicado. Bliss.

"I've got neighbours too,' I add. 'One's helping me bring all my cases down later. The other's an organic farmer. His wife's a ..."

I pause. What did Julie say Treena was? 'White witch' was one of the descriptions, but if I mention this Mum will freak out and imagine I've been kidnapped by a cult.

"An aromatherapist." The word pops back into my head. Phew.

"Well, that's nice," Mum says grudgingly. "I had a lovely aromatherapy massage at the health club the other day. Maybe you should book one? It's wonderful for stress."

"Maybe." I have absolutely no intention of doing this. I can't think of anything worse than some total stranger seeing all my flabby bits and rubbing oil into them. That's more likely to elevate my stress levels than lower them.

"So what will you do today?" Mum is asking.

I lean my head against the cool glass of the picture window. Go into town and buy a decent torch is high on the list. It's a long and very dark walk to the boathouse at night, and last night the iPhone's thin beam simply hadn't cut it. Once a few footsteps away from the fading interior lights of my car the darkness had intensified and a swathe of thick cloud extinguished any helpful moonlight. As I'd tripped and stumbled on the unfamiliar path the trees either side had seemed to press forwards as though eager to see what I might make of any rustling in the undergrowth, and blackness yawned before me. When I'd passed Oyster House an owl screeched, taking several years off my life and making my heart play pinball with my ribs. A big flashlight was called for, and I'd reached the boathouse with relief, and running rather than walking.

I'd lit the wood burner, made a hot chocolate and curled up on the sofa, reluctant to climb the steep stairs to my attic room. Cosy by the wood burner and with Breakspear slumped across my feet, I'd pulled one of the throws up to my chin and closed my eyes, only waking when soft fingers of sunlight caressed my face and the crying of gulls drew me from a deep sleep.

Life began early on the estuary, and as I'd watched the light filtering through the trees turning from pink to tawny to gold I knew it was going to be a beautiful day. The sun lifted the morning mist from the river and my spirits rose too. Warmed by the glowing embers of the fire and snug in my nest of throws, I felt I could laugh at myself for being so nervous. A new day meant a new start.

The tide was in and the river flowed lazily past the fringe of aspens and willows draped over the opposite bank. A herring gull bobbed on the glassy surface, and higher up a buzzard circled in the new day. I'd let Breakspear outside and made coffee, sipping it by the window and wondering whether the mysterious Gerald Snowe had once stood where I did now. Had he included this view in the literary masterpiece Selina Trewen described? I was certain he must have. It would be impossible to live here and not be inspired by the river.

"Lowenna? Are you still there? Hello?"

My attention has flowed away with the tide. Deep in thought about forgotten novels I've completely missed what my mother has been saying.

"Sorry. I was watching the river."

"When you can drag your attention away from it, I was asking what you're doing today."

"I thought I might go into Penhayes," I say.

The town is big enough to have a chandlery where I can find a decent torch. Of course, this is just an excuse, because what I really want to do is find Hamish Pendragon and spend hours in his shop, rummaging through second-hand books, sniffing the yellowed pages and running my fingertips over cracked spines. Is there anywhere more magical than a bookshop?

"Penhayes is very smart these days. There should be some lovely shops and probably an artisan deli too," Mum says approvingly.

I think of Trevellan's empty houses and Selina Trewen's sadness that the school has long been closed.

"Great. I'm all out of olives and what I could really do with is some organic hummus."

She sighs. "Could you still do with Granny May's box? Because I've found it."

"That's amazing, Mum! Thank you so much!"

"It's not me you need to thank. Your poor stepfather was in the attic for hours rooting around. Eric came down filthy and covered in cobwebs. I've no idea what he was doing up there for so long."

I suspect Eric was enjoying some well-deserved time out with the spiders and assorted junk.

"Tell him the drinks are on me," is all I say. "Oh, Mum, I'm so pleased. That's brilliant!"

"I'm glad you think so. It all looks like junk to me. I can't imagine why I kept that box all this time. It must be because Mother was so funny about it."

"She always said it was worth a fortune."

Mum snorts. "It's clear where you got your imagination from! There's nothing in that box but a load of old rubbish. I'll pop it in the post tomorrow. What's the address of this place you're renting?"

I hesitate. As much as I'm longing to see Granny May's treasures I don't entirely trust my mother not to *accidentally* pass my address on to David. She means well, but the very last thing I want is him to make a pilgrimage here, armed with flowers and empty promises.

"I'm not sure the postie makes it this far. Maybe the pub will take it for me?"

"Don't be ridiculous, Lowenna! You're in Cornwall, not the Congo. The postman will know exactly where to leave it. Now, what's the address?"

"The Boathouse, Oyster Shore, Trevellan," I say, already picturing her texting it to David.

"I'll send Eric to the post office first thing. He needs to pick up some pieces for dinner – we're having the Donaldsons over. Did I tell you Amy's got two children now?"

The Donaldsons are Mum's next-door neighbours. Amy and I might have grown up together, but all we have in common is parents either side of a party wall.

"Just a few times," I say, rolling my eyes at Breakspear and tuning out as Mum proceeds to tell me about Amy's new car and the house she and her husband are buying in Milton

Keynes. It's like hearing about somebody who lives on the moon.

Call ended, I take a quick shower before dressing in shorts, vest top and walking boots. The day is already warm, and a hike up to the lane will be hot work. A text arrives from Noah offering to meet me at the top to collect my bags, and I ping a reply arranging to do this in the afternoon. Then I lock the boathouse and watch Breakspear race ahead into the woods. I'm filled with optimism. Everything's going to work out beautifully. I have a subject for my book and headspace to work on it. Coming here was meant to be.

I sing along to the radio at the top of my voice as I drive to Trevellan. Today I reverse easily for other drivers, proof I'm practically a local, and my confidence soars. I pass clusters of cottages, post boxes mounted in crumbling walls and gateways hidden behind verdant grasses, all picture postcard-worthy and the cause of frequent stops to snap pictures (not so local after all, perhaps). Once on the clanking ferry I stop the engine, wind the window down and let the salty breeze fill the car and my lungs. Even this short time on the water is bliss. Sunlight bounces from the water and small pleasure boats are scattered all the way down the estuary and peppered across the bay. Children crab on pontoons, dangling lines with great concentration, and day visitors lean against the railings eating chips or posing for photographs to grace Facebook profiles or gather dust on sideboards.

Penhayes is a picturesque warren of narrow streets which hug the river and wind their way along to the main quayside. Between the houses narrow alleys frame perfect views of bright blue water. Some are cluttered with lobster pots and piles of weed-straggled nets while others, generally those running between immaculate houses with sage-painted windows and romantic names like Sea Thrift and Tide's Edge, boast weathered oars propped up artily beside lead planters brimming with bright blooms. In contrast to sleepy Trevellan, Penhayes is buzzing with activity and, just as my mother had predicted, shops that wouldn't be out of place in Chelsea.

The holiday atmosphere in the busy town is contagious, and once I've bought a torch and peered into several gift shops, Breakspear and I share a pasty while sitting on damp steps leading down to the water. The smell of salt and chips tugs me back through time until I'm a child again, happy in this place where there were no broken hearts or disappointments. If only we could stay that way and freeze time like a photograph to keep these perfect moments close for ever. Maybe that was what Gerald Snowe tried to do in his book? I hope I'll soon find out.

I brush crumbs from my bare legs.

"Let's find this bookshop," I say to Breakspear.

But Pendragon Books proves elusive, and I wander aimlessly up and down the street on the riverfront before retracing my steps to the pasty shop, where my enquiries are met with surprise.

"Don't you want a proper bookshop? Try in Fore Street, love. Left and first right."

"Proper bookshop?"

"Modern books. New ones." The shopkeeper leans forwards and lowers her voice as though inviting me into a conspiracy. "Like *Fifty Shades*. They had that. We all bought a copy of it. You might enjoy it."

I'm not sure what to say to this. Do I look like the kind of girl who's seeking whips and cable ties? Unless this carrier bag from the hardware store is a local code?

"I'm looking for a specific old book," I say hastily. "I was told Pendragon's sell second-hand books."

The capped head bobs agreement. "And third and fourth hand, I wouldn't wonder. Well, if second-hand's what you want, Hamish is your man. He's in Crumpled Lane, back along Fore Street and third alley off. It's unlocked, so just go in. Hamish won't mind."

I thank her, but even with her directions it takes me a while to find Pendragon Books, since Crumpled Lane is as squashed and as hidden as the name suggests. Eventually I find it, then spot a small slice of shop wedged between two others, white walls oozing in the fashion of cream in a sponge cake. Books are piled high in the window and pressed against the bulging panes of old glass as though seeking to escape. A black cat suns itself on the nearest pile, glaring balefully into the street with bold green eyes. Breakspear barks at it and tugs on his lead, and when the cat doesn't even so much as look up I realise the unfortunate creature is stuffed and placed artfully beside a selection of T. S. Eliot's poetry.

"Poor Macavity," I say. "You'd better behave, Breakspear!"

'Pendragon's Book Emporium' is picked out in swirling gold script above a narrow red door propped open with a listing pile of books. As I attempt to persuade Breakspear to sit and stay, I spot a nineteen-fifties world atlas, a well-thumbed copy of Katie Price's latest offering, and Beowulf. Odd neighbours I think, as I pick Beowulf up and thumb through it. Somebody has made neat pencil annotations in the margin. I wonder who they were and why their book ended up in a tiny second-hand shop tucked away in a Cornish fishing town? So many stories ...

"That's in the original Old English. For a translation, I wholeheartedly recommend Heaney's. It's superb."

The voice floats above me from the darkness of the shop. My first impression is of height and width, a giant with a mane of long silver hair and bright hazel eyes, framed in a hobbit-sized door which he ducks through. Not a giant, then, but a very tall man dressed in a rainbow-hued top and maroon cords suffering from alopecia. A very tall man, broad-shouldered and bare-footed, with skin as creased as the leather cover of the book I am holding. When he smiles a thousand more lines appear and his eyes sparkle with a zest for life that makes me smile too.

"I'm Hamish Pendragon," he says. "Welcome, young Beowulf reader."

"I'm not so young! And I'm not sure I could read this. I studied it ages ago," I confess, replacing the book and straightening up.

Hamish twinkles down at me. "You'd be surprised what the heart and soul recall. Take it, my dear, and welcome. Come into Pendragon's Book Emporium!"

He waves a hand at the dark interior.

"I'd love to, but I've got my dog with me."

"Doesn't your dog like books?"

I'm not quite sure how to reply. Hamish Pendragon sounds as though he's asking a serious question. Does my dog like books? I have no idea.

"He prefers dog biscuits."

Hamish crouches down and pats Breakspear.

"We supply those for our discerning canine readers. In my experience animals love books. It's just a case of finding where their tastes lie. My old lurcher, Sally, was a great fan of Tolstoy. Can't get on with him myself, but she had no issue with all the names. That cat, bless his soul, was a great fan of metaphysical poetry. We'll make a reader of you yet, won't we, boy?"

Breakspear barks.

"That's a yes," laughs Hamish. "Come on in."

Breakspear and I venture inside. I blink as my eyes adjust to the gloom. After the busy main street and press of tourists the tranquillity is blissful and I glance around with pleasure, for this tiny shop is, as Selina Trewen had promised, a treasure trove. Everything imaginable is crammed in here. There are hand-bound books, Bibles with age-worn covers and inscribed with family trees, old paperbacks with yellowed pages, and manuscripts bound with string. Gothic novels rub shoulders with Mrs Beaton. Mills & Boon snuggle up to Cicero and Pliny. There's no logic or order to this cataloguing, but the confusion only adds to the wonder of the place. I feel a tug of my heart that's just like falling in love.

"This is incredible," I breathe. "Are you a book dealer?"

"A book *collector*," Hamish corrects. "Like Doctor Dee before me, I love the alchemy of words and the power of language. I've travelled far in my time and I'm an unashamed devotee of car boots and jumble sales. This" – he sweeps his arm theatrically, narrowly missing a stand of nineteen-sixties Penguin classics – "is my life's work. It's my soul's calling, and I'm at your service."

As Hamish says this he bows, which, although it ought to be a ridiculous gesture, is oddly noble and brings to mind knights of the round table, quests and chivalry. With his long grey hair and regal bearing, Hamish fits his name, whether it's adopted or original. Maybe he'll fulfil my quest? If anyone knows about Gerald Snowe I'm certain it'll be this man.

"I'm Lowenna Scott," I say, holding out my hand

"Lowenna. A good Cornish name," Hamish remarks as we shake hands.

"My mother's family were Cornish."

"You have a Celtic look about you," he agrees. "You're dark-skinned and slight like Cornish folk, and your eyes are a wonderful colour. Not blue but almost violet, like a stormy sky in summer."

"Thanks," I say, startled and flattered by the romantic comparison. I turn a little pink under his scrutiny and focus on my quest. "I'm looking for a book. Maybe you can help? It's by a local writer called Gerald Snowe who I believe was writing at the start of the last century and set his only book here. Selina Trewen from Trevellan thought you might know more about him."

"*On Oyster Shore*," Hamish says, his voice so low that even in the stillness of the empty shop my ears strain to catch his words. Even the dust motes pirouetting in the shards of sunlight freeze, as though poised to hear what comes next.

"That's got to be it! I'm staying in the boathouse there. I heard a writer lived there years ago." I scan the crammed shelves excitedly, half-expecting the novel to leap out at me and flutter down like something from Harry Potter. "Do you have a copy?"

"I'm afraid not. That book's been out of print for over a century. I don't believe it even exists any more, and if it did it would be a very rare book indeed. It would be the kind of find that book collectors dream about."

"It would be valuable?"

"Very."

I'm confused. "I've never even heard of Gerald Snowe."

Hamish steeples his fingers beneath his chin. "Is worldly fame a measure of value?"

The answer to this, in the publishing world at least, is a resounding *yes*, because fame sells. Celebrity biographies, cookbooks, travel guides and novels shift huge numbers of books and command big advances for their authors. I look across at Katie Price's offering, currently doubling as a neon-pink doorstop, and reflect that although the literary value might be debatable nobody can argue that her books haven't sold in huge quantities.

I try again. "If it was a first edition of *Rebecca* I could understand it, but nobody ever talks about Gerald Snowe. I'd never heard of him until last night."

"Ah. You meant that if his work's so valuable, you would have expected to have come across it in some capacity?"

"Yes," I agree, relieved he understands. "Or at least to have heard of him. Was it a good novel? A success?"

"I have absolutely no idea. The first and only print run was relatively small. There may be some reviews somewhere, but if there are I've never seen them. I believe it was very lyrical and well-received, but it was published in the dark last days of the First World War and has been lost for decades."

"If he's unknown why would an existing copy be worth so much money?"

I think of the amounts that first editions of Harry Potter command or the value of an early folio of Shakespeare's work. These prices make perfect sense. You would have to live on the moon not to have heard of these writers. But Gerald Snowe isn't famous or even successful. Hamish considers my question.

"The antiquarian book world's a strange place full of wealthy individuals who like to collect the unique and the rare, and who are more than happy to pay handsomely for the privilege," he says eventually. "They may not be readers, but they like to own something nobody else has or can ever have. For them the joy comes in the possession rather than from the art which lies within the pages. Just as an art collector will long to possess the Mona Lisa or Guernica, so it is with book collectors. The value of *On Oyster Shore* lies in its rarity and the possibility of the ownership of a unique piece of literary history."

"But why were there so few copies? Surely the publishing house could have issued another print run?" In my world books go out of print all the time, but if the publisher holds the rights they can be reissued at any time. In this digital age it's as simple as the click of a mouse – but with Gerald Snowe that hasn't been the case: Google drew a blank and even the mighty Amazon hadn't been able to find anything. If I wanted an obscure author then my wish has been well and truly granted.

"Over the years there have been leads and rumours about existing copies, but they never materialise." Hamish offers Breakspear a Bonio then takes one himself, oblivious that it isn't a custard cream. "I've had a hunt myself, don't think I haven't. I've always thought somebody around here must have a copy tucked away in an attic or hidden in a cupboard. I've scoured boot sales and house clearances across Cornwall just in case, but I've never had any luck. It seems Gerald Snowe was instrumental in making sure that as many copies as possible were destroyed, and those that escaped probably fell apart many moons ago." His mouth droops with sadness. "A whole world lost, and words that were once everything reduced to dust. It breaks my heart."

This is a better story than anything I could have hoped for. All vague thoughts of a biography are suddenly replaced by the prospect of a genuine literary mystery, and it's so exciting that I feel giddy with the possibilities. There are so many ingredients here that I know will captivate readers: a beautiful Cornish setting, the crumbling Downton Abbey splendour of the lost Edwardian age, the pity and terror of the First World War, class rivalries, local fallouts, legends of curses and a young man's peculiar antipathy towards his greatest and only work.

"Why would Snowe destroy his work? Writers long for immortality, surely?"

I am back at Rosecraddick Manor, wandering through quiet rooms filled with glass display cabinets, splashes of red poppies and slowly falling dust while Kit Rivers' handsome face, dreadfully young beneath his army cap, stares out across the decades. Kit's poetry kept his story alive long after all living memory of him was lost, yet Gerald Snowe, his contemporary in age and class, strove to make sure his story was erased. At a loss, I delve for the only solution I can come up with.

"Could he have had shellshock?"

Hamish sinks into a battered leather armchair and motions for me to take its twin opposite.

"That would be a logical conclusion, except that Gerald Snowe has no war record. We can safely assume that he didn't fight, which was extremely unusual for a young man of his age and class. There seems to have been some kind of medical exemption for him, but unfortunately that's as far as I could get. So many archives and records were lost during the bombing in the Second World War."

"Are there any pictures of him? Or of when he and his family lived at Vyvyan Court?" I ask, recalling the exhibits at Rosecraddick Manor. Photographs of serious young men in cricket whites and boaters. Boys with fledgling moustaches on upper lips that are trying hard to be stiff as their owners pose in pristine uniforms. A lost world of tea on the lawn, hunt meets outside country houses, tightly corseted girls in white dresses with flowers in their hair. No longer individuals so much as relics of a time that exists now only in history books or period dramas.

"If there are, I've never seen any," Hamish says. "I imagine that when his family relinquished the lease on Vyvyan Court all their belongings went with them. It's strange, I admit, and I often think it's as though Gerald deliberately erased himself. Sometimes people need to do that, don't they? They want a fresh start. To leave their past behind."

His enquiring gaze meets mine. Although I'm certain Hamish is referring to himself, those eyes seem to reach deep into my soul as though he knows I'd rub out the past few years if I could. Suddenly I have huge sympathy with Gerald Snowe. Not everyone wants to hold onto the past, especially if you're not proud of it. But why wouldn't Gerald be proud of his success? I feel a frisson of excitement, an instinct which is whispering to me that this is the key to it all. For some reason he hated his book.

"But it gave him everything. Money. Literary success. Talent. Why would he want to walk away from that?"

Hamish lifts his broad shoulders. "Why do any of us do the things we do? Why would a bank manager from Coventry change his name to Hamish, run away to the West Country and become a bard?"

I caress Breakspear's silky head. I could pick up here with my own story, and I sense he's giving me an opening to do so, but my new life is like freshly fallen snow and I don't want to spoil it.

"Like his missing book, Gerald Snowe is also a lost

figure," Hamish continues, into his stride now. "The bare facts are that his wealthy parents rented Vyvyan Court in the early part of the twentieth century and Gerald spent much of his childhood here and presumably down at Oyster Shore. It was a favourite spot once for boating and other, less salubrious, pursuits."

"The Prince of Wales entertained his mistresses there," I supply. "Everyone knows that bit."

Hamish laughs. "Everyone loves a scandal! That would all have been long before Gerald's time, and certainly before everyone wanted central heating and mod cons! I think Oyster House was a little neglected even when Gerald was a child. The Trelyons used it to house their dependants, and I believe the last known resident was Lady Constance Trelyon. That poor woman would have been mistress of the entire estate had her husband not decided to break his neck hunting and had she produced a son rather than a daughter. Can you imagine? All that lost to a quirk of Fate and X chromosomes."

A daughter. An aristocratic little girl left to run wild on Oyster Shore. Princess Clementine, flanked by the two boys. Was she Lady Constance's child? The last of the Trelyons? And did my Princess Clementine know Gerald Snowe? The frisson of familiarity I have with this place makes the hair on my arms stir.

"It wasn't Fate as much as sexism," is all I say when Hamish looks at me enquiringly.

"Different times, dear girl, although I'm sure Lady Constance was sore about it. Human nature doesn't change. That's what makes Gerald Snowe so unusual. Most writers are thrilled with any success."

"Yes indeed – I worked in publishing for years. Most

authors court success and fame, no matter what they might say."

"But not Gerald Snowe. He actively sought obscurity, although if he hadn't done what he did he would have been very successful as an author and even wealthier."

"What do you think happened?"

Hamish sighs. "Truly? I have absolutely no idea, only theories. Nowadays we'd say he had a breakdown, but they didn't have a lot of time for mental health issues back then. Look at how they treated soldiers with shellshock. You only need to read Rivers or Owen to see there was little sympathy for anyone who couldn't cope. Success appears to have been too much for Gerald. He bought all the rights to his book and then withdrew it from publication. The story goes that he bought as many copies as he could find and destroyed them all. For some reason known only to himself he was determined to bury the novel."

"But that makes no sense at all!" If one of David's writers behaved like that, what would he do? He would flip and probably sue.

"It doesn't, which is why we can only conclude that Gerald was unwell. As time went by any existing copies of his books were lost and eventually his brief venture into the literary world vanished from memory. Perhaps he didn't think he deserved the success when most of his generation were slain."

"Survivor's guilt?"

"A version of it, although that's cod psychology and not fact. Anyway, there's little more to tell. Gerald never married and had no close family. He was very religious at the end, by all accounts, and died in a monastic hospital. Only obsessive rare book collectors have heard of him these days."

It's a sad story and a strange one. If I can help Gerald's voice be heard again so that his story is no longer lost, how incredible would that be?

"You feel it too, don't you?" Hamish says. "That sadness when authors are forgotten and their words no longer read? Their only way to reach immortality, lost. They may turn to dust, but their words live on, and each time we read them it's as though the author is resurrected and we hear their voice again, the quirks of personality, the concerns and the passions. The loves and the hatreds. If there is a written record nothing is ever forgotten. Nothing is in vain. I think it's why I love books so much."

I agree. When I was editing at Erasmus I was always conscious that I was tweaking someone's voice and strove to keep faithful to it. Yet something about this story is off-key, for writing a book is a hugely personal journey. The soul is poured onto the page and the heart dissected for all to see. Even fiction is a huge act of self-revelation, and all authors want their voices heard, for silence is what they fear the most. To willingly destroy your own book that has been laboured over, given up to an editor like a ritual sacrifice, and sent out into the world, is a very strange thing to do. It makes no sense.

"Something," I say slowly, "must have prompted him to want the book withdrawn."

"Undoubtedly. My guess would be if not shellshock, then there was a woman involved. In my experience love, and her twin sister jealousy, are to blame for all kinds of odd behaviour."

Like running away from everything you know, to live in a boathouse miles from anywhere? Yes, shattered hearts make you do all kinds of crazy things.

"But you said Gerald never married."

"I did – but I never said there wasn't a woman. I seem to recall a story about a lost fiancée, which is very romantic but could be a total fiction. It's not written anywhere that I know of. I think there was something about the shore being cursed too – again a local story, and probably one spread by those who wanted to use the river for their own nefarious purposes."

"Or did Gerald think the book itself was cursed? That might explain why he burned the copies?" I'm excited. A cursed book would make a great hook for a book pitch.

"He wrote an unlucky book, that's for certain," muses Hamish. "It never made him happy."

"Davey Tuckey, a fisherman, said Oyster Shore's haunted." I am happy to talk about this in the daylight and in company, although I'm not nearly as brave when night falls and I'm walking through the woods with only my dog for company.

"I've heard that too," he nods.

"You heard it from *me*, Hamish Pendragon! Don't you dare let Davey take the credit! I'm the only one who's really seen the ghost of Oyster Shore." A tall woman with vivid pink hair ducks beneath the door jamb and explodes into the shop. A diamond nose stud glitters in the sunlight which surrounds her like an aura.

Hamish jumps to his feet and hugs her, delighted by the interruption. "Treena! What fortuitous timing. You'll tell this to Lowenna far better than I ever could."

Treena? Is this the beachcomber, organic vegetable farmer and part-time witch? So who was it that I saw tracing the tideline yesterday? Who was that silent girl with bracken-red hair? Breakspear had growled and shrunk from her, and I feel cold all over.

Did I see the ghost of Oyster Shore?

Treena flops onto a pile of cushions and kicks off her lime-green crocs to reveal chipped red nail polish and a tattoo of stars on her left foot.

"I'll tell you about the ghost of Oyster Shore," she says to me. "I saw him once myself. So, what do you want to know?"

8

THE PRESENT

Cornwall

Lowenna

"I hope all this talk about ghosts and curses hasn't put you off?"

Treena and I are sitting on a bench, eating ice cream and watching the Penhayes ferry clank across the river. Hamish and Breakspear are down on the slipway playing a complicated game of stick which is only partially going according to plan inasmuch as Hamish is doing a sterling job of lobbing a stick into the water: Breakspear is sitting at the water's edge, all lolling pink tongue and tail beating against seaweed, and pretending not to understand 'Fetch!' while Hamish wades in to demonstrate. Both look as though they are having a wonderful time, even if Hamish's cords are soaked to the knees and one deck shoe has floated off to France. With the sunshine on my face and a mouth full of ice cream, I couldn't feel less worried – although it might be different tonight when I'm alone in bed, tucked up in beneath the creaking beams, and jumping at every groan and sigh the old boathouse makes.

Treena is only too happy to tell me all about the unquiet spirits of Oyster Shore, several of which she claims to be in frequent communication with. While Hamish makes tea so sweet my teeth almost give up the ghost at the first sip, she describes the figure of a man often seen walking through the woods, head bowed and shoulders stooped, who Hamish thinks must be Gerald Snowe. There's also a ghost dog, apparently only seen on a full moon, a headless horseman and even a phantom rowing boat. I wait for her to finish by telling me the *pièce de résistance* is a girl in white with bracken-red curls who haunts the shore – but Treena, reaching the end of her ghostly catalogue, is busy swinging a crystal over me. I feel oddly disappointed. It might have been something to have discovered I had an undiscovered psychic ability. Granny May had claimed to be able to read the tea-leaves courtesy of her Romany ancestors, but neither Marina nor I have inherited that talent.

Besides, we both use teabags.

"You have a spirit watching over you," Treena declares. "It's a woman who's from this place. She says she sent you."

I watched the crystal swing back and forth, feeling I could be forgiven for being cynical. Was it a tremor in her wrist that made the crystal jerk and change direction? It was hard to tell. I've always felt when it comes to psychics the jury is still out. I'd once edited the memoir of psychic who'd insisted her spirit guides had to have copy approval. Another had given my gay colleague an entire reading about his girlfriend's flaws.

"Maybe your granny's with you?" says Hamish, who was very taken to learn I had family roots in the area. He might be a Cornish bard, he sighs wistfully, but he doesn't have a drop of Celtic blood. Maybe in a past life though, Treena suggests kindly, and he perks up a little at this notion.

"Your guide says she's drawn you here," Treena says. Her eyes are closed as the crystal circles lazily. Then they snap open and hold mine. Her eyes are brown, intense and wide. "She's saying something about a box. The box is very important to you."

She has my attention at that, but I've decided not to mention anything about Granny May's treasures. There's no need to give Treena clues she could exploit. She seems nice enough, and Noah Wilson is certainly a fan, but the last thing I need is my neighbour descending on me with her tarot cards and crystals every five minutes.

I listen politely to more talk of energy and auras for a few more minutes before predicting my parking ticket is about to expire and saying I need to get back to the ferryside car park. This prompts Hamish to decide he wants an ice cream from the waterfront kiosk and Treena to cadge a lift back to her farm.

"It's literally minutes from Oyster Shore. Gareth's too busy to pick me up – he's working on the farm today with Noah, whom you've already met."

"Did the crystal tell you that?"

Treena threw her head back and guffawed. "That'd be something! I'd get it to do the bloody lottery numbers if it was that specific. No, Noah said he'd bumped into our new neighbour, Lowenna. No wonder he was in such a good mood to find *you*!"

I felt my face flame. I feel glad it's dark inside Pendragon's.

"He was kind enough to show me how to get the wood burner going."

"Noah can turn his hand to anything," Treena says warmly. "When he goes back to Oz, Gareth will be in pieces. We all will. Still, maybe Noah'll stay. If there's a reason to, I mean."

She dangles the crystal which began to swing from left to right.

"What's it saying?" Hamish demands, but Treena closes her hand around it.

"It says the future's not yet written and you're nosey!"

As I finish my ice cream and watch Hamish wade into the water for the umpteenth time, all pleas of fetch! ignored by my stubborn dog, I know I need to make it clear I'm not going to waste a moment fretting about ghosts or listening to magic crystals.

"I'm absolutely fine," I say firmly. "I like it at Oyster Shore."

Treena licks her ice cream, a pointed pink tongue dragging it into a white crest, and nods.

"The shore likes you too. It wants you there. The Universe always delivers us to the right place."

I haven't known Treena more than an hour, but I already know she talks in circular statements you can't disagree with or reply to.

I get to my feet and offer Breakspear, who's given up watching Hamish fetch sticks, the end of my cornet.

"Good," I say, "because I'm intending to be there for a while."

"And you are going to solve the mystery of Gerald Snowe?" Treena adds with more confidence than I feel. "I'll see if I can have a chat with his spirit once the moon's in the right quarter. It might help. What do you think?"

What I think is that I'm already planning to visit the main county library and see what I can find on microfiche. I'll also call in a favour with my teacher ex, Drew, whose wife works at the British Library.

"It's good to explore all avenues," I say tactfully.

Treena gives me a sideways look. "That's what a Virgo would say. I bet you're a Virgo."

She's right. I am. "Lucky guess," I say.

"Not a guess at all. I can tell." She holds her hand up and ticks points off on her fingers. "Can be cynical. Needs proof. Creative. Hard-working. Kind. Vulnerable. Compatible with Librans." She ticks these off on her fingers and shrugs. "You think I'm nuts."

"Of course not," I fib. She's clearly as mad as cheese.

Treena laughs again. "I don't believe you! I'd think exactly that, and maybe I *am* mad. Why else would a city girl shack up with a farmer, in a falling-down house miles from the nearest Starbucks! Lord, no wonder Gerald Snowe didn't stick around. He probably couldn't wait to get back to civilisation."

"Wasn't Penhayes *the* place to holiday back in those days?"

"You mean when the Prince of Wales was having his wicked way with all and sundry in your boathouse?"

"I'm thinking of a bit later, when Gerald Snowe would have been a young man, just before the First World War. Didn't fashionable Londoners come here?"

"They still do," Treena says darkly as, bang on cue, a group of women sporting huge sunglasses pushed into caramel-streaked hair and handbags the size of cars dangling from their skinny arms, sashays past. "They're the only ones who can afford this place. If Gerald was here now, he'd be on a powerboat, hogging the pontoon and unable to moor to save his life – just like that utter idiot!"

We watch the unfortunate man in question attempting to line his massive boat up with the pontoon and failing miserably. I imagine that apart from the speedboats and the rash of new-build houses on the top of the hill, this scene has hardly changed since the 1900s. Gerald Snowe would recognise the clustered cottages of Trevellan across the water and the wooded bluff concealing Oyster Shore from prying eyes. I don't mention to Treena that I'm hoping the elusive author might provide wonderful material for a book, but I'm quietly convinced I've found my subject and can hardly wait to be back at the boathouse with my laptop open so I can begin. My fingers tingle.

"I really hope you find something more about Gerald Snowe. It would really put Trevellan on the map if we had our own du Maurier," Treena says, unfolding her slim frame from the bench. Licking ice cream from her fingers, she adds, "Heaven knows we need all the help we can get with farming on its arse and everyone staying in Penhayes because a celebrity chef is there for twenty minutes a year."

"Is it that bad?"

Hailing from London, I've never thought too deeply about the realities of rural life. In the city farmers are an abstract concept, sometimes glimpsed on Country File or Midsomer Murders, and not people you bump into.

"We're luckier than most because we diversified early on and went organic. Gareth's brilliant with the veg boxes, and I supplement where I can with the aromatherapy and a bit of tarot reading, but some more people glamping on our fields would help. A Kit Rivers or Daphne du Maurier would really bring the tourists flocking. Apparently Rosecraddick's heaving these days."

I recall the monstrous car park at the rear of Rosecraddick Manor. It had been packed on the day I'd visited, and the attendants were flat out, playing a game of vehicular Tetris.

"Gerald Snowe would have been a contemporary of Kit Rivers," I say thoughtfully. "Maybe they knew one another. Families of their social standing would have attended the same gatherings. There could be something about Gerald in one of the documents at Rosecraddick Manor." I decide to drop Matthew Enys, curator of the Kernow Heritage Foundation, an email when I'm back at my desk. Maybe he knows something.

"That makes sense," Treena agrees as we reach the slipway where Hamish is wading out of the water with the stick held aloft and looking as though he's about to shake himself dry. "Everyone knows everyone around here because it's a small world. Take it from me, that's bloody annoying at times! Sometimes I long to get away from it all like Noah did. He left everything behind and ran to the other side of the world."

"But that was because of his mum."

I think of the sadness on Noah's face when he told me how she'd loved family history and how it ended with him. He really misses her.

Treena shoots me a puzzled look. "Don't you mean his wife? She's the reason Noah came to the UK."

Noah hasn't mentioned a wife. A swift and irrational flare of disappointment takes me by surprise. What is it with me and men who conveniently forget to mention their partners?

Now I'm imagining all kinds of scenarios. Treena and her husband enjoying cosy kitchen suppers with Mr and Mrs Noah, Noah telling his wife (who in my imagination looks a lot like Scarlett Johansson) about the mad woman renting the boathouse, Noah's wife annoyed he's taking his time delivering logs …

"I didn't know he was married," I say. Nobody in the pub thought to mention it either.

Treena sighs. "He'll always be married. Men like Noah love deeply and for ever."

Her words wrap themselves around my heart and constrict it so tightly that it aches. What must it be like to have love like that? Will I ever know? I swallow back a knot of sadness, unable to understand why I'm feeling so disappointed. Noah Wilson drank coffee with me for an hour. It was nothing more. It's fine.

I'm about to ask why Noah's wife brought him to Cornwall – I'm imaging she's English – when Hamish arrives with Breakspear in tow, desperately attached to the stick and refusing to drop it. By the time I've persuaded Breaky it really won't fit into the boot and said goodbye to Hamish it feels awkward, if not downright nosey, to raise the topic again. Treena doesn't expand on it and we spend the rest of the short journey chatting about her plans to grow the veg box business while the unspoken topic of Noah's wife rides along with us like an extra passenger.

"I can ask Gareth's grandad what he knows about Gerald Snowe," she offers as we pass Oyster Shore's gate. "I think his father might have bought some land from the Trelyons after the First World War. Grampy loves to talk about the past."

"That would be great. Thanks."

"And I think a Penwurthy married into Gareth's family at

some point, so I'll ask Grampy. Wouldn't it be fun if you were related to us?"

I nod, but my attention is focused on the enormous tractor bearing down on us. It's towing a trailer the size of a house. I tuck Polly the Peugeot tightly into the verge, such as it is, and pray. Maybe I should reverse? Although that thing is huge, Treena seems blissfully unconcerned that we're about to be squashed flat by John Deere's finest.

"May Penwurthy," she muses. "Grampy might have known her. He's ninety-eight."

"Mmm," I say. The tractor has stopped. It looks like the driver, a strapping man with dreadlocks and wearing a scarlet bandana, is blowing kisses. That's an improvement on the last driver we met, who'd given me a very different hand gesture when he had to reverse. I edge past as best I can, trying not to think about the paintwork while Treena blows kisses back.

"Is the kissing a Cornish thing?" I ask.

"Only if it's your husband! That's Gareth and he's been muck-spreading today. He'll stink now, and blown kisses will be as good as it gets for him!"

We squeeze by Gareth's tractor and as my car scrapes brambles and nettles I resign myself to scratched paintwork being part of my new life. Oblivious to the damage, Treena chats away about organic farming methods and sourdough starters until we arrive at the farm. A five-bar gate guards the entrance to a collection of industrial-looking sheds, hugely at odds with the chocolate-box house cowering in their shadow. The view reaches to Penhayes, and would be breathtaking – if you dared snatch a breath, for when Treena opens the car door the stench of manure is overwhelming.

"Home sweet home" she says, grimacing. "Pooh! Hold

your nose. It's totally organic, but Gareth'll need at least five showers before he comes near me!"

My eyes are watering and I hardly dare inhale. Poor Breakspear with his fine sense of smell must be having a terrible time.

"Thanks for the lift. Hopefully I'll see you about," Treena says, uncoiling her long legs and swinging out. "I often beachcomb past the boathouse, because you can find some really cool bits along that stretch of the shore. I found a signet ring a couple of years ago. Weird to think the last person who saw it was the one to lose it."

"I saw a girl beachcombing there yesterday," I say.

"That's unusual. Most people can't be bothered to wade along the shore because it's a bit tricky if you don't know the path through. Folks have got stuck in the mud before now."

I picture the lone figure I'd spotted, skirts held above the wet sand and dark red curls lifted by the breeze. She'd not seemed to have any difficulty navigating the mudflats, and must know the river well to move on so quickly. I decide not to say anything more about her. There's something about that encounter I'm still trying to process.

Treena shuts the door and I'm just about the attempt a three-point turn without ending up in a ditch when her silver-ringed knuckles rap on my window. I take a gulp of air before winding it down.

"I probably shouldn't say anything because it's none of my business," she says leaning in, "but I really think you should know."

"Know what?"

She leans in a little more. "Know about Noah."

"Noah?"

Treena hesitates, as though listening to somebody I can't

hear before her head dips in the smallest of nods as if acknowledging something or agreeing. "Noah does have a wife, Lowenna, but it's not what you think."

"I don't think anything," I say stiffly. "Noah's love life's none of my business."

"I think it *is* your business and so do my spirit guides. He's a widower."

"A widower?" I echo. "Noah? But he's—"

"Too young?"

This is exactly what I was going to say. The word *widower*, with its connotations of old men with sparse grey hair, eyes pouched with sadness and houses ringing with emptiness, is as far removed from the beautiful Noah Wilson of the golden hair and gilded skin as it's possible to imagine.

"I guess so," I say.

"He is too young, but cancer doesn't give a crap about age. His wife passed away a couple of years ago, and then he lost his mum too. Noah was so devastated he wanted to get as far away as he could," Treena says quietly. "You can't blame him."

I'm shocked. "But he said he came here because his mum had been researching the family tree."

"That's true," Treena agrees. "But I think the deeper reason is that it was far away from all the pain. It's unbearable, isn't it? God, if anything happened to Gareth I don't know what I'd do." Her voice quavers. "Seriously, Lowenna, that's all I know. Noah doesn't talk about it much, so the rest you'll have to hear from him. I just didn't want you to think he was a cheat or—

"Or conveniently forgetting her," I supply, thinking of David, who was very good at conveniently forgetting what didn't suit him. Like fiancées for instance.

Treena nods fervently. "*Exactly*. He's one of the good guys, is what I'm trying to say."

I think about Noah who has offered to help with logs and given advice on rudimentary fire-lighting and later will be delivering my luggage.

"He's definitely one of those," I agree.

Treena beams. "He is. He *really* is. He's loyal and fair and generous to a fault. All in all, I guess it's safe to say that Noah Wilson's a typical *Libran*."

And with this parting shot she straightens up and walks away, flowery skirts billowing, and even though I can't see her face I know Treena Trehunnist is smiling a wide Cheshire cat smile. And so am I because I hadn't realised how important it was to me for Noah Wilson to be one of the good guys.

And a Libran.

9

THE PRESENT

Cornwall

Lowenna

Later, after several fruitless hours googling Gerald Snowe, I set off to meet Noah. The tide is out, so Breakspear and I trail along the seaweed line, quietly picking our way cautiously through the oyster shells, ignored by wading birds. The weather is warm for May, and the air soft with the promise of summer. A tractor is growling in the far distance, perhaps Gareth muck-spreading, and as I follow the creek it feels timeless, as though Oyster Shore is a portal to another age, one when men wore striped blazers and women were squeezed into corsets. I half-expect to see Gerald Snowe walking towards me, flannel trousers rolled to the knee and boater held loosely in one hand as he plans his masterpiece, or comes across a gaggle of village children shrimping in the shallows. The soft alluvium beneath my feet is neither land nor sea but a shifting, liminal place where water is brackish and nothing is solid. It isn't hard to imagine the years peeling away with the ebbing water. Maybe all I need to do is wait and watch as Gerald's story unfolds.

As I go up past Oyster House, it regards me from beneath its veil of trees. Squinting against the light, I study the once-white walls, now streaked with verdigris as though a giant crayon-happy child has scrawled across them, and I wonder if it's just my imagination that makes the old house seem so familiar from this angle? I feel certain I've seen it before, only when it was smart and gleaming, the gardens neatly tended and the gravel paths raked smooth. There was no choking ivy, no boarded-up windows, and no wild garden of flowing greens and nettles hissing from abandoned flowerbeds or saplings sprouting from splits in the terrace. Now the house is drowning in greenery, and I wonder how long it will be until the walls succumb and sink beneath it.

Gerald Snowe would have known this place well, as would my great-grandparents. To them this house would have been a symbol of wealth and confidence rather a sad relic of a lost epoch and extinct line. Did Gerald write some of his lost masterpiece sitting in one of the bay windows overlooking this very stretch of shore? Did he glance up from the page and frown, puzzled by the sight of a woman dressed rather indecently (by his standards) and staring straight at him? Is there a place where it's possible to cross through the years and step into another age? Then the hairs on the back of my neck prickle because I could swear I see a shadow flit across an upstairs window and a white face swim forward from the darkness. I step back and in my haste stumble over a rock. When I look again the window is empty.

Of course it is. It was always empty.

"Too much *Outlander*," I scold myself. "Although who wouldn't be thrilled to be swept off their feet by a gorgeous highlander?"

Not even a week of living alone, and already I'm talking to myself. I'm half-amused and half-concerned at how alarmed I am to think somebody else is here. Perhaps they are. Lack of mobile signal or not, this is the perfect spot for a camp or a hideout.

Disconcerted, I turn away from the house and call to Breakspear, who's still digging down in the grey mud. Tail wagging furiously and rump swaying from side to side, he's intent on burrowing as deeply as possible, and is deaf to my cries.

"Breaky!" I holler, but my spaniel no longer has any recall skills, something which often happens when there are pigeons/other dogs/footballs in his vicinity. One day I fully expect to find myself a YouTube sensation as I shriek at the mad dog racing around in circles creating havoc and completely ignoring me. That dubious fame is coming closer by the day. Vowing to find a local obedience class, I make my way back down to the tideline. Sand spraying the air and much excited barking suggests a find, and I brace myself for something stinky which I'll have to wrestle away from him.

"What have you found, boy?"

Breakspear tugs at something tangled in seaweed and wedged beneath a large rock. I peer closer, expecting a dead seabird, for although Breakspear has never been near a shoot in his life his gundog instincts are strong. As I do, a dazzling kingfisher flash glances from his find as the sunlight hits it.

"What's that, Breaky?"

I crouch beside him to look more closely. Whatever my dog has found is wedged beneath what I now see isn't a rock at all but a mooring weight. It's hardly surprising a cocker spaniel can't move it. I tuck my fingers underneath and scrabble while Breakspear leaps around me and barks. Intrigued, I continue to try and work the item free, but the barnacled weight is reluctant to yield and it's all I can do to lift it even a few centimetres. Finally this is enough, and as I flex my fingers to make sure they haven't shattered Breaky snatches his prize and enjoys several canine laps of honour around me.

"Drop it!" I order.

Usually this is the point where Breakspear tears off with a putrid chunk of dead wildlife or stolen ball and I have to wrestle with him, but to my surprise he trots over and relinquishes his find at my feet. Pink tongue lolling, he watches proudly as I pick it up.

"Impossible," I breathe. "It can't be."

Knotted in bladderwrack and dusted with sand is an enamelled comb. Even with chipped paint and missing teeth it's the identical twin of the one Marina and I squabbled over all those years ago. The weight of it in my palm feels the same, and as I hold it to the light the ruby-red glint of the bird's beak and its bright sapphire wings are so familiar that I am eight years old once again, lolling on my stomach on Granny May's hearthrug while my sister spins stories.

"The blue bird comb," I whisper as my fingertips run over the enamel and caress the golden claws. Who dropped it, I wonder, as I trace the swirls of the wings and curve of the beak. How did my great-grandmother come across its mirror image? Were they both hers? Was she playing here with the children from the pictures? Or did it belong to somebody else entirely? A girl who was rowed downstream by Gerald Snowe and lost her comb when she leaned over to admire her reflection in the water? I hear her cry of distress and the gentle splash as the blue bird falls from the world of air to dive into the watery lands beneath the hull. She watches it sink and vanish, little knowing that it won't be seen again for over one hundred years – and then gives its twin to her maid ...

That's just one story, of course. It could have been stolen and later on disposed of by a servant (Granny May's mother is instantly in the frame), or perhaps the truth is far more mundane. Years ago people threw all kinds of rubbish into the river. Out of sight was definitely out of mind as past generations dumped remains of meals, pipes and broken plates into the water. The banks of rivers are layered with alluvial trash turned treasure, and mudlarking is the latest middle-class hobby. Friends of David's regularly spent weekends squelching along the muddy hem of the Thames searching for bits of clay pipe and old coins. But this is more than a random find, for what are the chances of finding another comb like the one Granny May had kept in her box? It feels as though this comb has been waiting for me to arrive, and its re-emergence into the world above the water and alluvium a reminder that the past only remains buried until it is ready to be uncovered. Hoping this is a good omen for my research into Gerald Snowe, I wipe it on my sleeve, then slip it into my pocket.

Abandoning the river, I trudge back up the steep drive with Breakspear tearing ahead. Although it's nonsense I have the strongest sensation that somebody is watching from the old house. If I turn around I'll see them at the window, sewn in by ivy and with their hands pressed against grimy glass as though pleading for rescue. I stare resolutely ahead, my eyes fixed on the path, and ignore the prickling on the back of my neck. Treena's ghost stories have affected me more than I realise. They were just silly stories, the kind told around the campfire on a late summer's evening when shadows pool, and are utter nonsense. But even so my pace increases, and I don't look back.

Noah is waiting at the top of the drive, leaning against his Landrover and texting with great concentration. Spotting me, he slides his phone into the back pocket of his jeans and holds up his hands.

"Before you come too close, I have to tell you that this isn't my aftershave!"

"Treena said you were helping with the muck-spreading – otherwise I might wonder," I tease, relieved to see a friendly face. My hurried walk up the drive feels foolish suddenly. I must get a handle on my imagination. It's gone into overdrive since my arrival.

"Ah. T warned you about Eau du Manure?"

"Yep. I'd stick to Chanel if I were you."

"Chanel? In my dreams. We struggling artists are lucky to afford soap."

Noah stoops to greet Breakspear, who's thrilled to see him. Glancing up at me, he adds, "I've actually showered twice but it's a hard pong to sluice off. You may prefer to walk back down rather than sit in a car with me."

His wet hair, wavy from the shower, is the colour of sun-bleached wheat. A fresh grey tee shirt, loosely tucked into the waistband of his faded jeans, clings to the still-damp muscles of his chest as though it's been painted on by an artist. With his strong shoulders, narrow hips and smile that chisels dimples into his cheeks, I know most women would willingly sacrifice their sense of smell for five minutes alone in a car with Noah Wilson. Unbidden, a jolt of longing snatches my breath, and as broken sunlight filters through the trees I'm lost in a dancing sea of green and gold, slipping deeper and deeper beneath the waves and unable to resist.

Noah straightens up. "Is everything okay, Wenna?"

I'm staring. Embarrassed, I drag my gaze away, not sure how to articulate my feelings. I am struck to the core with molten horror. Noah Wilson is a *widower*. He's grieving. He's another woman's husband. I shouldn't think of him *that* way.

"What's up?" he asks.

I can't reply, for how do I explain that my thoughts have drifted to a forbidden place? Flustered, I pretend to be engrossed in a bag hunt for my car keys.

"Just wondering where my keys are. I can never find them."

My hair tumbles over my face and I am glad for once of my wild mop because I can hide behind it now and mask my red face. In my defence widowers are usually sweet elderly men with grandchildren and gardens. They aren't smiley and sexy and sweet like Noah Wilson.

I pull the keys out with an exaggerated flourish.

"Here they are! Always at the bottom. Why do keys always do that? Go to the bottom of the bag, I mean, although being a man you probably don't have this problem and —"

"Wenna. Stop." Noah's voice is gentle but firm. "Take a breath. Stop panicking."

"I'm not panicking. I've found them." I jangle the keys. "Shall we load up? You must have lots to be getting on with, and I'm taking up far too much of your time."

Noah leans back against the Landrover and crosses his arms. "Someone told you, didn't they? About my wife."

What do I say? That it's none of my business and he doesn't need to say anything more, or talk about something that's painful? Or – and what my heart is telling me to do –

say yes, Treena did mention it, and I'm so sad to hear about his loss. I so don't want to say the wrong thing that my tongue is knotted. We're so hopeless at talking about death. We skirt around it, use euphemisms like *fell asleep* or *lost her life* and we do our utmost to pretend the only certainty we have in life is something that we can avoid.

"It's okay," he says quietly when I fail to reply. "That wasn't a trick question. It's not a secret."

"Noah, I'm so sorry. I don't know what to say."

"Of course you don't. Nobody does. *I* don't, and I'm the one in the middle of it all. I'm an aberration. I frighten people."

I'm thrown. "How do you mean?"

"Maybe that's the wrong word. I unnerve them? Bad luck can be contagious? Death is something that only happens to old people? Facing the truth, which is that life's bloody precarious, puts folk on edge, and I can't blame them. They're scared of saying the wrong thing, which either means they ignore the topic completely or they avoid me instead. That's excruciating because all I want to do is talk about it, or at first anyways. Am I making sense?"

I've been lucky so far to have never experienced a close loss, but when my parents split up nobody mentioned my father or talked about him for a long time. Mum had acted as though Dad had never existed. It was as though he'd been beamed up by aliens, which she would have probably preferred, and if Marina and I were grieving for our old life and missing him, we soon learned to keep quiet and live with the loss. It was a death in a way, and I imagine a therapist would have a field day with us.

"People don't want to cause upset or make things worse," I say.

Noah fondles Breakspear's silky ears. "I know that, intellectually at least, but it's hard. The widower word is a taboo. Everyone looks at you like you're a freak and you know they're brimming with questions. What happened? How did she die? Are you coping? Will you date again? Have you had sex since? Will you again? Do you want kids? Is it too late?"

He's right; I have wondered all of these things.

"And that's fair enough, isn't it, mate?" Noah says to Breakspear, who stares up at him adoringly. "We all have questions, but some of them don't have any answers." He straightens up and sighs. "I should have said something, but I guess I didn't mention it to you when we were chatting because I didn't want to make you feel awkward. You'd just arrived, I'd given you the fright of your life and it looked as though you had enough to contend with. Death isn't exactly an ice-breaker when you meet new people. Then you wonder if you ever dare raise the topic, especially when you're having a great time in good company. A big wallop of guilt usually follows soon after. Who am I to be having a good time? Does that mean I didn't love her? Don't miss her? Am I being disrespectful to her memory?" He presses the heels of his hands into his forehead as though kneading away these spiky thoughts. "It's a bloody minefield."

"I can't imagine what it's like."

"I'm glad you can't. Kim, that's my wife, would have handled this widower shit much better. She always knew what to say, but I'm not much use at all, I'm afraid. I'm bloody useless."

"I don't think there's a scale for how good you are at being widowed. It's not like exams," I offer.

Noah laughs bleakly. "Yeah. I guess that's the schoolteacher in me. I told you teaching was a family tradition, didn't I? I guess I want to grade everything to make sense of it. Kim was a teacher too. She was a great one for telling things straight and then getting on with it. Her students appreciated knowing she didn't put up with nonsense from anyone – and I include myself in that. She never let me mess about."

Noah introduces his wife naturally and with such love that any awkwardness dissolves. He's happy to talk about her, and he *wants* to talk about her because this way Kim is remembered. As Noah speaks about her I listen, moved by the love in his voice. Noah Wilson may be standing in a Cornish lane, but his heart's thousands of miles away with the woman he loved.

"Sometimes Kim would get an idea in her head and that was it," he continues, and then, more to himself than to me, "it was going to happen no matter what. Nothing could stand in her way. I came home one day and she'd decided to decorate the entire house. Jeez! Half the wallpaper was stripped and she'd made a start on every bloody room. The woman drove me half crazy!"

He raises his eyes to the blue sky patched through green trees. I feel sure Kim would have been very familiar with this expression of fond exasperation and would have also known that Noah loved her wholeheartedly. He wouldn't have minded if she'd painted the house pink as long as she was happy.

"Shortly after that she was diagnosed with breast cancer for the second time, and it progressed so fast I paid decorators to finish up. When Kim didn't protest I knew it was bad because she'd usually give me hell for interfering. I think we knew then that the end wasn't far away."

His voice tails off and we watch the river flow by, lost in its own mysterious rhythm and never-ending, just as life carries on in a relentless flow even when hearts are broken and lives shattered.

"Sometimes you can't stop the course of some things, no matter how hard you fight, and Kim wanted all the facts," he says eventually. "She demanded the full prognosis and she insisted on knowing the truth. Jeez! It didn't make her the easiest to live with sometimes, and we argued about so much, but it was honest. We always knew where we stood because we were a team. We had each other's backs – and I never let her go, Wenna, not for a single second. I was with her until the very end. I never left her side."

Is it wrong to envy Noah a little, in spite of all the grief and the pain? To have known such love is surely a blessing. I've never experienced anything close to this, but I know without any doubt that finishing with David was the right choice. I may never find the kind of love Noah shared with Kim, but I won't settle for anything less.

"Kim insisted I should get on with life once she was gone," Noah tells me. "That's easier said than done, and I wished I was dead, along with her, for a long time – but how could I refuse my wife's final wish? She made me promise I wouldn't become a hermit, turn her room into a shrine and drift about mourning for the rest of my days, because she hated that kind of thing. 'Mawkish' was the word she used, and she said she never had much sympathy for overblown melancholy. Apparently English lit is riddled with it. Especially the Victorian stuff. Yeah?"

"Just a bit," I say. When I'd studied Tennyson's *In Memorandum* at eighteen I'd thought lifelong mourning was a mark of great love, but Kim Wilson was wiser by far than Tennyson, or indeed many great poets. Love is wanting your partner to be happy even though your heart is breaking to be leaving. True love is wanting your loved one to love again. True love is wanting those you leave behind to be happy.

"Not being as brainy as you two, I'll just agree," Noah replies. "Anyways, Kim wanted me to live for us both. She said I should marry again, have children and make a new life; but it's not that easy. It's bloody impossible when all you want is the life you had, the children you should have had and the plans you'd made. Those are losses too, and I wanted our life together back so badly I thought I'd die from the misery. I went to pieces after she died, Wenna. I was an utter mess. Kim would have been furious."

"She would have been heartbroken," I say gently. "And she would have understood."

"Yeah, but it felt like I'd let her down by giving up. That was when Mum started to plan our trip to Cornwall. She had some weird conviction it was where I needed to be, and I guess it was something for me to focus on – but then I lost Mum too, and for ages I couldn't bear the thought of much at all."

"That must have been tough."

"Yeah," he says. "It was. They were strong women and left a big emptiness. There were too many gaps where voices should be, and the silences almost drove me mad. In the end, though, I knew I owed it to Mum and Kim to do something with my life. I had a gift they'd been denied, and it seemed an insult to them to turn my back on it. Besides, I was no use at work and my own art wasn't happening. It was time to shake it all up a bit, and so I came to Cornwall. I came here for Kim and for my mum because they both believed it was the right place to be."

"And was it?"

Noah shrugs. "I'm still here, so maybe. Oyster Shore

certainly has a special energy; there's something about watching the tides turn and the waters ebb and flow that puts life into context. Being close to nature helps too, I think. I can draw here and listen to the wind in the trees and the call of birds, and that calms my heart. I'm not as ragged inside or as wild with sadness as I was when I arrived, either – so yes, maybe the peace here has brought me some solace. It's a healing place, and I think if I ever won the Lotto I'd buy a spot just like this and tuck a few little cabins away as retreats for people who've been bereaved or wrung out after caring for someone right until the very end. You need solitude and beauty to learn how to breathe again when you're piecing your world back together. You need space and light and nature, time and space to rediscover yourself and recalibrate, solitude to read or paint or walk, and to be able to step into a new version of your life feeling if not stronger, then renewed. Yeah. That's what I'd do, because that's what Oyster Shore has done for me. I know just how much it means."

It's a beautiful vision. A place to heal and cry and to simply be. A healing space, to remember and listen and grieve. A place of renewal and hope. I've never met Kim, but my intuition tells me she would have liked this plan.

"That's an amazing vision."

He flushes. "I was thinking aloud, really. I've never said that to anyone before."

"Then I'm honoured. I think it's a wonderful idea."

"Thanks, although it's more of dream unless I become the next Banksy and make millions," Noah laughs. "One day maybe? When everyone wants my sculptures? Until then I'm here in my van, living my life day by day and doing my best to make Kim proud. I'm not quite in the state I was when I arrived, as Gareth and Treena will tell you. They've been great, and the locals are mostly friendly. You'll soon settle in."

"I'm sure," I say, although I'm not planning to be wildly sociable. Or, indeed, to brave scary Fi again.

"I really hope Mum knows I made the trip," Noah says. "It meant everything to her that I'd come to Cornwall. Although there is one thing I do know for sure – if she was here right now she'd tell me to stop yakking and get on with helping your get your cases home. Then she'd tell me off even more for being so rude as to not ask you anything about yourself! 'That's not how I raised you!' is what she'd say."

He's closed the topic and I understand. I feel privileged he's taken me into his confidence and shared his dream.

"Me? There's nothing to tell," I insist. "I'm quite dull."

Noah raises an eyebrow. "I don't believe that for a second. Coming to live here, all alone and in a falling-down boathouse, is hardly dull. Kim wouldn't have thought so, and neither does Treena. She's already busy inventing all kinds of exciting explanations for your appearance. So, tell me, is it witness protection, or are you really working for drugs barons and turning the boathouse into a cannabis farm?"

I laugh, but Noah is straight-faced. "I kid you not. That's what Gareth heard – he told me. Heaven only knows what they're saying in the village pub!"

"They all have good imaginations," I say, unlocking my car. "I'm afraid the truth isn't nearly as exciting. I'm just a freelance author looking for a quiet spot to write a book. I haven't travelled halfway across the planet to fulfil last requests and trace my family roots."

"Some might say that was running away too. Anyway, I've not done much in the way of continuing to research the family tree. I'm far too busy muck-spreading." He inhales deeply and then grimaces. "I hope the smell isn't too offensive. I've gone nose-blind, I'm afraid."

"I don't suppose you carry clothes pegs. I could always put one on my nose," I suggest, opening the boot and reaching in for my luggage.

"I'll remember that for another time. Hey, let me get those."

Noah reaches in and lifts both cases out as easily as though they were filled with feathers rather than books and boots and the assorted other detritus I thought I couldn't live without. I step back, not sure whether to be grateful he's doing the heavy work (I'd nearly dislocated my arms carrying them from the flat to the road) or jump on my feminist high horse because he's decided I'm a feeble woman who can't manage. On the other hand, he's almost a foot taller than me and the cases weigh a tonne. He's being a gentleman and I find I like this.

"Thanks," I say, delving into the rear seats and tugging out carriers stuffed with bedding and clothes. Oh dear. All my worldly goods make a rather pitiful collection."

"No probs, it's an awkward lift. Anyway, my mum, if she was here, would clip me round the ear if I didn't offer. It's not an Aussie bloke macho thing either, before you ask! Mum drilled us all when it came to manners." His voice is light but there's a sad note echoing through his voice and I realise he's thinking of her. "Talking of Mum, I'll pop her research over for you, if you like. It's only family stuff, but you never know, it could help with your book."

"That's brilliant. Thanks. I have the name of the author you mentioned too. He was called Gerald Snowe."

"Maybe he'll come up in Mum's research. You never know."

"Are you sure you don't mind lending me her work?"

"She'd be thrilled. It's not as though I'm going to do anything with it. Kim would be riding my case for ignoring it so long. It meant a lot to Mum; she really wanted me to finish what she'd started."

"Maybe I can help do that. Call it repayment for all the logs?"

"Sounds good to me," Noah says. "You're on!"

Once my belongings are in the Defender, Breakspear and I hop in. As Noah steers us down the drive, warning me that the car will skip over the ruts like a roo, I tell him what I've discovered about Gerald Snowe, thanks to Hamish Pendragon.

"Hamish is quite a character," Noah says. "Like me, he washed up here and stayed on. Sounds as though you have something really interesting to work on with all this."

"You think? I've wondered whether I'm getting carried away."

"Hey, people don't vanish from history unless there's a good reason. And Gerald getting his work removed from publication is plain weird. Seems to go against the whole point of being an author."

Noah guides the car around the tight hairpin bend and Oyster House is revealed in all its fading glory, basking in the sunlight in the style of Joan Collins reclining on a St Tropez beach. It's a stunning setting for a book, and I wish again that I could read Gerald's novel.

"You've not heard anything about ghosts or curses?" I'm wary of asking in case he sneers, but Noah looks worried.

"Is this because of something Treena said?"

"Sort of. She had all kind of stories about this place. You haven't heard anything about a drowning? A girl, maybe?"

Noah tuts. "Please don't take on board too much of what Treena says. She means well, but she doesn't always know when to stop. I've lived here for eighteen months and I've never heard anything unpleasant, I promise, or had any bad feelings. I think Oyster Shore's utterly beautiful. I could draw it for ever. It pulls you in, doesn't it? The endless way the water unfolds. I think it's healing, not haunted."

I know just what he means. The undulating water is mesmerising and the turning tides have a hypnotic quality. If I want to get anything done I may need to reconsider my idea of sitting in the window to write. I wonder how Gerald Snowe managed to get around this issue?

"It really does," I agree. "But the drowning wasn't Treena's story. It was something my granny told me about years ago. She came from Trevellan, and I wondered if it happened here."

"If the riverbank could speak it would have all sorts of tales to tell. The locals aren't much use. They stay away."

As we draw close to the house I recall the shadow I thought I'd seen earlier. All imagination, of course, but even so I shiver.

"But isn't that a bit weird? Wouldn't you expect kids to have made camps in the building? Or squatters to have moved in?"

"Too far to walk for kids, and not many people even know it's still here."

I twirl a curl around my forefinger. "I thought I saw ..." I stop abruptly. Shut up, Lowenna. You'll sound like a hysterical woman at best and crazy at worst.

"You thought what?" Noah dabs the brake, and the car slows, crawling past the weed-choked terrace. "What's worrying you? And don't say 'nothing' because I can tell that isn't true."

"It's daft, but when I walked past the house on the way up to meet you just now I thought I saw someone inside it, upstairs. It was probably a trick of the light ... No, it *was* a trick of the light. What else could it have been?"

Noah stops the car and pulls up the handbrake. "I'll go and check."

"You don't need to. Honestly. It was just my imagination."

"That's as maybe, but in case it isn't I need to check, because that house isn't structurally safe upstairs. Nobody should be up there. I'll go and look."

I'm mortified at inconveniencing Noah Wilson yet again.

"Please don't. Not on my behalf."

"I'm meant to be the maintenance man, so it's in my remit. Squatters wouldn't be safe because the whole place could come down like a pack of cards. It's only a whisper away from demolition." He throws the door open, adding over his shoulder, "Come with me. You can have a look at a place your author would have known. It might not look much now, but it could inspire you."

It's inspiring me now, yet something repels me too. The blank windows stare at us, affronted, and the ivy seems to cling even tighter. Even in such a dilapidated state the building is imposing and without the engine's grumble the place is graveyard-quiet. With Breakspear eager to escape, I follow Noah up the age-nibbled stone steps to the ugly security door which he unlocks with a series of keys. I wait, twirling my curl faster and faster. This was a place Gerald Snowe was only too keen to disassociate himself with. He worked hard to ensure that his name wasn't forever linked with this place. Was there something here that unnerved him? The curse? Bad luck? Or is this sense of unease an energetic residue of his antipathy?

The door swings open, groaning hinges protesting, and I follow Noah inside; even coated with dust and swathed in gloom the entrance hall is impressive. A staircase sweeps up, the return doubling back beneath a large window which must have once flooded the space with light. Today thick foliage presses against the glass and the place feels gloomy and unloved. The elaborately tiled floor is dark with years of dust and mould, lank strips of wallpaper peel from damp walls and the smell of damp makes my nose wrinkle. At the farthest end of the hall a large marble fireplace has pride of place, elaborately carved with blank-eyed nymphs whose garlanded and flattened heads bear the weight of the mantel, and I imagine how it must have once blazed and filled this vast space with warmth. Maybe Gerald Snowe warmed his hands in front of it? Or waited at the bottom of the stairs for the woman he loved to sweep down in a ballgown? Did he set his lost masterpiece in this house? Or was the Oyster Shore of his imagination more akin to the world of the boathouse?

How I wish I knew.

Six doors open off the hallway, and Noah steps into each echoing room, sweeping his iPhone torch into the emptiness. Satisfied there are no intruders, he cautiously makes his way up the staircase to check the upstairs although we both already know it will be empty. I wait below because the boards are rotten and as his steps pass overhead the whole house creaks and sighs like a ship in a gale.

"All clear!" he calls down. "I'll just check the attic."

He doesn't need to, though, because Oyster House is empty. Nobody's hiding here, swaddled in shadows and watching us from dark corners, and no unseen eyes follow me as I peek into each dark room. No graffiti tags taint the walls. Nobody has carved their initials into the rich panelling. Not so much as a sweet wrapper litters the floor. Just as I was told in the pub, nobody comes to this house any more. It's long forgotten. But why should this be? Even in its dilapidated state the elegant proportions and beautiful riverside setting are whispers of a once breathtaking property. What could have motivated anyone to abandon it?

"We're all clear." Noah is back at my side. He brushes cobwebs from his jeans and wipes his hands on the denim. "Nobody's been up there recently."

"Sorry. I told you I was imagining things."

"Don't apologise. It's good to check. Let's lock up and get the rest of your things moved in."

He starts to usher me forward, his hand in the small of my back, but I don't move. I can't move because I'm rooted to the spot, all my focus trained on the elaborate stained glass of the cupola far above my head. The glass, piebalded by old leaves and moss, would have gone unnoticed except that a ray of sunlight, permeating the knotted trees, is stroking the dome tenderly. As I gaze up it illuminates a design so familiar that I blink, not quite able to believe what I'm seeing.

High above me, with sapphire wings outstretched and crimson beak wide open in full song, is an unmistakable, and very familiar, blue bird.

10

THE PRESENT

Cornwall

Lowenna

I pull the comb out of my pocket and show it to Noah.

"I just found this on the beach. It's the same design, isn't it? Tell me I'm not going mad!"

He glances upwards. "If you are, then so am I. That's identical."

I run my finger over the chipped enamel, a pale echo of the glowing copy above. "My grandmother had a comb just like this. My sister and I used to fight over who got to wear it."

I'm transported to the sitting room with raindrops trickling down steamed-up glass, and Marina taunting me by holding the comb out of my reach. How did our great-grandmother come to possess this link to Oyster House?

Noah whistles. "Now I *am* a bit spooked. What are the chances of finding another?"

"My granny grew up near here. Maybe she found the other one when she was beachcombing? Perhaps they were lost at the same time?"

Noah takes the comb and weighs it in. his hand. "It's a beautiful piece, and I'd say it's art nouveau, which places it at around the turn of the last century. I don't think it would have been cheap, either. See that red eye? It's possibly a ruby, and the claws look like gold leaf."

Gold and rubies? Could it have been the jewelled comb, then, that the stranger had alluded to when he'd told my great-grandmother that the contents of his box contained a fortune? It might have made more sense just to tell her so; she could have sold it and bought her children shoes or enough coal to see them through the winter.

"But how is it that the same blue bird design is in the window?"

There's something just a fingertip's reach away, I can feel it. The woman who'd owned this comb must have been linked to Oyster House. Had she seen this window and asked a craftsman to copy the design?

"That's a phoenix, not a mortal bird," Noah says gently. "The phoenix is part of the Trelyon family's coat of arms. If you look around it's pretty much everywhere. It's on the hotel gates at Vyvyan Court and the memorial in the church. Most importantly, it's on the pub sign!"

Distracted by the pursuit of food I hadn't paid the sign a great deal of attention but on closer inspection it's obvious this sapphire creature with its fiery eyes and cruel talons isn't an ordinary bird.

"Whoever owned this comb had it designed to match her family's coat of arms, then? It beats my tatty scrunchie!"

"In Oz girls use elastic bands," Noah laughs.

I turn the comb to catch the light. The ruby eye glitters knowingly. What secrets is it keeping?

"A comb like this would have been worn on special occasions. Maybe for a party?"

"There were enough of those here once," Noah says. "Perhaps the owner dropped it. Or went swimming and it fell out. The tide turns so fast downriver it could have been swept away in moments."

Or perhaps she was in the arms of her lover who'd tugged the combs out before running his hands through hair the colour of bracken? I recall the slender girl in white, bent low over the sand as she scoured the tideline. Is she searching for lost combs rather than shells? Scanning the tideline for the crimson glimmer of a ruby eye?

"My mum used to say the past never stays hidden and that secrets always have a way of being uncovered," Noah says thoughtfully as, search completed, he locks the house up. His hand just hovering above the small of my back, he guides me down the uneven steps. "Watch that part, Wenna. It's loose."

My tread misses and he catches my elbow. As he steadies me, I feel the strength in Noah's arms, a strength which comes from physical exercise beneath the wide skies rather than from treadmills and the endless lifting of weights. It seems like the first time in ages a man has touched me, and I pull away as soon as I'm safely on the path.

If Noah notices, or is offended, the warm cadence of his voice gives nothing away. "I think that's why Mum liked working on the family tree. She said it made her feel like a detective and part of something more. When she found we had British roots on her side I thought she'd pop. That was a big surprise."

"You didn't know?"

"Nobody was really interested before. Dad's family were from Sydney and, like I said, if you want status Down Under it's all about being related to a convict. Mum was really into her research. I feel bad I haven't done anything with it."

"You've had a bit on yourself."

"Yeah, I guess. Anyways, if Mum was here she'd be desperate to know more about that comb. She'd be digging half the beach up looking for more treasure and buying a metal detector. Maybe you could get Treena to help? She'll bully Gareth into taking the digger down. Or swing her crystals to locate more loot."

"I don't need a digger or crystals to find treasure," I say. As we return to the car I tell him about Granny May's box. I can hardly wait for it to arrive.

"Sounds like you have several treasure hunts on with all your family stuff and Gerald Snowe," Noah says, opening his car door and helping me inside. I resist the urge to tug my shorts down. Climbing into a Defender is nowhere near as easy as Brenda Blethen makes it look on *Vera*.

Noah leaps effortlessly into the driver's seat. "I'll fish out Mum's notes. Hopefully they'll be some use. She'd be glad to think so, anyway."

"I can't wait to have a look," I say. "You never know what you might find when sifting through texts. I've worked with enough authors to know that nuggets are often hiding where you least expect them."

"I hope you find some." Noah lets out the clutch and the car lurches forward over the rutted ground. "Jeez! Hang on tight, Wenna. This part's rough."

The drive peels away and Oyster House vanishes as we turn into the woods. Moments later the boathouse emerges, drenched in sunlight and with the windows twinkling. My heart lifts. I hadn't realised just how oppressive I'd found the decaying old house. Added to Treena's talk of ghosts, curses and the strange tale of Gerald Snowe, it's no wonder I'm feeling on edge.

By the time the sun slips behind the trees and the river is a low line that mirrors the purpling trees and lilac grasses, I have created some semblance of order. Most of my belongings, carried into the boathouse by Noah – who'd flatly refused to allow me to lug up a single bag – are unpacked. The lamps are lit, Radio Four chats softly to itself and Breakspear snoozes by the wood burner. With my own things about the place the boathouse feels more and more like home. Even the gloomy bedroom feels friendlier with my duvet in situ and my to-be-read pile stacked on the bedside table. The atmosphere softens with the lamplight, and it feels as though the boathouse is pleased to be inhabited. The misgivings of earlier on are just fragments of a bad dream, and I can laugh at myself for being foolish. No more supernatural chat with Treena. I don't need to be distracted.

But Noah Wilson has the potential to be a very different kind of distraction, for my thoughts keep drifting in his direction. From his easy laughter to his kindness when delivering my bags, Noah's shown himself to be a thoughtful man as well. Recalling the heat of his skin on mine when he steadied me outside Oyster House, I know it's more than the wine making my head spin tonight, but risking my heart aside, I don't fancy taking scary Fi on.

I pick up my wine glass and wander to the window. A fat moon floats above trees while its twin drifts lazily in the inky water. I peer through my own reflection and see stars speckling the sky and the orange pinhead of Mars. The world of streets and corner shops feels just as distant as the red planet, and as alien: I feel as though I couldn't be any further away from the world I know.

The phoenix comb rests besides my laptop, its enamelled feathers glowing softly in the lamplight and its metal teeth snarling. I push it into my own hair and wonder about the last woman to do the same. Did this comb slide out unnoticed? Fall when she was stepping into a boat? Slip as she tipped her head back to smile up at a lover, skirts held up above feet buttoned into delicate boots as a he helped her into a rowing boat? In my imagination the man is Gerald Snowe, dapper in a boater and stripy blazer, and the combs tumbled into the water with a splash. Or maybe they were stolen, and fell from the thief's pockets as he scrambled across the shore before vanishing into the woods? So many stories. So many questions. So few answers.

I boot up my laptop to see if I have any replies to the emails I sent before I'd unpacked. One of the three in my inbox is from David, which I delete instantly. The second is from Drew, telling me he's never come across Gerald Snowe but saying he'll ask his wife to do some digging at the British Library. I fire back my thanks and ask after their twins, glad that we've stayed friends. The third email – the one I save for last because it's very exciting – is from Matthew Enys of the Kernow Heritage Foundation; it'll be a reply to my enquiry about Gerald Snowe. That was fast! I can hardly wait to discover what he knows.

I'd emailed Matt, an acknowledged expert on Cornwall during the First World War, asking whether he knew anything about Gerald Snowe or the Trelyons. They may have been known to the Rivers family, I'd suggested, and possibly attended the same social gatherings. It was a long shot, and imagining how busy Matt must be with Rosecraddick Manor and his burgeoning television career, I hadn't expected to hear back this quickly. I open the email and am thrilled by the genuine interest which rings through his reply. Even though he can tell me little more about Gerald Snowe than Hamish could, Matt Enys agrees with the theory that the enigmatic author and Kit Rivers were likely to have come across one another.

Cornwall's a small county, where everyone knows everyone, Matt writes. *At the turn of the last century that would have certainly been the case among the upper classes, who were expected to socialise, and later on marry, within a very limited social group. For Gerald Snowe and Kit Rivers not to have come across one another seems highly unlikely.*

Trevellan and Vyvyan Court are mentioned in several letters we keep here at the museum. In one, Kit mentions a Private Carew from Trevellan and his poem Dugout *describes an explosion hitting the trench and killing several of his men. I'm afraid, though, Gerald Snowe isn't mentioned in any of Kit's letters or notebooks. But Gerald may have been present on embarkation day to say goodbye to his friends and wish them luck. It would have been unusual for a man of his status not to have been there.*

I've recently come into possession of a wonderful collection of images taken by a travelling photographer working in Cornwall just before the First World War. It's possible this man was also commissioned to take portraits of the Snowe Family or even that the enigmatic Gerald appears in some taken at the social gatherings at Rosecraddick Manor. I don't know if you have any means of identifying him, but it may be helpful to look at this collection of photographs. I'll dig out anything I think may be of interest, and am free after four tomorrow, if that suits?

Best wishes,

Matt Enys

I don't need to think twice about my answer. If it suits? Of course it does! If I could, I'd drive there now!

I fetch another glass of wine and return to the laptop. I'm getting closer to finding out the truth about *On Oyster Shore.* Even the red eye of the phoenix comb seems to twinkle at me with approval.

11

THE PRESENT

Cornwall

Lowenna

Reposing at the end of a neatly raked gravel drive, Rosecraddick Manor snoozes in the afternoon sunshine like a stately dowager after one too many sherries. It's late in the day and the geometrically clipped topiary is casting long indigo shadows over the lawns, but visitors are still strolling through the grounds, eating ice creams. I'm tempted to buy one myself but having spent ages crawling here behind a tractor before struggling to find a spot to park, I'm running late and I don't even have time to enjoy another look around the museum. I'll have to save that, and a vanilla cornet, for another time.

Matt Enys is waiting for me on a bench in the walled garden, a sun-soaked spot where bees thrum and the air is fragrant with rosemary. I recognise him at once from his documentaries, and wave before realising he won't have a clue who I am. Luckily he joins the dots and waves back, and with his shy smile and warm manner soon puts me at my ease. Before long we're chatting away about Kit Rivers and war poetry, and I've forgotten that I'm in the presence of a TV star.

Unlike Oyster House and Vyvyan, Rosecraddick Manor has escaped the neglect and decay of the past century to become, Matt Enys says proudly, the jewel in the crown of the Kernow Heritage Foundation.

"It's been a labour of love, but I do sometimes wonder how many of our visitors actually think about war or read the poems. Most of them seem far more interested in the tearoom and gift shop," Matt confides as he shepherds me along a rosemary-hemmed path.

"I confess the last time I visited, ice creams and souvenirs were high on my list too. I think what you do so well here is to make the past feel real. Kit feels as though he's a friend and you could stumble across him at any minute."

Matt flushes with pleasure and it's clear how much the manor means to him. A quiet man, handsome in a dishevelled and slightly chaotic way that reminds me of David Tennant's Doctor Who, I soon fall under his spell as he tells me about the memorial garden and the discovery that changed everything for the manor.

"Sorry if I'm rabbiting on," he says. "You can probably tell this is my passion."

"It's absolutely fascinating. Thanks so much for giving me so much context."

Matt laughs. "Trust me, the pleasure's all mine. You've probably gathered that this isn't just a job for me. It's safer to say it's an obsession. I confess I feel rather ashamed that I've never heard of Gerald Snowe. As a contemporary writer he could well be a part of Kit's story."

"I think being unknown is exactly what Gerald wanted," I sigh.

"As you've said, very strange indeed. Writers usually long for immortality, and as shy as they are in person their work is often the vehicle for conveying a message they feel duty-bound to share: Owen's was the pity of war, Kit's the power of love in the face of annihilation. It's rare for a writer to achieve critical and commercial success only to retract it."

"More than retract it. A local bookshop owner, Hamish Pendragon, told me that Gerald Snowe destroyed every copy of the book he could find and withdrew all the rights to publication. Hamish was absolutely certain about that, and about Snowe becoming a recluse in later life."

"If anyone knows about literary Cornwall, it's Hamish," says Matt.

"You know him?"

"Of course! He's a member of the Gorsedh Kernow."

"What's that? A secret society?"

Matt laughs. "I'm afraid not, although Hamish would absolutely love that idea! The Gorsedh Kernow are Cornish Bards. They elect to their ranks only the few people they feel worthy of the honour, and their mission is to maintain the Celtic heritage and literature of the county. There's not much Hamish doesn't know about Cornish language and literature."

"Even he didn't know much at all about Gerald Snowe. Nobody seems to."

Matt Enys takes off his glasses and polishes them on his sleeve. "Which makes this even more interesting, don't you think? Gerald Snowe went to extraordinary lengths to remove himself and his great work from history. I wonder what he was hiding? Or what he wanted to protect?"

"I'm wondering the same thing."

"The fact that another young man was writing less than ten miles away from Kit – a young man he may have known and even shared his work with – is incredible." Matt bounces on the balls of his feet. "I hope you get to the bottom of it all. There are so many missing pieces in this jigsaw."

I teeter on the brink of telling him about the mysterious stranger who'd left a box of 'treasures' with my great-grandmother, but Matt moves on to discussing cataloguing the early work of Alex Evans, the travelling photographer he had mentioned in his email.

"Latterly a war photographer, and one of the very best there ever has been, Evans spent a couple of years working in Cornwall and undertaking private commissions. He may well have visited Vyvyan Court, since he attended most social gatherings in the vicinity and took portraits of the great and good. Evans was also the official photographer on several enlistment days."

"Gerald didn't enlist. Hamish said he had a medical exemption."

"All very unusual," Matt says. "Maybe somebody pulled strings to keep him away from the action? Used a spurious medical complaint to keep him safe?"

"Like an ex-president's bone spurs?"

He grins. "*Exactly*! Although we could be being very unfair to Gerald Snowe. He might have been desperate to fight alongside his friends but had a genuine ailment. Most of the young men flocked to enlist. You can tell that from Evans' photographs. It was like a carnival."

"Kit Rivers wasn't desperate to join up." I recall the part in the film where the young poet had bowed to the weight of expectations and enlisted. The scene where he'd broken the news to the girl he loved had made me cry buckets. How awful to know you had no choice but to leave behind everything and everyone you held dear. And what courage it must have taken to do your duty anyway.

Matt's mirth dissolves. "Kit understood his duty. He also had a military background, and by all accounts was an excellent captain. Unfortunately for Gerald, anyone left behind wouldn't have been seen in the same light as those who fought, even if they had a good reason not to go."

"He was ashamed of not fighting and didn't feel he deserved success?" I offer.

"It's a good theory. Maybe you'll be able to prove it. Anyway, thanks to you I've made myself sit down and work through lots of photographs. I've even managed to sort out some which may be useful, although how you'll recognise Gerald Snowe is anyone's guess. They weren't big on labelling pictures back then. The historians of the future are going to have a much easier time since we're all tagging ourselves on Facebook and Instagram, and blogging about our lunch. My kids are always going on about TikTok, too. I'm such a dinosaur I haven't a clue what they mean."

"I think you should pity the future historians. They'll have to watch lots of people doing strange dances, and be forced to study pictures of food," I say. "And not to mention all the squabbles about Brexit."

Matt winces. "I can't think of anything worse. I'll stick to analogue archives. Anyway, let me show you what I've found."

He ushers me through a small door, almost hidden beneath smothering ivy and wisteria. After the brightness of the afternoon, the interior of the old house is dark, and a hidden clock ticks in the gloom, sonorous and assured. We descend a flight of stairs and follow a subterranean passageway whose flagstone floor is worn into dips from centuries of trudging feet. It feels as though I'm travelling through time, a sensation which increases when we surface in the museum, where Kit and his comrades are forever young as they gaze out from enlarged photographs. The blinds are drawn, and low spotlights illuminate the exhibits and highlight smudged fingerprints on the glass cases. It's a little like entering a church, but with its holy relics of war, and its shrines decorated with the faces of lost young men rather than stained-glass saints.

"It's so different after closing time," I say, glancing around. "It's so still."

"This would have been one of the busiest parts of the house in Kit's day," Matt tells me as we walk through several connecting rooms. "This was the servants' domain, and these rooms mostly used for storage or preparing food. This was the servants' hall."

We're in a vaulted space lined with display cabinets and boasting a large table in the centre. It isn't hard to imagine servants jumping to attention when one of the bells rings from the row set high up on the wall. On the far side of the room is an exhibition featuring enlarged sepia pictures of long-ago staff. A cook. A butler. A stern-faced housekeeper. Maids. Valets. Footmen. Gamekeepers. An entire army of people whose existence here was for the sole purpose of looking after the Rivers family. I imagine my ancestors would have filled similar roles at Vyvyan Court.

"It really makes you think about how life was for most folk in a system that benefited the select and fortunate few,"

Matt says. "We've gone a bit fluffy and Downton in this room, but the visitors like it. Your chap, Gerald, would have known something very similar to this setup. If anything, Vyvyan's even bigger than this house; the Trelyons were a very wealthy family."

"I think they'd lost their money by Gerald's time."

"You're absolutely right. I've done a bit of digging – not a great deal, I'm afraid – but by the early twentieth century the Trelyon family fortune was certainly diminished. The estate was entailed, which meant—"

"Only a male could inherit," I say, unable to contain myself. "That's how Gerald's family came to be renting it. After the war, when most of the young men had been killed, the entail was broken, and the estate sold off."

Matt rolls his eyes at me. "I'm lecturing, aren't I? I drive my kids crazy."

"Don't apologise. It's fascinating. If I'm going to write a book about Gerald Snowe this context will really help."

Matt listens as I tell him about my publishing background, leaving out any mention of David, and if Matt senses gaps in what I say he's polite enough not to press.

"Erasmus House were interested in Kit's letters," he says slowly. "They weren't impressed when we went for a bigger publishing house, but we needed as much money as we could possibly get. The manor's a hungry beast to feed."

I recall how David had stomped around the office that day.

"I hope the publishers fight for mine," is all I say.

"For what it's worth, I think you have a fascinating subject," Matt says kindly. "Wouldn't it be great if you find a link to Kit Rivers? There could be an entire literary scene going on in this part of Cornwall that nobody knows about. Imagine that!"

I laugh. "That's the dream! In the meantime, I'd settle for knowing anything about him. I can find birth and death dates easily enough, and I've got a researcher on the case at the British Library, but Gerald's literary life seems to have been totally erased."

"Intentionally erased if the withdrawal of his own book's anything to judge by. It's fascinating!"

"I'd expect to find some more original manuscripts, as you have for Kit, but it's as though Snowe never wrote another word."

Matt frowns. "That's unusual. Writers usually leave notebooks or journals. They pen letters and diaries, too, because writing is a compulsion for them. It was certainly that way for Kit. There must be source material somewhere for Gerald Snowe. Or a copy of the book."

"No such luck. Hamish calls it a lost masterpiece."

"A masterpiece which came from nowhere, without a clear genesis or evidence of any literary aspirations from the author. That's compelling stuff! If I were you I'd see what I could find out about Gerald's early life. Did he show literary promise at school? Was he a reader? Did he write letters? Stories for his friends?"

"Yep. I've got a heap of research to do," I say.

It's feeling a little like a dead end. But Matt is excited. "I envy you! That's the fun bit. I always think of it as a treasure hunt; each new detail is another clue and a step closer to finding the truth. Let's start with what we *do* know; the Snowe family came to Vyvyan Court in 1904. That was the year the direct Trelyon line ended with a daughter and a distant cousin inherited the estate. Vyvyan Court was rented to the

Snowes until the early nineteen-twenties. After that it's all a bit murky."

"Any reason why?"

"Nothing sinister. Lots of documents were lost during the Second World War when Vyvyan was requisitioned by the army. Like so many of these great houses, after the military left it was in a bad way and was eventually abandoned. So even if she *had* been allowed to inherit in 1904, Madalyn Trelyon – that's the daughter – would have been forced to give it up by the forties."

Madalyn Trelyon. The name shivers in the air like a single note played on a violin vibrates long after the bow is lowered. Are they her combs? Is she the girl in white, trailing the shore that should have been hers? Have I glimpsed the past through a threadbare patch in time's fabric?

"It's very unfair that she couldn't inherit."

"Male heirs were all-important. It's only very recently, in 2011, that the Royal Marriages Act allowed a daughter to ascend the throne if she was the firstborn. But that doesn't mean that the aristocracy will follow suit – well, they haven't so far, at any rate; in nearly all of our noble families a daughter can never inherit the property or the title. But I don't suppose Madalyn would have questioned the way of the world, as she'd have only been about seven years old when the estate passed to her cousin. Her sole purpose in life would have been to marry well in order to support her widowed mother."

"And did she?"

"I've no idea. Like I said, there aren't a great deal of records, and I haven't had time to delve in any detail." Matt regards me curiously. "I thought it was Gerald Snowe you're interested in?"

I'm not sure how to explain my sudden fascination with Madalyn Trelyon. It's as though I've caught hold of a new thread, given it a tug and followed it to a new design in the tapestry.

"Would Madalyn have known Gerald?"

"Possibly, although her direct family wouldn't have been living here. Madalyn and her mother may have lived in the summer house, though – that's Oyster House. The family did retain it for their private use."

"I hope she became a suffragette, went to university and had a wonderful life," I say staunchly.

"I think it's far more likely that she married a man from her own milieu and became a dutiful wife. Maybe you can find out? In the meantime, have a look what I've been able to find." Matt gestures to the mosaic of photographs and documents set out on a table. "Hopefully some of it'll be useful."

I lean forward as he points out scenes and locations. Figures pose on croquet lawns, hunts meet outside stately homes, and family portraits are composed with painstaking attention to detail. Dressed formally, the subjects stare out unsmiling from a world as lost as the names belonging to their long-forgotten faces.

"I found this particular portrait with Alex Evans' early studio work. I believe it could be the Snowe family." Matt points to a photo of a woman in a huge cartwheel hat, a man with a bushy beard reminiscent of nineteenth-century Russian tsars, and a sullen dark-haired youth standing awkwardly outside a grand ivy-smothered house. My first impression is that none of the three seem to be at ease or feel they belong there.

"Look closely at the young man," says Matt. "He could be Gerald Snowe. He looks about the right age." Pale-faced and with a neat beard, the slender young man, clad in stripy blazer and cream trousers, holds himself with the air of superiority I used to see in David's public-school friends. The belligerent stare is familiar, and from the depths of my memory arises the image of a little boy in a sailor suit glowering at the camera with a similar dark intensity.

Henry.

Is it possible? Could the little boy in my grandmother's picture be this young man? Gerald Snowe?

"How can you tell who they are?" I ask Matt. The unsmiling trio could have been any wealthy family of the period, except that it was unusual that the couple appeared to have had only one child.

"The picture's taken outside Vyvyan Court. See the Trelyon crest above the door?"

I peer closer. Sure enough the phoenix emblem that adorns the combs and the cupola snarls above stony flames. The Trelyons certainly liked to mark what was theirs.

"The date of this image also fits with the dates you gave me. I'd place money on the young man being Gerald Snowe. The same lad's in this photograph" – pointing to another one on the table – "with a young woman. From the composition I'd say it's an engagement portrait."

"But Gerald Snowe was a bachelor."

"Maybe the relationship ended."

"Hamish thought there was a story about a broken engagement," I say slowly. Is this it? Is the reason for Gerald's loathing of his book something as simple and as complicated as heartbreak? His great book reminded him of the girl he'd lost?

I pick up the photograph and study it. A young couple stand before the same great house beneath the beady eye of the phoenix. The dark-haired young man, a little older now, sports a neat beard and lifts his chin proudly, as though commanding everyone to admire the girl beside him, her hand tucked into the crook of his arm. The pride he feels is understandable, for she is beautiful in the timeless way the very lovely always are.

I stare and stare. If I didn't know better, I'd swear that this is Princess Clementine grown up. Although her eyes have lost their boot-button boldness and are cast down modestly, she has the same heart-shaped face and rosebud mouth.

"Do you know who she is?" I ask Matt.

"I'm afraid I haven't a clue. I've never looked that closely at these particular pictures. They're an important part of the archive but I've been so busy with Evans's war photography that his early ones have taken a bit of a back seat."

"I think I recognise both of them," I say slowly.

"Really? How's that?"

I tell him about Granny May's box, how it was delivered by a stranger who'd made her mother angry, and his strange promise that it would make the family a fortune. I even describe the games my sister and I had made up about the children in the pictures, which makes him smile.

"My mother's sending the box to me, and I can't wait to see if Gerald's the same little boy from the photograph," I finish.

"That would be some coincidence. I'm afraid I haven't been able to find any more pictures which might be of Gerald, but feel free to look at the others. If nothing else they'll give you an idea of how life was back then. These on the left are the Trevellan Enlistment Day ones. I always find them so moving. Those boys didn't have a clue what lay ahead, and just as well."

The images are all of young men, proud and serious as they take the King's shilling. Two friends stand with their arms slung around one another's shoulders as they face the camera and the grand adventure ahead, blissfully ignorant that death is already breathing down their necks.

"M. Penwurthy and E. Carew," I read. "Hey! Marrick was my granny's father! That's my great-grandfather!"

"Seriously?"

I raise my hand to my own tangled curls which are identical to those squashed beneath the cap the young man wears. To see my own hair on this stranger is unexpectedly moving, and I'm close to tears. Scary Marrick wasn't always that way: he was once young and freckled, and close to his friends.

And he looked a lot like me.

"That's him. My grandmother often talked about her dad. He was a fisherman."

Matt picks up the picture and holds it next to my face. "I think I can see a similarity. Yes, it's in the chin and the hair. Definitely. That's incredible, Lowenna. Did Marrick make it through the war?"

"Yes. Granny May always said he was one of the lucky ones. All his brothers died at the Front. I wonder if his friend made it home?"

The friend is the same height, with a clear-eyed gaze set above high cheekbones. A lock of fair hair falls across his forehead and a dimple dances in his cheek. I have seen him before too.

N. OS. 1914

This is the young man from the sketches, I'm absolutely certain of it. Like Gerald Snowe, he too is linked to my family.

"That's Edward Carew from Kit's poem. You have a link to

literary history, Lowenna, if he's standing with your great-grandfather. He's recorded as lost in action, I'm afraid."

I stare at the patchwork of pictures on the table, faces floating in a sea of lost Cornish lads, poppies blooming like spilled blood where they fell in combat. Did Gerald Snowe consider himself lucky to have avoided seeing action? Or did he feel cheated of his chance to be a hero like my great-grandfather and Kit Rivers? And what about the girl beside Gerald in the photograph? Who was she? And who was it who had once sketched Edward Carew with such tenderness? My great-grandmother? A lost lover? Or even Marrick himself? Why not?

There are no answers, but later, as I drive back towards Oyster Shore with the manor house shrinking in my rear-view mirror and the sky behind it streaked peach and gold, I feel certain that when I discover why Gerald Snowe went to such lengths to make sure his great novel was lost, I'll be a lot closer to finding some of the truth. I can't wait for Granny May's box to arrive. I have the strongest feeling it holds the key to everything.

12

THE PRESENT

Cornwall

Lowenna

You have a link to literary history. Matt's words follow me home, riding shotgun through the darkening Cornish lanes and then floating alongside like will-o'-the-wisps as I hurry down the drive to the boathouse. As the shadows lengthen and the sky bruises, my pace quickens. Curses and hauntings can be laughed off in the daylight, but when dusk blooms it's harder to rationalise fear. Although the old house is behind me now, I can't help glancing over my shoulder just in case I spot the girl in white or glimpse a little boy in a sailor suit tagging behind his friends.

I let myself into the boathouse deep in thought, greeted with great joy by Breakspear. I tip biscuits into his bowl, switch on some lamps and make coffee without really registering, because all I can think about are two young soldiers, one fated to die in battle and the other destined to become my great-grandfather. One immortalised in poetry, and the other in a fleeting expression on my face or the twist of my curls. But for the quirk of Fate which took Edward's life rather his friend's, I wouldn't even be here at all. How everything balances on the head of a pin. It's so fragile it's dizzying.

I make toast and sit at the table, transfixed by the red gaze of the phoenix comb I've placed there for inspiration. While the laptop attempts to link to my mobile hotspot, Radio Four plays quietly to itself from the kitchen, as comforting and familiar as the buttered toast piled high on my plate. I'm too preoccupied to eat, still busy wondering whether my great-grandfather was Joe, the scruffy village lad who played with Henry and Princess Clementine on the banks of Oyster Shore. Is Marrick Penwurthy the missing piece of the puzzle?

My head starts to ache, and bizarrely I miss David. He was a good professional sounding-board and loved a literary puzzle – especially if he thought it might lead to something commercial. After the success of the Kit Rivers film, anything associated with the young war poet has become gold, and David wouldn't leave a stone unturned until he was at the bottom of the mystery. He'd be making calls, charging off to interrogate Matt, and charming my mum so beautifully she'd have shimmied up the loft ladder herself to retrieve the box. Then he'd be in the pub buying the locals drinks to lubricate their memories, and he'd even impress Treena Trehunnist with his interest in crystals and tarot. I've witnessed such charm offensives a thousand times. It's how he manages to win agents over and persuade big authors to sign with such a small publishing house. It's also why he's so hugely successful for, just like the river over the wet sand, David Blake is unstoppable when he has set his sights on what he wants. This recollection swiftly dispels any nostalgia, because I don't want him taking over my book any more than I wanted him doing the same with my career and my life. In contrast, though, I can't wait to tell Noah about today's discovery; he's as intrigued as I am, and I know he'll listen to my thoughts before offering his own suggestions.

I look up, startled. Why am I suddenly comparing my partner of almost four years with a man I've known only a few days? I flick through a plethora of reasons and shy away from each one. Solitude is doing strange things to me, that's all. I need to focus on my research and start to find some solid leads. Tomorrow I'll walk into the village and see whether Selina Trewen wants to have a coffee and a chat about the history of the area. She might be able to tell me a little more about Madalyn Trelyon and shed some light on the family's connection to Gerald's story. Selina's father could have mentioned something to her in passing, and she strikes me as a woman whose sharp mind misses nothing.

Eventually the computer and the iPhone hook up, and the bright screen becomes a gateway to information. I type *trench death Trevellan soldier Kit Rivers* into the search engine and am served up with *Dugout*, one of his more famous poems. A harrowing piece, widely compared to Owen's *Dulce et Decorum Est,* it is unsparing of the reader's sensitivities as it lays bare the horror of an explosion which shattered bones and lives in the blink of an eye. As I read, the violence of scattered flesh and the shrill of panic are immediate as the poet pares confusion and carnage into imagery as bald and as bloodied as Private Carew's mangled body.

I minimise the page. It's one thing to read the poem from an academic perspective, but another entirely when you've seen the face of the young man who was smashed to bits in this confusion of gas and guns and blood-soaked khaki. Keen to find more insights, I turn to literary criticism and read arguments about whether Carew is a Christ-like figure and metaphor of sacrifice or merely a construct to make a political point, but the intellectual point-scoring from the safety of universities and Oxbridge colleges is far removed from the noise and hellish confusion of trench warfare. I scan several articles and conclude there's nothing here that makes the Front more real than the original poem and the photograph of Edward Carew and Marrick Penwurthy. The two young men are real to me now, and no longer abstract names or unknown and unmourned relatives. They are just boys, boys with hopeful faces, with good humour and with the world ahead of them. Young men who will be robbed of optimism, hope and life. Young men who wouldn't be out of place in Trevellan today, surfboards under their arms and faces tanned from sunshine and wind.

I open the gallery on my phone and scroll through until I find the photo of the two friends with their arms draped across each other's shoulders, and thankfully with no idea that in decades to come professors will argue over their significance in the work of a great poet. Was my great-grandfather Marrick with Kit Rivers and Edward Carew when the shell exploded? Did he dig for his friend? Or was he trapped too, held close by the embrace of death and mud as the world exploded above him? Was this the point in time when that open-faced young man began to morph into the irascible father that Granny May had feared upsetting?

I place my phone down on the table to return to the laptop and the poem. No matter how harrowing the subject is, I owe it to my great-grandfather and all the other men who fought in the trenches to face the truth about the experience of the war. I read through the poem several times, and each rereading feels like a physical blow. Like most British schoolchildren, I've studied First World War literature. I know all about the naïve boys hoping for glory and adventure, the soldier poets, the mud, the doughty women who became nurses and ambulance drivers. I'm familiar with Owen and Rivers and Sassoon, with young men going over the top and into hell, aristocrats and butchers' boys levelled as they fought through mud and choked in gas. There are films and books and plays, too, that are a part of our culture. As in Kit's poetry, there is no noble sacrifice or glory, but only slaughter as an entire generation was sent to an abattoir of mud, shell-holes and barbed wire.

Yes, these are stories I must have heard a hundred times, but with the picture of Marrick and Edward in front of me and the visit to the manor fresh in my mind, it's a remote tale no longer, but real and terrible because these soldiers were *boys*. They were fledgling adults with their downy top lips and coltish limbs, real people who lived and loved, and whose end was mostly brutal and ugly. There was no sense or logic to any of it. No glory, and certainly no noble sacrifice. It all feels very bleak and I rub my eyes until I see stars, needing a break from death and despair. At the very least a glass of wine is required.

Feeling heavy-hearted I'm poised to log off when the unread email icon appears on the screen, and my heart lifts to see this is a message from Drew, telling me his wife has managed to uncover some information about Gerald Snowe.

Anna says there wasn't a great deal on Snowe. She's attached a copy of a review of his book from ***The Mail*** *in 1919 and a couple of obituaries from the same period that might be of help. She wasn't able to get her hands on a copy of Snowe's novel, which she says is* *likely down to the confusion of the inter-war years. A lot of information was lost then, apparently, and a great deal in the bombing raids of the Second World War. Anna says she's intrigued now too!*

Your man Snowe was published in 1918, the same era that Proust and Freud and Hesse were published, so he's in exalted company. It's intriguing that Snowe hasn't stood the test of time, especially since his novel appears to have been exceedingly well received, according to the review. Anna says check out the attachments – she hopes they are helpful.

I skim over the rest of the email, which is mostly about Drew's new job as Head of English at a big comprehensive school and his general despair at the ineptitude of senior management and the latest education secretary. I open the attachments, all thoughts of wine and exhaustion forgotten, and read the 1919 newspaper review of *On Oyster Shore* which, although brief, is crammed with terms I'd have been overjoyed to have applied to any of my authors' work.

Hardyesque, with a bleak purity of the soul, the novel is set in an Eden torn and tarnished by war but where Nature's ability to console is upheld even though the protagonist's loyalties are as divided as the channels of the river threaded through the silt beneath his boathouse home. Here, the ties between nature and imagination are questioned through a narrative classic in its simplicity yet antithetically complex in lyricism. In one sense a simple novel of a boy and a girl whose love for one another and doomed hope for the future haunts the memory, the novel also scorches the soul with its bleakness and unsparing details of mechanised warfare. A landscape of the imagination, Snowe's ***On Oyster Shore*** *is as powerful as it is original and a lyrical triumph.*

I read the review again, greedy for any details. Then I read it for a third time and then a fourth. On each reading the reviewer's admiration for Snowe's work is unmistakable.

"*Hardyesque,*" I say to Breakspear. "*A narrative classic in its simplicity yet antithetically complex in lyricism.* That's the kind of review writers dream about. So why would Gerald want to kill his book? And why did such a talented man never write again?"

I lean back in my chair and mull over what I've just learned. I have some idea now what the subject of this lost book may have been. The review implies that it's a love story, but one destined to end with a loss that encapsulates the inevitability of the turning tides. It's a lyrical and measured work, simple in style yet complex in the ideas it explores. It's a novel about how love is eroded by time and war, and how high emotion becomes muted by duty and class and death. The book sounds beautiful and I wish more than ever that I could read it.

Nature's ability to console is upheld even though the protagonist's loyalties are as divided as the channels of the river threaded through the silt beneath his boathouse home.

This sentence makes my skin tingle. I was right: Gerald Snowe *would* have spent time in this boathouse. Did he write his book sitting in this very spot, watching the river wind its way to the sea and the tides ebb and flow? He must have done, for his book appears to have had the river flowing through every word. The silent herons and the sprightly dippers must surely have made their way onto the page, along with the creaky pontoon and this strangely ornate boathouse, lost amid the trees and tenderly cupped within a forgotten meander.

The second attachment Drew has sent is Gerald Snowe's obituary, which is brief and provides no new information. It makes no reference to his writing, and reinforces the idea that he stayed well away from Cornwall, passing away at a monastic hospital in London. I save the piece to my desktop before clicking on the final attachment, this time a cutting from a local Cornish paper. Expecting another version of what I've already read about Gerald, I'm taken aback to discover this last file is an obituary for a very different person.

Trelyon, The Hon. Madalyn Rose 1898–1917

ONLY DAUGHTER OF RUPERT, the Viscount Trelyon (deceased) and Constance, the Viscountess Trelyon, of Chatton Place, London, and latterly Oyster House, Trevellan. The young lady was lost tragically in her 20th year and a private service held in the parish church of St Nun, where a memorial will be erected in her memory. The sympathy of all goes out to Lady Constance in her great sorrow and also to Miss Trelyon's fiancé, Mr Gerald Snowe of Vyvyan Court.

MATT ENYS' hunch was right! Madalyn Trelyon, the girl who should have inherited the vast Vyvyan Estate and Oyster Shore, was engaged to Gerald and she had lived at Oyster House. I find the image of the handsome young couple on my phone and examine the beautiful girl. If this proud young man is Gerald Snowe then logic dictates she must be Madalyn Trelyon, his wife-to-be. If Madalyn appears stiff and downcast, this might well have been more about having to pose for a formal photograph than about her feelings towards her intended, for Gerald is handsome, in a brooding Heathcliff kind of way, and very wealthy to boot. Madalyn, raised to marry money and restore her family's fortunes, was probably thrilled to have landed such a catch. Her work was done. Mission accomplished.

Whoever wrote Madalyn's obituary knew that she and Gerald were engaged. I'm grateful for Drew's wife's archivist skills, since the few facts I do possess about Gerald present him as a confirmed bachelor who died alone and largely forgotten. The engagement was probably a low-key one given the events taking place across the Channel and any awkwardness caused by Gerald's medical exemption. Grief for a fiancée associated with his book had probably led to Gerald Snowe's obsession with obliterating the novel and disassociating himself from it. Death affects people in all kinds of ways.

I chew the end of my pen, then write *Madalyn Trelyon – lost tragically* on my pad and underline the words twice. The phrase 'lost tragically' is vague in a way that's undoubtedly deliberate. Any death at that age is a tragedy. Why not state the cause? Illness? An accident? Murder? The more I consider this coy phrase the more I'm convinced that what's *not* said about Madalyn Trelyon's death is the important part of her story. The gaps swirl with possibilities, and my mind is busy selecting any which could fit. A murder would have made the papers. An illness was sure to have been mentioned. As was an accident. What would be so awful that it couldn't be mentioned? Was considered so taboo that the local paper would recoil from reporting it? Did Madalyn kill herself? Or – and this one requires a big leap of imagination but could be another explanation for his antipathy to his book – did Gerald kill her? A crime of passion? Or maybe she'd been lost in a dreadful accident? A drowning?

There's a sudden ripple in the atmosphere. Breakspear raises his head from his paws and stares out into the darkness where the river slides past, unseen and silent in the darkness. The intensity of his gaze makes the hairs on the nape of my neck prickle, and when he whines I have an urge to leap up and draw the curtains to shut out the yawning night. Is this where Madalyn Trelyon met her tragic end? Is Madalyn the drowned girl of Granny May's stories and the ghost Davey Tuckey mentioned?

"If Treena was here she'd swing a crystal and ask the spirits," I say to Breakspear, but my dog is too busy watching the darkness. He whines again.

"What is it, boy? What's out there?"

I stare outside into the emptiness, but all I can see is my own reflection swimming in blackness, pale-faced and wide-eyed. It's impossible to distinguish anything that may be lurking in the inky world beyond the glass. Although it's probably a fox creeping past that's caught Breakspear's attention, I draw the curtains swiftly, and the boathouse becomes a lamplit life-raft floating in the middle of the woodland ocean. I'm being a silly townie – afraid of the dark when there are no street lights and bright corner shops to chase the shadows away.

I pour a glass of wine and return to my work. Murder aside, since there's no evidence of that, what was taboo in 1917? Suicide seems the obvious answer. Wasn't it only recently that suicides could be buried in churchyards as against unhallowed ground? Taking your own life probably wasn't seen as a cry for help in early nineteen-hundreds. Suicide would have been considered shameful, so it would make perfect sense to keep one a secret, especially if it involved a high-ranking family like the Trelyons. This theory seems to hold together. Granny May's story about a girl who drowned is likely to have been based on the tragedy of

Madalyn Trelyon as her story slipped from fact into local legend. Selina Trewen was frustrated when we parted, because she was certain there was something she'd forgotten about Oyster Shore. Could this have been the story of a mysterious death?

I click the pen nib in and out in time with my volley of thoughts. The hypothesis makes sense. There's no ornate gravestone for Madalyn – just a memorial, which suggests no body – and no mention of a big funeral service befitting the daughter of a viscount. As she was the last in the direct line of a family which had held great influence in Trevellan since feudal times, it seems very odd that her death was brushed aside. A cover-up for a suicide makes perfect sense, and in the chaos of war people probably didn't ask too many questions.

Lassoing this theory is the easy part; tethering it onto the page with hard facts is the tricky bit. There's also the question I'm afraid to ask myself: who was the girl in white collecting shells on the tideline? The girl with bracken-red hair who drifted with the turning tides? Have I seen Madalyn's ghost? Or is it just my imagination, easily triggered in this atmospheric place?

Stick to facts, I tell myself sternly as I google "Madalyn Trelyon". Facts are the bedrock of biographies, not gut feelings or ghosts or intuition. I need to keep it factual. History is supposed to be factual, and there's a huge amount of history about the Trelyon family: they go back to the reign of Henry II and have held many exalted posts, their fortunes rising and falling with the monarchs they support, yet no matter how much I scroll and click through the knights and courtiers and members of Parliament up to the early years of the 20th century there's no mention of a Trelyon girl who was lost so desperately young. It's as though Madalyn has been erased from history.

My hunt comes to a dead end. Like Gerald's book, it's as though Madalyn never existed, a peculiarity which arouses my suspicions that somebody once worked very hard to eradicate both. Tangled up in this mystery is the curious link to Kit Rivers, Edward Carew and my own great- grandfather. I turn my attention to the picture of Marrick and his friend, certain that these young men are the key to unlocking the puzzle. Enlarging the image on my phone and zooming in, I spot something which adds an entirely new layer, and which makes me wonder whether my tired eyes are playing tricks.

"Impossible," I breathe, zooming in even more closely until the pixels dance and I have no idea if I'm hallucinating. I zoom out again and then try another close-up, but each time there's no change, and no mistaking what I've spotted in the time-dimmed picture. Held loosely between the thumb and forefinger of the ill-fated Private Edward Carew is none other than the bright-eyed phoenix comb.

13

THE PRESENT

Cornwall

Lowenna

I'd been expecting to suffer an unsettled night thanks to tales of ghosts, nightmarish descriptions of trench warfare and puzzles about combs, but I sleep surprisingly well and only wake up when sunlight pours through the skylight and warms my face. I drink tea on the pontoon, watching Breakspear tearing along the riverbank. A huge heron flaps skywards like an out-of-time pterodactyl, and when the sun is out and the birds are singing it's easy for me to laugh at myself for pulling the curtains closed so hurriedly the night before.

This morning a light breeze ruffles the river, and chiffon clouds scud across the powder-blue sky. A tractor grumbles from the far side of the valley and a flotilla of sailing boats from Penhayes stitch up the horizon. It's a perfect early summer's day, and once breakfast is over I set off for Trevellan, planning to visit Selina Trewen and ask her some questions about the Trelyons.

I climb the steep drive, envious of Breakspear zigzagging effortlessly in front of me, and console myself that I'm clearly getting fitter without a gym membership. Although I quicken my pace when I pass Oyster House, the place is benign in the morning light and the shuttered windows are no longer glaring eyes but twinkly and smiley. I know the tiled hall will be jewelled with light from the phoenix cupola and swords of sunshine will pierce the shutters and light the closed-up rooms. Even the rotting veranda is benevolent in the sunshine, the perfect spot to take breakfast. Did Madalyn Trelyon sit here, maids pouring tea from a silver pot while she watched the river slip by? And did she walk hand in hand on this shore with the dark-haired young writer who would have dropped onto on one knee and asked her to be his wife? Did she truly love Gerald? Was she happy? Or did she agree to marry him for his money?

So many questions and so few answers. I must make sure I don't get carried away and invent new stories. I must be methodical. Private Edward Carew could be holding the phoenix comb by a sheer coincidence. He might have found it. Or maybe he was a thief and was about to slip it into his pocket. That he has it in his possession doesn't mean he knew Madalyn, since a village lad like him would have been far below her in the social order. Perhaps he worked at Oyster House and had been given the comb by Madalyn for his own sweetheart? Maybe my chat with Selina will yield some answers.

I've been hoping Granny May's box might arrive today, but when I peep inside the old milk churn at the top of the drive, which is where the letting agent has assured me any post will be placed, there's no sign of anything – unless the postie delivers woodlice and fat spiders rather than letters. Maybe it will arrive tomorrow? Having to be patient for several more days is torture, and if Mum hadn't called to say she'd posted it, I'd have been tempted to drive back all the way to Harrow and collect it myself. I can't wait to see if my ideas are rooted in truth. Is Private Carew the young man from the sketches? Is Madalyn Trelyon my Princess Clementine? Sailor-suited Henry really Gerald Snowe? And what is the significance of the tattered novel? If my life was a Dan Brown novel that would be the only copy of *On Oyster Shore* in existence, and from what Hamish said, a copy would certainly make my fortune. A windfall would be very welcome, because my savings won't last for ever.

It's an unlikely outcome. If Granny May had been a child when the stranger had delivered the box, Gerald's book would have been out of print for only a short while. What makes it so valuable now is its rarity – but nobody would have known then that *On Oyster Shore* would become the stuff of antiquarian book mythology. It's far more likely it's somebody's favourite novel and has ended up in the box by accident. I seem to recall that Marina and I left a couple of Lego people in there too, and some drawings of our own. These are treasures, too, in my eyes, and I'm longing to see them again.

With my head full of memories, I walk to the village through sunken lanes which meander past ancient cottages, weathered Celtic crosses and lonely farmhouses. If it wasn't for the occasional car that passes by, forcing me to yank Breakspear's lead hard and flatten us both back against the wall, it could still be the nineteen-hundreds. In contrast,

Trevellan has been catapulted into the twenty-first century, and I arrive in the middle of refuse collection day. The ferry road is jammed with cars forced to wait while the lorry crawls along at tortoise speed, the chinking glass and cans an accompanying percussion to the rumbling engine and squealing brakes. Further up the lane BT Openreach is digging up the pavement by the village shop, and a double-decker bus waits at the only stop while the driver has a chat with a friend. Even the quayside is noisy, for the Trelyon Arms is in the middle of a delivery, beer barrels rattling over cobbles while the fishermen holler to one another and whiz about on a forklift truck. While all this activity takes place seagulls screech high above the rooftops of old cottages and divebomb any visitors naïve enough to attempt eating outside.

I observe the unfolding scene and enjoy the sense of life and energy before turning up to the church. The narrow lane, little wider than a cart, weaves its way through the heart of the village, past pastel-hued holiday cottages, the old police house and several bigger dwellings which are now second homes. The old forge is now all gleaming paintwork and ornate wrought-iron railings, and Range Rovers the only horsepower. Selina Trewen had implied her father was ashamed of his humble roots, and I wonder what he would think if he could see his place of work now.

"Wenna!"

Noah Wilson is waving from the garden of a small cottage. As he's clad in green overalls, unzipped to the navel and peeled away to reveal a honed torso, I do my best to focus on the strimmer balanced over his shoulder as Breakspear tows me up the lane.

"Morning," I say.

Noah lowers the strimmer and greets my excited dog.

"Afternoon now," he tells me as bang on cue the church clock begins to chime. He straightens up and passes a hand across his brow. "Some of us have been hard at work since the sun came up."

"Don't believe a word of it!" Selina Trewen emerges from the low doorway, her white hair a dandelion clock against the darkness of the porch. "This young man started at nine am on the dot, not a second sooner, and has been eating biscuits all morning. I could have done a quicker job myself and I still have a packet of digestives in the tin. He costs me more in biscuits than the job's worth, and I have no idea what he does out here all day. Flirting with the young ladies mostly, by the look of things."

Noah catches my eye and the corners of his mouth twitch. The lawn in front of the cottage is bowling-green smooth, the weeded flower beds immaculate and the box hedge neatly clipped. He's been working very hard.

"Flirting? I should be so lucky! Look at the state of me. Selina, you're a slave driver. I deliver logs and spread muck for a rest!"

"The garden looks great," I say admiringly. "Maybe I should hire you to clear around the boathouse."

"Are you trying to finish me off?" he groans.

"Don't be so feeble." Selina steps out into the garden, leaning heavily on her stick. "You'll be demanding another cup of tea next."

"Now you're talking!" Noah says. "I could murder a cuppa, as they say in these parts. To think I never drank the stuff until I came here."

"You're almost a Brit," I say.

"Strewth! You're right. I'll be eating Marmite soon rather

than Vegemite."

I nearly say this would make him my perfect man but fortunately stop myself just in time, flushing at the narrowness of this squeak. Luckily Selina and Noah think my pink face is courtesy of the steep hill.

"Very well. I'll put the kettle on if I must," grumbles Selina, but the brightness of her eyes betray how much she actually enjoys the banter. "Come on in, Lowenna, and the dog too – so long as he doesn't upset my cat."

I can't promise anything here. Breakspear doesn't know many cats and is likely to find meeting one very exciting. I tighten my grasp on his lead.

"Thanks, but I'm just on my way up to the church. Remember I was doing some research into Gerald Snowe? The writer?"

"I'm not gaga yet!"

Her tone is pure schoolteacher. I consider myself firmly reprimanded.

"I didn't mean–"

"Of course you didn't," says Noah swiftly. "Don't be so touchy, Miss Trewen. Wenna didn't mean it like that. Nobody thinks you're anything other than your usual grumpy self!"

I hold my breath, waiting for Selina to tell him off too, but she only smiles. "Sorry, my dear. I think the heat's getting to me today," she says. "I walked down to the shops earlier to buy biscuits, I've no idea why the tin's so empty, and walking back up's taken it out of me. It's a damn bore, getting old."

"It's a steep hill," I say. My legs are aching and I'm a third of her age.

"Did you find anything more on him?" Noah shrugs the overalls over muscular shoulders and tugs the zip up.

I pull my mind back to the topic. "Apparently Gerald

Snowe had a fiancée. Madalyn Trelyon."

"From Vyvyan?" Noah asks.

"She was the last of them, but the estate went elsewhere because she was a girl."

"I guess that was how it was back then."

"According to Matt Enys from Rosecraddick Manor."

"You spoke to Matthew?" Selina approves of this. "I taught his father, you know. Bright lads, both. Oxford men."

"He's been helping me fill in some gaps." I don't mention the link to Kit Rivers or my own great-grandfather. This is something I'm nursing closely until I have a better idea of what it might mean. "An archivist friend has found an obituary for Madalyn, where she's named as Gerald's fiancée. She died in tragic circumstances, which might explain Gerald's behaviour."

"It certainly would," Noah agrees quietly.

Selina hits her forehead with the heel of her hand. "*That* was what I wanted to tell you the other evening. What a *nuisance* it is getting old! My father once said his friend's sweetheart drowned in the river. That it was why he didn't want me and my brothers to play there. It was a tragic accident according to Pa. They searched Oyster Shore for days but never found her body. The currents can be deadly in some areas there, especially if you're not a strong swimmer."

"My grandmother used to tell us ghost stories about a drowned girl," I say slowly. "Maybe it's Madalyn your father was talking about?"

The pieces seem to fit, but Selina shakes her head. "My father always said it was his friend's sweetheart who drowned, and there was certainly no love lost between him and Gerald Snowe. I'd go as far as to say they were enemies. So it can't have been her."

"Why were they enemies?" Noah asks.

"Probably a childhood falling-out that carried on into adulthood. I imagine Gerald would have lorded it over folks here, and Pa was always sensitive about being the blacksmith's boy. People have long memories in these parts."

"So there were two girls who drowned during the same period? That seems some coincidence," Noah says doubtfully.

"We don't know that Madalyn Trelyon drowned. That's just supposition. All the obituary says is that she was lost in tragic circumstances," I point out.

"Sounds like a euphemism for suicide to me," Selina says. "Back in those days people didn't like to use the word because it was such a stigma."

"I thought that too," I say.

"And you're one hundred per cent sure your father wasn't friends with Gerald?" Noah mops his hot face with a towel.

"I never heard Pa say a good word about Gerald. I believe he was utterly delighted when the Snowe family left. I think most people were," Selina tells him. "It was long before I was born, of course, but I'd imagine there was some resentment that the Snowes' son didn't fight when so many of the villagers lost their menfolk in the war."

"In that case, what happened to Madalyn Trelyon that was so tragic?" I ask.

Selina shrugs her frail shoulders. "It was ancient history long before I was born, but I do know where her memorial is, if that helps. The Trelyons are buried at the east end of the south aisle. Pre-Reformation it was the Lady Chapel."

"Before your time too, Miss T?" says Noah, deadpan.

"Cheeky monkey!" Selina laughs and it's clear that Noah Wilson's charms work on females of all ages.

"Will you show me where it is?" I ask her. There can't be many people who know Trevellan better.

But Selina is tired after her trip to the village shop, so Noah volunteers to be my guide. Once he's tidied away the gardening equipment, stepping out of his overalls and pulling on a fresh tee shirt, we set off with Breakspear running ahead, ears flopping and tail wagging.

St Nun's is cool and quiet. Breakspear's claws click on the flagstones and seem terribly loud. The church is steeped in the cumulative prayers of generations of villagers, and very little can have changed here since Gerald Snowe and Madalyn Trelyon sat in their family pews while my Penwurthy ancestors were relegated to the back with the other villagers.

"I love this place," Noah remarks, surprising me since I associate him with open spaces and sunshine rather than cloisters and dim light. "I used to come here a lot when I first arrived. It made me feel closer to Kim."

"Was she a churchgoer?"

He laughs. "Nah! Kim only went to church at Christmas and for weddings like most of us. I don't think she had any great belief in the afterlife either, although she never said much about it. It wasn't a subject we touched on while she was doing okay. It felt a bit ..." He pauses and inhales deeply, as though this memory robs him of breath.

"Too close?" I offer.

He nods. "Yeah, I guess so. It felt defeatist to be talking about death while she was still fighting. The language of cancer is all about battles and wars and standing up to it, and anything else feels like you're letting the side down and giving in. When you're in the thick of it there's something almost taboo about surrendering to the reality that the final days are coming. You have the end-of-life meds safe in a cupboard, and the nurses on stand-by, but it isn't real. It's not going to happen. Not to you. No way. Never."

I don't know what to say. This is so outside my own experience that expressing sympathy feels banal and almost insulting, but Noah isn't waiting for a response.

"It's a liminal zone, that time between a terminal diagnosis and the very end," he continues softly. "Each day feels like walking over quicksand, and it's only a matter of time before you go under. You're still together, but parting's inevitable and although life looks just the same you sometimes catch a glimpse of it from another angle and then the enormity of what lies ahead is so overwhelming you can't breathe or move or even think. And when the worst happens? Then you have no idea how life can continue. You don't even want it to continue. You just want the whole world to stop turning."

What can I say to this? What can any of us say? Life is full of wonder but full of partings too, our days laced together with pain as well as joy. When Gerald Snowe's Madalyn died, did he feel like Noah does? Was her loss so devastating that his only recourse was to destroy the life and work associated with it, just as Noah Wilson moved across continents to heal his heart? People find coping mechanisms where they can.

"This church reminds me that we're all passing through," Noah says. "Whenever I come here I feel as though Kim's not so far away. So many people have been inside this church and believed in something more than we can see or know. I guess coming here gives me hope I'll see her again one day. Some might say that idea's nonsense, but it helps me. This can't be all there is. There has to be more than we can see."

He pauses beneath a stained-glass window emblazoned

with saints and angels huddling under the wings of a familiar sapphire phoenix. The walls are inlaid with tombstones, *mementi mori* and engraved tablets dating back to the Middle Ages dedicated to the Trelyon family. Madalyn had belonged to an ancient line.

"Pretty hard to miss, hey?" says Noah.

"This is hardly subtle," I agree, pointing to a life-sized effigy of a knight, forever frozen in chainmail and with his hands piously folded in prayer. "They've been here for ever. Where to start looking for Madalyn? There must be hundreds of memorials!"

Text rolls and swells in the dim light and the archaic spelling makes my eyes ache. So many Trelyons – but no sign of Madalyn. Not for her angels and swirling script, nor even a brass panel. I'm almost cross-eyed by the time Noah spots a small bronze plaque no larger than a bathroom tile and obscured by a table bearing a vase of flowers.

Madalyn Rose Trelyon
Beautiful. Beloved. Brief.
1897–1917

"The family didn't exactly push the boat out, did they?" Noah remarks as he moves the table aside so we can look more closely. "And this is just a memorial. It doesn't mark any final resting place. It's not even above the crypt. It's screwed in as though it's an afterthought."

"Perhaps Gerald had it placed there, rather than her family?"

"That's weird too, because he isn't mentioned and neither is her mother, which surely would be the norm? Kim has a small plaque in a memory garden back home which says she's a dearly loved wife and a much-missed daughter and sister. The relationships we have, the people we leave behind who miss us, are what's important. The love we leave behind defines us. It's our legacy. If Gerald was engaged to Madalyn, why wouldn't he have acknowledged his relationship with her?"

"And why wouldn't a mother place her daughter's memorial in full view and make it huge?"

I might not have children, but I can imagine how all-consuming the love you have for them must be. It's hard enough loving a dog, and if anything happened to Breakspear it would break my heart. Losing a child must be unbearable.

"Graves and memorials are for the living, because we're the ones who need them. Maybe after her death nobody was left who felt they needed a big memorial."

"Or maybe they didn't care enough to make sure she was remembered? She was only a daughter. She didn't even save the family by marrying well in the end," I say.

"Perhaps Madalyn's mother had her daughter buried elsewhere?"

"Wouldn't the obituary mention that?" I shake my head. "Noah, I think there's more to it. Something must have happened that they wanted to hush up. It's another mystery. There seem to be a lot of them round here."

Breakspear, who's had enough of being inside behaving himself when there are seagulls to chase and woods to explore, sighs gustily, and Noah pats him.

"I think we all need a change of scene. How about a drink at the pub and a sandwich? They do a great crab roll."

Right on cue my stomach rumbles and he laughs. "I'll

take that as yes. We can chat through some theories as well. You never know, it might help."

The thought of tucking into crab rolls is very tempting. It's worth braving the wrath of Fi for food, good company and the chance to bounce ideas.

"Lunch is on me," I insist. "I've taken up enough of your time lately."

"It's on me because it was *my* idea. Besides, you've been hired to help finish my mother's research. Buying lunch is way cheaper than paying someone to finish that off!"

Does Noah Wilson only want to hire my research skills or does he want to have lunch with me? It's alarming how one of these thoughts makes my spirits plummet while the other makes them rise like balloons. I need to be careful, for my bruised heart is vulnerable.

"In that case, consider me hired," I say. "And I'm more than happy to be paid in crab rolls!"

Noah beams. "Beauty! Let's head into the sunshine. You guys don't have much of the stuff. Better not waste a second of it!"

It's just lunch, I tell myself sternly as we walk into the village with Breakspear bounding ahead – just lunch, and a chat about history. Noah is a wonderful sounding-board, too, for the more we chat about the small memorial the more convinced I become that the truth about Madalyn Trelyon doesn't lie within the walls of St Nun's at all but is to be found much closer, guarded by the tides and mists of Oyster Shore. This is where I will find the answers that will solve the riddle. But as for the riddle of why my stomach turns cartwheels whenever Noah Wilson smiles at me ...

That's one puzzle I'd rather not attempt to solve today.

14

THE PRESENT

Cornwall

Lowenna

"What's this I hear about you having a lunch date with Trevellan's most eligible bachelor?"

Treena Trehunnist must move like a ninja, because I had no idea she was behind me in the queue. Having made the trip across the water to collect my parcel from the sorting office I'm sheltering from the rain in the kind of deli my mother raves about.

"I didn't mean to make you jump," Treena apologises when I almost leap into orbit. "Did you think it was Fi, coming to sort you out? You might be in Penhayes, but that isn't far enough to hide!"

"I'm not worried, because it wasn't a lunch date," I laugh. "Anyway, how do you know I had lunch with Noah? Have you got spies? Seagulls with secret cameras?"

Treena taps her nose. "You may well ask!"

"I am asking! Is the pub bugged?"

"Actually, the truth isn't nearly as exciting. You can't get away with anything in a small place like Trevellan, and you're new and therefore very exciting. Your lunch with Noah is the most exciting thing that's happened in that pub since Richard and Judy popped in for supper about a decade ago. Davey Tuckey's got a book running as to when you'll get engaged, and Fi's loading up her shotgun as we speak."

"Very funny."

"You think I'm joking? She's a crack shot. Gareth has her over to shoot vermin on the farm. Not very organic of him but he's too impatient to wait for me to charm them away." Treena rolls heavily kohled eyes. "Live and let live, I say, but apparently that doesn't apply to rats or rabbits. But never mind all that. Tell me about your lunch date with hot Noah!"

"It was grabbing a sandwich while helping with some family history," I tell her as I shuffle forwards in the queue. The bag for life holding Granny May's box bangs against my shins, and I wince.

"I'm only teasing. I'm glad he's got a friend."

A little glow of warmth spreads through me and my face heats up. I pretend to be hunting for my purse so Treena misses my blushes. The truth is Noah and I spent a lovely hour sitting in the sunshine, eating crusty rolls stuffed full of Cornish crab, sipping scrumpy and falling easily into friendship. We'd talked endlessly about Gerald and Madalyn, testing theories which all ended nowhere, before returning to the boathouse and spending another few hours drinking tea and swapping theories. It's been several days since I last saw him, the rain keeping me inside and farm work occupying Noah, but we've exchanged several text messages and he's popping over tonight with his mother's research. I've offered to feed him, hence my trip to the deli, but if Treena finds out Noah's coming for supper she'll read far more into it than a research meeting.

"I can't imagine what he's been through," Treena says sadly while I continue to rummage and attempt to compose myself. "It's lovely to see him out doing something normal."

"Aha! You spotted us, then? Not the village's spy network?"

"No, they failed miserably! I was on the ferry. I waved, but you guys were far too busy talking to notice me."

"We'd just visited the memorial of Gerald Snowe's fiancée. I think she may have drowned on Oyster Shore," I explain.

Treena looks curious but I've reached the counter and the shopkeeper, gloriously old-fashioned in a straw boater and stripy apron, smiles expectantly. Treena peers over my shoulder into the display cabinet.

"Please, please, please don't buy the last steak and ale pie! Gareth needs something proper for supper. He'll be eating Pot Noodle otherwise, because I'm a crap wife."

"I'm sure you're not," I say.

"She is," the shopkeeper assures me. "Gareth's on our darts team and the poor bugger's always hungry. He eats all the sandwiches. Why he puts up with you, Treena, is a mystery."

"I'm good in bed," she says cheerfully, which knocks the wind from his sails. "I'll have that pie, Jago, and two scotch eggs. And some potato salad. And the coleslaw."

Once Treena's finished and Jago's over his shock, I buy a camembert to bake and dip crusty bread in. Nibbles should be fine, I decide, as I follow Treena's yellow raincoat into the mizzle; it's not as though I'm attempting to impress anyone. Noah Wilson's just a friend.

"Let's grab a coffee." Treena takes my arm and steers me along the street. Cars swish past and soggy seagulls huddle sullenly on chimney pots, looking as fed up as the drenched holiday-makers. I'd forgotten how the Cornish rain can soak you to the skin in mere moments, and the thought of a hot drink is very inviting.

We find a table in Presto Pasty and before long are seated in a vast squashy sofa with hot chocolates set in front of us, piled high with whipped cream and marshmallows.

"I'll put on a stone just drinking this," I grumble, but reed-thin Treena plops three sugar cubes in her drink. Life is so unfair.

"Not walking up and down from the boathouse, you won't. How's that going, anyway?"

"I only need to stop twice on the way up now, so I must be getting fitter."

"Great. Sounds as though it's suiting you."

"It's wonderful, and I think I can really write there. If I can get to the bottom of why Gerald Snowe did his best to destroy his book, I'll have something very special to work with."

Treena stirs her drink and sucks the cream off the teaspoon. "We could try a séance."

"I'll pass on that, thanks. My editor won't see a chat with a ghost as valid source material."

Treena waves a hand. "No probs. Now! Come to mama!" She bites into a cupcake, and livid pink goo squelches out as she tucks in with gusto. This is pretty much how Treena approaches life in general; I wish I could be the same, but I'm one of life's worriers. I'm fretting about Noah coming over now, because although Treena was teasing he's slipped into my every thought so quickly that it's taken me by surprise. Is he just interested in history, or is there something more pulling us together? Does he feel the same way about me? And do I want him to?

Men like Noah love deeply, and they love for ever.

Of course he doesn't. I sip my hot chocolate and settle back into the sofa. After a flurry of customers when another downpour of rain sends everyone scurrying for shelter, there's a lull and the coffee grinder ceases to growl. I exhale and start to relax. Noah Wilson is a friend and no more. It's the family history project that is drawing us together. Anything else is just my imagination.

"That's a big sigh," Treena says through a mouthful of cake. She mops her chin with a paper napkin. "What's up?"

"I was thinking about all the questions I need to answer if I'm to get my book off the ground," I reply. It's half-true.

"I spoke to Grampy about your Granny May. He's a bit muddled but he did remember her. He said she was a bit older than him but very pretty, with dark curls. All the village boys fancied her, apparently."

I think of stout Granny May with her grey perm, house-coat and sturdy ankles. It's strange to think of her as a girl with a host of admirers.

"He said that?"

"Well, not exactly," Treena admits. "He said they were all sweet on May Penwurthy, and that her father was very strict. Grampy still remembers being yelled at for messing about with fishing nets and he says he never did it again: Marrick Penwurthy was a hard man, and apparently his wife didn't suffer fools."

I think of the young man in the photograph, laughing at

the camera and with his arm slung around his best friend's shoulders. That version of Marrick Penwurthy was carefree and fun-loving. Then the war came, his friends were slaughtered, and his heart was hardened.

"Did Gareth's grandfather say anything about Gerald Snowe?"

"No. Grampy was born long after Gerald left. He did say his father had no love for the Snowe family, because none of them fought in the war."

"Selina Trewen said something similar. There seems to have been a lot of resentment towards men who didn't fight."

"Can't have been easy for your Gerald, then. Grampy also mentioned someone called Ned, who was his father's friend. He thought Ned fell out with Gerald about something but he couldn't remember what it was."

"Ned? Who's that?"

"No idea, but Grampy gets so muddled. He said Ned was a war hero, but he couldn't remember anything else about him."

Was Ned a war hero? Could he be Private Carew from the Kit Rivers' poem? Could he be the other young man in my great-grandfather's enlistment photograph? And is he the young man drawn over and over again in the sketch book? Granny May's box, resting in the bag at my feet, presses against my ankles as though urging me to open it. My hands are trembling as I reach into my bag and place it on the table. Sent second class, I notice wryly. Mum didn't want to spend money on Granny May's junk.

"My grandmother's box has been sent to me," I tell Treena. "It's been in our family for years and I think it's got something to do with all this, and maybe even the young man, Ned."

"The war hero one? How come?"

"I think he's Edward Carew, who enlisted with my great-grandfather. Ned could be short for Edward, couldn't it?"

Treena's eyes are saucers. "I guess. What's in the box?"

"Nothing that makes much sense. Photos and marbles and sketches of around here and maybe Oyster Shore too, although it's been years since I saw them. The contents were going to make the family fortune, according to Granny May anyway, although I've no idea how. My mum says it's all junk."

Treena's ringed hand flutters to her mouth. "Blimey! You must be gagging to open it."

I was, but now the box is here, placed on the low table in front of me and surrounded by cake crumbs and empty plates, I'm reluctant to unwrap it. What if Mum was right and it *is* all junk inside? Or I find that my memory has been playing tricks on me and I've been kidding myself making links and seeing patterns that don't exist? I hear David's voice, filled with faux concern as he makes a comment about my instincts being no more than an overactive imagination. Well, I wasn't wrong about his cheating, and my instincts are telling me I'm not wrong now. There is a link.

"I was going to wait until I was at the boathouse," I say.

"I'd totally pop if it was me," says Treena. "In fact, *I'm* going to pop if you don't open that package right now!"

"It won't be very exciting. Just old pictures and drawings, really, that mean nothing to anyone apart from me – and even I don't know what they are."

"But you might find somebody here who can identify them. Especially if they're of local people and places. The Penhayes History Society is run by the local librarian. And don't forget Hamish. He knows everything about this area."

"Taking my name in vain, Mrs Trehunnist?" A tall figure wearing sodden blue robes which cling to his skinny legs beams down at us. With a steaming mug of coffee held in one giant paw, he drips gently onto the tiled floor and steams in the warmth.

Another coincidence? Or is this, as they say, God's way of getting my attention? I can't shake the feeling that somebody wants me to keep pursuing this mystery, but who? Ned? Madalyn? Or Gerald Snow himself?

"I've just been giving a talk to the WI." Hamish shakes out his grizzled mane and pulls off his coat. Droplets rain onto the coffee table, and he picks up a paper napkin to dab his face. "I got caught out by the weather, and at my age you can catch your death if you don't dry out. May I join you ladies?"

"Please do," I say, moving up to make space beside me on the sofa. "And actually, Hamish, since you're here, there's something I'm hoping you might be able to help with ..."

15

THE PRESENT

Cornwall

Lowenna

The contents of Granny May's box don't look like much, but seeing them again is like meeting old friends after decades apart. The stranger who delivered the box, my great-grandmother and Granny May are long gone, but this odd collection of items has outlasted them all. It may well endure long after I'm forgotten, too, which feels like standing on the edge of a precipice and peering into infinity. It's not surprising I feel lightheaded.

"Take your time," Hamish says gently.

I'm eight again, squabbling with Marina about who wears the blue bird comb and gets to be Princess Clementine. When we're bored with that game, with the rain still trickling down the windowpanes and spluttering from guttering choked with moss, I'll entertain myself by filling a glass with water and dropping marbles in, loving the way the submerged globes loom large and mysterious. As I gaze at the postcard of the old house, the photograph of children in old-fashioned dress who eyeball the camera with such serious intent, the enamelled glint of the comb, fraying spine of a battered sketch book and the dog-eared old paperback, I could be back in my grandparents' cottage. I'd expected to be disappointed and to have had tricks played on me by my memory, but the opposite is true. Everything is *exactly* as I remember.

"Let's start with these." I arrange the photographs and the postcard on the low table. Hamish pulls out spectacles and examines each image intently.

"The stately home is definitely Vyvyan Court."

"The postcard?" asks Treena.

"Yes. It's an amateur photo printed on postcard paper, which was a popular thing to do in the early part of the last century, especially when a place was a local landmark. If you look closely, you can see the Trelyon phoenix in the masonry above the door."

"These children are standing in front of Oyster House, aren't they?"

I recognise the location now, even though the building I'm familiar with is an unloved echo of the pristine dwelling in the old picture. Joe, Henry and Princess Clementine stare back at me pityingly. *You're so slow*, I hear Henry say in his clipped and imperious voice. *Don't you know who we are yet? When will you twig?*

"Yes, that's the very place," Hamish says. "Wasn't it something special back then? I don't think I've ever seen a picture of it in its heyday. No wonder the Trelyons kept hold of it when they rented out the big place. What a wonderful spot."

"Is it possible Madalyn Trelyon might have lived there?"

"I imagine so, or at least she may have holidayed there. The entire estate would have gone to her if it hadn't been entailed, so letting the family stay there seems like a small thing to do, especially since Madalyn and her mother were pretty much left penniless." He shakes his grizzled mane. "She needed to marry well."

I fish my phone from my bag, scrolling through the image gallery until I find the pictures I'd taken of the photographs Matt Enys had selected. Just as I'd known they would be, Gerald Snowe and Madalyn Trelyon are positioned on the steps of the house from the postcard. With Gerald's wealthy father and blossoming literary career, Madalyn had certainly fulfilled her destiny when she'd become engaged to him – yet not long after this picture was taken she'd perished in mysterious circumstances and Gerald had turned his back on writing.

Perhaps just as well none of us knows what lies ahead.

"That little chap in the sailor suit could well be Gerald Snowe," Hamish says. "The clothing would suggest high status."

I show him the engagement photograph.

"According to Matt Enys it's definitely Gerald outside Vyvyan. It's the same boy, but grown up, isn't it? His hair falls the same way."

Hamish squints at the screen. "I'd say that's also the same girl, grown up too. She has a rather determined look about her, doesn't she?"

I'm delighted he thinks so. "That's just what I always thought when I was a kid. My sister and I called her Princess Clementine."

"Grown-up Gerald looks proud as punch to be standing

next to her, and who can blame him? She's absolutely beautiful," Treena remarks.

Hamish is staring at my phone and frowning as though puzzled. "She really reminds me of somebody, but for the life of me I can't think who. There's something so familiar about her."

"But who was the other little boy?" I wonder.

"With his bare feet and rolled-up trousers, he looks like a village boy," says Hamish.

"Could he be your great-grandfather?" Treena says.

I only wish I knew. Did my great-grandfather play with Gerald back at a time of life when who was best at climbing trees and catching fish was far more important than social class?

"I'd guess he's one of the local children," I say. "Granny May always called him a ragamuffin."

"Whoever he was, they must have been friends to pose together like this, and whoever took it wasn't worried about the class disparities either." Hamish is thinking out loud. "I find that most intriguing. I wonder who they might have been? Cameras were rare back then."

I touch the boy's face with my fingertip. His mouth is curly, the freckled face is kind, and he has a thatch of fair hair. He looks like the sort of person who could laugh and have fun, and the type of boy who makes friends easily and inspires love. Even in a faded photograph he's a stark contrast to the dark Gerald with his surly expression and pinched pale face.

Hamish turns to the picture of my great-grandfather in his uniform. "Ah, an Alex Evans photo. So this is a local man."

"That's my great-grandfather, Marrick Penwurthy." I scroll

through the pictures on my phone and hold it up. "Here he is with his friend Edward Carew. Kit Rivers writes about Edward in—"

"*Dugout*," Hamish breathes. "He's the young man from the trench. Good Lord! Your grandfather was friends with him. They enlisted together."

"I think all the village boys enlisted that day. Selina's father did – and, and Gareth's great-grandfather," says Treena. "All the young men went to war except for Gerald Snowe. No wonder they'd have bloody hated him. What else is in that box?"

I place the comb, the marbles and motheaten bag of sea glass on the table. They're no more than bric-à-brac, but for me each item glitters with childhood magic. If only I knew what their significance was. They must have been important. The sketch book is at the bottom of the box and feels fragile. Is the young man within it really the one who Kit Rivers immortalised in poetry? I'm almost afraid to look in case my memory is playing tricks, but when I turn the page and those wide eyes meet mine once again, I know beyond all doubt that this is Private Edward Carew. Edward. *N. OS 1914.*

Ned.

Just as I remember, he sprawls on a riverbank, shirt-sleeves rolled up to the elbows and head thrown back as he laughs at something the artist is saying. In other sketches he leans against a tree with his blond head bent over a note-book, lies on the grass with a book splayed across his face, and lounges in a rowing boat, oars loose in the rowlocks, and one hand trailing the water. Each pencil line is exquisitely simple yet powerful in conveying his energy and joy and – I realise now that I am an adult – resonates with the artist's overwhelming love for him.

Did Gerald draw these? Is the secret that Gerald Snowe loved Edward Carew and when Madalyn discovered the truth of her fiancé's true affections she took her own life? It's only a theory but it could hold. Overwhelming guilt might, then, explain why Gerald would go on to behave so oddly, as would his grief after Ned had been lost in battle.

Treena points at the page and whistles. "He was gorgeous! I so would! Any idea who he was?"

"I think he's the young man Kit Rivers writes about in *Dugout*. Edward Carew," I say.

"That's the war hero guy Grampy mentioned. The one, he said, whose family was treated badly by the Snowes." Treena says excitedly. "Hey! That's so cool you have pictures of him!"

"And he's definitely the same man from the enlistment photograph." I turn the pages of the sketchbook and pausing at the page where Edward, or Ned as I'm already thinking of him, is lying on a bed, propped up on one elbow and smiling at the artist. It's a tender smile which speaks of intimacy, lingering lovemaking and a thousand delicious joys. Above his blond head dark beams arch upwards, and leaves press against a small window. I lean closer and to my amazement realise he is beneath the same beams I look up at each night. Ned Carew was in the boathouse! He was in the bedroom with this artist, whose identity is key to the whole mystery.

"He grew up a right looker, didn't he?" Treena says admiringly.

"Who did?" I ask.

"The little boy in that photo of the children. The one with the bare feet." She leans forward, picks the picture up and passes it to me. "That's him, isn't it? The same chin and dimple. Few more muscles when he grew up though."

I can't believe I hadn't spotted it myself. The little boy

with the bare feet and cloth cap clutched tightly in his hands, the Joe of my childhood games, is without any doubt a younger version of the handsome young man from the sketch book.

"They all knew each other as children," I breathe.

Hamish looks sad. "What a shame that life and class divided people. I can't imagine that once Gerald or Madalyn were adults either of them would have given that humble village lad the time of day."

But I'm not so sure. One member of this trio wanted the links between them to be preserved. This friendship had meant *everything*. Was it Gerald Snowe himself who had put these keepsakes into my great-grandmother's hands? And where does my great-grandfather, Marrick Penwurthy, come into the narrative?

Ma tried to slam the door when she saw the visitor. She was furious but he pleaded with her to take in a box he'd brought and said something about it making our fortune. Ma was hissing like a cat and wouldn't give him house room. She had a fierce temper on her, my mum. Nobody ever crossed Elizabeth Penwurthy!

But as angry as she was, Elizabeth Penwurthy kept the box and passed it on through the family and down the generations. Something about its contents had compelled her to hold onto it.

"Have you any idea what the other things in the box mean?" Treena says.

"Childhood treasures?" I suggest. "Like the Lego men I put there! Somebody collected shells and sea glass too."

"There are drawings of shells in the sketch book." Hamish tilts a page to show me. "The artist had a huge talent, whoever they were."

"There are no sketches of anyone in uniform, and no war

scenes. Could Gerald have been the artist? He didn't fight," I offer.

"You could be right, but be careful not to make connections where none exist," Hamish warns. "I'm sure Matt Enys would say the same."

"Ned Carew is holding the phoenix comb in his enlistment photograph. Did Madalyn give it to him? Did Ned know her as an adult?"

"But if she did that why is it in the box now? And how would it have got there?" Treena asks. "Who drew him?"

Hamish is still thumbing through the sketches. "I would guess somebody who loved him very much and who was very gifted. And what else do we know about this Ned Carew except that he died during the shelling?"

I shake my head, because I have no answers only a heap of clues that seem meaningless. This must be what Matt Enys meant by a treasure hunt.

"If he was a local lad it shouldn't be too hard to find out. You should ask Selina too. She's very well-read and may know more about the background to *Dugout*," agrees Hamish. "You have some good places to start exploring, Lowenna. Your grandmother's box has been very helpful for your quest."

"Has it? I've got more questions than ever."

"But there are answers, too. You know who the children were, and you've identified the subject in the sketchbook," Hamish points out. "You've also got some credible theories to explore. I'd say it's been a very good day's work."

"But what I want to know is how any of this is meant to make your family's fortune," Treena says.

"Don't get your hopes up there! Granny May always said it was just a silly story."

"I think the box is a collection of evidence," says Hamish slowly. "The contents might make no sense individually but when placed in context they point the way to the answer. But what that is, who knows?"

"A first edition of *On Oyster Shore* hidden somewhere? Tell me it's there at the bottom of the box," begs Treena.

I laugh. "This isn't a Dan Brown novel! There *is* a book – but not that one, sadly."

The final item I show them is a slim paperback, its plain green cover torn and the edges of the pages speckled with mildew. When I pass it to Hamish the musty scent of my grandparents' old cottage brings a lump to my throat.

"*Soldier's Return*," he reads, "by Anon. Did you ever read this book, Lowenna?"

"Afraid not. It had no pictures and way too many words for an eight-year-old. Marina tried, but she said it was boring."

A memory swims to the surface. My sister sprawled on the sofa, tossing the paperback aside in disgust. "Why hasn't Granny got any decent books? Like *Sweet Valley High*?"

Marina's version of decent books and mine had been very different. She'd wanted to read about Californian high schools and cheerleaders and jocks, while I'd been mad about Enid Blyton.

I'd looked up from my game of marbles, desperate to placate her as always. "What's it about?"

"Something about a soldier coming back from war. It's *bor-ing*. He's only got one leg, and he goes away again without doing anything. Literally nothing happens. He just leaves."

"Without saying hello to his mum?"

"You're such a baby," Marina had said scornfully. "He's a grown-up, and he's in love with some soppy girl and she doesn't love him anyway. His friend tells him that. Nothing happens. Not like at *Sweet Valley High*. Jessica would make sure there was a big party."

"Doesn't he go and see his girlfriend?"

My sister had shrugged. "He might have done, but somebody's scribbled stupid numbers all over the words. I can't be bothered to read any more."

I'd felt worried. "That wasn't you, was it? We'll be in big trouble if you did."

"I don't scribble in books. I'm nearly twelve," Marina had said loftily. "Now shove up and give me those marbles. It's my turn to have a go."

Something about a soldier coming back from war. In love with some soppy girl and she doesn't love him anyway. His friend tells him that.

Excitement loops the loop in my stomach. There's a connection here. I can feel it.

Hamish weighs the book in his hands. His touch is as tender as though it's a baby bird, and I can tell he's wishing for cotton gloves to protect the old pages.

"It's nothing special, so don't worry about harming it," I begin, but his shaggy brows draw together.

"Books are all special. They're the essence of who we are. They're spells and wonder and magic. Books are our only hope of resurrection."

"Can you resurrect this one?" Treena asks through a mouthful of cake. "Why is it anonymous? Was the author ashamed of it? Is that why they didn't want their name on it?"

"Sometimes an author wants to hide their identity for a personal reason, especially if the topic is sensitive. Like Belle du Jour did with *Diary of a London Call Girl*," I say.

"Yeah, fair enough. You'd want to keep that from your

parents," Treena says. "But this book doesn't even have a pen name. Why would that be?"

"Sometimes names are lost in the sands of time – Beowulf for example, or if the writing is a collective effort." I'm thinking hard, but Treena isn't persuaded.

"That was years ago. This book isn't that old."

"Writers were often anonymous if they were writing something controversial like erotica or homosexuality," says Hamish carefully. "The desire to remain in the shadows is also found with books about corruption or politics. Sometimes it's simply safer for an author not to be in the public domain."

Treena looks incredulous. "And not be famous?"

"I always think the best books are where the author's identity is a mystery for years and we are all kept guessing, but that's hard to do these days. Besides everyone wants to be famous. Why else would you go on *Naked Attraction*?" he says.

She giggles. "To find love, of course! Thinking of trying it?"

"You didn't see my episode?"

Treena covers her eyes with her fingers. "Some things really are better left to the imagination. Not that I've ever imagined!"

While they banter, I recall the authors I've worked with who dreamed of tube and bus posters, and longed to be featured in magazines. I can't think of any who wanted to hide away like this author. Or like Gerald Snowe ...

Like the glint of scales beneath the water the thought surfaces. But it dives and is gone before I can grasp it.

"I can't see a publishing house on the cover. Is there anything inside?" Hamish asks.

I open the front cover. The inside is covered in batches

of numbers, as though somebody has been trying to do some complicated maths, and there's a contents page but little else. The back cover yields even less information – just more of the scribbled series of numbers, which continue over the pages, in gaps in the text, all through the book.

"Nothing." I'm deflated.

"Self-published?" Hamish muses.

"Did they do that back in the olden days?" Treena asks him.

"They certainly did. Self-publishing isn't anything new. Charles Dickens self-published *A Christmas Carol* when he couldn't get a publisher to take it on. Indie authors, as they're now called, could make great livings. E. L. James started off as one."

"E. L. James!" Treena screeches. "I should have a go. I could write about *real* filth. *Fifty tonnes of muck*! I'm sure G has cable ties, and there's lots you can get up to in a tractor! Once in the cow shed we—"

Hamish holds up his hands. "Stop! All you need to know, Lowenna, is it's perfectly possible that if the author of this book stumped up enough cash they could have published this tome themselves. Maybe it's Gerald? Now *that* would make some money if you could prove it, Lowenna! A second Snowe? There's your fortune."

"I'd better get reading!" I say.

"Please hurry. I'm dying to know what it's about. I can always pop over this evening and help with some research. I'm a quick reader," Treena offers excitedly.

"I'm having supper with Noah tonight. He's bringing his mum's research over." The words tumble from my tongue before I can stop them.

"You kept that quiet." Treena looks surprised and a little hurt.

"It's no big deal," I say, although under her stare it feels like the exact opposite. "It's just my way of repaying him for all his help."

"Maybe he can have a look at these items as well? He may come up with something we've missed. Noah's got a sharp mind," says Hamish.

"It's not his *mind* most of us notice," Treena grins.

I decide not to comment. It feels inappropriate.

As Hamish and Treena carry the plates and mugs to the counter I replace the items in the box. An obscure self-published book, old pictures and some odds and ends may not seem a great deal to most people, but I can't wait to pore over them again in the peace of my home.

It's only once I've said goodbye to Treena and Hamish and am on the ferry that I realise I'm calling the boathouse home. Home is no longer Hanwell or David's flat or my mother's Harrow semi, but a tumbledown dwelling nibbled by the tides and hidden in a tangle of woods. Home is a place where herring gulls cry, mobs of rooks caw and skies tremble in water.

Oyster Shore, lonely, beautiful and a little melancholy, has become my home and it feels as though life has never been any other way.

16

THE PRESENT

Cornwall

Lowenna

"It's looking good in here." Noah presents me with a bottle of wine and glances around the boathouse with pleasure. "You've made it really welcoming, especially on an evening like this."

Although it's still daylight the world outside is murky and dim. The mizzle drifts down onto the river which seethes below the pontoon, and scarves of mist are wrapped around the overhanging boughs on the opposite bank. Very soon the trees and the sky will dissolve into one as the shore is steeped in mist. In the fashion of a lighthouse keeper warding away danger I've lit the lamps and stacked the wood burner, and fairy lights glow from the dim depths of the kitchen, making the shadowy space more cheerful. With cushions and throws scattered over the chairs, pictures hung up and family photos placed about the room, the small house has taken on a different persona altogether. With each tiny change the darkness lurking in the corners has receded, and the aroma of bread warming in the oven completes the sense of homeliness. Any sense of abandonment has dissipated, and the boathouse is a welcoming bolthole in the gloom, just as it was when a handsome young man reclined against rumpled sheets and an artist's pencil flew across the paper.

"And *you* certainly look as though you've settled in, mate!" Noah reaches over the back of the sofa to pat Breakspear, who's sprawled across the claret-red throw. As my dog rolls over to have his tummy rubbed by Noah's strong tanned hands I imagine the same hands caressing me, and turn my attention to opening the wine. It's the candles and the warmth playing tricks on me, I tell myself – but the image of Ned Carew replete and naked beneath the beams of the room above us causes my hands to tremble as I attempt to unscrew the cap. The two men blur together in my mind, and now I'm not sure whether Ned's features truly rhyme with Noah's or if my mind is playing tricks on me. There's definitely something about the line of Ned's jaw and the way his hair falls that is familiar, and I can't quite push it away. Unlike the tragic figure in *Dugout*, my Edward Carew is young and virile and adored by whoever drew him and helped rumple the bedsheets. That person placed sparkles in Ned's sleepy turned-down eyes, eyes that are so very like the green ones twinkling at me right now. They look the same ...

The bottle slips and I almost drop it.

"Here, let me help with that!" Noah relieves me of the wine and unscrews the cap deftly. "Sorry it's not an expensive one with a cork, but the village shop didn't have a great range."

"This is great," I say, still unable to drag my attention from his face. Is that dimple in the same place? The hairline falling the same way?

He looks surprised. "It's *not*, Wenna! It's dreadful plonk!"

"It's wine," I say. "I'll fetch some glasses. Help yourself to nibbles."

Help yourself to nibbles?

I have never, ever used this expression in my life. *Nibble* suggests a teasing, gentle nipping sensation of teeth teasing the soft skin of a throat before straying lower and lower. Ned Carew of the sketches has been nibbling somebody, and his heavy-lidded eyes and secret smile imply the action was reciprocated. He was a man well nibbled.

Nibbles? I cringe as I search the kitchen for glasses, because I may as well have said *'Put your car keys in the bowl'*. Heat sweeps up my neck and I open the fridge on the pretext of retrieving some butter for the sliced French bread. The window beyond is as blank as an unseeing eye, and as the river creeps closer to the boards beneath my feet and the sea fret presses in on the walls, it feels as though we're the only two people in a rubbed-out world. We're shipwrecked on a shore where nothing exists except for us. The rules and usual life have been suspended. Anything is possible.

"Is all this stuff from your granny's box?" Noah is standing by the table. "The box you told me about?"

"Yes, it is. None of it makes much sense alone, but I think that linked together it will. I just have to see the pattern."

Noah nods. "You will, I'm sure. Ah, glasses. Let me pour."

Once we're both holding wine glasses, heavy bottle-green goblet affairs, he raises his. "To the sheila with the cleanest boathouse in Cornwall!"

"Trust me, the lamplight hides most of the dirt," I say as we chink glasses.

"Even so, I can tell how busy you've been. Have you had any time to work?"

I shake my head. "Not really."

After walking Breakspear and tearing around the boathouse cleaning, I'd spent the rest of the afternoon trying to make sense of the box's contents, and reached the conclusion that the only way to make any progress was to approach this book as I would any other research project. I would have to regard the characters as subject matter and not become emotionally involved. Ned, Madalyn and Gerald weren't my friends; I didn't know them any more than I knew what Selina's father was like, or whether Kit Rivers was really a good officer or just another titled toff.

Fired up, I'd spent several hours typing up notes on my meeting with Matt Enys and rereading Kit Rivers' poetry. I'd written up Hamish's contributions, and documented Selina's memories along with the snippets of hearsay provided by Treena and the assorted drinkers in the Trelyon Arms. I'd printed these pages out and scribbled my own thoughts over them, highlighting some parts, and scrawling questions and areas worth exploring. My next step is to create my own version of a police incident board, and add in photographs and items as well as a rash of post-it notes. These I'll link to one another with lengths of the fraying string I'd unearthed in one of the kitchen drawers. Absorbed in my work I found the day had slipped away from me when I'd glanced up at the vegetable clock and realised Noah was due any moment. I'd whirled around in a frenzy, switching on lamps and putting out food, and this is why I'm still wearing jeans and an ancient hoody and have my hair skewered on the crown of my head with a biro. I wasn't planning to dress up but, catching my wild-haired reflection in the picture window, I wish I'd at least dragged a brush through my curls.

"Can I help with anything?" Noah's green eyes, deep and dark, meet mine in the glass. With the world blanked out it feels as though a thousand new realities are poised to splinter away, and our reflected selves as are as insubstantial as the mist. I feel my shadow self urging me to slide my arms around his waist and rest my cheek against the angel wing of his shoulder blade. Nothing more than holding him close. It would be a release to feel his skin, and the sweetest conclusion to a long journey I hadn't even known I was on. The salt-damp of the house, the soft lighting and the murmur of the radio suspend us in a moment already seared into my memory; a moment where everything could change if I allowed it to ...

I step away quickly. "It's fine, thanks. I've got it in hand."

"Cool. Shall I fetch my mother's research from the car? We can get stuck in, and I can tell you what I know."

"Let's eat first," I say, tugging the curtains together swiftly so the cosy reflected scene and the eerie blankness beyond are no more, and all the possibilities which hovered between two worlds are lost.

"Food sounds good," Noah says, bending over the table for a closer look. His hair, damp from the mist and worn loose, brushes the shoulders of a newly pressed blue shirt, and although he still smells of muck, it's combined with Sauvage and woodsmoke and male skin. He's utterly delicious. Yet again the sketches of Ned Carew, bare-chested and gloriously unabashed, dart into my mind and raise my pulse.

"There's lots of it," I say, scuttling to the kitchen to distract myself with French bread and the baked camembert.

Noah laughs. "Beauty, I'm starved. But Gareth's a machine – he doesn't even stop for lunch!"

"Good. I must have bought my own body weight in bread and cheese."

"We should make a fondue. I know a great recipe. And let's face it, this wine could be better used in that," Noah says wrinkling his nose in disgust. "Jeez. That's awful."

"Fondue? I thought you were an Aussie."

"So I should be barbecuing something meaty on the beach in my cork hat? You *have* looked outside, right?"

"Ah. Good point. Does it get misty a lot here?" There's a quiver in my voice and Noah picks up on it at once.

"Nah, not that often, and then the forecast's looking better for tomorrow. All this will blow away by dawn. I quite like it. Everything's so quiet you can feel time turning, you know?" He returns to the photos on the table, stirring them around with a forefinger as though meaning might appear. "When it's like this it could only be minutes since those kids were playing on the shore. If the mist lifted we might see them right now."

I understand exactly what he means. Oyster Shore is timeless.

"Maybe to each child it seems as if they left only moments earlier," he says almost to himself as he studies the photos. "They never missed their companions. Were never lonely. Never missed one another. Never mourned."

His words thrum with emotion and I know he's thinking of Kim. What must it be to have loved that deeply? Wonderful and terrifying, I should imagine, but worth everything.

"So, which kiddo is Gerald?" Noah asks me.

"The one in the sailor suit."

"Doesn't he look an aggro little guy? And that's Oyster House, and that's Vyvyan."

"Check out the sketchbook."

He picks it up and flicks through. "Hey! These are good. Really, *really* good."

I feel a glow of pride on the behalf of the unknown artist. "They are, aren't they?"

Noah nods as he points out examples of the artist's skill, exclaiming over what he sees and holding up pages to illustrate his points.

"The proportions are exquisite. See the veins in his arms? And the sketch of this heron? The simplicity is so deceptive. It's powerful and bold. Almost modernist in composition."

"Look at the last one," I say. "Hamish worked out that he's Edward Carew, the soldier from the Kit Rivers' poem about a trench that gets shelled."

Noah turns the page and whistles. "Trenches are a way off. That's a man who's just had a wonderful time in bed!"

The sexual heat of the sketch sweeps from the page, up my neck and flood my cheeks. I long to look away from Noah, to scuttle into the kitchen and pretend to be checking the food, anything but stand here discussing the rumpled bed and the tousled beauty of the young man sprawled across it. Above our heads my own bed is made up, neat and cushion-covered and untouched beneath those very beams, because nobody has held me close and made love to me beneath the listing roof or looked at me as tenderly as that young man, the ill-fated Ned Carew, once looked at the unknown artist.

Maybe they never will?

There's an ache below my breastbone and I push the feeling down to the hidden place I don't like to visit, the place where all my mother's warnings about being in my thirties lurk, along with biological clocks and being picky. It's the place where, circling like sharks, are doubts about true love and the fear I'm an idiot for believing in more.

Noah scrutinises the sketches. "Any idea who drew these? The style seems familiar."

I pull my thoughts back to the here and now. *Focus, Lowenna*. "Was it a popular style of drawing?"

Noah shakes his head. "I wouldn't say so. The style is unique to this particular artist, although there are influences on the work for sure." Noah turns the pages over and over.

"Maybe it's Gerald's work? He lived and wrote here, and the bed the man's in is …" Warmth ripples through me. I take a big mouthful of wine, preferring to blame alcohol for the watery sensation in my knees and the curling sensation in my belly when Noah looks at me questioningly.

"Go on."

I swallow. "It's my bedroom here. The window, the beams and the way the light falls are just the same. He was in bed here. Maybe he was with Gerald? That would be a reason for wanting everything hushed up."

"A secret love affair with a male servant would certainly explain why Gerald might have kept a low profile," Noah agrees. "Especially since he was engaged to be married. There's a hypothesis for you."

"As if I need another one," I groan. "I also wondered if that was how the box could have made my great-grandmother rich. Maybe she had an explosive secret that she could use as leverage against the Snowes?"

"That would explain a lot. Did Madalyn find out, so Gerald had to cover the truth up? Did he drown her? People do strange things when they feel cornered, frightened."

I shiver. "I really hope not, but the mystery's certainly

deepening. To be honest, I feel as though I'm looking down more blind alleys than I know what to do with."

Noah replaces the sketchbook. "Hey, don't look so down. My mum always said nothing's ever solved on an empty stomach, so why don't we eat and then you can tell me what you've come up with so far? You never know, I might be able to help figure something out. I've got all her notes too, and there could be something in them."

"That'd be great," I say. "And food's definitely a good idea."

"It will soak up this disgusting wine," he laughs. "Next time I'll bring something more palatable. My cousin Elliott has a vineyard in Victoria – he'd disown me if he knew I was buying plonk like this!"

There's going to be another time when we eat together and share a glass or two of wine? What does it mean that he's talking like this? Is it proof that we're becoming good friends, or does he want more? Treena's teasing aside, I sometimes catch Noah studying me with an intensity that makes the heat pool in my belly, and I can't deny I'm attracted to him.

"I'm apologising in advance for guzzling." Noah scoops kettle chips from the bowl and lowers himself onto the sofa. "Muck-spreading's hard work!"

I choose the chair opposite and reach for some bread. "Maybe don't bring that up when we're about to eat?"

He wrinkles his nose. "I've had three showers and even I can still smell it! Don't get too close, or if you do then hold your breath!"

"We won't smell anything once I've cut into this camembert," I say, and Noah laughs.

"Do it fast! My aftershave's losing the battle!"

As we eat the simple bread and cheese supper we talk

easily and no longer about Oyster Shore and the past but about our own lives and the quirks of Fate that have brought us both to this beautiful place. By the time the wine is finished and most of the French stick and cheese has been consumed, any awkwardness has passed. I brew coffee and when I carry it through Noah is reading the paperback book from Granny May's box with an adoring Breakspear beside him, head resting on Noah's knee and paw prodding him now and then for attention. Noah, deep in the book, strokes him absently.

"Any good?" I ask, setting down the mugs and tearing open a packet of biscuits. Noah takes one and munches absently.

He points to the inside cover. "What do you make of these numbers? They're a sequence, aren't they?"

"I haven't really had a chance to look closely," I confess. "My sister didn't think much of it. I was going to have a proper read when I have a moment, but from what little I have seen it isn't very well written. It looks like a vanity project to me."

"Vanity project?"

"Somebody wrote it and paid to have it printed for themselves."

"Wouldn't that have been expensive? Before Amazon and the Internet?"

"Yes, I think so. Whoever did it would have had money to spare."

"They must have really wanted to do this and been able to afford it in that case. Maybe the author is the soldier in the story? And the book itself is part of a bigger message? Lots of the items in your granny's box don't seem to make sense on their own but perhaps they do when put together?"

"I think so too," I say slowly. "But wouldn't my great-grandmother have known what they meant?"

"Who says she didn't? Your granny told you her mother was angry. Maybe she understood exactly what that box and its contents signified, but chose to ignore it?"

"Granny May always said it was given to her mum by a stranger."

"He might have been a stranger to your gran, because she was a child – but her parents could have known him very well. It's unusual to be angry with people we're indifferent to, isn't it?"

He's right. What if the man hadn't been a stranger at all but somebody who had once been a friend, or more? This might mean my hypothesis of Gerald Snowe being the gentleman at the door with the box might be worth pursuing.

"What if the man who visited your great-grandparents had brought them a collection of items that would only make sense when put together by somebody who understood their significance?" Noah continues thoughtfully. "But out of anger your great-grandmother hid the box, and once she and her husband passed away any meaning it held was totally lost. It became no more than a strange collection of junk."

"Junk that was meant to make our family fortune."

"And perhaps it would have done if the significance hadn't been lost. Hey, I feel like we're on the edge of something here."

"Insanity?" I joke.

But he's serious. "I can't help thinking," he says, "that it's all connected with Gerald Snowe and Oyster Shore. Your family has to be linked to his."

"I don't see how. The Penwurthies were fishermen. They

wouldn't have had anything to do with the Snowes apart from selling their catch to the cook."

"How about illegitimate children, then? Could your granny have been Gerald's daughter?"

"Calm down, Jeremy Kyle! You'll be talking paternity tests and lie detectors next!" I say. "But no, I've never heard any talk of that, and anyway we all have the Penwurthy curls and stumpy legs."

"Bang goes that theory, then," Noah says. "And your legs are absolutely perfect, by the way."

He's noticed my legs? I've been wearing shorts a lot since I arrived, but even so my short and milk-bottle-white legs can hardly be described as perfect. I stare at him.

"Anyway, back to this." Noah seems suddenly flustered. He peers hard at the paperback with more intensity than it truly requires, and I know he's startled himself with the comment. Something shifts between us, and even Breakspear looks up.

I return to the safe topic of the book. "From what I can gather the story's about a soldier who returns from the First World War and finds his world has changed. His sweetheart's run away with another man and his injuries have made him useless in the eyes of society. It's not exactly cheerful and, from what little I've seen, not very well written." I'd flicked through the paperback earlier on, dismayed by the clunking prose and awkward choice of language. The pathos seemed third-hand too, as though the author was struggling to identify with the protagonist and had cobbled together several accounts and stitched them up with hearsay. Any faint hopes that this novella might be a lost Snowe masterpiece were soon dashed. If this book had landed in my slush pile at

Erasmus it would have been treated to a very swift rejection slip.

"Not a lost masterpiece, then?" Noah asks.

"Sadly not."

He weighs the book in his hands, a small frown scrunching his forehead. "Gerald didn't go to war, and your great-grandfather Marrick came home, married and continued going fishing, so the story doesn't link to him. I suppose lots of his friends died, and those who survived wouldn't have been the same. Like the returning soldier in this book, some were even rejected by their loved ones."

"Matt Enys has written a paper on facial disfigurements and the early attempts at plastic surgery during the Great War," I tell him. I'd read this online and been moved to tears by some of the accounts it explored. "They called themselves 'broken gargoyles' and lots of them committed suicide. It's heart-breaking."

"So not only did they suffer in the trenches, but their homecomings were no picnic either because they weren't the same men who had left, either physically or mentally. How could they be after what they'd been through?"

"Granny May always said her father had a dreadful temper," I recall. "He used to shout and scream at night. She said he terrified her."

Noah nods. "Shellshock or what we call PTSD nowadays. I guess back then it was just a case of *chin up and get on with it* for the poor guys who made it back. Not a great thank you for their sacrifice."

"Different times. In their poems Kit Rivers and Wilfred Owen write about injured young men who survived the war but were left on the edges of society."

"Is it possible that this book was written by somebody

who'd witnessed something similar and wanted to document it but who didn't have the literary talent of Rivers or Snowe?"

"That's certainly one theory," I say. "But who *was* he?"

He wags a finger. "Or she!"

"Yes," I laugh.

"But since we're drawing a blank on the author's identity, what about the numbers written down inside the covers and over the text? They must mean something. Shove up, Breakspear! Let your mum see." Noah gently pushes the dog towards the arm of the sofa and pats the empty space. "Plenty of room."

Plenty of room for Kate Moss, I think as I do my best to breathe in and ignore the sensation of Noah's tautly muscled thigh pressing against mine. If I suck in my stomach I may just fit.

"This book has to be significant, badly written or not." Noah presses the tips of his thumbs and forefingers between his brows as though trying to massage the answer into his mind. I see the muscles in his arms swell and ripple, and this causes an exquisite ache deep inside of me, so I distract myself by studying the number sequences, which must be a puzzle of some kind. Scrawled in a faded blue ink and written in a cramped hand, a century has passed since they were scribbled down, but the paper is still indented, such was the writer's urgency.

"I can't figure out what these numbers mean," I say. "Birthdays don't work."

"Nor do dates, unless the stranger was a time traveller!"

"That would send the Internet *crazy*. I'd have a bestseller on my hands for certain!" I laugh. "This looks more like a jumble of grid coordinates to me. Maybe we should find a map? And hunt for treasure?"

"That's it, Wenna!" Noah says. "That's *exactly* what these numbers are. It's a treasure map written in code. Whoever wrote this knew that the recipient, your great-grandfather, would be able to break it. Would it have been a game he played as a kid? Kids love codes and secret clubs."

I chew my pen and drill my focus down. "A schoolboy code would be pretty simple, wouldn't it?"

"I think so ... Hey! I've got it. Can't believe I didn't see it straight away. The numbers only go up to 26, and it's a matter of matching the alphabet to the numbers reversed, so A is 26 and Z is 1."

He's right, and the task is only onerous because there are so many sequences of numbers crammed inside the front and back covers and squeezed between the words of the story. I work through, painstakingly jotting down each sequence with the corresponding letters beneath it before moving on to the next, while Noah transcribes the words into a notebook. It's slow work and not helped by dim light and eyes heavy from wine. When the jumble on the page starts to blur I take time out to brew some very strong coffee.

"This looks like nonsense," Noah says, curling his hands around his mug and looking disheartened. "Maybe I was wrong?"

We have pages of random words which seem to make little sense no matter how hard we try to rearrange them, and which make a mockery of our earlier certainty that we had cracked the code.

"They wouldn't have been racing to recruit us at Bletchley Park," I say as I pore over the random words.

"I reckon it begins here: *Mother. And. Right. Return. Instead. Cold. King.*" He blows on his coffee. "But it's not making sense."

I gnaw my pen. I'd been so certain I was onto something and, disappointed, I screw up my eyes and will the words to rearrange themselves. There's a message here. I know it.

Mother. And. Right. Return. Instead. Cold. King.

The letters blur and dance. The text shifts again as the first letter of each word steps forward from its fellows to stand alone, and instantly the solution is so obvious I can't believe I hadn't spotted it sooner. I pick up my pen and underline the letters of the first seven words. *Mother. And. Right. Return. Instead. Cold. King.*

"*Marrick*!" I breathe. "That *must* be the beginning, then. The message was intended for him. This is written to my great-grandfather!"

"My God," says Noah. "That's it!"

I picture the writer, head bent as he painstakingly translates the words he is compelled to say into a series of number sequences intended to be read by my great-grandfather. Who was the author? Would it have been Gerald, speaking to me across the decades and sharing the secrets of his lost masterpiece?

Noah helps me for another hour, but he's had a long day working with Gareth, and after several huge yawns surrenders to his exhaustion. He fetches the two carrier bags containing his mother's research before stepping into the misty night, after making me promise to let him know what else I find. His headlights sweep behind the curtains and his taillights stain the room crimson for a few seconds. Then he's gone and I'm alone. Now, though, the silence doesn't gnaw at me. It's a pool of peace I can dive into as I begin my task.

I focus my attention on the task in hand. As I pluck meaning from the mire of letters my excitement grows with every word I decipher. It doesn't matter that the fire dies down and the boathouse grows cold. All that matters is completing the task, and by the time I put down my pen I have filled three sheets of A4 paper. I sit back for a while ...

I rub my eyes. A few lingering stars straggle as daylight chases away the last traces of darkness. The mist is just a memory as I open the door for Breakspear and watch him bound into the sharp-edged air. A heron rises silently from the pontoon and somewhere a rook caws, a sound ringing with emptiness and loss. This is a place where farewells have been said and where hearts have broken. A deciphered message trembles in my hand, a living entity shaking with the enormity of what it contains, for it grants the reader a choice: confessor or executioner? Absolution or punishment? If my great-grandfather Marrick had been given the choice, what would his response have been? And what should *I* do?

I sink onto the steps and rest the pages on my knees. The river is in flood, grey mudflats swallowed by a hungry tide, but I barely notice because my head reverberates with the voice of the one who had written the instructions I hold in my hand.

A century after he had put his fountain pen down, Gerald Snowe's voice is heard once more on Oyster Shore.

Marrick,

I know you will decipher this message easily and I pen it above your old hiding place in the boathouse, seated here in the window and watching the river slither past. I write it in the code you and Ned devised, for this message is for you alone. How do I know your secret code? Oh, Marrick, you and Ned always underestimated me. Excluded me. Scorned me. You never guessed I spied on you from the shadows and knew where the hiding place was. Watched you lift the tile by the window and hide your treasures. Who did you think took things? Slipped into the boathouse like a ghost when you left it unguarded? Stole the comb and the letters and so much more? Taking what wasn't mine is a habit I fell into from a very early age. It has led to my destruction. It led to Madalyn's death.

The poor novella containing this coded message is my version of the events which led to that terrible final event. It is my true magnum opus, a confession of how I am to blame for the loss of Madalyn. It has no literary merit, but it is honest. In the box are the items I stole from your hiding place and which I return. Theft is a sin, but how I loved lifting that tile and delving for your treasures. Did you ever suspect?

After I failed to save Madalyn I fell gravely ill. They said it was a malady of the mind as well as the body, for I was never strong, as you will remember, and I almost died. I wish I had, for living with the knowledge of what I did is my own personal hell. I have recovered, but I am not the same man, Marrick. God has told me that the rest of my life must be lived in penance. Ned and Madalyn are lost, and I cannot make recompense to them for my sins, but I can do my utmost to make things right for you at least.

The manuscript is in the old hiding place. No printed versions remain. This original draft is the only copy. Like its namesake it has cursed me. What shall it profit a man if he shall gain the whole world and forfeit his soul? And my soul is lost unless God, and Bess, forgive me. All the money the book earned has been placed in a secure trust for Ned's next of kin. The three-mile stretch of Oyster Shore, Oyster House and the boathouse are also theirs in perpetuity.

How I hate this stretch of water! My loathing increases with each turning tide. I will never return. Now Ned is gone, **On Oyster Shore** *belongs to Bess. In the hiding place you will find all the letters and documents that prove this. Do with this knowledge as* *you wish. Tell the world of my crimes. Destroy me. Say nothing and deny me absolution. The choice is yours. You and God are my judges now.*

Gerald M. Snowe

I struggle to make sense of the strange letter. It alludes to events and places known only to my great-grandfather, and although contrite and pious at first reading, the author's voice contains undertones of petulance. The thinly concealed malice makes me uneasy, and I glance around the boathouse as though I might spot the author observing me from the shadows.

This is the voice of Gerald Snowe, and I recoil from this new version of him, unconvinced by his pleas of penitence and unsettled by his confession of a crime I don't understand. No wonder my great-grandmother Elizabeth, or Bess as she seems to have been known to the author, sent him away and shoved the box under the stairs. She must have known what an odd character Gerald was. She'd wanted nothing to do with him. Was she unconvinced by Gerald's apparent change of heart? Unmoved by his sorrow? Or did she have a good reason to detest him and want him nowhere near her family?

Bess Penwurthy may have silenced Gerald Snowe's voice, but her great-granddaughter has awoken it. I have lifted the lid on Pandora's box, and now his unquiet spirit urges me to uncover his secrets. Gerald Snowe wants his story to be told, and as the last of the Penwurthies I know what I must do; I must open this old hiding place and see whether he was true to his word.

I drag the table away from the window and carry the chair to the side of the room. The floor at this end of the boathouse has been covered up with one of the large rag rugs I'd brought with me, but underneath are the elaborate black and red tiles I'd admired when I first arrived. Although beautiful to look at they are chilly to walk on – the Prince of Wales might have invested in some underfloor heating, I'd thought, as I placed my own rug over the intricate design – and a couple of tiles had risen; it was only a matter of time before I tripped and, miles from the nearest hospital, the last thing I'd needed was to head-butt a tiled floor, no matter how aesthetically pleasing it was.

But now I can't pull the rug up fast enough. Whether or not the floor is cold and hazardous, I have to locate that loose tile beneath which schoolboys once hid messages. I sink onto my hands and knees, hardly daring to breathe. The intense emotion of the confession is so fresh in my mind it's as though the urgency of the writer is embedded in my hands. Two little boys crouch beside me, faces bright with excitement, oblivious to the resentful child spying from the shadows as they hide treasures and make plans.

But then I hesitate; some secrets are best kept, aren't they? My hand hovers above the tile. I'm nervous, sensing that something is waiting beneath that will change my life for ever – but I can't turn away. Gerald is desperate to confess his sins, Madalyn Trelyon and Ned Carew have stories to be told, and my great-grandfather's voice is calling out to me. Even Kit Rivers is here in his officer's uniform, as much a part of this story as the troubled Gerald Snowe. Their tale is unfinished, and something I can't explain has drawn me to Oyster Shore. Even the beautiful and broken Noah has been pulled here by an invisible cord. We are a part of something more. Something bigger than us.

I have to see what lies beneath. There's no other option.

My nails scrabble for the edge. The loose tile lifts easily, as though it had been replaced only moments ago, revealing a dark void beneath this room and below it the struts of the platform below upon which the entire construction balances. The whole building is an elaborate façade, never seriously intended to house boats. It is a glorified stage set built to look like as though it should be found on the banks of the Thames, and the dank space where tackle and ropes and oars would ordinarily be stored was rendered obsolete in a prince's love nest. This small opening is the only way into a secret and long-forgotten space. No wonder the schoolboys had loved it.

I fetch my new torch and shine it into the void. Cold rises upwards and brushes my face with icy fingers. Was Gerald Snowe the last person to peer into this place? Or was whatever he'd left in it discovered long ago and spirited away by modern grave robbers? There's also the possibility that he was playing a cruel game and there was never anything here at all. The bitter voice of the letter strikes me as belonging to the kind of person who would find such a practical joke amusing.

Giving him the benefit of the doubt, I lower my arm into emptiness and try not to think about rats. I lie on my stomach so I can peer in, and the torch beam reveals a cavity no more than a foot square, which has been carefully lined with metal in order to create a watertight box. This isn't the work of schoolboys. Schoolboys hiding marbles and silly notes and humbugs don't worry about damp or fret about mould. Their treasures don't have monetary value and, from what I know of my nephews, they seldom leave things long enough to worry about decay. This work was obviously carefully and deliberately commissioned by somebody who wanted to make certain that whatever they hid away was preserved from vermin and damp.

It was something that they felt was so valuable it couldn't be risked. Something like a precious manuscript.

My heart thudding, I stretch my arm down and my fingers grope blindly until my fingertips brush against something tactile. It's the dry skin of a leather case, and straining every muscle I stretch until my fingers close around a handle. Crawling backwards across the floor, I drag my find to the surface. Breakspear watches from the corner of the room, but seems reluctant to venture any closer. Does he sense something here that is better left alone? Is Gerald Snowe drawing closer?

Finally a schoolboy's satchel rests on the tiles, above the dank hiding place for the first time in a century. Its leather is dry and worn from years of bumping against a jacket. The handle is smooth, the edges battered, and the leather stained with dark marks that look alarmingly like blood-splatters. I'm being over-imaginative, because these marks are more likely to be something a child once spilled. Hiding place aside, this could be any normal satchel. I take a steadying breath and flick the catches open and lift the flap. Instantly the aroma of leather and chalk conjures memories of primary classrooms, ink-stained fingers, and long-forgotten teachers.

There's a name written on the underside of the flap. The ink was gulped up by thirsty leather long ago but I'm still able to distinguish the ghostly remains of a childish hand.

E. Carew

Edward Carew. Ned. Ned of the Kit Rivers poem. The Ned of whom Gerald was jealous and who was best friends with my grandfather. Ned who was naked in the room above my head. Ned who knew Madalyn Trelyon. This was his satchel.

Ned Carew had carried it on his back to school when he was a little boy with no idea of what lay ahead for him in France or that he would be immortalised in poetry.

This puzzle has always been about him, for this is Ned Carew's story, not Gerald Snowe's.

My hand slips into the satchel. It's stuffed with letters, loosely bound with faded ribbon and written in a hand I don't recognise. There's a photograph of three men in a trench – one of whom I am certain is Kit Rivers – yellowed newspaper pages, what looks like a legal document and a lock of bracken-red hair tied up with an emerald ribbon. But what makes my heart thump is a leather-bound notebook. Dare I hope this could be the original draft of a long-lost book and that Gerald was telling the truth when he told Marrick the original manuscript was here? But why would he hide it? Why pass his greatest work to my great-grandparents?

I know the answers are here. I take a deep breath and turn the first page of the notebook.

On Oyster Shore

I can hardly breathe. This is it; the find of a lifetime. I am holding the original manuscript of *On Oyster Shore* in my trembling hands.

My eyes flick to the clock. It's still far too early to call Noah or Hamish, which means his treasure is exclusively mine for a stutter in time. It's mine to hold close. Mine to marvel at. While the world slumbers I'll read the story that once captivated the literati and which Gerald Snowe did everything he could to destroy. This is the book he blamed for Madalyn's death and the curse he believed was on him.

The dark secrets that he kept for a lifetime nestle within these pages and urge me to set them free.

I haul myself to my feet, place the items reverently on the table, and curl up on the sofa with a blanket pulled over me, prepared to lose myself in a story that has slipped from history and into myth. Then I turn the page and begin to read.

It ended as it began, on Oyster Shore ...

17

MAY 1904

The School House, Trevellan

Ned

"Violet Tuckey says the big house has been let out," Ned's mother announced over the breakfast table. "She could hardly draw breath, she was so excited. Apparently the new people are taking on some staff, and she thinks there might be a position for Timmy. Vi's convinced he could start off as a footman and work his way up to butler."

Edgar Carew spluttered into his teacup, drenching his toast and only missing his newspaper because it was propped up against the chipped blue teapot. "Is this the same Timothy Tuckey I'm unfortunate enough to teach? The boy who dropped the entire milk crate *twice* when he was the monitor and practically pours ink all over his exercise book? *That*

Timothy Tuckey is to be loose with a silver platter and armed with a gravy boat?"

Matilda Carew laughed as she fetched a dishcloth from the sink to mop up the mess. She was used to her husband's fond despair over his pupils at Trevellan School, and the family often enjoyed his tales of their latest antics. Timothy Tuckey, blessed with a handsome face and two left feet, was often the subject of a drama.

"Yes, my love," she said, "the very same! Who am I to disillusion a doting mama? Vi is certain Timmy's face will be his fortune."

"I can assure you it won't be his brains," said Edgar, pushing his spectacles up the bridge of his nose and helping himself to another slice of toast. "He tests my ability as a pedagogue even more than you do, young Ned."

Ned grinned. He knew his father was teasing him. His schoolwork was exemplary and, unlike his best friend Marrick who struggled to string his letters together – an issue owing more to his habit of missing lessons to go fishing than a lack of ability – Ned found that learning came as naturally as breathing. It helped having Trevellan's schoolmaster for a father and a home crammed full of books: before he'd even started school he had learned his alphabet by looking at the names of the authors emblazoned on the spines of the tomes in Edgar's study and had learned to write by copying them out, seated at his father's desk with his feet swinging in the air and his brow furrowed in concentration. A voracious reader and Oxford graduate, Edgar Carew delighted in reading to his children, and Ned and Bess Carew grew up with Austen and Chaucer and Dickens as their friends. By the age of almost nine, Ned had held out his bowl with Oliver, quaked when Magwitch loomed above the tombstones and had his dreams haunted for weeks by the pale face and gory fangs of Dracula. Bess, who was all for Heathcliff, often had nightmares about windswept graves and hanged dogs.

"You shouldn't let them read such books," Matilda often scolded her husband after nights of being interrupted by screams. "They're not suitable for children."

Edgar disagreed. Words were knowledge and knowledge was power, he pointed out, and Edgar wanted his children to have the ability to harness that power for themselves. Matilda huffed and said it was all very well for *him*! Edgar wasn't the one who had to stay up in the small hours until a terrified child fell asleep once more – but she'd not argued much, and Ned knew she was secretly proud of her clever husband and (he hoped) her clever children.

Ned loved words with a passion. Like his father's, his eyes were often pink in the mornings because he'd read late into the night by the faintest trickle of moonlight. Was there anything better than being transported by a story? Anything more magical or more wondrous? A writer could shipwreck you, take you on a voyage to another land, even whisk you back in time. Words were enchantments, and the more of them Ned read the deeper his seams of knowledge became and the more he longed to mine them to build stories of his own.

One day Ned would study at Oxford just like his father, but his dreams were not of teaching in a small country school or even of becoming a don, for Ned Carew knew he was destined to be a writer. Like his hero Charles Dickens, Ned would write books to be sold all around the world and he would tour the globe giving readings. Everyone would know his characters and his stories as well as he did. This was Ned's most cherished ambition, and he had already filled a dozen notebooks with fledgling novels. These were mostly tales of derring-do, featuring heroes with violet eyes, freckles and shocks of sun-streaked hair who looked rather like the author. The similarities didn't end there either, for Ned's brave heroes also lived on the south Cornish coast, where they sailed and swam and made camps on the deserted banks of wooded estuaries. They found treasure, explored abandoned boathouses and invented fiendish secret codes that the villains had no hope of cracking.

Ned read these stories to his friends, who all begged for more, and even his sister, inclined to be scathing about anything her brother did, would clamour for the next instalment. Filled with the joy of creating something that sparked excitement in others, and longing to know himself what might happen next, Ned often slipped away to find a quiet spot to write. Although the Carew family home was a happy place, filled with friends drawn to the warmth and laughter there, it was not always the best location for great works of literature to be penned. Wordsworth had communed with Nature, and so, inspired after reading his Lyrical Ballads, Ned had taken to packing a notebook and pen in his satchel and seeking out solitude in the natural world. This was when he first fell under the spell of the slumbering grandeur of a place the locals called Oyster Shore.

Ned had grown up playing on the shingled hems of the St Wyllow estuary, paddling in the shallows and catching shrimps when the tide turned. Several miles along the meandering river, and shielded by a bluff, was a secret dwelling presiding over its own stretch of riverbank. Although it was locked up with its shutters tightly nailed, when Ned peered through the cracks he glimpsed furniture shrouded in dust-sheets and floorboards deep in dust. *Miss Havisham*, he'd thought with a frisson of fear, or perhaps Dracula's lair. Ivy cast a net over the white walls and the briars played a stealthy green-fingered game of grandmother's footsteps. Once a place where the wealthy Trelyons had enjoyed summer parties and river picnics, this was also where, according to Marrick, who was a source of local gossip, the King had stayed with his concubines long before he'd become the King.

"What's a concubine?" Timmy Tuckey asked one sunny morning when Ned and his friends were catching their breath on the riverbank. The water chattered away with more stories, all told to the sky and trees, while out at sea a small yacht leaned away from the wind. How Ned longed to sail with it and into adventure!

"It's like a hedgehog," Sammy Trewen declared with the utter confidence of being the blacksmith's son and the biggest boy in the class. "But lots bigger."

Ned laughed a lot at this, which earned him a hefty rugby tackle from Sammy. When he could breathe again Ned explained what the word actually meant (reading *Don Juan* had proven to be far more *educational* than Matilda Carew had realised), and Marrick made some very coarse comments about the King's behaviour, which Ned supposed he'd heard his father come out with. Everyone in Trevellan knew Dick Penwurthy had a mouth like a privy after he'd been in the pub. Ned was glad Bess wasn't with them.

"So why don't they come here now? The concubines?" Sammy demanded. He glanced around, looking crestfallen at not spotting Mrs Keppel flouncing along the tideline.

"My ma says fashionable people prefer Penhayes," said Marrick, whose mother took in washing from the town across the river. "And there's no gas to this house. Who wants to stay somewhere like that?"

"There isn't gas in *your* house," said Timmy. He wasn't being unkind, just pointing out a fact in his usual blundering fashion, but Marrick punched him anyway. He was sensitive about his family.

"They don't come because there isn't anyone living here any more," Ned explained to Timmy once he had got back up again. "There's nobody to give parties any more, not since the old Lord died. I don't think the new one comes here much. And you were right about the gas and electricity, Tim. My father says Vyvyan Court doesn't have either of them, so the new Lord found it inconvenient and old-fashioned."

Timmy brightened at Ned's praise. It was rare for him to get something right.

Edgar had explained to Ned that the previous Lady Vyvyan had lived on at the house as something of a recluse until she had passed away a year after her husband. There were tales of ghosts and curses, and it was true the Trelyons weren't the luckiest of families since the main branch had died out. Only a baby great-granddaughter had remained; the previous viscount's son had come to a very sticky end, whatever that meant. Ned had pressed his father for more information, but his mother had shaken her head at Edgar and the subject was closed. Closed but not forgotten, because whatever it was that had happened was clearly *pas devant les enfants*, which made it even more intriguing, and wonderful story material.

Ned had told Timmy as much as he knew, and he wished he knew more, but he supposed Timmy wouldn't really be that interested. All the same, Timmy asked, "Is that why he let the old lady stay on there?"

Ned could see that Timmy was already itching to join the others in a wrestling match. Ned sighed. He often felt as though he didn't quite fit in. "I expect so," was all he said.

Edgar had also explained how the Vyvyan Estate was entailed, which meant it could only pass to a male heir. This had made Bess very angry, and Edgar suggested she study a little more diligently so when she grew up she could play her part in changing such rules.

"There will come a time when women can vote," he told her, his eyes bright with zeal. "Be the one to change the world, Bessy."

But Bess wasn't interested in changing the world. She was far too busy swooning over Timmy Tuckey and whispering with her friends about her plans to be crowned May Queen. Sometimes Ned really envied his sister, just as he envied his friends wrestling on the riverbank like puppies rather than becoming melancholic because the days of elegant parties and boating were fading shadows. The other boys weren't moved to tears by how the years came and went, or wistful that there were no longer ripples of laughter or floating notes of music at Oyster Shore. They didn't fret that in a hundred years the house would be smothered in the woodland, walls fallen in and rooftops folded in upon the beams.

Maybe one day in the future somebody would fall in love with the spot, Ned thought. They would rebuild the house and walk along the shore, collecting shells and gathering oysters. Glasses would chink once more and skirts whisper over the grass. Perhaps when he was a famous author he would return to Trevellan in triumph and buy the place himself…

"Ned! Come on! Or are you chicken?"

Marrick's shout hauled Ned back to the present, and

shaking off his dreams he followed the other boys down to the shore, where they stripped off to launch themselves into the water like otters.

"Last one in's a *girl!*" yelled Marrick, curly head bobbing, and Ned, never one to resist a challenge, doubled his speed, only to be tripped up by Sammy and last into the water. A strong swimmer, Ned soon restored his honour by beating all the others to the opposite bank. By the time the boys had flopped back onto Oyster Shore all teasing was over and they basked in the sun, kings of their own secret realm.

The village children weren't supposed to play on Oyster Shore. Technically they were trespassing since the land belonged to the Vyvyan Estate, but the isolated stretch of riverbank was so overgrown and neglected it seemed to belong to Nature rather than a faceless Trelyon. The gates at the top of the drive had been chained up for as long as Ned could remember, and the elaborately paved paths were weed-smothered and carpeted in moss. The carcass of a fountain stood forlorn in what must have once been a clearing, now tangled in brambles and filled with rotting leaves and pools of brackish water where frogspawn wobbled like amphibian tapioca. The salt-damp house with peeling white paintwork, curtains half-drawn and dustsheets over its furniture, was surely long forgotten by the Trelyons, and gradually Ned and his friends claimed Oyster Shore as their own, a secret land shared only with motionless herons and the restless tides.

Around a meander in the river and hidden in a huddle of trees, a boathouse on stilts balanced above the tideline. The boys seldom ventured this far, preferring to swim and fish, but one raw January the door was blown open by a storm and Ned and Marrick, caught in the rain, crept inside to explore. Unlike the big house this building was empty except for a brass bedstead marooned in the grimy attic. Thick cobwebs were draped from the beams, and rich velvet curtains had been shredded to ribbons by rodents. Dust twirled in the air and it seemed to Ned that the room was watching the intruders closely.

"Satis House," he whispered. Shivers licked his arms. He couldn't move.

But Marrick had no such inhibitions. He leapt onto the bed and filled the room with puffs of dust. His corn-coloured curls and dark brows were soon grey, and Ned glimpsed the glowering fisherman he would become.

Unnerved, Ned blinked and the image melted. Marrick was himself once more.

"What house?" Marrick demanded in between bounces on the ancient mattress.

"Satis House. You know, Miss Havisham's place in *Great Expectations*. It's Dickens."

"Not *books* again. You're such a girly swot!" Marrick started jumping higher and faster. "Girly! Girly! Big girl's blouse! Ned's a big girl's blouse!"

Ned was used to this particular brand of teasing, and it seldom lasted long since he was as good at sport and tree-climbing and fighting as he was at his schoolwork. After leaping onto the bed and pummelling Marrick until the other boy was spluttering and begging for mercy, Ned returned to making comparisons of the old boathouse and Dickens settings while Marrick swung from the low beams like a monkey. Ned wanted to tell him to stop because this felt disrespectful, but he didn't want to prompt another torrent of name-calling. Besides, experience had taught him that his friend would soon move on to something else. Marrick was brimming with energy and never settled at anything for long. It was a mystery how he had the patience to go fishing.

Ned studied the attic room. There was something about its low ceilings and the green light filtering through windows packaged with ivy that he found pleasing. As the rain fell from the sealskin sky and pattered on the slates he imagined curling up here with his notebook. Maybe he would write his first proper novel here? Not another boys' adventure, but something serious and grown up. He could slip away far more easily than Marrick, and the other boys seldom ventured this far. Ned shivered again, utterly certain this place was going to be important. His whole life would begin on Oyster Shore. He could *feel* it.

Ned's mother often had feelings about things and was forever listening to her intuition. Sometimes Matilda's feelings were spookily right, like the time she had warned Marrick's father not to put out to sea, a warning he'd ignored only for a storm to blow up which had almost resulted in the boat being sunk. At other times Matilda's words were vague and she had only nebulous feelings to guide her. Edgar always teased her, saying she would have been burnt at the stake in another era, and Matilda would counter this with a quotation from his beloved Shakespeare.

"*There are more things in heaven and earth, Horatio, than are dreamt of in your philosophy*," she would point out tartly, which silenced her husband, since not agreeing with the Bard was unthinkable in the Carew household. Besides, Matilda would add, with a toss of her dark locks, these things were in the blood and she was part Romany. With her inky curls and striking beauty, Matilda Carew certainly looked the part, and so did Bess – but it was Ned who had inherited, along with her wide violet eyes and easy laugh, the tendency to feel atmospheres and sense echoes of the past. Old houses shared secrets with him, standing stones beckoned him forward, and even the wind seemed to murmur his name. Sometimes Ned wondered where his stories really came from: did they spring from his imagination, or were they whispered to him from some other unseen place? Muttered by the river and sighed by the sea? Were they even his at all?

Matilda Carew might not have been an Oxford graduate, but she was as sharp as one of Marrick's gutting knives as well as very beautiful, and Edgar adored her. Family legend had it that the young undergraduate had fallen head over heels in love from the very second he'd first laid eyes on Matilda in a Truro teahouse. Edgar hadn't been able to eat a mouthful and he'd not been able to think of anything else except for how beautiful the serving girl was. It was love at first sight, like Romeo and Juliet as Bess once said, which had made their father laugh.

"I don't recall Romeo was eating macaroons when they met," he teased, swinging her around before turning to ruffle Ned's shock of blond hair. "And besides, their story didn't end well, whereas Mama and I have had a very happy ending, wouldn't you say?"

Ned and Bess would. Their parents were always laughing, and often held hands which, although they pretended to find it embarrassing, both children secretly liked very much. The Carews might not have many possessions, but their children were always warm and well fed, and although the schoolhouse was small it was a happy place to be. Matilda was usually singing as she baked, while Edgar was most contented when preparing his lessons. The schoolhouse was filled with visitors, and Marrick, whose father spent most of his time in the Trelyon Arms, was like another sibling.

Although Marrick screwed his nose up at Edgar and Matilda's affection, saying they were soppy and only sissies believed in love, Ned understood that his friend was envious, and didn't react to the provocation. Unlike Mrs Penwurthy, Matilda Carew never sported a black eye, for Ned's parents were the best of friends and the schoolhouse was filled with love. Being well-read and accustomed to the violent side of village life, Ned knew this was a very rare thing indeed.

One day, Ned thought, when he was much older and had written the book that would make him famous, he would very much like to meet a girl who would become his best friend. She would like reading and poetry, walking beside the river looking at the birds, and maybe even sailing. She would be clever and beautiful, and they would have lots of children and live in a big house with roses like pink cabbages scrambling around a porch with barley-sugar pillars and a smart flight of stone steps. Ned couldn't quite see her face yet, but he was certain that when he met this girl he would know her instantly. Shakespeare wouldn't have got that part wrong.

Bess had come close to the truth, though, when she'd mentioned Romeo and Juliet, for there had been a huge family estrangement caused by Edgar marrying Matilda. It might not have been a blood feud which stretched back generations, and as far as Ned knew nobody had been murdered or banished, but the Carew children had never met their paternal grandparents, and Ned had once overheard Matilda telling her friend Jenny Trehunnist how Edgar had been cut off without a penny.

"A serving girl wasn't a suitable match for their son," Matilda had explained, pouring tea into the cup Jenny held out, her blue eyes as wide as the saucer beneath it. "Especially not one with a murky family background."

"Was he really a gypsy, your pa?" Jenny leaned so far forward that the tea sloshed onto the table and Ned, peering through the crack of the kitchen door, held his breath. He quite liked the idea he was part Romany. It was far more romantic than being a fisherman's son or, as much as he hated to say it, the goody-two-shoes son of a schoolmaster. A gypsy's life held a glamour that chalk dust and marking didn't, and in his mind's eye Ned saw brightly painted vardos pulled by horses with feathered feet, and the leaping flames of a campfire.

Matilda laughed. "Ah, so that's what the villagers believe, is it? A silver-tongued gypsy who stole my mother's heart?"

"Is it true?" Jenny whispered. Although her face was set in a sympathetic expression, Ned could tell the farmer's wife was relishing every word of this scandalous story and already looking forward to retelling it in the grocer's shop. By the time it reached the butcher, the narrative would be more fanciful than anything Ned could have penned.

Matilda shrugged. "After a fashion. His grandmother had been born a Romany, I believe, but my dad was quite ordinary, I assure you. He was a groom at Rosecraddick Manor, where my mum was an under-housemaid. She said he could do anything with horses. I never really knew him, because he died when I was very young. Sorry to disappoint you, Jen, but it's all very dull. No tea-leaves or clothes pegs!"

"Oh yes, of course not," Jenny said quickly, although Ned thought she did sound rather disappointed. "I just thought that might be why Edgar's parents didn't … don't …" Her words dried up like the school inkwells in the summer holidays.

"Didn't accept me marrying their only son?" Matilda supplied. "That's exactly it; Edgar's parents wanted him to marry somebody of his own class, not the daughter of servants."

Jenny tutted and made sympathetic noises, but Ned imagined she was trying to decide quite what class this might be. He wasn't certain himself. It was difficult sometimes being the son of the village schoolmaster, because it clouded your social standing. Were you a village lad? Or were you a gentleman's son? Or neither? Was Edgar a working man, albeit a highly educated one, or was he something else again? He dressed and spoke like a gentleman, but lived in the tiny schoolhouse which came with his job as schoolmaster. He owned a library of beautiful books and could read Latin and Greek, but his clothes were patched and the family's accounts in the village shops were regularly in arrears. Perhaps they were genteel poor, like the Bennets in *Pride and Prejudice*?

So, were the village children his equals? Ned didn't much care as long Marrick and the others didn't rib him too much about his la-di-dah accent or tease him for being a swot. He could run as fast as they could, was the best swimmer, and was widely admired for his tree-climbing skills. Helping people with their schoolwork made him very popular, and he was as much a whiz at marbles and conkers as he was at chess. What did anything else matter? Ned didn't care a jot that Marrick's father was a fisherman or Sammy Trewen's a blacksmith. So why did he always feel as if they saw him differently?

Edgar said birth was no more than an accident of Fate. He insisted there was nothing clever about being born to an old and wealthy family, and was adamant that a time was coming when nothing would count except the person you were. Ned wasn't so certain. In a small village like Trevellan accidents of birth mattered a great deal. Here the Trelyon family were second only to God; their phoenix emblem was omnipresent, they owned huge swathes of land, and most people in the village worked for them in some capacity. Reverend Tullis was next in the pecking order of things, Ned decided, and after that it was a scramble between the farmers and shopkeepers for precedence. People in service and gamekeepers followed, and the fisherfolk were definitely at the bottom.

Where Edgar Carew fitted in was anyone's guess.

"And that was why Mr Carew left Oxford? Because his family cut him off?" Jenny breathed, hands clasped to her ample bosom.

Matilda nodded. "But wasn't that Trevellan's gain? Edgar's a wonderful schoolmaster. I can't imagine another school in the whole land has one as well educated."

Jenny Trehunnist made a noise that could have been agreement or chewing, Ned couldn't tell. She was desperate to pursue the topic, but he knew from his mother's tone of voice that the conversation was over.

Ned had also hoped to hear a little more, but Matilda skilfully steered the conversation to Jenny's sons, swaggering boys with whom Ned regularly scrapped, and the apples of their mother's eye. The Trehunnist twins were blond, built like brick privies and filled with their own importance – but luckily for him Ned was lithe and quicker, both on his feet and with his words. Unable to stomach their praises being sung by their doting mother, he wandered off with his head full of new ideas for stories and a growing understanding of why his father had abandoned a lofty academic career to become a humble country schoolmaster.

It was wonderful material for a story, and Ned's notebooks were soon filled up with new ones. Maybe his rich grandfather would come looking for him, like Magwitch had for Pip. Or would Ned run away to join the gypsies and become a famous horseman? This was unlikely since Ned had never ridden, but he did like the costermonger's pony and often gave it an apple, so maybe horsemanship was in his blood. Or would he seek out the cruel Carews and wreak vengeance upon them in the style of the Count of Monte Cristo? This was a somewhat long-term plan, requiring a nature that held grudges and brooded, and since Ned was a cheerful boy who looked for the good in everyone and never kept a score of wrongs (luckily for Marrick), it wasn't one he dwelled upon for long. Busy with schoolwork, friends and his writing, Ned had plenty to occupy him.

And best of all he had Oyster Shore as his private kingdom.

The isolated stretch of riverbank had become the place Ned retreated to when he craved solitude. When scrapping with his friends became too much or Bess was squabblesome, he would thread his way through the tangled trees and briars to sit above the waterline, his back resting against the rough bark of a gnarled tree and a pen held loosely in his hand. Watching the water advance and retreat calmed his soul, and whenever he hid here his words flowed with the tides. The boathouse, where he liked to shelter when it rained, listening to the relentless drops beating a watery rhythm on the tiled roof, was his favourite place, and one he shared only with Marrick. The boys had fashioned a hiding place in an alcove beneath a loose floor tile where they would store their treasures or leave coded messages as part of the complicated games Ned had invented. Ned also hid his notebooks there inside an old satchel, and as much as he enjoyed making camps with Marrick his favourite times were when his friend was at sea and he had the boathouse to himself.

Then Ned would sprawl on his belly across the tiled floor, propped up on his elbows with his pen flying across the page, as swift as the kingfishers which darted along the water's edge. Ned and Marrick would row along the estuary and moor on the pontoon and fish before making a campfire to cook mackerel and boil up shrimp. The namesake oysters were rampant here, neglected and malevolent to bare toes, and Marrick would prise them from the rocks before splitting each tight treasure open with his knife. The flesh inside glinted like wet sand, and tasted of salt water and secrets when gulped from the shell. The two boys dined well on Oyster Shore.

So, to discover over breakfast that the Trelyons had rented out their estate made Ned's heart freefall. Would he be exiled from his Eden? Like Adam and Eve in *Paradise Lost*?

"Is the whole estate being let out? Even Oyster Shore?" he asked, trying his best to sound nonchalant, and failing.

Edgar regarded his son over his half-moon spectacles.

"I would imagine so, Edward – but what difference does that make to you? You assure me you never trespass on their property."

Ned crossed his fingers under the table. He wasn't fibbing anyway, he told himself. Oyster Shore didn't really count as part of the property. How could it when it was so neglected and so different from the rolling parkland and grandeur of the big house?

"I just wondered," he said, pretending to be intent on buttering his toast, but the effect was ruined by the lack of butter on his knife. Bess sniggered until Ned kicked her on the ankle. Then she yelped.

"Enough," said Edgar in the tone of voice which would instantly silence a playground full of noisy children. To Ned he added, "I'm well aware you and Marrick consider Oyster Shore to be your own property, but if there are new tenants in situ that has to end. I won't have it said that the schoolmaster's son is trespassing. You are to stay away from Oyster Shore. Do you understand me?"

Ned's throat went all tight and funny. Stay away from the boathouse? The willow-fringed shore? The special tree he always climbed? The thought made him want to cry.

"Ned?" repeated Edgar, sternly.

Ned swallowed a lump of misery. "I understand, Papa."

He didn't promise to stay away, though, and held his breath in case his father realised and made him agree properly. Ned couldn't lie to his father. Edgar was his hero.

"Who are the new people?" Bess said quickly. She caught Ned's eye and gave him a conspiratorial wink. His sister might be a pain and a girl, but she wasn't all bad, Ned thought. He owed her a piece of liquorice at the very least for distracting their father.

"Violet says a wealthy family from London have taken the place. Mary and Arthur Snowe. Something to do with soap, she thought. Vi was in quite a lather herself!" Matilda laughed.

Edgar groaned. "I can imagine. She'll be door-stopping them until they employ Timmy."

"Snowe? Like Snowe Soap Suds?" Bess asked, wide-eyed. "*The white way to wash whites*?"

The slogan was familiar. Like an apparition, Ned saw a picture of a jolly washerwoman in a mob cap (who looked nothing like Marrick's raw-knuckled and scowling mother) with her arms deep in a tub of suds, from which bubbles in the shape of snowflakes rose towards a washing line pegged with bright white sheets.

Matilda nodded. "I imagine so. They're Trade, Vi says – but very rich."

The compensating 'but' quivered in the air. Class again, Ned realised. It was so confusing. The Snowes were rich, but a busybody fishwife like Violet Tuckey still turned her nose up at them. What was the problem with making money?

"Maybe there'll be a daughter with a pony," Bess said hopefully. She was always drawing pictures of horses, and longed for one of her own. She'd been in trouble several times for attempting to ride the vicar's pony bareback, and although Matilda had scolded her she had been sympathetic. Their Romany heritage must be to blame, she'd whispered.

"I think there's a son," she told Bess now, "but I can't imagine he rides much. Vi said he's the sickly type. The doctors have prescribed sea air and exercise, which is why they've taken Vyvyan."

"How on earth does she know all this?" Edgar asked, astounded.

Matilda tapped the side of her nose. "Women have a way of finding things out. You'd be amazed what we know."

"I'd be terrified," he said. "Tea-leaves? Crystal balls?"

His wife laughed. "Nothing so exotic, my love. Her cousin's married to the head gamekeeper. Violet took tea with them yesterday and got all the news. She's hoping they'll put in a word for Timmy."

"He's a nice lad with a good heart. I'm sure there's a place for him somewhere as long as it doesn't involve coordination," Edgar said. Folding up his paper, he added almost reverently, "A soap magnate in the big house. Times really are changing. You see, children? If you set your mind to it, you can be whatever you wish."

Ned nodded, but his heart was still set on being a famous author. It seemed a loftier aspiration than selling soap.

"Why would the Snowes *rent* Vyvyan?" Matilda asked, pushing back her chair to begin collecting the dishes. "If they're so wealthy, why not buy a house? Or build one? Plenty of people do."

"You can't purchase or create a Vyvyan, my love. It's more than a house. It's an entire history and possesses a social cachet money can't buy. A house like that comes with access into the highest levels of society."

Matilda rolled her eyes. "That sounds like something your father might have said."

"Indeed, but he knew exactly how the world operates," Edgar said. "At Vyvyan the Snowes can entertain all levels of society in high style. It validates them and buys them entrée to a very exclusive club. Trust me, my love, it's only a matter of time before the important local families are calling on Arthur Snowe. In return, his wife and son will be invited to the cream of the local gatherings and accepted into the smartest circles. Invitations to soirées and dinners, Ascot, Henley, Covent Garden boxes and the like, will all follow – and *that's* why Arthur Snowe's renting Vyvyan. He wants to enter society and for his son to be accepted into its upper echelons, which is no easy feat for a man whose background comes from industry."

Edgar was speaking from experience, and not for the first time Ned found himself wondering about the life his father had stepped away from when he'd married Matilda Jago. He knew Edgar Carew would be just as at ease at the opera as he was in the Trelyon Arms. As happy dining at Rosecraddick Manor as he was eating a pasty on the quayside. Papa would be accepted in those upper circles – but where his children fitted in, Ned wasn't so sure. He was neither one thing nor the other, and if Oyster Shore was out of bounds, then where could he go to be himself?

Staying away was simply impossible. It was unthinkable.

Feeling mutinous, Ned pocketed the last slice of toast for the swans on the river. It was a small but satisfying rebellion, and as he set to work clearing the table and fetching pails of water to heat on the range he knew he wouldn't be forsaking his special place, no matter what his father had bidden. The boathouse and the riverbank belonged to him in a way he couldn't explain. His destiny lay on Oyster Shore, and Ned Carew couldn't have stayed away even if he had wanted to.

18

MAY 1904

Vyvyan Court, Trevellan

Gerald

The house was old and shadowy, and Gerald hated it. It nestled at the head of a steep-sided valley and was approached by means of a long drive which twisted and turned like a serpent. As he peered through the window, wiping away the mist with his sleeve, Gerald already knew that even if he hadn't been feeling carriage-sick and headachy from the long train journey he would still have loathed Vyvyan Court on first sight. He was marooned in a waterlogged world. The rain had been falling from the moment the train had crossed Brunel's marvellous bridge; pewter clouds pressed down onto the façade of the old granite building, and the incessant rainy tears weeping on the glass made Gerald feel depressed and claustrophobic. Even the hills seemed to press inwards, and he slumped against the seat, already homesick for London with its parks and people, and missing the elegant townhouse he'd always known.

"Sit up, Master Gerald," Nanny barked. "And stop looking like a wet weekend. Your mama and papa don't want to see a long face when they greet you."

Gerald thought his parents wouldn't much care what he looked like. In fact he would have been shocked if Arthur and Mary were waiting for him; it was past seven o' clock, and they were bound to be otherwise engaged with a dinner or some social event. No doubt he would eat cold cuts in the nursery and then go to bed without laying eyes on them. Being in Cornwall wouldn't change this. But he sat up anyway and did his best to look interested. Nanny had a way of making a boy wish he hadn't looked miserable or dared to complain when he was so blessed and fortunate – a way which usually involved cod liver oil.

As the carriage crunched towards the house, Gerald tried his best not to imagine that Vyvyan Court was crouching in the gloom as though waiting to pounce or that the triangular topiary loomed like tombstones and the giant phoenix above the grand entrance was poised to snatch him up in its sharp talons. He told himself it didn't matter if the windows were unlit or if the façade seemed to glare into the murk, or even if the door, a vast slab of ancient oak bristling with studs, was more suited to a fortress. This house was grand. It was magnificent. It was exactly what his papa deserved.

Vyvyan Court was on a scale that even Gerald, who had lived all his nine years in houses considered splendid, had never encountered first-hand. With a mile-long drive lined by stately oak trees and undulating parkland dotted with deeply wooded sections, this was a house designed to make all visitors feel humbled and which spoke of importance and wealth and gravitas. It was a house perfectly suited to a man as successful and important as Arthur Snowe. Vyvyan was a house which matched their standing. It was fit for a king, or in this case a man as rich as a king.

Gerald knew all this because his father had told him so many times. He knew off by heart how important it was to show the world how successful the Snowes were. He understood that appearance and propriety were everything, and that being linked to trade was somehow shameful and a stain on their name. If he hadn't already known this, the boys at his prep school had also made it clear, and Gerald had lost count of the times he'd been held down and made to eat soap or had his head held under in the bath. He did try to tell Mama, and cried himself sick each time the holidays were over, but she only said he was being ungrateful. Didn't he know how much money it cost to send a boy to St Hugh's? How lucky he was? The opportunities he was being given? Didn't he want to go to Harrow? And then to Oxford?

Actually, no. Gerald didn't. Not at all, if St Hugh's was a taste of what was to come. If prep school was hell he couldn't begin to imagine what his life would be like at public school. He didn't like rugby, he hated being called Soapy, and he lived in terror of the other boys. At night he did his best not to cry, but sometimes the tears refused to listen to the silent orders of his frantic mind and just slid out regardless, slipping from the corners of his eyes and drenching the pillow. The other boys jeered at him and found a thousand different ways to make his life a misery. As animals will hunt down the weakest in the pack, so Gerald's peers knew he wasn't really one of them. He might be rich, but his father's wealth came from factories. They called his mother a washerwoman, stuffed their dirty laundry into his face and sometimes even left excrement in his bed. Ashamed, and knowing that telling was the worst way of breaking the schoolboy code and would only make his life even more miserable, Gerald bore it all in silence, but he brooded on revenge and promised himself that when he was older anyone who dared to oppose him would be sorry.

It might have helped if Gerald had been good at sports, but he had a weak chest and was regularly to be found in the San, head bent over a bowl of steaming water as he spluttered and coughed. Thin and wheezy, he hated playing rugby and was always squashed at the bottom of a scrum, frozen with terror as soon as he possessed the ball, and unable to run. His lack of coordination made fives and tennis impossible, and to make matters even worse he wasn't academic either. Latin declensions sent him into paroxysms of terror and, in what he felt was a very bitter irony, he had lost count of how many times he had been caned for his poor arithmetic.

"Soapy Snowe has soap for brains!" the other boys would jeer, and one master even fashioned a dunce's hat for him, much to the delight of all the pupils. Gerald had sat alone in the corner with the cone of shame upon his dark head, and a seed of hatred had taken root in his heart, watered by the tears he dared not shed but pushed down deep inside. When he was a grown-up nobody would dare to mock him. Everyone would respect Gerald Snowe. Nobody would make jokes about soap or mimic his father's Yorkshire accent.

Arthur Snowe didn't know about any of this, and Gerald suspected that even if he had told his parents about his misery at school they wouldn't be particularly interested. Arthur wanted a son to take over the business, and he wanted to boast about Gerald's achievements. He wanted a son who could hunt, play rugby and take his place in society. It was what he was paying for, by heck! St Hugh's was an exclusive school, he would brag to anyone who might listen, and it was attended by the sons of dukes and earls and baronets. Their sons and his son were equals and friends. Arthur Snowe's boy would take his place in the world alongside the best of them. He would have invitations to the greatest houses in the land. He would hunt and shoot and fish at the best estates. He would attend soirées and balls, and one day marry the daughter of an old and established family. Through his son, Arthur Snowe would take his place in high society.

Gerald didn't want to disillusion his father. It was true that he shared a dorm with the heir to the Duke of Cirencester and sat with the son of the previous Lord Chancellor in lessons, and that the young Earl of Cressex was his house captain. However, it was also true that they were chief among his tormentors and more likely to fly to the moon than invite him to stay at their family seats. Gerald didn't foresee much changing in this regard either unless he miraculously became super-bright, or discovered a hidden flair for sport, or woke up to find his sallow face was tanned and handsome and his lank hair thick. At night he would lie on the hard bed in his dormitory and pray to God for these things. He would bargain with the Almighty and promise to be a better, kinder, more generous boy if he could only be a little more sporty or brainy or a tiny bit popular; but his prayers went unanswered and Gerald soon learned that even God didn't have time for a miserable specimen like him. After the episode with the dunce's cap he'd given up on God entirely.

Gerald Snowe was on his own.

There was no point explaining any of this to his father. At only nine years old Gerald had learned far more about the intricacies and pitfalls of polite society than his parents ever would. He knew that people sneered at his father and that his mother was only invited to society events because her husband was rich and her own hospitality generous. Even if his father was eventually knighted, as was his dearest hope, the Snowes would always be Trade. They would never be accepted into polite society. It didn't matter that Henry Cressex's father had bankrupted the earldom or that the Honourable Rupert's father was a gambler with debts and mistresses all over London; they hadn't made their money selling soap.

Vyvyan Court wouldn't change a thing, Gerald reflected as he stepped into the vast hall and studied the vaulted ceilings, coats of arms and suits of armour. His father was mistaken if he thought it would make the great and good accept them, because all this grandeur was borrowed. It wasn't theirs. Nobody would be fooled by it. Even if his father were to have rented Windsor Castle it wouldn't change anything. There were some things in life money couldn't buy, and for Gerald Vyvyan Court was already a constant reminder of this. It was his own shortcomings set in grim Cornish granite.

This house, and the status contained in every stitch of tapestry and every knowing stare of the ancestral portraits covering the walls, was a stage set. The Snowes were frauds, and Vyvyan Court, ancestral home to the Trelyons, knew it. As Gerald explored the draughty corridors, wandered up and down staircases, and pushed open doors to vast saloons filled with chaise longues, upholstered footstools and velvet sofas piled with fat cushions, he felt the glassy eyes of long-dead stags watch him and sneer. The staff, local people newly appointed by his mother, were all polite and deferential, but Gerald, used to hiding in the shadows and listening, had overheard them whispering and knew they were judging the new occupants and finding them lacking. He burned with resentment.

His parents, oblivious to the snobbery of the servants, soon set about redecorating Vyvyan Court to their own taste. Gas lighting was installed and the plumbing updated. Mary Snowe purchased new furniture and curtains for the drawing room, declaring the Trelyons' antique chairs and drapes to be old-fashioned and dirty, and ordered the servants to store everything she didn't like in the attics. Gerald caught the look of disdain on the butler's face and filed this away with the hundreds of other small grudges he carried on his narrow shoulders. One day everyone who laughed at him and his family would be sorry, he promised himself as he trailed through the house listening to whispered conversations and smothered laughter. They would pay.

It was no better out on the estate. Arthur harboured plans to fill the stables with highly strung hunters and was set on establishing a pack of foxhounds by the autumn, even though he could hardly ride. Gerald, who hated every fear-drenched moment in the saddle, was already dreading October. A shoot was being organised, too, and Gerald cringed to see his father striding across the park dressed from head to foot in brand-new attire and with a twelve-bore he had no intention of using slung over his shoulder. The boys at school would crucify him if they ever saw that. What would it be like when his parents decided to invite the neighbouring families to the house? Colonel Rivers from Rosecraddick, a terrifying man with gimlet eyes and a walrus moustache, and whom

Gerald had met once when Mama had taken him to call upon the neighbours, would see through his father's pretensions in an instant, and the colonel's son, Kit, a small blond boy who'd smiled shyly at Gerald, would also look on him with scorn. Coming to Cornwall had made everything a thousand times worse, Gerald decided, and he loathed the place. The house, and the world it represented, was the embodiment of all the taunts he suffered at school.

It was therefore rather ironic that his family had only chosen to rent Vyvyan Court because of Gerald. Never a strong boy (his nurses were amazed he survived infancy and Nanny Snowe swore he'd only made nine years old because of the bracing walks and cod liver oil she'd administered) the cold dormitories and poor food and utter misery of St Hugh's had weakened Gerald's health so badly that when scarlet fever swept through the school he had come close to death. But in a dark answer to his desperate prayers, Gerald had been sent home to London to convalesce, and although he had recovered, he was even thinner and frailer now and suffered palpitations and breathlessness to boot. On the plus side this meant he was unable to return to school (Gerald *might* have exaggerated some of these symptoms a little, as it seemed only fair he should get some payoff for feeling so ill), but on the minus side he had become Nanny's prisoner and was placed under house arrest. His father bought him books which Gerald pretended to read, and his mother drifted by the sickroom from time to time to mop his brow, but mostly he was left alone in the nursery, where he brooded on the wrongs done to him at school, and filled notebooks with plans for elaborate revenge on each perpetrator. All in all, life was peaceful and, constant doses of cod liver oil apart, very pleasant. He could, Gerald decided happily, spin this state of affairs out until he was too old for St Hugh's and maybe even Harrow.

Although rather distant figures in their son's life, the Snowes had understandably been concerned about their son's health and engaged the services of a top Harley Street physician. To Gerald's great surprise a full examination revealed he was as sick as he could ever have hoped, although the prognosis of heart failure if he overexerted himself was very alarming, as was the talk of bloodletting and isolation. Returning to school would be impossible, the doctor had added just as Gerald was opening his mouth to protest that he felt far better; Master Snowe would need to be tutored from home indefinitely. Gerald had closed his mouth quickly. Maybe he still believed in God after all.

"I recommend fresh sea air and good food to build this young man up. The very worst thing for him is city air and smog," the doctor had declared. "I recommend Cornwall. I have a country place in Penhayes, and there's nowhere better on God's earth for salt breezes and gentle exercise. That's what this young man needs to recover."

Gerald had been perfectly happy with the town house and bustle of city life. If exercise was required then he would bowl his hoop along the paths of Hampstead Heath while Nanny gossiped with her friends, but his parents had other ideas and within weeks they had taken Vyvyan Court. Gerald didn't see how this place could possibly be better for his health than the London house, since it was draughty and speckled with black mould. Any restorative salt breezes were laden with damp, and since their arrival in Cornwall a battalion of storms had advanced up the Channel to hurl salvos of rain at the windows. At night the darkness was so thick it felt as though it was pressing down on him, and the old building creaked and groaned. Sometimes Gerald heard heavy footsteps pass his room, stopping by the door as though listening, and he would freeze beneath the covers with his breath held until they continued on their way. It wasn't Nanny – he could hear her snores rumbling from the nursery – and the servants' wing was above them, so it could only be something restless and spectral. Perhaps it was a long-dead Trelyon pacing his ancestral home in an attempt to drive out the imposters. It soon became just as hard to sleep at Vyvyan Court as it had been at school, and a measure of just how much Gerald hated the place that he was actually missing St Hugh's. Why had his parents insisted on coming here?

Then one morning he awoke to a world drenched in sunlight. The sky outside the bedroom window was Wedgewood blue, the parkland a tessellation of greens, and the slice of sea beyond the wooded hills sparkling like his mama's diamonds. As though a bad spell had been broken, the winds and rains had vanished, and when Gerald pushed his window open the air was soft and sweet. It was impossible to feel glum when the world was all new and shiny and waiting to be explored. As he ate his soft-boiled eggs in the nursery and dutifully took his morning dose of cod liver oil, Gerald struggled to sit still, because he was suddenly brimming with energy and excitement. There were woods and a beach here. All kinds of excitement beckoned and he could hardly wait to explore. Maybe he would even climb a tree? He'd always wanted to do that!

But unfortunately for Gerald, Nanny had other ideas. Her charge had been close to death's door, she reminded him, and it was more than her job was worth to let the young master excite himself or catch a cold. And what about his weak heart? To his consternation Gerald was bundled up in a coat and forced to perambulate up and down the parterre under Nanny's beady eye. He'd seen a couple of young footmen watching him, and one of them, a tall boy with blond hair and a merry face, said something which made them both laugh. Humiliation flooded Gerald in a molten tide. He knew they were laughing at him, the pathetic namby-pamby rich boy supervised by his nanny and wrapped up like a sissy in his winter garb even though it was May. He kicked the flowers in one of the ornamental beds viciously and petals fluttered to earth like confetti. Gerald wished it was those boys he was kicking. He longed to make them sorry they'd ever dared mock him. Biting the inside of his cheek so hard that it bled, he vowed to add the young footmen to his long list of people to get even with. One day, when that boy least expected it, Gerald would make him pay. The metallic tang of blood on his tongue sealed it.

After this incident Gerald hadn't wanted to venture outside much. He would rather stay indoors than be ridiculed again, so he took short walks alone in the garden and didn't stray far. He certainly didn't wander anywhere near where the footmen and gardeners might lurk. Yet day after day dawned bright and sunny, the Cornish air teased colour into his face and coaxed his appetite. Soon Gerald began to plot an escape from Nanny and venture further afield than the mocking parterre.

His chance came one Saturday afternoon on her half-day, when she had planned to visit Bodmin to purchase knitting wool and more supplies of the dreaded cod liver oil. Gerald's mother was taking tea with Lady Rivers at Rosecraddick Manor and his father was in town on business. Gerald was tasked with reading in the library, a neglected room filled from floor to ceiling with depressingly thick tomes he had no hope or desire of ever ploughing through. For once, nobody would be supervising him and Gerald knew he would soon be forgotten. Being quiet and unremarkable paid dividends after all. This was his chance. This was his time to explore.

His book abandoned with the pages splayed, Gerald stood at the window with his nose pressed to the glass and his breath misting the pane. He hardly dared lift his hand to wipe it in case he was spotted and a servant dispatched to watch over him. He knew if he waited long enough the coast would be clear, and sure enough the dogcart soon appeared, Nanny perched beside the groom. Gerald ducked behind a dusty curtain and held his breath as the dogcart bowled down the drive and turned out of the gates. Nanny's best straw hat bobbed above the clipped hedges for a few moments before it vanished, but Gerald didn't move; she'd been known to return unexpectedly before, 'waterworks' being the usual explanation, so he counted to ten and then counted for ten more just to be on the safe side. When the straw hat did not return his heart soared. This was the moment he'd been waiting for, Gerald thought jubilantly as he slipped from the library. He was free!

It wasn't difficult to leave the house when you were the sort of person who was easily overlooked. Gerald had often envied other boys for being golden and glorious, and longed to be the type of child adults admired. To be small, pale and generally unremarkable was a knife-blade to the soul when your classmates were praised for their prowess on the rugby field or in their lessons. He had lost count of the times when he had been passed over for praise. When the other boys came looking for him to taunt him, Gerald had learned to sink into the shadows and shrink against the walls to render himself invisible. These accomplishments were far more useful than Latin or rugger he now decided, as he slipped past the housekeeper and crept through the gunroom. Even the spaniels dozing in their baskets barely lifted their heads from their paws, and as Gerald slid the bolts on the door he glowed with pride at his stealth. He had a skill after all. He was the unseen presence in the shadows, the eyes watching from the dark corners. Who knew what he might see and what he might learn this way? And what he might be able to do with that knowledge? Nobody would laugh at Soapy if he knew their deepest secrets.

They wouldn't dare.

The garden stretched before him, a green yawning wilderness filled with salty air and possibilities. Gerald glanced over his shoulder, half-expecting Nanny to reappear and summon him back, but the windows of Vyvyan Court were shrouded in drapes and the staff were occupied elsewhere. He stood on the terrace, overwhelmed by the glorious freedom that was now his. Where should he go?

The straining rumps of two gardeners digging in the formal gardens rendered exploration of that part of the grounds tricky. The orangery and vegetable gardens held little appeal, and anyway Gerald was more interested in the woods beyond the deer park. He'd studied this cluster of trees from his room and was intrigued by them as well as a little frightened, because they seemed to stretch on for ever, blanketing the steep sides of the valley and plunging towards the river. Apparently there were secret houses set within their leafy depths, ruined now and with wild gardens filled with forgotten fountains. Vyvyan had been visited by the King back when he was Prince of Wales, or so Papa had said until Mama had shot him a sharp look over the dinner table. Why the King would want to have come to such an isolated and miserable spot Gerald had no idea, but when he'd asked his father about this Arthur had changed the subject. Gerald was intrigued.

So how could he resist exploring the woods and looking at the King's secret house? As he walked through the deer park Gerald's spirits were high. He raised his face to the sun as though drinking in the light could make him strong and turn him into the kind of boy who ran and jumped and climbed trees rather than one who lay in bed and drank cod liver oil. He hopped over the ha-ha, scurrying through the rougher pasture because the long grass scratched his legs where his socks had fallen down, and climbed a fence. Feeling a little uncertain he followed this boundary for a while until he found the ghost of a path, once neatly raked gravel but now moss and leaves and earth. It twisted and turned, and as he followed it the trees on either side seemed to grow thicker, jostling for space with the encroaching brambles and looming rhododendrons. Weeds and grasses crept forward, and Gerald realised he was in the woods. Somewhere in the invitingly dark depths a branch cracked like a pistol shot as an unseen creature fled. Gerald's heart thudded with terror for a moment and he thought he might swoon like a girl before he caught sight of the white tail of a deer bobbing through the trees. Was that all? A stupid deer?

"Bang! Bang!" he cried, pointing his fingers at it and giving chase. "I've got you! I'll shoot you dead!"

He dashed through the trees after his prey, whooping and yelling as he pretended to fire guns and arrows at it. In this green wilderness he was no longer a sickly little boy in a sailor suit waving a stick, but a big game hunter on the plains of Africa. The fearful flight of the animal filled him with a dark and savage joy, for now he was strong and powerful. He could kill it if he chose, and the deer knew it. It was afraid! It was afraid of *him*.

Afraid the deer may have been, but it was fleet of foot and familiar with the woods, and it swiftly vanished. Exhausted, Gerald bent double and paused to catch his breath. The chase had taken him deep into the heart of the woods, where the trees pressed even closer and the canopy was so thick the sky was all but blotted out. Ivy crawled across the floor and thick roots bulged from the dank earth like veins. His breathing sounded ragged in his ears and terribly loud against the stillness. Gerald straightened up, frowning. Which way had he come from? Which way was the house?

He looked around hoping to see an obvious path, but the briars and undergrowth were a thick tangle of green. Onwards then, Gerald decided. Downhill towards the river. Wasn't that where Papa had said the King's secret house had been? On the river? He would very much like to see the river and the house, Gerald decided, as he pushed his way through the undergrowth, barely noticing in his excitement that the brambles were tearing his clothes and scratching his bare legs. It could be fun to have a boat and learn to swim. How he would love that! Gerald had once asked his mama if he could have lessons in the men's bathing pond on Hampstead Heath, but she had been so horrified by the mere notion of cold water that Gerald had quickly understood this was not to be. But maybe here, in the fresh sea air everyone seemed so keen on.

Pleased by this idea he continued on his way through the woods until he found himself on a riverbank fringed by willows and yellow laburnum. The tide was out and the sand glittered in the sunshine. Gerald stood for a while like somebody caught in a dream as he watched pools of water glisten as golden as sovereigns while long-legged wading birds picked their way through. It was a beach! His own very beach!

A wild cry broke his lips, and he kicked off his shoes and tugged off his socks with excitement, before running over the rough grass and leaping onto the sand. Who needed the fuss of a bathing hut or a silly knitted costume? He was going to run down the water's edge and paddle. At long last he was going to have some fun!

But the smooth sand of the beach was deceptive and in moments all Gerald's hopes of fun trickled away like the receding tide. More silt than sand, the beach shifted under his weight as dank mud oozed between his white toes. Gerald scowled as he lurched forwards, gasping at the cold and grunting with the effort of pulling one foot at a time out of the sucking mire. He was determined to reach the river and paddle, but no matter how hard he tried the ribbon of glittering water seemed to grow no nearer but remained forever ahead of him like a mirage. The further he trudged the softer and deeper the alluvium grew. Submerged oyster shells nipped his heels painfully and the cold mud chilled his toes. Gerald was bitterly disappointed. Just his luck his father had chosen a house with a rotten swamp for a beach. He didn't want to paddle in the beastly river anyway. Paddling was for girls. He was going back.

Gerald tried to turn round, but as he attempted to lift his right foot his left leg sank into the riverbed until it was almost knee-deep. His belly somersaulted when the same happened as he tried to heave his left leg out. The grey mud sucked him down, and with each effort he made to free himself he sank a little deeper. No matter how hard he tried it was impossible to turn around, and after several minutes of frantically straining to pull free the awful truth dawned; he was stuck in the riverbed. And he could see the water rising with the incoming tide. He'd learned about that in his schoolbooks, but it was different when you were faced with the reality of it.

"Help!" Gerald shouted, panic fizzing through his bloodstream like sherbet. "Somebody! Help me!"

But his frantic cries were muffled by the wooded valley and snatched away by the soft wind.

"Help! Help me!"

Gerald looked around frantically, hoping desperately for a small boat to sail down the narrow channel or perhaps a doughty gamekeeper to appear on the opposite bank, but the shore was deserted and the bank opposite was wooded hillside. The only answer to his desperate calls was the mocking cry of gulls. Fear's wings beat in Gerald's chest. Nobody knew where he was. Who would think to search for him on the riverbank? Nanny wouldn't even notice he was missing until suppertime, and by then it would be far too late because the tide would have risen until the water drowned him.

Tears pricked Gerald's eyes. He was going to die. The cold water would creep closer and closer, rising inch by inch until it reached his chest, his chin, his mouth, his nose and finally closed over his head. It would be just like when Henry Cressex held his head under the water in the bathroom, only this time there was no Matron to bustle in and tell them to stop messing around. He was going to die today, stuck in the riverbed, and nobody would know. Gerald had often thought he wanted to die – he'd pleaded with God on many occasions to take him when he fell asleep like all the dead children he'd read about on tombstones – but now that Death was breathing down his neck and sharpening his scythe Gerald realised he didn't actually want to die at all. In fact, he very much wanted to stay alive.

"Help!" he cried again.

"Help! Help!" laughed the gulls, wheeling in the blue sky. "Help! Help!"

All alone and stuck in the mud, Gerald began to cry. With nobody to see him and jeer he cried big choking sobs. He wept for the terror of what was going to happen and for the unfairness of a world where boys were bullied and made fun of and left to die alone. Gerald wept for his mother and father and even for Nanny, and he cried for all the things he would never see and do. As the sun began to duck behind the wooded valley and the water crept closer he thought he would faint from dread. At least that way he wouldn't be aware of drowning.

"Hey! You! Don't move!"

The shout came from behind him and for a moment Gerald thought he must have dreamed it for who would be passing by such a lonely spot? As for not moving, he couldn't have budged an inch even if he'd wanted to, for he was stuck fast. A tear rolled down his cheek and splashed onto the mud.

"Help!" he sobbed. "Please! Help me!"

"Don't panic. I'm coming!"

He hadn't imagined it. There *was* someone. A boy, by the sound of it, and a well-spoken one at that.

"I can't *move*!" Gerald wailed.

"Don't try! Stay still. If you panic it'll make things worse." There was a crack like a branch breaking. "Don't struggle!"

"But I'm stuck and the tide's coming in!" Gerald howled. "I'm going to drown."

"No you're not," replied the boy. He sounded very certain.

"We've all got stuck here before, haven't we, Marrick?"

"Yep," agreed a second voice which possessed the same rich accent as the staff at Vyvyan Court. "The riverbed has a few marshy places on this stretch, see. It's easy to get stuck if you don't know where they are. That's why we all avoid walking on this bit."

Gerald felt rebuked and he bristled. "I didn't know that."

"How could you if you hadn't been told?" said the first voice kindly. "Anyway, we'll get you out. You need to fall backwards and turn onto your stomach. Then you can crawl towards the bank and grab this branch. We'll pull you in."

Gerald was terrified. The mud would suck him under and fill his mouth and nose. "I'll sink," he whimpered.

"No, you won't," said the first boy firmly. "You think you will, but your body has a greater surface area this way, and will spread your weight more evenly across the mud. It's basic mathematics really. You'll be able to crawl on your belly to the edge quite safely, I promise."

"You're such a brainbox, Ned," said the other boy. He didn't make this sound like a compliment.

Gerald gulped his terror down. He didn't much like the thought of flopping into the mud, but the boys sounded very confident and he didn't really have much choice. He didn't want either of the boys to think he was a baby. Closing his eyes, he launched himself backwards with a plop. The sun-warmed mud was warm and not unpleasant.

"Turn onto your tummy," Ned ordered and, eyes still closed, Gerald did as he was told. When he opened them he saw to his enormous relief that, just as Ned had promised, he wasn't sinking into the mire but was sprawled across it. On the bank two boys, one with a mop of curly hair and the other with a white-blond thatch, were lying on their bellies too, and clinging onto an enormous branch which they were holding out for him to grab.

"Now crawl!" the curly-haired one yelled. "Come on! Hurry!"

Gerald wasn't accustomed to taking orders from working boys, but today he didn't argue. He started to swim his limbs and little by little inched his way towards them until his fingers grasped the leafy tips of the outstretched bough.

"Hold tight," said Ned. "Ready, Marrick? One, two, three!"

Together they began to pull the branch towards the shore with Gerald clinging to it for dear life, beyond caring that his sailor suit was ruined and his face raw from crying. When he felt shingle scrape his belly and rough grass tickle his face, he cried even harder because he was safe and hadn't drowned in the river. He swiped his eyes with the back of his hand, but only succeeded in filling his vision with mud.

"Here, have this," said the white-blond boy pressing a hanky into his hand. It was freshly laundered and smelled of violets, Gerald noticed, as he mopped his face and blew his nose. Once he'd rubbed away the tear tracks he tried to pass it back, but the boy, Ned of the mathematical mind, waved it away.

"I think you need it more than me."

Ned was still panting from his exertion, but his voice was kindly and he looked concerned, unlike Marrick who was laughing.

"I'll say! You're plastered in shit! You should see yourself!"

Gerald glowered at him. Although still shaken and glad of the rescue, he was not inclined to be teased by a common boy in patched corduroys and hobnail boots.

"It was an accident," he snapped. "I didn't know the riverbed was marshy. I've not lived here long."

"Then how could you have possibly known?" Ned said easily. He held out his hand. "I'm Ned Carew, and this is Marrick Penwurthy. We've always lived here."

Mollified by Ned's easy manner, Gerald shook the proffered hand. Ned's grip was firm and filled with an assurance that Gerald instantly envied. Marrick didn't offer his hand, though, presumably because he knew he should be doffing his cap to his betters. Wrong-footed by his own stupidity, Gerald decided to pull rank.

"Thank you very much for your assistance," he said stiffly. "I'm Gerald Snowe, of Vyvyan Court. You shall be rewarded."

"Don't be daft," said Ned. "You'd have done the same for us."

Gerald wasn't so sure he would have done. He suspected he would have been frozen with indecision.

"You're from the family who're renting the Trelyon estate," said Marrick.

Gerald bristled. He didn't like the way this common boy with his patched trousers and rough hands said 'renting'. It seemed to imply the Snowes were somehow less worthy than their predecessors and indicated a distinct lack of deference. It was time to make sure these village boys knew where they stood in the pecking order.

"I'm Gerald Snowe. I didn't think anyone else was supposed to be here. It's private property," he said haughtily. The implication was clear.

Ned and Marrick exchanged a swift glance.

"Bloody lucky for you we were, then," said Marrick. "Else you might be nearly underwater by now. Or worse."

All three boys stared across at the river. The spot where Gerald had been stuck only five minutes earlier was covered by creeping water. Feeling sick, Gerald looked away.

"You never know when it might help to have folk around," Marrick continued thoughtfully. "Especially when you're exploring a new place and don't know it so well. There are deadly currents here, and mine shafts and ghosts. You could've come a right cropper."

"Ignore him. There are no mine shafts," Ned told Gerald, his unusual violet eyes crinkling. "And the strong currents are only toward the river mouth where nobody really swims. Just keep on the shingly parts of the riverbed here and you'll be fine. You won't sink or get caught in a rip."

Gerald waited for him to say there were no ghosts either, but Ned didn't and Gerald shivered. Suddenly the riverbank was filled with dangers, and Gerald decided he didn't like this place at all. This was a spot where bad things happened, and where bad things would happen for years to come. Maybe even to him? Gerald could feel it in his bones, and as he sat shivering it was all he could do not to start crying again.

"Your folks don't know you're down here, do they?" Marrick asked.

Gerald raised his chin. "Of course they do."

"So why didn't anyone come looking for you?" Marrick picked a blade of grass, pressed it between finger and thumb and blew it to make a loud razzling noise while Gerald struggled to think of a sensible answer. He knew how he must appear to these two lads; a feeble cry-baby who couldn't even explore the riverbank unsupervised, and a wave of humiliation broke over him. How he hated Marrick for making him feel such a fool!

"I think you've given your folks the slip and gone exploring," Marrick continued slowly. He pointed to Gerald's muddy sailor suit and the smart shoes with silver buckles and the white socks he'd left neatly on the riverbank.

"Nobody would come here dressed like that if they'd planned it. I think you made a break for freedom."

Gerald was impressed by Marrick's deductions. He also rather liked the idea of being the kind of boy who made a break for freedom and gave adults the slip. It made him sound interesting and rather daring. Soapy Snowe who wheezed and blubbed and was the punchbag of the form seemed very far away.

He gave a nonchalant shrug. "Very well, you're correct. They can't watch me all the time, can they? I saw my chance and I took it."

"Won't they have missed you by now?" Ned was regarding him admiringly, and Gerald basked in the unusual sensation. "Will they be angry? Are you in trouble?"

The truth was that nobody would have even noticed his absence. Nanny would still be on her way back, and his mother, full of excitement about the Rivers family, wouldn't have given him a second thought.

But this didn't make for a good story, so Gerald thought hard. "They'll think I'm in the gardens. Or the library."

Ned's eyes widened. "You have a *library*?"

"Of course," said Gerald airily. And very dull it was too, with all those dusty books, he almost added, but Ned was looking impressed so he held his tongue. Having a library made him important in this boy's eyes, and when you were covered in mud and feeling foolish every little thing helped.

"Bloody books," said Marrick rolling his eyes. "Ned's a real swot, Gerry. He's teacher's pet!"

Gerald opened his mouth to point out it was 'Master Gerald' to the likes of him, but Marrick and Ned were far too busy wrestling to listen to anything he had to say. Gerald watched them rolling about in the grass, fists flailing and legs kicking, and by the time Ned was sitting astride Marrick and forcing him to apologise, the moment had passed. It was probably as well. A little in awe of these lively boys, he didn't want to sound priggish.

"My father's Trevellan's schoolmaster," Ned explained once he'd clambered off Marrick and was lying on the grass. "That's why I read a lot. I'm going to be a writer when I'm older."

"He really is," Marrick panted. He flopped on his back. "Ned writes great stories. He'll be the most famous writer of the twentieth century."

He said this with such conviction that Gerald was in awe. Ned Carew was confident, clever, sporty and talented. He knew the riverbank, had a handsome face and could wrestle. He also had a best friend who admired him. In short, Ned was exactly the sort of boy Gerald longed to be. He could hardly stop staring at him.

"My pa's a fisherman," Marrick added proudly. "I'll be one too, I expect. All the Penwurthies fish."

"My father ..." Gerald paused, frowning because ... what exactly *was* his father? At school the other boys ragged him because he was in trade, but something told him these two lads wouldn't do that. He tried again. "My father owns factories."

"I thought he made soap," said Marrick.

Gerald glared at him. "He's a businessman, actually."

"My father says he's an industrialist," Ned said diplomatically. "He says men like your father are the future."

Gerald liked the sound of this, and it was good that Ned and his family knew Arthur was very important.

"And he's rich," grinned Marrick. "We all know that, since he's got Vyvyan, and half the village are working for him."

Gerald liked this even more, but he knew a gentleman didn't boast. Besides, he could afford to be magnanimous now the two boys knew their place.

"As I said, he'll reward you for helping me today," he told them graciously. In his imagination he saw the two boys, faces scrubbed and caps in hand, standing at the back door of Vyvyan Court, where he and Arthur handed them a few shillings and the staff clapped admiringly. The vision made him feel all warm and tingly. The minor issue of his father discovering what he'd got up to and being furious with him ... well, he'd worry about that later.

"Good," said Marrick. "Can it be a sixpence?"

Ned shot him a sharp look. "We don't need a reward, thanks. Anyone decent would have done the same."

Marrick looked as though he disagreed, but Gerald could see how he deferred to Ned.

" 'Spose so," Marrick muttered.

Ned turned to Gerald with a smile. "Anyway, you said you're not supposed to be here, so your father would be angry, and we don't want you to get into trouble with him. You never know, he might not mind you coming down here to play and fish eventually. We could show you all the best places to find bass, the climbing tree and our secret boathouse."

Gerald's eyes widened. So it *did* exist!

"It's where the King used to take his women," grinned Marrick. "The dirty devil!"

"What for?" Gerald couldn't imagine why ladies in corsets and who carried parasols would want to visit this lonely spot. His mama could barely walk from her dressing room to the carriage, her skirts were so heavy and her corset so tight.

"For spooning, of course," Marrick said, as though this

was obvious, but Gerald was none the wiser.

"For parties mostly," Ned explained. "The Trelyons were famous for their summer parties. They had a garden house just along from here. It's all shut up now, but we can show you another time, if you like. There's not much about Oyster Shore we don't know."

"Oyster Shore?" Gerald echoed, and the sliced soles of his feet seemed to throb at the mention of the name. Hateful place. Hateful oysters. Hateful river. Hateful Cornwall.

"That's the local name for this part of the river on account of the wild oyster beds," Marrick said. "You need to watch out for those, but you've probably worked that out now, Gerry. Your feet look a right mess."

Gerry was better than Soapy, Gerald decided, and Marrick was right. His feet were in agony.

"Oyster Shore is private land. It belongs to Vyvyan Court, so if you're the new tenants it's your father's now," Ned told him, looking awkward. "We shouldn't really be here."

Gerald couldn't argue with this. "You're trespassing," he said.

"*You're* not meant to be here, either," Marrick pointed out, "but if you don't tell your father about getting stuck and meeting us, he'll never know anyone was where they shouldn't be. He can't mind about what he doesn't know, can he? You could come back again if you wanted. And if you didn't tell him about us we can come back to meet you and show you everything here. Like where not to paddle for a start."

Gerald nodded. He could see the sense in this suggestion, although he wasn't sure he ever wanted to see the hateful riverbank again. On the other hand it was fun to be here with Marrick and Ned, watching them play-fight and listening to their chatter. They were also very useful to him because he'd already learned about the hazards of mudflats and how to navigate them. Now he was determined to find out what spooning was. Gerald suspected it was something illicit, something the boys at St Hugh's would snigger about, which was why Nanny wouldn't tell him. His only hope of learning all the important things he needed to know was to be friends with Ned and Marrick, however common they were.

"I could join you? You'd show me about?" he asked cautiously. Used to rejection, Gerald was prepared for Ned and Marrick to laugh and tell him to get lost.

"Of course," said Ned. "There's sometimes a few more of us. Even my sister and her friends when the sun's out. If you don't mind us being on your father's land, you could join us. If you like."

Gerald stared at Ned, not quite able to believe what he was hearing. In four years at St Hugh's no boys had ever asked him to join in with their games. Suddenly Gerald wanted nothing more than to be like Ned and Marrick. He wanted to know where the rip tides and the hiding places were. He wanted to climb trees and wrestle. In his imagination Gerald saw himself no longer skinny and frail but strong and tanned as he ran through the woods and sliced through the river. He would sail and swim and climb, and all the local boys would look up to him because he owned Oyster Shore. They would have to do what he said if they wanted to play there. They would admire him hugely, and eventually he, not Ned Carew, would be their leader. Gerald would be a better choice for that role because he was a gentleman. That was right and that was proper. All he had to do was keep it a secret that the boys played here, and everything he'd ever wanted would be his. Where could be the harm be in keeping this secret? It wasn't as if his parents would ever choose to explore the woods or perambulate along Oyster Shore. They didn't know this place existed, and if they did they wouldn't be interested.

"Will you keep mum about us being here?" Marrick urged. "Cross your heart and hope to die?"

Gerald nodded. "If you show me all the places, I won't tell anyone you come here. It can be our secret."

"Cross your heart and hope to die. If you ever betray us you're cursed to death," Marrick said. It was schoolboy stuff, but Gerald shivered.

"All right. I swear," he said.

"So we're friends, then?" Ned's smile was open and guileless, and Gerald wondered how it was possible to believe everyone was a friend and the world was just one big adventure. He wanted to sneer at Ned for this, but the truth was he rather envied the other boy.

"Friends?" urged Marrick, holding out a grimy hand. "Shake and swear."

Could they be friends of a sort? Should he keep this meeting a secret? Even if he managed to sneak back and explain away his absence and the ruined clothes, did he want to see these boys again? They weren't the right sort of people, but they might prove useful. The entire riverbank seemed to hold its breath as it waited for his answer. Even the gulls fell silent, and Gerald had the oddest feeling that the rest of his life was poised to pivot on this moment; how he chose to answer the question would change the course of events for ever. There would be no turning back.

Gerald took a deep breath and shook their hands. "Friends," he said firmly. "Cross my heart, hope to die and may I be cursed if I ever betray you."

19

JULY 1904

Trevellan

Ned

"I'm not coming. I'm busy."

Marrick stood on the deck of his father's lugger, one hand shading his eyes against the afternoon sunshine as he peered up at the quay. Ned, perched on a pile of crab pots, frowned.

"Doing what?"

He was genuinely perplexed. The tide was out, leaving the pebbly bed of Trevellan's small harbour naked save for a few fronds of seaweed draped coyly over the rocks. It was a Saturday afternoon in the school holidays and although the weather was beautiful a nor'westerly had whipped white horses into a gallop across the sea out in the fishing grounds and the fishing fleet was tied up. All the ropes on the boat were neatly coiled, the deck was scrubbed, and the nets were mended and stored for the next trip out. Marrick's father had been in the pub since it had opened while his mother was in the schoolhouse chatting to Matilda over tea, trying to pretend she didn't have another black eye. There was nothing for Marrick to do here, Ned said, so why didn't he want to come down to Oyster Shore?

Marrick shrugged. His eyes slipped from Ned's. "Just stuff."

Ned tried again. "Can't it wait? I've dug up some worms and I thought we could crab from the pontoon and maybe cook what we catch. Gerald said he's got a new fishing rod, too, and we can use it if we like."

"Bully for him," said Marrick. "And I don't want to use his fishing rod, anyway. What's wrong with ours? Or aren't they good enough for Lord Gerald?"

Ned bit back a sigh. Marrick was like this a lot lately. He was always sniping at Gerald, who, it had to said, was equally cool towards him. Since the three boys had started spending time together Ned had increasingly felt as though he was having to keep the peace.

"Of course they are," he said. "I think he was excited to try this new one, that was all. His father bought it in London."

"Well, that makes it far better than ours, then," Marrick said sourly. "The King probably has the same one."

The King could have, since Fortnum's was the origin of the new fishing rod, a fact Gerald had been keen to impart the last time he and Ned had met up on Oyster Shore. Ned decided against sharing this detail with Marrick, who would see it as yet another example of Gerald Snowe showing off. In fairness to Marrick, Gerald did boast a great deal and never missed an opportunity to remind the boys that they only enjoyed Oyster Shore on his good graces, but Ned, who had spent a lot of time with Gerald this summer, understood that his bragging was a cover for his insecurities.

Gerald Snowe might be wealthy but he was hopeless at climbing trees, couldn't swim a stroke, puffed like a steam train when he ran and didn't have a clue which berries and mushrooms would poison him. The skills Ned and his friends took for granted were as alien and as complex to Gerald as the quadratic equations set by the Reverend Tullis, now tutoring him, and which Ned had taken to solving for Gerald. In return Gerald lent Ned books from Vyvyan's library and kept mum about the village children playing on Oyster Shore. Ned had spent hours patiently attempting to teach Gerald to fish and climb trees, but neither activity had proved a success. Fish seemed to give Gerald's hook a wide berth, and since he was dreadfully un-coordinated Ned's stomach lurched every time the other boy's foot slipped on a bough or his hands flailed through thin air when he tried to catch a branch.

No wonder Arthur Snowe had given up appointing masters to teach his son to shoot and ride, Ned had thought wearily as he watched Gerald struggle to reach the lowest limb of the old horse-chestnut tree in the heart of the woods. Marrick and Ned could scale the branches easily and perch at the very top of the leafy canopy like kings of the world, but Gerald had yet to reach even the first boughs. His face grew puce with rage at each failed attempt. On the last he'd kicked the truck so hard in rage that he'd made himself cry and then threatened to have his father fell the tree. It had taken the alarmed Ned a long while to calm him down.

Marrick had gone home in disgust. "Fancy blaming the

tree because you can't climb it," he had remarked pityingly over his shoulder. "You might as well blame the river because you can't swim. The only person to blame is you, Gerry. Buck up."

Gerald, still kicking the tree in temper, didn't reply, but Ned caught sight of the ugly look he threw in Marrick's direction and felt very uneasy. Gerald Snowe, Ned was quickly learning, held grudges, and although he owned everything a boy could ever desire he seethed with resentment. If Ned hadn't craved the solitude and beauty of Oyster Shore so very badly, he might not have chosen to spend *quite* as much time with Gerald.

Once the summer holidays began and weeks of glorious freedom stretched ahead, the other boys joined them in the woods, and sometimes Bess and her friends would wander down to make daisy chains and paddle in the shallows. Ned and the boys would swim in the river, diving and darting through the water like minnows, before collapsing breathless and dripping on the riverbank to dry off in the sunshine. Ned thought this was the most tremendous fun in the world, but Gerald, who couldn't swim, hated being left out and would glower from his perch on a fallen tree, refusing to peel off his thick woollen stockings and dip so much as a toe in. No matter how many times the other children tried to encourage him Gerald would only shake his head and pretend to be bored. He must have been unbearably hot in his Eton collars, knickerbockers, garters, woollen socks and heavy boots, Ned thought sympathetically. It must have been torturous watching the other boys fling off their flannel shirts and loose shorts to dive into the cool water, but no matter how hard Ned tried to encourage Gerald to join them the other boy refused. Ned suspected

Gerald was secretly afraid of the water and didn't want to lose face.

"There's nothing to be afraid of," Ned said gently one afternoon when they sat on the riverbank watching the others. The warm air was split with shrieks and splashes and Ned longed to join in, but felt duty-bound to keep his new friend company. "It's very shallow here and the riverbed won't give way, I promise."

Gerald flushed. "I'm not afraid."

"So come on. then!"

Gerald shook his head. His dark brows were drawn together, and his top lip curled in distaste. "I don't want to swim with *village* boys."

Ned was stung. "*I'm* a village boy."

"Not like the others. You're the schoolmaster's son. Your father went to Oxford, and you said he's the son of a gentleman."

Ned had indeed said so, but now he wished he'd kept mum. The boys had exchanged stories about their families, and Ned had boasted about Edgar because he was proud of his clever papa and wanted Gerald to understand why he loved books and wanted to become a writer. He hadn't been trying to claw at respectability or raise himself socially above Marrick and the others, and now he felt quite hot with shame that Gerald might think this the case.

"I live in the village and that makes me a village boy," he said firmly. "Come on, Gerry, be a sport. Take your socks off and have a paddle at the edge. You'll enjoy it."

There was a whoop from the bank and huge splash as Marrick hurled himself into the river. They watched him strike out for the far bank, Sammy and the Trehunnist brothers powering after him, their brown limbs slicing through the water. Gerald's scowl deepened.

"You can teach me to swim when we're alone," he said. This was actually a command, and they both knew it because when it came to Oyster Shore Gerald had the upper hand. This place belonged to his family now, so if Ned and the others wanted to enjoy it they had to tiptoe around him. Gerald was prickly and sometimes the sunny-natured Ned felt exhausted trying to second-guess the mood his friend was in or avoid doing something that Gerald might perceive as a slight. Ned had also learned very early that Gerald hated to fail at anything, and considered this an embodiment of inferiority; to be less skilled than common village children was a huge affront to his pride. Ned often tried telling Gerald that swimming and sailing and tree-climbing came as naturally as breathing when you grew up in Cornwall, and did his best to placate him by pointing out that none of the village children knew Latin declensions or which knife to use at dinner.

"*You* know all those things," Gerald countered, and glared at Ned as he said this, as though furious that Ned could swim and climb as well as observe social niceties and ace a Latin translation. Something in his expression unnerved Ned, and he'd swiftly joined his friends in the river, diving beneath the surface in the hope that the water would wash away his unease. Gerald just had a chip on his shoulder. He didn't mean any harm.

Still, Ned was dreading trying to teach him to swim. Gerald was either going to drown or demand that Arthur Snowe had the entire river dammed if he couldn't manage to reach the far bank after five minutes. Or maybe he would blame Ned for his failure and cause all kinds of trouble. Ned would be in deep water if Edgar knew he was still frequenting Oyster Shore, for Arthur Snowe had made it very clear that the Vyvyan Estate was private property. Anyone who tried to snare a rabbit there would be in big trouble, and the gamekeepers were kept very busy securing fences and tending pheasant pens in preparation for the October shoots. What if Gerald said he'd never given the boys permission to play on Oyster Shore and Ned was hauled in front of the village policeman? Nobody would believe Ned and Marrick over Gerald Snowe.

His pa would be so ashamed – but Ned pushed this worrying thought away. Gerald had a temper, and he was often jealous of the daftest things. The boy didn't have a very happy life, that was all. He'd often told Ned how he was unhappy at prep school and he had been dangerously unwell. Since so many of the villagers worked at Vyvyan these days Ned knew Mr and Mrs Snowe were often away, leaving Gerald alone in the big house with its long echoey corridors and with only his elderly nanny for company. Timmy Tuckey, now an under-footman to his mother's delight, said that some nights Gerald screamed the house down with nightmares. Matilda and Timmy's mother had once discussed this at length when they hadn't known Ned was listening in, and the general consensus in Trevellan was that the poor boy was sorely neglected. Ned's kind heart went out to his new friend, and he often wished he could bring Gerald home, where there was always laughter, cake and somebody to talk to. Of course Gerald would see the schoolhouse as terribly beneath him, but Ned was convinced that a few hours in the company of Edgar and Matilda would do him no end of good. Ned had told Gerald a little about life at the schoolhouse, described the fun the little family had together, and recounted the deep discussions on literature and science that Edgar encouraged over the dinner table. Gerald had looked wistful.

"Mama and Papa usually dine out," he'd said. "And if they are at home, my mother's usually occupied in the drawing room and my father's busy with the business. I don't spend much time with them."

Ned gleaned from the little Gerald did say that most of his time was spent either with Nanny, the terrifying old battle-axe they sometimes saw shopping in the village, or studying under the beady eye of Reverend Tullis. The afternoons and weekends were when Gerald was supposed to be reading or walking in safe confines of the park, his health apparently still a major concern, and these times were when he was able to slip away to meet Ned. Ned would leave him messages on the boathouse door – not, though, the special coded ones he left for Marrick in the secret place where the notebooks and treasures were hidden – or they would meet on the terrace of Oyster House. Ned would invent elaborate games and tell stories, which Gerald loved listening to. If the other boys were with them they would make camps or play at being Robin Hood and his outlaw band. This was Gerald's favourite game, and he liked to be Robin, ordering everyone around. Marrick, who said Gerry would have made a far better Sheriff of Nottingham, would often give up and go home, saying he was needed to help on the quay. As July slipped by, Marrick joined the children less often, and Ned missed him. He also missed Bess, who was no longer so keen to play, either.

"Come with us. You can be Maid Marian," he pleaded with her one sunny afternoon. "Bring Polly and Annie too if you like."

Bess glanced up from the book she was reading. "Is *he* going to be there?"

"Who?" Ned asked, although he knew exactly who his sister was referring to. His heart sank.

"Your new friend, of course. Gerald."

He scuffed the kitchen floor with the toe of his boot "I expect so. Why?"

"I don't like him," Bess said bluntly. "The other day he tripped Polly up on purpose. *Polly*, Ned. Why would he do something like that?"

Polly Polmartin had suffered polio as an infant and wore a calliper leg brace. All the village children doted on her.

Ned couldn't quite look his sister in the eye. "I don't suppose he meant to."

"Yes he did," said Bess. "He stuck his foot out and laughed when she fell. He did it when none of you were there to see. He tried to pull my plaits too, but I punched him in the stomach and that jolly well stopped him."

Ned imagined it had. His sister might look like a delicate slip of thing, but Bess Carew could hold her own with anyone, as Marrick, whom she'd once wrestled to floor for calling her names, would testify. Bess Carew's temper was famous in Trevellan.

"He wouldn't dare do that to Sammy or Marrick," she added. "Gerry's spiteful, and he says unkind things. I can't bear him."

Ned sighed. "He thinks people are laughing at him."

"Nobody cares enough about what he's doing to laugh at him," declared Bess, a statement of fact which Ned knew would mortify Gerald. The only thing worse for him than being laughed at was not being noticed at all. He was obsessed with not being left out or excluded. If Ned and

Marrick wanted to leave messages or access their secret hiding place they had to work hard to lose him.

"He watches people, too. He reminds me of a spider in a web, weaving away and gloating over all the flies getting stuck," Bess added. "Don't feel too sorry for him, Ned. I don't think he's a nice boy at all."

Ned shivered, for his sister was right; Gerald watched people closely, as though studying them for a weakness or a vulnerability he could exploit. Tugging a girl's pigtails was playground behaviour (Ned had to confess to tugging a fair few in his time) – but tripping a girl up was something very different, especially a girl who wore a leg brace.

"I don't know why you still play with him." Bess said stood up, book in hand, and looking determined. "I certainly don't want to."

Ned wasn't sure how to explain the pull of Oyster Shore. How could he make Bess understand how the eternally flowing water and watchful seabirds called to him? How the trees whispered stories and the calling gulls made his heart swell with emotions he had yet to name? He had to go there to write, for this was where his great novel would be born. Ned could no more stay away from it than he could cease breathing.

"His father owns Oyster Shore," was all he said.

Bess tossed her dark curls. Her violet eyes were scornful. "So that means he can order us all about, does it? Be the Lord of the Manor?"

Ned sighed. He supposed it did. Gerald Snowe was only tolerated by anybody because his father was the tenant of Vyvyan.

"He doesn't mean it, Bessy. He feels awkward."

Ned sometimes felt caught between his new friend and

the village boys. He felt the sting of Gerald's disdain for them just as he flinched for Gerald when somebody laughed at him for tripping on a tree root or screeching at the approach of a wasp. Being in the middle was no fun.

Bess snorted. "He didn't feel awkward when he tripped Polly up. He *laughed*, Ned. Gerald thought it was funny – and then he pretended it never happened. He tells lies. You can make excuses and play with him if you like, but I'm not going to."

This conversation troubled Ned greatly, because there was truth in what his sister said. Gerald could be very funny, but his humour was cruel. He was a wonderful mimic and his impression of Reverend Tullis, a man who suffered hayfever and spent all summer blowing his nose like a trumpet, made Ned and Marrick weep with laughter. As for lies, Gerald often told tall stories which he genuinely seemed to believe, and became quite angry when challenged. One rainy afternoon when he and Gerald had been sheltering in the boathouse, listening to the hammering of heavy drops and the ping of water landing in pails, Ned had shared an idea for a new game with his friend – only to hear Gerald explaining it in detail a few days later to Sammy, and claiming it for his own. Ned hadn't said anything but he'd been deeply hurt, and from that moment had decided never again to allow Gerald into his secret world. Instead, Ned made sure that all his notes and stories were tucked away in the secret place below the boathouse floor. Neither boy had divulged this hiding place to Gerald, and they never would. Even though Ned wanted to help Gerald fit in, he didn't trust him.

~

"I've written another chapter of my new book," Ned said to Marrick now, while the weather made fishing impossible, as he stood on the quay and did his best to persuade his friend to join him to go to Oyster Shore. Marrick was always clamouring to hear more from his latest novel, a thrilling tale of boys who battled pirates on a desert island, and Ned was looking forward to sharing the latest instalment. "I was going to read it to you in the boathouse."

"Like I said, I'm busy. Dad's left me some nets to mend, and when the tide's in I'm going to row out and set some pots. Come with me if you like."

Ned was tempted. He loved going out to sea in Marrick's little wooden boat, but he was also longing to listen to the call of the seabirds and wander along the shell line. There was a special poetry on Oyster Shore that his heart yearned for.

"The tide won't be in for hours. We can do that later," he said. "After crabbing."

"No thanks." Marrick began lifting nets, pouring mesh from one side of the boat to the other. The discussion was over as far as he was concerned. "Have fun with Gerry. Don't let him get stuck up a tree. He'll blame you."

Ned gave up. When Marrick Penwurthy set his mind on something there was little hope of changing it. Anyway, he didn't blame Marrick for being fed up with Gerald. The last time the boys had met up they had busied themselves damming a stream and Marrick had gently ribbed Gerald about getting his pristine sailor suit dirty. It was a joke, and he'd teased Ned about being filthy too, but Gerald had retaliated with a sarcastic remark about what else were washerwomen for but scrubbing the clothes of their betters? Marrick, protective of his mother, had come dangerously close to punching Gerald, and only Ned stepping between the two had saved Gerald from a well-deserved bloody nose.

"We'll go alone another time," he promised Marrick.

"If you like," said Marrick.

Ned sighed. Marrick was still upset, and once again he, Ned, was caught in the middle. Gerald's arrival had certainly complicated matters. As he walked along the wooded footpath which hugged the estuary Ned realised he was looking forward the arrival of autumn when school started again. Gerald would be back at St Hugh's, the keepers on the estate would be distracted by shoots and hunting, and it would be safe for the village children to roam Oyster Shore again.

As arranged, Gerald was waiting for Ned by the old fountain. Although it was a warm day Gerald was dressed formally in a tweed suit with an Eton collar and a bow tie, and his feet were laced into sturdy boots. Ned felt hot and bothered just looking at him, and after they'd spent a happy hour trying to catch the frogs that lurked in the fountain's murky depths, he suggested they made their way down to riverbank. There would be a breeze here and although the tide was out the boys could peel off their shoes and socks and walk out across the cool sand to dip their toes into the icy strands of the river which twisted across the centre of the channel.

Gerald, puce and sweating, was amenable to this plan and followed Ned through the woods, past the climbing tree he had yet to master and down the path to the boathouse. Invisible choirs of songbirds gave concerts from the trees and as they walked the boys tugged off their jackets until they were in their shirtsleeves. When they broke through the undergrowth the heat seemed to press down on them while the gauzy white clouds massed above. The air, heavy with the threat of storms, trembled, and the naked riverbed glittered where the waters parted. The whole world was poised on the brink of something, and before Ned even caught his first glimpse of the girl in white who stood by the shell line, everything he was and would ever be already knew she had arrived.

It was her. The girl he was made for. It was as though he'd known her all his life, and now she was here.

She stood on the flat sand, a slender figure dressed in white and alone in a world that sparkled like diamonds and where all colour had been drained by the thirst of the hot air. Some of her full skirts were tucked into her waistband but the rest trailed behind her, skimming the wet sand and caressed longingly by the icy fingers of the veined channels. Her face was turned away, and she studied the riverbed with such intensity that, recognising total immersion into the world of creativity, Ned caught his breath. That her hair was the same burnished red as the conkers he and Marrick collected each October, and her eyes the same brilliant green as rock pools and her skin as rich as clotted cream were all details he would notice much later, for these came second to the wonderful and joyous recognition of a kindred spirit. Her wild beauty was as much in the concentration with which she held a shell to the light as it was in the perfection of her face.

Ned stared, transfixed. This unknown girl who traced the river's memory on Oyster Shore, this girl without a hat to shade her complexion or cotton gloves to protect her hands, was lost in the eternal whirls of seashells. Her breath rose and fell with each frond of seaweed which stirred with every sigh of the distant ocean. She was transported by the world of the senses to the magical place where poetry and music and art was born, and Ned knew she was as much a part of this place as the solitary herons, silent mists and turning tides. She was made for Oyster Shore.

"*Oh she does teach the torches to burn bright*," he whispered, unable to pull his eyes away. The line from Shakespeare, the one Edgar always said had popped into his mind the first time he'd seen Matilda, had never seemed to hold meaning before this moment. Ned had privately thought a cake shop a banal setting for such a powerful sentiment, but now he understood perfectly because it was how familiar a stranger *was* that captured the heart and soul.

"Who's that?"

Ned was startled to hear Gerald speak. Lost in wonder, he had forgotten he wasn't alone, and it was something of a shock to find himself standing on the riverbank with the other boy. Gerald was staring too, but his forehead had corrugated with outrage.

"She shouldn't be here. This is private land."

"Maybe she doesn't know," Ned said, unable to look away. "It rather seems as though Oyster Shore belongs to her."

Gerald nodded, displeased. "She's very bold. Is she from the village?"

Ned shook his head. The village girls didn't dress in white or wear silk ribbons in their hair unless it was May Day, and there was nobody in Trevellan who looked like this girl. Was she even real? Had the shimmering heat conjured her? Or was he lying fast asleep on the riverbank with Puck playing tricks on him as he slumbered?

"I've never seen her before," he said.

The girl, too far away to hear their conversation, continued to pick her way over the sand. She held a pail loosely in one hand and every now and then would crouch down to scoop something up and raise it to the light before placing it inside. She was beachcombing, Ned realised. Not in the merry way his sister did, but with a measured consideration as though she was selecting subjects for careful study.

"Hello, Miss?" Gerald called, waving his hand. "Hello!"

The thick heat muffled his words, but some sound still carried. Plucked from her task, the girl turned around, long tresses floating like seaweed and the bucket swinging. Startled, she slithered on the shingle before slipping over and landing heavily on her hands. This part of the riverbed was razored with sharp oyster shells and Ned's warning cry came far too late. Although she made no noise, even from the bank he could see crimson petals flower on her pale skin.

"Stay there," he called, although whether to the girl or Gerald he wasn't certain. Both maybe? Not that Gerald appeared inclined to move anywhere; he was far too busy watching the disaster unfold.

"See what happens when you trespass?" he said smugly.

Ned was too busy kicking off his shoes and tugging off his socks to rebuke him. Leaving Gerald behind, Ned splashed across the wet shingle and sand until he reached the girl, who was nursing her left hand. Splashes of blood speckled her dress and bloomed into roses on the skirt where the muslin had been drenched by brine.

"That looks nasty," Ned said.

The girl looked up at him. Her eyes, green as the rock pools, shimmered with tears which she was trying hard to blink away. Having lacerated his hands and feet on oyster shells many times Ned knew what an effort it was taking not to howl. She was brave, he thought with admiration.

"At least it isn't my right one," she said shakily. Her voice was as polished as the sea glass that filled her bucket, and although she was in pain and her dress was ruined, she held herself like a princess. Ned felt as though he was a humble knight from Mallory, rescuing a damsel.

"Would that make a difference?" he asked.

"Of course," the girl replied as though this was obvious. "If it was my right one I wouldn't be able to draw."

"You're an artist." It wasn't really a question. Hadn't Ned known this from the first moment he'd seen her?

She nodded and the deep red curls nodded too in confirmation. "I'm collecting subjects to sketch."

They both looked at the bucket, which was filled almost to the brim with sea glass and shells and tiny triangles of ancient ceramics.

"I'll need to use this bucket to wash your hand, Miss ..." Ned faltered, because this girl, with her proudly tilted chin, beautiful clothes and an accent which made even Gerald sound as though he came from a family of tin miners, was undoubtedly a lady. He resisted the urge to kneel and swear fealty.

"Madalyn," she said.

Ned bowed. "I'd shake your hand, Miss Madalyn, but it seems to be in a bit of a poorly state."

She laughed, which made her nose crinkle and her freckles dance and the merry sound made Ned's mouth lift in response. "Madalyn is fine. Miss makes me sound about one hundred. I'm actually eight."

"I'm almost nine," said Ned proudly. He thought this sounded very elderly although ten would have been even better.

"I'll be nine next month," Madalyn declared, and they smiled at one another, bonding over their advanced ages.

"I'm Ned," Ned said when he eventually stopped grinning. "Edward Carew."

"Sir Edward," she corrected. "A gallant knight who rescues damsels in distress."

She had read his mind, and Ned blushed to the roots of his hair. With her pale skin and flaming hair Madalyn could have come straight from the verses of Sir Walter Scott, and he knew then that he would gladly lay down his life in her service.

"May I have the bucket?" he asked, and for the first time her composure faltered.

"Do you really need it? I've spent ages collecting all these and I was so looking forward to sketching them."

Ned understood at once. Just as he stored rich words and snippets of imagery in his notebooks ready to weave into prose, so Madalyn had selected the items that sang to her and which she longed to capture on paper. He pulled off his cap and tipped the contents of the bucket into it.

Madalyn gasped. "It'll be ruined."

Ned thought it would be worth a thousand ruined caps to see her happy. "It'll dry out. I'll just fill this bucket with water to wash your cut. Then we can walk to the riverbank and bandage your hand."

"You have bandages? How organised you are." She raised her eyebrows, and he knew she was teasing him.

"Mother always makes me take a clean hanky." Ned patted the pocket of his shorts. "That will do until you can have your hand looked at properly."

He carried the bucket to the deepest channel where he swilled it out with clean water before filling it to the brim.

"Do you want to be a doctor? You seem to know a lot about tending wounds." Madalyn said to Ned, as they picked their way over the sharp shells and stones to the bank where Gerald was watching. Ned had torn a strip from his shirt and wrapped her hand in it but was alarmed to see blood creeping through.

"I've cut my feet a lot here. You get to be quite good at patching yourself up." He paused, uncertain as to whether he should carry on, but there was something about the way Madalyn was looking up at him, her wide green eyes filled with interest, that made him brave. He took a deep breath and a leap of faith. "I actually want to be an author. I come here to write whenever I can."

Madalyn didn't say how wonderful or that he must be clever or even ask what sort of book he was writing. "But you're one already, then! A writer's like an artist; not something you become, but something you are. One day I shall be very famous. I shall have exhibitions of my work and travel all around the world."

Ned admired her confidence, and as he followed her onto the riverbank he realised he didn't doubt her for a moment. This little girl had an air about her that inspired total belief and loyalty.

They reached the riverbank, where Madalyn sat down, arranging her bedraggled skirts around her as though she was a queen settling down for a riverside banquet.

"Hello," she said to Gerald, peeling off the bloodied rag that had once been a shirt-tail and holding out her hand imperiously to Ned. Crimson droplets ran down her pale forearm and splashed onto the grass. "I'm ready for my bandage now."

"You're bleeding," said Gerald faintly. His pale eyes bulged at the sight of the blood and he looked a little green. Ned had seen Gerald look faint when the other boys gutted fish and hoped he wasn't about to swoon.

"I am rather," agreed Madalyn. "Lord, you *are* a funny colour. You should look away if you're scared of blood."

Gerald gulped. "I'm not scared of blood."

"Just as well," said Madalyn cheerfully. "There's been quite a lot of it so far. My dress is utterly ruined."

"The cold water makes bleeding look worse than it is," Ned said, taking her hand and dipping it into the bucket. At least he hoped this was true. If not, the little girl was in a bad way. Maybe he should ask Gerald to fetch help. On the other hand, Gerald looked as though he was in a worse state than Madalyn: perspiration beaded his forehead, and as Ned washed Madalyn's hand, impressed at how she scarcely flinched, he noticed Gerald was swaying.

"Are you all right?"

"I'm fine," snapped Gerald, his gaze anywhere but on the pink water in the bucket. "I'm not the one bleeding."

Madalyn's eyes glittered. "No, but you're the one turning green. Don't faint, for heaven's sake ... Ouch!" she gasped as Ned dabbed her hand. "That really stings."

"Sorry," said Ned. "It'll feel better in a minute."

Scowling, Gerald fanned his face. "I'm not going to faint. What rot. I'm just hot."

"I'm not surprised if you're wearing tweed. Why are you dressed for shooting, anyway?" said Madalyn, perplexed. "Everyone knows that's months away. You must be melting. This time of year you should be in tennis clothes or cricket whites, not plus fours. Nobody wears plus fours in the summer since you can't stalk."

Ned winced, for Gerald was indeed dressed in his brand-new shooting outfit. It had arrived last week, along with a shiny gun, and he'd been strutting around in it for days, showing off and not realising he was making a fool of himself. Nervous of Gerald's temper, and knowing his sensitivity for perceived slights, Ned hadn't dared remark upon the absurdity of Gerald's attire. His awe for Madalyn was increasing with each passing second.

Gerald's eyes narrowed balefully. "I don't know who you think you are, but you shouldn't even be here. This is a private estate. I could actually have you thrown off if I chose. It belongs to my father."

Pleased with this threat, Gerald waited to see what response it would have. Ned suspected he would be hoping for tears. That had been the result when he'd told some of the village girls they would have to carry his shoes and socks or he'd tell the estate manager they were trespassing. Marrick had told Gerald he was pathetic for picking on girls, and Ned had agreed. Gerald would never dare speak to the Trehunnist brothers that way.

But Madalyn laughed. "How absurd! This estate doesn't belong to your father."

Gerald's face turned almost purple. He hated being contradicted, and to be laughed at by a girl was a huge insult.

Hoping to distract him, Ned said quickly, "Gerald, would you fetch me some of that moss from over there by the laburnum? My mother says it helps to stop bleeding."

But Gerald couldn't have cared less if Madalyn bled to death on the riverbank. He was far too furious. "It *does* belong to him! It does! Oyster Shore is our private land, and you're trespassing. I could call for the constable and have him take you away if I chose!"

Ned, horrified at this lack of gallantry, flushed. "Gerald! Madalyn's not done any harm."

"She's trespassing!" Gerald hissed. "This is my father's estate, and she has no right to be here."

But Madalyn was unperturbed. "Don't be so ridiculous," she said. "This estate doesn't belong to your father – as well you know! It belongs to my second cousin twice removed, St John Trelyon, and I presume that your father rents the big house, which means he's *our tenant*. This part of Vyvyan, Oyster Shore, is kept as my cousin's own private residence, and isn't included in your father's arrangement. It certainly isn't available for tenants, because the house is kept as a family home – *my* family home – and I think you'll find *you* are trespassing on *my* property. I'm Madalyn Trelyon. Who might *you* be?"

Was it possible to fall in love when you were only eight years old? Ned felt certain it must be, for at that moment he worshipped Madalyn Trelyon with all his heart – unlike Gerald, who was slack-jawed and lost for words. Ned almost felt sorry for the boastful boy, for Madalyn made the dilapidated summer residence and overgrown stretch of riverbank sound very grand indeed, as she spoke with the innate confidence born of generations of privilege. Gerald might have a wealthy father, but Madalyn's social status was something he could never possess.

"Well? Do you have a *name*?" she demanded.

Gerald flushed. "I'm Gerald Snowe. My father rents this estate."

"Doesn't he have one of his own?" Madalyn asked.

Gerald's mouth closed as tightly one of the oysters on the riverbed. A livid scarlet stain spread across his face and to the tips of his ears. If hair could blush, Ned thought that Gerald would now have locks the same colour as Madalyn's.

"His father's an industrialist," Ned supplied, taking pity on him.

"Oh yes! Mama said something about that," Madalyn

recalled, while Ned bound her wound with his hanky and stepped back to admire his handiwork. "When we arrived last night she mentioned that St John had let the big house to someone who was in trade. So that's your family?"

"You're staying here?" Ned asked quickly, and before Gerald could combust, *Please, please say yes,* he added silently. It was so satisfying to see Gerald unable to pull rank, and Ned had a feeling that life on Oyster Shore with Madalyn Trelyon present would be very interesting.

She nodded. "St John says Mama and I can have Oyster House for the summer or longer. It's only fair really, since my father should have inherited the whole estate. If it wasn't for the beastly entail I'd be ordering you off my estate, Gerald Snowe!"

Gerald stared at her. He could tell she meant it, and a flicker of admiration crossed his face. "If that's true, why didn't you inherit the estate?"

"You *do* know what an entail is?" Madalyn asked haughtily. "You're not such a clot that you don't have a clue?"

Ned knew that Gerald didn't and although his friend had been dreadfully rude he couldn't bear to see him so humiliated. Gerald was sensitive about lagging in his schoolwork and being behind Ned.

"Of course he knows," Ned said firmly. "It means the estate legally has to go to the next male in the line. Like in *Sense and Sensibility* when the Dashwoods have to leave Norland Park."

"Yes!" Madalyn said, turning to him with bright eyes. "Exactly like that! Or the Bennets with Longbourn. It's not fair!"

"Of course it is. Girls simply can't inherit like men," said

Gerald who, unable to join in the literary discussion, resorted to being spiteful.

"What about the old Queen?" Madalyn countered. "She was just a young girl when she ascended. And how about Queen Anne? Elizabeth the First?"

"That's different," muttered Gerald. Debating was not his strength.

"How?" Madalyn demanded. She was not a girl who was prepared to back down any more than she could make a fuss over a cut hand, Ned realised. She was magnificent. "Well?"

Ned decided to intervene. "It's a silly law and it won't always be like that. My father says a time is coming when things will change, and so does my mother. They both support women's suffrage – and Father says women will have the vote too, one day."

Gerald snorted. "What rot! Only men can vote. Women must do what their husbands tell them. That's the law and it won't change."

Now it was Madalyn's turn to glower. "No husband will tell *me* what to do. I intend to never marry."

"*Never marry*?" echoed Gerald. He stared at her as though she'd fallen from the moon. "But what will you do without a husband?"

"I shall paint and become a great artist," declared Madalyn as though it was a given fact.

Gerald was struggling. "Ladies don't work."

"Of course they do," she said. "Who do you think scrubs your floors and cooks your food?"

Gerald kicked a tree root with the toe of his boot. "I meant *proper* ladies. Not old scrubbers like Marrick's ma."

"Don't let Marrick hear you say that," warned Ned. "He'll give you a bunch of fives."

"He can try," said Gerald puffing out his chest. It was all talk to impress Madalyn, for Ned knew Gerald would die of fright if Marrick chose to fight him.

"My father says women can do anything men can," Ned told Madalyn. "He's a teacher and he says girls are just as clever as boys."

"Oh! Maybe he can teach me," said Madalyn. "I'm dreadfully behind. Mama had to let my governess go because we couldn't pay her any more. We don't have much money."

Gerald was shocked. "But you're a Trelyon!"

"A good name with no money. Papa lost the lot," she said, as matter-of-fact as though discussing the weather. "St John inherited the estate, and he got landed with Mama and me. We're the poor relations, but he knows deep down the estate should have been mine. That's why when Mama needed sea air he said we could have Oyster House. He couldn't really refuse us since he's the interloper."

She was a princess from a fairy tale, Ned thought. Denied her castle and true inheritance, she was living in a shabby house on a lonely riverbank where she would draw the birds and wait for rescue, although he had to admit there was something about Madalyn Trelyon which suggested she was far more likely to rescue herself. She would make a wonderful heroine, and Ned couldn't wait to liberate his notebook from the hiding place in order to spend the afternoon writing. He was desperate to immortalise her in fiction.

"Mama says I have to marry money and save us, but I don't want to do that at all," Madalyn was telling the agog Gerald. "If I'm not a famous artist by the time I'm old, say twenty, I shall be an explorer instead and find us riches and new lands."

Ned could picture her standing in the deck of a sailing

ship, telescope pressed to her eye as she spied a new shore, or trekking through the jungle brandishing a butterfly net. She would be glorious!

"Girls can't be explorers," muttered Gerald, but he no longer sounded quite so certain of his own opinions.

"Says who?" Madalyn wanted to know.

He shrugged one shoulder; a gesture Ned knew meant he didn't have an answer. "Anyway, there's nowhere left to discover."

"How do you know?" She tilted her head on one side. "Have you ever left England? I've been to Paris and Prague. Papa was in India for five years and he found a diamond mine. One day I shall go and claim it."

Gerald was checkmated. A soap factory couldn't compete with a diamond mine, and it was very clear that neither boy could compete with the agility of Madalyn Trelyon's mind.

"You could go to the stars," Ned blurted. She could be one herself because she shone so brightly.

"Yes! – why not?" Madalyn said thoughtfully, and she smiled at Ned, a warm smile that said they shared the same way of thinking. "One day I'm sure people will go there. So why not me?"

Ned couldn't think of any reason, and unusually Gerald didn't make a snide comment. Instead he was staring at Madalyn with an intensity which made the hairs on Ned's forearms ripple. There was no logic to the unease seeping through him, or rational explanation for the compulsion to keep her away from the other boy, but Matilda had taught him that feelings should be listened to – no matter how irrational they might seem.

"How's the hand?" he asked Madalyn quickly, and as he had hoped, Gerald looked away.

Madalyn wiggled her fingers. The bandage held and no blood seeped through the cotton. "It's sore but I'll be fine. Thank you, Sir Ned, my gallant knight!"

Ned flushed. He didn't really want this to be the last he ever saw of Madalyn Trelyon. "Do you need us to walk you back?"

She laughed. "How kind, but I think I can find my way."

"You could come up to Vyvyan for afternoon tea, if you like," offered Gerald. "There's always a fine spread. Bread and butter and two types of cake."

The invitation didn't include Ned, but Ned understood why. He wasn't Gerald's social equal, or at least not as far as Gerald was concerned, and he certainly wasn't Madalyn's. Ned could fight dragons, go on quests and worship her from afar, but he couldn't share sandwiches and cake with her. It was the way of the world.

But Madalyn didn't seem to care about any of this. "Why don't you bring some food down tomorrow afternoon? We could all have a picnic and then you can both show me all the best places. That way I might *just* forgive you for trespassing and decide to let you come back." Madalyn's face was serious, but Ned saw the twinkle in her eyes.

"You're blackmailing us? Cake in return for coming to Oyster Shore?" he asked.

Madalyn held up her bandaged hand. "*You* can come to Oyster Shore as much as you like, Sir Ned. You've saved the day."

"What about me?" said Gerald, not liking being left out. "Can I come too?"

Madalyn tilted her head to once side, considering the question. "If the cake's good, then maybe," she told him. Then, and with a wave of her good hand, she jumped to her feet and walked away into the afternoon haze. Ned and Gerald stared after her as though trying to hold onto a fading dream. Her silhouetted figure was seared into the memory of each boy, and Ned's Romany sense of foretelling whispered to him that from this moment neither of them would ever be able to see anyone else again.

The arrival of Madalyn Trelyon had changed everything.

20

LATE JULY 1904

Vyvyan Court

Madalyn

"Sit still, Madalyn! You'll crease your dress," Lady Constance hissed as the trap bowled through the parkland. She leaned forward and prodded her daughter in the solar plexus. "Don't slouch, and do stop scowling. Whatever will Lady Rivers think? Or Mrs Snowe?"

Who cares? Madalyn thought, irritably. Why did it matter so much to Mama what strangers thought about them? *You're a Trelyon and we have the family name to uphold* would be the next remark, accompanied by much sighing and a pained expression. This meant that although everyone knew that Lady Constance and her daughter were as poor as church mice and lived on St John's charity, whispering behind gloved hands about Madalyn's father, the scandalous viscount who gambled and drank his way into an early grave, it was still imperative that the two behaved as though the imposing house looming towards them with its endless deer park were still theirs.

"And you're a *Trelyon*," Constance added sharply. "Do you want everyone to think we've lost our manners as well as our fortune?"

In truth Madalyn didn't give thruppence what the neighbours thought, and anyway the Viscount Trelyon's wife and daughter *had* lost their fortune. Everybody knew it. Why else would they be living in a damp house without gas and only a handful of servants to attend them? Although Madalyn thought Oyster Shore heaven on earth, she was aware that it was her mother's very private hell. In another life, the one she ought to have led, it would have been Constance presiding over the silver teapot at Vyvyan as she graciously invited her neighbours for afternoon tea. The granddaughter of an earl and wife of the heir to one of the finest estates in England, Constance Trelyon had never expected to find herself in such reduced circumstances. No wonder she spent most of her time confined to her bedroom with a headache.

"Well?" Constance snapped when her daughter failed to reply.

"No, Mama," Madalyn said quickly. The last thing she wanted was to agitate Constance or cause her to become so concerned that she would sell the last of her jewellery in order to hire a governess. That would ruin the wonderful freedom Madalyn had enjoyed since she'd arrived in Cornwall. The thought of sitting indoors conjugating French verbs while the boys had all the fun filled her with panic. She loved climbing trees and wading through the shallows, and was learning to row in a little wooden boat that belonged to Ned's fisher-lad friend. Already, she was a hundred times better at rowing than Gerald, who could still only manage to go in circles. It made Madalyn smile to recall how furious he'd been that she was able to dip the oars in and out of the water with ease, although her smile slipped a little when she recalled how Gerald had snatched an oar from the rowlock and hurled it into the water before jumping into the shallows and wading to the bank. He had looked as though he'd wanted to lob her in after it, and for a second Madalyn had almost been afraid of him. There was a nasty temper simmering behind that pale and watchful façade.

"That's Marrick's oar!" Ned had said called after him. "Fetch it back!"

"Fetch the stupid oar yourself," spat Gerald. "Stupid boat. Stupid oars!"

Ned's violet eyes met Madalyn's, and a look of mutual exasperation passed between them before he jumped in to retrieve the oar, pulling the boat after him while Madalyn reclined on the wooden seat.

"You look like the Lady of Shallott," Ned had said, and then flushed, looking away swiftly to mask his embarrassment.

Madalyn sat up. "Wasn't she dead?"

"I didn't mean that. I meant you look like a princess."

Then it had been her turn to blush. Anyway, it was nonsense, because Madalyn knew full well princesses had long golden locks and lily-white skin; all the paintings and storybooks showed this. Princesses didn't have unruly red curls which knotted in the salty wind like the briars tangling the banks and knees scraped from tree-climbing, and they certainly didn't have tanned faces speckled with freckles. Madalyn thought it was just as well that Mama could no longer afford Nanny or Mam'selle Marsaud, who would have had a dozen purple fits at the wild hoyden she was becoming. Thank goodness her mama was far too busy being an invalid to notice what Madalyn got up to when she was supposed to be reading and sketching. In fairness, she was sketching all the time, but rather than the still life compositions her art master had suggested, Madalyn's sketch books teemed with wildlife and were replete with the wanton curves of the river.

"Well, I'd be quite dead if I fell overboard," she said, to change the subject and melt away the strange awkwardness. "I can't swim a stroke. Mama did say we might go sea-bathing at Penhayes, but I don't think she'll be well enough for an excursion, and bathing huts are very expensive."

"You don't need to go to Penhayes to swim. I can teach you here," Ned said.

Her eyes widened. "Without a bathing hut?"

He trailed his hand through the water and splashed her with icy cold droplets to make her shriek. "Bessy and I never used a hut. Have you got a bathing costume?"

Madalyn didn't think so, but that wasn't going to stop her. Suddenly there was nothing she wanted more than to twist and turn in the cool river with her hair spreading over the surface like a mermaid. Mama was bound to have a bathing costume folded away somewhere. She had brought three trunks of her own clothes to Cornwall, clothes from her glorious days of balls and opera and when she had been the toast of the season. Somewhere there must be a bathing costume.

Ned tugged the boat to the pontoon and tightened a line around the cleat. "If you find one I'll teach you to swim. We can start right here. The water's a good depth when the tide's in and the riverbed is firm."

She nodded and was about to agree when Gerald butted in: "You said you were going to teach *me* to swim."

"I am. I will," Ned promised. "I can teach you both. It'll be fun."

Gerald didn't look as though he thought it would be fun. His face was thunderous.

"Worried I'll be better than you?" Madalyn teased, but Gerald wasn't amused.

"I don't want to swim with a feeble girl."

"Bess swims as well as I do," Ned said. "I don't think being a boy makes one a better swimmer, Gerald."

"Like climbing trees," Madalyn added, unable to resist. Gerald really was insufferable at times and the queerest boy, always seething over some perceived slight. He had been consumed with envy yesterday when she had finally joined Ned at the top of the climbing tree, both children swaying high above in the canopy as they surveyed the green ocean of foliage and the watery blue one beyond. Gerald hadn't congratulated her, or even had another attempt himself, but had slunk away to stamp on ants and sulk.

Ned Carew, Madalyn had soon discovered, was the polar opposite of Gerald Snowe. Consequently, she turned to his easy company as naturally as flowers do to sunshine, and did her best to avoid Gerald, who glowered and made mean comments whenever she was around. Madalyn ignored him. Although she hadn't known Ned very long, and he was just a village boy, she had already decided he was destined to be her best friend in the whole world and (a very secret thought) she was quite set on marrying him when she grew up. He would write books and she would illustrate them, and they would travel the world together, discovering new countries and having marvellous adventures. When they were very rich they would return to Oyster Shore and St John would be so delighted to have such famous relatives that he would give Oyster Shore to them.

It was becoming her most cherished dream.

The day after she'd first met the boys, Madalyn had returned to the riverbank with a fruit cake and three bottles of lemonade stoppered with marbles, pilfered from the pantry when the housekeeper's back had been turned. When she got there she found Ned amusing himself by blowing on a blade of grass pressed between his hands to imitate a curlew's cry, but there was no sign of Gerald. Madalyn hadn't been sorry; his high-handed manner had annoyed her, and although it had been fun to pull rank and take the wind out of his sails she had no desire to make Ned feel awkward. And what use was it being a Trelyon, anyway, if you didn't have a bean to your name and had to rely on the charity of a distant cousin? Madalyn had decided long ago that being a Trelyon wasn't much to brag about.

Gerald was with his tutor, Ned explained, when she asked if the other boy would be joining them. Although it was the summer holidays, Gerald still had lessons because he had to catch up on his schoolwork after being ill.

"He's going to Harrow," Ned finished. "Like Byron."

"Mad, bad and dangerous to know?" Madalyn replied before she could help herself, and clapped her hand over her mouth, horrified to have been disparaging about Ned's friend.

Ned grinned. "Gerald will be thrilled to hear that! Have you read any Byron? My father has 'Childe Harold' and 'Don Juan' at home."

Madalyn was impressed. Mama had a copy of 'Don Juan'

somewhere, but it was meant to be racy and most unsuitable for ladies – rather like the poet himself.

"I haven't read anything of his, but he was at school with my grandfather," she said.

Ned stared at her, and Madalyn felt a gulf start to open between them. To bridge it, she said swiftly, "So, are you going to show me all the best places?"

"Is your hand up to it?"

"Of course! I can hardly feel anything," Madalyn fibbed. It still stung dreadfully and clenching her fist was painful, but she would rather die than admit weakness. "I thought you were going to take me to the boathouse. And the climbing tree?"

"You still want to go? Even though Gerald hasn't come with afternoon tea?"

Madalyn held up her wicker basket. "I have supplies."

"And I have your shells," Ned said, jangling his pockets.

Madalyn was delighted. "Then we can swap," she said, and Ned, gallantly taking the basket, agreed readily.

Now, and as the carriage grew closer to Vyvyan Court, Madalyn's thoughts drifted back to the first afternoon she and Ned spent alone on Oyster Shore. He had shown her the place where kingfishers nested, and told marvellous stories of smugglers and pirates. Turning away from the water, they had picked their way around a densely wooded bluff to the place where the hidden boathouse nestled in the trees, and picnicked on the weed-slicked pontoon, sipping lemonade, eating cake and talking until the shadows grew in length and the air chilled as the evening fell. It had been the best day

Madalyn could remember, and she hadn't been sorry that the peculiar little boy with the pale face and watchful eyes had been otherwise engaged. When she and Ned had parted at the fork in the path which led to Oyster House, she hoped Gerald would be busy all summer.

Unfortunately, this wasn't to be, for Gerald soon joined them, his resentful presence an awkward third wheel in her easy friendship with Ned. Sometimes village children played on Oyster Shore too, and Madalyn soon discovered just how much it irked Gerald that he could no longer order them about or decide who to favour by allowing them to stay. The boys would join in with the swimming and climbing, and Madalyn noticed that Gerald always stood apart from them, observing everything with a hungry look on his pale face.

Ned's sister, Bess, and her friends often played in the boathouse, but always wanted to set up imaginary afternoon tea parties which Madalyn, regularly forced into the real thing, shied away from in favour of beachcombing and mudlarking. She also realised that the village children were uncomfortable around her, uncertain of what the etiquette might be when playing with one of the illustrious Trelyons, and she hated making them feel awkward. Worse, they perceived her reticence as disdain, and before long their visits stopped. Ned said that they were needed by their families to work, but Madalyn knew he was being kind. Her presence put the other children on edge, and soon there were only three playmates on Oyster Shore. Madalyn wished there were only two. When it was only her and Ned the hours would gallop by as he wove magical stories and her pencil flew across the page capturing shells and wildfowl, but when Gerald joined them she hid her work, not trusting him to refrain from making a scathing remark or even snatching the sketchbook and tossing it into the river. Gerald would say this was an accident, but Madalyn knew the truth; she'd watched him tease the girls, and once he'd even untied the rowing boat when Marrick wasn't watching and let it drift away. Gerald Snowe, Madalyn had soon realised, was a boy who liked having the power to hurt people.

He would never hurt her, she decided as the carriage pulled up in front of Vyvyan Court. There was nothing Gerald Snowe could do that would make Madalyn Trelyon cry – but how she wished she wasn't having to take tea with him and his family. It was a glorious afternoon, and she was longing to explore the shore looking for shells or enjoy her first swimming lesson. Madalyn longed to feel cold sand against her bare feet rather than cotton stockings and button boots. She was all hot and bothered in her best dress, and would have to sit on the terrace with her back straight, sipping tea and nibbling dainty sandwiches with the odious Gerald, his mother, and the son of some very important and wealthy neighbours.

Why couldn't Mama have had one of her famous headaches today?

"Stop scowling, Madalyn! You look quite plain when you pull faces."

Constance's words were like a slap. Madalyn knew that appearing plain was the worst crime she could ever commit – far worse than cutting her hand or snagging her skirts on brambles. Plain girls with fortunes still made advantageous marriages. But plain girls with a good name but not a penny didn't. Madalyn toyed with telling her mother that one day women would vote and not need husbands at all, but thought better of it, for then Mama might show a rare interest in who she was keeping company with and put an end to any playing on Oyster Shore. Madalyn bit back a retort and attempted a smile.

Constance shuddered. "Dear Lord, that's even worse. Just be polite to Lady Rivers and Mrs Snowe, and don't speak unless spoken to." She leaned forward and smoothed Madalyn's hair, starting to curl in the heat, and straightened her hat. "Remember, if your father hadn't decided to die *we* would be the ones receiving guests here. Don't let the Trelyons down."

Madalyn had heard this a thousand times. She was certain that Papa, a hazy figure who smelled of horses and cognac, hadn't died on purpose. Drink had killed him, or so she'd overheard her nanny telling the new governess, although Madalyn wasn't quite sure how this had occurred. Drowning in a vat of Malmsey, as featured in *Richard III*, had given her nightmares for a while, but now she was older she knew the reality was far less exciting.

The carriage drew to a halt. Footmen helped the Trelyon ladies alight, and a pretty maid took their hats and coats before the butler showed them through. As Madalyn crossed the great hall, her ancestors observed her disapprovingly and the chilly corridors seemed to echo their displeasure that she was reduced to a visitor's status. She felt rather glad that she didn't have to live here, though, because the vast house was an echoey labyrinth of switchbacking passageways and shadowy alcoves housing blind marble busts and sinister statues without arms. The red-eyed phoenix emblem glowered at her everywhere she turned – and at Vyvyan he seemed a very different creature from the jaunty chap up in the cupola at Oyster House. That version twinkled and danced in the light but his Vyvyan doppelganger looked as though he wanted to devour her. Even the monstrous fireplaces, guarded by giant bare-breasted and flat-headed nymphs, yawned like flaming maws. Madalyn shuddered. Her papa had grown up here. How had he borne it?

She was suddenly very thankful for the simplicity of Oyster House with its plain walls, swollen sash windows and pools of sunlight which rippled like the river over polished floorboards. The rugs might be threadbare, the wallpaper faded and the servants always complaining about the lack of gas lighting, but the house was friendly and warm. At night owls called, and in the morning plump ducks waddled onto the terrace, quacking noisily for the crusts of bread Madalyn had taken to feeding them. It was a humble spot, far removed from the splendour of Vyvyan, but as she studied her ancestral seat Madalyn didn't share her mother's regrets. She wouldn't want to live here. This huge and forbidding house hadn't brought her family any luck, and it made her feel on edge. For the first time she felt a twinge of sympathy for Gerald, who had to live in such a mausoleum.

To Madalyn's relief afternoon tea was taken on the terrace, away from the oppressive grandeur, and at an elegant table facing over the balustrade and across the manicured gardens. A team of gardeners toiled on the parterre and she recognised one of them as a friend of Ned's. The footman, a handsome but clumsy boy who almost dropped a tiered plate of cakes as he crossed the terrace, was another. Although she tried to catch their gaze and smile, both looked steadfastly through her as though embarrassed, and Madalyn felt hot with foolishness for thinking she had friends here. These boys could never be her friends: at Vyvyan, Ned's father's hope that one day rank wouldn't matter seemed little more than a dream.

She gulped and fixed her gaze beyond the ha-ha, struck

by a bolt of misery. Would Ned also ignore her if he was here, hoeing a flower bed, or would he catch her eye and give her a secret smile which spoke of shared dreams, collecting seashells and weaving never-ending stories? Madalyn felt certain Ned would be her ally no matter where he was, and her heart lifted.

Gerald was already seated at the table. Dressed in a crisply laundered sailor suit, and with his hair slicked into a dark cowlick across his forehead, he looked every inch the Lord of the Manor even if the plump woman beside him presiding over proceedings kept patting her hair and biting her lip. She had the same bulging blue eyes as Gerald, and her greying hair was as limp and fine as his. She must be Mrs Snowe. Madalyn was surprised, for although Gerald's mama was the mistress of the Vyvyan Estate she didn't look at all grand, unlike her own mama, who was resplendent in a pearl choker, a frilled afternoon gown (painstakingly made over from her Parisian trousseau) and ivory combs in her thick brown hair.

Seated opposite Mrs Snowe was an upright woman clad in an immaculate gown of frothing lilac lace; her waist was pulled in so tightly that Madalyn couldn't imagine she could eat a morsel. Dreading the day when Mama decided she would have to wear a corset, Madalyn resolved to eat as many cakes and sandwiches as possible. Madalyn was also determined to hide some of them in the little bag which swung from her wrist in order to share them with Ned later on.

"That's Lady Rivers," Constance told Madalyn *sotto voce*. "She's the wife of Colonel Rivers of Rosecraddick, and very well connected. The boy beside her is their only son, Kit. He has wonderful prospects, and will inherit a fortune."

The subtext was clear: this angel-faced boy, already rising

politely to his feet at the presence of ladies, was a suitable match, and Madalyn was *not* to mess this up. She sighed but supposed it could be worse; at least Mama wasn't intending her to marry Gerald. She'd become a nun first!

Madalyn took her seat at the table while the introductions were made and maids scurried around with hot water in silver pots. Gerald said little, but Kit Rivers was friendly and as the adults chatted he did his best to draw the younger boy out, asking whether he enjoyed sailing or riding. But Gerald was monosyllabic to the point of rudeness, and eventually Kit admitted defeat and turned to Madalyn.

"This seems like an awful lot of food for six people," he said. "I do hope you're hungry."

The table was laid beautifully with snowy white linen, ornate silverware and bone china platters heaped with delicate cucumber sandwiches, triangles of bread and butter, a huge sponge cake oozing cream, and piles of warm scones. Dishes of scarlet jam and thick clotted cream attracted the attention of hopeful wasps, which made Mrs Snowe flinch if they buzzed too close, and call for a footman to shoo them away.

"I'm ravenous," Madalyn said to Kit. Hopefully, if he thought she was greedy little girl he wouldn't question how much cake she ate, which would make taking some for Ned much easier. The clumsy footman served her with sandwiches, several of which almost landed in her lap, then two scones and a slice of cake, which made Mama frown at such unladylike gluttony. While the grown-ups were distracted by their conversation, Madalyn slipped her haul into her bag. Then she took several more sandwiches to join her stash.

"Golly," said Kit, spotting her empty plate. "I'm impressed by your appetite. My friend, Rupert, can eat five macaroons in a sitting, but I don't think even he could eat that many sandwiches."

"She's not eating them. She's stealing them," piped up Gerald. "I've been watching her slip them into her bag."

The accusation made colour flood to Madalyn's cheeks. "I'm *not* stealing! I'm saving them for Ned, since he wasn't invited!"

"Of *course* he wasn't invited," said Gerald nastily. "That wouldn't have been fitting."

Kit looked from Gerald to Madalyn with interest. "Who's this hungry chap?"

"Just a village boy," Gerald said.

"Who's our friend," Madalyn corrected sharply. Gerald was the most dreadful snob, and she bit back a cutting remark about soap makers, which would have put him in his place very swiftly. Just because he was cruel didn't justify her being unkind too. She turned away from him and smiled at Kit. "Ned's father is the schoolmaster in Trevellan. He knows everything."

"Goodness," said Kit. "I wish I did."

"Gerald and I sometimes play on the riverbank at the other side of the woods. It belongs to my family, and it's called Oyster Shore. Ned knows everything about it, and he's teaching us to swim." She took a deep breath before adding, "It seems very unfair he's not invited to tea. He's the cleverest person I know, and our best friend."

Gerald snorted. "One doesn't invite the plebs to afternoon tea. Isn't that right, Rivers?"

Kit ignored him.

"I think it's jolly unfair he can't come," Kit said to Madalyn. He selected three cucumber sandwiches and passed them to her. "Here, take these for Ned. Friends need to look out for one another, don't they?"

Madalyn beamed at Kit. The son and heir of the most important family in the area agreed with her. *That* put Gerald in his place. His sour expression could have turned the clotted cream to cheese.

"They do," she agreed. "Oh, I wish you could meet him, Kit! He tells the most wonderful stories. Ned wants to be a writer when he grows up."

Kit lit up like a November bonfire. "I do too! Well, not a writer exactly, but a poet."

"Then you *have* to meet him," said Madalyn. "It will be such fun for you to meet another writer."

"Who's a writer?" Lady Constance's cut-glass vowels cut across their conversation. She had an uncanny instinct for sniffing out anything Madalyn might attempt to keep secret. "Madalyn. Of whom do you speak?"

Madalyn glanced at Gerald in panic. He wouldn't say anything, surely? He could be spiteful at times, but he enjoyed playing with Ned as much as she did. Gerald wouldn't want to lose Ned Carew's friendship.

"Well?" Constance repeated.

Madalyn's mouth was dry. She didn't know what to say, and as she searched for inspiration Gerald leapt in.

"I'm a writer," he said, his voice ringing with confidence. "I intend to be renowned when I'm older. People all across the globe will feel that they are familiar with my worlds and that the characters who people them are their very dear friends. I want to transport my readers to new places and give their lives a sprinkling of magic."

This speech was word for word what Ned had told Gerald and Madalyn one rainy afternoon when they sheltered in the boathouse waiting for a break in the clouds. Madalyn's mouth fell open because she hadn't thought Gerald had been listening. He had a habit of interjecting his own ideas and opinions without showing any interest in what anyone else might say or think. To hear Ned's heartfelt dream borrowed and repeated with such conviction was a shock and a little sinister. Shivers rippled up her arms.

Mrs Snowe looked up, a laden scone poised halfway between plate and lips. "Do you, darling?"

"Of course," Gerald said firmly. "It's what I've always wanted, Mama. The work of Mr Dickens first inspired me, I think. His language is so detailed and vivid. I can only dream of coming a poor second, but all that I am in *here*," Gerald laid his hand on his heart and held his mother's gaze, "tells me I must try. It's not a choice, Mama, it's a calling. Like it was for Wordsworth and Coleridge, so it is for me."

These too were Ned's words, words he had stuttered out, cheeks pink with self-conscious embarrassment, when he'd explained his dream. "It sounds so pretentious," he'd said ruefully, "but it's how I feel."

Madalyn understood. "I feel like that that about becoming an artist. It's in me. I have to draw."

"How about you, Gerald? What do you want to do more than anything?" Ned had asked, seeking, as always, to draw the other boy in.

Gerald screwed up his nose. "I don't want to do *any*thing. Gentlemen don't work, and neither do their wives."

"Which is why I'm never going to be a wife," Madalyn said.

"And I'll certainly never be a gentleman," Ned laughed.

Recalling this at the tea table, while the ladies cooed over how marvellous Gerald was, Madalyn felt uneasy. The

Honourable Kit Rivers, so at ease in his own skin and gilded with every blessing life could offer a young man, had validated Ned's dream and made it so desirable that Gerald wanted it for himself. The more Gerald parroted Ned to the delight of the women, the more Madalyn realised he was starting to believe what he said and even claim the feelings as his own. It was bizarre and a little frightening, and the more the adults smiled indulgently at Gerald the worse Madalyn felt.

Kit reached below the table and retrieved a small box. "Forgive me, Mrs Snowe, but I was wondering whether we might be excused to walk in the garden and use this?"

"Is that a Brownie camera?" gasped Gerald.

Kit nodded. "It's Papa's, but he kindly said I could borrow it. I thought it might be fun to take a composition."

"How wonderful," said Mrs Snowe. "Of course you must, my dear. Oh, I do wish Arthur was at home! He was talking about investing in a company that makes these only the other day. He says there's money in photography."

Gerald shot her a dark look and Mary Snowe flushed at her *faux pas*. Fortunately Lady Rivers and Lady Constance were far too polite to show any reaction to this mention of trade, and Kit was the sort of boy who didn't seem to care a jot about such matters. Chatting easily about composition, he arranged them all around the table, adjusting cake stands and teacups to his satisfaction, before taking several shots. Everyone sat very still and did their best not to move or flap at wasps. When Kit was satisfied, he and the other children were excused from the table while the ladies moved indoors out of the sunshine.

"Marvellous! I think we have an hour or so before Mama calls out the search party." Kit slung the Brownie case onto his shoulder. "I'd really like to see the river and meet your friend Ned."

Gerald screwed up his nose. "He probably won't be there. How about I show you the fishponds?"

"He'll be there. He said he was going to write by the boathouse," Madalyn said firmly. She was proud of Ned and couldn't wait to introduce Kit to him. "If we take the path through the woods it's not far at all. Oyster Shore is Vyvyan's summerhouse, you see. It was built for bathing and picnics."

"And spooning," said Gerald, showing off. "The King took ladies there."

Kit looked shocked.

"That was ages ago," Madalyn said quickly, "when he was the Prince of Wales and my grandfather was the viscount."

Reassured, Kit followed Madalyn and Gerald through the parkland and into the woods. The path to Oyster Shore was well worn now, which Madalyn was grateful for because Tilly, their maid, was clearly growing tired of mending tears in her skirts. As they walked, Gerald explained where the old fountain was and the climbing trees and the best places for fishing as though he owned the place and was granting Kit access to his realm. This rankled, but Madalyn remained silent. Gerald's moods were volatile and she wasn't certain whether he would tell about her taking the sandwiches. It was best not to provoke him.

They found Ned sitting on the pontoon with his bare feet dangling above the water. He had a notebook balanced on his lap and was writing furiously, his forehead scrunched up and his eyes narrowed against the sunshine which bounced from the river. Hearing them approach he looked up and his expression was confused, as though he had found himself somewhere unexpected.

"I've brought you some sandwiches," Madalyn called, bunching her skirts up and running over the tussocky grass. "Like I said I would!"

Ned slid the notebook into his pocket and stood up with a smile, but when he spotted Kit he looked alarmed and Madalyn realised he was wrong-footed by the arrival of an upper-class stranger. This shiny-faced boy with his floppy blond hair, pristine cricket whites and Box Brownie slung over his shoulder wasn't from the village, and Ned probably feared he was about to be ordered off the land.

"This is Kit. He wants to be a poet," she said, proud to show off her new friend.

"Kit *Rivers*," added Gerald pointedly, "from Rosecraddick Manor."

Ned swallowed nervously, and Madalyn realised he was well aware of who Kit was. Why did Gerald have to go out of his way to make people feel uncomfortable? Kit didn't seem bothered in the slightest about being the son of the Lord of the Manor, and wore his rank as lightly as the camera which bumped against his hip. He held out his hand.

"Hullo, there! I hear you're a writer?"

Ned gathered himself, taken aback by the warm greeting. He shook Kit's hand and the two boys smiled shyly at one another.

"I'd like to be."

"You're already one," Madalyn said stoutly. She was very proud of her friend. "Ned writes wonderful stories, Kit."

"I wish my poems were wonderful," sighed Kit. "I struggle with rhyme sometimes. Love and dove. Heart and cart. It's awful. When I read my latest attempt to my friend, Emmy, she laughed until she cried. I need an advocate like you, Madalyn."

Kit was so self-effacing that Ned relaxed at once. "Maddy's very kind," he said. "I just make things up and she listens."

"I write too," Gerald butted in. "I write my own stories, Kit. Next time you come for afternoon tea at Vyvyan I'll read them to you."

That should give the little fibber time to write a few, Madalyn thought. Or maybe Gerald would ask Ned if he could borrow one of his. She couldn't imagine Gerald sitting down and writing anything, though. She'd never even heard him talk about reading a book, let alone writing one.

"That sounds super," Kit told Gerald politely.

"Have a sandwich before they curl," Madalyn said to Ned, changing the subject before Gerald could monopolise the conversation yet again. "I thought we could show Kit the riverbank. He could take a few photographs."

"We don't have long," Kit said, consulting a smart silver pocket watch. "Mama will be wanting to call the carriage at five."

"Let's eat on the hoof, then," Ned suggested. "I'll give you a tour, and there are some super spots for pictures. You could look at them later and write a poem."

"Image poems," said Kit slowly. "That's a brilliant idea, Ned. Thank you."

Sandwiches in hand, the children explored Oyster Shore and shared the food Madalyn had slipped into her bag. Away from the house her appetite mysteriously returned, and even Kit found room for one more scone. But Gerald, still sulking, muttered about stolen food and refused to join in. Ned showed Kit the boathouse once frequented by the King, the ruined fountain (which Kit was hugely excited about and insisted on photographing) and the climbing tree, which Madalyn demonstrated to Kit's applause. As they walked back to the path Ned and Kit were deep in conversation about books while Gerald trailed behind with a sulky face.

"It's not appropriate," he muttered, kicking the ground. "Kit's the heir to Rosecraddick Manor. He oughtn't to be so familiar with Carew."

He meant that Kit should be giving *him* the attention, Madalyn thought. "Do buck up, Gerry. If the wind changes you'll be left looking like that, and then who will want to marry you?" she teased.

"*You* will, because I'll be very rich," he said. "Then you can live at Vyvyan and your mama won't have to wear old dresses and worn shoes to tea. Mama noticed, you know, and so did Lady Rivers. It must be very humiliating for you both to be so reduced."

Madalyn felt a cold tide of horror sweep through her, swiftly followed by another of hot shame for Mama.

"I'd rather drown in that river than marry you, Gerald Snowe," she said.

Gerald curled his lip into a sneer. "You say that now, but you'll change your mind. You'll see."

The sun slipped behind a cloud and the water turned to steel. Sharp-edged waves spiked the estuary.

Madalyn was about to tell him she would rather be a nun than Mrs Snowe, but Kit and Ned, who'd reached Oyster House, were waving and telling her to hurry. Kit held up the camera and pointed to the terrace.

"I've got an idea for a poem about fountains and childhood! It's just come to me!" he was saying excitedly. "You all need to stand on the terrace, with Oyster House behind you."

"I don't know," Ned protested. He glanced down at his bare feet and twisted his cloth cap in his hands. "I'm not exactly dressed for a portrait."

"It doesn't matter what you look like. The whole point is that it this is a moment caught in time. Youth's fountain won't run for ever," Kit said earnestly.

Gerald was puzzled. "What fountain?"

"It's a metaphor," Ned explained.

Kit beamed. "That's exactly it, Ned! A metaphor."

Gerald crossed his arms and glared at Ned. "I knew that. I was joshing."

Madalyn's patience finally frayed. What a fraud he was! "You didn't, or you'd have said so. If you want to be a writer, Gerry, you really need to swot up on your imagery," she snapped, pinning her hat into place and smoothing down her dress.

Gerald said nothing, but as he stood beside her on the terrace Madalyn felt the anger radiating from him, and he pinched her arm while Kit was taking the photograph, knowing full well she wouldn't dare move or cry out. It wasn't an accident. He did it on purpose..

Once the picture had been taken, Madalyn rubbed her arm and allowed herself to shed a few tears now nobody was looking. There would be a big bruise, of that she was certain. A bruise would fade, but Gerald's brooding resentment would only grow. Unchecked, it would turn into something dangerous. As they turned back for Vyvyan, Ned and Kit chatting easily while Gerald glowered and kicked tufts of grass, Madalyn was unnerved by a gathering unease she couldn't name and didn't understand.

21

AUGUST 1904

Oyster Shore

Ned

The summer of 1904 was the hottest Ned could remember. The heat pressed down on Trevellan like a living entity, and the river flowed listlessly as though oppressed by the heavy air. On the Trehunnists' farm the crops ripened earlier than in living memory, and as the grass yellowed and the wheat toasted the whole world seemed gilded. All the village children were called upon to help gather the harvest in, and they peppered the fields for days trailing the horse-drawn reaper to rake up the crop and bind the sheaves.

The Carew family always took part in the harvest. It mattered little in Trevellan that Edgar was the schoolmaster rather than a farm labourer, for harvest time was when the whole village came together; even Reverend Tullis rolled up his shirt sleeves and joined in. It was Biblical, he told Ned and Bess, for hadn't our Lord told the parable of the sower? And did not Isaiah say that mortal flesh would be cut down like grass? Ned wasn't sure that he liked the sound of this, but he did like being a part of something bigger than himself and usually enjoyed being in the fields with his friends until the dusk smoked from the hedges and the pink moon rose.

But this year time spent helping with the harvest meant time away from Madalyn, and Ned found himself itching to escape. That Gerald could be on Oyster Shore with her when he could not was hard to bear, almost as hard as biting his tongue when Gerald had declared he was going to become an author. Whether this was because Gerald had been so impressed by Kit Rivers or simply because he wanted to best Ned was anyone's guess. Maybe a mixture of both, Ned had decided. He wouldn't usually mind – after all there were enough words and stories in the world for them both – but being accustomed to writing on the river bank all morning while Madalyn sketched or gathered shells, it rankled to know that Gerald was enjoying her company now, when he couldn't.

There was also something about Gerald's behaviour that made Ned uneasy. Madalyn hadn't said much, but he knew she didn't relish the other boy's company and often made excuses to return home when he joined them. She flatly refused to swim if Gerald was there, which Ned hadn't understood since Madalyn was far more accomplished than Gerald, who shrieked if a strand of weed so much as brushed his big toe. It was hard work being a teacher. His father was a saint.

"I don't want to swim with Gerald," Madalyn said.

"It's perfectly proper," Ned assured her. "You have a bathing costume."

Madalyn certainly did. Woollen and heavy, it was only suitable for paddling. Whenever she tried to swim it become waterlogged and threatened to sink her, so she'd taken to swimming in her shift, which Gerald thought quite scandalous. During their last swimming lesson he'd stared at her so openly that Madalyn became so self-conscious she sank every few strokes. Disheartened, she'd retreated to the boathouse to dry off while Gerald showed off, doggy paddling up and down with a great deal of splashing.

"Wear the costume if you feel happier," Ned said quickly, seeing she was close to tears. "Honestly, Maddy, with a bit more practice you'll be swimming like a fish. You are so good at holding your breath. How about we try again tomorrow?"

"Only if Gerald isn't here. He splashed me last time."

"He's jealous because you're better at swimming. It makes him feel he's not very good at it if a girl can catch him up." Ned was still inclined to be generous to Gerald. He felt sorry for him sometimes.

Madalyn drew her legs up against her chest and wrapped her arms tightly around them. "It's not the same when we're here without you, Ned. I try to sketch and play games as usual, but he doesn't join in. He just chews his nails and watches."

"He's just shy."

"No, Ned. He's cruel. The last time Mama and I took tea at Vyvyan, I saw Gerald kick his mother's lapdog."

Ned was shocked. Mrs Snowe had a fat pug which grunted and snuffled and was always tucked under her arm. It would be hard to imagine a more harmless creature.

"It happened the last time we saw Kit, before the Rivers

family went to London, and when Kit gave me the photograph he took of us," Madalyn said quietly. "Gerald didn't care that Kit had bought him a beautiful book to write new stories in – he wanted the photograph too. But Kit was adamant it was for you, because it accompanied a poem you'd talked about."

"*The Fountain of Youth*," Ned said. Kit had enclosed a first draft with the photograph, apologising that it was rough, although Ned had thought it quite brilliant even if a mountain in Cornwall required quite a stretch of imagination and was in truth only there to rhyme with 'fountain'. Proud to have been taken into the other boy's confidence and allowed to read his work, Ned had tucked both the poem and the photograph into his secret hiding place and left a coded note for Marrick asking him not to touch it. Lately, though, his friend seemed to be moving things and losing them. The marbles had gone missing and so had a sketch Madalyn had given him. Marrick swore blind he hadn't touched anything but there was nobody else it could be since only Marrick and he knew the hiding place existed. Ned was perplexed and Marrick was offended. They hadn't quite restored their old accord, and Ned felt bad. Maybe he was going mad?

"THAT WAS when I saw him kick poor Henry," Madalyn concluded. "Kit didn't notice, but I did."

"Maybe Gerald tripped over Henry?" Ned offered. "Little dogs do get under people's feet."

Madalyn was exasperated. "Of course he didn't trip! He deliberately kicked the poor little dog when he thought nobody was looking. I think he wanted to kick me. He doesn't like me at all."

"I don't think that's true," Ned said. "I think it's because he can't tell us what to do on Oyster Shore and that makes him angry. Gerald likes to be in charge."

Madalyn tossed her fiery curls. "He's never going to be in charge of me. *Nobody* is."

Ned believed her; Madalyn Trelyon was a law unto herself. He'd never met a girl who was so determined, so brave or and so pretty. Madalyn was prettier even than Tamsyn, the innkeeper's angel-faced daughter who was always crowned May Queen.

"I like it best when he isn't here," Madalyn admitted. "I know he's your friend, Ned, but he's hard to like."

"He's awkward, but I don't think he means any harm," Ned protested. He found Gerald hard work at times, but he understood that the other boy struggled to keep up and felt these perceived shortcomings keenly. Still, Madalyn was right; Gerald wasn't easy to like, and when he was detained at Vyvyan Ned and Madalyn were able to sit quietly, sketching and writing and blissfully happy in one other's company. Gerald was an uneasy third, always agitated and desperate to compete. They usually ended up playing a game where he set the rules and they did their best to follow them. More often than not, though, Madalyn would soon go home and Ned would plead it was his suppertime.

Today, as Ned gathered corn into stooks, his attention drifted from his task. Even being allowed to have a go at steering the brand-new reaping machine didn't compensate for time lost when he could have been weaving new stories for Madalyn to illustrate. Her darting pencil brought to life places and people that until that moment existed only in his own imagination. He had never written as much or so easily, and the pair were determined to work together one day. They would visit Egypt, Madalyn told him, where Ned would write stories about Pharaohs and lost treasure while she would paint the pyramids and the bulrush-hemmed banks of the Nile. This dream was far more appealing, and he could hardly wait to write the next instalment of his new story. Being with Madalyn at Oyster Shore was better even than sliding down haystacks or wrestling with the village boys, and as soon as the day's work was over he had taken to slipping away to the river on the pretext of a swim. If the other boys wondered why he didn't join them in the harbour, they never mentioned it.

Toiling in the fields was hot work and when Edgar decided it was time for the Carew family to go home for the day, Ned could hardly wait to dive into the river. Bess tried to persuade him to swim in the cove with Marrick and Sammy, but Ned craved the stillness of Oyster Shore. He ran all the way through the woods and didn't even stop to remove his shirt and trousers before kicking off his shoes and plunging into the river. The cold water made him gasp, but it was heaven to slice through it. Ned drifted on his back for a while until he spotted two figures on the riverbank and struck out for shore.

The tide had turned while he was swimming, and Madalyn and Gerald were wandering along the bank, legs pale beneath tucked-up skirts and rolled-up trouser legs. One red head and one dark head were close together and in harmony for once. Joining them, Ned saw they were examining a discovery. Sometimes the mud and shingle spat out treasures, things once loved and lost long ago, and Ned always thought there were stories beneath the shore waiting to be revealed.

"What have you found?" he asked.

"You're dripping on me," said Gerald, stepping away. His fist was clenched around something and his fingers were dark with silt.

"Show him!" Madalyn said. "I found it, anyway."

Gerald glowered at her. "You didn't. *I* saw it first."

"What is it?" Ned said, sensing a fight was about to erupt.

"A necklace. I think it's Roman." Madalyn was breathless. "I wanted to draw it, but Gerald says he's taking it."

"It belongs in a museum," Gerald said piously.

"Show him!" Madalyn said again, and Gerald opened up his hand, one finger at a time, to reveal a round brown lump on a piece of green chain.

"*De puella perdidit monili,*" Ned breathed. It was indeed a necklace, very old, no doubt about that, and the haughty profile etched onto the amber bore the imperial arrogance of a Caesar. Who had lost it? he wondered. A girl paddling in the river back in the times when villas and mosaics were commonplace and slaves worked the land he had toiled on earlier? Tunic tucked into her waistband as she played, perhaps she didn't notice it slip until later, when she raised her hand to her throat and encountered the absence of the chain. Or had a slave snatched it in a desperate bid from freedom, his breath coming in harsh gasps as he tore through trees, baying dogs hard on his heels, the river his only hope of evading capture and a cruel death? Did the necklace tumble from his shaking hands as he stumbled over boulders and slipped in the mud? No matter what the truth of its origins, this necklace had been part of Oyster Shore for a thousand years. What would it say if it could speak? Ned itched to pick up his pen.

"I shall ask Papa to take it to the British Museum," Gerald said importantly, closing his fingers again. "He's a great benefactor, and they'll be obliged to look at it."

Madalyn looked disappointed. Ned knew she had been hoping to keep the necklace, and would have sketched it until her candle burned down and her eyes were sore.

"Good idea," he said briskly to Gerald. "Maybe they'll have a dig. Wouldn't that be exciting, Maddy? Perhaps they would let you help, since it was found on your land. They'll probably call what they find here the Trelyon Trove."

That was one in the eye for Gerald. Ned started to count: one ... two ...

"Probably isn't Roman anyway. Have it if you *really* want," Gerald sniffed, passing the necklace to Madalyn.

"Thank you," she said, surprised. "That's kind."

Gerald turned crimson and for once didn't say a word.

"I wonder what else is hidden in the riverbed?" Madalyn said to Ned as she tucked the necklace into her pocket.

"You find all sorts here," he replied. "Whenever we go mudlarking we always come home with something. Once I found an inkpot and Marrick came across a clay pipe. It makes you think, all the people who've lived here and dropped things over the years. It makes you feel pretty tiny. If we drop something in people will wonder about us one day."

"Let's do that!" Madalyn clapped her hands. "Let's all throw something in for the people who come here in the future to find!"

"Such as?" Gerald asked.

"Something they can look at and study in the years to come. Something that'll give a clue about us and who we were." She reached up into the thick masses of curls which were secured on the crown of her head by a pair of phoenix combs. "I'm going to throw one of these in because it's the Trelyon phoenix. That way somebody might find out about me."

"Isn't that valuable?" said Ned, worried.

Madalyn shrugged and pulled the combs out. Red curls spilled down her back like lava. "Probably, but they're heavy and really ugly. They were my grandmother's. I'll tell Mama it fell out if she notices – not that she will; she's always in bed these days. It's her nerves, you see, because she's a woman."

Ned didn't know what Madalyn meant. *His* mother wasn't nervous in the slightest, and neither was Bess – but it was a fact that Lady Trelyon was always in her bedroom. When the children sat on the terrace to drink lemonade they could see that her curtains were always drawn, and Tilly, the Trelyons' maid, said they had to be very quiet. Ned thought women were very mysterious. Bess and Polly were always giggling about something. Thank goodness Madalyn was as open and as easy to read as the sky.

"I'll throw this in. It's very expensive." Not to be outdone, Gerald tugged a crested signet ring from his middle finger. "What about you, Carew?"

Ned dug his hand into his pocket. His fingers closed around a large marble he'd won from Marrick.

"This is all I have."

"That's a beauty," Madalyn said admiringly. She liked to put marbles in jars of water and sketch them, unworldly and looming large as alien planets. "Now, as we throw the items in, we each need to make a wish. Take care what you wish for! It'll come true."

Ned didn't need asking twice. As he hurled the marble

into the middle of the river he wished with all his heart he could write a book that would capture readers' hearts and which people would still be talking about a hundred years after he was dead. As Madalyn threw her comb, the ruby eye glinting balefully before the phoenix sank into the watery underworld, he knew she was wishing to be a great artist – but as for Gerald, whose face was screwed up tightly as he tossed away the ring, Ned had no idea what the secretive boy was wishing for.

"There," said Madalyn, satisfied. "Our wishes are made, and the river will be sure to grant them."

Gerald was unconvinced. "Really?"

Madalyn thought about this. "It will if your wish is pure. If not, it will rebound on you a thousand times and become a curse. The curse of Oyster Shore."

Gerald snorted. "What utter *rot*!"

"Is it?" Madalyn said. "We'll see, won't we? Our futures will reveal the truth. One day somebody will find those things and bring us back to life by working out who they belonged to. We'll be immortal." She held her second comb out to Ned. "This needs to be kept safe now it's alone. Will you take care of it? Have it as a talisman?"

"I can keep in my father's safe. That's a much better place," Gerald offered quickly, almost snatching it away. "It's very secure, and he takes it everywhere he goes. Even when he travels to America by ocean liner."

Madalyn shook her head. Wild curls fell over her shoulders. She looked, Ned thought, like a Celtic warrior princess.

"Best it stays in Cornwall where it belongs, not far from its twin. One day they'll be together again because they belong together. What's meant to be together can never be separated. Here, Ned. Take it. It'll bring you luck. I know it will."

Her green eyes met his, and Ned knew she was talking about herself and making a promise that only he understood. One day a wealthy man would come along who could lock Madalyn Trelyon away in a safe marriage, a man who could keep her in luxury and far away from water and tides and shifting sand, but Madalyn didn't want this. She was telling Ned she would always choose the freedom of the riverbank and the endless sky over anything else, because she belonged here with him, just as he belonged beside her. Even though they were only children she understood she was his destiny and he was hers. There would only ever be Madalyn Trelyon for Ned Carew.

As he slid the comb into his pocket, the teeth biting into his fingers, Ned knew they had made a pledge as solemn and as binding as any that could be made in a church. He would cherish that comb and keep it safe for ever, just as he would cherish and protect Madalyn Trelyon. Even though he was a child Ned understood that he would do this for the rest of his life, no matter how long or how short that time might be, because Madalyn was his muse, now and for ever more, and there was nothing Ned Carew wouldn't do for her. Absolutely nothing at all. All he had and was and would ever be was hers.

He loved her with his soul.

22

AUGUST 1904

Vyvyan Court

Gerald

Gerald had scarcely slept a wink. As he lay in bed, hearing Nanny Adam's snores rumbling from her room, he relived the events of the previous day. Vivid images of combs, necklaces and bright blue sky captured in shining water whirled before his vision like a kaleidoscope, and when dawn's grey fingers poked beneath the heavy curtains he was prickly with exhaustion and resentment.

Why had Madalyn given her comb to Ned and not to *him*? The question was like a splinter trapped in Gerald's mind, and like a splinter it festered and irritated him because there was only one answer: she preferred Ned. Of course she did. Ned was strong and confident. He climbed trees easily and darted through the river like an otter. He could sail and fish and name the stars. Ned's hair was thick, bleached white from sunshine and salt water, and he was as brown as a nut after hours of working in the fields. Gerald didn't envy *that* – everyone knew gentlemen didn't work the land – but he was bitterly jealous of Ned's popularity with Marrick and the other boys. They were only common village children, Gerald reminded himself. He would have been degraded by any association with them. Even so, the fact they never attempted to offer him friendship smarted. He would have liked to have had the choice of snubbing them.

As he tossed and turned in the lumpy nursery bed, Gerald brooded on how Ned and Marrick kept secrets and deliberately chose to exclude him from their silly codes and secret hiding place in the boathouse. Ned might be clever, reading all those dull books Gerald had lent him from the library, but he wasn't nearly as bright as he thought he was, otherwise he would have realised weeks ago that Gerald had followed him and discovered the hiding place. If Ned was really clever he'd know that none of his stories and secret writings were really his at all, because Gerald could take them all any time he chose. So far Gerald had been careful, only taking one thing at a time, and it was fun to think that Ned must be puzzled, or blaming Marrick. Gerald felt like a god, toying with the mortals for his own amusement. The sense of power was addictive.

It also gave Gerald a great deal of satisfaction to know he had one over on Ned. The stolen marbles were hidden under his bed along with some sea glass that Madalyn had given Ned in a black velvet bag. Pathetic treasures really, Gerald had thought scornfully as he'd plucked them from the void, but these items were impregnated with huge value because they had been gifts – gifts that hadn't been given to him. Well, they were Gerald's now, and for as long as he wanted to keep them, so there! Maybe, he thought as he kicked back the covers and padded to the window to stare out over the garden, he'd take the stupid comb too. It was right that he did really, for it was valuable and Madalyn should have offered it to him rather than a village boy. She was a Trelyon of Vyvyan Court, and Gerald was the wealthiest boy in the county, so that was the proper order of things. Didn't Madalyn understand as much? Or was this a subtle insult?

Gerald returned to bed, where he spent a restless hour planning how he could make Madalyn sorry for not favouring him. He could pull her plaits or duck her under the water when Ned wasn't watching, he supposed, or perhaps he could make certain that her mother would discover just how unladylike Madalyn was. Climbing trees and splashing about in her undergarments was hardly suitable behaviour for the daughter of a viscount. He could pen an anonymous letter filled with concern for the Trelyons' good name. Gerald liked this idea very much. He could easily have it delivered to Oyster House. The clumsy footman could take it once night fell, for if he dared refuse Gerald could threaten to break a vase and blame him. The mere thought of Madalyn's mother reading the shameful contents over breakfast, her haughty face paling as she discovered the extent of her daughter's inappropriate behaviour, was so delicious that Gerald had been tempted to a start straight away. This letter would ensure that Ned was also in trouble for encouraging Madalyn, which would mean the end of him roaming on Oyster Shore as though he owned the place. Then Madalyn would only have Gerald to play with.

Only the fear that he would be implicated in Madalyn's wrongdoings stopped Gerald from writing his letter. If his mama discovered he was climbing trees and swimming, however badly, she would have hysterics, and that would be the end of his hard-won freedom. Gerald only managed to spend so much time on Oyster Shore because Nanny believed the fresh air was doing him good since his appetite was so improved. Gerald knew she enjoyed having her afternoons free for gossiping in the kitchen and drinking nips of sherry, and he was loath to return to hours spent cooped up in the nursery or being forced to play croquet with his mother.

No. That wouldn't do at all.

Anyway, Gerald concluded as he screwed his eyes up and tried to sleep, he didn't want Madalyn to hate him. He wanted her to look at him the way she looked at Ned. He wanted to be the one who she gave shells and sea glass and combs to, the one she climbed trees and rowed boats with, and the one whose stories she listened to and illustrated in her sketchbook. But if Madalyn thought Gerald had got her into trouble with her mama, she wouldn't do any of these things. If Madalyn Trelyon was to be his best friend Gerald had to be cleverer than this. Telling tales wouldn't work. He'd have to do something that would impress her. Something which made him as good, if not better, than Ned Carew.

When they had tossed their treasures into the river and made wishes Gerald knew exactly what the others were wishing for. Ned would be wishing to be a famous writer and Madalyn that she would become a famous artist. They were so transparent, so trusting with their simple dreams, that Gerald envied them. He was glad that nobody could tell what he had been wishing for, because how feeble was it to wish you could be like somebody else?

When Gerald Snowe had thrown his signet ring into the

river he'd wished with all his heart that he could be just like Ned Carew. Although Ned was only a village boy, he was everything Gerald secretly longed to be. Ned was strong and brave but also kind and gentle, not in a way which made him a sissy but one which made everybody want to be with him and to be admired by him. Had Ned been at prep school he would have been the rugby captain and head boy, as well as excelling in lessons and having scores of friends. Nobody would ever pick Ned last for a sports team or refuse to sit with him during prep. Nobody would call him names. Even Kit Rivers thought Ned, a boy so far below him, was marvellous. It was sickening.

Ned's parents adored him and they adored one another. Gerald had observed the Carew family together at church and noticed how Ned's father had ruffled his son's hair fondly while his mother had rested her hand on his shoulder as they shared a prayer book. What must it be like to have Matilda Carew as a mother? She was beautiful with her hourglass waist, thick dark curls and mesmerising violet eyes, and Gerald had noticed how the gaze of many men in the congregation, from his own father to Reverend Tullis, strayed to her as though enchanted. Matilda didn't seem to register their attention at all, though, but sang and repeated the liturgy piously, although she and her husband often caught one another's eye and smiled as though sharing a wonderful secret. Gerald had studied his own parents at length and soon concluded that bar *pass the salt* or *the weather is set fair* they barely spoke. They certainly never smiled at one another, and he seldom saw them together. Ned was always talking happily about his family, and it was clear from the way the villagers flocked to speak to the Carews after church that they were exceedingly well regarded. But although people raised their hats and nodded respectfully to the Snowes, nobody wanted to talk to them. Nobody liked his family much at all.

Was Gerald jealous of Ned's family? A schoolmaster for a father and a wild gypsy-looking woman for a mother? Did he long to play with a sister? Eat at a rough table in a tiny schoolhouse? Gerald searched his heart and realised that despite all those things he was indeed bitterly jealous. His own parents were far too busy and important to spend time with him, and Nanny didn't love him; she was merely doing the job she was employed to do, and when she came at him with the cod liver oil Gerald suspected she actually rather disliked him and in fact children in general. Even Reverend Tullis had passed the burden of tutoring him to the new curate, who obviously bore the task with Christian fortitude. Ned's stories of reading with his father and discussing literature over supper were like tales of a foreign land – one that Gerald had never visited, but for which he was instinctively and most dreadfully homesick.

It wasn't just his parents who shunned him. Even Henry the pug avoided Gerald now. The cowering dog was a constant snuffling reminder that Kit Rivers, too, preferred Ned to Gerald, for it was Ned that Kit had talked to about poetry, Ned that Kit had insisted should keep the photograph, and most galling of all, Ned's stories that Kit admired, even though he believed they were Gerald's ...

This deception had started by accident. Gerald had taken one of Ned's stories from the hiding place, intending just to read it. It was a detailed piece about a boy who became lost in the mist and wandered into a strange land where a russet-haired princess needed to be rescued from her own fears and led safely through a maze filled with dangers. Gerald read it in one sitting, utterly transported to the vivid landscape Ned had created. His breath caught when the hero seemed certain to fail, and his heart soared when all was well. The writing was beautiful and sad, and Gerald had wished it was his own work so much that a knot twisted in his stomach. Without pausing to think about what he was doing, he crept into the library and copied the story out in the notebook Kit Rivers had given him, signing his own name beneath it with a flourish. When Kit and Lady Rivers next visited on a rainy day, Gerald read Kit this story as a distraction. What did it matter who the author was? Kit would never know the truth. Nobody would.

Kit shook his head with wonder when the story concluded.

"You have a rare talent, Gerald. That was beautiful! I could picture everything. Lord, I feel rather embarrassed about my own work now."

It was wonderful to bask in Kit's admiration, even if the praise was borrowed, and Gerald brimmed with happiness. He'd borrowed several stories since then, and painstakingly transcribed each one before returning the originals to the satchel beneath the boathouse floor. Was Ned confused when items vanished and reappeared? Did he even notice? If he did, Gerald hoped Ned would blame Marrick. Then the two would fall out and maybe Ned would stop visiting Oyster Shore as much. And then Madalyn would have no choice but to spend more time with him.

Gerald didn't like it that Madalyn preferred Ned to him. Her family might be *impoverished*, as his mother often said, wrinkling her nose as though the mere word smelled bad, but Madalyn was from the oldest and most respected family in the area and was the daughter of a viscount (even one who had come to *a bad end*), and was a good prospect. Gerald could do a lot worse for himself than marry such a girl one day. Gerald had filed this information away although he thought girls rather silly. Bess and her friends were always whispering, and he was sure they were laughing at him. They'd soon stopped sniggering when he knocked the lame one over. That had shown them. If Madalyn did what she was told and behaved like a lady, then maybe he would marry her and save the last of the Trelyons from poverty. Gerald liked to imagine how grateful Madalyn would be. At least she couldn't marry a village boy like Ned – the one thing Gerald had over him.

The sun poured through the gaps in his curtains, promising another fine day, and Gerald decided it was time he won Madalyn over. It was a Thursday, which meant the curate wouldn't be calling, and Gerald would be free once he'd made a pretence of swotting in the library. Ned was needed in the fields for harvesting, leaving Madalyn alone, sketching. If Gerald asked Cook nicely she might make him up a picnic. He could share it with Madalyn, and maybe she would give him some sea glass or a hair slide.

It was a good plan. Perking up, Gerald soon forgot about his restless night and bad temper. He polished off two bowls of porridge and some kippers, and even the Latin translation the curate had set wasn't too onerous. Today felt like the sort of day when nothing could go amiss. The weather was glorious. Cook had made the picnic and he set off for Oyster Shore with the laden basket on his arm. Gerald was full of optimism.

Madalyn was sitting on the pontoon, skirts tucked up to her knees as she dangled her bare feet in the river. It was an exceptionally high tide, a spring tide Ned called it even though it was high summer, and the river looked fit to spill over onto the grassy bank. She wasn't wearing a hat, and her long red hair lifted in the warm breeze.

"Madalyn!" Gerald called, waving. "Hello!"

Madalyn started and a fleeting expression darted across her face when she saw him. It looked a little like disappointment, and Gerald was hurt. Couldn't she see how much effort he'd gone to?

"I've brought a picnic." He set the wicker basket down and sat beside her, taking care that his boots didn't dip into the brackish water. Salt water ruined leather; everyone knew that.

"A picnic?"

"That's right. I've got a game pie, hardboiled eggs and half a fruitcake. There's some lemonade too. I thought we could go to the old fountain and eat it there, where it's cool." He fanned his face, hot in his tweed jacket and thick stockings and already longing for shade. "What do you think?"

But Madalyn shook her head. "I'm waiting for Ned. He said he'd take me out in the boat this afternoon and show me where the otters are. I'm going to sketch them."

Ned. Always Ned. White-hot fury flared in Gerald, but he swallowed his anger. "Ned has to work in the fields, I'm afraid."

Her face fell. "Oh no. I was so hoping to sketch the otters. Are you sure he isn't coming? Why else would the boat be ready?"

"So I can take you."

She stared at him. "But you can't row."

"That's what you think. I've been learning. In secret."

Sometimes when he tumbled into a lie Gerald found himself almost believing it, and as he looked down at the boat, bobbing gently on the turning tide, it seemed to him that maybe he could row after all. How hard could it be? He'd watched Ned do it enough times, and lots of the boys at St Hugh's rowed. Surely it was just a matter of timing?

"Really?" Madalyn said doubtfully.

"Really. We can take the picnic with us and eat it on the way."

"And you know where the otters are?"

"Of course."

How hard could it be to find the otters? If he couldn't spot them Gerald supposed he could always say they must be elsewhere. Otters were a law unto themselves, surely?

He jumped to his feet and the pontoon swayed, which made him feel a little queasy. Bracing his legs as he'd seen Ned do, Gerald held out his hand. "Coming?"

Madalyn glanced over her shoulder as though Ned might appear from the woods. "This isn't a joke? You really will take me to see the otters?"

"Why would I joke?"

"Sometimes you do. And you say cruel things. Ned never does."

Ned again, thought Gerald. The other boy was practically a saint. "I don't mean to," was all he said. "Sometimes I just get angry."

"Like when you kicked Henry?"

"That was an accident. I tripped. You know what he's like. Come on,puff Madalyn. Don't you want to see the otters?"

He saw she was torn between wanting to see otters and staying on the riverbank in the hope of seeing Ned.

"What if Ned gets away and we've gone without him?"

"He isn't coming," Gerald repeated as he untied the boat. "Stay here if you'd rather not see the otters. It's up to you."

"I want to see them, but only if you really can row. Neither of us can swim properly yet."

"I can row," said Gerald, with great confidence. "It's far easier than you think."

He jumped down into the boat then helped Madalyn in. Once she was seated and her hat pinned back in place, he cast off from the pontoon and pulled in the painter just as he'd seen Ned do. Perching on the narrow seat opposite he picked up the oars and pulled on them gently. For once luck was on his side and the oars slipped through the water as easily as a hot knife through butter, dipping in an out with a gentle splash. The boat, carried more by the outgoing tide than Gerald's prowess as an oarsman, drifted gently down-river and Madalyn trailed her hand in the cool water. A flotilla of ducks passed them, paddling hard in the opposite direction and overtaken by two swans gliding past with ease. As Gerald rowed he felt that for once everything was going in his favour. The golden day, the flowing water, the sunbursts of gorse on the headland, the heat haze scarfing the land – it was all magical, and he was the beneficiary of every imaginable blessing. The rowing boat moved on his command, the river flowed exactly as he willed it. Even Madalyn was smiling at him.

"So where are the otters?" she asked eventually.

"Just around the bluff," Gerald said. One oar slipped in the rowlock and he struggled to regain it. Sweat greased his palms and he was sure he felt the beginnings of a blister.

A frown creased Madalyn's brow. "Past Oyster House? Are you sure? I thought they were upstream?"

Gerald grasped the oar tightly. It was heavy and slithered through his sweat-slicked fingers. "No. They're definitely this way."

Oyster House loomed over his shoulder. A frill of sand appeared at the edge of the riverbank, and the wooded bluff which shielded the secret shore from Penhayes was approaching fast.

Madalyn sat up, no longer languid and smiling. "Gerald, they're not downriver. They live where the riverbank's overgrown and there are pools of deeper water. This part widens out to where it joins the sea, and Ned says there are strong currents. We should turn back."

There was a note of fear in her voice. Gerald, feeling the oars pulled deeper and of the water's volition, felt it chime in his own breast. He pushed his misgivings aside. He *would* take Madalyn for a picnic. "It's fine. We'll be there soon. I know the perfect place to moor."

"Turn round, Gerry!" Madalyn ordered, and her voice rang with centuries of Trelyon authority. "I want to go back right now!"

But Gerald didn't know how to turn the boat. What did Ned do? Left oar? Right oar? Both, but in different directions? The tug on the oars grew stronger and his fingers started to throb.

"Stop making such a fuss. We're almost there," he panted.

"I said, turn around!"

"Or what? You'll row instead? Or will you jump overboard and swim to the shore?"

"You know I can't swim properly!" Madalyn's face was so white her freckles stood out like a rash. "Oh! Why are you always like this?"

"Like what?"

"Like you know best all the time. Like you're so much better than anyone else! Well, you're not, and you can't row either. Don't even try to pretend you can. You'll drown us both if you don't turn around now."

Her voice was shrill with fear. The emotion was contagious, and Gerald, frantically tugging on the oars, feared he would drown in it long before the sea claimed him. What if they drifted right out to France? Or these sharp waves spiking the water now that they were leaving the shelter of the meander capsized the boat? Madalyn was right; they'd drown! His mouth parched with terror.

"I want to go back! Please, Gerry!" Madalyn said.

The boat was parallel with Oyster House and only minutes away from rounding the bluff and entering open water. The river sucked at the oars and Gerald's arms hurt with the effort of keeping hold of them. There was no way he could attempt another stroke without losing them. Gerald tugged on the left oar to sweep the boat around in a circle as he'd watched Ned do but his poor skills were no match for the tide. The oars rattled in the rowlocks, and he almost lost one over the side as the boat pitched.

"Careful!" Madalyn cried, gripping the side of the boat for dear life. "If you drop the oars we'll drift out to sea."

Gerald doubled his efforts, but his shaking arms were no match for the merciless tide, and the small rowing boat continued to drift downriver.

"Help me row," he gasped. "Take an oar, quickly! Before I drop them both."

Madalyn stood up, but in her haste she forgot about the balance of the boat and the vessel lurched sideways, spilling her over the side and into the deep water. Her skirts spread out around her in a white circle and Gerald realised that the fabric was filling with water. Soon it would become so heavy it would drag her beneath and straight to the bottom of the sea. Madalyn's head vanished for a few dreadful seconds before she surfaced, spluttering and gasping. Her limbs thrashed frantically as she made her very best attempt to swim, but the waterlogged fabric dragged her beneath the surface once more. This time she did not emerge, and Gerald felt the blood drain from his body. Madalyn Trelyon was going to drown! He would be in such trouble! What would they do to him?

"Gerald! Throw her the painter! Now!"

The voice came from the shore, where a figure was running along the riverbank, the sun lighting his blond hair like a halo. Ned was waving and shouting, but Gerald, frozen with terror, hardly registered a word he was saying.

"Help!" Madalyn had surfaced, spluttering and her arms flailing. "Help!"

"The rope, Gerald! Throw her the rope!" Ned yelled. "If she goes under again, she won't come back up!"

Shocked into action, Gerald abandoned the oars and staggered forward to toss the bow rope in Madalyn's direction. For once his aim was true and she clutched it tightly, gasping and coughing.

"Pull in the oars so you don't hit her!" Ned was yelling. "Don't lose them! You're still drifting!"

"Hold on," Gerald said to Madalyn, heaving the oars over the side. "Let me pull you in."

He leaned over to haul on the rope, but the boat rocked and almost spat him out. Gerald clutched the side with a whimper and started to cry. This was all Madalyn's fault for making such a fuss about the otters. Why couldn't she have been content with a simple picnic on the shore?

"Hold on, Maddy! I'm coming."

There was a splash as Ned leapt into the river. Gerald

gulped back his tears. There was little more he could do other than wait to be rescued, for he didn't have the strength to haul her into the boat. What if Ned only rescued Madalyn and left him behind? Would he float away to France all alone? Die of cold and thirst? And would anyone really care?

Ned's strong crawl sliced through the water and made light work of the current. Even in his miserable and frightened state Gerald felt a twinge of envy at the other boy's skill. When Ned reached the boat, scarcely out of breath, Gerald looked away, ashamed of his panic and filled with bitterness at his lot in life.

"It's all right, Maddy," he heard Ned say. "I'm here now. Put your arms around my neck and hold on tight. I'm going to pull us into the boat. You can let go of the rope. I've got you. Trust me. I won't let anything happen to you."

Madalyn was too out of breath to reply but she loosened her grasp on the rope and wound her arms around Ned's neck, clinging to him like a baby monkey while Ned trod water furiously and held onto the boat with one hand.

"I'm going to pull us both in," he said. "Gerry, grab me!"

Gerald stared at him in horror. "The boat will tip over."

"It won't if you're quick," Ned said. "Our weight will topple it back. Ready?"

Gerald didn't feel ready at all. He wanted to pretend he couldn't hear. Madalyn and Ned could hold on until somebody rescued them. Someone must be boating in the estuary today, for Penhayes always teemed with pleasure craft.

"Gerald! Now!" Ned ordered. "Hurry!"

Ned clawed at the side of the boat as he heaved himself and Madalyn upwards. Gerald staggered forward to grab Ned's shirt. The boat lurched, his boots slithered on the wet deck and he heard himself cry out in terror but he didn't let go. He pulled with all his might before toppling backwards when Ned and Madalyn followed. All three children lay on the deck, gasping like landed fish.

"Why are you in the boat?" Ned asked Madalyn once he'd recovered his breath. "Why didn't you wait for me?"

Madalyn was too exhausted to speak, but she glared at Gerald and he knew that as soon as she caught her breath she would tell Ned exactly what had happened. Would Madalyn tell her mama? Gerald felt sick at the mere thought.

"Sit at the front," Ned ordered Gerald. He obeyed, watching miserably as the other boy took the oars and swung the boat around deftly. Although the outgoing tide was strong, and Ned must have been exhausted from his swim and the effort of clambering into the boat, he managed to wrestle the oars against the current, and the shore soon grew closer. The shingle beach glittered in the sunlight, a far wider band than when Gerald and Madalyn had set sail, but there was still enough water for the boat to reach the pontoon. None of the children spoke on the way back to Oyster Shore, but as soon as Ned had tied the painter into a bowline and helped Madalyn onto the pontoon he turned to Gerald.

His usually sunny face was dark with fury. "Why did you take the boat out? You can't row, and you know Madalyn can't swim properly! You could have both drowned!"

Gerald shrank from Ned's anger but his instinct was to defend himself rather than to apologise. "Don't shout at me, Carew! Remember who I am."

"I remember all right! You're a bloody *idiot*!" Ned roared. "What were you thinking? Neither of you can row or swim."

"Madalyn insisted on seeing the otters!" Gerald spat, clawing for a scapegoat. "And I *can* row."

"Quite clearly *not*!" Madalyn hissed. She was shaking

with cold, but her eyes were a furnace of scorn. "It's another of your lies. Like the otters! I told you Ned was going to show me where they were, but you said you knew. You said he wasn't coming today and you'd take me."

"I *don't* lie," Gerald cried, his cheeks flaming.

"You *do*!" Madalyn shook her head and her curls bobbed furiously. She looked like a sodden Medusa and Gerald flinched. Her voice was so cold he got goosepimples and he couldn't look at her; he would surely turn to stone.

"You're a liar, Gerald Snowe!" she said. "A nasty little liar who kicks dogs and sneaks about. No wonder nobody likes you."

"Maddy, don't," Ned said softly, and Gerald wasn't sure what was worse – the pity in Ned's eyes or the scorn in Madalyn's. "I'm sure Gerald never meant this to happen. He underestimated the strength of the tide, that's all. This stretch of Oyster Shore can be really dangerous on a spring tide."

Madalyn looked from Ned to Gerald in sheer disbelief. "Why do you always make excuses for him? He's nothing but a horrible little liar, and I've had enough of his tall stories. He says he can row. He can swim. He can write. He can climb trees. Bt the truth is he makes everything up because he can't do *any* of it. He's pathetic!"

Gerald felt a wave of rage building inside him, an anger that was bigger and darker than anything he'd ever felt before. How dare Madalyn Trelyon laugh at him? A girl with no money, and a father who'd died in shame and scandal? And how dare Ned Carew, the lowly son of a schoolteacher, pity him? He'd show them both. Nobody doubted Gerald Snowe's word.

Nobody.

He leapt to his feet. "I'll show you. You just watch!"

Fuelled by the energy of wrath, Gerald leapt to his feet and tore along the riverbank towards the woods. His feet were nimble for once, leaping snaggled roots and barely touching the hardened earth. The path twisted and turned before growing steeper as it rose towards the clearing where the old fountain slumbered in the half-light and the big horse-chestnut tree reached upwards to the sky. *Come and climb me*, it seemed to say. *Show the others you can do anything they can.*

Gerald craned his neck and gazed upwards, sickened by the mere thought of height. His palms tingled and his pulse raced at the sight of the ancient tree soaring into an eternity of sky and greenery. How would it feel to reach the top? How would it feel know you were as high as it was possible for a boy to be? As he studied the gnarled trunk it seemed to Gerald that each branch was calling to him and every bough beckoning him to make the ascent. He could do it, for how many times had he watched Ned and Marrick scale this very tree with an easy confidence he longed to feel? Even Madalyn had conquered it, and she was only a girl. Then again, how many times had he scraped his hands and knees attempting to make it to just the lowest branches while the world whirled and his stomach churned? How many times had he given up while the others played?

You're a liar. No wonder nobody likes you.

Madalyn's accusation rang in his ears. It was impossible to block out, because deep down Gerald knew it to be true; he did lie. He lied about being happy at school, about not being afraid of the dark, and of not caring whether people liked him or not. He lied about not minding when his father was looked down upon by the Rivers and the Trelyons. He lied about not being able to understand his prep. He lied about being able to write stories which drew people in and made them marvel. He'd lied today about being able to row and where Ned was. But most of all Gerald lied to himself because he wanted people to like him – however much he pretended not to care or told himself he was superior.

Well, he would never again care what other people thought. He'd show them all, when he was richer and more successful than any of them. And most of all he'd show Madalyn and Ned. They'd be sorry they'd ever doubted him.

He reached up and grasped the first branch.

"Gerald! Wait!"

The sound of footfalls galvanised him, and he heaved himself into the tree. Anger lent his climbing a new edge, and he soon found himself on the second bough. Rage drove him higher, gifting him with a bravery and a recklessness he had never known before. Gerald climbed with a grim determination, his limbs fuelled by the need to prove the other two wrong. He would get to the top of this beastly tree, and then Madalyn and Ned wouldn't be able to call him a liar. They'd know Gerald Snowe could do everything he claimed, and they would have to apologise.

"Gerald! Come down!" Ned's voice was shrill.

Ned was obviously scared Gerald was going to beat him. Ned wouldn't look quite so marvellous now, and neither would Madalyn, because it was just a silly old tree. Whatever had they all made such a fuss about? Gerald stretched for the next branch and hauled himself upwards. Although his stomach lurched when the bough trembled, he continued to climb. He wouldn't stop for anyone. Not now.

"You're cold and tired," Ned shouted up, as he began to climb. "Come down now! Let's do this another day."

Gerald ignored him. He was shaking, but from exhilaration rather than cold. He could do this! He could really do this!

"I *told* you I could climb," he called down jubilantly, while his fingers clawed for the next hold. His feet slithered before they recovered their purchase against the stout trunk. But he was undeterred: "Look how high I am! *Now* call me a liar, Madalyn Trelyon! I dare you!"

"I didn't mean it! I was angry and frightened," Madalyn cried. "Oh! Please do come down, Gerry. You're really high."

"I know!" Gerald called back.

Madalyn's voice was high with fear. "Please come down. I'm sorry I teased you!"

"I'm going to the top!" Nothing would stop him now. Elation, not fear, made Gerald giddy, for he was the king of the woods. Of Oyster Shore. Of the whole wide world! "Watch me!"

"We know you can do it," Ned shouted. "Come back down and warm up. We can have that picnic if you like."

Gerald, halfway to the top of the tree, was not interested in picnics, but he would look down and enjoy his achievement; it'd be amusing to see their stupid surprised faces. He dipped his head and then the world turned inside out. His mouth tasted metallic and filled with saliva, for Madalyn was at least sixty feet below and far smaller than he could have imagined. She was so far below him that her face was no more than a flesh-hued smudge as she stood there looking like one of the paper dolls Nanny used to make for him to colour in. But just as he was revelling in his achievement the view suddenly cartwheeled and Gerald's stomach was plummeting to earth. His legs, so deft only seconds earlier, turned to rubber, his hands buzzed with pins and needles and his face was numb. Oh Lord!

He was so high. So high it made him feel quite dizzy. Gerald shut his eyes, but even in the dark he felt the earth turning upside down and there was a strange buzzing in his ears.

"Gerald! Come down!"

Madalyn's voice was a half-remembered echo from a faraway place where silly things mattered like squabbles and impressing people. Gerald clung to a branch and started to cry. He couldn't move as much as an eyelash, and he was sure he was about to pass out.

"He can't," he heard Ned call down to Madalyn. "The height gets some people like this. Sammy Trewen can't jump off the quay to save his life. He literally freezes."

"What are we going to do?" Madalyn was crying. "Get a ladder?"

"He might fall while we fetch it. I'll help him down," Ned replied. "Hold on, Gerald. I'm nearly there."

There was the sound of rustling and the creak of branches as Ned climbed higher. Gerald's arms, already aching from the rowing, were starting to twitch, and his hands were dead hunks of flesh – but he couldn't let Ned rescue him again. The shame would be unbearable, and Gerald thought he would rather plummet to his death.

"I'm fine," he croaked. It was another lie, and they all knew it.

"Can you lower your foot onto the branch below?" Ned sounded closer. "Keep your eyes shut and feel your way, Gerry. It's only a few inches."

"Can you come up here?" whispered Gerald. His eyes were screwed shut so tightly he thought they might never open again.

"The branch isn't strong enough to take us both, but I'm

right below you. If you get your foot to the branch below I can guide you down. We'll do it one step at a time."

Gerald's left foot tapped thin air. When his right foot slipped on bark his stomach dropped away and his brain began to swirl inside his skull.

"Hold on!" Ned shouted. "And don't look down! Keep your eyes shut."

But Gerald was consumed with a terrible compulsion to look earthwards again. Once he lowered his gaze everything began whirling until the blue sky, the green leaves and the girl in white below became hazy. Round and round they all went like a merry-go-round until all the colours blurred. He no longer knew which way was up, and it was exhausting. Even looking at the whirl of colours was too much effort, and his vision was turning black around the edges. He felt so sleepy. Fuzzy. And whoever knew snowflakes could be black?

"Don't let go! Hold on! I'm here! Don't faint, Gerry! Breathe deeply!"

Gerald heard Ned's desperate command, but it was drowned by a scream that seemed to fill his entire head and reverberate through the whole valley. It was a scream which froze the blood and which was, he realised with a peculiar detached interest, coming from deep inside his own head.

Then there was only silence. Nobody was laughing at Gerald Snowe now.

23

MAY 1914

Oyster House

Madalyn

Madalyn had never expected to see Oyster Shore again. As the motor car crawled down the rutted drive she held her breath in anticipation of the sudden revealation of bright water diamonding through dense greenery. The summer spent here was no more than a mosaic of hazy memories sprinkled with splashes of remembrance, yet the remembered imagery of the senses was so vivid that it often felt more real to her than the monotony of life at Miss Millingdon's Select Seminary for Young Ladies.

The dip of oars. A smiling freckled face. Sand smooth and chilly beneath bare feet. Clear water. Keening gulls. The sickening thud of bone and flesh on root-twisted earth ...

"Will this journey ever end?" Constance's weary voice

interrupted Madalyn's thoughts, and Madalyn turned her attention back to her mother. Her eyes closed above hollowed cheeks, Constance's pale face seemed more a *memento mori* than a living woman. Madalyn bit her lip. Would the Cornish air prove to be the cure the physicians promised? Or was there some canker eating away at her mother that even salt breezes and sea-bathing couldn't cure?

"We're almost there, Mama. Just at the bottom of this drive," she promised.

Constance grimaced as the car bounced over a rut. "I dread to think what condition Oyster House must be in. It was bad enough before. I don't know what St John was thinking, suggesting we reside there. He has a perfectly nice place in Dorset. I could have convalesced there just as well."

It was on the tip of Madalyn's tongue to point out that St John Trelyon didn't owe his distant cousins anything, but she said nothing. It wouldn't do her mother's fragile health any good if Constance became agitated about the cruel twist of Fate that had robbed her of the life she'd been born to live. It certainly wouldn't do her own peace of mind any favours to listen to another bitter tirade about her father's fecklessness and the misfortune of Madalyn being born a mere daughter. As if, Madalyn thought, she hadn't wished enough times herself that she'd been born a boy! Apart from never having to wear a corset or spend eight miserable years at boarding school learning to speak French, embroider and arrange flowers (again, courtesy of St John, who would have been well within his rights to have turned a blind eye to the education of his dependant's daughter) she would have been the heir to a fortune and, most importantly, the mistress of her own destiny. Nobody could tell the Viscount Trelyon whom he should marry or impress upon him that making an advantageous match was paramount. If the Viscount Trelyon longed to be an artist and to travel to Paris to study, nobody would stop him.

The injustice of it all, combined with the sense of being trapped in a life she had no desire to live, made Madalyn's heart beat like the wings of a trapped bird. So Constance's latest illness, and this enforced stay in Cornwall, was a welcome respite from all the plans for the upcoming social season. There was only so much taking tea with dowagers and their clearly uninterested sons, fittings at dressmakers for gowns they couldn't afford, and furtive trips to jewellers to pawn what was left of the family treasures to pay for it all that Madalyn could bear. When St John offered Oyster House for an indefinite stay, Madalyn sensed freedom as a prisoner might when glimpsing the stars through a barred window.

"It was very kind of him to offer the house to us, Mama. The air there will do you good, I'm sure, and Tilly and William, even though he's so old, will have made the place fit for our arrival. It'll be more than comfortable," she said firmly.

A small frown puckered Constance Trelyon's brow. "That, my dear Madalyn, is a matter of opinion. By all rights we should be at Vyvyan."

There was nothing Madalyn could say to this. Her mother might as well argue that the tides should cease to turn. This was how life was, and as unfair as it seemed there was nothing to be done. Madalyn had read about women's suffrage and felt a spark of excitement that in the future things might change, but watched closely by Constance she had been unable to attend any meetings. If only she could have attended art school or university! How wonderful it would have been to explore these new ideas, and how exciting to be a part of something bigger than herself and her own narrow world. Oh, it was so frustrating!

"There's the house, Lady Trelyon," the chauffeur said over his shoulder. "We're there now."

Sure enough, Oyster House appeared through the foliage, a splash of white amongst innumerable greens and mirrored in the river along with eiderdown clouds and weeping willows. Madalyn's gloved hands were folded neatly in her lap and her face reposed in a neutral expression but beneath her stays her heart was soaring, for it was all exactly as she remembered.

Although a dangerous fever followed by months of illness made the long-ago weeks on Oyster Shore seem little more than another delirious dream, Madalyn was often filled with a savage longing for this place. Her ears rang with the echoing voices from the past and the cries of her soul's longing to return. Sometimes she flicked through her oldest sketch books, and although she winced at the crude nature of her early work, her breath would catch at the energy in the pencil lines. Wonder was captured in every sketch, and each drawing brimmed with an intensity she had never known since. Wading birds stood in the shallows, shells spiralled to infinity, and a merry-faced little boy fished from a pontoon and walked barefoot along the tideline.

Ned, Madalyn whispered to herself as the car drew closer to where it had all begun. Ned Carew. Her childhood friend. Her best friend. In truth her only real friend, since the pupils at Miss Millingdon's had not wished to associate with a girl who had few prospects, no matter how good her breeding or how noble her name. Little village boy Ned hadn't cared a jot for such things. He had shared her dreams, taught her to climb trees and saved her life. He was the truest friend she had ever known.

Madalyn often wondered what had become of Ned Carew. Was he still here? Or had he followed his dreams and become a writer? She had never heard from him again after that terrible day when the boat had drifted down the river and Gerald Snowe had fallen from the tree. She had written to Ned but there had never been any reply. Village people tended not to move far from where they were born, so presumably Ned had ignored her, which made her heart constrict with sadness even all these years later. Most likely he was still in Trevellan, fishing perhaps, or working as a pupil master. Maybe she would see him again at Church. Would he remember her if she did? Or had Ned Carew chosen to forget those heady days of mudlarking and picnics because their final day had been so dreadful? She supposed this was one explanation for his silence over the years.

Madalyn wished she could forget that last day on Oyster Shore. In the weeks that followed Gerald's accident – weeks in which she later learned she had come close to death from pneumonia – her dreams were haunted by the figure of a boy silhouetted against the blue sky and tumbling to earth like Icarus. He lay on the ground with his leg twisted and as silent and motionless as any effigy in St Nun's. Madalyn would sob and moan in her sleep, twisting her sheets into knots as she relived the scene repeatedly and watched herself crouching at his side while Ned ran for help. His dash to Oyster House seemed to take an eternity, and Madalyn had been so afraid that Gerald would die. She'd never prayed as hard as she had at that moment, and had made all kinds of bargains with God if he would spare the boy's life. Madalyn couldn't recall what she had promised the Almighty but by the time the servants arrived with a sheep hurdle and blankets she was almost incoherent with fear and her teeth were chattering so ferociously she couldn't speak.

After this point her memory of that day was a blank, but Madalyn knew she was ill because fever filled her dreams with terrors, and she was racked with fits of coughing. Once she was able to sit up and sip a little broth she discovered she was in London, with the best doctors in attendance. Her homeward journey and medical care had been taken care of by Arthur Snowe because, Madalyn had later learned from Tilly, Gerald had admitted full responsibility for her soaking. Tilly thought there had also been some altercation regarding a village boy's involvement, and from what Madalyn could gather Ned Carew had shouldered the lion's share of the blame. Once she recovered, Madalyn tried her best to find out more, writing letters to Ned, care of Trevellan School House, which she asked Tilly to post. When no reply was forthcoming Madalyn could only assume he wanted to forget all about her. Shortly afterwards she found herself packed off to school, and as the years passed the events at Oyster Shore faded until they seemed little more than a childhood story.

Gerald Snowe thankfully survived the fall, but his leg had been badly broken – smashed to splinters according to Tilly – and this was no exaggeration, for St John Trelyon had said the boy had been in danger of losing it altogether.

"He'll be lame for the rest of his life, of course," he'd sighed while visiting on the pretext of enquiring after Madalyn's health but in reality breaking the news that the house they were presently occupying was required for his son and that Lady Trelyon would be moved to a smaller dwelling on the less fashionable side of town. Madalyn recalled that

Constance had been far more upset by this news than by poor Gerald's injuries.

"The boy has to learn to walk again," St John had added, "and he'll always need a stick. It's a damned shame. He won't even be able to attend school this year. He'll never play rugger or hunt either. Still, as we all know, he was lucky indeed that he didn't break his neck."

Madalyn knew how much Gerald loathed St Hugh's and sport, and imagined this prognosis wouldn't upset him in the slightest – he'd always become so angry when she and Ned ran faster than him – but how dreadful that he would struggle even to walk. Gerald would certainly want to punish somebody for his misfortune. Did he blame her? Or Ned? Would he want to get revenge on them? Madalyn feared he would, for Gerald Snowe struck her as the sort of person who wanted old scores settled and any perceived wrongs righted. She had felt very glad to be miles away from him.

In spite of Gerald's accident the Snowe family had remained at Vyvyan Court, and now over a decade had passed since the accident. It was all ancient history, Madalyn told herself, as the motor car rounded the final curve in the drive. She hadn't heard much about them since then, but presumed Gerald had recovered sufficiently to live the life of a wealthy young man about town. Madalyn hoped he was happy – although the recollection of his brooding manner made her doubtful of this. He'd never struck her as the sort of person who was inclined to be happy – unlike Ned, who had been all smiles and laughter and generosity.

What would either boy make of her now the long and miserable years at school had dulled her sparkle? Madalyn no longer ran or skipped but walked slowly, with her back straight and chin up as her skirts brushed the ground. She hadn't paddled in a stream or attempted to swim since that lost summer, and her ivory complexion was jealously guarded from the sun these days by wide-brimmed hats. Even her wild curls were tamed, tied back and arranged by Tilly into elaborate plaits and loops, and her dreams of exploration and of becoming an artist were equally tethered. Inside, deep down in the secret part of her heart where nobody else could see, Madalyn still cherished those dreams, and she sketched and painted whenever possible. She was talented – her art masters all said so – and could have exhibited at the Royal Academy, but she knew this was not to be her fate; she had to marry well and support Constance. Her mother's health was poor and it was up to Madalyn to take care of her. When the Season began Constance would launch her into society and pray very hard that a good name and pretty face would make up for lack of wealth. It was the only plan and the only hope they had.

But this was all a long way in the future, Madalyn reminded herself sharply, as the familiar stomach plummet began – a long, long way in the future. For now, she was safe at Oyster Shore and the whole summer stretched ahead in a golden haze of sunny days spent sketching on the riverbank and swimming at Penhayes. Marriage and duty were problems for another day.

The car pulled up in front of the house. As the chauffeur helped Constance alight, Madalyn stared up at the familiar white walls, purpled with wisteria today and rippled with dancing reflections from the river. The house was just as she remembered it and once inside, with the jolly phoenix twinkling down at her from the cupola, the sense of familiarity was overwhelming. While William collected the cases and Tilly took their hats and gloves, Madalyn wandered through the rooms half-expecting to pass her eight-year-old self, sketch book and pail in hand, as she crept out to explore. The views of the river, greenery and shore were still framed like artwork by the generous floor-to-ceiling windows, and even the smell was the same, a wonderful blend of beeswax, salt and age. The long-case clock continued to tick away the hours from its place at the foot of the stairs, and catching sight of her reflection in the hall mirror, Madalyn wondered how many minutes it had counted since she last stood in this spot.

"Will you take afternoon tea, your ladyship?" Tilly asked Constance, who flapped a languid hand.

"I'm far too tired. The journey was utterly exhausting."

Madalyn suppressed a disbelieving sigh. They had only travelled from Plymouth, having broken the journey the previous night, and today's ride in the Snowes' Rolls Royce had been far more comfortable than any carriage. Unlike her mother, Madalyn was brimming with an energy she had almost forgotten existed after the ennui of her life in London. She was hoping desperately that Constance would retire for several hours and leave her free to revisit her old haunts. With a skeleton staff running the place, and Tilly occupied with her mistress's demands, Madalyn would be free to walk and paddle and sketch. She could scarcely wait.

"Sir Arthur Snowe has sent an invitation to dine at Vyvyan Court this evening, your ladyship," Tilly told Constance, gesturing to a card on the mantelpiece. "His man said they would send the car back at seven."

"You'll be far too tired for that, Mama," Madalyn said quickly. She couldn't think of anything she would rather do less than make small talk with the Snowes, and the thought of bumping into Gerald, injured and more resentful than ever, was not a happy one. "We're here for you to convalesce."

But Constance had brightened at the news of an invitation to Vyvyan. "A rest this afternoon will restore me, Madalyn. It's only polite that we dine with Sir Arthur and thank him for his kindness in sending the car for us."

It was *Sir* Arthur Snowe nowadays.

"Send one of the boys to Vyvyan to tell Sir Arthur and Lady Snowe we are delighted to accept," Constance told Tilly, turning for the staircase. "Lay out Miss Madalyn's French gown once you've attended me. She looks particularly fetching in that."

Madalyn opened her mouth to point out that the fashionable green dress required her corset to be laced so tightly she wouldn't be able to eat a mouthful (even if Gerald wasn't present to put her off her food), but Constance was ascending the stairway and the determined set of her shoulders suggested she wouldn't be argued with.

Madalyn's heart sank. There was only one reason her mother would want her to look fetching; Gerald might well be present, and as the heir to the now Sir Arthur's fortune, Constance would consider him quite the catch. The image of a wheezing little pug shrinking into the shadows drifted up from Madalyn's memories, and she shivered. No, thank you.

I'd rather be a nun, said her eight-year-old self, and Madalyn agreed.

Madalyn retreated to her old bedroom to gather her thoughts. To her delight the room had scarcely changed in a decade. Now the windows were opened wide, the floral curtains still billowed in the breeze and sunlight rippled on the worn floorboards. Madalyn leaned on the windowsill and tilted her face up to the sunshine, ignoring all warnings about freckles and ruining her complexion. Beyond the terrace was the river, a silver ribbon of promise, and even though she had been away from it for over half a lifetime Madalyn sensed that the tide was turning. Very soon the soft, worm-casty sand would be revealed as the water peeled back like an unravelled stocking, and there would be shells and the ribs of old boats and all manner of wonderful things to sketch. There would be nobody here to remind her that young ladies required parasols and didn't go barefoot. Once she was around the meander which divided Oyster House from the boathouse she could even unpin her hat and pull off her shoes and stockings. How wonderful it would be to feel the breeze in her hair and the grass beneath her bare feet!

Since Tilly was busy with her mother, Madalyn abandoned any hope of changing into lighter attire so she just took off the jacket and plumed hat of her travelling suit. The fine lawn blouse was perfect for a sunny afternoon, and the navy skirt could be tucked into the wide belt if she wanted to dip her toes into the water. Selecting a straw boater which she rammed onto the top of her auburn curls and stabbed into place with a hat pin, Madalyn fetched her new sketchbook – pages upon pages of cream parchment simply begging to be filled with the yet-to-be sketched events of summer 1914 – and a felt case filled with sharpened pencils. She tucked these into the deep pocket of her skirt, and before anyone could find a task for her or a reason why she was needed indoors she flew down the stairs and out through the front door. Madalyn knew that young ladies oughtn't to run, but she couldn't help leaping down the three steps which led from the terrace to the lawn. She was free!

As though her feet had a memory of their own, Madalyn walked across the lawn before following the path which led to the old boathouse. Kingfishers darted along the bank and a heron watched her from an ancient oak tree on the opposite shore, its grey bulk almost too motionless to belong to a living creature. Fighting the impulse to run, Madalyn walked on steadily until Oyster House had vanished and she was free from watchful eyes and disapproving stares.

The peace after London was wonderful, the only sounds birdsong from the woods and the distant call of gulls. Madalyn sat on a fallen tree to unbutton her boots, rolling off her stockings and curling her bare toes into the grass. Emboldened, she removed the boater and then, so fast that she almost tangled the elaborate braids, she unpinned her hair to let the curls tumble to her waist. It was wonderful to feel the heat on her skin and the wind lift her hair and, feeling as though she was a child again, she tucked her skirts into her belt and scrambled down the bank to the glistening riverbed.

The tide had always turned swiftly at Oyster Shore, and the pebbled beach was growing wider with each passing minute. It was irresistible, and Madalyn found herself drawn to the shell line where sea glass and treasure were waiting to be liberated from the cold sand beneath her feet. As she stooped to gather them she wondered whether the phoenix comb was waking up and urging a lost signet ring and a giant marble to make ready.

Hands sandy and her pockets laden with seashore treasures, Madalyn followed the river until she reached the boathouse. The small dwelling was exactly as she remembered, a fairytale building with diamond-paned windows set at the top end of a sturdy pontoon, and she was swept away by a sudden cascade of memories: three children stood on the end of the pontoon dangling fishing lines; Gerald was complaining that his hook wasn't working; she was more interested in the way their reflected selves wobbled in the water than she was in fish; and Ned was busy reeling in a flapping pollock. Where had those children gone? Did they still exist somewhere in the magical place where time stood still and nobody ever had to grow old?

Madalyn was about to return to her beachcombing when she noticed a plume of smoke rising from the boathouse chimney. Now she looked more closely she noticed white shirts hanging out to dry on a makeshift line strung across the porch and logs stacked neatly by the door. A vegetable patch had been created from the grassy slope by the porch, and tethered to the pontoon was a wooden boat, which lolled on the sand like a dog tied up outside the grocer's shop.

The boathouse was occupied. She was not alone after all.

Conscious of her bare head and naked legs, Madalyn brimmed with an unreasonable rage that the solitude of her magical place was violated by an interloper. The freedom she'd been dreaming of for so long felt as though it had been snatched away before her fingers could even grasp it, and her throat tightened with disappointment. If St John Trelyon had given this place to another impoverished dependant, all her hopes of paddling and sketching barefoot and bareheaded would be dashed. Even now somebody could be watching her and feeling outraged by her lack of modesty. They might already planning to write to the Viscount and complain. Constance would be mortified and insist upon leaving – and then what would Madalyn have to look forward to except London, and her mother's suffocating expectations of a suitable marriage? Oyster Shore would be lost all over again.

This thought filled Madalyn with despair. Perhaps, though, it wasn't too late to avoid detection. If she could reach the bank and slip away into the trees without being spotted nobody would know she had ever been here. No damage would be done. She would confine her paddling and freedom to the upper part of Oyster Shore and the woods.

Madalyn turned, taking care to pick her way along the harder, gravelled patches of the riverbank to avoid the sucking mud, but she was out of practice and it was slow progress. By the time she reached the river bank her calves were aching and her face was hot. She bent to catch her breath, hands resting on her knees and hair swinging in front of her face, before straightening up and gasping when she realised she was staring into the violet eyes of a young man standing on the boathouse steps.

"Hello, Madalyn," said Ned Carew.

24

MAY 1914

Oyster Shore

Ned

At first Ned thought his imagination had conjured into existence his heart's most secret and deepest longing. He rubbed his eyes and told himself he had been working too hard; digging the vegetable plot in the hot sun after writing into the small hours must be making him hallucinate because this simply couldn't be. It was utterly impossible. This russet-haired girl tracing the tideline, skirts tucked up to reveal shapely calves, was no more than a mirage. She wasn't here. She *couldn't* be.

He rubbed his eyes for a second time but to no avail; the girl was still there. No matter how many times Ned blinked or pinched himself she didn't vanish. The sun turned her hair to flame, and although her back was to him Ned knew her eyes were the same deep green as the seaweed kissing her bare toes. He knew she was brave and funny and determined, just as he knew she was talented and sensitive and the other half of his soul.

It was Madalyn. She had come back at last, and Ned knew he'd been waiting over half his lifetime for this moment. Everything he was and would be had led him to this ripple in time. Why else had he taken St John's offer of a groundsman's job on Oyster Shore rather than becoming a pupil master at the school? He could tell Marrick that it was for the free lodging in the boathouse, persuade his mother that the inspiration the creek offered meant more to him than an academic career, even convince himself he enjoyed keeping the woods clear and that the abundant fish and game compensated for fiscal rewards – but the truth was he had always been waiting for Madalyn Trelyon to return. And now here she was at last, as beautiful and bright as an angel; and with his heart in freefall Ned knew he worshipped her as utterly at eighteen as he had at eight years old.

Until the moment Madalyn stepped around the bluff and back into Ned's life it had been a perfectly ordinary afternoon. Contrary to any book he'd ever read or attempted to write, there had been no signs that his world was poised to turn upside down. His work done for the day, he'd just settled into the old armchair that he and Marrick had carried through the woods to the boathouse. With this positioned in the boathouse window, pen in hand and a fresh page of his notebook open, Ned was ready to write, because if ever a spot had been created to pen a story, this surely was it. All he needed to do was find his elusive muse, and he would be up and running. It was only a matter of time.

"No excuses not to write that masterpiece now," had been Marrick's comment once the chair was in situ. The two friends were sharing a beer on the pontoon, their legs dangling over the water and reflections fragmenting just as when they had been knock-kneed schoolboys. "Make sure I get my cut – I think I've buggered my shoulder for good, lugging that bloody chair down here."

Ned laughed, but Marrick had been right – the chair was heavy. A big leather affair, arms worn bare and seams oozing stuffing, it had once enjoyed pride of place in Edgar's study, and whenever Ned sat on it he felt closer to his father. When the stunned and grieving remainder of the Carew family had left the schoolhouse for the final time on that bleak November day, Ned insisted the chair accompany Matilda to her new lodgings at the Rectory, where she had accepted a post as housekeeper. Now it reposed in the window of the boathouse and had become the place where Ned wrote. With the ever-changing picture of tides and foliage, accompanied by the tranquillity and solitude, he was certain it was here that he would write his masterpiece, and it seemed fitting he would sit in his father's chair to do so.

Edgar Carew might have been gone three years, but the creak of the leather and roughness of the worn hide beneath his shirtsleeves transported Ned back to being a little boy sitting on his father's lap and listening to tales of knights and dragons and noble quests. All was well in the world when Edgar told stories. The world where he resided over the classroom and smoked his pipe in his study was a world where all was as it should be. Matilda would be baking in the schoolhouse kitchen, Bess giggling with her friends, and Ned set to follow in his father's footsteps and go to Oxford. In that world

Ned wouldn't be a gardener, Bess wouldn't be in service at Vyvyan Court – and Matilda certainly wouldn't have married Reverend Tullis.

The thought of this made Ned's head ache and his heart twist. Couldn't Matilda have stayed on as the Reverend's housekeeper? Why did she need to remarry? And so soon? Did Edgar mean so little to her? Hadn't she loved his father after all?

"Women's choices are never easy, my love, and marriage isn't always about love," was all Matilda said when, filled with outrage on his deceased father's behalf, Ned expressed his feelings. He'd been utterly mystified. Why would Matilda – beautiful and bright Matilda who loved Edgar so utterly and laughed with him every day of their marriage – want to marry a dry old stick like the vicar? It was unthinkable at best, and disrespectful to Edgar at worst.

Matilda's decision had made Ned question whether his cherished ideal of love truly existed. Should he hold out for it, like a gallant knight of old, or should he (as Marrick always insisted) enjoy the charms of the local girls? Tamsyn, the innkeeper's blonde and buxom daughter, was certainly a tempting proposition, but inspired by his parents' love, and the memory of a girl with flame-hued curls and rockpool eyes, Ned had kept aloof. Marrick said, rather enviously, this drove the girls even more wild and he could take his pick, but Ned believed there had to be more to love than a quick tumble in the net loft, surely? People died for love. They gave up *everything* for it. From Romeo and Juliet to Anthony and Cleopatra, what was more noble than sacrificing yourself for true love? Love, Ned had always believed, was *everything.* So why would his mother marry a man she didn't love, a

Casaubon to her Dorothea? It made no sense and it threw everything Ned had always believed in into confusion.

"Choose not to marry him!" he pleaded with Matilda. "You don't love him, Mama. Not like you loved my father. Why marry him?"

His mother shook her head sadly. "Oh, Ned. Your father left us with nothing but books and debts. His family cut us off years ago and we're all alone. Michael Tullis is a good man. He'll keep Bess and me in a respectable state. Without him, what do we have?"

"You have lodgings and employment," Ned said stubbornly. "Bess is fine working at the big house, and I'm at Oyster Shore. We don't need him."

But Matilda's dark eyes were filled with sadness. "Don't you understand? Your sister and I *do* need him. We need respectability and security, and Reverend Tullis is offering us exactly that. He's even said he'll help you to enter the Church by taking you on as his curate. I know it's not Oxford, my love, but it'd be a good profession. You should consider it."

Ned stared at her in disbelief. "You want me to settle for the Church? When I have no vocation for it?"

Matilda's head drooped, and his heart had broken to see the dark hair streaked with grey.

"Plenty of men do, and it would be a good living," she said quietly. "I loved your father with all my heart, but he was a dreamer and you can't live on dreams. Dreams don't keep you safe. They can't fill your stomach or pay the grocer and the baker. Dreams don't put shoes on your feet or pay the doctor's bill. Tell me, how did Edgar's dreams keep us safe when he died? We lost our home overnight. We lost everything. That must never happen again, Ned. It's the worst thing a man can do to a woman, leave her poor and vulnerable. Once she's sold everything else what currency does she have but herself?"

Her words hit Ned like a punch. In order to settle the doctor's bills after Edgar's illness, and indeed to pay off their creditors, Matilda had pawned her wedding ring and been forced to sell most of Edgar's precious books. The few Ned did manage to save resided on the bookshelf he had built out of orange boxes and placed beneath the window in the boathouse. They were a sad reminder of their lost companions, and sometimes he found it hard to even look at them.

"Think about the Reverend's offer to you, Ned. Don't be too quick to dismiss it," Matilda urged. "You'll need to make your way in the world. It would be a good start for you."

"Can you really see me as a churchman, Mama?" Ned asked.

The worried expression on his mother's face told him she couldn't. "I only want to do my best for us all. Bess will marry, I have no doubt of that, and will have a husband to take care of her. So will I. But what of you? I worry, my love. You need so much more."

She looked so sad that Ned's anger slipped away. "I'm going to be a writer, remember?" he said. "I don't need any other profession, and you don't need to worry about me. I've got my work at Oyster Shore to keep me, and a place to rest my head while I write. I can catch prawns at the slack of tide, and grow vegetables, and I dine on oysters whenever I choose. I'm a lucky man, and no mistake!"

Then, not wishing to cause Matilda any more distress, he'd hugged her and had given her his blessing.

Her wedding took place, a small affair followed by afternoon tea and dancing in the village hall; beautiful Matilda

Carew became the vicar's wife, a role she filled as effortlessly as she had once presided over the schoolhouse. Bess, delighted to leave service, moved into the Rectory and seemed settled enough, but Ned felt as though he was adrift in a small and leaky boat, no longer belonging anywhere and floating far away from the family life that had been his anchor and his safety. If it hadn't been for Oyster Shore and his conviction this was the place where he was meant to be, Ned often thought he might have left Trevellan to seek his fortune elsewhere.

In the meantime, he was happy at Oyster Shore. Largely left to his own devices, he made sure the woods were managed, the paths kept clear, and any poachers warded off from the Trelyons' remaining foothold in their once-great estate. In the winter he assisted Sir Arthur's gamekeeper, beating and picking up for the family and their house guests during shooting parties, while doing his best to avoid Gerald. Not that Gerald was often in Cornwall, and even when he was he couldn't walk well enough to shoot for very long. After the tree-climbing accident the Snowes had whisked him away to London for the best medical care. Gerald walked with a stick now, an elegant silver-topped cane that probably cost more than most villagers earned in a year, and on the rare occasions when Ned did see him Gerald made it plain that a mere gardener was too far beneath him to even acknowledge. Ned understood that this was the way of the world, but he longed to tell Gerald he was so sorry about his accident and the terrible injury. If he could have suffered in the other boy's place, Ned would have done so in a heartbeat.

Ned's stomach still fell away when he recalled how Gerald had attempted to scale the tree, and the sound of the cracking bones would haunt him until the day he died. The thrashing Edgar had given him certainly haunted Ned's backside for weeks, and he'd been kept indoors for the rest of that glorious summer, writing out Latin declensions until his hand cramped and his vision swam. Ned had tried to send notes to Gerald and Madalyn by bribing Bess, but they were all returned unopened. When he was finally freed to walk down to the river he discovered Oyster House locked up once again and Madalyn long gone. He heard she had been ill, for Violet Trehunnist had whispered to Matilda with ghoulish delight about the Trelyon girl 'catching her death of cold' and almost dying. Ned thought he would die of misery at the loss of his friend but he understood his unhappiness was nothing in comparison to Gerald's suffering. The village doctor said Gerald had shattered his leg and pelvis and was lucky not to have broken his neck. Other than this, all was silent and it was as though the summer friendship had never happened. Ned had never heard from Madalyn again and he could only suppose she blamed him for what had happened that final afternoon on Oyster Shore.

The years passed in the slow yet galloping way years do when one is growing up, and now, ten years later, the long-ago summer seemed like a story he had read about another boy. Sometimes he caught sight of Gerald in the motor car and would tip his hat, but Gerald would look straight through him. Bess, who had worked at Vyvyan Court, said Gerald walked with a limp and was as miserable as ever even though he had taken his place at Harrow and was set to go up to Oxford. Sometimes when Ned checked the old hiding place in the boathouse it seemed to him that the air had been stirred and the place took on a watchful air, but nothing was ever moved or appeared any different and there was no other sign that someone had passed through. Even the light-fingered ghost of yesterday had deserted him.

Oyster House, closed up and unloved, continued to decline. The Snowes avoided the place and even the Trelyons appeared to have forgotten it. The wooden terrace warped in the wind and the sunshine, and ivy wrapped her fingers around the balustrades, tugging at the soft wood until paint flaked onto the weed-knitted garden like gentle tears. Inside the house, dust dulled the floorboards and settled on the shrouded furniture, and Ned often thought that the house, like him, was pining for a girl with autumn curls and sea-green eyes.

He stayed away from the house itself as this was not in his remit, but he maintained the grounds as St John had instructed, and looked after the boathouse and pontoon. He kept the drive as clear as possible but it was a Sisyphean battle, and Ned often asked himself who he was maintaining it for: St John Trelyon, ageing and arthritic, lived in Brighton, and the Snowes, quite understandably, detested the river-bank. Was he doing it for Madalyn? Did he scythe and mow and chop in anticipation of her return?

Maybe, for she was Ned's Viola. His Juliet. His Isolde. She had climbed trees with Tom Sawyer and ridden through the greenwood with Robin Hood. Madalyn was the Queen of the Round Table and the Cathy to his Heathcliff. She was the heroine of every novel he had ever attempted to write. Was he counting the days until she returned to be his muse and he could truly write the book of his heart?

Maybe, for Ned knew he was marking time. Sometimes he went out to sea with Marrick, hauling nets and pots in return for a few mackerel or a lobster, or helped Sammy Trewen at the forge. Afterwards the young men would enjoy a drink in the Trelyon Arms, where Ned would flirt a little with Tamsyn, but before her warm glances and slow smiles reeled him in like one of the flickering fish on Marrick's line, he would slip away to walk through the darkening woods back to the boathouse, where he wrote by candlelight into the small hours.

Oyster Shore was the home of his soul. Ned found poetry in the cadences of the turning tides and a rhythm in the slowly moving water. Kingfishers darted like inspiration, hard to spot and impossible to hold, and thought was alluvial, for who knew what was buried in the mud and the past? Somewhere in the riverbed were the treasures of childhood, sunk from sight and into memory but as real as the day they were tossed away, just as deep down inside Ned was the boy who'd climbed trees and loved Madalyn. Life was simple here, and he was content with furniture built out of driftwood, happy to wash in the creek and eat mud-flavoured mullet for supper. The damp, the leaking roof and the candlelight didn't lower his spirits. At night he slept on an old brass bed beneath the sloping eaves, listening to the call of owls or the patter of raindrops on the roof. He sat in Edgar's chair, and stories flowed from his pen just as the river flowed past the pontoon, but Ned knew that the greatest of them all was still waiting to be written.

And now, as he watched the slender young woman turn towards the boathouse, he understood that everything in his life had led to this very moment. His greatest work could only ever be written here, on Oyster Shore, and with Madalyn Trelyon beside him. This was his time.

As though pulled by an invisible current, Ned abandoned his writing and walked into the sunlit afternoon and the rest of his life.

"Hello, Madalyn," he said.

Madalyn was bent double, hands resting on her knees as she caught her breath from the effort of pulling her feet from the sucking sand. As she straightened up her green eyes grew wide with disbelief.

"Ned?" she whispered, and so quietly that the breeze seemed to tease the words away to drift them across the valley. "Is it really you? Or am I dreaming?"

The joy in her voice and the wonder in her eyes were all Ned needed to know that Madalyn's heart still mirrored his. They smiled at one another and Madalyn pointed to her sand-splattered skirt. "I would have dressed up if I'd known this'd be a social occasion!"

Ned's gaze strayed to her slim legs and up to the curve of her waist and the swell of her breasts beneath the sheer cotton blouse. The glorious red hair tumbling past her shoulders should have been pinned up beneath a hat, and already the sun was sprinkling freckles across the bridge of her nose and planting roses in her cheeks. Although she was still Madalyn, his dearest childhood companion and best friend, she was also not Madalyn, for this new incarnation was so utterly beautiful that he, who loved words and knew so many, was totally and utterly lost for them.

"You're perfect as you are," was all Ned said, for it was true. With the afternoon sun turning her hair to fire and her blouse to sheer gossamer, she was Botticelli's Venus – albeit a muddier version, surrounded by sharp oyster shells and seabirds rather than blossoms and ethereal beings.

"I'm not sure my mother would agree," Madalyn sighed, glancing at her bare feet and soiled skirt. "I suspect she'd say all my years at Miss Millingdon's have been well and truly wasted. St John will demand a refund instantly if anyone sees me!"

"Then we'd better get you cleaned up before they do," said Ned. "The herons can be trusted to keep their beaks shut, but I'm not so sure about the gulls. They'll be gossiping all over Trevellan."

"Lord. I'll be in such trouble!" Madalyn held out a hand so Ned could pull her up onto the grass. "Hurry! Before I'm discovered!"

He took her hand and as he drew her towards him, Ned drank in the scent of warm skin and the faint echo of something sweet she must have dabbed on her wrists. His senses reeled.

Madalyn smiled up at him, tucking a curl behind an ear. "What?" she asked, self-consciously. "Have I got mud on my nose?"

"That's probably the only place you don't have it," Ned said with a grin of pure joy from ear to ear.

"What's so funny, then?"

He squeezed her fingers. "Nothing's funny. I'm just so happy to see you again, and I can't believe you're here. Are you sure I'm not dreaming?"

Madalyn slipped her hand from his and pointed to her feet. "I can prove I'm not a dream if you like, Ned Carew! I'll make muddy footprints all around your house."

He laughed. "Do you remember how muddy we used to get? Marrick's mother was always taking in our washing and complaining. I think we must have paid for the Penwurthies' new boat that summer. If it's all the same with you, Miss Trelyon, I'll boil up some water for you to wash your feet in. I take it your hat and shoes are on the riverbank? Same as always?"

Madalyn's eyes danced up at him as she tipped her head back to study his face.

Of course, Ned realised, he was much taller now, almost six feet, while she was petite. Long gone were the days when they had been of equal height. Ned's arms were corded with sinew from physical work, his legs were well-muscled, and even his hands, rough from chopping wood and hacking at undergrowth, seemed to have doubled in size. His hair was longer and thicker, a pelt of white-blond almost brushing his shoulders, which Matilda was always suggesting he cut. Now Ned wished he'd listened to his mother, for Madalyn Trelyon was a lady. What must she think?

But Madalyn didn't seem horrified by his unkempt appearance, and she certainly didn't seem very ladylike when she wiped her hands on her skirt and unhitched acres of fabric from her belt.

"Where else?" she said. "I simply couldn't help myself. Oh, Ned! I've dreamed about being back here for so long. It hardly seems real. Are you sure this isn't a just another dream?"

"I'm not an expert on Dr Freud but I don't believe mud comes into dreams," Ned said.

Madalyn raised an eyebrow. "No, I don't believe mud is one of the preoccupations he's concerned with."

Ned laughed. She hadn't changed a bit!

"In any case I had better get cleaned up," Madalyn was saying. "I don't want Mama getting another headache over the state of me and deciding I need to stay indoors and do embroidery."

"God forbid," said Ned. "We can't have that."

He led the way into the boathouse, settling Madalyn into his father's chair and placing a pan of water on the pot-bellied stove. While they waited for it to boil, he pulled a stool over and sat beside her, still unable to believe she was here.

"I always loved this little place. You've made it into a beautiful home," Madalyn said warmly. "And books everywhere, of course!"

Ned flushed at this praise. "I think the only reason I took the job here was because the Viscount said I could live in the boathouse. It's where I love to write."

"I know," she said. "It always was. I had no idea you still lived in Trevellan. I thought you'd have gone away to Oxford by now. Wasn't that your dream?"

Ned shrugged. The loss of Oxford still cut deep. "Balliol wasn't for me."

"I don't believe that." She pointed at the notebook, splayed on the arm of the chair. "You still write, though, don't you?"

"I do, and I still want to be a writer. That dream has never changed. How about you? Do you still want to be an artist?"

"I *am* an artist!" Madalyn said, with a flash of her old fire. "My tutor said I could be a Royal Academy Member if I was a man. Just my beastly luck again. But you're a man, so what's stopping you? If I were a man nothing would stop me. Why aren't you at Oxford? Why didn't you go?"

"My father died."

Ned looked down at the tiled floor. Suddenly the gulf in their social classes was a gaping chasm and he wondered whether Madalyn would comprehend the implications of Edgar's death for the Carew family.

"Oh, Ned. I'm so sorry. How awful."

Madalyn placed her hand on his arm and her eyes were bright with tears. Ned knew then that she understood everything. Of course she did, for who would understand better than Madalyn Trelyon how the death of a father changed everything? There was no need for him to explain further, but as he fetched the water and a towel Ned found himself telling her about the changes the past ten years had brought to the Carew family. While she washed the mud from her legs he listened in turn as she confided in him about her mother's illness and their increasingly reduced circumstances. He and Madalyn were the same. How could he ever have doubted it? They were two halves of one soul, and what she felt Ned felt too. It had always been that way.

"Gerald was always so jealous of your family," Madalyn reflected once they had caught up as much as possible and Ned was watching the kettle, his heart still overflowing with happiness to learn that Madalyn was staying at Oyster House all summer.

"Jealous of me? I don't think so."

"Oh Ned! It ate him up. It's why he climbed that silly tree, wasn't it? To prove that he was as good as you?"

"But he looked down on me. Why would he have been jealous of a village boy?"

Madalyn huffed with exasperation. "Because of how you are."

"How I *am*?" Ned was mystified. Gerald saw him as a pleb. A common working man. A nobody. It seemed unlikely.

"Oh! You *must* know!" Madalyn's face was pink and she could hardly look at him as her words tumbled out on top of one another. "You're clever and brave and strong. Everyone liked you best." She paused. "*I* liked you best."

Ned, spooning tea-leaves into his pot, almost tipped in the entire contents of the caddy. "Did you?"

"Of course I did!" she cried and as she spoke the light

turned her hair to a sunburst. It dazzled him. *She* dazzled him.

"I liked you the best too," he said softly.

"And now?" Madalyn asked. Her eyes were as dark as moss as she held his gaze. "Do you still like me?"

Ned's heart raced. He wanted to tell Madalyn Trelyon how he felt. He wanted to let her know not a day had gone by when he hadn't thought about her. He wanted to tell her that he'd looked out for her every day, had tried his utmost to wish her into appearing, and that she was the apparition of his heart. Most of all he longed to take her in his arms, hold her tightly, and never let her go, because he loved Madalyn Trelyon. He always had and he knew he always would.

"I do," he told her. "I always will. Never ever doubt it, Maddy."

The old name was the breach in the dam of separation and time. Madalyn exhaled as though she had been holding her breath for a decade, and suddenly it no longer mattered to Ned that she was a lady and he just a gardener. He was Ned and she was Maddy. They were the best of friends. They knew the secrets of each other's hearts and shared all their hopes and dreams, and there was no need to explain anything. There was no awkwardness between them.

"Why didn't you write back to me?" Madalyn asked. "I sent you so many letters, Ned. When you never wrote back I was so afraid you blamed me for what happened. Did you?"

The hurt rang through her voice and wrapped around his heart. Abandoning the tea-making, Ned crouched at her feet and reached for her hands, raising each in turn to his lips then pressing them to his cheek.

"Never, Maddy. Never! Of course not! And besides, I never had any letters from you."

She looked shocked. “Are you sure? I wrote lots.”

“I would have *treasured* them,” Ned said fiercely. “I’ve kept everything you ever gave me! The comb and the glass and the sketches are hidden here, but I would have carried your letters everywhere and read them over and over until I knew them by heart.”

Tears spilled over her cheeks. “I thought you blamed me. For years I’ve thought that.”

“Never! If anything, I blamed myself for showing Gerald the boat and the climbing tree in the first place. Of course he wanted to row and climb the tree right to the top. Who wouldn’t? His parents, and mine, certainly blamed me for the accident. I had the thrashing of a lifetime that night. I didn’t sit down for a week.”

“That wasn’t fair! It was all his idea. And he almost drowned us all.”

Ned shrugged. “Maybe, but I was the one who should have known better – and I wasn’t even supposed to be on Oyster Shore, remember? My father almost lost his job because of it all. The Viscount was furious, and Sir Arthur was calling for justice. It didn’t help, either, that Gerald had lent me a pile of books from Vyvyan which his father accused me of stealing. It all got very ugly.”

Madalyn was horrified. “Gerald didn’t tell his father he gave them to you?”

“To be fair, he wasn’t in a fit state to tell anyone much at all, and I imagine that by the time he was it was the least of his problems. He had to learn to walk again.”

Madalyn fell silent. Ned could feel the rise and fall of her chest against his arm and the heat of her body through the thin blouse. Their closeness made his head swim. He’d never felt drunk on another person's proximity before. It was overwhelming, terrifying, and utterly wonderful.

"Gerry could have said something later on," she said finally. "He didn't, though, did he?"

"No," Ned said quietly, "but I never blamed him. Gerald had a rough time of it. Even now he walks with a stick. He was angry and wanted someone to blame. Who wouldn't?"

"You?" she suggested. "You always were too kind to him, Ned. Gerald was a spiteful boy. I remember him kicking that poor pug something wicked."

"I felt sorry for him," Ned said. He recalled the hungry way Gerald used to watch him as a boy, and the bleak expression in his eyes. Despite all the riches and advantages that life could offer, Arthur Snowe's heir had been an unhappy boy. "Maybe he's changed? It was all so long ago."

"Mama and I are dining at Vyvyan Court this evening, so I'll be able to tell you if Gerry's changed – but I doubt it somehow. Have you changed? Have I?"

Ned cupped her cheek in his hand. "Yes, Maddy, you have. You're even more beautiful now."

A flush stole across her throat. "I'm not beautiful."

"But you are," he said quietly. Her skin was like silk beneath his fingers, and Ned longed to press his lips to it. He burned to hold her. To touch her. To worship her. To love her. The torrent of emotions was overwhelming. Ned hardly knew where they ended and he began.

"How can I stop telling the truth?" he whispered. "You're bright as the daylight, Maddy. You're the sunlight on the sand. The diamonds in the water. The flash of a kingfisher's wing. You're the birdsong and the breeze in the willows. You're everything that is beautiful and true."

Madalyn rested her forehead against his. "I'm not a

weaver of words. That's your gift, not mine – but you're in every line I've drawn and every line I will ever draw. Do you know how many times I've sketched this place? Or you? How I've longed to see it, to see *you*, once more? You meant everything to me as a child, and you still do. How can it be that hasn't changed? Is this place magical?"

He raised her chin with his forefinger, and when her eyes locked with his, Ned knew beyond all doubt that everything he felt was echoed by Madalyn.

"It is a very special kind of magic," he told her softly, "and an enchantment that will never end. Now you're here again I know I'm going to write something special, Madalyn, something incredible that will last for ever, because you'll be in every line I write. Every piece of imagery will be because of you, and for you. Every word and every sentence is inspired by you. I can feel it here, where you are. Where you've always been. Where you'll always be."

He pressed her hand against his chest. Could Madalyn feel how his heart raced beneath the linen of his shirt? As he delved for the words he knew she must hear, the words he knew he had to say, she nodded, and Ned knew her heart raced in tandem.

"Maddy, I know I have nothing to offer and I know you should marry a wealthy man —"

Her head jerked up. "Do my duty, you mean? Sell myself to the highest bidder to pay my mother's debts? Class and titles for money? All the talk of being an explorer or painting in Egypt was just a silly dream. We've always known what my future holds."

"It was abstract then, Maddy, and so far in the future it was like a story about somebody else. It wasn't about *you*."

"But it *is* about me. Mama's depending on my making a good match. She's been telling me so my entire life."

The thought of Madalyn being married to a man who wouldn't love her spirit, or know or even care that she could climb trees, skip pebbles and draw, filled Ned with a savage anger. It would destroy Madalyn. She was far too precious to be sacrificed on the altar of family name and duty. Madalyn had to know there could be more to life – if she chose another life. He looked down at his hands, calloused from work and engrained with dirt, and took a deep breath.

"But it's your life, not hers. You're worth so much more than a financial transaction."

Madalyn laughed bitterly. "I'm not. I'm just a useless girl, remember?"

"You're far from that! You're *everything*." Now she was here Ned could no more hold back from telling her how he felt than the flooding tide could be prevented from racing over the riverbed. "Maddy, I've loved you since the day we first met, and I've loved you every moment since. Not a day has passed when I haven't thought of you and missed you."

"You love me?" she whispered. "Truly?"

"With all that I am," Ned promised. "I don't have anything to offer you except my heart, but that's yours, and it will never belong to anyone else. I promise I'll love you every moment for the rest of our lives and all the moments beyond. I'll love you until the very end of time."

A tear slipped down her cheek. "Oh, Ned."

Although his hands were shaking and his heart racing, a sense of lightness overcame Ned as he spoke. At last he could articulate his feelings, and even if she were to walk away Madalyn Trelyon could be in no doubt as to how much she meant to him. "I love you, Maddy. I love the way you study the shells. I love the way your tongue pokes through your lips when you sketch. I love how you are brave and funny and determined. And I love how when I'm with you everything is magical and possible. I want nothing more than just to be at your side. There's nothing in life that could bring me more joy than to be with you."

Madalyn held up her left hand with its silver whisper of a scar. "I've never stopped thinking about you either, Sir Edward, my gallant knight," she said. "That summer was the happiest time of my life, and it broke my heart to leave. You were my best friend and I think I knew even then you were my destiny. We're meant to be together, aren't we? No matter what? Fate brought us together, then and now, and I know I love you too. Oh! If only it was all that easy and we could stay here in the boathouse for ever!"

Ned kissed her hand. "Why can't we? We can eat oysters for our supper! Or boil up prawns!"

"And you can write, and I'll paint! Just like we always did!"

"But no tree-climbing!" he warned.

Madalyn grimaced. "And no boating either! I still can't swim."

"I'll teach you again. You'll be like a mermaid by the end of the summer."

"This summer can't end. I won't let it," Madalyn said. But a shadow crossed her face and Ned knew that even after everything he had said she was still thinking of the approaching London Season and her duty. She tightened her grasp on his hands. "Don't talk about endings, Ned. It feels as though a dark cloud will come over us if we do. Let's enjoy the time we have now."

Ned understood. It wasn't the time to speak of endings,

not when they were lost in the wonder of rediscovering their friendship and exploring their blossoming love. But dark clouds were on his mind more than ever lately, for Reverend Tullis thought there would be a war. From what Ned gleaned from the newspapers the situation on the Continent was fraught. But war? The idea seemed unlikely, especially when woodpigeons called, the sky was cloudless, and wild garlic bloomed in the woods. How could there be a war when the world was beautiful and he was in love?

"The summer has only just begun and it's going to be wonderful," he said – but for some reason his promise felt hollow. Was this Matilda's gift of presentience? Was war creeping towards them? Ned shivered.

Madalyn hadn't noticed the shadows creeping closer. She was smiling and making plans. "We have days and days ahead. Isn't it bliss!"

"Bliss," he said, and kissed her hand.

"But bliss or not, I ought to go back up to the house now," Madalyn sighed, "because I'll need to dress for dinner at Vyvyan. If I stay here much longer I'll be missed, and Mama will send out a search party."

The tide had turned and the river was beginning to flood. The sky above the treetops was still a vivid blue but shadows were starting to lengthen across the grass and swallows were arrowing over the river, feasting on a supper of insects. Ned knew it was time for their unexpected reunion to come to an end, and the thought made him feel bereft.

"We can't have your mother worried. If a search party find your shoes they'll think you've vanished."

"Or that I went swimming and drowned! Oh, I wish that would happen! Then nobody would think to find me here, and I could stay here for ever," she cried.

For the second time in mere minutes shivers dusted Ned's forearms and stirred the hairs on the nape of his neck. Talk of drowning was unlucky. Fisherman Marrick would have been horrified, and Ned had absorbed enough local superstitions over the years to feel uneasy at hearing Madalyn's words. Matilda would have said it was tempting Fate, and Ned fought the urge to cross himself. How he wished he didn't have these strange premonitions.

"There's no need to wish that. You can come here any time you wish," he promised.

"I'd like that more than anything," Madalyn said.

Pushing aside his unease, Ned pulled her into his arms. She fitted exactly beneath his chin and against his heart. Madalyn and he had been made for each other. This was meant to be.

"Madalyn," he murmured, and her name was a prayer, a wish, a blessing on his lips. "Madalyn. My Madalyn. My love."

"Yes," she said. "I am *your* Madalyn and you are *my* Ned. We are each other's. We always were and we always will be."

In answer, Ned brushed his mouth against hers, and as softly as the opening of a butterfly's wings, Madalyn kissed him back. Ned had kissed girls before, but nobody had ever consumed him this way or filled him with the longing to hold her closely and keep her safe. It was an overwhelming torrent of sensation, and he hardly knew where Madalyn began and Ned ended. He only knew that Fate had brought her back to him at long last. His beautiful, glorious Madalyn. His best friend. His soulmate. The girl Ned had loved from the moment he'd first seen her on Oyster Shore.

No matter what the summer held, nothing would keep them apart, Ned thought as, laughing and kissing, they made their way along the woodland path to rescue Madalyn's abandoned shoes and hat. They had come home to one another. And as words and new stories and imagery flowed through his imagination in a joyous torrent, Ned knew beyond all doubt that Madalyn Trelyon would be the inspiration for his greatest work, for she was the reason for every breath he would ever take.

25

MAY 1914

Vyvyan Court

Gerald

Gerald didn't look forward to his parents' dinner parties. The guests were generally dull and the conversation less than scintillating. If tonight's guests hadn't included Madalyn Trelyon he would have pleaded his leg and retired to his rooms.

But Gerald didn't want to miss tonight's gathering. He was curious and oddly nervous at the thought of seeing Madalyn again. His memories of the summer she had spent in Cornwall ten years ago were bold colours in an otherwise monotone palette, and had carried him through the grind of school and misery of all the doctor's appointments. The time when his leg didn't drag behind him belonged to a golden age, one where the world brimmed with possibilities and a little boy called Gerald could still run and climb and swim –

however poorly. That boy had been lost a long time ago, but sometimes it was a shock to see the thin countenance with neatly trimmed beard peering out from the looking-glass. Who was this smart young gentleman with the limp and the silver-topped cane? Where was the man Gerald Snowe should have become?

Ned Carew had stolen him. Ned Carew, with his lion's mane, crinkling violet eyes and no physical impairments, had killed the person Gerald should have become as surely as if Ned had physically pushed him from the tree. It was Ned who had encouraged Gerald to climb and row and swim that summer, so it stood to reason that Ned should bear the responsibility for the accident. Gerald had only taken Madalyn rowing because Ned had shown him the boat, and he had only climbed the tree to prove that he was Ned's equal. Ned had been punished for trespassing and whipped for stealing books, and St John Trelyon had come close to exercising his right to dismiss the village schoolmaster. Only Edgar Carew's good standing in Trevellan had saved him; but he'd died a few years later a broken man, or so Gerald had heard, and the family had gone into service – which was exactly where they belonged.

He'd spotted Ned amongst Vyvyan's gamekeepers, and his bold sister had been a housemaid for a while, but the bonds forged in childhood had been severed long ago and Gerald would have sooner broken his other leg than degrade himself by acknowledging their old friendships. If Ned was now tall, broad-shouldered and handsome enough to make the housemaids giggle whenever they glimpsed him, Gerald could live with this, since Ned Carew would never be a gentleman. He would certainly never be a writer now that his unrealistic dream of an academic future had been taken away from him.

Ned Carew's future lay, fittingly, in physical toil rather than in literary salons, while Gerald's was destined to be glorious and golden. The balance was restored. Libra was satisfied.

As his valet brushed the shoulders of his dinner jacket, Gerald studied his reflection in the looking-glass and admired the well-groomed young man who gazed back at him, eyes filled with superiority and the happy knowledge that he was the heir to a fortune and soon to take up a place at Balliol. It was not his lot to work the land for pennies.

"Which ones for this evening, sir?" Gerald's valet was offering him a choice of cufflinks. Picking plain gold discs, Gerald moved towards the window for them to be fastened in the daylight. While the valet straightened his cuffs and adjusted the jacket, Gerald's attention was caught by a monogrammed notebook and expensive fountain pen set out upon the writing bureau placed beneath the window in hope of capturing inspiration. Soon he would fill the blank pages with flowing prose; it was only a matter of time before he composed a story that would propel him to literary fame. If he was still rehashing Ned's stories, this was because he had yet to discover the brilliant idea that would make his name. Before long Gerald Snowe would be as celebrated in literary circles as Dickens and Austen. Then Ned Carew would know he had been bested; his dreams would be ground to dust and revealed as arrogance above his station.

Gerald still sometimes showed extracts of his work to Kit Rivers, who was still attempting to write poetry – most of which was in Gerald's opinion overcomplicated and rather worthy. Gerald, meanwhile, had yet to complete more than a few pages of his own novel and struggled for inspiration. Tonight this would change, for Gerald was certain that

Madalyn was the key to unlocking his creativity. She would be his muse.

He'd never stopped thinking about her. After his accident Gerald learned she had almost died from pneumonia and been taken away to a sanatorium. He'd wondered whether she would return to Oyster House once she was better, the sea air being the panacea for all ills, but she had been packed away to school and never returned. Years later, when Gerald was able to walk with his cane and had returned to London, he might catch sight of a slender figure with red hair, and his heart would leap – only for the illusion to dissolve when the lady in question turned around. There were also fragments of dreams that haunted Gerald when he least expected it: frightened green eyes calling to him to turn around; hair like seaweed spreading in deep water; a pale face lost beneath the waves. Sometimes he relived his fall through the air, the time it took stretched grotesquely from seconds to hours, or felt the sickening roll of a small boat carried out towards the open sea by a merciless tide. These dreams always woke him with a racing pulse, bedlinen rank with sweat and a murderous anger towards Ned Carew, whose fault all these things were.

"That'll do!" Gerald shook the valet away impatiently, wishing he could do the same with these memories, and turned back to the mirror. His appearance was perfect. Expensive dinner suit, neatly trimmed beard which hid a chin he secretly feared was weak, and the smart silver-topped cane. A pine-fresh cologne scented his handkerchief, and pomade smoothed down his dark hair. He was groomed and wealthy and, he thought, not wholly unattractive. Would Madalyn Trelyon be as beautiful as he remembered her? Or had she bloomed early, puffing up like a peony and collapsing inwards? How disappointing it would be to discover his muse was flawed. He would regret, then, agreeing to attend his parents' dinner party, and have to plead a painful hip.

Satisfied with his escape plan, Gerald made his way to the drawing room, his cane tapping its way along the draughty corridor and down each treacherous stairtread. Long-dead Trelyons eyed him from their gilded frames with the now familiar scorn, Madalyn's green eyes and bold gaze reaching out across the centuries to judge him and his family just as the great and good of south-east Cornwall would do this evening. Why Sir Arthur insisted on arranging these ordeals was anyone's guess: a rather pitiful longing to be socially accepted, Gerald supposed, which he could have told his father, knighted or not, was never going to happen. The miserable years at school had taught Gerald far more than the Classics, and even though his father's money had bought him access to the upper echelons of society he was painfully conscious of the ever-present snide comments about trade. The society of Cornwall was no different to the schoolboys who'd made his life a misery, and Gerald knew the Snowes were only tolerated because they were wealthy.

He often wondered whether his mother would ever realise their neighbours only dined with them out of good manners and because Sir Arthur kept one of the finest cellars in the county. This was much appreciated by Lord Julyan Pendennys, a notorious drunk who usually passed out by the time the cheeseboard was offered, and who was only invited because his daughter, Emily, was the sole heir to the family estate. Lady Snowe was desperate to match Gerald with a blue-blooded young woman; his money for their breeding was considered a fair exchange, and he suspected that his mother was grateful that her crippled son was still considered marriageable. For the past year she'd attempted to throw as many suitable young women into his path as possible. No doubt any of them would obligingly produce a son and heir for the Snowe Soap Empire and assure the future of the line, but Gerald couldn't have been less interested, because not one of them could hold a candle to Madalyn Trelyon. It was her or nobody, Gerald decided as he crossed the hall towards the laughter rippling from the drawing room, and she would be his, because everyone knew the Trelyons were penniless. They would bite his hand off for a marriage offer.

Madalyn aside, Gerald had to admit that Emily Pendennys had come closer to his ideal than most girls. A fearless horsewoman with curves that would tempt a saint, she was often invited to Vyvyan to hunt, but since she frequently witnessed Gerald's less than glorious escapades on the field, he found himself wrong-footed with her. She was a girl who thought nothing of leaping enormous banks and ditches while he sought desperately for an open gate; Gerald was sure he'd seen Emmy smother a smile at such times, and his heart had blackened against her. To add insult to injury she clearly preferred Kit Rivers' company, talking to him all evening at gatherings and blatantly ignoring Gerald. During last month's dinner party at Rosecraddick Manor, Gerald had seethed all the way through the pudding course. Who was the Hon Emily Pendennys to turn her nose up at him? She might be able to trace her lineage back to the Norman conquest, but everyone knew her father had gambled away the family fortune and was poised to lose the lot. She ought to be begging Gerald Snowe to notice her.

The thought of the haughty Emily tear-stained and

pleading made Gerald feel a little better. As he paused outside the drawing room to compose himself, he indulged in a delightful fantasy where he bought Pendennys Place and turned Emily out onto the street. Then she'd be sorry she'd shown him up on the hunting field and laughed at him. Nobody laughed at Gerald Snowe. Nobody.

"Gerry? What are you doing skulking outside? Come in, son!"

His father's booming voice plucked Gerald from these dark thoughts. As always he winced at the flat northern vowels, but composed his features into an expression of mild politeness as he stepped into the drawing room.

The scene was familiar; a cluster of guests dressed in their evening finery seated on chairs or standing at the polished table where servants had set out drinks which Sir Arthur, oblivious to convention, was pouring out himself for his guests, in generous measures. Colonel and Lady Rivers were chatting with an elderly couple whose names evaded Gerald; Kit was leaning on the mantelpiece, deep in conversation with his fat London friend, Rupert Elmhurst, about the tensions in Prussia; and Lady Snowe was fussing over a frail woman sitting in the window with a shawl draped over her bony shoulders. Something about the set of her head and the sharp angles of her cheekbones were familiar to Gerald. But it was the sight of the slender figure with her back to him that made his breath catch.

It was Madalyn Trelyon. She had returned at last, and even Vyvyan Court seemed to know she was in her rightful place, for the evening sun streamed through the window and bathed her in gold. How was it possible that Kit and Rupert weren't staring at her? Or his father? The Colonel? Did they not realise that they were in the presence of a goddess?

Although he couldn't see her face Gerald knew instantly that Madalyn was far more beautiful than he remembered. Her chestnut-red hair was scooped into an elaborate arrangement and pinned with hothouse flowers, and her shoulders, rising above a dress of deepest forest green, were smooth as scoops of cream. Her waist was so tiny even he could have circled it with his hands, yet the hips below swelled out in a way that was both wonderful and terrible. Gerald's mouth dried and he stood rooted to the spot, transported hopelessly back to that awkward little boy in the sailor suit who trailed behind, unsure and unwanted. He closed his eyes, loathing the old twist of nerves, but when he opened them again Mary Snowe was waving him over.

"Gerald! Darling! You must remember Lady Constance and her daughter Madalyn?"

Lady Constance, Gerald realised, was the invalid in the chair. She had been a shadowy presence back then, always confined to her room with a headache or a chill, but now she had become a wraith of a woman, as insubstantial as moonlight in comparison to the blinding sunlight of her daughter. Wait! Shouldn't he be writing this down? It was the most poetic thought Gerald could recall having, and he felt a punch of excitement. Hadn't he known that Madalyn Trelyon would be the catalyst for great things?

Gerald crossed the room to greet the new arrivals, cane tapping the Persian carpet, walking slowly to avoid a stumble. How he hated being lame. He longed to stride across the room as he sometimes saw Ned cross the stable yard, confident in his strength and power like a young god. Gerald was glad Madalyn's attention was trained on something in the garden, for he would hate her first impression of him to be of someone crippled and weak.

"Lady Constance, what a pleasure." He took the withered hand, kissing it as though she was a queen, and enquiring solicitously after her health. What she said in return Gerald couldn't tell since his attention was pulled towards Madalyn as iron filings to a magnet. Everything about Madalyn's presence threatened to overwhelm him, from the rosepetal blush in her cheeks and the floral scent she wore, to the softness of her skin when he took her hand in his, and the sparkle in those bewitching sea-green eyes. Madalyn Trelyon was a living, breathing poem, and in the sunlight of her presence every other woman was eclipsed.

"Gerald," Madalyn said. Her smile was as taut as piano wire. "I hardly recognised you without a sailor suit."

"I've grown out of that, Madalyn. It was an age ago." Gerald knew he sounded curt, but he wasn't a poet like Kit or a natural wordsmith like Ned. He was no use at flirting either – if indeed this was flirting. It felt more like a reminder of the foolish boy he had once been, trailing after Madalyn and wearing shooting gear out of season. An ugly flush mottled his neck.

Mary Snowe, always on edge around people she still referred to as gentry, laughed nervously.

"You *are* a tease, Madalyn, my dear! Gerald's quite the young gentleman nowadays. He's off to Oxford in the autumn."

Madalyn's green eyes met his. "And will you be rowing for your college?"

The barb hit home and he flushed.

"Gerald can't row, Madalyn dear. Not since his terrible accident," Mary Snowe said, a small frown creasing her brow as she looked from Gerald to Madalyn.

"Oh yes, silly me." Madalyn pressed her fingers to her

temples. "The memory's a little hazy. Still, I believe I was quite unwell after catching cold that day. I was sorry to hear you were so badly hurt, Gerald."

Mary Snowe was delighted by this evidence of Madalyn's regard for her son. "Why, he's quite better now, Madalyn. You must take a turn around the garden with him after dinner."

"Indeed," Madalyn said slowly, her unblinking gaze still holding his. "We have a great deal to catch up on."

Gerald knew Madalyn was telling him that she remembered the accident and thought it had been his own fault. Although a decade might have passed, her allegiance still lay with Ned. Anger surged through him, the perfect antidote to fear, and Gerald remined himself that he was the heir to a fortune and the son of one of the most powerful men in the county whereas Madalyn was a penniless young woman with an ailing mother. She was *nothing*, and if she was wise she would soon reconsider where best to place her loyalty.

"Enough of the old chin-wagging," Sir Arthur boomed, offering his arm to Lady Constance. "Let's go through to the dining room. Gerald, you'll bring Miss Trelyon. You two must have a lot to catch up on."

Gerald nodded and Madalyn placed her gloved hand in the crook of his arm as he escorted her into the dining room. She said nothing more and played her part beautifully, allowing him to settle her in her chair before the footmen spread napkins and set out drinks. Gerald was seated beside her and as the dinner progressed he made sure Madalyn's wine glass was constantly topped up. She ate little, pushing food about her plate and staring dreamily into her glass with a secret smile playing on her full lips. He wondered what she was thinking about. Was it another man?

Was it Ned Carew?

This thought made his stomach curdle, and suddenly he felt unable to face the rich dishes and sauces. Surely not? The Trelyon party had only arrived that morning – his father's chauffeur had collected them from Plymouth – and Madalyn wouldn't have had a chance to see Ned yet. Besides, Carew was a servant now, and Madalyn, so beautiful in her silks and pearls, was every inch a lady. She understood how the world worked and that she needed to marry well. She wouldn't be so foolish as to squander herself on a lowly groundsman.

No, Gerald decided as he gulped back his wine and set the glass down with a thud, she was probably tired from her journey and thinking about whatever it was women thought about, for who knew what mysteries went on inside their heads? He pushed his anger down deep and talked to her about London and mutual acquaintances. Now and then he caught a glimpse of their reflections in the large mirror above the mahogany sideboard and thought what a handsome couple they would make. With a woman as beautiful as Madalyn as his wife, who would dare to sneer at Gerald Snowe or cast pitying looks at his injured leg? He would be the envy of every man, and she would do well to land him. His mother's measured smiles from the far end of the table suggested that her thoughts were travelling along similar lines.

The dinner progressed slowly. Madalyn turned to Kit's friend, a plump young man who was apparently a brilliant legal mind, and they made small talk about the local area. Bored, Gerald held up his glass for a footman to refill while tuning into the conversation taking place between Colonel Rivers and his own father.

"Mark my words, war's coming," the Colonel said, sounding delighted at the prospect. "It's inevitable. The

Germans are overweening and their assurances utterly worthless. We need to protect the integrity of our great nation and take them down a peg or two. By George, if I were younger I'd be the first to show them."

"Hear, hear," said Arthur Snowe. "We can't have our hand forced by the Krauts. A short, sharp lesson is what they need, and who better to teach it to them than us?"

"I shot a few Boers in my day. I'm sure I can shoot a few Huns," slurred Julyan Pendennys.

"I'll help you," said Arthur. "I have a well-stocked gun room."

Gerald was amused by this. His father had no military experience whatsoever, and if there was a war, he and Colonel Rivers were far too old to be anywhere near a battlefield.

Kit Rivers' blond head had snapped up at the mention of war. His expression was troubled.

"Let's hope it won't come to that, Father, and that Mr Asquith can accept their assurances of peace," he said gently. "War benefits nobody except maybe a few politicians and the manufacturers of weapons."

"Nonsense," barked the Colonel, moustache bristling. "Utter nonsense! It's what you youngsters need to buck you up. Nothing like a bit of action on the battlefield to make a man of a boy. When war comes – and believe me it *will* come – I'll be expecting you to represent the Rivers family and make us proud."

"He'll be at Oxford, my dear," ventured Lady Rivers, but her husband snorted.

"There's no hiding behind books in the Rivers' family. Real men fight for their country."

"They do indeed," agreed Arthur. "Unless they're unable

to, of course, like my boy. His leg, you see. Damn shame he'd miss the show, but it can't be helped."

Gerald wanted the floor to swallow him whole. Even Madalyn shot him a sympathetic look.

"I'm perfectly capable of fighting," he said tightly. Gerald didn't know whether this was true or even if he would want to fight if this hypothetical war did occur – but he did know he couldn't bear to be considered less than the other young men at the table.

"Real men follow their conscience, Papa," Kit said quietly. "I believe true courage comes from heeding what that tells you. Any fool can follow orders blindly."

There was a lull in the conversation. Everyone's attention was trained on Kit, who coloured. Lady Rivers looked stricken, and even the Colonel was lost for words. Gerald couldn't help admiring Kit. Colonel Rivers was a notoriously violent man who probably wouldn't be averse to strapping his son, no matter how old. Kit's poetry might be drippy, but he had guts.

Kit's London friend, Rupert, reached across the table for a bread roll. "Lord, I hope they don't want *me* to enlist," he drawled, breaking the roll in two and slathering each half with butter. "Apart from the fact I'm far too fat to dazzle the ladies in my uniform, no matter how much they say girls love a soldier, my eyesight's shocking. I'd probably shoot the wrong side or something."

His self-deprecating comment shattered the awkward atmosphere, and relieved laughter rippled through the dining room. The moment passed but Gerald noticed that Kit stayed silent for the remainder of the meal, deep in thought and oblivious to the ugly glances his father threw at him. Happily, the talk of war was replaced by a discussion of the latest local gossip, and before long the plates were being cleared and the ladies were rising to adjourn to the drawing room. Madalyn was with them and Gerald's heart lurched. He couldn't allow her to leave before he'd had a chance to speak to her.

He rose to his feet, bowing to his companions. "Excuse me, gentlemen. I need to get some fresh air."

He reached for his cane and made his way through the dining room and into the hall where a swirl of green skirts swished towards the drawing room. Gerald increased his pace to a speed that would have astounded his physicians.

"Madalyn."

Madalyn pressed the heel of her hand against her breastbone. "You made me jump." She carried on, into the drawing room.

"Will you take that turn in the garden?" he asked, following her.

She shook her head. "I'm helping Mama to get comfortable."

Lady Constance flapped a languid hand. "I'll be fine, Madalyn. Go and enjoy some fresh air with Gerald."

"You're exhausted, Mama. I need to make sure you have some tea and maybe a little of your headache tincture. Perhaps we should ring for the trap and return to Oyster House?"

"Stop fussing, Madalyn. I'm perfectly fine," snapped Constance.

"I've rung for tea and a cool lavender cloth, my dear," added Mary Snowe. "I'll take very good care of your mother. You two young people enjoy the fresh air. The roses have just bloomed. You should show Madalyn, Gerald. They're exquisite."

"Of course Mama, although they can't possibly compete with her beauty," he said gallantly.

The two mothers exchanged a conspiratorial look and Gerald smothered a smile. He was right: they'd already decided he and Madalyn were a good match, which was half the battle. The rest he could take care of.

He offered Madalyn his arm and, defeated for the time being, she walked with him into the twilit garden, where lamplight trickled onto the terrace and the first stars speckled the sky. They strolled silently past the dining room, where the remaining menfolk were wreathed in smoke, and descended the rough steps to the lower lawn. Beyond the box hedges and parterre, darkness smoked from the woods and the faint glint of silver betrayed the whereabouts of the evening river. The night air was sweet with the scent of mown grass, and above the gables of Vyvyan bats flickered through the shadows.

Madalyn's skirts sighed across the grass. The closeness of her body and touch of her hand on his arm was all he could think about. Gerald thought he wanted her more than he'd ever wanted anything. She was utter perfection.

When they were far enough through the rose garden to melt into the dusk and vanish from prying eyes, he halted. "Madalyn. I need to speak to you."

"You're not about to offer to take me rowing, are you?" she said. "If so, the answer's no."

Leaning on his cane, Gerald gazed down into her face, which was as pale and lovely in the blooming dusk as the moon rising above Oyster Shore. Madalyn Trelyon was so beautiful she took his breath away. What did it matter that she was penniless or had once preferred the company of a common village boy? He deserved a beautiful wife, and he wanted her. Gerald knew she was poor, and he was confident money would win her hand even if her heart lay elsewhere.

"I want you to marry me," he said.

Gerald hadn't expected to speak these words so soon, but they tumbled from his lips of their own volition.

"Don't be ridiculous!" Madalyn laughed.

Her mirth was like a slap. Didn't she realise what he was offering her? How fortunate she was?

"What's so funny?" he said, wounded to the quick.

"You," she said, shaking her head. "Apart from not wearing a sailor suit you haven't changed at all, have you, Gerry? It's always about what *you* want. Never mind anyone else."

"I'm serious, Madalyn. Marry me."

He reached for her hand, but Madalyn took a step backwards. She was still laughing. "You'll be telling me you can row next! Lord, if you try to climb a tree I'll be really alarmed! What's the matter with you, Gerald? Have you consumed a little too much wine?"

"Forgive me if it seems forward, but I'm proposing marriage," he said with exaggerated courtesy. "You should be pleased. It's what everyone wants."

Madalyn's mirth drained away. The breasts beneath her green bodice rose and fell as her breathing quickened. "Pleased? I'm utterly confused. Why would you think I'd agree to marry you? We don't even know one another."

Gerald had forgotten how difficult Madalyn could be. He bit back his rising impatience.

"We've known one another since we were children, but that's by the by," he said. "You need to marry money, that's no secret, and I'm wealthy. I can look after you and your mother, settle all the debts and keep you both in comfort. That's why you should marry me. It makes perfect sense."

He stepped towards Madalyn, thinking to hold her in his arms, but his cane was in the way. By the time he had untangled it and tucked the damn thing under his arm, Madalyn had edged further back until she was almost in the flower bed and the roses were snagging on the silk of her skirts.

"It doesn't make any sense because I don't love you," she said. "And I know you don't love me."

Gerald swallowed rising irritation. Love? What did that have to do with anything? Women had some funny ideas.

"Love often follows marriage," he said sagely, and as he spoke he thought he might even believe this. Madalyn was so beautiful, and no girl he'd ever met since could hold a torch to her. He wanted her to be his. He wanted to keep her away from the eyes of all others. He wanted to possess her. That was love, surely? "And I do love you. We were friends once, weren't we?"

Madalyn's gaze was fixed on the darkening line of the trees which hemmed the valley and shielded Oyster Shore. "That's not how I remember it, Gerald. You were unkind. You pinched me when Kit took the photograph, and you nearly drowned me."

"I'm sorry about that. I was a silly schoolboy," he said. "I was trying to get your attention the only way I knew how. I was quite revolting, I imagine."

"You were unkind," she said. "Ned was never unkind. Not even when you deserved it. You let him take the blame for your fall, Gerald. Why did you do that?"

Gerald's grasp tightened on his cane as he fought to keep his temper. Damn Ned to hell. Would it always be *him*? A servant. A nobody.

"I was a child, Madalyn, and I was unconscious for days. I don't even remember the accident." This was an utter fib, but nobody could prove it and Gerald pressed on. "I nearly died after that accident. I live with the legacy of it every day."

"So does Ned," she countered. "It haunts him too."

Gerald's eyes narrowed. She *had* seen Carew.

"You've spoken to him?"

"He works on the shore for St John. He tends the grounds and keeps the drive clear."

Gerald was relieved to know she hadn't sought Ned out and that he was a servant there these days. It was good that Madalyn had seen Ned reduced to chopping wood and scything.

"That's all in the past. I have no grudges against Carew," he lied, "but I also know now that it wasn't an appropriate friendship. Children don't always understand these things, do they?"

Madalyn looked as though she wanted to argue but something clearly held her back. Probably knowing he was right.

"On the other hand an engagement between you and me would be fitting," he continued when she remained silent. "There's no point in being coy, Madalyn. We both understand how the world works. Think how delighted your mother would be to see you as mistress at Vyvyan."

"We don't even *know* each other," she said.

"Of course we do. We grew up together."

"We spent one summer together, and the last time I saw you I almost drowned."

"That wasn't my fault."

"So it was mine?"

Gerald opened his mouth to say that this was Ned's fault, but it was time to pick his battles if he was to win the war.

Hadn't Chaucer written something about women wanting nothing more than their own way? Gerald seemed to recall as much, anyway.

"You're right, it was my fault and I'm sorry," he said, hanging his head. "I was just a boy and I wanted to impress you. I suppose I still do, because inside I'm just that little boy who couldn't row or climb or keep up. I could never keep up with you, Madalyn, because you're as far above me as the stars – but I swear that if you marry me you'll want for nothing. Neither will your mother. I promise. All her troubles will be over."

He waited for Madalyn to protest, but she didn't. So her mother was her weakness. That was useful to know. It was time to press his advantage.

"Wasn't marrying well what you always said you'd need to do? You once said it was your duty."

She nodded reluctantly. "Yes. I did say that."

"So let me help you. It's what our families want and the perfect solution. Why, I imagine our mamas are plotting the very same thing at this very moment. We could make everyone very happy."

He thought she was about to accept, but a shadow flitted across her face. "I'm sorry, Gerald, but my answer's still no."

Christ, but she was stubborn. Gerald fought to hide his irritation. "At least consider my offer. I know I was a little beast when you last knew me, but I'm not that boy any more. And I swear I have never, ever kicked a dog since."

He was hoping this would raise a smile, but Madalyn's face was stony. "I'm not going to change my mind. Please don't ask me again, Gerry."

She was rejecting him? Madalyn, who was penniless and

ought to have been on her knees in gratitude? It made no sense.

"Is there someone else?"

She turned away, the roses clawing her skirts as though trying to hold her back, and he heard the fabric tear as she snatched it from the thorns.

"I'm cold. I'm going back inside."

"I said, is there someone else?"

"I don't answer to you!" Madalyn stepped away so abruptly that she staggered backwards into the rose bed. "This conversation is over. I never want to talk about this again."

Beads of blood, dark against her pale arms, traced where the thorns had caught her tender skin, but she didn't appear to notice. She was too busy ripping her skirt away from the roses before retreating to the house, back straight and head held high.

Gerald didn't follow. She hadn't answered his question – which was, Gerald decided, all the reply he needed to tell him her heart was elsewhere. He pulled his cigarette case from his dinner jacket pocket and lit up, drawing smoke deep into his lungs along with his suspicions.

Was Madalyn still sweet on Ned Carew? Surely not. Ned was a servant. A nobody. His dreams of studying were in ashes, and he was as likely to fly to the moon as he was to write a literary masterpiece. Carew wouldn't dare aim so high as a Trelyon, especially since for Madalyn an association with him would demean her and condemn her to poverty and shame. Nobody else could offer her what Gerald could, and eventually she would realise this. Until then it was just a matter of patience. His opportunity would come.

"You will marry me, Madalyn," he said quietly, "because if

I can't have you then I swear no one will. And certainly not Ned Carew."

The evening breeze shivered in the trees and carried his smoke-laced vow over the woods and down to Oyster Shore where Ned Carew, unaware of the drama unfolding only a mile away, sat in an old leather chair as his pen flew across the first page of a brand-new notebook.

"It all ended as it began, on Oyster Shore ..."

26

JUNE 1914

Oyster Shore

Madalyn

"Don't move! I'm still drawing."

Madalyn's pencil darted across the page. Her eyes flickered from the subject, reclining against the pillows with his sun-toasted arms a golden contrast to the white bed sheets she had kicked off just minutes earlier, before returning to her drawing. Oh! But this was perfect, just perfect. The light fell in exactly the right way so that his long lashes feathered his cheeks and shadows carved out the planes of his beautiful face. The cloth draped across his legs moulded to the muscle and sinews that lay beneath in a testament to the wonder of his strong body, and hinted at potency and masculine power. She needed to work fast before the light shifted or Ned had had enough and pulled her back into bed, but if she could capture this moment with her pencil Madalyn knew that something wonderful from this glorious, golden summer would remain caught for ever.

"Your tongue's poking out again," Ned said. "Do you think Michelangelo stuck his tongue out when he was carving David?"

"Michelangelo never had such a fidget for a life model," Madalyn retorted, her pencil cross-hatching the dip of his hipbone and the shadow of the lean flank beneath. He was so perfect it made her breath catch. The artist in Madalyn, rather than the woman who loved Ned Carew so much, thought Michelangelo would have killed to draw such a subject.

"Or maybe he did?" Ned was wondering as he stretched and yawned. "And that's why poor David is rather *lacking*? The artist had his revenge in the end!"

"If you don't keep still I'll do the same to you," she threatened, pointing her pencil at him. "And then, when I'm a famous artist and this sketch is hanging in the Louvre, you'll wish you'd kept still for just five minutes!"

Ned laughed. "Why do you think I'm keeping the covers up to my waist? I know how cruel artists can be. Look at you, sitting all the way over there and too far away from me. Come back here!"

Madalyn was sorely tempted. She was sure her love and longing for Ned Carew must flow through her pencil and pool onto the page in a flood of desire, and anyone who looked at her work would surely know the artist had adored this man. Had worshipped him. Lived for him. Even as she sketched, Madalyn fought the yearning to toss her work aside and curl up beside Ned, tracing the cords and sinews of his golden body with her lips and fingertips and threading her fingers into his thick hair as his arms closed around her and his mouth sought hers.

She and Ned had discovered heaven this summer, and the old brass bed under the boathouse eaves had become their very own paradise. It was where they honoured the promises made that May afternoon when she had come up out of the soft sand to discover Ned Carew waiting for her on Oyster Shore, and it was where they found a happiness that neither had ever imagined possible. Ned was everything to her. He was her life, and now she had found him once more Madalyn could no more imagine being parted from him than she could envisage not breathing.

Following Gerald's shocking proposal, Madalyn had been afraid to seek Ned out again for fear of bringing trouble to his door. She knew of old how vindictive Gerald could be, and how he hated losing something he considered his. Of course she never had been his, and never would be – but they were no longer children, and if Gerald suspected her feelings for Ned the consequences could be catastrophic. She hoped Gerald's bizarre proposal had sprung from an excess of alcohol rather than a sincere design. He hadn't mentioned it since, but there were more social gatherings at Vyvyan Court on the horizon and Madalyn feared he was merely biding his time. Her mother certainly seemed full of optimism and had developed a habit of taking tea with Lady Snowe most afternoons. Madalyn suspected they were plotting a match and the thought filled her with dread.

She would rather drown herself in the river than marry Gerald, Madalyn vowed. There was something about him that unnerved her. He possessed the same air of watchfulness she had noticed as a child, and although he was courteous to her and perfectly gentlemanly, his presence made her uneasy.

When he sent her orchids from Vyvyan's hothouse the cloying scent sickened her, and his visits to Oyster House, on the pretext of enquiring after Lady Constance's health, were filled with awkward silences. While Madalyn poured tea and acted the part of perfect hostess, she replayed Ned's kiss over and over again and dreamed of how life could be if she was free to follow her heart.

"What's the matter with you, Madalyn?" her mother said in exasperation, picking up a bouquet of lilies, another gift from Gerald which Madalyn had abandoned on the veranda, the smell reminding her of death. "Have you no idea what an alliance with the Snowe family could do for us? It's everything we could wish for and the answer to all our problems." She passed the flowers to Tilly with a pained expression. "Put these in water and display them on the mantelpiece in the morning room. Mr Snowe will want to see that we appreciate his kindness."

But Madalyn wasn't appreciative, not in the slightest, and no matter how many hints her mother dropped about marriage she was determined to avoid Gerald at all costs. Maybe, she found herself thinking one morning as she walked along the river – not in the direction of the boathouse, since she would quite dissolve with longing and loss – maybe she could hurl herself into the river and catch pneumonia again? By the time she was recovered Gerald would have left for Oxford and she would be safe from his unwelcome attentions and the machinations of their families. This was a rather dramatic plan, but sometimes Madalyn felt like one of the butterflies pinned in the glass cases that lined Vyvyan's corridors; trapped, skewered, admired and lifeless. She was a thing. A commodity. A prize. Did nobody care what she wanted? Did nobody care about *her*?

Ned cared, but he was as out of reach as the boats that sailed over the horizon. His love for her would only bring him unhappiness, and Madalyn would rather break her own heart a thousand times over than cause him any pain. She knew Ned would have been waiting for her to return, and she hated to think he might believe she'd abandoned him. Several times she started to pen a note pouring out her heart, but whom could she trust to carry it to the boathouse? Tilly was loyal to Constance, and the other servants would be in dreadful trouble if they were caught. Maybe it was best Ned believed that their kiss and heartfelt words had meant nothing to her and that she'd chosen to turn her back on him. That way would be safest for him.

She had glimpsed Ned fleetingly in church, but their eyes met only briefly as she passed him on leaving the church after the service. Madalyn had read a thousand messages in their violet depths. Sadness and confusion and love were written there, and it had taken all of her willpower to stare unblinkingly ahead as she walked through the nave and into the churchyard. Gerald walked several steps behind with his parents and his gaze burned into her back while Madalyn clutched her prayer book. Her only petition to the Almighty was that she didn't betray her true feelings. *Keep Ned safe*, she prayed as the Snowes' chauffeur helped her into the car, *keep Gerald away from him*.

Knowing that Ned was only minutes away along the tree-fringed path from Oyster House was torture. Every morning Madalyn rose and walked onto the lawn to watch the river flow by, and felt envious it had reached the boathouse and been so close to him. Once, as dawn's rosy smile spread over the world, she saw him row past, and the longing to throw open the window and call his name was so strong she had to clamp her hands over her mouth until the boat and Ned were lost from view. Madalyn had wept, silent tears that trickled down her cheeks and dripped through her fingers. Then she had forced herself to take a deep breath, wash her face, and join Constance for breakfast. But Madalyn hadn't been able to eat a mouthful, and she looked so dreadful that when she pleaded a headache Constance didn't argue. Left in peace to dream of Ned while her mama visited Rosecraddick Manor, Madalyn drew her beloved's face over and over again in her sketchbook, and wept until she really did have a headache.

In direct contrast to Madalyn's state of mind, June 1914 was sunny and bright, the sky a perfect powder-blue and the verdant Cornish banks and hedgerows overflowing with foxgloves and daisies. Numb with misery, Madalyn hardly registered the beauty as she looked after her mother and attended endless luncheons and garden parties. Each engagement seemed to blend into another; the men were all full of the talk of war and, from what Madalyn could glean from listening in, the tensions in Europe were increasing daily. Troops were mobilising on the Continent, and the Kaiser was apparently not to be trusted, but in their little corner of Cornwall life continued in a genteel round of social engagements and sunny afternoons spent taking tea on the terrace of Oyster House. All threats of war seemed little more than a story from another world.

A FORTNIGHT after their return the Trelyon women had been invited to a luncheon party given by the Rivers at Rosecraddick Manor. Lady Constance had talked of little else for days but Madalyn couldn't think of anything worse. Trussed up in her white lace gown and with a hat skewered onto her curls, she was already wilting. Her stays were so tight she could hardly breathe, and her head was pounding.

"Mama, I need to lie down," she said, and Constance, laying her hand against her daughter's brow, hadn't argued.

"You're very hot, dearest. I do hope you haven't caught a chill sitting out in the evenings. The cool air can be dangerous."

Madalyn had taken to watching the red sun sink behind the trees as night fell. She knew Ned would be watching the sunset too, his pen capturing the scene with language just as her paintbrush would with colour. She felt closer to him when the sky was streaked pink and peach and the sun set to rise again, for there was a sense of hope that a new day would dawn, one filled with possibilities and where she might catch a glimpse of him once more.

"Maybe you should stay here, and I should stay with you?" Constance continued, frowning. "You do look rather pale."

Madalyn, longing for a few hours alone with her sketchbook in the shade, thought swiftly.

"It's nothing to worry about, Mama, but a little rest will help. I'll be better for church tomorrow."

In a hurry to depart, Constance agreed Madalyn could stay behind, and instructed Tilly to bring up some mint tea. Her mother safely gone for the afternoon, Madalyn lay on her bed, watching the curtains blowing in the breeze and listening to Tilly giggling downstairs with Timmy, the clumsy but well-meaning manservant. The two were walking out, and Madalyn burned with envy because her maid's romance was so uncomplicated. Why couldn't she be free to choose like Tilly? To be with the man she loved? Why was she a prisoner here? Why was she to be punished for her father's lack of financial acumen and by the entail? None of these things were of her doing. It was so unfair!

And it was at that moment Madalyn knew she'd had enough. The bedroom door wasn't locked. Nobody was watching her. She was at liberty to pick up her sketchbook, step outside and wander wherever she chose. If her walk just so happened to take her past the boathouse then so be it. She was tired of obeying everyone else's rules. Whatever had happened to the little girl who climbed trees and swam in the river? The girl who had challenged Gerald, tried to learn to swim, and tossed an heirloom into the water? How bitterly disappointed that little girl would be with the cowed and obedient creature she'd grown into.

She was done with being the dutiful daughter. She was done with being unhappy. The only chains binding her were those in her mind, and Madalyn was free to be with Ned if this was what she chose. Nobody could stop her – unless she allowed them to.

As though in a dream, Madalyn slipped away from Oyster House and melted into the woods, her feet seeming to barely touch the ground as she hurried along the path. It felt as if she was watching another girl run through the woods, red hair flying and white skirts bunched into her hands, and no more than an observer as that girl leapt up the boathouse steps and flung open the door, startling the young man seated by the window.

"I'm sorry, Ned," Madalyn sobbed. "I'm so sorry."

Ned didn't move. He appeared almost afraid, and Madalyn understood at that moment just how much he had suffered too, for their kiss had meant everything to him too. He had laid his soul open only for her to vanish, and she had shattered his heart. The thought of this was enough to break hers all over again.

"Why didn't you come back?" Ned said.

She hung her head. "I was too afraid."

"Afraid? Of me?" Ned sounded horrified. "Because I kissed you? Did I frighten you? My God, Maddy! I wouldn't hurt you."

"No! Never of you! Never!"

She ran to him then, throwing her arms around his neck and pressing kisses onto the crown of his head. He smelt so wonderful, of salt and warm earth and his own delicious scent, that she began to cry with the sheer joy of being close to him again. Her person. Her heart. Her *everything.*

Ned's arms closed around her. He pulled her onto his lap, rocking her tenderly and murmuring words of love, until the torrent of weeping slowed. He reached into his pocket and tugged out a hanky. "It's clean, I promise. Marrick's mother still takes good care of me."

Madalyn laughed through her tears and blotted her eyes with the soft cotton. "Thank you."

"My pleasure," Ned replied, and then shook his head. "Not that seeing you cry is a pleasure. Quite the opposite; it breaks my heart. But what were you were frightened of, Maddy? Was I too forward?"

Madalyn knew there was only one way to convince him that his fears were groundless. She raised her hand to his cheek, brushing golden stubble with her fingertips and kissed him, a kiss that would tell him all he needed to know about her feelings. As Ned kissed her back, tentatively at first and then with growing urgency, all the misery of the past weeks vanished, and Madalyn wondered how she had ever managed to stay parted from him.

Ned brushed the damp curls from her face and kissed away the tears from her eyelids and her cheeks. "Can you tell me what it was that upset you?" he asked. "I never want us to have any secrets, Maddy, and I promise that nothing you say or do will ever change how I feel, because I love you. I love you so much."

"I love you too," she sobbed. "That's why I stayed away. I was afraid of getting you into trouble. Of letting Mama down. Afraid of how I felt. But I was *never* afraid of you! I missed you so much I thought I'd die. Oh Ned. It's been unbearable. I can't be without you. I *can't*!"

And the words were tumbling out and she was telling him everything. Ned listened without interrupting, although when she described Gerald's proposal a muscle clenched in his cheek. By the time she had talked herself to a standstill he knew her deepest fears and most secret hopes. He knew everything.

"You can't marry Gerald just because your mother wants you to," Ned said carefully. "Marriage is about so much more than duty. You must live your life in a way that's true to your heart. You'll die inside if not. You'll be just a shell."

It sounded so simple when he put it like this.

"But Mama *needs* me to marry well, Ned. I've always known that. Gerald's the answer to all her prayers."

"But is he the answer to *yours*?"

"Of course not!" Madalyn cried. She was outraged Ned would even need to ask. "He frightens me, and he could really make life hard for you."

"Gerry can't harm either of us," Ned said firmly, his arms tightening around her. "He's jealous and he's resentful, but he can't hurt me or force you to marry him. There's nothing to be afraid of. He can't do anything."

But Madalyn wasn't so certain this was true. "He could tell St John to dismiss you."

Ned shrugged. "He could, and then what? All his power would be lost. Far better to let me sweat. That's what Gerry enjoys, the poor bugger! Besides, if you were to marry me I'd need to offer you more than a shack by the river, so he'd be doing me a favour by forcing me out."

Madalyn's heart skipped a beat. Was this a hypothetical proposal? Unlike her last proposal, this time she longed to hear the words again. Her answer would be a resounding yes!

"But what would you do without this job?"

Ned kissed the tip of her nose. "Do you even need to ask? I'm going to finish my novel. I'm already several chapters in, and it's the best thing I've ever written. It really is, Madalyn! It has that special magic, I can tell, and it's going to make our fortune. Do you know why?"

She laughed, swept away by his excitement and conviction. "No! Why?"

"Because I'm writing it for you! It's *your* novel, Maddy, and it's our story. Every word I write is there because of how I feel for you. You're my muse. You're my everything!"

Her heart rose like a hot air balloon, and the world seemed full of hope. When Madalyn was with Ned everything felt possible.

"In the meantime, and until I make our fortune, we could elope," Ned continued, kissing her throat, the hollow of her collarbone and the soft skin above her bodice until she was melting for him. "I have an uncle in Australia. We could go to him. Or how about America? That's a world of opportunity. Or the stars? Wherever you want to go!"

Madalyn kissed him. "I'll go anywhere with you!"

"We'll be poor," Ned warned once their kisses paused.

"Writers are notorious for living in garrets and having no money."

"Artists also need to suffer to be great," she pointed out. "Maybe we should elope to Paris and find that garret. I can paint and you can write."

"And we can eat crepes, walk by the Seine and drink coffee beneath the Eiffel Tower," Ned declared. "I can teach English when I'm not writing, and be a schoolmaster like my father. What a life we shall lead, Maddy! Won't it be marvellous?"

He was on his feet and she was in his arms being twirled around and around as they laughed and shared their dreams. They would be together from now on. Nothing could come between them again. Ned swung Madalyn into his arms and carried her up the narrow stairs into the bedroom below the eaves. As he laid her down on the old brass bed, she smiled up at him, marvelling that such strength could be found alongside tenderness and beauty. She wanted nothing more than to hold Ned as close as anyone ever could and love him until there were no more sunsets and the stars were all burnt out. She never wanted to let him go. She never wanted to be without Ned Carew again.

They spent the rest of that afternoon beneath the eaves, holding and loving each other, lost in a world of sensation and wonder where words no longer existed and a whole new language was spoken. As she trembled and the world span, Ned wrapped Madalyn up tenderly in his eiderdown while he brewed tea which only went cold while they made love again. Eventually, exhausted from passion and happiness, Madalyn must have dozed for a while and when she opened her eyes again, Ned was propped up on one elbow and looking down.

"What did I do to deserve all my dreams coming true?" he whispered, curling a lock of her hair around his finger and pressing it to his lips. "How did I ever live without you? I love you so much, Maddy. I love you with everything that I am, and I always will."

There were no words that could express the tidal surge of love she felt for him then, so Madalyn kissed Ned and let her body speak instead. Only the lengthening shadows and realisation that evening was approaching had stopped them from losing themselves once more. Although parting was excruciating, when Ned kissed her goodbye at the end of the path this time Madalyn knew their separation was only temporary: Ned Carew was her other half, the keeper of her heart, and nothing could keep them apart.

After this Madalyn and Ned snatched time together as often as they could, which was difficult since he was usually working and she was increasingly busy with social gatherings at Vyvyan Court and Rosecraddick Manor. These occasions were still torturous to her, but with the wonderful secret of her love for Ned tucked deep in her heart, Madalyn could endure each long minute with grace, even managing to be civil to Gerald when she couldn't avoid crossing his path. Gerald hadn't mentioned marriage again, but he often engineered a seat beside her at dinner, and Madalyn suspected her mother was still busy plotting. Well, let Constance Trelyon and Mary Snowe plot! Madalyn and Ned were making their own plans for the future, and as soon as the summer was over they would marry and begin the rest of their lives. Ned was certain that Reverend Tullis would look kindly upon them, for Matilda's sake if nothing else, and confident that everything would work out. He would find work as a schoolmaster and find a publisher for his book. Their future would be glorious.

"Just imagine, Maddy," he would say, gesturing at his leather-bound notebook, half the pages now covered with his beautiful looping script. "This book could make our fortune."

"It *will* make our fortune," she'd say, never doubting Ned's talent. Gerald, who still styled himself as an author yet seemed to do little actual writing, would seethe if he knew how truly gifted Ned was. The little she had seen of the book was beautiful.

As June stretched her hand out to July, Ned and Madalyn continued to glean as many precious hours together as possible. When Constance slept in the afternoons Madalyn would slip away to the boathouse. They picnicked in the woods, and sometimes Ned rowed them out into the middle of the river, where they lay back on blankets and watched the clouds race overhead. The best times of all were when they hid away beneath the eaves and lost themselves in lovemaking. Afterwards, when Madalyn lay in his arms, Ned would share parts of his book and hold her close to his heart as he read. His imagery transported Madalyn to a world she knew so well, a world where the tides turned, long-legged sea birds picked their way down the shell line and lovers yearned to be together. His prose was so beautiful it hurt, and Madalyn often turned her face away so that he couldn't see the tears in her eyes. How would the story end for his lovers? With happiness? Marriage? Or with a parting? Sometimes she feared his book was prophetic and that the ending he chose would seal the fate of them both.

Ned wasn't the only one inspired to capture the golden days, for Madalyn had soon found she was sketching more than ever before as her love for Ned opened the floodgates of creativity. She knew her own work was flourishing and maturing, and this excited her hugely. She collected shells and sea glass for still life work, and she still sketched the oystercatchers and terns endlessly, but most of all she loved to draw Ned. Or at least she did when he stayed still or wasn't carrying her back to bed.

"I'm warning you, Madalyn Trelyon! I'm not sure I can keep away from you a second longer. Put your pencil down right now – I'm coming to get you!"

Ned kicked the sheet away and leapt from the bed, striding naked across the attic bedroom to the window seat where she was perched with her sketchbook, and all thoughts of art were soon forgotten. When he lifted her into his arms all Madalyn's fears were no more than half-remembered nightmares, for once Ned's novel was finished and this summer was over, they would be married. Nobody would keep them apart once God had joined them, and their life together would truly begin

She could hardly wait.

27

JULY 1914

Oyster Shore

Ned

"I'm just going to come out with it," Marrick said over his pint glass. "I want to marry Bess."

Ned spluttered into his drink. Warm liquid sloshed onto the bar, and Tamsyn, who always hovered nearby whenever he drank in the Trelyon Arms, mopped the spill up, and slanted her blue eyes at him invitingly.

Oblivious to her charms, Ned stared at Marrick. "What?"

"I said, Bess and I want to be married. I'm asking for your blessing because you're her brother and the head of the family."

Ned wondered if this was some kind of joke. In a moment Marrick would bellow with laughter, slap him on the back and gloat that Ned had fallen for it. He waited, but his best friend wasn't laughing.

"Do I have it?" Marrick demanded. "We can have the banns read over the next few Sundays and be married soon after. Reverend Tullis will do that much for his stepdaughter."

Ned didn't think he'd ever known Marrick so serious. His arms were folded over the coarse blue fabric of his fisherman's smock, his eyes were filled with sincerity and even his blond curls, crushed beneath a woollen hat, were subdued.

"You've only been courting five minutes," Ned pointed out. He'd been surprised when Bess had announced she was walking out with Marrick and, knowing how his friend liked to play the field, a little concerned. He'd tried to warn his sister but Bess had snorted at him.

"He's lucky to have me," she'd said. "I'm the vicar's stepdaughter these days, remember? I could aim much higher than a fisherman. If Marrick Penwurthy knows what's good for him he won't look at another girl as long as he lives!"

Ned had almost felt sorry for Marrick. Bess was a determined girl and her fiery temper was famous in Trevellan. His friend's days of carefree womanising would be well and truly over if he courted her, but to the surprise of most villagers the new relationship had blossomed. Marrick had been far less in evidence in the pub, and Ned hadn't heard any reports of less than gentlemanly behaviour. His friend had been at sea continually, working hard to put money aside in order to buy his own lugger.

"We've been walking out for nine weeks," Marrick said patiently. "That's long enough to know I love Bess and want her to be my wife. Who puts a time scale on love? You're a writer, so surely you know that?"

Ned couldn't argue with that. But, "You haven't mentioned marriage before," he said.

Marrick shot him a sharp look. "I've not seen much of you lately to mention anything, have I?"

Disapproval laced his words. Marrick knew about Ned's relationship with Madalyn. It would have been impossible for Ned to hide it from him when the two friends had been in the habit of drinking beer on the pontoon most evenings and fishing together, so it would have been simply a matter of time before Marrick had arrived when Madalyn was at the boathouse. He was sworn to secrecy, and Ned trusted him with his life, but Marrick, deeply suspicious of Madalyn, hadn't held back from making his feelings known.

"She'll change her mind," he'd warned. "Girls like her don't marry lads like us. She's playing with you before she marries some toff like Gerry. She's born to marry money, that one."

"Not Madalyn!" Ned insisted.

Marrick shrugged. "She'll cost you your position if you're discovered."

"Madalyn's worth it."

"If you say so – but it'll feel a whole lot different in November when you're having to go to sea with me in a force seven. Can't you choose someone else? Madalyn Trelyon's never meant anything else but trouble for you."

"I love her, Marrick," Ned replied, quietly. "I've always loved her. You know I have."

Marrick rolled his eyes. "Plenty more fish in the sea. I should know!"

"Very funny."

"I'm serious, boyo. Tamsyn's wild for you and so's Polly. Even Amy Trewen, and she's a picky cow. Forget Madalyn Trelyon, Ned. She's pretty, I grant you, but she's not for the likes of us. A girl like that only brings trouble."

Marrick would never understand because he didn't see *Madalyn*; he only saw an upper-class girl, and Ned had fully realised then that the barriers of birth and class Edgar had once talked about affected everyone. Would this system really change one day, as his father once dreamed? It felt like an impossibility, for what could shake the world so much it turned everything upside down?

"I love her," Ned insisted.

Marrick shook his head. "I can see there's no talking sense to you. I'll keep my trap shut, don't worry about that, but watch out for good old Gerry. If he finds out about this, you're in big trouble. He won't like it."

"Gerald's all right," Ned protested. He still felt bad about Gerald's accident.

"Now I *know* you've lost your marbles. Snowe's a nasty bastard. He always was. I'd put money on it that he used to steal things from our hiding place."

"Come on, Marrick! There's no proof of that. We probably just mislaid things. We were little boys."

"Mislaid your stories? Or those marbles we treasured? Maddy's comb? They mysteriously reappeared too, remember?" Marrick placed his glass down with a thud, a clear signal that as far as he was concerned the matter was settled, and his merry face clouded. "Be careful, Ned. Gerry's not a resentful little boy now, but a wealthy man with the power to follow his grudges through. You watch your back."

Ned had taken Marrick's warning on board. It was true that as much as he sought to reassure Madalyn that Gerald was harmless, Ned had turned cold in church last Sunday when Gerald's gaze settled on him. Did Gerald blame him for the accident that crippled him? Did he curse Ned with each stumble and every painful step? Or were these fears the whispering manifestations of Ned's own guilt? Ned often blamed himself for the events of that fateful day. Although he hadn't forced Gerald to take the boat or climb the tree, Ned had always known how excluded the other boy felt, and understood better than anyone his desire for Madalyn's approval. Maybe if Ned had been a little kinder when he'd rescued Gerald and Madalyn, if he hadn't torn a strip off Gerry, things might have been different? Gerald wouldn't have felt the need to prove himself, and the accident wouldn't have occurred. How odd it was that the whole course of the future hung on what word you uttered or a split-second decision. Ned decided to tread carefully, for Madalyn too had pointed out that Gerald had held grudges as a boy and she said there was no evidence to suggest he'd changed.

"Don't trust him," she had said, and Ned had felt her tremble as he held her close. "He's angry and he's just biding his time. You don't see the way he looks at me, Ned. It feels as though he could devour me."

Ned kissed the crown of her head. Her curls were soft as thistledown and smelt of summer and sunshine. He hated her feeling so afraid. "Gerald's all right really."

"Why do you always stick up for him? Even now? When are you going to wake up, Ned? Not everyone's as good as you."

Her skin was peach gold in the light, her limbs long and luscious, and her eyes burned with a fire that was all her own. Madalyn Trelyon took his breath away, and Ned longed to pick up his pen and pin her beauty to the page. What similes and metaphors could ever do her justice?

"I pity him," he said quietly. "I pity any man who can't be with you, Maddy, for I'm in heaven but they're doomed to always be outside looking in. How must that feel? It must be unbearable. It must be hell."

"Don't pity *him*," she said, but her anger was diffused and she slipped back beneath the eiderdown and twined her limbs around his, clinging to him so tightly Ned thought she would squeeze the very air from his lungs. It was as though her sheer willpower would keep him safe.

"Watch out for him, Ned," she whispered. "Be careful."

Ned had agreed to be very careful, but Madalyn's lips were on his and her soft skin pressed against his chest and he would have agreed to anything at this point. Anyway, once he and Madalyn were married there would be no need for her to worry about Gerald. When his novel was finished they would marry and leave Trevellan for a new life. Maybe they would settle in London once he found a publisher. Ned's novel was writing itself now and, inspired by his love affair, he was scribbling late into the night and during every spare moment. He knew he had never penned anything better. *On Oyster Shore* was the book that would make his name. Ned knew this as surely as he knew he loved Madalyn. He also knew that without her he would never be able to write with such passion and power. Madalyn Trelyon was his muse. His reason for living. His soulmate. His *everything.*

It would have been impossible to explain any of this to Marrick. He dealt with the tides, winds and seasons. His work was physical, not cerebral, and he would have scorned the idea of a muse. Marrick thought Ned was mad to risk everything for Madalyn Trelyon, and his antipathy towards her had inevitably driven a wedge between the two old friends. Ned couldn't recall the last time he'd spent more than an hour with his childhood companion, which was why he'd been so pleased when Marrick called at the boathouse to invite him out for a drink. Now he understood why Marrick wanted to see him in person. This was not about healing their ailing friendship but about marrying Bess.

"Well?" pressed Marrick. "Do we have your blessing?"

"Nine weeks isn't that long," Ned hedged.

Marrick shot him an amused look. "Says you. Madalyn's only been back five minutes and you're bloody Romeo and Juliet."

Ned felt chilled by the tragic comparison. "We're not talking about me."

"You're right, we're not," his friend agreed. "We're talking two people who've known one another almost since birth, and who have everything in common. Bess and I grew up together. We went to school together. We're the same class. We have the same friends. I know she has a mean right hook, and she knows I hate liver. There won't be any surprises."

Ned couldn't argue with any of this, either. "You're marrying my sister because you know she won't cook liver?"

Marrick held out his pint glass to Tamsyn. "So it's agreed that I'm marrying her?"

Neatly cornered, Ned nodded, and Marrick punched the air.

"Pour another one for Ned, Tam! He's going to be my brother-in-law! I'm marrying Bess!"

There was a ripple of excitement in the pub. Several fishermen clapped Marrick on the back, and Tamsyn's father declared drinks were on the house.

"Bess said you'd agree," Tamsyn told Ned, working the beer pump and batting her eyelashes. "A woman always gets her way in the end, Ned Carew!"

The invitation was unmistakable. The sooner he was married to Madalyn the better, thought Ned, because in a minute Tamsyn would make her move and then he'd have some explaining to do, for no man in Trevellan would turn Tamsyn down without good reason.

He turned to Marrick. "Have you spoken to my mother?"

"Not my place. Bess said once I've talked to you I can ask your ma officially."

Bess had it all planned out. Ned admired his sister for her determination and envied the ease of this match. If only he could be open about his love for Madalyn and celebrate how he felt. That would make Ned the proudest and happiest man on earth.

"We want to be married as quickly as possible. By harvest time at the very latest. Sooner if we can," Marrick was saying.

"Why so fast?" Ned grabbed hold of Marrick's arm and pulled his friend closer until their eyeballs were almost touching. "Is there something else you wanted to tell me?"

Marrick yanked his arm away. "Don't be so daft. She's not in the family way, if that's what you're asking. We want to get married before war's declared. That way, when I enlist Bess will be able to have my wages."

"What are you talking about? What war?"

"Come on, Ned! You're surely not so loved up you don't know there's a war coming? There's been talk for nothing else for weeks. Certainly not since the Archduke was assassinated. It's only a matter of time before the Germans make a move on Serbia. Then we'll be in the game – everyone thinks so."

The pub floor, beer-sticky and worn into dips from the years of booted feet, seemed to shift beneath Ned. He'd heard conversations about the turmoil on the Continent, but with his thoughts occupied by Madalyn and his book, he hadn't paid a great deal of attention.

"How do you know all this?"

"Bess, mostly," Marrick admitted. "Your sister's as sharp as a knife and she reads the vicar's copy of *The Times* every day after he's read it; it gives her a chance to learn about what's going on. She knows all about it. Practically an expert."

Ned smiled. "Sounds like my sister. She should have been a man."

"She bloody shouldn't!" said Marrick. "Anyway, Bess says since Archduke Franz Ferdinand was shot in Sarajevo, the Germans and the French are poised for conflict, and we'll soon be called to fight the Germans along with the French. It looks like we'll be at war sooner rather than later. When we are, I'm signing up to fight for my country."

Madalyn had mentioned how the talk at Vyvyan was all of war and had recounted Kit River's repugnance at the jingoistic posturing. His thoughts filled with writing and love, Ned had dismissed the military rhetoric as bluff. Apparently, he was wrong.

"You're a fisherman, Marrick. You're not a soldier," he said.

Marrick knocked back his drink and wiped his mouth on the back of his hand. "I know – but if war comes I'll do my bit for King and Country. We all will, won't we?"

Ned felt a cold clutch in the air, as though something unearthly was breathing down his neck. He turned to see if a sea fret was creeping into the pub, but the sun was shining through the window and the door was closed. This icy sensation came from inside him. *Someone walking over my grave* was how his mother had often described it, and it never boded well.

Ned felt uneasy. "I suppose so," he said slowly. "But I hope you're wrong and it doesn't come to war."

"Don't look so glum," Marrick said. "It'd be a bit of an adventure, don't you think? I'll get to see the world and have much better pay than fishing. I'll be able to earn enough to buy my own lugger and really care of your sister."

Not if you don't come back, Ned almost said, only just stopping himself in time. Such words felt unlucky as mere thoughts; to speak them out aloud would lend them an unholy power.

"You should join up," Marrick suggested. "Save a few bob until you sell that great novel of yours."

"You'd look so handsome in uniform, Ned!" Tamsyn piped up, bright-eyed. "All the girls swoon over soldiers!"

Ned laughed. "I'll stick to writing, thanks! You keep fishing and make sure you take care of my sister, Marrick Penwurthy, or you'll have me to answer to."

Marrick held out his hand. "I won't let you down, Ned. Your sister will never want for anything. I swear I'll take care of Bess for the rest of my life."

Ned clasped his hand. The strong and true grip he'd known all his life brought a lump to his throat. "I know," he said. "She's a lucky girl."

They left the Trelyon Arms soon after, Marrick keen to find Bess and share the good news, and Ned longing for the peace of Oyster Shore, where conflict, archdukes and uneasy nations had no place. But Ned's thoughts darted with the shifting patterns of light on the woodland path and refused to stay still. There wouldn't be a war, he told himself; how could there be when the sun was bright and the world ripe and full of hope? Marrick was allowing himself to be carried away, and all would be well. Nobody wanted a war. Least of all Ned. All he wanted was to be with the girl he loved.

"Marrick thinks war is coming," he said to Madalyn the

next time they were together. The weather, glorious for weeks, had suddenly broken, with a volley of thunderstorms, making it impossible for her to slip away. The six days since their last meeting were torturous for Ned, rendered even more unbearable now he was aware that the idyllic hours spent sketching and writing, splashing from the pontoon and making love beneath the beams of the old boathouse, were most likely numbered. If there was a war, Ned knew he would have to enlist and go away. There would be no other choice.

After talking to Marrick, Ned had made a point of visiting his mother and stepfather at the Rectory, where he had read the paper and spoken at length with Reverend Tullis. By the time he held Madalyn in his arms once more Ned had come to realise even lovers couldn't escape the stormclouds massing on the Continent. Even as the Trehunnists mowed the long grass for hay and the corn ripened, the shadow of war was lengthening over them all. Something dark was approaching, and Ned knew in his heart that he had sensed this for a long time. Maybe even all of his life.

It was early evening. Ned and Madalyn sat on the pontoon with their legs swinging above the water and their reflections floating lazily beneath. Swallows skimmed the river, gorging on flies, and the shadowy forms of mullet moved through the depths, as stately and mysterious as deep-sea monsters.

Ned squeezed Madalyn's fingers. He was holding her hand tightly as though she was all that tethered him from spinning away and into despair. "Maddy, did you hear me? I think we're going to be at war very soon."

Although Madalyn turned her face away, Ned knew she was close to tears. "They talk of nothing else at Vyvyan," she said. "And Reverend Tullis thinks it's inevitable. He says that without any assurances on Belgian neutrality we'll have no choice."

These repeated words sounded stilted to Ned's own ears. What did they even mean? The politics of war were an entire world away from turning tides, shifting waters and the girl he loved. What did he know about Germany or Serbia, or Belgian neutrality?

"Colonel Rivers seems excited about it, and so does Sir Arthur. Even Gerald joins in – but it's all right for him, isn't it? He won't have to fight, not with his leg." Bitterness filled her voice.

"It can't be easy for him, because he'll be left behind if it happens," Ned said. "Marrick's really excited, though. He says it'll be an adventure – a chance to make money and see the world. He thinks it'll all be over by Christmas, anyway."

Madalyn turned to face him. Her green eyes were filled with fear. "And what do you think, Ned?"

He raised her chin with his forefinger. "I think the only adventure I ever want is the one we're going to share."

He kissed her softly and Madalyn kissed him back, but it was a kiss filled with sadness, and Ned knew her heart was already breaking for he hadn't given her the answer she wanted to hear. Madalyn knew what Ned would do if war was declared.

"You'll enlist." It wasn't a question.

"I'd have to. It'd be my duty. What else could I do?"

"Plenty! What about your duty to me? What about all your promises? Our plans? Your great novel? Or was that just a dream too? Has all of this, you and me, just been another one of your stories? A fiction? Something made up to pass the time?"

Ned stared at her, aghast. "Of course not!"

"So you say. But now you're telling me you'd leave me and go to fight some stupid war far away. You'd rather play soldiers than be with me. All those promises you made! How could you?"

"That's nonsense," Ned said. "And you know it."

"Do I? I'm not sure. Maybe I should have married Gerald after all. At least I already *know* he's a *liar*!"

She spat the word before leaping to her feet and tearing down the pontoon. Ned watched her storm through the long grass of the bank and plunge into the woods, and his heart ached for her. He didn't attempt to follow or beg her to come back, because he understood fear was making her cruel. Part of him even wondered whether Madalyn was right; had he broken his word to her? Should his loyalty belong to the woman he loved, the woman he had made so many promises to, rather than to some abstract notion of King and Country?

Ned groaned. If war was declared how could he *not* enlist? If he didn't play his part in defending his country and his home, in defending Madalyn, then he wouldn't be a man who deserved her. He wouldn't be much of a man at all. The more he thought about what was coming, and the more he understood of it, the more convinced he was that enlisting was the right decision even if doing so would break both their hearts.

Following his conversations with Reverend Tullis, Ned asked himself over and over what his decision would be if war was declared. He hoped this question would remain hypothetical, but feared that by August war would become a reality. Ned wondered what Edgar would have had to say on the matter, and he missed his father more than ever, longing to hear his words of advice just one more time. Would Edgar say he should let others fight and stay with Madalyn? Or would he advocate doing your duty even when this smashed your heart into pieces?

Ned thought he knew the answer; Edgar would have said a man had to be true to himself, no matter what it might cost him. Although Ned longed to marry Madalyn as soon as possible, perhaps fleeing with her to his uncle in Australia and starting a new life far away from the spectre of war, he wouldn't respect himself if he allowed Marrick and his friends to fight while he stayed safe. Guilt and self-loathing would follow, killing their love and their hopes for a future as swiftly as any war. There was no choice for Ned Carew. If war came he would enlist and he would fight for his country.

Ned hauled himself to his feet and edged his way along the pontoon. The rickety structure rocked beneath his feet in sympathy with his whole world. The deep water glinted through the gaps in the planks, cool and inviting and whispering that he could lose himself in it. Ned unlaced his shoes and tugged off his shirt and dived in, gasping at the icy sting of the river. It was impossible to think when the water was so cold, and Ned sliced his way to the far bank, losing himself in the rhythm of his arms as they powered him across. Once there he floated on his back, watching clouds scrawl chalk marks on the bright blue, before turning over and gazing back to Oyster Shore. His eyes were so dazzled by the sun that for a moment he thought he saw an angel stepping across the grass, hair a halo and white skirts spreading around her as she walked across the water. Blinking away the sun's imprint and drops of water, Ned realised this was Madalyn, up to her knees in the river and wading deeper.

"Maddy! No! You can't swim!"

The river was deep enough to launch a boat here. She could drown. She *would* drown.

"Don't go any further! I'm coming!"

Ned struck out for the bank. Madalyn was already waist deep and only her bright head was visible, bobbing up and down as her hair spread out like seaweed and her pale arms tugged at the water. "I'm swimming, Ned!" she called. "I'm swimming!"

Madalyn was in the middle of the river and finally Ned was beside her. He trod water, hardly able to believe what he was seeing. She was spluttering and splashing but undoubtedly swimming, and Ned was confused. Maddy couldn't swim, so how had she managed this?

"I'm sorry! I'm so sorry. I didn't mean it! I was frightened, Ned. I love you so much!"

Madalyn was breathless from her efforts and caught hold of his shoulders, pressing her cold lips against his cheeks, his eyelids and his lips while he kept them both afloat. He held her and their limbs tangled in the water, white and ghostly beneath the surface, as they clung to one another. Tears mingling with river water, their mouths met in a kiss that told each everything of the other's fears.

"I didn't mean any of it," she sobbed. "I love you, Ned. So much."

"I know. I know," he soothed. "And I love you too, Maddy. I'll always love you. No war will ever change how I feel for you, or stop us being together. I promise."

He knew what she was thinking; that this was a promise he couldn't keep no matter how much he might believe it.

"Are you surprised by my swimming?" she said instead. "I've been practising when the tide's in. I was waiting to show you when I was a bit less splashy, but when you swam away just now all I could think about was reaching you and telling you I was sorry, that I never meant those awful things —"

Ned stopped her words with a kiss. His own heart was pounding from terror as much as from exertion. He had truly thought she would drown, and it had been horrible because as she sank into the water it had seemed almost pre-ordained, as though Madalyn Trelyon was always meant to end her life beneath the river as it flowed towards Oyster Shore. It all ended as it began, on Oyster Shore ...

He pushed the notion away. That was fiction, not a premonition.

"I'm surprised all right," he told her. "Although maybe 'shocked' is a better word. I had no idea you could swim or hold your breath underwater."

"A girl has to have some secrets! And try 'proud'! That's better than surprised!"

"I'm always proud of you, my beautiful, brave Madalyn," Ned said, stroking her face tenderly while he trod water for them both and she clung to him. "And you *are* brave. Much braver than you'll ever know."

Her mouth trembled. "I'll try to be, Ned. Whatever happens, I'll try, and that's a promise."

He kissed the tip of her nose and thought he loved her more at that moment, wet and bedraggled, than he ever had.

"You're getting cold. Let's swim back, side by side."

"Always side by side," she said with her old determination. "No matter what may happen, Ned Carew, we'll always be side by side. Nothing's going to change that."

Slowly, and with much splashing, Ned and Madalyn made their way back to the shore and collapsed onto the riverbank where, hidden by swathes of long grass and legions of rag-taggle daisies, all thoughts of war were forgotten as kisses sealed a promise their hearts would keep for ever.

28

LATE AUGUST 1914

Oyster Shore

Gerald

As far as Gerald was concerned Trevellan was little more than a collection of hovels clustered around a tatty quay. He preferred Penhayes with its sailing club and elegant hotels. Apart from the obligatory Sunday visit to St Nun's he avoided the village, for the merest glimpse of Ned Carew was enough to fill him with a most unchristian rage.

If it hadn't been for Carew, Gerald would be stepping out smartly through the village this morning, resplendent in an officer's uniform as he encouraged the menfolk to enlist. These soldiers in scarlet uniforms, marching past in perfect time, the brass band and the coloured bunting, would have all been in honour of him. The clapping children would have admired him. The village girls would have shyly offered him posies of wildflowers. Each flag which fluttered in the breeze would have celebrated his bravery, and when the sergeant-major climbed up onto the steps of the Trelyon Inn and gave a rousing speech about joining up to stop the Hun, Gerald's chest would have swelled with pride, for everyone would have looked his way.

"Look at Sir Arthur's boy!" they would have whispered admiringly, nudging their sons. "He joined up straight away. Isn't he a fine officer? You need to follow his example and do your bit. You need to be as brave as Gerald Snowe."

The dream was a pleasant one, but it was evaporating by the second as the sergeant-major called out that the King needed each able-bodied man to fight for him and their country. He pointed into the crowd of gathered villagers, seeming to look into the eyes of each man there, as he implored them to do their duty and fight for their country.

"Our brave boys in France need you! Your country needs you! Who'll join up today and take the King's shilling? Who'll do his duty and make his family proud?"

Gerald, standing with his parents at the back of the crowd, wished he could melt into the floor. Why had his father insisted they attend the recruitment drive? Didn't Sir Arthur understand how humiliating this was for Gerald as the young men of Trevellan stepped forward to much cheering and clapping? Amid the drumming and brass band music there would be people whispering that Sir Arthur's son was holding back like a coward. Not for him the admiration of the girls and the pride of the older people, but humiliation and the cold sweep of shame.

"You and I might not be able to fight, but by Jove we'll support those who do," Sir Arthur had declared over breakfast. He'd mopped his mouth enthusiastically with a napkin, a gesture which always made Gerald wince. "Hearts of oak, our village boys, and we'll cheer them on."

Gerald had considered pleading a bad leg or a headache, but something about the glint in his father's eye decided him against this, so he'd accompanied his parents to Trevellan, where the army was recruiting on the quayside. Having already heard about the recruitment drive in Rosecraddick Gerald wasn't looking forward to a carnival atmosphere where photographers would ply their trade as the brass bands belted out 'God Save the King'. He would much rather have stayed in the library and attempted (yet again) to begin his great novel.

War had been declared three weeks earlier, something which came as no surprise to Gerald since his father had spoken of little else for weeks, but until today little seemed to have changed. Life at Vyvyan Court had continued in its well-oiled pattern of leisurely breakfasts and afternoon teas on the lawn, but the conversation at the dinner parties was wholly focused on the best way to show the Germans a thing or two – something Colonel Rivers and Sir Arthur held strong opinions on. The war would be over by Christmas, because the Huns would soon realise they were bested, the Colonel predicted, although Gerald suspected that his father, currently negotiating a contract to supply soap to the troops, hoped it might last a little longer.

"We might not be able to fight, my dear boy, but we Snowes will still play our part and keep the troops clean," Sir Arthur would boom, clapping Gerald on the shoulder. "No shame at all in that. There's more than one way to win this war."

Gerald, who possessed no real desire to enlist other than

looking dashing in an officer's uniform, had done his best to look disappointed during the dinner parties, but here in Trevellan it was different as the young men began to surge forward. The band struck up 'Tipperary', and there was a big cheer when Marrick Penwurthy became the first lad to sign up. Marrick was married now, Gerald recalled, to Ned's sister Bess, she of the sharp violet eyes and even sharper temper. Where was Ned? Gerald craned his neck for a glimpse of blond hair and strong shoulders. Was Ned going to enlist with his friends, or was he hiding on Oyster Shore, scribbling stories and dreaming of Madalyn?

It irked Gerald that Ned lived in the boathouse. There was an element of frustration too, for now it was nigh on impossible for him to slip unseen into the boathouse and lift the tile that concealed the old hiding place. This was where Ned had always hid his writing, and Gerald would have given anything for a glimpse of what he was working on these days.

"Well done, lads!" boomed the Saul Trewen the blacksmith, scrubbed clean for once and beaming at his son who was in the line of local boys queuing to enlist. "We'll show 'em!"

"It's every man's duty to fight when his country calls," said Reverend Tullis piously. "We are on the side of what is right, and it's God's will that a man obey his King."

Neither man was addressing Gerald, but to him their rallying words felt like poisoned darts of shame. As village lads and farmer's boys jostled one another in the line, faces bright with zeal, Gerald leaned heavily on his cane and fought the urge to return to the motor car. Were they all looking at him and laughing? Crippled Gerry who couldn't climb trees and who couldn't go to war? Did they think him a coward?

"I hope *you know who* joins up, Polly! Wouldn't he look fine in uniform?" giggled a voice at his elbow.

Glancing down, Gerald saw the innkeeper's pretty daughter with a friend. They were laughing together, and their words were obviously aimed at him, highlighting his lack of uniform. His hand tightened on his cane.

"All the nice girls love a soldier, Tamsyn!" said her friend. "I'll give a kiss to Sammy Trewen when he's in uniform! He'll look very handsome!"

Linking arms, they moved on through the crowd. Gerald watched them wave to some boys in the queue and call their encouragement. Could he enlist with a limp and a stick? Possibly, and it was very tempting. Even the podgy lawyer, Rupert Elmhurst, had acquired a certain panache since enlisting, and Gerald saw how the female servants giggled and blushed when they caught sight of Kit Rivers in his elegant mess kit. Did Arthur's blustering comments about the Snowes still playing their part suggest there was shame in having a lame son who couldn't 'join the show' in France? Were his parents secretly wishing they could boast about which regiment their boy had joined? And did their neighbours sneer at them even more because of this?

This was yet another humiliation caused by Ned Carew, and another piece of evidence to add to the towering pile he'd collated over the years to prove that the village boy needed to be put in his place. Just thinking of Ned with his easy laugh, his strong tanned limbs and his alchemy with words made Gerald's fist clench on his cane again. Madalyn might not say as much, but her thoughts were always elsewhere, and her face was freckled in a manner which must have betrayed to everyone how she was once again abandoning her hat to roam like a gypsy with her old companion.

Gerald knew this for sure; he was paying a village lad to spy on Madalyn, and he said she often met Carew at the boathouse. Gerald suspected the two were lovers. The notion made him seethe with jealousy.

Since her return to Cornwall Gerald had taken to observing Madalyn carefully at the dinner parties and soirées they attended. Although she was polite, dancing with him or taking his arm for a turn around the garden, she was distant and said little. On one occasion a travelling photographer had been hired to take portraits of the Snowe's guests and Gerald and Madalyn posed for a photograph on the steps of Vyvyan Court. With her small hand resting on his arm and the heat of her body against his skin, he felt she had belonged beside him and for a few blissful moments Gerald imagined a world where she was his fiancée.

"What a handsome couple they make!" his mother declared, clapping her hands. "Don't you agree, Constance?"

Lady Trelyon's eyes, the same clear sea-green as Madalyn's but as cold as the English Channel, swept over them. "They do indeed," she said, nodding slowly. "A very handsome couple."

Madalyn had tensed at this remark, but remained in position as the photographer, a red-haired young man who all the great and good were raving about that summer, exposed the frame and instructed them to remain still. Madalyn gazed ahead, but Gerald knew she understood as well as her mother did that a match between Lady Trelyon's daughter and Sir Arthur's heir was the obvious course of action. Breeding combined with money – it was the way of the world and the right thing to do. Gerald understood very well that *he* wasn't the cause of Lady Constance's approval, for who knew better than he did that he was undersized and lame? No, it was the positioning of her daughter on the steps of the ancestral home that caused the older woman to smile so warmly at him. Like the Snowes, she believed it was only a matter of time before Gerald and Madalyn were engaged and the Trelyons assumed their rightful place.

It was fortunate indeed for Lady Constance that she was ignorant of her daughter's scandalous behaviour, Gerald had thought as he raised his chin and stared haughtily into the camera. Lady Trelyon wouldn't be nearly so proud if she knew how her daughter was behaving behind her back. Madalyn might resemble an angel in her white dress, but it was all an illusion. If Gerald chose he could ruin them both, and jolly thoroughly too. He could reveal such a scandal that nobody in polite society would want to associate with the Trelyons, never mind offer marriage to a fallen daughter. St John would throw them out, they would be forced into poverty, and Madalyn would wish with all her heart that she had been nicer. Then she would beg Gerald to take her on. She would weep and plead for his forgiveness and a second chance. He would grant this – of course he would, because he had loved and wanted her since they were children, and it would also be an extra pleasure to take her away from Ned – but he would make her grovel to him first.

That Madalyn would choose to associate with Ned when she'd been offered marriage to a gentleman stung, but Gerald could overlook this. He kept the information to himself, turning it over and over in his mind and brooding upon it like a bird with a clutch of eggs. Sooner or later he would know what to do with the knowledge, and he revelled in the fact that until then Ned and Madalyn had no idea their secret had been uncovered. Madalyn thought she was so clever by playing the lady and looking demure, but Gerald knew the truth.

And that gave him power.

If he exposed their love affair, the scandal alone would ruin Madalyn, and Ned would be sent packing from Oyster Shore. With his rival removed, the way would be clear for Gerald to marry Madalyn and rescue the Trelyons from shame. He often lay awake at night chasing this scenario around and around, but as satisfying as it was, there was one unavoidable flaw – Madalyn could well choose Carew over her mother and leave with him. Gerald's other plan was less initially satisfying but could ultimately be far more successful: he could play the long game and befriend Madalyn slowly. He knew she hadn't forgiven him for the boating incident and didn't trust him, but with time he could charm her and persuade her otherwise. Once she was won over Gerald could woo her slowly. Then she would see that he and not Ned was the better man.

The biggest problem was that Madalyn was strong-willed and had already chosen Ned. While Carew was still on the scene the brightness of his presence would blind her to all else, just as the sun dazzled the vision of all who looked at it and diminished the cooler beauty of the watchful moon. Yes, if Ned had to leave Trevellan because Gerald revealed the love affair all would be lost, since Madalyn was stubborn enough to choose poverty and love over financial security. What Gerald needed was a way to remove his rival that could not be blamed on anyone at all. Then, once Ned was safely removed from the scene, he could win Madalyn over, and with her mother on his side it would only be a matter of time before Madalyn would cave in. As he watched the young men of Trevellan line up to take the King's shilling, Gerald almost laughed out loud because Fate was about to play right into his hands. Ned Carew wouldn't shy away from doing his duty. No matter how much Ned might love Madalyn, he was the kind of man who wouldn't be happy if he thought he had been dishonourable. What an idiot, Gerald thought scornfully. How stupid Ned was if he couldn't see how his ideals and so-called honour left Madalyn vulnerable. When Ned lost her to the better man, he'd only have himself to blame.

Then, and as though his thoughts could manifest men into existence, Gerald spotted a sun-bleached mane amongst the clustered heads. Ned Carew had joined the queue to enlist. It was all happening exactly as Gerald had hoped.

"Late to the party, aren't you?" somebody called.

"Better late than never," Ned replied. "Anyway, I had to fetch something."

"What?" Marrick was elbowing his way through the crowd and slung his arm around Ned's shoulders. "What kept you from the fun?"

"Something I need for luck," Ned replied and held an item up to show his friend. It was obscured by his hand but when the sunlight caught it the flash of red and gold was so familiar Gerald gasped. Ned had been to the boathouse to retrieve the phoenix comb Madalyn had given him all those years ago. He felt a stab of the old jealousy that she'd preferred Ned even then. Gerald knew he should have kept that comb as a trophy. He should never have returned it. Once Ned was gone, he would visit the boathouse and take it back to add to his collection of treasures extracted from the old hiding place.

"Bloody hell, you've got it bad. Don't wear it when we

have our pictures taken. The sarge won't like that," said Marrick.

"Don't panic. I'll hold it," Ned replied, tucking the comb into his pocket. "I may be enlisting, but this shows where my heart belongs."

"You're a soft git," said Marrick. "I suppose you'll wear it next to your heart when you go into battle."

Ned laughed. "It's far too valuable to risk taking anywhere. It can wait for me in the usual place."

While the band played and the contagious excitement spread throughout the village, Gerald watched Ned Carew edge closer to the table where an officer was doing the paperwork. He wondered whether Ned truly believed all that nonsense about King and Country and Germans coming to ravage good Englishwomen and raze houses to the ground? Surely not. Gerald detested Ned, but he knew the other man was intelligent and well-read. Ned would know that the Germans were fundamentally no different to the English. He would recognise the hollowness of patriotic rhetoric when he heard it.

But Ned was fighting for a very different reason. Not for him glory or money or even the King. Carew was fighting for the world he knew. The world of Oyster Shore, where tides turned, where hulks rose from the sand like the ribcages of mythical beasts and where a girl in a white dress found treasure at the tideline. He was fighting for the peace of this place and to protect the people he loved, but most of all he was fighting for Madalyn. When Ned sat at the table, leaning over the paperwork with a pen held loosely in his ink-stained fingers, Gerald held his breath, knowing that once Ned signed he had lost the most important battle in a very private war. The natural order would be restored. It was only a matter of time before some faceless German took care of the rest.

Gerald was sure now that Madalyn Trelyon was as good as his, and as soon as he visited the boathouse, so was the phoenix comb. And once he'd got it, how long Ned Carew would last without his talisman was anyone's guess.

29

APRIL 1915

Oyster Shore

Madalyn

"There's a caller for you, Miss Madalyn," Tilly said.

Madalyn glanced up from her sketchbook, frowning at the interruption. She was on the brink of perfecting the lone heron on the far bank; now he'd be bound to move and her morning's work would be ruined. Why, she thought irritably as she put her pencil down, didn't anybody listen when she told them she didn't wish to be disturbed? There was so little time to spare from nursing Constance, whose health seemed to decline daily. Only the faithful Tilly and a daily woman from Trevellan worked at Oyster House, and the running of the household had fallen to Madalyn. Since the gardeners and footmen had all enlisted, tending the vegetable garden was also down to Madalyn, and the days of worrying about freckles and rough hands seemed as though they had belonged to another life.

Madalyn was glad to be kept occupied. When her daylight hours were spent digging, polishing and hanging out washing she would fall into bed exhausted and then her thoughts couldn't flee to the aching place in her heart where the darkest fears for Ned dwelt. The brief moments she snatched to sketch glimpses of Oyster Shore were a welcome respite from the dread that stalked her every waking moment and caused her heart to race whenever she caught sight of the telegram boy.

Madalyn's drawing was also precious, because these sketches were intended for Ned. They were her small way of sending him a glimpse of home while he was at the Front. In his treasured letters, much of what he wrote had been redacted by the army's censors with ugly black lines, Ned often said her drawings transported him to Oyster Shore in a way even his writing couldn't. He was still penning his book, he told her, but sometimes it felt as though it belonged to a lost world and it was hard to return to the water and dancing light. Was there still a place where barbed wire didn't bristle for miles? And was spring still a time for new life and soft greens instead of death and mud and gunfire?

It gives me hope that, away from this trench-sliced mud and the pocked wasteland, beauty can still exist, he had written in his last letter, *and I dream of walking along the riverbank with you once more, Maddy, just as I dream of holding you close and loving you. The fields here should be tangles of spring grass and knotted with wildflowers, not shell craters and mire which is bound with barbed wire and mutilated by man. In your sketches I see beauty and I know that there is something more than this, something worth fighting for and which is greater than any conflict. One day this war will be little more than a footnote in a history book, but Oyster Shore is eternal, leaves flagging the blue sky as the trees peel away to the place where tides turn like moods. My book will capture that place for ever, and long after you and I are forgotten it will weave its magic. Until I see you there, know I think of you always. Each night, before I close my eyes, I kiss the lock of hair you gave me and pray that the time soon comes when I will hold you in my arms once more.*

Madalyn was glad Ned had something of her with him. A curl of her hair, tied with a red velvet ribbon, was a small thing, but it made her feel closer to Ned and as though she was watching over him. How she wished she could! How she missed him!

Their parting had been agony, and Madalyn claimed a headache afterwards, lying on her bed and turning her face to the wall to weep until there were no more tears left to fall. How could she live without Ned? How could she face a world without him or pretend that all was well when her heart was filled with terror? Madalyn had gleaned enough of the horrors of the Front to tremble for Ned. She knew this was no jolly game or a boy's outing.

It was carnage.

Ned was fighting for her and for Oyster Shore. He had no argument with any Germans, but he did love his home and he would fight for that, he had said. He would defend their way of life, one where boats put out to sea and men hauled nets, kingfishers darted along the shallows and girls in white dresses took tea on the lawn, and Madalyn knew that if not for men like Ned and his comrades, who was to say that the conflict wouldn't cross the water and wreak devastation across their own country as well? Lacerate this shore with trenches and bind it with the barbed wire Ned described in his letters? Without men like Ned, birdsong might be replaced by shell blasts. Craters could pit Vyvyan's lands just as they pockmarked France. She would glance up from his letters to stare across at the river, so timeless and so peaceful, and it seemed impossible that the horrors Ned described could exist in a world that contained such beauty.

Madalyn read each of Ned's letters over and over until the paper was worn and in danger of disintegrating along the folds. They were her lifeline, her reason to haul herself from her bed each morning as well as her own private torture since Ned, true to his art and the honesty that had always been between them, never held back. He told her funny stories about the other soldiers, described football matches in the mud and recounted tales of a week spent taming a rat the size of a cat. He spoke of Marrick and Sammy, who'd enlisted alongside him, and sang the praises of another soldier called Alex, who was a photographer and set upon documenting everything.

The army isn't keen on soldiers having cameras, Ned wrote, *since they prefer to stage scenes that are deemed more suitable for the general population to see, and boost morale. It makes sense, but is it truth or the perpetuation of lies? Alex says his calling is to tell the truth of war through his camera images, and his work is truly incredible. Ugly and harsh, for certain, but devastatingly brilliant and bold. I only wish I could do the same with prose, but it isn't my gift to write of war in an overt way. Is my way to paint way through imagery and allegory? Maybe, but I know it's chaps like Kit Rivers who possess a true gift for stripping this truth to the bone and laying it bare in verse.*

Madalyn had been glad when she'd learned that Ned had joined the same regiment as Kit Rivers. She had only met her neighbours' son a handful of times, but she knew Kit wasn't seduced by delusions of glorious battles or heroic deeds. He would do his duty, and do it well by encouraging and inspiring his men, and Madalyn was comforted by knowing that Kit fought at the side of the man she loved. Marrick and Sammy would look out for Ned, too, just as they always had as boys, and with this knowledge Madalyn knew she had to be content.

The war hadn't been over by Christmas as Colonel Rivers and Sir Arthur Snowe had believed, and the news from the Front grew bleaker by the day. Reverend Tullis preached long sermons imploring men to do their patriotic duty, and each week the pews emptied as, one by one, each remaining able-bodied man enlisted. The farms were run by women now, the blonde and long-limbed Trehunnist daughters driving the few old ploughhorses the army hadn't taken, and the Vyvyan Estate, lacking staff, was neglected. Abandoned pheasant pens toppled in the woods, emboldened deer invaded the rose garden and sly brambles encroached on the lawns, beckoning the nettles and bindweed to follow. There was talk of Vyvyan Court becoming a hospital, and Madalyn thought she would have liked to become a nurse and do her bit for the war effort, but Constance was weak, and would have been unable to manage alone. It seemed Madalyn was doomed to wander the riverbank alone as she longed for Ned or attempted to prevent Oyster House from falling into further decline. She haunted the boathouse, weeping silently into the pillows of the old brass bed beneath the eaves and curling up in Ned's chair to reread his letters, which she kept hidden in the old hiding place with their treasures. Sometimes she felt as though someone else might have been there, and the phoenix comb and her sketch book seemed to have vanished, but this was probably her imagination. In her misery,

Madalyn decided she had mistaken what Ned had left hidden.

The boathouse, now unlived in and damp, had mould crawling across its walls, and Madalyn thought it fitting that without Ned's touch the place was as desolate as she felt. The path through the woods became choked with brambles, and by the end of the summer would be rendered impassable. She could hide away there, Madalyn thought. She could stay lost in the scrambling ivy and tangled bracken until Ned cut his way through to rescue her like a prince from one of their childhood games.

Oyster House was in danger of suffering a similar fate. If it hadn't been for Sir Arthur occasionally sending elderly gardeners to help, the drive would have vanished months ago as moss-jacketed trees crept forwards and fountains of ferns erupted on either side of it, while brambles were lacing the house into a green corset. This didn't matter much to Madalyn, since Constance's declining health prevented her from leaving and visitors seldom called. Their pony trap was long gone, for the army had taken all the horses, and although Sir Arthur kindly sent one over each Sunday so Madalyn could attend church, she always walked up to the main gate to meet it, in order to spare the coachman a bumpy drive down. There was also something about the sense of isolation that Madalyn enjoyed when she was able to steal an hour to walk along the riverbank; it seemed possible that she might have journeyed back in time, so that when she rounded the bluff smoke would be rising from the boathouse chimney and Ned would be waiting for her on the steps, a book held loosely in his hand and his dear face wreathed in smiles.

But Ned was gone, taking her heart and soul with him, so until he returned Madalyn preferred to live in seclusion with her mother. She seldom left Oyster Shore, and Tilly, engaged now to her footman sweetheart but due to his absence as unhappy as her mistress, ran errands to the village while old William trundled deliveries of food and other essentials down to the house in a handcart.

Recently Gerald had taken to visiting in the motor car, bearing gifts of fruit from the hothouse to tempt Lady Constance or a book he thought Madalyn might enjoy. These small kindnesses had taken Madalyn aback, and she was suspicious at first, fearing Gerald had returned to press his suit now that he was one of the few young men remaining at home. She'd spent his first few visits braced for a repeat of the dinner party episode, but to her great surprise Gerald seemed to have put all notions of marriage from his mind and only made small talk. He genuinely seemed to want nothing more than company, and as the months passed Madalyn had found she was no longer on edge when he called. In fact, she was even pleased to see him, for with Gerald she could reminisce about their childhood days by the river and mention Ned without it appearing odd. Speaking his beloved name aloud was the greatest joy Madalyn knew in his absence, and if Gerald's presence was a way of bringing Ned back to her, she was willing to be thankful for the visits. He still had a way about him which made Madalyn a little uneasy; his pale blue eyes were just as intense and watchful as they had always been, but Gerald had proved to be kindness itself and the old dislike of her childhood had ebbed away. She supposed the war had forced them all to grow up.

Madalyn was sitting on the terrace sketching, when Tilly came up to her. "Mr Gerald usually doesn't call until the afternoon," Madalyn said, closing her sketchbook. "If you show him into the morning room, Tilly, I'll join him there. You may bring us some tea."

Tilly shifted from one foot to the other. "Begging your pardon, miss, but it's not Mr Snowe. It's Mrs Penwurthy."

Madalyn's head snapped up. "*Bess* is here?"

It was out of the ordinary for Ned's sister to call, for although Ned's letters arrived via Bess, who surreptitiously passed them to Madalyn after church and collected the ones she penned for him, Bess's disapproval of Madalyn was always made abundantly clear by her stony expression. Bess Penwurthy might have been taken into her brother's confidence and reluctantly agreed to act as a go-between, but she neither liked or trusted Madalyn. Knowing the trouble their childhood friendship had caused for the Carews, Madalyn couldn't blame her, but she dearly hoped that one day she could prove to Bess just how much she loved Ned.

One day, when she was his wife.

"Miss Madalyn?" Tilly pressed when, lost in dreams of apple blossom and white dresses, her mistress didn't reply. "I'd usually show a visitor to the morning room, but since it's Mrs Penwurthy I suggested she waited outside the kitchen."

The unspoken remainder of this sentence implied this was exactly where a fisherman's wife belonged, and Madalyn sighed, fearing another black mark in Bess's book. Even as children she had been wary of Ned's sister's sharp tongue. Why was Bess here? What could be so urgent that it couldn't wait until Sunday? Unless ...

Fear washed over her in an icy wave and the world became a whirl of lime and sage and moss green. No. Not that. Please, God, not *that.* Suddenly Madalyn's mind was flailing just as her limbs had all those years ago when she thought she would drown. Terror closed over her head like water as she clutched desperately for alternative explanations. Maybe Bess had a message that couldn't wait? Or perhaps Ned was returning on leave? Or had other news?

"She's followed me into the garden!" Tilly exclaimed, exasperated. "The bold creature! I'm so sorry, Miss Madalyn. I *did* ask her to wait at the back door."

Bess Penwurthy wouldn't wait for anyone, Madalyn knew that, and sure enough she was walking across the lawn towards them, skirts rippling the unmown grass behind her like wake as she strode towards the riverbank. Madalyn rose to her feet. She knew why Bess had come and why she wouldn't wait at the kitchen door. This terrible certainty wasn't because Bess's face was taut or because she was wearing black. A young woman dressed in mourning in 1915 was hardly an unusual sight, and Bess had often looked at Madalyn with suspicion. No, it was none of these things. What sent the blood whooshing into Madalyn's ears was seeing the leather-bound notebook Bess was clutching tightly to her chest.

It was *On Oyster Shore.*

"No," she whispered. "Not that. Please, not that."

"Miss Madalyn? Are you unwell?" Tilly stepped forward to take her arm, but Madalyn brushed her away. If anyone showed kindness she would disintegrate into dust.

"Leave us, Tilly," she said, her voice brittle. "I'll speak with Mrs Penwurthy."

"Here, Miss? Maybe you should sit in the shade?" Tilly turned her engagement ring around and around as she spoke, a nervous habit which now seemed to Madalyn almost superstitious, a wartime equivalent of touching wood perhaps. She was filled with the desire to laugh hysterically. What use was superstition now?

"No, here, Tilly," she said. "Please don't disturb us."

Tilly flung a furious look at Bess. "Since you've taken it upon yourself to come into the gardens, you'll have to do without refreshment, and mind you don't stay too long. The sun's strong today and Miss Trelyon can't be expected to stand out in it with the likes of you."

Madalyn thought the sun could burn with a thousand times the intensity and she would still feel cold to the marrow.

Once the maid was out of earshot, she turned to Bess. "It's Ned, isn't it?"

Bess's red eyes met hers and Madalyn knew she was right. There was a rushing in her ears and she thought she might fall to the ground.

"Yes. Mother's in a terrible way so I can't stay long, but I thought you should know at once. He loved you, heaven help him, he always did. I know his last thoughts would have been of you."

His last thoughts. The words were so terrible it was all Madalyn could do not to wail. Unable to stand, she sank down onto the grass and pressed her hand against her chest.

The rushing in her ears grew louder. "Are you sure?" she whispered.

If Ned had been killed, Madalyn always thought she would have known. When she gazed up at the stars in the night sky, she surely would have seen him there, shining down at her from the heavens? Or she would have noticed, when the sun shone, that there was less radiance in the world and less warmth in its rays? It was impossible Ned Carew could have left the world and she'd not felt it. When Ned was dead, how could Madalyn continue sketching and beachcombing and worrying that Constance might be outraged by bread and jam served for afternoon tea?

Bess nodded. "The telegram arrived last night."

"Telegrams can be wrong," Madalyn said staunchly. "It must be confusing in the heat of battle."

"There's no confusion. Marrick's letter and Ned's belongings arrived this morning too. There had been a delay in sending the telegram for some reason, but there's no doubt. Marrick saw everything. He says Ned saved his life." Tears spilled over Bess's cheeks and she made no effort to wipe them away. "My brother gave his own life to save my husband."

Madalyn clutched Bess's arm. "What happened? Tell me."

Bess reached into the pocket of her skirt and pulled out a crumpled letter, ink-smudged and heavily scored with black in the redacted parts. Unfolding it with trembling hands, Madalyn saw shaky writing and ink blurred where the author's tears had dripped onto the paper.

My deerest and most bootifool Bessy

She glanced up, moved by the love contained in his child-like spelling. This was a letter written between husband and wife. It wasn't for her eyes. Maybe she should ask Bess to read it to her?

"Marrick was never one for book learning," Bess said defensively, misunderstanding Madalyn's hesitancy, "but he tries his best. This letter tells you exactly what happened. I think it's best you read it for yourself. You'll be as proud as we are, since you loved him too."

Loved. Bess's use of the past tense felt like a slap.

"I'll always *love* him," Madalyn said quietly. "That'll never change."

Bess nodded. "I know he loved you. We all told him he

was mad, and Lord know I did my best to talk him out of it, but Ned wouldn't listen. For him, it was always you. Read Marrick's letter. That'll tell you what happened."

Feeling dazed, Madalyn turned her attention to the letter. At first it was a struggle to decipher Marrick's poor spelling, but before long his voice broke through the stumbling prose and she read first-hand an account of the events which had taken place over three weeks previously.

It was late March, but the weather was still wintry and the earth the soldiers had carved up to strengthen their defences was iron-hard. The men staggered under the weight of the duckboards and sandbags they carried to the communication trenches, and at night patrols ventured out into no man's land to ascertain the security of the lines and make sure all the barbed wire was repaired. Some men enjoyed the night patrols, Marrick said, because there was an excitement in venturing away from the safety of the trench and a reckless thrill when snatches of German conversations were overheard. It made a change from spending long hours below the dripping earth where boots were always sodden and hands grew wrinkled. By day the men played cards, ate bully beef (which Marrick loathed) and brewed tea. Captain Rivers would write his reports during this time or scribble poetry, sometimes sharing his work with Ned, who was still working on his novel when he wasn't writing to Madalyn. Sometimes Kit and Ned would have literary discussions that Marrick couldn't follow, so he would drowse instead, knowing that the night was when a man needed his senses to be sharper than the kiss of a bayonet.

It was a quieter-than-usual night – which, looking back, should have made Marrick uneasy. His commanding officers believed the Germans were drawing closer to the Allied line, and it made Marrick's blood boil to think they could be creeping closer while he and his mates just had to wait in the dugouts like sitting ducks. As always, the guns were rumbling like distant thunder, and the thuds of shells to the north were no more disturbing than pebbles tossed into the harbour. It was funny what a man could get used to when he had no choice, Marrick had written: maybe this was no worse than being miles out at sea and wondering whether you'd make it back to shore. He had to admit there were similarities, and as a fisherman he was able to deal with being away from home and hardship better than most. What he couldn't handle was inactivity.

Marrick had hurt his wrist the previous evening, tearing it on wire as he crawled through the mud and shale that mired the emptiness between his company and the German lines, and Captain Rivers had ordered him to stay back from tonight's patrol, a decision that filled Marrick with impatience.

"It's fine, sir, just a scratch," he protested, although his arm ached like stink and his fingers tingled. "I'm fit for duty."

"That's my decision to make, Private Penwurthy," Kit said. "There'll be plenty of other patrols. We might be fighting a war, but that doesn't mean I take risks with my men."

"With due respect, sir, I'm the best you have."

Kit smiled wearily. "Which is another reason not to risk you tonight. Or the others if you were to make a mistake because of your injury."

"I won't make a mistake," Marrick flared. Who did Rivers think he was, telling him what to do? They weren't in Cornwall now.

"You're to stand down and that's an order. You're dismissed, Private."

Marrick glowered at Kit, but he didn't argue. Nobody ever did. Captain Rivers was fair and courageous, but he wasn't a soft touch and the steel in the officer's voice said the matter was closed. If Marrick pushed it he would find himself being disciplined.

"What's wrong?" Ned asked, when Marrick stomped into the dugout and flung himself onto his bunk. Ned was sitting at the table and poring over his leather-bound book. It was the great novel, finally finished apparently, and poised to make Ned's fortune – if they ever escaped this hellhole, Marrick thought darkly.

Over by Christmas, his arse.

"Rivers says I can't go out on patrol," he grumbled. "Typical bloody toff, telling me what to do."

"He's our commanding officer, and besides, you're injured," Ned pointed out, closing the book and placing it in his satchel. "The Germans won't win the war just because you stay behind for one night."

"They might do. Anyway, there's a place I wanted to investigate. That old ruin. Near the sheep track. It's the perfect spot for the Huns to hide a gunner. I would if I was them."

"So we'll take a look tonight," Ned said patiently. "Just rest for a while and make the most of a reprieve, you lucky sod. Besides, I can't have Bess thinking I don't look after her husband. She'd make the Germans look positively friendly if she thought I let you go out when you're hurt."

"It's just a scratch," Marrick scoffed, although in truth the wound felt hot and itchy. Maybe Kit had a point, and it was best he stayed behind? He had a headache too. Still feeling tetchy, he closed his eyes.

He must have slept for a while because when he next sat up, groping for his cigarettes and blinking blearily into the gloom, night had fallen and the dugout was quiet. The others must have headed out on patrol, leaving only him and a soldier with a dose of gutrot in the dugout.

"How long have I been asleep?" Marrick asked, grinding his knuckles into his eyes until he saw stars.

"Long enough for me to pity your missus if you snore like that at home!" said the other soldier.

"I pity yours if you stink this much at home. Place smells like the khazi," shot back Marrick.

The other man grinned, putting his cigarette out and swinging his long legs out from over his bunk. "Just wait until you get this, pal. You won't be so fragrant yourself. How about I light the stove and brew us some tea. Then we'll—"

But whatever it was he'd thought they'd do next Marrick never discovered, for this was when the shelling began. The air was filled with acrid smoke and the darkness was lit with flashes and pea-green flickers. Both men flung themselves to the ground as a shell flew overhead and exploded behind them. The earth was heaving as though wanting to vomit them out of the trench and Marrick flattened himself. Earth and dust rained down upon him, and his chest heaved in panic as his nose and mouth filled. So this was how it would end. He was going to be buried alive in this godforsaken foreign quagmire. So much for making the money to buy a boat and look after Bessy. Who would take care of her now she was a widow?

Another shell hit, yards from where he lay, and the earth rose and fell again. He could hear the other man groaning and the rapid stutter of machine-gun fire around them. For a moment his heart quailed as he thought of Ned and the others out on patrol, before the earth convulsed once more and all was darkness. He drifted a while, waking to booted feet stamping on the duckboards in a staccato beat that kept time with the rat-a-tat-tat of the guns. Clods of earth fell onto his face and crept into his nose. When earth sealed his eyes, Marrick knew he was done for.

"They're both inside," he heard someone – Ned? – cry.

"Ned!" Marrick tried to shout, but his mouth was filled with mud and his voice was just a whisper. Were his lungs already filled with clay? Was he returning to the earth, just as Reverend Tullis had always promised? He wished he could pray, but Marrick had given up believing in God a long time before. There was no God here on the Western Front.

"Ned," he croaked. "Ned!"

"Stay back, men!" This was Kit Rivers. "Wait for stretcher-bearers! Carew! Evans! Follow me."

There were more footsteps, followed by another explosion and a warning cry. Then, and like a miracle, Ned was beside him in the hellish smoke and hailstorm of debris.

"You take Simpson, sir!" he heard Ned yell to Kit over the gun fire and explosions. "I've got Marrick. Come on, Marry! You always were slow!"

Arms were lifting him, and even in the thick smoke Marrick knew this was Ned and they were no longer in a dugout in an alien land but little boys and best friends once again on Oyster Shore, daring one another to leap into the cold water or climb the highest tree.

"Ned ..." Marrick's voice was no more than a croak, and he felt Ned stagger as they stumbled through the swirling blackness. "Ned."

Then there was another explosion, evilly and beautifully bright as a fallen angel, which threw Marrick face first back into the cold mud while Ned flew upwards, hands outstretched and eyes wide with surprise, as though ascending to heaven. When Marrick was able to see again he was sprawled besides the bloodied remains of a severed leg and chunks of gore. Reposing in the devastation was a leather notebook speckled with blood. Marrick turned his head and vomited. Then, mercifully, all was dark once more.

The next time Marrick woke up he was in the field hospital with his head bandaged. The nurses said he was one of the lucky ones, for his line of trenches had all but been obliterated by the surprise attack, but Marrick hadn't felt lucky.

"Where's Ned?" he asked one of the Red Cross nurses, clutching her sleeve desperately as she passed his cot. "Private Carew? Where is he?"

The nurse, a fresh-faced young woman who reminded him of Trevellan girls from another life, pushed him back against his pillow. "Try to rest, love. You've been unconscious for almost two days."

"I can't rest until I know Ned's safe!" Marrick cried, frantic with terror. "He's about my height and he has blond hair. You can't miss him. He's a handsome bugger."

"I'm afraid he isn't here."

A memory floated before Marrick's vision. Unsure whether it was the remnant of a bad dream, he tried again. "He may have hurt his leg. Did you see a soldier with an injured leg?"

"Only you came in. Somebody was watching over you."

She was right; somebody *had* been watching over Marrick, and it had cost that man his life. Marrick wept bitterly for Ned. How could he face Bess knowing Ned had died to save him? How could he celebrate his own miraculous escape from death if Ned Carew was now no more than a name on the list of the missing? How could he live for the rest of his days without his best friend? If Marrick hadn't hurt his hand when out on patrol, Ned wouldn't have risked returning to the trench when the shelling began. It was all his fault Ned Carew had been killed.

Once declared fit by the MO, Marrick returned to the dugout, now little more than another scar in the mire. There was no sign a man had sacrificed his own life here. No sense of wonder or awe, and no clue that his best friend had hurtled into the jaws of death to save his life. It all felt utterly meaningless, and as he listened to the guns fired by men killing men they had no personal enmity with, and who in another world they would have played cards and drunk beer with, Marrick was filled with the blackest despair. What was this all about? In a hundred years' time would anyone know or care about this conflict? What the hell were they all dying for?

Captain Rivers stood beside him and for a while they contemplated the desolate moonscape of craters where grim-faced stretcher-bearers carried corpses back to ambulances. A pair of Red Cross stretcher-bearers staggered through mud and shale with their heavy load. When one man stumbled a marble-white hand slipped from beneath a thin grey blanket and swung pendulum-like. Marrick looked away.

"They've managed to salvage some of Ned's belongings from the rubble," Kit said, resting a hand on his shoulder. "I've put them aside for you as his brother-in-law."

Ned's satchel rested on the table in the officers' quarters. Marrick picked it up and withdrew the leather-bound notebook, relieved that the cover bore only faint traces of blood. Somebody had wiped it carefully and placed it inside the bag. Somebody who knew what that book had meant.

"Thank you, sir," he said to Kit.

"He read some to me. It's sublime," Kit replied. "I hope it's published one day. His was a rare talent."

With trembling fingers, Marrick turned the page.

It ended as it began, on Oyster Shore...

But it hadn't ended on Oyster Shore for Ned Carew, had it? His life had been blasted away in a rat-infested dugout in France. Marrick slid the novel back into the satchel and fastened it. This book didn't belong to him. It belonged to the person who had inspired it, and Marrick had known his friend's heart well enough to accept that Madalyn Trelyon was the reason for everything Ned had ever written.

She was his muse, and that book belonged to her.

"I'll send these things back to my wife," Marrick told Kit, and then returned to his new quarters where he drank a bottle of Scotch and wrote into the small hours, pouring all his grief into a letter to Bess. He couldn't write like Ned, Marrick thought, but he could tell Ned's sister and the girl Ned had loved of the selfless bravery which had ended his life and allowed a far lesser man to live on.

Give the book to Maderlin. I know she wood have been the last thort he had. She was in every thort Ned had.

Madalyn wept then, wishing she could join Ned wherever it was he had gone before her, and she felt Bess reach for her hand. The young women clung to one another until the tide turned and the river began to ebb. How Madalyn longed to hurl herself into it. How she yearned for the cold water to close over her head and carry her far away to the place where Ned was waiting. *On Oyster Shore* lay on her lap, the opening line she knew by heart telling her that Ned had written the ending of their story a long time ago.

Madalyn closed her eyes. As though in sympathy the sun hid behind a cloud and the whole world turned grey. A world without Ned Carew would never have colour, she realised, because he was the sun and the moon and the stars to her. He was the birdsong in woods. The spangles in the sun-glazed water. The warm sand beneath her feet. Ned Carew had been everything, and without him the world was empty and her own remaining years a prison sentence. How could Ned have left her? He'd promised to stay with her for ever, a promise that he had foreseen couldn't be kept. Ned had always known with that Romany magic that it would end here for them both. Their fate had been sealed long, long ago.

Madalyn stayed by the river long after Bess left. She was still there when dusk began to smoke in from the secret heart of the woods and the bats flickered from the trees. Then, knowing that Constance would need her, she wiped her eyes on her sleeve and pressed the book against her heart. It was all she had left of Ned, and her most treasured possession. This book was Ned's voice, and Madalyn swore she would do everything within her power to endure it was heard once more. *On Oyster Shore* would be Ned's legacy. It would make his name known across the world.

She rose to her feet and stared at the darkening river.

"It all ended as it began," she whispered, *"on Oyster Shore."*

30

SEPTEMBER 1917

Allington House, The Cotswolds

The patient

The patient sat on the terrace, his hands folded neatly in his lap and his gaze trained on the hillside. When the year slipped from summer into autumn he liked to study the colours, naming as many as he could before writing them down into the notebook Dr Bell had given him. He narrowed his eyes and watched the hues blur into a glorious haze of ochres, bronzes and clarets, stitched with gold and edged with apricot. Shadows rippled as gilt-edged corn blew in the wind, an inland sea sailed upon by ploughmen with billowing shirt sleeves and groaning harness rigging, and closer to the old house limes yellowed and conkers swelled in spiked cases high in the chestnut trees.

The nib of his pen scratched the paper. Somewhere in the

depths of his confused mind, cobwebbed in the shadowy room the doctors said he had locked away, the patient knew he had written about these streamers of lemon and peach clouds before. There was water too, a mirror reflecting chalk-stick clouds and where trees kissed the shallows and brambles stippled with blackberries guarded cool and secretive woods. These images came to him unbidden, but like smoke from a snuffed-out candle they dissolved before he could grasp them or remember their origin.

How many colours were contained in the glossy plumage of the handsome cock pheasant strutting along the edge of the flower bed? And how could the nasturtiums tumbling from the mossed containers possess so many orange hues? Sienna. Turmeric. Chilli. Mustard. Terracotta. All these and more jostled side by side, their brightness accentuated by emerald leaves and scrabbling ivy, and the patient's pen danced over the page, trailing loops and swirls as ornate as any carved into the planters and urns.

"Writing again?"

He looked up to see Dr Bell standing behind him, half-moon glasses glinting in the sunlight.

"Sorry, old boy. Didn't mean to make you jump." The doctor caught the back of a chair and pulled it around to seat himself down at the table. "Anything useful coming up, Will?"

Will Shakespeare. That was what they called him here on account of when he was first brought in and, caught in a hinterland between dreaming and waking, had been declaiming soliloquies from Hamlet. Dr Bell, a newly arrived Freudian, had recognised the verse and given him the nickname since nobody knew his real identity. Almost eighteen months on, and much writing, in the hope of unblocking his subconscious, later, they were no closer to uncovering his true identity, so Will Shakespeare he had become. The patient often thought it strange that although he had no inkling of his own name it still jolted him to be called by another. The locked-up part of him that Bell insisted spoke through dreams and images was adamant this wasn't his name, and it seemed quite offended that he had dared to assume a new identity.

Will dearly wished his subconscious would spit out his real name, for he was tired of being a jigsaw of a man. Sometimes a piece fell into place, but there was no way of knowing when this would happen or what might prompt it. Once he'd overheard another patient speaking and the deep West Country lilt brought to mind a man's freckled face. This was someone he knew well, because his heart leapt with pleasure and the name was only a breath away before silence had settled over the memory like a snowfall. On another occasion he had picked up a poetry anthology and discovered he knew a great deal of it by heart. Verses flowed from his tongue and, excited by this development, Dr Bell had shown him into Allington's vast library and encouraged him to explore. As his hand caressed the spines, the swell of embossed lettering familiar to his touch, Will realised he'd read many of these books already and knew them well. He saw a fleeting image of a man seated in a leather armchair reading to the small boy who sat on his knee, and his throat ached with grief for a loss he couldn't recall.

There was a river flowing through his dreams which often receded to leave a babbling channel edged with emerald-green weed where a girl trailed the tideline, white skirts dragging over the wet sand as she collected shells. Whenever this dream ended Will woke with tears on his cheeks, and the ache in his heart was more painful than the ache in his ghostly leg.

He clung to these clues because without them he was fated to be Will Shakespeare, a phantom of a man with no past and his left trouser leg sewn up at the knee. He knew he was an educated man with a friend from the West Country, and he had lived near a river. It was a start, but his brain was miserly with memory. Was the girl his sweetheart? Will thought she must have been, since he longed for her with every waking moment. Did she think him lost and weep for him? Or was she just a fragment of his damaged mind, no more real than the dreams of shells and smoke and gunfire that caused him to wake screaming?

Will sometimes forgot how long he had been at Allington, for at the beginning of his rehabilitation one day had seemed very much like the next. Once his dreadful injuries had healed, and he'd mastered walking with the aid of crutches, he had left the military hospital in France and been transferred to Allington. This was a place for convalescence, the VADs had told him, and he was a lucky bugger because Allington was a cushy number, but the patient had wondered what they could do for him there. He had no memory of who he was or what he had done before he had been a soldier, and with his injuries it would be hard to find work. A half-man like him would have been better off not surviving.

While still in the military hospital, when his body had arched in a rictus of pain and his breathing had come in harsh gasps, Will had wished many times that he'd died on the battlefield. It would have been a kinder fate.

"That's no way to talk," one of the nurses had scolded when he'd expressed this sentiment. "You're a miracle. God himself must have a very special purpose in mind to have spared you."

How she could talk of God and divine purpose while the guns still rumbled and the sky was lit with flashes the patient had no idea. He had even less conviction there was a God of any description when he saw an endless procession of men arrive on stretchers, their bodies mangled and their faces contorted in agony, but whether one believed in a higher power or not, Will knew his survival was miraculous. When he finally swam to the surface after his morphine dose was reduced, Will had learned from the nurses how he'd been amongst the bodies flung into no man's land following a shell attack on British lines. During a short and unofficial truce called for both sides to collect their dead, his body had been placed in a cart and was en route for a battlefield burial when one sharp-eyed Red Cross orderly saw fingers curl into a fist.

"They'd taken you for dead," a nurse told Will, lifting bandages to check his wound and narrowing her eyes at whatever lurked beneath. "Hardly surprising, the bad way you were in. If not for that orderly's observation you wouldn't have lasted the night, and it's thanks to him they took you to the base hospital."

Will was to hear this tale many times over the course of his recovery and little by little he gleaned details which he hoped could be the key to his true identity. He had been wearing a private's uniform rather than an officer's when they found him which, although he was well-spoken and well-read, suggested he was a working man rather than gentry. Although he wore no wedding ring he'd carried a lock of beech-red hair tied with a red ribbon in his breast pocket which must belong to a sweetheart, the nurses thought, because he wasn't such a bad-looking fellow. One of the nurses, a pretty girl who always blushed when he spoke to her, had said that his broken nose made him even more attractive. Will wondered if his lack of interest in her was evidence that his heart was already spoken for. Was there a wife waiting for him somewhere, and children too? It felt unlikely, but what did he know? He couldn't even say what his favourite food was, or which colour he liked the most.

Some of the fellows they brought in from the field hospital tossed and turned on their pallets and yelled out as fever's bonds tightened. Grown men cried for their mothers. Others called the names of sweethearts, and one tortured soul even coughed out a confession of murder amid the chaos of blood, ripped flesh, and urgent shouting. Will wondered whether he too had spoken while in the grip of delirium, and whether his own words contained clues. A sweetheart's name? That of the flame-haired girl? Or even his own?

He was to be disappointed, for the Red Cross orderly who had saved him had nothing to report, and the field surgeons had administered so much morphine when they operated that he hadn't spoken for days, drifting in and out of a blizzard of pain. One of the nurses did recall that he'd accused them of being insane, shouting 'mad' repeatedly whenever the pain relief wore off.

"Hardly surprising, love," she said. "It's bloody bedlam here, that's for sure. You'll feel better when they move you to Allington. Who can even think straight, never mind recover, this close to the Front?"

Will had eventually been sent back to England. The voyage to Kent had been so rough that most of the other men invalided home had spent the whole journey vomiting, but he hadn't been among their number. Although the boat had roiled and heaved as the winds strengthened and the sea grew rough, Will had sat on the deck and watched the waves rise and fall without so much as his stomach churning. Was this another clue? Had he been a seafarer in another life? Or lived near the coast? The coils of rope on the deck and the way the mariners threw lines seemed familiar to him. Perhaps he had sailed for pleasure? Will tried his hardest to haul up his memories but the more he delved the deeper they seemed to sink. Dr Bell said it was best not to push himself or feel under pressure to remember. He believed memory returned in its own time.

Allington was a forward-thinking institution dedicated to the recovery and rehabilitation of injured servicemen. Once Will had settled in, sharing his room with a man called Foster who shouted out in the night and hallucinated such hellish visions that Dante would have paled to hear them, Will worked on learning to walk again and on strengthening his weak arm. It was only once he was able to climb and descend the stairs independently that the true business of Allington became clear – it was a place which specialised in treating injured minds as well as injured limbs.

The majority of physicians at Allington House, a honeyed Cotswold pile masquerading as a war hospital but in reality a holding pen for men with neurasthenia, were mystified by Will. He had no memory at all, and no apparent trauma save his physical injuries. He didn't scream in the night or scrub himself raw, or seem disturbed that he had been left for dead in a pile of corpses. In itself, they agreed, Will's lack of obvious distress was fascinating and posed an intellectual argument they never tired of debating over dinner or including in research papers.

Unlike some of his other colleagues, Bell was a devotee of

Dr Freud and a firm advocate of exploring the hidden parts of the mind to cure all manner of physical ills. He argued that Will was suffering most dreadfully and only by unlocking his memory could the man be healed fully. He encouraged his patients to paint and draw, believing that their subconscious would use these pursuits to access and cure the afflictions they suffered, and took time to know each man as an individual. The patient liked Bell and he thought that in another life they could have been friends, but he was certain there were no afflictions, secret or otherwise, that he needed cured. All he wanted was his memory to return. Then he would be well and whole.

"It's the strangest thing with you, Will," Bell said thoughtfully one day when they were nearing the end of a therapeutic session. "Normally I want my patients to work through what they've suffered so they can begin to forget and move on, but with you it's the complete opposite. You, my friend, are a medical mystery!"

The patient laughed. "I would've thought that makes me the ideal case study, and an even better soldier. If it wasn't for my leg, I could be sent straight back to the Front to carry on. Job done, I would've thought!"

Bell looked troubled. "Is that what you think we do here? Mend men simply so they can be sent back to war and bring up the numbers?"

"Isn't it? We're losing more men than I dare to imagine. The more you can send back to carry on the better, surely?"

The patient held the doctor's gaze.

Bell looked away first. "In a manner of speaking, you're right. But although we're a military hospital first and foremost, our work here is about far more than replenishing troops. I want to understand more about the working of the mind and how it can have to power to bring a man to his knees when physically he's fit and healthy. Psychiatry is about healing the whole man, not just the mind, and I believe it's the least understood branch of medicine there is. You've seen the men here, Will. Look at Gregory for instance. He constantly scrubs himself raw, which is —"

"A manifestation of his guilt," Will supplied. "He's killed, and wishes to wash himself clean. Very Shakespearean."

"Out, damn'd spot," said the doctor. "Poor bugger looks like an Egyptian mummy."

We'll visit Egypt. You can write stories about Pharaoh's curses and lost treasure while I paint the pyramids and the Nile.

The voice was so clear and loud that the patient turned around. For the briefest stutter in time, he thought he saw a small girl with hair the colour of embers and wide sea-green eyes grinning at him. He blinked.

"Mad—"

The word died on his tongue. There was more, but the memory fragment abandoned him as swiftly as it had arrived.

"That's not a word I'd choose," Bell said reprovingly.

The patient shook his head. "I saw something ... someone. A girl."

The doctor leaned across his desk. "A memory?"

"Maybe. It was swift but it was there. She's somebody I used to know."

"A sweetheart?"

The patient frowned. "No, she was a little girl. Seven years old, maybe?"

"Daughter, then? Does it feel as though you have a family?"

Will thought hard, starting out of the window and down to the garden where patients in bath chairs were parked on the terrace to admire the view whether or not they wished to, while others hobbled or dragged their way along gravelled paths.

Will buried his face in his hands. "I don't know."

"You know she exists, and that's a breakthrough," Bell said firmly.

"But why can't I remember? Why has this happened to me?"

"You suffered a severe blow to the head. That would be enough without the trauma of what followed."

"I don't feel traumatised. Not like Gregory or the others. I don't remember a bloody thing."

"My point exactly," Bell said in his most patient and professional tone. He pulled out his pocket watch and consulted it, his habitual precursor to ending a session. "You were lucky to make it through at all, Will. Not many men would have done, but you fought hard, so there must be something worth fighting for. Hold on to that. Piece by piece your memory will come back."

"But you can't say for sure, can you?"

"Maybe not. The mind is far more complex than we can possibly imagine, but keep the faith, my friend. Sometimes all it takes for memory to return is the smallest trigger. It could be a scent or a song that provides the key. I've seen many such cases, and there's no reason to believe you'll be the exception."

The doctor rose and patted his patient on the shoulder as he crossed the room to hold the door open. Will took his cue and stepped outside.

"You've done really well today, my friend. You must be exhausted," Bell said.

"Exhausted? From just talking?"

"That's work, my friend. Talking is our work."

Will thought he knew somebody who would have scoffed at this, but the name and the memory were shy and wouldn't come any closer. He sighed and walked along the long corridor which led to the refectory, his head full of questions that he feared even the physicians couldn't answer.

After that session Will had been determined that his memory would return and for the next few days waited patiently for more images to play before his mind's eye like a mental magic lantern. He tried listening to music on the gramophone and even asked the nurses if they could bring him hankies dipped in perfume in case these prompted a memory but as obliging as they were (and rather embarrassingly keen to let him sniff wrists and necks) his mind appeared disinclined to oblige. Will Shakespeare's past was a much a blank page as any his namesake might have taken a quill to.

The days washed into one another just as tides lapped forgotten riverbanks, becoming weeks and then months. Eventually it seemed to Will that he had always been here, taking slow walks in the grounds, talking with Dr Bell and teaching some of the other patients to read and write. Will was a natural teacher, Bell said, warm and encouraging as he allowed each pupil time to sound out words, however halting their reading, and full of praise when they succeeded. Will read to them too, and before long groups of men would cluster around him in the evenings demanding the next chapter of *Great Expectations* or *Silas Marner.* Eventually Bell persuaded the senior physician to turn one of the neglected drawing rooms into a schoolroom with several tables and a wobbly chalkboard on wheels, where Will was able to teach his pupils with greater ease.

"You're a natural, Will," Bell once said, after watching the patient deliver a lesson. "When you leave us you should become a schoolmaster. Maybe you were one before you enlisted?"

Will nodded. He enjoyed teaching the men, and there was a huge joy in seeing somebody understand a concept after struggling with it, and enormous satisfaction in knowing you had given the lifelong gift of reading to another. Bell also was right in his observation that teaching seemed to come naturally, and the classroom setting felt as familiar to Will as his own face. It was possible that he could have been a schoolmaster, he supposed, yet something deep inside told him this hadn't been his calling. There was something else he'd always been drawn to ...

It was lost. Would he find it again? Will despaired, and his only solace was writing his own stories, narratives he could control and take in any direction he chose. He wrote dark fairy tales of children lost in a forest of tangled thoughts, which Bell read with excitement, muttering about the forest of the unconscious mind.

Will, who grew protective of this earnest doctor who gave his all to the broken men he worked with, was happy to share some of his work with Bell. That Bell thought his work good was pleasing, but there were other pieces of writing he kept hidden, feeling these were too precious to be subjects for psychoanalysis. He wrote of a river that turned with the tides and where egrets picked at seaweed, and wooded hills as richly curved as a woman's body. This world was the key to who he was, since it felt more real to him than Allington. When he was well enough to leave the hospital, he would travel the length and breadth of England until he found it. Until then Will would continue to sift through the silt in his mind and devote himself to his new role as a teacher.

A stream of broken men flowed through the hospital, many finding sanctuary in the classroom. Some lost themselves in Keats and Dickens, others purged their experiences through writing, and many learned to read for the first time. Each man made progress except for Will, whose memory remained as blank as the blackboard he wiped clean at the end of each day. His physical wounds were long since healed and he was agile on his crutches. Even the scars on his burnt hands were silver echoes. Once a prosthetic limb had been fitted Will would be well enough to be discharged and free to make his way in the world – however he could do that even now: Dr Bell said there were grants and funds set up for maimed men, and offered to look into these unless, he suggested hopefully, Will would be prepared to stay at Allington officially as their schoolmaster.

"The work you've been doing here is invaluable. We'd hate to lose you," he said. "You're an asset to Allington, my friend."

Will was touched. He also knew Bell's quiet encouragement of his teaching and writing had played a huge part in his own rehabilitation. He might not know his true identity, but he did know the nature of the man he *was* in his heart and soul.

He was a wordsmith and a teacher.

But to teach for his living? Did he dare to hope this was possible?

"You don't know anything about my background. I have no idea how much of an education I had. I could be anyone," he pointed out.

Bell leaned back in his chair, hooking his thumbs into the pockets of his claret-hued waistcoat, and shook his head.

"Oh, you're not just anyone, of that I'm quite certain. I may not know who you *were*, but I know the man you *are*, and I don't believe the essence of you has ever changed. You're intelligent, patient and honourable, and above all you're a wonderful teacher and writer. The men here are lucky to have you, and you've helped them more than you can ever know. Consider the last year your schoolmaster's apprenticeship, for if you'd like to stay we'd be delighted to have you as an official member of staff. I'm speaking with the full support of the Chief MO and the board of trustees too." He held out his hand. "What do you say, Will?"

The patient was quiet for a moment, sensing that this was a moment when his life was poised to change for ever. There had been other moments like this, he felt certain of it. The memory of a little girl with red hair, pale bare feet ghostly beneath cool river water, filled his mind. Was this a sign? Was she telling him that accepting this position would lead him back to recovering more memories? It was a hope he would cling to. Besides, he liked Bell and Allington. He might even grow to like being Will Shakespeare, schoolmaster and aspiring writer. Until his old life returned, Will decided he would embrace this one.

He shook Bell's hand. "Thank you, Doc. I'd like to stay on and teach the men, I truly would."

Life settled into a pattern, and it soon seemed to Will as though he'd always been at Allington. By the time the summer of 1917 put on the melancholy cloak of autumn he was resigned to his new identity and contented in his work. His own writing was fitted into any spare moments he might have, and his favourite spot for this was a bench at the far end of the terrace with views over the lake.

He was generally left uninterrupted here, so when Bell took a seat beside him on this golden afternoon Will felt a frisson of irritation. He'd never been disturbed in the boathouse. It had always been the perfect place to work. Wooded hills running into the sky like inkblots, and water lapping the banks as his pen scratched the paper, he'd always written his best work here ...

His nib veered, bleeding ink across the page. *Boathouse*? Did he have a boat somewhere? Was he a sailor after all?

"I think something may be coming up," he told Bell, snapping the cap onto his pen. "I just recalled a boathouse."

"Fascinating. You said you thought you sailed, so that must be a link. Maybe you hail from the Thames? Lots of boathouses there. Or perhaps Cowes?"

"No, I don't think so. The place I see is wilder and on a tidal river," he said, perplexed. "I often describe it when I write. Then it feels more real to me than here."

"You've not shown me those pieces." Bell failed to keep the hurt out of his voice.

Will exhaled wearily. "I haven't shown anyone because it makes no sense. It's a strange place with slow silver water and sand that shines like stars when the sunlight hits it. There are shells everywhere, jagged as shark's teeth, and they snarl all the way along the shore. They'd cut your feet to ribbons if you didn't watch for them."

"You must mean oyster shells," Bell said easily. "They'd be sharp if you came across them on the shore."

Will stared at the doctor. The terrace seemed to lurch.

"What did you say?

"Oysters," repeated Bell. "Those are the shells you mean, Will. You often find wild oysters on the shore in places like Cornwall."

The garden blurred. The bench bucked beneath him.

"Will, what's wrong?" he heard Bell ask, but the doctor's voice came from a very faraway place. "Will?"

Will pitched to his knees, hands clawing the stone flags for purchase while the world turned inside out. "Oysters," he gasped. "Oysters."

"Nurse! Fetch water!" Bell cried. "Mr Shakespeare is unwell. Hurry, woman!"

People were running. Hands reached for him, voices called, and faces filled with concern peered down. Will didn't see them. He only saw the river, clear water shining like a thousand suns and defended by endless battalions of shells.

"Oyster Shore," he whispered. "*It all ended as it began, on Oyster Shore.*"

Memories raced in, a flood tide tearing up an estuary, and the patient was swept away, dragged beneath the surface by currents of recognition and rip tides of remembrance. If this was drowning then he welcomed it, because she was beneath the water too, the girl with hair like flame and sea-green eyes he'd dreamed of. An angel in his watery heaven, she turned to smile at him with such love he could scarcely breathe, because it was really her! His love. His best friend. His dearest childhood companion. How could he ever have forgotten her for a single second? How could he not have known her name? He had kept the lock of hair next to his heart from the moment she had given it to him.

"It's you!" he cried. "It's really you!"

"Of course it is," she laughed. "Didn't I promise I'd wait for you? I was here all the time, Ned. You only had to look."

She held out her hand and as he took it, his heart soaring with the gulls circling above, Will Shakespeare stepped aside for Ned Carew, Madalyn Trelyon and Oyster Shore.

31

OCTOBER 1917

Vyvyan Court, Cornwall

Gerald

Gerald often thought it ironic that a war which had brought untold misery to so many was the harbinger of his greatest happiness. Legitimately unable to fight, he was able to feign sorrow at not being able to actively serve his country while accepting sympathy from older men like Colonel Rivers and Julyan Pendennys. Not for Gerald the white feathers and scorn endured by others. Instead, as a young man of marriageable age and one whose fortune increased daily after the family business had won lucrative contracts to supply soap to the troops, Gerald found himself very popular with all the mamas and their single daughters. In contrast to the horrific injuries suffered by his contemporaries a twisted leg and awkward gait were as nothing, and if his heart hadn't been set on Madalyn Trelyon all the unaccustomed attention would have quite turned his head. However, Gerald was content to turn down invitations to dinner parties and exchange London society for Cornwall. Here he would wait patiently for events to unfold in his favour because although he might lack sporting prowess, Gerald Snowe knew how to play the long game.

The long game suited him. Having played it for most of his life, overlooked while the popular boys were lauded on the rugby field or praised in the classroom, he had learned to watch from the shadows and had mastered the art of patience. His opportunity might come when another pupil left a treasured item unguarded which Gerald could spirit away and plant in the desk of the boy who had wronged him months previously. He was skilled in stealing exercise books and dribbling ink over a page of arithmetic to earn the unlucky owner a caning. While so many of his contemporaries were being cut down like the wheat that the Trehunnist girls were reaping, Gerald had slowly set about winning the trust of Madalyn Trelyon. She'd been wary at first, still suspicious of him after his clumsy and much-regretted proposal (it never did to show one's hand too soon) but she had thawed gradually, and now Gerald believed she even looked forward to his visits. He certainly lived for them.

The art of winning Madalyn around lay in not showing so much as an eyelash's flicker of romantic interest. Instead, Gerald kept their conversation light and made a big fuss of bringing flowers for Constance or a cake from the Vyvyan kitchen to tempt Madalyn's wan appetite. He sent gardeners to clear the flowerbeds, and after spotting the cobwebs draping the cornicing and the thick dust on the mantelpiece, arranged for maids from Vyvyan to visit Oyster House twice a week. As much as anything else, Gerald had no desire to spend time in a house that was less than spotless. Lady Constance's health was deteriorating and he offered to collect them in the motor car on Sundays so she and Madalyn could attend church. It was all very time-consuming, but Gerald never doubted that the ultimate prize would be his.

Madalyn Trelyon would be his.

As soon as he'd spotted Ned Carew lining up to enlist, Gerald had felt sure it would be only a matter of time before the news came that his childhood companion had been lost. As time went by the reports from the Front became increasingly bleak, and each week the list of casualties in *The Times* grew longer. It was a numbers game and Gerald hadn't long to wait, for by the spring of the following year Reverend Tullis and his wife were in deep mourning and Bess Penwurthy was wearing a black armband. Gerald had bowed his head respectfully while the names of Trevellan's fallen were read out in the church, but his heart had pounded to hear Ned's name listed among them. Missing in action. That was as good as dead. Everyone knew what that dreaded phrase really meant. At long last the way was clear for Gerald. The golden brightness of Ned Carew had been extinguished for ever.

Gerald's eyes slid across the aisle to Madalyn, white-faced and as achingly beautiful as he'd ever seen her. He knew this was his chance to win her once and for all. Heartbroken and unable to speak of her grief, what could be more welcome to Madalyn now than a confidant? Somebody who had known Ned and who shared their past. Somebody with whom she could talk freely about Ned. Somebody who would whisper that he'd guessed how she had felt and who would offer sympathy. Gerald Snowe would save her from the loneliness of loss. He would win her trust and her heart. The memory of

Carew would fade away as the years passed, and one day all Madalyn would see was him. They would marry and she would be the mistress of Vyvyan. It was practically predestined.

Yes, Gerald had decided with growing confidence and with his head bowed in prayer, their shared loss was the perfect way to win Madalyn's approval. She was headstrong and stubborn, both traits he fully intended to curb when they were married, but with Ned Carew safely beneath the mud of France there would be no obstacles to their match. She could have no real reason to reject him, for he was rich, their families would approve, and above all he was her friend who understood her secret sorrow. He would be the only one she turned to.

Gerald had waited for five days, a decent enough period he felt for Madalyn to deal with the tears and hysterics women always exhibited at such times, before gingerly driving the Rolls Royce to Oyster House. The drive was in danger of vanishing beneath the undergrowth, and he made a mental note to order their elderly head gardener to deal with it better. Gerald had no intention of scratching the shiny blue paint of the car on future visits, and he wasn't inclined to walk either. Once they were married Madalyn would move up to Vyvyan, he decided as he guided the car around the bend in the drive and glimpsed the old house peeking out of the trees, and St John could close this place up. Maybe even pull it down. It was inconvenient and damp, and contained far too many memories. Better still, they could move to another county altogether. Gerald thought, as he parked the car and pushed his driving goggles into his dark hair. He liked Surrey. It was more civilised than Cornwall and much closer to London. He could buy a country estate where the ghost of Ned Carew couldn't haunt him. He and Madalyn could start their new life in a place where the only memories were the ones they made.

The Trelyons' maid took his hat and gloves and showed him into the small drawing room. While he waited for Madalyn, Gerald walked to the window and leaned on his cane and watched the river flow by. He had to admit that there was something mesmerising about the water. Kingfishers darted along the far bank, wings no more than a flash of blue and as out of reach as the last butterflies in the long grass, while beaten-metal light spread over the water as the sun peered out from behind the clouds, the watery hues shifting from pearl to gold to brightest blue. The part of Gerald that dreamed of writing ached with longing and regret. He could never capture this beauty. He would never write like Ned Carew.

I *am* a writer, Gerald reminded himself sharply. One didn't need to possess the lyrical skills of Ned Carew to be considered such. Who wanted purple prose these days, anyway? Gerald had recently penned the opening chapters to a comic novel, *Chin Up*, in the style of a new and widely admired author, a certain P G Wodehouse the literary world was fawning over. Gerald was rather pleased with his efforts, and an old school acquaintance whose father owned a publishing house had agreed to look at it. Literary success was just around the corner and Gerald could hardly wait. Kit Rivers and Ned Carew could keep their complicated poems and stories. Gerald Snowe would be the man of the hour. All of London would toast him.

"Miss Trelyon, sir," announced the maid.

Madalyn stood in the doorway, one hand resting on the door frame. With the light streaming from the cupola in the hall, her hair was a rich as the beech leaves in the woods, and the blue silken dress she wore was so sheer that Gerald could see the curve of her hips and the lines of her slender legs through the fabric. He couldn't look away, for she was more exquisite today than ever. Even the violet shadows beneath her eyes, huge in her pale face, emphasised their sea-green hue. There were deep hollows beneath her collarbones, and he could see a pulse fluttering beneath the porcelain skin of her throat. How fragile she was. Gerald thought he had never desired Madalyn more than in her vulnerability, and it took all his self-control not to blurt out another proposal.

Softly, softly, catchee monkey, he told himself. If he alarmed Madalyn she would bolt like a deer into the depths of the woods, and all chance of winning her would be lost.

"This is an unexpected visit. We weren't expecting you, were we?"

He swallowed his rising desire and arranged his face into a concerned expression. "I apologise for visiting unannounced, but had to come. It's dreadful news."

Madalyn's brow creased. "What is?"

Gerald wasn't prepared to have this conversation with a servant present. He inclined his head towards the maid. "Some tea, perhaps?"

The girl's eyes flicked to Madalyn for affirmation of his order and Gerald was irked. In the future he'd ensure the staff would know who gave the orders and paid their wages.

"Tea please, Tilly," Madalyn said. "And some of the seed cake if there's any remaining."

Once the maid had departed, Madalyn swept into the centre of the room, skirts swishing around her. "I assume you're referring to Ned?"

Gerald hoped he looked suitably grief-stricken and was

surprised to discover that part of him was truly sad. Since boyhood his thoughts had been as much occupied by his rival as they were by Madalyn, so maybe he had loved Ned too in his way. He had certainly wanted to be just like him. In losing Ned, Gerald wondered if he'd also lost a part of himself? The better part he had aspired to become?

"Let's not waste time pretending," he said gently. "I know how you felt about Ned. I've always known you loved him."

Surprise and horror flittered across Madalyn's face. She'd thought it was a secret, and was shocked that another could have guessed the inner secrets of her heart.

Had she given herself to Ned, Gerald wondered. The rose-pink stain on her throat and cheeks suggested as much, and his spy had certainly thought so – Gerald had clipped the boy's ear for making such crude remarks about a lady. Gerald waited to feel jealousy's pincers bite into his heart, but there was nothing. It didn't matter what had come before, he concluded, because Ned was dead. His rival was no more, and whatever had passed between the two lovers was dead too. Madalyn's compromised honour might even work in Gerald's favour, for not every man would accept a wife whose virtue was in doubt. Without family money to keep her, a good marriage was all Madalyn had left to hope for. She needed Gerald. He was the prince who would finally rescue her.

"There's no need to say anything," he said. "Or explain. Not to me. We all grew up together, didn't we? You two were always a pair and it was inevitable you would stay that way. I realised that when we met at Vyvyan and I proposed. Lord, I felt a fool for not twigging sooner! Soulmates, isn't that what they say? You and Ned were soulmates."

Madalyn was silent. Gerald knew she was keeping herself in check, but it was only a matter of time before the floodgates opened. A tear slipped down her cheek and he delved into the pocket of his waistcoat to offer his handkerchief to her.

"I can't pretend to understand what you're feeling, Madalyn. Ned and I weren't on good terms towards the end, but I would never have wished this on him." He stepped back while she pressed his handkerchief to each eye in turn, the cotton soaking up the grief and the tears poised to spill. He knew she hadn't been able to speak of her loss until now, and his mentioning Ned had breached the dam of restraint. There would be torrents at first but eventually the reservoir of tears would run dry. She couldn't mourn for ever. She would be happy again. He could give her the world. There was nothing he wouldn't buy her.

"How can everything still exist if he isn't here? How can it go on?" Her voice was the faintest whisper. "I can't believe it."

"The world's a lesser place without him. He was the best of us," Gerald said.

To his great surprise a lump filled Gerald's throat as he said this, for he knew it was true; Ned Carew had been the best of them all. This was why he'd envied and hated Ned so deeply. In the end such a powerful emotion was love in disguise. It consumed you, drove you, obsessed you and filled your every thought. Hatred was the flip side of love's coin – night to day, winter to summer. Why else did Gerald keep the stolen childhood treasures? The sketch book? Old photographs? The phoenix comb? Gerald had taken that as soon as Ned had left, the relief it had been returned to the hiding place rather than carried to France making him lightheaded when he glimpsed the red eye in the darkness beneath the tile. Its protective power was his now, and without it Ned was vulnerable. He was laid bare. He was not coming back without the protective power of his talisman.

Of course, this was childish nonsense, but when Ned had been listed as missing in action Gerald had felt a prickle of unease. Was this his doing? Was it his appropriation of the comb that had killed Ned rather than a shell or a bayonet? Had the Almighty watched him reach his arm into the dank gap beneath the boathouse floor and logged it as a crime? Would there be a reckoning for him?

Sometimes thoughts like these made his heart race, and he felt judgement breathing down his neck. Gerald didn't believe in God, not the way his mother did or with the certainty of Reverend Tullis, but the crawling guilt that made him wake in the night after dreams of mud and shattered bone sometimes trailed him into the morning. Gerald shook this off as weakness. He was close now to winning. He had to hold his nerve. Without Ned Carew to define him, he was free to be the man he'd always wanted to be. He could rewrite their childhood and cast himself in Ned's image. He could be the man that Madalyn wanted.

As Madalyn wept, Gerald did his best to murmur words of comfort. Some of them he even thought he might mean, but beneath his sombre exterior Gerald was jubilant. His time was coming. There was nobody to eclipse him now. He was going to be the man Madalyn wanted. He would be the best of them all now.

The months passed slowly. Autumn shivered into winter, which melted into spring before summer once splattered the hedges with campion, yolk-yellow buttercups and foaming cow parsley. The year turned. More men departed for the Front never to return, and it felt as though the war had always been a part of their lives. The sight of women wearing mourning was no longer uncommon, the last of the Snowes' hunters were sent to France, and the newspapers were filled with increasingly gloomy news. Reverend Tullis tried his best to preach sermons filled with soaring rhetoric about serving King and Country, but since Matilda had died, some said from the grief of losing her only son, the vicar's words lacked the ring of conviction and he was a sad and shrunken figure. By 1917 hearts and losses were heavy in Trevellan, and each Sunday as he sat in church Gerald felt the eyes of widows settle on him. Their scornful gaze suggested that his old injuries were nothing compared to what their menfolk were suffering, and he burned with shame because in his heart he knew this to be true. The war had brought him only wealth and happiness. Would he pay another way? Was God watching him and waiting to deal out retribution at a later date? Surely not, Gerald told himself sharply. This was all nonsense, the kind of cautionary tale Nanny used to trot out alongside Hilaire Belloc's terrifying stories. It was all superstition.

Madalyn mourned Ned deeply, and Gerald knew he had to be careful with any overtures he made towards her, but little by little he felt sure she was coming to care for him and value his friendship. It might not be the passion she'd felt for Ned, but there was a new regard between them.

And then one day, when they were walking along the riverbank, she tucked her hand into the crook of his arm as though it was the most natural thing in the world. "Thank you," she said.

"For what?"

"For being a friend. For listening to me talk about Ned. For not judging."

"I'd never judge you," Gerald said, and to his surprise he meant it.

"Lots of people would," Madalyn looked across to the boathouse and he knew she was thinking of Ned and the hours she'd spent there with him, hours only mentioned in passing but which Gerald suspected meant everything to her.

"I love you, Madalyn." The words fell from his lips and he couldn't claw them back because this was the truth. What had started out as a challenge to win Ned's sweetheart for himself, to have what was Ned's and to best him, had developed into something else entirely and something Gerald had never expected. He had fallen in love with Madalyn.

Madalyn's hand fell from his arm. Gerald wanted to tell her he was equally shocked by this emotion, explain that it had crept up on him, laid siege to all his plans and breached every defence he ever had. This was no longer about settling old scores or enjoying a victory over his childhood rival. It wasn't even about allying his family with one of the oldest dynasties in the country. He wanted to marry Madalyn because she was perfect for him.

"I shouldn't have said that." Gerald looked away from her, because he would be crucified to see distaste in her expression – or, worse still, pity. "I know you love Ned."

"I'll always love Ned. I've never made any pretence of that."

"And I know that. I respect it," Gerald said. He wanted to add that Ned was gone, but he bit his tongue. Madalyn was drawing her own conclusions and he didn't want to interrupt.

"The truth is I don't know whether I can ever love again. That part of me died with Ned, I think." Her head drooped. "I'm dead inside, and can't be the person you want me to be."

"I don't want you to be anyone else." He reached for her hand. "I want you just as you are. You're perfect."

She shook her red curls. "Oh, I'm far from that."

"You're perfect to me," Gerald insisted. "If you marry me, Madalyn, I promise I'll never ask for anything more than your friendship. I won't expect you to love me as you loved Ned. I won't lay a finger on you unless you want me to – but I *will* look after you and Constance. I promise you'll want for nothing."

"Except for the most important thing," she said sadly. "Except for love."

"There are different kinds of love, Madalyn. I know our marriage wouldn't be born from grand passion." Not on her side anyway, Gerald thought, but what did this matter since he loved her enough for them both? "Love can grow from friendship and respect, don't you agree?"

She looked up at him doubtfully. "I suppose so."

"I know so. Let me look after you as a friend and a husband. Let me make sure your mother's comfortable and safe too. Let me take care of you both. I can take you away from the struggles and the worry. I can send Constance to a sanatorium in a warmer climate. Whatever you need, Madalyn, I swear you'll have it."

Raising the subject of her reduced circumstances was a low blow, but Gerald was desperate. Unable to compete with her love for Ned, he had played his biggest ace. Would this prove a winning hand?

"But I love Ned," she said. It was her mantra; Gerald had heard it so many times the words no longer held any meaning. But Ned was gone. He was never coming back.

"Ned would want you to be safe and cared for. He wouldn't want you to struggle, would he?" Gerald pressed.

"He's gone, Madalyn, and we have to accept that. Let me honour his memory and make up for the things I did as a boy by taking care of you and your mother. Let me take care of you for Ned."

Madalyn turned from the boathouse abruptly, as though unable to bear looking upon a place where she had known such happiness, and they retraced their steps to Oyster House in silence. When they rounded the bluff and the boathouse was lost in the trees, she exhaled wearily as though reaching the end of a long, arduous journey.

"Yes," she said. "All right."

"Yes?" Gerald echoed. He wasn't quite able to believe what he was hearing. "You'll marry me?"

Madalyn nodded. "You might look a little less aghast. I thought that was what you wanted?"

"It was. I mean, it is!" He took her hands in his and raised them to his lips, pressing kisses onto them over and over again. "You have made me the happiest man alive! Oh my love, thank you!"

He felt Madalyn flinch when his mouth brushed her knuckles, but she didn't say she had changed her mind. She had made it clear she didn't love him or want him in the slightest, but she was willing to trade herself for wealth and status just as women had always done. Gerald felt slightly disappointed. He supposed he must have harboured a secret dream that Madalyn would realise she loved him too and just as much, if not more, than she'd loved Ned Carew. That, of course, was storybook nonsense. Who could love him? Even his own parents were disappointed in their weakling of a son.

Once again he would have to content himself with the crumbs from his old friend's table, and he supposed he ought to be glad that he'd managed to survive the twentieth century long enough to still be present to collect them. As he and Madalyn returned to Oyster House, arm in arm and planning the best way to announce their engagement, Gerald searched for the warm glow of triumph he'd anticipated, but it eluded him. This was baffling, because he'd beaten Ned in the end and nobody was laughing at Gerald Snowe now. Who cared about climbing trees or rowing or even books? Madalyn Trelyon was to be his wife

The Snowes were delighted with the happy news and Gerald thought nothing he had ever done in his entire life pleased them so much as this union with the Trelyons. Sir Arthur considered it evidence of his acceptance into the very best levels of society, and Mary Snowe could talk of nothing but the engagement party she would hold for the couple at Vyvyan. Constance duly posted the announcement in *The Telegraph*, and one sunny Saturday in July Gerald slipped a huge diamond ring onto Madalyn's left hand. It was a little loose – she seemed to have lost weight in recent weeks – but everyone agreed it was a magnificent piece and she was a lucky girl.

Madalyn nodded and smiled, but the light didn't reach her eyes and as she turned the ring over and over Gerald knew she was wishing Ned was the man who had placed it there. In the past this would have filled him with rage, but since Ned was dead Gerald found he didn't care as much as he had imagined, for Madalyn belonged to him now. In November she would become his wife. He could hardly wait for that moment, for he still feared she would slip through his fingers like river water.

Madalyn never pretended she loved him, and although this stung Gerald accepted that she had accepted his offer of marriage to provide security for her mother, and perhaps for herself as well. He shrugged this off, choosing to see it as another piece of evidence that Fortune was well and truly on his side, for without Ned Madalyn didn't seem to care overmuch what became of her own future. St John Trelyon had passed away the previous winter, bequeathing the estate to yet another distant male relative who possessed no attachment to his newly inherited dependents. The timing of this engagement was perfect, for even if Madalyn did have second thoughts, as he sometimes suspected, these circumstances would certainly make her reconsider. There was already talk about breaking entails and selling off the estate, and without St John's charity to protect them the Trelyon women were vulnerable. Gerald thought the phoenix comb was looking after him admirably.

"It would break my heart to leave Oyster Shore," Madalyn confided one afternoon as she and Gerald took tea on the terrace. The low tide was flirting with the notion of returning and she studied an oystercatcher as it picked its way through strands of lime-green weed, her top lip pressing down on its full-bottomed twin. "I really hope the estate stays whole so we can still visit it once we're married."

Gerald had no attachment to Oyster Shore. Quite the opposite. Some of his worst memories were of the place, and he certainly had no desire to glimpse the shade of Ned Carew around every meander, in each keening gull's cry or in the splash of a boat's oars. His preferred habitat was London, where the noise of the city and whirl of social engagements chased away all the ghosts of the past, and the more he thought about it the more he fully intended that once they were married he and his new wife would reside in town, and hold house parties in the luxurious country seat he'd envisaged in Surrey. But because he loved Madalyn so much

Gerald couldn't bear to think of her being unhappy, so if Oyster Shore made her happy, he was determined to ensure she never lost it. He secretly made enquiries into the possibility of buying a three-mile stretch of riverbank and the old house; it would be a wedding present to her. He would have Oyster House torn down and rebuilt with all modern conveniences, and they would use it in the summer for their house parties and elegant gatherings. The negotiations with the new Viscount's solicitor were completed –the turmoil of war meant that many bothersome details such as entails could be trodden into the mud as well – and Gerald planned to present Madalyn with the deeds on their wedding night.

This gift would surely open her heart to him. Madalyn would be so happy she would give herself to him as he knew she had done to Ned. It was the final part of his victory.

There would be one condition to this gift; the boathouse would be pulled down as well. Knowing it had been the setting for her trysts with Ned, Gerald had developed an aversion to the place. He hadn't set foot inside it since he'd taken the comb, but he knew Madalyn often visited it because he still had the village lad following her.

"She sits in a chair and reads. Then she kneels on the floor and puts something under it," the boy had said. "I can look if you want, sir. When she's gone. It looks like a big schoolbook. It goes in a satchel."

Ned's writing! It had to be. Somehow Madalyn had acquired it.

As always, Gerald's pulse quickened at the idea of Ned's treasures waiting beneath the tile. A novel would be a glorious treasure indeed, for there was no denying Ned's gift, and Kit River's long-ago praise still rankled. If there were more stories in existence Gerald wanted to read them. He *had* to read them! He couldn't rest until he knew what tales slumbered beneath the tiles. His curiosity festered until it was a monstrous boil of restlessness which could only be lanced by knowledge.

But he couldn't face returning there himself. The thought of God watching and judging him haunted Gerald more the older he became. Maybe it was all the talk of death, or the seances his mother insisted on attending, but the fear of divine retribution often kept him awake until the small hours. The Bible story of David and Bathsheba, retold last weekend in a particularly fiery sermon by Reverend Tullis, haunted him too – for was not Ned Carew like Uriah? Fighting for the king while David stole his wife? Did Tullis suspect what Gerald had hoped might be the outcome of Ned's loss, or was Matilda Carew, perhaps, speaking through her husband somehow when he stepped into the pulpit? There had always been whispers in the village that she was a gypsy ...

Utter nonsense! Gerald pushed these superstitious misgivings aside, but decided he would pay the boy to steal whatever was beneath the tile. That way his own hands would be clean of the deed.

"I'll pay you a shilling to bring me that satchel, and another to hold your tongue," he said.

Money was the solution to most of life's problems and the boy's eyes lit up like church candles. By the end of the day Gerald was in possession of a leather-bound notebook filled with Ned's looping script, and the lad had two shiny silver coins in his grubby fist. Once dinner was over Gerald retired to the library where, door closed and large brandy clutched in a trembling hand, he turned the first page.

It all ended as it began, on Oyster Shore...

The sun cast the world in molten bronze as Gerald read, and by the time he had closed the notebook the sky was rose and peach above the dark smudge of woods. His eyes were gritty and his head thick with lack of sleep, but Gerald hadn't been able to bring himself to stop reading because the novel was exquisite. Ned's imagery flowed like the river which coiled its way through the narrative, transporting the reader to a world of passion and obsession and beauty. Janus-like, the prose turned to war in parts and then was unsparing with the reality of splintered bone and congealing mud. Gerald shuddered for the protagonist and flinched at the vivid scenes which unspooled before his imagination. The ending left his eyes damp and his heart aching. As he placed the notebook on his father's desk he knew without a doubt that this novel was a masterpiece. Gerald felt bitterly ashamed of his own paltry efforts: *Chin Up* was no more than a weak pastiche, a pale imitation of something else, and not even a very good one. They would be laughing at him at the publishing house, wouldn't they? *Poor old Gerry*, his friend would say, *he never was good at much and he can't even write for toffee. Better send it back with a polite rejection.*

Even in death Ned Carew had bested him. It was bad enough that his own fiancée loved a dead man more than him, but worse again that a single sentence of Ned's work contained a thousand times more promise than his own stilted prose. It was beyond unfair.

Ned. Always Ned. When would it be his turn?

Looking back, Gerald wasn't sure what had possessed him to do it. Temporary insanity maybe? Jealousy? Or perhaps exhaustion combined with six brandies had blurred his judgement? Whatever the reason, he'd strode to his father's desk and withdrawn a thick sheet of embossed writing paper and a fountain pen. The silver nib had scratched the paper as Gerald had written words which flowed from his bitter heart as readily as the ink. He had sanded the page, folded it and slipped it into an envelope to accompany a package the exact shape and weight of the word-filled leather-bound notebook.

On Oyster Shore was a book his old school friend, Henry Fortescue, would want to publish, there was no doubt in his mind, and as the footman had set off to catch the post Gerald was drunk from brandy and triumph. This was his chance. Now everyone would call him an accomplished author and they would admire him and want to include him in salons and soirées. Nobody knew the name Ned Carew. Ned Carew was dead and would be forgotten, but Gerald Snowe would be famous. He was giving Ned immortality of a sort, wasn't he? And he was taking care of the woman Ned had despoiled and abandoned. Gerald was doing a noble thing. It was practically an act of charity!

After such a long and brandy-fuelled night Gerald slept most of the following day. As the weeks passed the episode took on the semblance of a dream. Had he even read the book at all? Sent it to Henry? If Madalyn ever discovered the manuscript was missing she never mentioned it. By the time Fortescue & May Publishing wrote offering a sizeable advance Gerald had almost forgotten the episode.

It was too late to admit what he had done in a moment of drunken madness. Besides, the admiration of his peers was seductive, and that he was believed capable of such work was a balm to Gerald's soul. Henry gushed over dinner about the versatility of an author who could veer so readily from the 'ridiculous to the sublime'; a rare find indeed. His father was delighted, much back-clapping and handshaking had ensued, and Gerald couldn't bear to disillusion him. How could he explain or justify what he had done? At best it was stupidity and at worst grave robbery, for the reality was that Gerald Snowe had stolen a dead man's work. When he woke at night with a racing heart and an increasing sense of dread, Gerald wondered whether Ned was in a shadowy corner, watching him from the afterlife. Would he be punished? And would that punishment come in this life or the next?

In the daylight it was easy to dismiss his night terrors as foolish fantasies. When the sun streamed into the study at Vyvyan and Gerald sat at the big desk and checked through his proofs, he had even been able to laugh at his fears. Ned was dead and buried, and ghosts and spirits were the stuff of novels and women. *On Oyster Shore* was his now, and nobody would be able to say otherwise. Madalyn was the only difficulty here, but Gerald felt certain he could persuade her that he was doing this for Ned's sake. And if she argued? He pushed this concern away and reminded himself that by the time the novel was published she'd be his wife, and her loyalty would lie with him. She wanted security and comfort for her mother – Gerald was under no illusions as to why Madalyn had agreed to marry him – and it would not be in her best interests to create a scandal. The shame would kill Constance Trelyon.

This aside, Madalyn showed little interest in his work. Previously this had irked Gerald, since he recalled how she had provided Ned with illustrations and made plans for joint ventures, but now he felt relieved by her indifference. If Madalyn found out what he'd done she would end the engagement in a heartbeat, and he couldn't have borne that. The best way was to keep mum until after they were married, by which point she'd have as much to lose from a scandal as he would. Gerald would tell his family he wanted the book to be a surprise, and since she took no interest in his business ventures Madalyn would remain oblivious until it was too late for her to cause a fuss. He would tell her it had been a drunken error of judgement that had gone too far and then argue that this was a way of keeping Ned's work alive.

Gerald suspected, though, Madalyn would want Ned's name on the cover, and then he would have to exert his authority as a husband. This thought brought him no joy. Another argument was that since the book was hers and she was his wife, it belonged to him, as did she. Even if the law said otherwise, it was a moral right, surely. With the additional threat of Constance's future to make Madalyn see sense, Gerald felt sure he could contain the situation. Anyway, Ned was dead, so what difference did it make who claimed the book?

But as the weeks passed his deception took on a life of its own and Gerald soon regretted not telling the truth from the very start. He was also starting to sweat at the thought of having to produce a second novel, something his publishers were very keen he should do since they were so certain that *On Oyster Shore* would be a success. Fear of discovery stalked Gerald constantly, and it was fortunate that most people who would recognise Ned's work had fallen in battle. He was willing to wager that Bess Penwurthy wouldn't have read it – and Marrick, against the odds still alive in France, was practically illiterate. Who would take their word, anyway, over Gerald Snowe's? They were common folk, and their home and livelihood depended on his father's good graces. All would be well.

By the time the autumn arrived preparations for the wedding were in full swing and the publication of *On Oyster*

Shore was just months away. As he drove the Rolls back from Rosecraddick Halt after a very successful meeting with his publisher, Gerald reflected that but for the quirk of Fate which had sent him tumbling from a tree he too might have fallen in Flanders. Even worse, he could have returned maimed like the unfortunate figures he'd seen in the city or the crippled man ahead of him who was making his cumbersome way along the lane. Dragging a leg and stooped beneath the weight of the kitbag slung over his shoulder, the fellow made Gerald shudder. He'd read enough about the injuries sustained at the Front to know what he was looking at. The station had been full of such men.

He squinted into the low sunlight. Who *was* this beneath the hat? Why was he on the road to Oyster Shore? The man wasn't in uniform like the soldiers he'd seen in London. Was he a Trehunnist? One of the fishermen? Or maybe stranger hoping to pick up employment? If so, Gerald was determined to send the man on his way. They didn't want vagrants here.

He slowed the Rolls Royce to draw parallel with the man and pushed his goggles up. "Can I help you?"

The stranger turned around. "Gerald?"

The shock was akin to plunging into iced water. Gerald's hands gripped the steering wheel as though it was all that prevented him from tumbling into a chasm of pure terror. Was this a ghost? A manifestation of his guilt for stealing *On Oyster Shore*? The punishment he feared when he lay awake during the small hours?

"Gerald! It's me! Ned!"

The sun darted behind a cloud. No longer dazzled, Gerald saw the glint of gold hair beneath the cap and the shine of violet eyes. His stomach dropped into his shoes. "Ned? Good Lord!" Gerald was amazed that his voice remained steady, because his heart was beating a wild tattoo against his ribs.

"I may look a little different but it's definitely me," Ned laughed, pulling off his cap. Thick blond locks tumbled to his shoulders and a dimple danced in his cheek as he smiled at Gerald. Gerald didn't return the smile. He was far too shocked. With shoulders and arms well-muscled from using crutches and skin tanned from sunshine, Ned looked as vital as he always had. This was no phantom. Ned Carew had returned from the dead.

"But ..." Gerald gasped for words and failed. Everything he had worked for, everything he wanted so badly, was turned to ashes in a heartbeat. "It's not possible!"

"Don't look so worried. I'm not a ghost!" Ned laughed. "It's a long story, but there was a mix-up at the field hospital. I can't wait to tell everyone what happened."

Gerald thought he would vomit from sheer panic. Ned mustn't be allowed to see anyone, especially not Madalyn, for then all would be lost. She would fall into Ned's arms and forget all about the engagement and wedding plans. And what about *On Oyster Shore*? Gerald would be ruined. His father would be furious. His peers would despise him. In the blink of an eye everything Gerald held dear was in the balance, ready to be snatched from him, and his thoughts whirled like sycamore seeds. A cold sweat of dread made his shirt cling to his back.

"I thought you were dead," he said.

"You weren't the only one. They had me in the meat wagon at one point."

"Meat wagon?" Gerald echoed.

Ned pulled a face. "Tommy slang for the cart that collects the corpses. Our dugout was caught in enemy shelling and I was in the thick of it. They thought I was goner, but luckily for me a sharp-eyed Red Cross orderly spotted I was still alive. I was in a bad way and lost my memory. For two years I had no idea who I was."

Gerald stared at him in disbelief. This was like one of Ned's stories. The returning hero had come to claim his princess prize.

"Two years?"

Ned nodded. "It's been a slow recovery. I only regained my memory yesterday, but I set off for Trevellan at once."

Gerald did some swift mental arithmetic. As it was wartime a letter wouldn't have arrived in this short time, and he was pretty sure Ned wouldn't have sent a telegram to Madalyn, because that would have alerted Constance and so ruined any hopes of a romantic reunion. Ned would have wanted to surprise the girl he loved and sweep her into his arms like the hero of a novel.

The thought of Ned touching Madalyn Trelyon, *his* fiancée, made Gerald feel quite savage. Would anyone know if he ran Ned down? Or care? A wounded soldier might easily stagger out into the path of a motor car ...

"I couldn't wait a moment longer," Ned was saying, blithely unaware of Gerald's murderous thoughts. "I caught the first train to Rosecraddick, hitched a ride with a carter as far as the Trehunnists' farm, and here I am. I'm almost home!"

The longing in his voice was palpable and Gerald almost faltered. Only the thought of what he stood to lose kept him from weakening and feeling sympathy. Ned's arrival would ruin everything. It would destroy him.

"Does Bess know you're here?" he asked. If she did, all was lost.

Ned shook his head. "Nobody does, except you. I'll see Bess soon enough. There's someone else I need to see first."

Ned was on his way to claim Madalyn. He would steal Gerald's hard-won happiness and push him back into second place. Gerald knew Madalyn didn't love him; she had told him so enough times, and he had yet to even steal a kiss. Gerald had been patient, believing he had all the time in the world – but he had been wrong. Madalyn had only ever been on loan to him.

His thoughts raced. There had to be a way to recover the situation. There had to be a way to keep Ned away from Madalyn. He flicked his eyes downwards in Ned's leg. Would a lover want to see an injury like this? Would Madalyn be disgusted? Would she reject Ned now?

"You've lost a leg?"

"That's why I'm walking slowly!" Ned laughed, and Gerald realised his rival was not beaten by injuries. Why would he be? There had always been more to Ned Carew than his physical prowess.

"You can hardly walk at all," Gerald pointed out. Fear made him cruel, but Ned's smile didn't slip.

"But I'm still walking, and that's more than enough. Trust me, losing a leg is a small price to pay for having made it through. Not everyone was as lucky as me."

It was an odd definition of luck, thought Gerald, watching Ned switch his kitbag onto his other shoulder and lurching as the weight shifted. He was a cripple, a burden, and Madalyn deserved better. Gerald would be doing her a kindness by saving her from a life shackled to a man like this. Ned was being selfish.

"That's more like it," Ned said once his bag was in place. He held out a hand. "It was good to see you, Gerald."

"You're going to see Madalyn, aren't you?" Gerald blurted. Panic swelled beneath his breastbone. Unless he thought fast this was where it would all unravel. Madalyn would always choose Ned over him, whole or injured. He was going to lose her. He was going to lose *everything*.

"I am," Ned said.

"But why?" The question sounded more like a wail. "You're a cripple."

Ned gave him a curiously pitying look. "I'm still me. I lost my leg, not my heart, and I love Madalyn, Gerald. I've always loved her, and she loves me. What else can matter but that?"

Madalyn, Gerald thought, was *his* fiancée! She wore *his* ring. She was marrying *him*. She was *his*! Outrage flooded through him. Ned could not just ride in like some knight errant and carry her away at the eleventh hour. It wasn't fair. He wouldn't allow it!

"You're crippled, Ned. She won't want you now."

"I think that's for Madalyn to decide," Ned replied. "*Love is not love which alters when it alteration finds.*"

Gerald almost exploded with the pent-up rage of a lifetime. How dare a common man like Carew stand here quoting Shakespeare and declaring love for *his* fiancé? A village oaf! A nobody! It was insufferable. It was not to be borne. Gerald longed to kick Ned's crutches from under him and leave him sprawled in the dust where he belonged, but he fought the urge. He had to stay in control. They were men now, not boys, and he had to be cunning if he was to checkmate his old rival. He would need to convince Ned that walking away from Madalyn would be the action of a man who truly loved her. Ned's love for Madalyn was his weakness, and Gerald would exploit it to prevent his own world from imploding.

"How can you support her now? And her mother?" he asked. "Or do you think Madalyn should support you? Is that it? Do you intend her to work? A seamstress, maybe? Or a washerwoman?"

Ned looked shocked. "Of course not. I'll write to support us both."

"That's a dream, Ned. You must realise that?"

"Perhaps," Ned said quietly, "but without our dreams, what are we? I've written a book, and I'll teach. It's what I've been doing at the hospital and I'm sure they'll give me a reference. I'll become a schoolmaster like my father."

"You expect a highborn lady to be the wife of a *schoolmaster*?" Gerald sneered, but Ned didn't rise.

"There's no shame in being a schoolmaster – my father taught me that – and Madalyn and I love each other, which is all that matters. We can make a wonderful life together. We don't need a palace to be happy. We just need one another."

Gerald had feared as much, and he knew Madalyn would agree with Ned. She would live in a hovel with Carew. He pushed down his rising panic and forced himself to remain calm. He had to keep the lovers apart or he'd be ruined.

"Utter nonsense!" he scoffed. "What will become of Lady Constance? Will she live at the schoolhouse too? Can you support her? Pay her bills? Will you keep her as she expects to live? Or will she scrub floors and take in washing? What about her staff?"

Uncertainty danced across Ned's face. He'd never been able to hide his feelings. An open book in all senses, Gerald thought scornfully.

"Madalyn and I will take care of her," he said staunchly. "I can support us all."

"You're a fool – a fool who's going to ask Madalyn to give

up everything on the chance that you might write a book and sell a few? That's a pipe dream. She'll be staking her security and future on a dream! She'll live in poverty because of you!"

"That's her choice, Gerald."

Gerald chose to ignore the familiarity. There had always been something rather socially ambiguous about Ned Carew. He'd never spoken with the deference owed to his betters.

"She's not some village fishwife, Carew. She's a Trelyon. A lady. She deserves the best."

"And I'll give her everything." Ned's eyes shone with conviction. "All I am is hers, and all I ever will be."

Gerald shook his head. "And what use is that? You're a cripple, man. You'll always be a burden. If you loved her as much as you claim, you'd turn around and leave her be. She has a wonderful new life where she wants for nothing. Madalyn's engaged to be married, and she's happy. You're dead to her now, so if you love her leave her be."

Ned was pale. "That can't be true. Madalyn wouldn't marry another."

"It's true," said Gerald. "Ask anyone in Trevellan, they'll all tell you. Lady Constance is delighted her daughter's future's secure. Madalyn will want for nothing once she's married, trust me on that. She'll be taken care of, and restored to the rank and fortune she was born to.

"It's you, isn't it? You're engaged to her."

Gerald had waited a lifetime for this moment. "Yes. We're to be married on All Saint's Day. Over time we've grown very fond of one another and become close. It was a natural progression, you understand, because we're equals, and it's a union that has delighted both our families. Madalyn's very happy now, and busy with dresses and flowers and all the things a young bride desires. You know how women are."

Ned swayed on his crutches. "I can't believe she wouldn't have waited for me. You're making this up, Gerald. It's one of your stories."

Gerald shrugged. It was time to call Ned's bluff. "Believe what you like; it's true. Go to see Bess. She'll tell you. Or ask your stepfather, since he's been reading the banns. You were dead and buried, Ned. Did you really think Madalyn should mourn for ever? Did you want that for her? To be an old maid without a house and family of her own? To live in poverty?"

"Never. I only want her to be happy. She's everything to me."

Ned was teetering on the precipice of despair as the reality of his new life became clear; all Gerald needed to do was watch him fall. What use was a crippled soldier to a girl like Madalyn Trelyon? A man with a head full of dreams was no match for the heir of a wealthy industrialist. Gerald took a deep breath. This was his last chance to salvage his future.

"She is happy. Very happy, because I am giving her a life most women only dream of. With me she'll have everything – but what could you truly give her, Ned? Oh, before you say a word I know you'll say 'love', because you believe love conquers all, and somehow you think can support a wife and a family. But the reality is that you're crippled and penniless. We both know Madalyn will overlook such details now – but one day, many years from now, she'll pause and wonder what her life could have been like. When her hands are raw from washing and scrubbing and the last of the money is gone, when she's aged prematurely from hardship and toil, that's when she'll wonder why she chose the life she did. She'll wonder if it was worth it. Maybe she'll even come to hate you for it. You'll have done that to her, Ned, and you'll both know it. Can you imagine the resentment and the bitterness? Your selfish determination to have her, come what may, will destroy Madalyn. Her mother's family will disown her and polite society will turn their backs on her, because you'll have degraded her, down to your level. There's no security for a woman like Madalyn with somebody like you. There's only a spiral to despair and poverty. Life with you will mean misery for Madalyn. Is that love? Is that how much you truly regard her?"

"I love Madalyn," Ned said quietly. "She's everything to me."

"Then you'll walk away. Let Madalyn believe the man she loved died a hero fighting for King and Country," Gerald said. "Don't ruin the life she's built by shackling her to a crippled man who can't take care of her. Don't steal her future because you're clinging to the past. *I* can give Madalyn the world. *You* would take everything away from her. If you truly love her as much as you claim, turn around right now and leave her at peace with her loss. Or is your love selfish, Ned, and about what *you* want rather than what's best for Madalyn? I can care for her. Let her go. Set her free."

The world seemed to stop as though waiting to see what Ned would answer before continuing its journey around the sun. Ned was looking doubtful, teetering on the brink. One more nudge would be all he needed. Gerald sensed victory was close.

"It's your choice," he said. "Madalyn's future is in *your* hands, because we both know she'd choose you. So, poverty or wealth for her, then? Hardship or comfort? In a decade's time, will she wonder if she should have taken a different path? When hardship has broken her would you be able to live with what you had chosen to do to her? Would she wonder about the life she could have had? The security her children could have enjoyed?"

Ned said nothing but he paled, and Gerald knew he had touched a nerve.

"If you walk away now, Madalyn won't be forced to have to choose one life over another or be obligated to choose you," he continued. "Her future is *yours* to decide."

It was a gamble. Ned might insist on speaking to Madalyn, and then everything would be over. Gerald had rolled the dice and now he had to wait. Would Ned behave true to form, or had war and suffering recast him into a more selfish version of the man he once was?

Ned exhaled slowly. His shoulders slumped and the kitbag slipped to the ground.

"Swear you'll make her happy." His voice was hoarse and his violet eyes dark with anguish. "Promise me you'll worship her every day for the rest of your life, that her name will be the first thing on your lips when you wake up and the last thing you'll say when you leave this world. Swear that she'll be everything to you and you'll live your whole life making her happy. Swear it on your soul."

Gerald loved Madalyn. He'd bought Oyster Shore for her, which would make her happy. He could give her anything. That would make her happy. His love was worthier of her than Ned's had ever been, and so it was easy for him to agree to what his old friend was asking.

"I will," he said.

"Swear it." Ned demanded. "Swear on your life you'll make her happy and take care of her. Go on. Swear it on your life and soul."

"I swear," said Gerald quickly and firmly. He wanted

nothing more than to see Ned Carew turn away and never return.

Ned's eyes held his. They were as hard as Cornish granite.

"If you break that oath God help you, because crippled or not I'll hunt you down and kill you with my own hands. I swear that on all I hold dear and on my love for her. If you hurt Madalyn Trelyon you'll be cursed, Gerald Snowe, do you understand? My mother was a gypsy, remember? Our line knows how to carry vengeance forward. If you betray Madalyn you'll never know a day's peace again."

A cold wave of fear broke over Gerald. Matilda Carew's wild lineage had always been a cause for gossip, and he didn't doubt for a moment that Ned meant every word.

"I swear I'll take care of her," he said, and his voice quivered with nerves. "But she must never know you came here or spoke with me. You must never tell her."

"Do you think I want to break her heart? Let her know that I forsook her? Broke every vow I ever made to be with her always?" Ned stooped for his bag, waving Gerald away angrily when he attempted to assist. "You've got nothing to worry about. You'll never see me again."

"Let me help with your fare."

"Don't you *dare*!" Ned's growl of rage took him by surprise and Gerald stepped back hastily. Ned might have lost a leg, but he was still taller and stronger.

"Come on, man. You must need funds to reach Australia."

Ned's lip curled in contempt. "There's no price on my love for Madalyn. You'll never understand, will you? I'm leaving because I love her more than anything. More than myself. More than life. More than my dreams. If you want to salve your conscience do so by loving Madalyn more than yourself – if that's possible for you."

Ned Carew turned away, and the final impression Gerald had of him was a melancholy tableau of a stooped figure strung between his crutches and limping a retreat, broken in body and spirit yet still filled with dignity and strength. Gerald remained by the car, gazing at the empty lane long after it was deserted, and puzzled by his own lack of jubilation. He was safe, he had won, and Madalyn Trelyon was his. The book was his. Victory was his. Everything he'd ever planned for was his. He should be celebrating, because at long last he was safe.

But as Gerald started the car and drove back to Vyvyan, he didn't feel safe at all. As Ned's gypsy warning rang in his ears, Gerald was gripped by the strongest conviction that he had just poisoned the rest of his life.

32

OCTOBER 1917

Oyster House, Cornwall

Madalyn

She'd been dreaming of Ned again, vivid dreams which left her sobbing and with a racing heart. These dreams were so real that on opening her eyes Madalyn was greeted anew with his loss and would weep into the darkness until dawn blushed the sky and turned the river to gold. Her beloved Ned was gone. He would never return. He would never hold her against his heart again, pressing kisses against her eyelids, lips and throat as he whispered words of love, and they would never sit on the riverbank in silent harmony, writing and sketching as dragonflies danced along the banks and ducks squabbled. The short few weeks they had shared had been the happiest of her life, and Madalyn sometimes wondered how she even continued breathing without the other half of her soul. She often lay in bed willing her chest to stop rising, and pleading with her aching heart to cease its ready beat, for how could she live a lifetime without him? It was unbearable.

How Madalyn wished she'd died in the trenches alongside Ned. The person she used to be had certainly perished when Bess broke the dreadful news, and the old Madalyn who had turned her face to the sun, who had drawn and laughed and walked for miles along the tideline, was gone for ever. Even now, eighteen months after hearing of Ned's death, Madalyn truly thought she would die of grief. On several occasions she had found herself standing on the pontoon by the boathouse, with no recollection of walking there, praying for the courage to hurl herself into the water so the current would drag her under. The river would wrap her in a cold embrace, kissing her and filling her like a deadly lover, before carrying her to the place where Ned was waiting for her. She would tug off her shoes and pull off her hat – only to glimpse a flash of golden hair in the boathouse window or a whisper of movement. Hope would flare and she would run to the boathouse and fling the door open, only to find the place deserted and his writing chair empty. Her courage and the moment lost, she would trudge back to Oyster House with damp cheeks and a heavy heart, knowing that an existence without Ned was no more than a living death.

Was it Ned who drew her back from the brink each time? Madalyn knew he wouldn't approve of her impulse for self-destruction, and the only thing during those first dark days that prevented her from finding a way to join him was the realisation that while she was alive so was his memory. As long as Madalyn Trelyon lived to walk along the riverbank and think of him, Ned Carew wasn't entirely lost. Her thoughts and her love would keep him alive.

Ned's writing would keep him alive too, and one day when she could read his words without sobbing, Madalyn would do her very best to find a publisher. Then Ned's voice would still be heard and he would never be truly lost. This thought comforted her, for she now considered herself the guardian of Ned's work. *On Oyster Shore* was beautiful, and the world deserved to share it. When she felt strong enough she would set it free.

Ned's novel had broken her into a thousand pieces. She had read it soon after she'd been given it, in just over a week, eking out each chapter and savouring every turn of phrase as she curled up in the old armchair, losing herself in Ned's world. It was a place she knew as well as she knew the softness of the hair at the nape of his neck, the warm hollow of his collarbone and the swell of the muscles in his smooth back. Ned painted with words the turning tides and molten copper sunsets he'd loved, and as his novel followed the journey of a young man's forbidden love affair with a girl who drew and paddled and laughed, Madalyn had smiled and cried in equal measure as she recognised their own love story. Yet there was more than a love story here, for Ned had turned his narrative to the fragility of life in a world where senseless wars tore lovers and flesh apart and generals sent thousands of young men to be cut down like summer wheat. His descriptions of battle were so harrowing they had haunted Madalyn for weeks and the novel's sweeping conclusion made her sob with both happiness and the soul-aching emptiness of knowing that the ending that Ned had written, and had hoped would come true for them, was marooned for ever in fiction.

The parallels in the novel were so overwhelming and painful for her to read that she had put the book back again.

She kissed it farewell, placed it in the satchel and slipped it into the old hiding place, frowning when she couldn't find the phoenix comb and her old sketchbook and letters. Had Ned taken those items to war? Madalyn was certain he hadn't. Was there a thief skulking in the shadows? Or had Bess sent Marrick to retrieve her brother's belongings?

Madalyn didn't want to make any decisions that might upset Bess. She truly believed the future of Ned's book had to be a joint decision. It was his legacy, and as Bess was his next of kin the book, and any money it might generate, belonged to her. Deciding she wouldn't read it again while her heart still felt as though it was lacerated with the barbed wire Ned had described so powerfully, Madalyn was set on retrieving the novel one day and doing her utmost to make Ned Carew's name equal to those of Dickens and Tolstoy. Until that time came, the manuscript would slumber in the old hiding place. One day she would be ready to share Ned with the world, but until then Madalyn needed him to be hers for a little longer.

As the seasons turned, Madalyn's grief became less of a knife-blade in her heart and more of a dull heaviness. She bore her sadness silently and reminded herself that she was not unique, for most of her contemporaries dressed in mourning nowadays and wore engagement rings destined never to be joined by a golden band. The woman she might have been, and the life she might have led, had died with Ned. Even her dreams of becoming an artist and travelling the world seemed faint echoes from another existence. Gerald spoke about Ned from time to time, but Madalyn suspected this was to humour her rather than because he wanted to, and as the months passed she resigned herself to the emptiness of a future without the man she had always loved.

Gerald had surprised her with his quiet friendship, and to her surprise Madalyn eventually came to believe she had misjudged him. He was no longer the spoilt boy she'd disliked, but a quiet man who was kindness itself to Constance and generous to her. Madalyn had no strong feelings for him, but when he proposed for the second time she concluded that if she must marry it might as well be to him. Gerald accepted that she still loved Ned and he wouldn't expect her to love him. He was wealthy and would take care of Constance, and as his wife she could stay in Cornwall and close to Oyster Shore. If Madalyn couldn't be with Ned, then what did it matter if she married Gerald Snowe? What did it matter what became of her?

Her forthcoming wedding was all anyone in Trevellan could talk about and her match with Sir Arthur Snowe's heir was considered a huge success amongst Constance's circle. Little caring what became of her, Madalyn allowed herself to be carried along like flotsam on a flood tide, drifting to dress fittings and appointments to choose flowers while paying little heed to anything else. Yet the closer the wedding day grew, the more vivid the memories of the man she loved became. Madalyn would be at a fitting, set high on a table while the seamstress adjusted a hem, and would suddenly be blinded by an image of Ned hunched over his notebook, face intent and golden hair falling into his eyes. She would feel sick with a wave of loss and have to bite hard on the inside of her cheek to recover herself sufficiently to comment on a choice of trimming or tightness of bodice. Why did Ned feel closer than ever? Was his spirit telling her not to marry Gerald? Was he angry?

"Ned," she whispered as she lay in bed staring at the cracked ceiling as hot tears slid into her hair and ears. "Oh

Ned. It should have been you. Why did you have to leave me?"

It was a gloomy day, the final glorious burst of autumn fizzling out in a succession of rainy days and storms mustering across the Channel. The trees in the woods dripped dismally, the grey sky bulged with rain and the river was grey and sullen. The whole world was in mourning for Ned and the life she should have led, the life buried in an unmarked grave in a foreign land alongside the man she loved.

And she had loved him. Madalyn had loved Ned Carew so much that she had once thought the sheer intensity of their passion would make her combust. When he kissed her and loved her Madalyn felt a firework display of desire ignite in her belly. She had ached for Ned and longed for his touch. She had craved him, adored him, worshipped him. Those things would never change, but now Madalyn had chosen another path, for tomorrow she would marry Gerald. It was time to pack away the past and lock up the memories of the man who had been her twin soul. The emotion she had for Gerald was nothing like love. Madalyn supposed it was gratitude and friendship rather than passion. Gerald wasn't her lover, but he was a friend of sorts, and one who was as much a part of the background of life on Oyster Shore as the keening gulls and restless tides. Even though he knew she could never love him, he had offered to take care of Constance and of her, so that was surely a type of love. Could she grow to love him as a wife should love a husband, Madalyn wondered? Could she bear him to touch her? To make love to her? Could she give to him what should have been Ned's and Ned's alone? The idea alone made her skin crawl with betrayal. It was nonsense for Ned Carew was dead and the whole world as grey as the sky beyond the window. There would never be any colour in it now.

"I love you, Ned," she whispered. "I'll always love you."

But there was no reply, only the cries of seabirds and the rustle of wind in the wisteria, and Ned's face faded. Madalyn prayed he wouldn't leave her once she was married to Gerald. She could bear a great deal, but she could not bear that. She needed Ned's image to be as vivid now as it had been the day he kissed her goodbye and promised to return, a promise which he hadn't been able to keep no matter how much he'd hoped to.

It was the only promise he had ever broken.

As she breakfasted, doing her best to eat at least a little under Constance's critical eye, Madalyn was haunted by the remnants of her dream, and her longing for Ned snatched what little appetite she did possess. While Tilly poured tea and her mother's knife scraped over the toast, Madalyn gazed out of the window and watched two swans glide downstream, and she thought her heart would break with envy. Even the wildfowl could be with their mate for life. Why not her? Why had Ned been taken away?

"Do try and eat a little more, dear. We've had the seamstress take in your wedding dress twice already. There isn't time for any more alterations," Lady Constance said. "Tilly, bring Miss Madalyn some scrambled eggs and a kipper. And more toast. With butter."

Madalyn's stomach heaved. She felt sick enough without the smell of kippers. How could she marry Gerald when she still loved Ned so much? It was as though her heart, drunk with grief, had been numb to anything else when she had accepted his offer and was only now beginning to awaken.

She couldn't marry Gerald Snowe! She didn't love him! How could she possibly go through with this wedding?

"Porridge too," added her mother. "With a little cream."

"Oh no, Mama. Toast is quite enough."

"Nonsense, you need to eat. Nobody wants to see the bride faint away at the altar," snapped Constance. "Pull yourself together, Madalyn. I don't know what's wrong with you."

No, thought Madalyn darkly, of course you don't, because you've never asked. All you want is to sell me to the highest bidder. It's all you've ever wanted.

"It's wedding jitters, milady," said Tilly sagely, sploshing tea onto the cloth. "My sister was just the same. She couldn't eat for days. Nigh on faded away."

Constance frowned. The truth was that Madalyn had been losing weight for weeks. If these were wedding jitters, they had started very early on. It was clear to everyone that Madalyn Trelyon was not an eager bride.

"Pay attention to the pot, Tilly. When I require your opinion, I'll ask for it," she said. "The eggs, please."

"Yes, milady. Sorry, milady," said Tilly, backing from the table, teapot clutched to her chest. "I'll fetch the eggs right away. And the porridge."

"What's the matter with you?" Constance asked Madalyn once the maid was out of the room. "Are you sickening for something?"

Madalyn looked down at her left hand. The huge diamond ring, chosen by Gerald at great expense, was looser than ever and reminded her of a line from Shakespeare about giant's robes hanging on a dwarfish thief. This ring had no place here. It had no right to be on her finger. Only Ned Carew's ring should sit on her wedding finger.

"I don't think I can do this," she whispered, clasping her trembling hands in her lap.

"Of course you can. It's only a kipper and some eggs," said her mother briskly. "Do perk up, Madalyn. *I'm* meant to be the invalid in this household."

"I don't mean breakfast, Mama. I was talking about marrying Gerald. I can't marry him."

Constance's knife clattered to the plate. "Of course you can marry him. The banns are read. It's all arranged."

"I don't love him, Mama."

There. She had said it and the truth was unleashed. Madalyn waited for her mother to reply but Constance picked up her knife and concentrated on cutting toast into perfect triangles. When this was done to her satisfaction, she fixed Madalyn with a sharp look.

"What has love got to do with this?"

"A great deal, I should imagine," said Madalyn, feeling bolder than she had done for a very long time. She would call this wedding off, hide in her room and wait for the gossip to die down. Gerald would understand because he knew about Ned and knew she could never love him. All would be well.

"Don't be a fool," said Constance. "Do you think I loved your father? Do you suppose Lady Rivers married the Colonel for love? People like us don't marry for love. You're not a housemaid, Madalyn, so please refrain from talking like one."

Madalyn didn't recall much more about her father than the smell of horses and brandy. As for Colonel Rivers and his big moustache? She shuddered.

"Love is for the lower classes," Constance continued, taking a sip of her tea. "It's for servants and fishwives and shopkeepers. The upper classes marry for alliance and family and duty. Love follows – if one is lucky. This match with Gerald Snowe is everything we'd always hoped for you."

"I don't want to marry for money, Mama."

Constance placed her cup on the saucer and dabbed the corners of her mouth with a napkin.

"This isn't just about what *you* want, my dear. This is about us and the future of our branch of the family. The marriage will keep us safe now we're alone in the world since St John passed. It's only a matter of time before the new Viscount asks us to leave. Then what will we do? Where will we go? How will we live?"

"I don't know," whispered Madalyn.

"Do you think I should seek employment as lady's companion perhaps? With my delicate health I wouldn't last a month. Is that what you'd prefer so you can gad about and find *love*?"

Constance almost spat the word. Somewhere Madalyn thought she heard a door clang shut. Was it Tilly with the kippers? Or a cell door in the prison of her future?

"Of course not, Mama, but —"

"There's no 'but' about this. If you jilt Gerald you're wilfully choosing to destroy us both. We'll be untouchable. No decent man from a good family will consider you." Constance rose to her feet. "I don't understand you at all, Madalyn. This is a good marriage to a young man, and one that *you* have chosen. A young man who is, I am reliably informed, on the brink of huge success as a writer. When he's published Lady Mary says you'll be richer than you could have ever imagined."

Madalyn had never once imagined being rich. Her dreams had all been of a life with Ned, one where they made love beneath the eaves, drew and wrote, and might one day paddle in the river with their own children. These were all the riches she had ever asked for. But that Gerald was on the brink of huge success as an author was a surprise. Madalyn had rarely seen any of his work, but the little she had read was truly dire. *Chin Up* was probably the worst of the lot, and she couldn't imagine that any publisher would have touched it.

"Are you sure?"

Her mother nodded. "Lady Mary said Gerald's been quite insistent upon it being a surprise for once you are married. It's been quite the secret. He'll be the toast of London and you'll be invited to all the very society gatherings."

Madalyn's stomach knotted like weed on a mooring. Something felt off. Why hadn't Gerald mentioned this? He usually loved a chance to boast.

"You'll be back in your rightful place at Vyvyan, which is all we've ever dreamed of," concluded her mother, bestowing Madalyn with a proud smile. "You'll be the wife of one of the wealthiest young men in the county. You're a very lucky girl."

"I know I am," Madalyn said miserably. Her good fortune was undeniable. Constance reminded her of this daily.

"So, enough of this nonsense. Gerald is coming at eleven to drive you to Vyvyan. Lady Snowe needs you to choose your wedding bouquet from the hothouse and wants to you to pick a tiara from her collection. Now if you'll excuse me, I feel one of my headaches coming on."

Her mother swept from the room. Madalyn placed her head in her hands. Everything was spinning. Books. Flowers. Secrets. She would have to marry Gerald tomorrow, for Constance was right; they would want for nothing, and it was indeed an exceptional match.

After breakfast, and even though the sky was the washed-out colour of old dishcloths and the trees smudged into a blur as rain blew in from the sea, Madalyn pulled on a coat and gumboots and walked along the river bank. She followed the old path around the bluff and through the woods to the boathouse, needing to bid a silent farewell to the setting for her greatest happiness, because once she was married her visits to this place would cease. The untarnished memories of the time she had spent with Ned beneath the eaves were too painful and although she had yet to even kiss Gerald the thought of being intimate with him made her queasy. What had been so beautifully and willingly given in love should never be bartered in a marriage of social convenience. The notion was a perversion of all that love should be. Her marriage would be a farce, too, but she was trapped, pinned down as tightly as the dusty butterflies in the display cases at Vyvyan; and like them she would become lifeless and brittle.

Madalyn blinked more tears away and felt glad the weather was as dreary as she felt. The drizzle pattered on leaves and pimpled the river, and even the bobbing ducks looked fed up. The sky to the west was bruised purple, and as she followed the old path a sudden spurt of chill wind blew up the estuary, bullish with the threat of storms to come.

The old pontoon was rotting away from a combination of high tides and neglect, but as she approached it, Madalyn was surprised to see a small rowing boat was tied up. Who was here? Two rooks cawed against the stillness, disturbed from their chimney nest by an intruder, and drawing closer she noticed the door was open. Somebody was in Ned's house! How dare they intrude!

Without pausing to consider the wisdom of it, Madalyn tore up the steps, her heart slamming into her ribs when she saw a man sprawled across the tiles, his right arm swallowed by the void as he delved into the old hiding place. Ned had been right all along! There *was* a thief.

"What are you doing?"

The intruder leapt up at her cry.

Madalyn slammed to a halt, shocked. "Marrick?"

"Surprised I'm not dead in France?" he said.

Madalyn shook her head. "Tilly said you were back on leave. I meant what are you doing *here*? In the boathouse?"

He jerked his shorn head in the direction of the void. "I've come to fetch Ned's things for Bessy. I thought you'd look after them but I got that wrong. If you're marrying Gerald you're not fit to keep Ned's book. Where is it?"

"In the cubby hole," she said.

"It's empty. Look for yourself," Marrick replied, his eyes hard.

He stepped away from the void and Madalyn dropped to her knees, delving into the gloom for the dry leather of the handle, but Marrick was right. It wasn't there. Somebody had taken the satchel and her precious letters. Somebody who knew where she and Ned and Marrick once hid things. Somebody who had been watching this place for a long time and who was skilled in biding his time. A dreadful suspicion began to gnaw at the edges of her mind.

"His book's *gone*," she said.

Madalyn sat back on her haunches, brushing dust and grime from her hands. It felt as though she was losing Ned all over again, for *On Oyster Shore* was all she had left of him. Every word of that book had been written with love, and the narrative held her in its heart. The book contained Ned's innermost thoughts and was a distillation of how he saw the world and his own place within it. *On Oyster Shore* was Ned's great work, and Madalyn had sworn his legacy would be protected. Where had it gone?

"Did you give it to Gerald," Marrick asked coldly, "since you're his fiancée now?"

"I wouldn't give it to *anyone*," she said.

Marrick loomed over her. Madalyn had never thought of him as a violent man, but war had changed him and he was no longer the boy she'd known. She was suddenly afraid of him.

"Swear on your life, Madalyn, and may God strike you dead if you lie!"

"I swear," Madalyn said. "Things have gone missing from the hiding place before. The comb. My old sketch book. Pictures. I thought Bess might have taken them to punish me."

"Punish you?" Marrick echoed. "What for?"

She looked at the tiles rather than into his accusing eyes. "For agreeing to marry Gerald."

"Ha!" Marrick's bark of laughter made her jump. "That's your own punishment, I'd have thought. Gerry's a nasty piece of work, and he'll make you pay a thousand times over for loving Ned first. You marry him if you want to. It came as no surprise to any of us *common folk*. You're two peas from the same pod."

Madalyn didn't know what to say. She only knew she hated the way Marrick had always viewed her with suspicion. What did he know of the pressures she was subject to? Who was he to judge her? She wouldn't rise to his taunts. She hadn't as a child, and she wouldn't now.

"Things used to go missing from here years ago," she reminded him.

Marrick took off his cap and scratched his shorn head.

"Aye. Things always did go missing from there. When the sea glass and the picture of the fountain vanished, Ned accused me of hiding them. I thought he took my marbles in retaliation. I even thought it might have been you playing games. I was really angry when he showed you our hiding place."

"It wasn't me," said Madalyn, "but I think we can both guess who it was."

They looked at one another, united by a dawning realisation.

"Gerald," Marrick said bitterly. "He must have spied on us. I bet he got a right kick out of playing games and taking our things." His gaze slipped to her left hand. "He always did like taking what belonged to Ned."

Madalyn felt ashamed of the huge diamond ring because Marrick's glance made her engagement, so celebrated by society, feel tawdry. Fake coin. A mere business transaction. This hot wash of shame also came from knowing deep in her heart that Marrick was right; her engagement was all these things. She had thought Gerald had changed. Was she wrong? Had he been biding his time to obtain both Ned's book and the girl he loved? It seemed impossible, yet the manuscript was missing, and with it everything which proved the genesis of the story.

"What good is Ned's book to Gerald?" she said, almost to herself.

"He's publishing a book," Marrick said. "Bessy heard it from Violet Tuckey, she's working at the big house now, and Vi overheard Sir Arthur boasting. Guess what it's called?"

Madalyn couldn't speak. She would have told Marrick he was wrong if Constance hadn't also mentioned this.

"*On Oyster Shore*," Marrick declared. "Bessy recognised it straight away."

Madalyn's hand flew to her mouth, and for a second or two she thought she might vomit. This claiming of other people's ideas was Gerald through and through. Ned knew Gerald had stolen the credit for games he invented and had suspected that Gerald had borrowed his stories, shrugging off the betrayal by insisting that the tales he'd created were always meant to be shared. Madalyn had hated hearing Ned's ideas parroted and passed off as Gerald's own. Maybe Gerald even believed they *were* his own, for he had always struggled to distinguish lies from truth. By now he probably even believed he'd written *On Oyster Shore*. It was exactly what he used to do when they were children.

"I won't let him steal Ned's book," Madalyn said.

"You don't deny he could have done it?" Marrick asked.

Madalyn closed her eyes. Ned had suspected his stories had been taken before, and Kit Rivers had certainly thought as much.

"It's the sort of thing he used to do as a child, isn't it? Take other people's things and hide them? He hasn't changed at all."

Madalyn was so weary. Pretending to be a happy bride-to-be was exhausting. She didn't want to marry Gerald. She didn't love him. She couldn't marry him. What had she been thinking? No matter how dire her family circumstances, she couldn't marry a man she didn't love. Madalyn had been sleepwalking through life for far too long; now it was time to wake up and fight for Ned and his work. It was the one thing she could do for the man she loved.

"I won't let Gerald steal *On Oyster Shore*," she said.

Marrick barked a harsh and mirthless laugh. "You can't do anything about it."

"I *can*," Madalyn said. "I'll tell everyone. I'll tell his

publisher. I'll swear it in in court if I have to. Gerald isn't going to take Ned's writing from him."

"By the time it's published you'll be married to Gerald," Marrick pointed out. "That means you won't be able to do a thing. Once you're his wife you'll belong to Gerald in law and in practice. He'll not allow you to say a word – and anyhow the law won't allow you to testify against your husband. I wouldn't put it past him to lock you up if he had to. Nobody gets in Gerald's way."

Madalyn recalled Henry the pug and shuddered. "I won't marry him now. I should never have accepted his proposal when I still love Ned so much."

Marrick stared at her. "What do you mean, you still love Ned?"

"Exactly that. I never stopped loving him, Marrick."

Marrick hawked onto the tiled floor. "If you love Ned so much why send him away? A cripple wasn't good enough for you? Funny kind of love *that* is."

Madalyn was confused. Who was crippled? "What are you talking about?"

"Ned, being crippled and you sending him packing."

Madalyn wondered if this was shellshock. She'd heard the war affected men in many ways. "Is this some kind of joke?"

"Hardly a laughing matter when man comes back from war to the woman he loves only to be sent away again because he's no longer as he was," Marrick snarled.

This made no sense. Madalyn opened her mouth to interrupt but Marrick was in full flow. "Bess knew Ned would go to you before anyone else, even his own family, because he loves you so much. It was always you for him, but he's no longer enough for you, is he, now he's crippled? Well, let me tell you, Madalyn Trelyon, none of us who've been fighting this bastard war will come back as we were. We're all crippled in some way and Ned may have lost a leg but he'll always be more of a man than that little weasel, Gerald Snowe."

Madalyn couldn't believe what she was hearing. She staggered to the chair, grasping it for support. "Ned's alive?"

Marrick halted in mid-tirade. "Of course he's alive. Who *else* was it? A bloody ghost? Do ghosts have crutches and wooden legs?"

Madalyn thought her legs would give way. Ned was alive? He'd been here? "He's still alive? He didn't die? He was here? In Trevellan?"

It didn't make sense. Why hadn't Ned come to her?

"You know he was. You saw him."

"I didn't, Marrick. Ned never came to see me. Do you think I'd have let him out of my sight again if he had? Do you truly think I'd care that he was injured so long as he was alive? Is your love for Bess so shallow? Or hers for you?"

Marrick's hand rose to his scarred face. "Course it bloody isn't."

"Neither is mine for Ned!" Madalyn cried. "I wouldn't have cared what he looked like or how hurt he was, as long as he was alive! He must have known that! How could he walk away and leave me believing he was dead? How could he *do* that to me, Marrick? How?"

This news hurt Madalyn so much she thought she'd die. How could Ned have not raced straight to her side? Did he no longer love her? Didn't he care how dreadfully she had missed him? Did all his words of love mean nothing? Was there someone else? A nurse perhaps? A tender Florence Nightingale who had nursed him back from death and won his heart?

It was a preposterous thought, and so against Ned's nature that Madalyn almost laughed out loud. Ned would never forsake her.

"Oh Christ," said Marrick, ashen. "Bessy assumed you sent him away because you want to marry Gerry. She thought that was why Ned was so cut up. He didn't breathe a word of why he was leaving, only made her swear she'd never mention he'd returned. I had to winkle it out of her because she's been so upset."

"Why didn't he come to *me*?" Madalyn no longer cared if she was weeping in front of Marrick. She didn't think she'd ever care about anything again. She wiped her eyes on her sleeve. "Nothing would keep me from Ned. I was *waiting* for him. I told him I'd always wait. We promised we would wait."

Marrick was shocked. "You really didn't know, did you?"

"I'd be with him now if I had!" she cried. "You saw him die, Marrick. You told Bess you were there when the shell killed him."

Marrick drew a tin from his pocket and pulled out a cigarette. "I was wrong," he said flatly. "Want one? It's good for the nerves. Wouldn't get through being at the Front without these."

But Madalyn was too distraught to even think of trying to smoke. All she could think about was Ned. He was alive and that was wonderful – so wonderful she'd have been turning cartwheels if not for the dreadful bewilderment of his rejection. Why hadn't he sought her out? Come back for her? Then she glanced down at her left hand and groaned. Ned had heard about her engagement and walked away, believing she loved Gerald now.

Ned must have thought she'd forgotten him. He must have been devastated.

"When was this?" she asked shakily.

"A month or so ago." Marrick drew smoke deep into his lungs and blew two plumes out through his nose. "Bess was shocked, thought she'd seen a bloody ghost, she said. Ned had to fetch smelling salts."

Madalyn could have done with some smelling salts herself. She felt lightheaded and as though she might float away. She sank into the armchair and pressed her hand against her chest, forcing herself to take some steady breaths. "I don't understand. Bess had an official telegram, and all his belongings were returned. He died, Marrick. Reverend Tullis even read his name out in Church."

Marrick drew heavily on his cigarette. "That's what we believed. Ned was badly injured in a shell attack back in '15. He pulled me clear and saved my life, but I don't remember much more than blood and bodies. The boys didn't find him, but in all the confusion that isn't unusual. He was listed as missing, and we all know what that really means. Only in this case Ned really *was* missing. He was collected with the bodies, but somehow he was still alive."

Madalyn was devastated. "Was he badly hurt? Is he all right?"

"He lost his leg and has to walk with crutches nowadays. He and Gerry are quits now, aren't they?"

But Madalyn wasn't thinking about Gerald. She was too upset that Ned could have let her believe he was dead. It was beyond cruel. Didn't he love her any more?

"Why didn't he write to me?"

"Ned lost his memory," said Marrick. "The field surgeons had no idea who he was, and neither did he. Trauma does funny things to a man's mind out there, Madalyn. I've seen all sorts of things I wouldn't want to ever see again. Ned was a patient at Allington Manor in Oxfordshire for almost two years. That's a hospital that specialises in shellshock and psychiatric disorders."

Madalyn's heart ached for all the lost months spent believing Ned was dead when he was ill and had needed her so badly. Hadn't her heart always told her he was alive? Why hadn't she trusted it? While Marrick described how Ned had worked as teacher at Allington, she wept to know he had been so close for all those dreadful lonely months. If only she had known! She would have raced to his side. She would have done anything to help him with his recovery, no matter how long it took or how badly he was hurt, for Madalyn would have waited a thousand years for him to return to her.

Surely Ned would have known this? They were soulmates. Twin souls. Everything to one another. What could have made Ned believe he was no longer loved or that she would no longer want him? Wooden legs and crutches were nothing to Madalyn; she'd have been the happiest girl alive to see his beloved face again and hold him tightly. She would never have let him go again. What did it matter that he was injured? It was *Ned* she loved. The essence of the man he was held her heart, and had done since she was a child. She didn't love him for his handsome face and strong body, but for the magical wonder of *him*. The loyalty. His honour. His kindness. His humour. His imagination. His slow smile. His gentleness. His tender heart. She loved everything that was Ned, and would have gladly given up engagement rings, grand estates and wealth to be with him. Ned must have known this – so what could possibly have made him think otherwise? What would have made him walk away from her. Unless ...

Unless somebody had reached Ned first and persuaded

him to believe otherwise? Somebody who wouldn't have been pleased at all to discover Ned Carew had returned from the dead. Who would have a vested interest in persuading Ned he would be nothing but a hindrance? Who knew him well enough to exploit the honour and generosity and selflessness that were the hallmarks of his nature? And who might be horrified to see a soldier hero return to claim the girl who loved him?

"Gerald," she whispered. "*Gerald* must have seen Ned before he could reach me."

"Aye," agreed Marrick. He tossed his cigarette onto the tiles and ground it out with the heel of his boot. "I reckon you're right. Sounds like the sort of thing he'd do. He's always been jealous of Ned. Ned wouldn't say anything but he was so cut up that Bessy just assumed you'd said you didn't want a crippled husband and were sticking with Gerry. We all know he could give you the moon on a bloody stick and you're about to marry him, so you can't blame Bess for jumping to conclusions."

"I'd always want Ned no matter what happened to him," Madalyn said. "Gerald knows that. My feelings for Ned were never a secret."

"So Gerry had a vested interest in sending Ned away, didn't he? Apart from knowing you'd leave him for Ned, he'd also have a lot of explaining to do about *On Oyster Shore* when you went to retrieve the book. He'd have done whatever it took to get Ned out of the picture."

Madalyn nodded. This made sense. Gerald had seen Ned first and somehow convinced him to go away. Even though he knew how much she loved Ned, how she mourned and missed him every day, Gerald had deliberately concealed the news of Ned's return. He had lied to her and betrayed her in the worst and most hurtful way possible. If not for seeing Marrick this morning – an accident of Fate if ever there was one – she would have married Gerald with no idea that the man she loved was still alive. Gerald would have been happy to let her live the rest of her life unaware that Ned was still alive.

The thought of her fiancé made Madalyn's skin crawl with repugnance. How *dare* he? This wasn't a childhood game or petty point-scoring. Gerald had played God with her life and done his utmost to destroy all her hopes of her happiness with the man who meant everything to her. Gerald Snowe hadn't changed a bit. His empathy and kindness had been nothing but an act to draw her in and blind her to his true nature. Hadn't she always likened him to a spider, waiting for the hapless little fly to become tangled in his web? Madalyn had almost been that fly, and the devious spider was only a day away from devouring her. She shuddered.

Marrick cleared his throat. "I'm sorry about Bess and me. We shouldn't have jumped to that conclusion."

"None of that matters now," Madalyn said. Nothing did, except finding Ned and resting in the shelter of his arms. She was filled with determination, for she would find him. She'd put this right. "I need to see Ned. Where is he?"

Wherever it was Ned had gone, Madalyn would follow. She would walk all the way if she had to.

Marrick shrugged. "He didn't say. Bessy pleaded with him to stay but he wouldn't. He could be anywhere. Maybe he went back to Allington. They might have helped him. He mentioned Australia, too."

"He used to talk about his uncle there," Madalyn recalled. "I think you'd better tell me exactly what you know. Then I can find him."

But Marrick looked doubtful. "Not if he doesn't want to be found."

Madalyn raised her chin. She felt like herself once more, and as though she'd finally woken up after being asleep for a long, long time. She was back to being the headstrong girl who climbed trees and swam in cold water. She was the girl who made love to the man she adored beneath the beams of a higgledy-piggledy boathouse. And now she was the woman who would search the whole world to find the man she loved.

"I'll find him," she vowed. "Even if he's on the other side of the world, I *will* find Ned, and I won't rest until that day comes. And I'll make sure Gerald regrets stealing *On Oyster Shore*. I swear on my life that he won't know a minute's peace until he returns that book. I'll come straight to you and Bess once I've packed a bag. I'm not staying here a moment longer. I'm going to find Ned."

The storm was blowing in earnest now and the sky was the colour of damsons. Marrick turned to Madalyn.

"Best I leave before this gets worse, but if Gerald turns funny come straight to us. He's a nasty piece of work and I don't trust him."

Madalyn nodded. Until a few hours ago she would have argued that Gerald was a changed man and there was no malice in him, but now she had stepped through the looking-glass it was plain to see that the direct opposite was the truth.

The river was spiked with saw-toothed waves as the wind grew stronger. Madalyn watched Marrick cast off and row out into the middle of the river before allowing the current to take hold of the boat and carry it downsteam. She shivered, recalling how that same current had once dragged her and Gerald towards the open sea. She'd been caught in a current with him ever since, only she hadn't seen it for Gerald had been trying to drown Ned in his wake since they were children. Well, no longer. Today was where it all ended. Madalyn Trelyon would leave Oyster Shore and she'd find the man she loved – no matter where he was. Nobody would ever part them again.

The wind blew the rain in needled arcs. Rooks rose like burnt paper from the trees calling their displeasure at the weather, and it was a relief to step into the woods and the shelter of dripping trees. Although she quailed at what lay ahead, Madalyn's heart was singing because the world had Ned Carew in it and a man like him didn't just vanish, for he was too colourful and talented to melt away. Wherever he went people would be drawn to Ned, for he was a man who inspired love and devotion just as Gerald, his mirror image, repelled it. All Madalyn needed to do was follow the glittering trail Ned left behind him and she would find him.

Madalyn rounded the bluff and paused by the ash trees to catch her breath. Oyster House was a white smudge in the rain and the path along the bank no more than a faint line in the long grass. Madalyn laughed as the rain stung her cheeks and flattened her curls to her scalp. It was washing away the past two years and all the mistakes which, deadened with grief, she had made. It was a baptism to end her old life as Madalyn Trelyon, and welcome the new one where she would become Madalyn Carew.

She ran across the lawn to the house, buoyed by optimism. All would be well. Nothing would part Madalyn Trelyon and Ned Carew again. Nothing and nobody.

"Where have you been, my love? You're late." Gerald was standing on the veranda, checking his pocket watch and looking disgruntled. "Lord, the state of you, Madalyn! We were supposed to meet my mother almost an hour ago to choose the flowers for the church. Where have you been?"

Madalyn looked him in the eye. "I've been at the boathouse. Something's missing."

Gerald's gaze slipped. One hand tugged the small beard he was so proud of, a nervous gesture she had grown accustomed to and, she now saw, an unconscious betrayal of guilt.

"I do wish you wouldn't frequent that place, my love. It's falling down."

"How would you know? I thought you never went there," Madalyn retorted. She felt strangely elated to be speaking like this to Gerald. How had she not realised that she was always careful and polite with him? Solicitous of hurting his feelings and always beholden to him for marrying her and saving the Trelyons. She raised her chin. "I was looking for a manuscript. I don't suppose you've come across it have you, Gerald? It's called *On Oyster Shore.* I hear it's considered quite remarkable."

His tongue flickered out and whetted his lips. "I have no idea what you're talking about. Do come in out of the rain. You don't want to catch a cold for the wedding." He walked down the steps, cane tapping, and holding out his hand to help her ascend. Madalyn ignored the gesture. She'd rather be drenched to her undergarments than be anywhere near Gerald Snowe.

"It's a beautiful book written by a man who was injured at the Front. His sister gave it to me for safe-keeping," she continued. "But you know that already, don't you, Gerald? Just as you know he's still alive because you saw him yourself. Don't deny it."

Two spots of colour bloomed across Gerald's cheek bones. "Madalyn, I —"

She held up her hand. “Don’t lie to me, Gerald. It’s pointless. I saw Marrick at the boathouse.”

“You’d believe him over me? A *fisherman*?”

“I’d believe *anyone* over you!” Madalyn cried. “You’re a liar, Gerald! A despicable, spiteful liar. You always were, and I can see now that you never changed. You saw Ned and sent him away because you knew I’d choose him because I love him. I’ve always loved him, Gerald! I told you that!”

Gerald didn’t deny her accusations, but Madalyn could see he was shaken. “He’s got nothing in comparison to what I have.”

“You’re so wrong,” she said quietly. “Ned has *everything* that truly matters. He has integrity and kindness and a heart full of love. It’s you who has nothing, and the tragedy is that you’ll never understand that. You have to steal everything from others because you can’t achieve anything on your own merits. You stole his book, didn’t you, because you thought you could pass it off as your own! You’re nothing but a liar and a thief.”

Gerald’s held out his hand. “You’ve caught a chill and you don’t know what you’re saying. Come inside, dearest, and we’ll forget all this nonsense.”

Madalyn ignored him. “Ned’s worth a thousand of you. He always was and he always will be, and everyone will know it when I tell them what you’ve done!”

“You’d be sorry if you do that, Madalyn. You and your mother,” Gerald said. The mask had slipped and she saw that the jealous and spiteful little boy she’d so disliked had been lurking beneath all along.

“I’m not afraid of your threats!” Madalyn cried into the rain and strengthening wind. “You’re rotten to the core, Gerald Snowe, and everyone’s going to know it. Your lies will be over just like our engagement. Then I'll find Ned and we'll be together just as we were meant to be. You can't keep us apart any longer."

She went to pull the engagement ring from her finger, but Gerald struck out like a viper and gripped her wrist. "If you do that, you and your mother are finished, do you hear me? I'll destroy you both and the Penwurthies with you. Rest assured of that. I'll have them out on the streets. Carew's gone and he won't be back. You should forget him. Trust me, he was willing to forget you."

"Let me go!" Madalyn attempted to wrench her fingers away, but Gerald was wiry and held her tightly, yanking her towards him until her face was only inches from his own.

"Do you hear what I said? If you breathe a word of this, I'll turn the Penwurthies out of their cottage, and you and your mother onto the street. I'll finish you all."

"Bess and Marrick can have the boathouse. You can't turn them or us out, because Oyster Shore belongs to the Trelyons," she said. "I told you that the day I first met you."

"Not any more. I've bought it."

Madalyn laughed at this preposterous lie. "Hardly. It's entailed."

"Entails can be broken if you have enough money for a good legal team. Oyster Shore belongs to me now, and I can turn your mother out any time I choose – and believe me, Madalyn, if you run after Ned Carew, or breathe as much as a single word about books, that's exactly what I'll do. There won't be a great deal of sympathy for you once the word's out about your carrying on with a gardener. Your mother will die of shame – if she lives that long."

The façade had well and truly slipped.

"You mama's income is so pitifully small I can't imagine

she'd be able to rent a house or afford to keep Tilly on," Gerald continued. "She'll have to find work or ask for charity once you desert her."

"What has Mama ever done to you?" Madalyn whispered. Constance was her weakness, and Gerald knew it. The spider was dragging the fly closer to the centre of his web.

"Maybe she could take a room in a boarding house. Or seek work while you search for Ned. There's always the workhouse, although I don't imagine Constance will fare so well there. The shame alone would kill her. Really, it's best all around if we just forget this silly squabble, my love. Once you and I are married she'll be well cared for and comfortable for the rest of her life. What daughter would want less for her mama?"

Gerald always had been skilled at turning a situation to his advantage. Madalyn was trapped and he knew it. If she didn't marry him and dared tell the truth about his book, Gerald would have his vengeance through hurting her mother. How could Madalyn allow this to happen? It might take months to find Ned, and by the time they returned for Constance it would be too late. Madalyn was cornered, or so she would let Gerald believe.

"You win," she said coldly. "I won't say a word about the book."

His hand fell away from her wrist. Madalyn rubbed the red bracelet mark of his fingers, branded on her pale flesh by his forceful grip.

"And you'll forget this nonsense about chasing after Ned. You'll marry me tomorrow. I'll be the one you choose."

Gerald had finally sprung the trap set long ago during childhood. He would have possession of *On Oyster Shore* and the girl Ned Carew loved.

But Madalyn *couldn't* let him win. There had to be a way she could escape marriage to him and keep her mother safe. A way that meant Gerald wouldn't lose face or take his anger out on Constance.

Think, Madalyn told herself. *Outwit him. Think*!

The rain was growing heavier and the wind was buffeting the trees like an invisible fist. As she turned to look at the river Madalyn saw how the surface had changed from silver to gunmetal grey flecked with the manes of white horses galloping in from the bay. Oyster Shore had many moods, and today it shared her anger. *Ride us!* called the white horses. *Gallop away! You've thought of it before! Hurry! This is your time!*

And this was when Madalyn knew what she had to do. There was no more time to think it through. This moment was all she would ever have.

"Everything you touch is cursed, Gerald," she said. "None of it will ever bring you any happiness. You'll live the rest of your life wishing you could change your past. You'll die wondering if you can ever be forgiven."

Before he could reply, Madalyn turned for the river. Her boots squelched across the lawn and several times she almost fell when her skirts tangled around her legs. She didn't dare look back but ran on, blinded by rain and strands of wet hair. She slithered down the grassy bank and teetered on the brink, mesmerised and repelled by the churning water at the tips of her boots. The storm-surge had made the river rise higher than she could ever recall, and her own face swam up at her, a pale and wide-eyed premonition already drowned in the churning depths.

It had to be now. This was Madalyn's only chance to make everything right, and now the time had arrived she knew part of her had always understood that this moment would come. How often had she longed for the cold caress of the water and the seductive pull of currents down to the mysterious depths? The river's siren call had wooed her since she was a child, and now it sang of a place where there was only blissful silence and deathlike ease. It was a place where Gerald Snowe held no power and no claim. If Madalyn was brave enough to visit that place Constance would be safe and Gerald would never be able to threaten either of them again.

One step more was all it would take.

"Madalyn! Don't be a fool!"

Gerald was gaining on her. There was no more time to waste. No more seconds to ponder on what had passed or to bid farewell. Hadn't Madalyn always known the river would lead her back to Ned? He had written of it and dreamed of it, and somewhere he was waiting for her. This last swim was a farewell to all she had ever known and everything she had ever been. The river was death and resurrection. The river was her only friend, and it was urging her forward with promises of freedom.

"I'm sorry I sent Ned away. I only did it because I love you!" Gerald's voice was high with panic.

"You know nothing about love!" she yelled, and the gale snatched the words away. "Nothing."

Madalyn knew this was her time. If she was to step into her power, escape marriage to Gerald and keep her mother safe there was only one thing to do; she had to die and Gerald had to bear witness to her death. There was no other way.

Madalyn stepped from the bank into the deep river. Shock and cold stole her breath and her ears were filled with the rush of fast-flowing water. Her wet skirts grew heavier and heavier, pulling her down and down until the sky was lost and the world above the surface was silenced, and the water closed over her head. The river flowed on and betrayed no evidence that she had ever been there at all. Only the young man standing on the riverbank, the young man shouting for help and weeping with despair, knew she had leapt in of her own accord. Only Gerald knew that he had driven her into the treacherous water as surely as if he'd pushed her. As he pulled off his jacket and kicked his shoes away, he knew Madalyn Trelyon was no more because of his actions, and the weight of this knowledge spurred him forwards as he called out to her and begged her to reappear. He would do anything she wanted, Gerald cried, anything at all if she would only come back.

But Madalyn Trelyon didn't hear his pleas. She had vanished from the world of fact into folklore. She was lost to him for ever and no amount of bargaining with God could bring her back. As he waded alongside the riverbank trying to see her, Gerald Snowe realised that Ned had been right all along; it was all ending just as it had begun, on Oyster Shore.

Without Madalyn Trelyon, everything was over.

33

THE PRESENT

Oyster Shore

Lowenna

A few hours ago I lifted the loose tile in the boathouse floor and tumbled into the past. Since then I've lived a lifetime with Ned, Madalyn and Gerald. Oyster Shore a century ago feels more solid than it does in the present, and the faces of its long-ago occupants are as real as the passions which consumed them. Their lost world has drawn closer with every word I've read, and voices silenced for over a century have called for the truth to be told.

The sun is creeping up by the time I finish reading the final document. I glance around the boathouse and see the same tiled floor, narrow staircase and beams that Ned and Madalyn knew, but also absences which seem shocking. Where's the precious armchair saved from Edgar's study? The pot-bellied stove where Ned brewed tea? Who removed the big brass bed where he made love to Madalyn and, drowsy with happiness, reposed while she sketched him? These modern pieces are imposters, and I expect to see Gerald creeping in to raid the hiding place or Marrick bounding onto the porch demanding that Ned comes out for a drink on the pontoon. Returning to the present feels disorientating and more than a little out of step with time.

Absorbed by my reading, I'd allowed the wood burner to die down, and the chill of a newly minted morning has been creeping into the boathouse just as secrets have been drifting from the old hiding place. I'm the new keeper of those secrets, and the only living person who knows the truth about a decades-old literary crime. Yet this isn't my secret to tell, and Ned's novel doesn't belong to me even though I'm the one who's found it. The truth is that *On Oyster Shore* belongs to someone far closer to Ned Carew and Madalyn Trelyon than me.

I toss another log onto the fire and poke the embers into flames before calling Breakspear and flinging open the porch door, where I'm greeted by a mother-of-pearl world. My dog hurtles through my legs and plunges down the steps, bounding along the riverbank and sending ducks flapping upwards, quacking their displeasure. Madalyn and Ned would have known such mornings when they walked hand in hand along the riverbank, their feet leaving dark green echoes in the dewy grass. Maybe they visited the lost fountain, smothered decades ago by brambles as thick as a man's thumb, where they talked about Kit's early poems and recalled the day when he took their photograph. Gerald must have known these quiet times too, for they are perfect for slipping unnoticed through the world. Maybe it was a morning like this when Ned's novel was stolen and the events set in motion that led to Gerald's lonely and unmourned for end?

Ribbons of mist hang over the river and a pair of swans glide by without so much as a ripple. I wander along the pontoon, lulled by the slap of waves against the pilings and the stillness of the sleeping world. Ned swam here, the tide carried Gerald out to sea, and the silver water closed over Madalyn's head during her last desperate bid for freedom. This river is a conduit for past and present to merge, and as the water swirls beneath my feet I know voices whisper here to anyone who pauses long enough to hear them.

"I'm listening," I say. "Is it time for the truth to be told?"

I'm not sure what I'm expecting. If this was a film Ned's ghost would appear, or maybe Gerald's shade (which I imagine would be weighed down by Jacob Marley-type chains) – but the only answer I receive is the shrill call of a seabird, so with this I will have to be content. The sun is rising above the trees of the far bank, and as I raise my face to its light the warmth feels like an affirmation. Are Ned, Madalyn and even Gerald giving me their blessing to tell the story of *On Oyster Shore*? Are they telling me Ned's novel must be returned to its rightful owner if any of them are to rest in peace?

The mist swirls on the far bank. Trees loom through the veil. Past and present overlap here just as faces lost from memory slip over the features of those now living. When the mist rolls in it's not hard to believe the village children still play on the shore. Ned, his face as brown and as freckled as a hen's egg, sprawls on the grass and writes furiously. Marrick wrestles with Sammy Trewen. Gerald sulks and Madalyn sketches. I know it's a trick of the light combined with tired eyes, but as the sunshine glints from the water I think I glimpse the whisk of white skirts and a flash of chestnut hair.

"Madalyn?" Is it her I glimpsed before? Is she the mystery girl on the tideline?

"Madalyn?"

Breakspear barks, more ducks beat their wings into flight, and she's gone. Maybe I tumbled back to her time, I think, as I call my dog to heel and return to the boathouse. Isn't there a theory that the past, present, and future all run concurrently? I like this notion, because otherwise time feels bittersweet, with our lives only an eye-blink. Seasons turn and years pass, hurts and loves fade, voices fall silent, and we all become images in dusty albums – but I'd like to believe that somewhere we continue as we always were, alive and vibrant and young. Is that heaven? Immortality? What writers hope to achieve if their words continue into the future? If something remains of who we were and what we felt, that brings us back to life. It might be the love conveyed in a simple sketch, the sadness in the eyes of soldiers photographed in a trench, or even the lines of an exquisite novel which enable who we are to resonate throughout the decades. Immortality is found in all manner of things.

There's another way we live on.

While I wait for the sun to gain courage, I feed Breakspear and brew more coffee. Then I fetch my laptop and sit down with all the paperwork spread around me. My coffee grows cold as I lose myself once again in letters penned between Bess and Marrick, including Marrick's account of the trench shelling Bess had allowed Madalyn to read, and my pen flies across the page as I make notes and links. By the time there's heat in the ribbons of light unfurling across the riverbank I know I must see Noah and tell him what I've discovered.

"Fancy a walk, Breaky?"

My dog thumps his tail. Breakspear loves his new Cornish existence. London with its streets and pavements must feel like another life for him, and I think he's even forgiven me for dragging him away from his beloved garden. How can that small grassy patch compete with acres of land and long country walks? It'll break his heart to leave Oyster Shore, and I think it'll break mine too, because I belong here. Who I am is rooted in the rich Cornish earth as deeply as the willows and the ash on the riverbank. I have no desire to rip these out or dismiss them, because I want to burrow into the past, into the incredible story I've uncovered. When I dreamed of Cornwall as a child it was Oyster Shore I yearned for. How could it not be when my family belong to this place? I'm beginning to understand that along with our hair and eye colour and a thousand other family traits, we also inherit deep memory.

It was in the early hours of the morning, and I had been beyond tired after speed-reading novels and trying to decipher faded handwriting, when I'd cried out with excitement. Breakspear, rudely awoken, barked reprovingly.

"Sorry, boy," I'd said. "But if Bess Carew was Elizabeth Penwurthy, my great-grandmother, that means Ned was Granny May's uncle. He's my great-great-uncle! How amazing is that? And Marrick and Bess were my great-grandparents!"

Unimpressed, Breakspear had placed his head back on his paws and returned to dreams of riverbanks and rabbits. His owner might decide sleep was optional, but a spaniel needed his full eight hours. I couldn't have slept a wink – I was far too excited by thrill of my discovery. I was related to

Ned Carew from the famous poem. Ned the war hero, who had saved his best friend at such huge personal cost. Ned of the tender sketches drawn by a girl who had loved him so dearly. Ned the gifted author who had sacrificed his great novel and his own heart so that Madalyn would be safe and happy. Ned was my blood. He was my family. He was a writer like me!

That Marrick Penwurthy was my great-grandfather had come as no surprise since I'd grown up listening to Granny May's stories of her father. With his black moods and violent rages, Marrick had always been a fairytale ogre of a man, so encountering him as a little boy who had played truant to go fishing made him human. As I read Ned's book and the letters he'd exchanged with Madalyn, my great-grandfather was no longer a shadowy figure but a determined young man who had married his childhood sweetheart and fought for his country, and whose life had been saved by the bravery of his dearest friend. If it hadn't been for Ned Carew I wouldn't have even been here. That was some thought.

Through these letters and documents I had been given the gift of seeing my great-grandfather as a real person, and I'd pounced on every mention of him, desperate to learn more. The uncertain temper and bad dreams of his latter life most certainly stemmed from PTSD, and it was his injuries sustained in the trenches which had eventually forced him to sell his boat and give up fishing. He had died an angry man, as Granny May always said, but now I understood why, and my heart went out to him and all the other men of his generation who returned home broken in ways that were not always visible.

Ned's violet-eyed and dark-haired sister Bess, she of the hot temper and ready fists, became the stern mother who

Granny May recalled. Bess Carew, later Elizabeth Penwurthy, was the furious woman who had turned a troubled stranger away from her cottage – except that this visitor hadn't been a stranger at all but Gerald Snowe, desperate to atone for the death of his fiancée and return the book he'd stolen. No wonder Granny May had quaked while her mother shouted, for how Bess must have loathed Gerald. He'd stolen Ned's work, cheated him, threatened the Penwurthy family and robbed her of a beloved brother. Ned Carew, settled into a new life in Australia, might as well have been on the moon, for how could poor fisherfolk like Bess and Marrick ever afford to go there? Bess must have known she'd never see Ned again. She would have known that if she'd told Gerald where Ned was he would have paid her passage readily to get rid of her, but Bess would never dream of breathing a word about her brother's whereabouts. She couldn't. There was too much at stake.

My own research had already revealed that Gerald Snowe became more reclusive and religious as the years passed. He inherited the family business as expected, but sold it for vast amounts in the nineteen-thirties and retreated to a life of prayer and solitude as a lay brother in a monastic order. Seldom seen outside its London seminary, Gerald Snowe died as he lived, alone and unloved, and bequeathed his fortune to the holy order. His efforts to retrieve and destroy all the copies had been successful, his brief literary career was forgotten, and *On Oyster Shore* drifted into obscurity. Nobody dreamed that one of the twentieth century's literary treasures had been bequeathed to a Cornish fishwife over forty years before, or guessed it had been stolen from the true author.

Now that literary treasure rests on my table. The find of a

lifetime is literally at my fingertips, and my biographer's mind is already sifting and sorting to structure the narrative I've freed from beneath the boathouse floor. This is a phenomenal find, the career-making discovery all biographers dream of; but I'm hesitant, because the book doesn't belong to me. I might have found it, and my branch of the Penwurthy family plays a huge part in its story, but the novel belongs to someone else entirely.

I select the pieces of evidence which prove my theory, and place them into the sturdy bag for life Fi gave me the last time I braved the village shop. The notebook, letters and books are delicate, so I wrap them up in a sweater and place this bundle inside my rucksack. All the rest Noah can collect from the boathouse and read in his own time – and I have a feeling he'll want to do this very soon.

Breakspear and I walk through the quiet woods and up the winding drive. As we pass Oyster House I recall how Madalyn watched the tides while fearing for the man she loved so far away in the mud and carnage of the Western Front. It was also here that my great-grandmother, unaware of the truth, had broken the news that Ned was missing in action and had unwittingly begun a chain of events that would change the course of so many lives.

I arrive at Noah's caravan brimming with the kind of jagged energy which follows no sleep and too much caffeine. Noah is sitting on the step basking in the sunshine, with his still wet hair spilling droplets over his bare shoulders. Rivulets trickle towards narrow hips covered by a towel and I look away hastily, hoping he doesn't think this is some crazy bag-for-life version of a booty call.

"G'day!" Noah says. "You've missed the early morning

swimming, I'm afraid, but you're both in time for a bacon sandwich."

Right on cue my stomach growls.

"Sounds like you need some tucker!" Noah stands up as Breakspear bounces up and down in delight. "Give me a sec to get dressed and I'll see what I can do."

"I haven't come to cadge breakfast."

"Don't tell me – you want to try muck-spreading?"

I wrinkle my nose. "Not in the slightest. Sorry for calling on you so early but you did say to let you know if I found anything. Well, I have. I know what happened to the book and to Madalyn Trelyon. It's been right in front of us all the time!"

I'm shaking, although this could be from drinking coffee all night long.

"Take a deep breath and say that again," Noah suggests. "And maybe without looking like you're about to pass out?"

"I *will* pass out if I don't tell you soon!" I say. "Your mum was almost there herself. A few more weeks and a visit here, and she'd have worked it out too. I know she would."

"Hey? What's my family tree got to do with your mystery writer?"

"Just about everything. Your family's story *is* the story of Oyster Shore. It always was, only somebody chose to hide the truth and steal it for themselves. That's why I have to tell you first, Noah, and before Matt Enys and Hamish and everyone else!"

"How about I throw on some clothes and make breakfast while you tell me everything, then," he says, propelling me into the caravan. "Pop the kettle on and make some tea. Isn't that what you poms like to do?".

"We're always making tea when we're not playing cricket or disturbing our neighbours."

"A beautiful woman calling around to see me is never a disturbance at any time of day," Noah replies, gallantly.

"If one comes by, I'll be sure to pass that information on to her," I shoot back.

He rolls his eyes and heads to the small door at the far end of the van before turning and smiling at me, a slow smile which makes me feel as if I might be just a little bit beautiful after all.

"No need, since I've already told her. Just don't let on to my mates that I put my clothes *on* when she visits. They'll say I'm not fit to be an Aussie bloke!"

"That will be your English roots. You know how uptight we are."

"Jeez! I'm more of a Pom than I ever realised!"

Far, far more than you realise, I think, as I dig out teabags and fill the kettle. While I wait for it to boil my phone vibrates in my pocket and I fish it out, feeling the familiar cloud of dread descend when I see a text message from David.

You've made your point. Call me.

His text is a missive from another life, one as wrong as that which Madalyn could have lived had she married Gerald. I delete the text and erase David's number from my contacts list. As his details vanish, I wonder what has taken me so long. What was I afraid of when it was so simple in the end? Like Madalyn Trelyon before me, I have leapt into freedom, and today really is a new start in more ways than one.

By the time Noah returns, jeans and tee shirt clinging to his damp body and his eyelashes still spiky with water, I've made two mugs of tea and spread all my artefacts out on the caravan's table. What Noah chooses to do with what I tell him next is out of my hands. He sits down and I start to explain, knowing I'm gabbling but unable to help myself as excitement flows out of me like water tumbling over rapids. Noah listens carefully, and I see amazement in his beautiful green eyes – eyes which once gazed out at the world from another heart-stopping face.

Some researcher I am! The biggest and most important piece of evidence had been under my nose from the moment I arrived on Oyster Shore. The truth was here all the time, only it wasn't to be found in museums, or antiquarian books or even coded confessions, but in a dimpled smile, green eyes and artistic talent – because Noah Wilson is the answer to the riddle. He's the conclusion to the story, and he is Ned Carew's greatest legacy.

The clues were everywhere, and many of them Noah had given to me himself. His white-blond curls. His artistic talent. His generous heart. His deep and abiding love for Kim, the woman he knew he would marry as soon as he met her. His Cornish heritage. His relative from way back who had sold an engagement ring to buy a passage to Australia. The family tradition of teaching. Even Noah's mother's obsession with the Wilson family tree was never about the past, but about the future and finding a place for her beloved son in a world without his wife and his mother. Noah is the reason why Gerald Snowe can finally rest in peace.

Immortality isn't only found through art or worldly fame. We can be found in the faces of those who follow us. They too carry our stories into the future for our children, and the families we create are legacies as well. Ned and Madalyn live on in far more than the pages of a lost novel and a handful of letters. They continue in the family they created.

Once I'd made the connection in the small hours I was buzzing. I read the novels again before perusing all the letters Ned and Madalyn had exchanged while he was away at war. Then I examined the documents painstakingly collated by Noah's mother, which included the passenger list for ships to Australia in 1917, a brief newspaper report of Madalyn's tragic accident, and several accounts of the work done at Allington Hospital. With the contents of Granny May's box all the evidence is here, just as Gerald had promised long ago when he'd given it to Bess Carew. There can be no doubt of the genesis of *On Oyster Shore* or the identity of its true author, and the literary world will know the truth about the novel and why Gerald Snowe grew to hate it. They will know he was trying to hide a theft, but they will also see that he was hoping to be forgiven for what he'd done. Gerald Snowe went to his grave knowing that Madalyn had drowned herself because of his actions. He spent his whole life believing he had as good as killed her, and ended his days tortured by guilt. You would need a heart of stone not to pity him.

"Talk me through all this again, and from the very beginning," Noah says, reaching for his mug. He takes a sip of tea and as the muscles in his butterscotch-smooth throat contract I wonder how that skin would feel against my lips and am shocked by how much I long to find out. Dragging my eyes away, and blaming these thoughts on sleep deprivation, I dive back into the story of forgotten friendships, love and childhood grudges that grew into a bitter rivalry and a serious theft. Noah listens carefully, sometimes picking up a picture and studying it or reaching out to caress the phoenix comb. When his hand alights on the leather notebook his green eyes are moist.

"And this is it?" he says wonderingly. "This is Ned's book?"

"It's *your* book now. Ned Carew was your great-grandfather, which means it belongs to you as his next of kin. It's your great-grandparents' story and your legacy. *On Oyster Shore* is yours."

Sometimes as a biographer you wander accidentally into uncharted territory. It can be a diversion from the set path which leads to quicksand and despair, or it can be a breathtaking off-piste slalom into an entirely new landscape filled with a myriad of possibilities. I've researched and worked on enough projects to recognise when I reach a blind alley, but I also know the chills of pure excitement which herald a breakthrough, and as I read on through the small hours these dusted my arms and made my pulse race.

Madalyn Trelyon hadn't drowned that day. Her death by drowning was a theory not a fact, and this is where the story became muddied, just as she must have hoped. Madalyn might have been remembered as *Beautiful. Beloved. Brief* – but there had never been a body recovered from the river and never been any solid evidence of her death, just an assumption that she had drowned and her body had been washed out to sea with the tide. The cloud of suicide had settled over her watery plunge, and explains why no more was ever said about the matter. I'd accepted the theory – it was neat enough and fitted the facts – but what if it was totally wrong? What if Madalyn had managed to hide underwater or behind reeds from Gerald's frantic gaze, then swim across the river, haul herself out and flee from Oyster Shore? Vanishing would have been the perfect solution to her dilemma, and Gerald, knowing she was a weak swimmer, would never have suspected otherwise. If he believed she was dead he wouldn't dream of looking for her, and would never want anyone to examine too closely what had taken place during their final exchange on the riverbank. He would certainly take care of Constance as his lost fiancée's mother.

But Madalyn Trelyon could swim. Ned had written about this in the letters they'd exchanged recalling an afternoon when they swam together before making love on the riverbank with their sun-toasted limbs tickled by long grasses and framed by the arc of blue sky. Madalyn had taken her chances with the bad weather and strong tides, striking out for the opposite bank, and praying the currents didn't sweep her out to sea. Once she reached the far shore my guess is that she turned to Marrick and Bess for shelter and help finding Ned. This hypothesis is substantiated by a document unearthed by Noah's mother – a 1917 embarkation list recording one Elizabeth Carew setting sail for Sydney. This had confused me at first, since my great-grandmother never even left Cornwall, let alone emigrated to Australia. Then I joined the dots.

"Of course!" I said aloud and my voice had echoed around the boathouse. "Bess lent her identity to Madalyn, so nobody could trace her, and her engagement ring from Gerald was sold to buy the passage to Sydney!"

Madalyn Trelyon journeyed to Australia, risking high seas and U-boats, to find Ned, by then a schoolteacher in northern Queensland. There she had remained for the rest of her life, where they were free to build a family and make a new life.

"But my great-grandmother was called Lyn," Noah says. "Or at least that's what I thought. She signs her work LC."

"I'm sure you'll find she was really Madalyn Trelyon. Lyn, short for Madalyn, was probably a name she used professionally. They wouldn't have wanted anyone to dig too deeply. They had a new life and a new start."

"New starts can be hard won," says Noah slowly, and I know he isn't just thinking of Ned and Madalyn. Then he frowns. "Hey! Does this mean we're related?"

"Third cousins once removed or something. It's really distant," I reply rather too quickly. I've already googled this – purely for academic purposes.

"You've already worked it out?" Noah is amused. "Any reason why?"

"Research, of course. I'm very professional."

"Of course," Noah says gravely, but his eyes crinkle. "No other reason?"

"What reason could there be?"

He laughs. "We'll think of one."

I blush, because I really hope we will.

While I drink tea and pretend my face isn't doing an impersonation of an Edam cheese, Noah leafs through the sketchbook, shaking his head wonderingly.

"My great-grandmother was a really respected artist in later life. She had exhibitions in Sydney and Cairns, and became quite collectable. I thought these looked familiar. It's her early work, isn't it?

"I think so, yes."

He holds up the picture of the young man reclining on the bed. "And you reckon this is Ned?"

"It *is* Ned. He looks like you."

His green eyes narrow. "A little maybe, but really far more like my Uncle Joey, God rest him. He had a mane of hair like this. And you said Ned was the son of a teacher?"

"He was. Haven't you told me many times you come from a long line of schoolteachers?"

"Much longer than I thought! I had no idea there was even an Edgar Carew or that my great-grandfather had once taught in a military hospital." He lays the sketchbook down on the table and sighs. "I feel bad I never asked Mum anything much about her family, but they never seemed like real people to me. I'm a Wilson, good Aussie stock, and her side of the family were just names from long ago."

"That's nothing to feel bad about. It *was* a long time ago. How many of us ask about our great-grandparents? They're pretty shadowy figures."

"They feel real to me now – Ned and Madalyn, I mean. They could be people we know and like. Friends even. I can't quite believe all this happened so long ago. It feels so ..." He pauses, searching for the right word. "So real. So vivid."

"Wait until you read Ned's book and all your mum's notes. Then it's even more real."

"I can't wait," he says. "Wow! My family came from right here. They saw the same things I see. The tides. The swallows. The patterns of light on the water. They loved the places I love."

"You're the continuation of their story," I tell him, because when I look at Noah, this gentle and kind man who brims with artistic talent, it's as if I'm looking at the two young people who fell in love all those years ago on the banks of Oyster Shore. Noah Wilson is a beautiful blend of Ned and Madalyn. It is from them that he has inherited his white-blond curls, green eyes and fiercely loyal heart as well as his vocation for art and teaching. He is the best of them. How I wish they could know he's returned to the place where his story begins.

"We know from my own family history that my great-grandparents lived quietly in Oz," he says. "No bestselling novels or fame for them, but just a low-key life, a happy marriage and a daughter; true riches they would have thought, and I totally agree. But what about Gerald Snowe? Do you know anything else about what happened to him?"

"There doesn't seem to be a great deal of detail, because he was so reclusive. He converted to Catholicism and joined an order as a lay monk," I say. "I'd go as far as to say he spent the rest of his days paying for his actions and regretting them. He certainly believed he drove Madalyn to her death and that seems to have pushed him to the edges of sanity."

"Poor bugger. He was just a kid really, wasn't he? They were still all just kids – the same age as the seniors I used to teach – and who knows anything at that age? We all mess up, but most of us are lucky enough to get the chance to put it right. Gerald never had that. He never knew absolution."

"He escaped the war too, and I don't think anyone ever forgave him for that."

I recall the pictures of the hopeful boys in their unforms. Madalyn and Gerald on the steps of Vyvyan. Kit Rivers leading men into battle when he was longing to be penning verse. They were all so very young, and when I think about Gerald it's impossible not to feel a twinge of sympathy because he loved Madalyn too, albeit with an unrequited and twisted love that corroded his soul and brought untold misery. I can only conclude that the guilt of her death, compounded with the crime of stealing Ned's work, drove him to madness. Or had Madalyn really cursed him? For Gerald's life certainly appears to have fallen apart.

I picture that small boy in the sailor suit who trailed after the other children and longed to be accepted. What an unhappy life he'd led, and what a tragic waste. Cursed with a jealous and vengeful nature, Gerald had made all the wrong choices, which led him to steal Ned's book and end his days in despair. Small wonder he'd grown to loathe Oyster Shore, and had done his utmost to dissociate himself from the novel he'd stolen. Had he lived in fear that his secret would be exposed? Or might he have hoped the theft would be uncovered so he would have the punishment he deserved? Was he disappointed when Bess and Marrick seemed to ignore his bequest?

Noah's mother, a thorough and methodical historian, had collated several contemporary newspaper accounts dating from the time of Madalyn Trelyon's disappearance. Each one contained vague details about how the couple were enjoying a romantic stroll when the young lady slipped and tragically fell into the river. None of them speculated that it was unusual to walk in such bad weather, but there must have been talk. According to one report Gerald, a weak swimmer himself, jumped in after his fiancée but to no avail. He'd contracted pneumonia and almost died, and it's at this point that he appears to have had a religious conversion. Another piece describes him as a tragic figure who knelt for hours in the village church and haunted Oyster Shore as he scoured the riverbank for Madalyn. Was it his ghost Treena claims to have seen? Does Gerald's unhappy spirit still haunt the place he grew to hate?

Constance Trelyon remained at Oyster House for another two years before she died, and the Snowes continued to rent Vyvyan Court until Sir Arthur's death in the mid-nineteen-twenties. After this, Lady Mary returned to be near her family in the north, and the estate, like so many other great estates of the day, was sold off piecemeal. I imagined this was also the time when Oyster House was locked up, the furniture draped in dustsheets, the gardens abandoned to brambles and woodland creatures, and the boathouse left to the lapping river and the encroaching undergrowth, as forgotten and as enigmatic as its owner.

Exactly where Gerald Snowe went once his family had quit Vyvyan is unknown. Noah's mother had made copious notes about possible religious retreats in France and Spain, but all these jottings are accompanied by question marks, and his life story contains more gaps than facts. I can fill in one gap, though, because I know for certain Gerald Snowe did return to Cornwall, trying to put things right, when he visited my great-grandmother.

In my mind's eye I see Gerald in later life, a stooped and frail figure, washed out with sickness and guilt. I watch him limp up the lane to Cobble Cottage, screwing up all his courage as his fist rises to knock and his heartbeat drums in his ears. I hear Bess berate him and tell him to leave them alone, the hatred of a lifetime and the grief of losing a brother to the far side of the world ringing through her furious words while Gerald pleads with her and tries to make amends. By giving the original manuscript to Bess and Marrick he must have hoped he had managed this, for Bess had the power to put everything right. She could return the manuscript to Ned, wherever he was, or she could choose to reveal Gerald's crime and destroy him. He might have longed for that to happen, feeling it was what he deserved, but it was a reckoning which would never come. Did he wonder why? I'll never know.

But even if Bess had passed the box and its coded message to her husband, Ned would never have been able to reclaim his novel without revealing the truth about Madalyn's survival. From what I know of Bess's nature I also suspect she would have wanted Gerald to suffer far more than she desired wealth. So she'd never have breathed a word to Marrick, leaving Gerald's guilt and the long-ago theft slumbering beneath the boathouse floor, never dreaming that over a century later her great-granddaughter would reach into the darkness and resurrect the past.

"Gerald tried to put things right," I tell Noah. "And maybe it's not too late for him to make amends."

Now I know why Hannah Wilson was so keen for her son to come to Cornwall and complete her quest. It wasn't a long-lost novel she was looking for or a fortune, but the family and roots that she knew her heartbroken son would need to comfort him in the years he'd have to face without her and his beloved Kim. Hannah Wilson's search wasn't about her past. It was always about Noah's future.

"Ned's direct line continued," I say. "That was what your mother had found out. He and Madalyn had a daughter, your maternal grandmother, and a son who died in the Second World War. You're the last of Ned's line, just as my sister and I are the last of Bess's. Gerald returns the book to Ned's next of kin, which means it's yours – as is the truth about *On Oyster Shore*. Oh, Noah, it's amazing! This is the type of story biographers dream of uncovering. It was here all the time, just waiting to be told."

"It wouldn't be told without you. You're incredible at what you do, Wenna. Don't ever let anyone make you doubt that."

I think of David and how he'd found a thousand subtle ways to fissure and crack my confidence, both personal and professional. He'd led me to believe I wasn't good enough to research and write my own books, and used my insecurity to keep me close. Distance and time and unpicking the story of Gerald Snowe has taught me this was about David's own fears, and in time I'll forgive him – I'll pity him, even – but for today it's enough for me to like myself once again.

"No wonder you feel like somebody I've always known," Noah adds. "Now it all makes sense. My God. What an incredible story. I wish Mum was here!"

I haven't even told him the most incredible piece of information. That's in my bag, still nesting in the yellowed envelope. Should I give it to him now? I slip my hand into my bag and curl my fingers around it. So small yet so powerful, the contents of this envelope will change everything for Noah. They'll anchor him to this place. Will Noah want this? Or does he long to return to the land of heat and sun and golden beaches, the *Home and Away* landscape of my teenage years?

"I have a feeling she already knew," I say. "But she ran out of time to finish what she'd started."

"It's overwhelming," Noah says. "I never expected this. Not in a million years."

Then the rest will blow your mind, I think. It's the stuff of books and movies and fairy tales, not real life. The sort of wonderful, incredible luck you might read about in a novel and accompany with a quiet eye roll because things like that never really happen. But they do, and one is happening right now. I withdraw the final document from my rucksack and slide it across the narrow table, knowing Noah Wilson's life is poised to change for ever.

"What's this?"

"It's Gerald's final act of atonement. I think this is what your mum was looking for. She must have suspected."

Noah cradles the envelope in his hands as though it's an unexploded bomb. In a way it is, for the contents have the power to blow his life apart. I watch him withdraw the papers and there's no explosion, only the last act of contrition from a man who died alone, tortured by regrets. As Noah scans the yellowed paper I hold my breath, not for the man opposite but for Gerald Snowe. Will Noah accept his gift and use it to make good the sins of the past?

The paper shivers in Noah's hands. "Is this what I think it is?"

"If you think it's Gerald Snowe's Will, then yes."

"*The rest and residue of my property, real and personal, which I may own or have the right to dispose at the time of my death, I give, devise and bequeath to Edward Carew. Should the preceding person die before me, I give, devise and bequeath the said property in equal shares to the issue of Edward Carew and in perpetuity their issue.*" Noah looks up, troubled. "I don't understand. Gerald Snowe's been dead for over fifty years."

"His estate was held in a charitable trust to be managed until the heir came forward. You, Noah."

"Me?"

"As the only one of Ned Carew's direct line alive, you're his heir. Gerald wanted to put things right with Ned and restore what he took."

"So why not trace Ned? He was a rich guy, right? He could have afforded to hire detectives."

"I imagine he must have tried but this was long before Facebook and Ancestry made it easy to find people, and letters were slow. Anyway, Gerald's estate, or what's left of it, has been managed by a trust ever since he died. It's been waiting for Ned's heir."

Noah runs a hand through his curls. Madalyn's curls with Ned's blond sheen. Even the way he bites his bottom lip is a gesture I know was hers. It's incredible.

"Hit me with it. What's the estate? A zillion bars of soap? Jeez, I'll be clean!"

I laugh. "The soap business went a long time before

Gerald's death, and most of the family fortune was given away to charities during his final years."

"So, what's this one about?"

"Gerald bought a wedding gift for Madalyn, but one which linked him to her loss and the masterpiece he stole. He grew to hate that gift, which is why it's been abandoned for so long. It's tangled in briars, neglected and unloved, and waiting for Ned and Madalyn to return. And if not them, then their descendants. Oh, Noah! Can't you guess what it is?"

"Oyster Shore? Seriously?"

"Seriously! Your mother must have realised where her trail was leading. That was why she insisted you finished her quest. If the Alzheimer's hadn't been so swift she'd have cracked it sooner rather than later, because this was about far more than a family tree. You're the only one who can put things right, Noah, and the only one who can help Gerald Snowe rest in peace. It's up to you what happens to Oyster Shore and to Ned's book."

"I already know exactly what to do," Noah says. "And I've told you already, back when we first met. This is a healing place, remember? A place where people can come for peace and to put themselves back together when life's thrown just about everything it can at them. This has been my healing place – and yours too, I think, Wenna?"

He's right. I have healed here, and in more ways than I ever expected.

"This place has been a haven for me after losing Kim and then Mum." Noah wipes his eyes with the back of his hand. "I really think it saved me. Perhaps it can do the same for others."

Noah's vision is one of such beauty and selflessness it

takes my breath away, as does the circularity of the bequest. This man, whose loyal heart loves without reservation, is the perfect guardian of Oyster Shore and all its secrets, because he is the best of Madalyn and Ned. He is their legacy, the most fitting memorial to their love, and their greatest creation.

If anyone can right Gerald's wrongs and lay the past of Oyster Shore to rest, it's Noah Wilson.

34

MAY 1918

Mount Jera, N. Queensland

Ned

No matter where you were in the world, schoolrooms were always the same, Ned thought. The odour of boiled cabbage and sweaty feet mingled with floor polish and chalk, exercise books Pisa-towered on the master's desk awaiting marking, and the shrieks of children at play in the yard were universally known to the pedagogue. If Ned closed his eyes he could have been back in Edgar's classroom once again, the familiar smells and sounds transporting him to when he sat behind a wooden desk with his booted feet barely touching the floorboards. The shrieks in the playground were made by Marrick chasing Sammy, or Bess and Tamsyn skipping, and the ticking behind his bent head the big classroom clock. This heat searing the back of his neck was thrown from the pot-bellied stove his father battled to keep alight all through the winter. Even the scratch of his nib could have been Edgar marking books with his hallmark thoroughness.

If Ned closed his eyes he could have been in Cornwall, where the air was soft with damp, the autumn filled with gold and russet, and the fields ridged with rich ploughed earth. The smell of burning would come from fires as the Trehunnists razed the stubble, and when he stepped outside Ned would pull his hat over his ears to keep the chill away and muffle the cries of gulls. As winter crept closer, its preamble the dew on the grass and taint of melancholy in the air, the trees in the woods turned to gold, and with their fallen leaves would offer a place to lose yourself in contemplation. How Ned missed those ancient trees and the solace they offered, for to wander in the bristling scrub of his new home meant risking death from the savage heat or poisonous creatures.

When he was alone at the schoolmaster's desk, Ned often closed his eyes and willed his imagination to transport him from the stench of mine chimneys, the heat of an unyielding sun and the mocking laughter of bush birds back to the land of his childhood. Sometimes this trick worked, and then he could breathe easily and move through his day a little less heavily, but on other occasions nothing would ease the yearning for home and the life that would never be his. Ned was hollowed out by homesickness, and he had privately named the yearning for his old life *the claw* because it ripped through him with sharp talons and left his heart as bloody as anything he'd seen at the Front. Ned sometimes thought it might have been better to have died on the battlefield; his physical injuries were as nothing to the pain of losing Cornwall, his writing and Madalyn.

If he'd had the chance to live his life again, would he have chosen the same path even though it led to this injury, this foreign land of heat and searing loneliness? And would he still have chosen to love Madalyn Trelyon only to walk away from her for ever so that she could live happily without him?

Ned knew the answer; nothing which led him to Madalyn could ever be considered a mistake. No matter what it had cost him, he knew he'd do it all again and gladly. He would do anything for her, and there was no sacrifice he would not make to ensure her happiness. Loving Madalyn as he did, how could he force this hard new life onto her? How could he expect Madalyn to give up the place and the people she loved for exile with him, a crippled man who scratched out a living as a schoolmaster in a rough mining town on the edge of the Northern Territories? Ned could never inflict such a hard life upon the girl he loved. He loved Madalyn too much to expect such a sacrifice, and knowing she would always choose him, he'd had no option but to walk away. Every step that took him further from her side had hurt as badly as the first steps he'd taken with his prosthetic leg, for knowing she was so close yet out of reach for ever had been agony. Only the knowledge of the hardships Matilda Carew had endured when his father had died, and recalling how she had been forced to go into service to support her family, stopped him from turning back. Ned couldn't expect Madalyn to struggle like that to keep him. He never wanted to see her exhausted and broken.

Ned loved her too much for that, which was why he would let Gerald give Madalyn the life he never could.

In Ned's dreams his pen flew across the notebook while the wind amused itself by rustling leaves and swaying branches. The heavier boughs reached arthritic fingers into retreating water to ruffle it and the pages were flipped forward as though thumbed by an invisible reader eager for an ending as yet unwritten. Ned watched his one-time self look up from his work with a start, recognising the momentary confusion which comes to an author when one world is abruptly superseded by another. It was like most days now; he could be in one of the rough bars the miners frequented, exchanging banter and downing rough beer, then hurled without preamble into the past by the flash of conker-bright hair across the room. His heart would soar with joy only to plummet because it could never be her.

Ned Carew was mourning his old life. In time he knew this savage grief would fade, and one day this harsh land with its glaring light, burnt-umber earth and savage inhabitants, animal and human, would feel like home – but he also knew his longing for Madalyn would never leave. She was his soulmate, his other half, and the only woman he would ever love. Ned would long for her every day.

After his encounter with Gerald had made Ned see that his love for Madalyn would destroy her, Australia had been his only option – for how could he live on the same continent as Madalyn and resist visiting Trevellan in the hope of catching a glimpse of the woman he loved? As with the amputation of his leg, parting from Madalyn had to be brutal and final. Ned could never return to Oyster Shore, and he could never reclaim his novel, for if she knew he was alive she would fly to him. He could never let her go then, so it was better to let her believe he'd died long ago. Ned truly thought it was kinder that way for her, and he prayed that Madalyn's life would be filled with love and children and joy. The nagging suspicion that Gerald Snowe was incapable of love was the only concern Ned ever had regarding his decision, and he hoped his old rival had changed. He hoped Madalyn was happy in her new life.

On Oyster Shore was hers now. She was written into every word of it, and Ned hoped she knew it was his hymn to their love. He would never publish it now, and he knew that Bess would never breathe a word of his whereabouts, because he had sworn her to secrecy. Ned remembered little about his last night at his sister's cottage, because he'd downed a bottle of Marrick's whisky and passed out. He'd come to while it was still dark, and slipped away as the stars were fading. He would never see his sister or his home again, and he had wept bitterly as he'd turned east.

Ned fled the village with little thought for where he was headed. Without Madalyn, he little cared whether he lived or died. Only knowing he had been plucked from the jaws of death when so many of his friends were slaughtered had stopped him filling his pockets with stones and stepping into the sea. What was there to live for? He no longer cared about literary fame or being a great writer. Compared to what he had witnessed at the Front these seemed vain and childish fancies. Battle and loss had changed him, Ned realised, and if words ever chose to flow for him again they would be penned in private and for his eyes only, since every single one would be a homage to Madalyn and a eulogy for the life they should have shared.

Venturing to a place from which few returned wouldn't ease Ned's longing for Madalyn, but it did remove the temptation of seeking her out again. Australia was a young land with the promise of opportunity, and one where many Cornishmen had ventured before him. Matilda's brother, Fernley Carne, had left as a boy to be a miner, and as a lad Ned had heard tales of life in Australia where it was said people walked upside down and a man could make his fortune. His uncle hadn't made a fortune, nor did he walk on his head, but he was comfortable enough in the small mining town of Mount Jera and had become its mayor. A tentative telegram from Ned enquiring after work met with a swift reply saying the town's schoolmaster had been lost at Gallipoli in 1915, and inviting Ned to take his place. Dr Bell had written a reference and paid his passage, waving Ned's promise to repay him away and arguing that the price of a berth to Sydney cost far less than paying a master to run the hospital's thriving school.

"There will always a place for you here," Bell said, when they shook hands for what both men knew would be the final time. "If you ever change your mind, we'll be delighted to welcome you back."

But Ned had known he wouldn't change his mind. How could he remain in England where every change of season and line of poetry was filled with Madalyn? As the hospital dogcart carried him away from Allington to the station, he watched the stately old house recede, knowing there was no future here for him. The life he'd hoped for was dead and buried.

The long voyage to his new life passed in a daze. There had been sea-sickness, but Ned was a good sailor and, unlike many other passengers, didn't suffer. Aware that travelling across the ocean was dangerous in a time of war, he cared little whether the ship made port or not, and spent most of his days on the deck beneath blankets watching the water yawn into sky. Sometimes Ned tried to write, but the words refused to come and he threw his work overboard. His gift had died with the man he used to be.

Mount Jera was a small mining town on the edge of the bush, days and days away from anywhere by road or by rail, and an entire world away from the salt breezes and mizzle of

Cornwall. It was a rough place populated by the flotsam and jetsam of humanity, and mining had been its lifeblood ever since the discovery of copper and zinc had created a mineral rush. Prospectors and miners had flocked to the remote part of Queensland from as far away as Cornwall, for didn't the old saying go that wherever there was hole in the ground you were bound to find a Cornishman at the bottom? Ned was welcomed with open arms by his uncle and the other Cornish immigrants, and there was comfort in the clotted cream accents and tales of home. Gradually he had settled in, and the schoolroom reminded him of Edgar, which was a great comfort.

But if the people and his classroom were familiar, the landscape was alien. The scrubby vegetation was needled with spiky trees and tufty bushes, and the arid ground was cracked and piled high with boulders the size of carts. All this sweltered beneath a harsh sun which seared the skin and baked the red earth to iron, and which could fell a man if he wandered too far. There were no cool woods or wide river valleys here, only vast canyons filled with rocks balanced precariously as though by a giant hand, and pepper-potted with termite hills. When the sun set it drenched the thirsty land in every shade of crimson from soft peach to paprika to blood-red, before the world plunged into darkness and the night sky became splashed with so many stars that Ned felt drunk staring up at them. It was a beautiful if unforgiving landscape, but it was here that Ned Carew found a place to settle, and it was here that he told wide-eyed children stories from another world where the trees were green and a wide river flowed past a boathouse ...

Ned's Queensland classroom possessed some similarities to Edgar's Cornish one, but there were some marked differences. Here the sounds of children at play were carried not through open windows but beneath slatted blinds lowered to shut out the merciless sun. Ceiling fans stirred the soupy air. Pens slipped in sweaty hands, shirts stuck to clammy skin and everything was viewed through a miasma of orange dust from the mine. Each evening when Ned returned to the schoolhouse, his furniture and bedding were lightly veiled in orange dust, and even his tanned skin bore a layer. No matter how many times he washed in the sink he was never able to escape the gritty dust, and soon accepted it as much a part of life here as the heat.

It was late one afternoon, when the pupils had departed into the heat and their master at his desk was working his way through a pile of books, that his thoughts turned longingly to Oyster Shore. The memories were proving intrusive and kept nudging him, clamouring to be heard. Ned closed the book he was grading and wiped his face with a hanky. He needed fresh air, or what passed for it here, if he was to finish correcting such *interesting* spellings.

His cane rested by the desk. The crutches were no longer needed, and Ned often thought it ironic that to the uninitiated eye he appeared no more of a cripple than Gerald. His pupils had been alarmed when they first spotted his cane, fearing stern punishments, but Ned had allayed their fears, and they had been fascinated by the workings of his false leg, taking it in turns to click the button which hinged it and begging to hear the story of how he had been hurt. Ned never did tell that tale, though, for it was far too painful. Instead he distracted them with Cornish folklore, which he embellished and made his own, delighted to discover he still possessed a talent for storytelling, and he had a very appreciative audience. Nobody at Mount Jera School ever needed the cane nowadays, for the thought of missing one of Mr Carew's stories was an even worse punishment.

His work abandoned, Ned stepped onto the veranda. Although it was late afternoon the heat was still intense. The air shimmered and the street took on the appearance of a mirage, a frequent occurrence which tricked the eyes into seeing what couldn't possibly be there. This was one such time, for as Ned leaned on the balustrade and squinted at the hazy road it seemed to him that a young woman was walking towards the school. Her skirt trailed in the orange dust, a case swung from one gloved hand, and she wore a large hat which cast her features into shadow. It was just a mirage, a trick played by the sun on the heat-crushed mind, and Ned closed his eyes. But when he opened them once more the figure was still approaching and her hair blazed so brightly in the sunshine that Ned was dazzled.

"Impossible," he whispered, clutching the door frame as his world turned a somersault. "It's impossible!"

It was the heat playing tricks, nothing more. Or perhaps the shock of his wartime injuries catching up with him, because it wasn't her. It couldn't be. Ned didn't dare allow himself to believe for a second that it was possible, for she would vanish soon and he would lose her all over again. He blinked again, but the figure still continued to walk towards him, and when she reached the shade thrown by the schoolhouse, Ned saw to his disbelief the beloved green eyes, heart-shaped face and fiery curls he'd adored since he was a boy. He couldn't speak.

"Hello, Ned," Madalyn said.

"Madalyn?" Ned whispered, afraid his voice might break this enchantment. "Is it really you?"

"Of course it's me!" Madalyn said, laughing and crying all

at once. "Oh Ned! I thought I'd never find you again! Australia's so *very* far away!"

His stick and injury quite forgotten, Ned tore down the steps as Madalyn was leaping up them with her old abandon, her suitcase tossed into the dust, her hat tumbling back and her skirts kicked up in her haste. Then she was in Ned's arms at last and he was raining kisses onto her upturned face, unable to believe he was holding her once more and after such a long time apart. Their tears mingling, they kissed and clung to one another, both unable to risk letting go.

"Don't you ever leave me again," Madalyn sobbed, burying her face in his shoulder. "Do you hear me, Ned Carew? Don't you *ever* leave me again!"

"I love you so much, Madalyn," Ned choked, pressing his lips into her hair, the scent and softness so familiar that he thought he might drown in it. "Can you ever forgive me for leaving you behind? I was so badly injured, and I wasn't the man I was or the man you deserved. I thought it best I went away. I thought —"

"Shush!" Madalyn said fiercely, grabbing the fabric of his shirt and pulling him closer. "There's nothing to forgive, and there's no need to explain. I know everything, and none of it matters now I've found you again. None of it!"

"But my injuries," he began; but she stopped his words with kisses.

"Oh Ned, don't you understand? All I ever cared about was *you!* All I ever wanted was you. The book, your injuries, where we go and what we do – none of that matters as long as I have you beside me. I can face anything if I'm with you. You should have known that. You should never have doubted me."

Ned gazed down at her, at the beautiful woman he'd

loved his whole life, and understood she had always been the wisest of them all. He might have read the great novels and poems that praised love, had even written a novel of his own in celebration of it, but he'd never truly understood what love meant, not in the instinctive and unwavering way Madalyn did. She had always known, and she had crossed the world to show him.

"*Love is not love which alters when it alteration finds*," he whispered, and Ned's tears fell in earnest now as he wept for all the heartache he'd caused through failing to believe that the strength of her love was equal to his. The sacrifice he'd made on her behalf had never been his to make. Soulmates, dear friends and lovers should always make their decisions as one. "Oh Maddy, what a fool I've been. I've wasted so much time, and you've had to travel so far, and when it's so dangerous." The thought of U-boats and the danger she had faced to find him made Ned tremble. "I've put you in such peril."

"The risks were mine to take, and facing them was my choice – as was whether or not I could live with your injuries! Don't you see? I love you, Ned Carew," said Madalyn, smiling through her tears. "I'd go to the ends of the earth to find you. In fact, I think I already have! What *is* this place? I'm turning orange!"

Ned laughed because Mount Jera was certainly as close to the ends of the earth as it was possible to get. It was as far away from Cornwall as a place was possible to be – but now that Madalyn Trelyon was by his side the writer in Ned saw the beauty in the peach and sienna wastes, and his soul was moved by this wide sky lanced by startling splashes of colour. The colourful birds and bright flowers made this place their Eden. It was their promised land. Their whole new world.

"I love you, Madalyn," he whispered, tenderly kissing her

wet eyes, the tip of her nose and her trembling mouth. "I'll love you every moment and be at your side for the rest of my life. I promise I'll never leave you again."

"*It all ended as it began, on Oyster Shore*," Madalyn said softly. "Remember, Ned? I think you always knew that. Our old life ended there when Bess came to tell me you were dead. And everyone at home believes it's where I drowned. I think part of me did die there when Bess said you were lost. Oh, Ned. We've missed so much of each other's lives. We've lost so much time."

Ned bowed his head. "It breaks my heart that we'll never be able to have that time back. What I wouldn't give to rewrite the past. If I only I could do that with my pen."

"You don't need to rewrite the past, because there's a new chapter to write now," Madalyn said. "Our new story, set in a new world."

Ned raised her hand to his lips, kissing it before pressing against his heart, the place where she had always been even when war and oceans had divided them.

"A new story," he agreed. "And it begins right now."

Then, hand in hand and unable to be apart a moment, Ned Carew led Madalyn Trelyon out of the schoolhouse and into the rest of their lives.

35

THE PRESENT – ONE YEAR LATER

Cornwall

Lowenna

Noah stands by the jaunty red ribbon Treena has strung across the top of the drive. Scissors dangle from his hand. "Is everyone here?"

I nod. "All present and correct. You can start any time you like."

Noah pulls a face at me. "This feels like taking assembly. I hope they don't muck about and throw paper planes."

"I can't see the Mayor of Penhayes doing that, or our MP. They're all rooting for you, because this is your moment. You've worked so hard for it."

"*We've* worked hard for it. I couldn't have done this without you. If you hadn't come along, Wenna, with your hopeless reversing and mad theories, I'd still be muck-spreading, and Mum's research would be festering in a carrier bag under the bed. This is your day, too, right?"

A warm glow spreads through me – but, happy or not, there is one issue I must address, because a girl has her pride, after all: "My reversing is *not* hopeless."

"Tell that to Polly the Peugeot's paintwork!"

"We need to cut the brambles more," I shoot back. "That's the problem. I can't see clearly."

The entrance drive to Oyster Shore has been stripped of brambles and nettles, the trees that grew so densely they blotted out the sun are neatly sided up, and now when any visitors come round the first bend they will enjoy the breathtaking reveal of an elegant house and a glittering river. Although I am a little sentimental and miss the romance of the listing gate and knotted greenery, the approach to Oyster House is as smart now as it was when the Prince of Wales visited the Trelyons all those years ago. Gareth has cleared and levelled an area at the very top of the drive for cars to be parked, since no noise or vehicles must disturb the tranquillity of Oyster Shore, and today this provides an ideal spot for the guests to leave their cars and assemble.

There must be at least fifty people gathered to celebrate the opening of The Haven at Oyster Shore. The *Western Morning News* has sent its star reporter, lots of Trevellan's villagers are here, all keen to have a good look at what's going on (and about to be very disappointed to find that rather than the rumoured hot tubs, bunny girls and nudist bathing, The Haven is a quiet retreat where heartsore folk can rest and recharge in rustic cabins set in woodland clearings), and even my mum and Marina have made the trip down from the city. They're still stunned by the revelation that Granny May's box of junk really *was* the key to unlocking a fortune (and, in Marina's case, totally gutted that it was Noah's side of the family that had hit the jackpot) but they're delighted to be part of a story that has made the national news and touched so many hearts. Mum can hardly stop boasting about *me* to the neighbours now, which is a turn-up for the books, and since she met Noah – who has the benefit of being both a distant relative and a man of means since he inherited the remainder of Gerald Snowe's estate – she has forgotten all about David. Having left my stepfather at home because the garden needs watering and the neighbours can't be trusted, she's currently flirting with Hamish and working her way through one of the bottles of fizz I'd set out for toasts after the formal speeches. If I don't stop her soon she'll be rolling down the freshly gravelled drive.

"Can we please make a start?" asks Treena, colourful in a bright orange and purple kaftan which billows over her hugely pregnant belly. She plops onto a chair and fans her face with a swollen hand, all rings long removed. "My guides are saying Andromeda's going to be born this evening. Typical! A day too late for me to enjoy all this free booze. I'll have words with her about that one day."

"We're *not* calling our daughter Andromeda," says Gareth firmly, but Treena shrugs. "Children choose their own names, G. Her spirit called it to me the second we conceived. You're lucky it wasn't Nigel."

I catch Noah's eye and his lips twitch. "I'd better make a move before you go into labour, T," he says. "It looks as though we're all here and the sun's out for at least five minutes, which is kind of a record in the UK."

"Any more champagne?" Mum asks, weaving towards us and waving her glass. She catches her heel on the gravel and my sister dives to grab her elbow.

"Or nibbles?" Marina says hopefully. "We haven't eaten since Reading Services, and that was hours ago. Mum will be pissed as a newt if we don't get her to the buffet soon."

"Please start," I beg Noah as my mum and sister start to squabble. "Before Mum passes out or Treena gives birth!"

Noah nods and does that magical teacher thing where a small shift in stance and tilt of the head signal that all attention must be instantly focused on him. As he welcomes everyone to Oyster Shore and introduces the concept of The Haven, I let my attention drift over his shoulder through the leaves and to the patches of river. This is where Ned and Madalyn once held one another in the long grass, whispering promises and words of love, and it's where Gerald Snowe thrashed around in the water over and over again in a fruitless search for the fiancée he believed he had driven to take her own life. Children played here. Vows were made and hearts were broken. So much history. So many secrets kept, and so much sorrow. The mists sometimes roll in, and with them there's a melancholy that I sometimes think must be Gerald's. Will what Noah has chosen to do with his legacy break the curse Gerald believed was placed on him? Heal a place so steeped in sadness? I believe it will, and so does Noah. This is a new beginning for Oyster Shore, and the final chapter in the story of the three childhood friends.

Further down the drive the woodland's haircut reveals the river in all its splendour, just as the original architect and garden designer had intended. The drive winds downwards through lush foliage, threading its way through greenery to arrive the wedding-cake façade of Oyster House. Twelve sustainable cabins are tucked away in the woods, each one with its river glimpses and backing track of birdsong an oasis of serenity where hearts can heal, tired minds find balm, and tears can dry. Noah's vision of a healing place has become a reality, and I couldn't be more proud of what he's achieved.

After explaining in detail the concept of The Haven and how it will be funded through the royalties from Ned Carew's novel – purchased by a major publishing house for a dizzying sum – Noah smiles out at his audience.

"Most of you already know what today means to me. It's the fulfilment of a cherished dream for sure, but for those of you who aren't familiar with the whole story, The Haven at Oyster Shore is also a tribute to my late wife, Kim, and Hannah, my late mother. They never made it here, but they knew all about this place and insisted I visit it when my time caring for them was over. Mum especially wanted me to finish her research into her family tree, and you all know where that led."

"And if you don't, you can read all about it in Lowenna Scott's biography of Gerald Snowe. She's my daughter, you know," Mum says loudly, and I'm touched by the pride in her voice.

"It's also available in a very good bookstore not so far from here," chips in Hamish, pointing in the vague direction of Penhayes. "In fact, I do believe the lovely author's doing a book signing next week!"

There's a ripple of amusement at his shameless plug.

Treena nudges me. "Free publicity's always good, hey?"

"I'll send any literary tourists straight to you guys for bed and breakfast," I promise.

"And then to Rosecraddick Manor for a tour," adds Matt Enys, not to be outdone. "There's a wonderful new exhibition there, or so I hear!"

"Stop touting for business. Noah's trying to speak!"

Matt's girlfriend pulls a despairing face, but Noah just

grins. The two men have become firm friends since piecing together Ned Carew's childhood meetings with Kit Rivers and their shared time fighting in the trenches. Rosecraddick Manor's Dugout exhibition has been a huge success, and there's talk of a film weaving Ned's story with that of the famous war poet, which led to a bidding war as publishers fought to secure *On Oyster Shore.* There was a flurry of excitement over my biography of Gerald Snowe, too, which David had been certain was honour-bound to go to Erasmus.

His fury when I told him I'd decided to publish it myself knew no bounds. "You're making a big mistake," he hissed down the phone. "You can't squander books like that on self-publishing. That's for failed writers."

"It's called independent publishing now," I shot back. "And thousands of indie authors do very well. Besides, why should I trust anything to you?"

David had fallen silent. Although I couldn't see him I knew he was pinching the bridge of his nose so hard the flesh was turning white. He exhaled sharply before naming a figure so astronomically high that I needed oxygen to even imagine it.

"No," I said.

"Don't be a fool, Lowenna! Put you and me out of the equation. Erasmus will take care of it all, and you'll do well. You know you will. You'll be rich beyond your wildest dreams."

"I'm already rich in ways you can't begin imagine," I said quietly, looking out of the window to where Noah was sitting on the pontoon and sketching. Noah, like his great-grandfather before him, would give everything he owned if it helped another. Nothing could ever equate to the value of this gentle man.

"For Christ's *sake*, Lowenna! This is business. Don't be irrational and make it personal. Be professional for once, will you?"

Powerless on the end of the line, David was incandescent with rage, and I pictured everyone in the office quaking as he shouted down the phone. I'd also quaked when he was angry – but not any more.

"Goodbye, David," I said. "Don't ever call me again."

I ended the conversation and blocked the Erasmus number. I would never sell out to him. I knew exactly how David liked to take care of things, although a better word might have been *control*: he would take everything away, repackaging Ned and Madalyn and Gerald *his* way, which would be the most efficiently commercial way possible, ignoring all the nuances and grey areas in favour of a narrative that was saleable and sensational. Gerald would be painted as a cartoonish bad guy and his tragedy would be ignored, when it's what makes the whole story so poignant. My skin had itched at the very thought of such interference. David Blake had tried to control me when I was his fiancée, and there was no way I was allowing him near my book.

I was free of him at last.

Noah had given me carte blanche to retell the story of Ned Carew and Gerald Snowe, and while he waded through trusts and wills and was busy with lawyers, I spent ten intense months lost in research and wandering the riverbank with the people of the past. At some point during this time Noah came to the boathouse for supper and never left, our life together beginning as naturally as the flowing water and breathing tides. Now I write and undertake research with the help of Selina Trewen, who is an incredible assistant, while Noah works on the plans for The Haven and helps Gareth at the farm – although happily the muck-spreading has been handed on to someone else.

Somewhere between Noah's meetings with solicitors and council planners, and my endless typing and pilgrimages to visit war graves on the Continent and old war hospitals, we fit in making love, cooking hearty soups and stews which we eat cosied up on the sofa while gales roll in and winter rain hurls itself at the windows, and we walk Breakspear for miles through the woods and along the shoreline. Scary Fi, who turns out to be a descendant of Madalyn's housemaid Tilly and who isn't scary at all, has totally forgiven me for stealing Noah, and so we often visit the Trelyon Arms for supper, the place where Ned and Marrick drank and where my great-grandfather had asked Ned for Bess's hand in marriage.

When *On Oyster Shore* was published, Noah held the launch party there, which thrilled the landlord and the owners of all the B and Bs in the village. Journalists and publishing executives flocked down, all the accommodation was booked up, and when Ned's great book flew up the best-seller lists across the globe Trevellan was well and truly on the literary map. With my book and the possibility of a film in the pipeline, interest has remained high and Fowey with its du Maurier links soon had a run for its money, at least according to Hamish. The shadow cast over Trevellan by trendy Penhayes also began to recede as the balance of attention shifted.

How to handle Gerald's side of story was something I'd struggled with as I began to write his biography. No matter how sympathetic I tried to be there was no denying his behaviour was appalling. As a boy he was spiteful and cruel. He stole Ned's work, lied and cheated, and he tricked Madalyn into believing the man she loved was dead. He was hard to redeem, even harder to like, and as I wrote about him my prose stuttered and all I felt for him was dislike. No wonder Bess, my great-grandmother, had given him such short shrift and not believed a word he had to say. She had probably thought Gerald's visit and his pleas no more than a ruse to hunt Ned down and ruin his new life. No amount of money or promise of literary fame and fortune would entice her to betray a beloved brother.

The more I found out about Bess Penwurthy the more I liked her. Maybe it's fanciful but I saw in her my own determination and family loyalty, just as I recognised Marina's hot temper and lack of patience. We're all a tessellation of the people before us who've paved the way. It's only when we step back and examine ourselves from a distance that we see the patterns and colours laid down by the past and understand how we're a mosaic composed of far more than ourselves. We're part of something far greater, and I like that. It makes me believe there's more to life than we can see. Something brought me to Oyster Shore and wove me into the design my family had begun over a hundred years ago. It brought me to Noah, and it made certain Ned's novel found the recognition it deserved. Was this Madalyn? Gerald? Or was it just a coincidence that I clicked on the webpage for the boathouse rental that day? I'll never really know, but I like to believe there was something greater at work.

Mysterious matters aside, Gerald Snowe was still proving tricky to sympathise with as I wrote my first draft, because I actively disliked him and risked losing my biographer's impartiality. Two early drafts of my book were quickly spiked, Gerald becoming more unsympathetic with every word I typed – and one morning I slammed my laptop shut in frustration, whistled to Breakspear, and headed into the woods where Noah was working on two cabins. One reposed at the foot of the big oak tree where once upon a long ago a little boy had forced himself to scale the highest branches, a sailor-suited Icarus who never even glimpsed the sun before plummeting to earth. The second cabin was beside the old fountain, rescued from the brambles and home to a teeming nature pond, and famous now as the inspiration for Kit Rivers' earliest poem. Whenever I visited these places I felt as though children were running ahead of me, boots kicking up leaves and cries of excitement splitting the stillness. They would never be far away now.

It was a late autumn day and the pale disc of a sun shone coyly through the gathering mist. Falling leaves twirled in an ochre and russet ballet, and rowan berries popped beneath my boots. Noah was working on the Fountain cabin, and I perched on a pile of timber to watch him, struck by the peace of the spot with its mossy floor, whispering leaf canopy and river glimpses. Noah's dream of a haven where broken hearts and troubled minds healed in nature was taking shape because of Gerald's legacy, and there was a sense of circularity that a man who'd caused such pain and spent the rest of his life broken-hearted and unhappy would be the vessel for providing such solace for others. Only with Gerald's bequest could Noah's cherished dream have become a reality. Surely that must be absolution of a sort? That Gerald had finally put things right?

While Noah sawed and hammered, Breakspear snuffled in the undergrowth and I turned the thorny problem of my unlikeable subject over and over in my mind. There had to be a way in. What did I know about him? I knew Gerald had been bullied at school and neglected by his parents. He had been lonely and insecure. Unloved and unlovely. He had been very ill, and was behind his peers who, as children so often are, were unforgiving and cruel. He'd been shaped by his early childhood, and without the right soil to grow in had become stunted and bitter. His own nature, unchallenged and unmoulded, was the curse he had been under from an early age.

Ned Carew, in contrast, was the product of a happy home. His parents had loved their children, and Edgar had nurtured his Bess and Ned as diligently as Arthur Snowe ever did his business empire. Ned and Bess were Edgar's greatest work and his greatest triumph, and honesty, courage, integrity and kindness were the values he instilled in them. Nature versus nurture, I thought. Who might any of us become given different circumstances? Was Gerald, jealous and insecure, already too damaged by the time he met Ned Carew for there to ever be any other outcome? Was stealing Ned's book and living a life of misery and regret always his destiny? Are we all products of Fate and chance? Do our lives hinge on the families we are born to and the paths they pick for us to follow? Or is it the people we become that define us rather than our past?

It was exactly when I had this thought that a ray of sunshine filtered through the leaves, brushing my face and dappling the earth. Maybe it was coincidence, perhaps my Carew imagination was galloping away with me, but it felt like a blessing, and I knew this was my answer. I'd been looking at things back to front. Rather than focusing on the youth and his crimes, maybe I should start at with Gerald's end and work backwards. The elderly Gerald, the one who took holy orders and died longing for forgiveness, is the point where my version of the story will begin. His lonely end could be accompanied by an account of the creation of The

Haven, my journey to Cornwall and Noah's mother's quest. These starting points set the course for my journey into the past as I explored the mystery of *On Oyster Shore* and examined Gerald's early life. Social history would add layers to the facts as I explored his world. This would be the story of a lonely and insecure little boy who fitted in nowhere. An adolescent who committed an impulsive crime he'd spend the rest of his life trying to put right. With a shift in perspective, Gerald Snowe's story can be viewed as one of redemption and hope, things we all need to believe in, for who hasn't made a mistake? Woken up in the small hours haunted by regrets? Wished they'd acted differently when they had the chance?

I have the belief now that life offers wonders when we least expect them. I'd fled to Cornwall with the intention of hiding away and burying myself in work. Falling in love wasn't on my horizon and it's been as unexpected as it's been wonderful. Noah and I have slotted together so easily, at peace living and working in this magical place where water shifts and seabirds cry and the air is fresh and salt-laced. We are contented in each other's company and there are no psychological games played. No need to coerce and control. No fights to assert one will over another. If I had to describe our life together I'd use the word 'peaceful', because Noah and I are embarking on the later passage of life's voyage. We may not have the fire and urgency of Ned and Madalyn's romance, but they were little more than teenagers when Ned fought for his country on the Western Front and Madalyn broke her heart for him. I've learned that passion is tempered by age and experience, and with Noah I'm in the calm harbour of my life – although trust me when I say there's passion too! I guess what I'm trying to say is that we're happy, we belong here, and we belong together. That's more than enough.

From what we've managed to glean of their life in Australia, Ned and Madalyn's latter years were gentle and filled with contentment, sunshine and love. They had one surviving daughter. They lived in a small house in the suburbs of Sydney and lived a quiet life where Ned's work as a schoolmaster, and latterly Madalyn's painting, kept them in comfort. Hannah Wilson's research suggests they lived happily and quietly until they were elderly, dying only three weeks apart as though unable to be divided. That's a true love story, and what we all hope for. They are together now in a small churchyard overlooking the ocean, and I like to think the water flowing past Oyster Shore will one day reach their resting place, whispering to them all its memories of turning tides, keening gulls and the young people who had once walked hand in hand along the riverbank and loved one another enough for a thousand lifetimes.

They may be gone, but Madalyn and Ned are not lost and they are not forgotten. Ned's novel is restored to him, a testament to his great talent and his even greater love for Madalyn Trelyon, and there is a consensus in the literary world that had he continued to write Edward Carew would have become one of the greatest authors of the twentieth century. Did Ned write another book? That remains a mystery, for nothing else has come to light. Maybe *On Oyster Shore* was his one and only. Maybe the experiences of the war and the memory loss submerged that part of him.

I'm certain Ned would have continued to write, though, because language flowed through him like the river past Oyster Shore. Perhaps it was enough to write for himself? Certainly neither he nor Madalyn, both so talented, sought fame, and as they wanted to leave their old life behind it would be a logical choice to keep a low profile. Or fulfilled by one another and their family, perhaps they no longer needed greater recognition. Dreams can change – and happiness, unlike high emotion and grief, doesn't necessarily create great art. As with so many of their lost generation, their secrets are kept for ever and we can only guess, but I do know love doesn't end. We take it with us, and like energy it is never truly gone. Wherever they are now, Ned still loves Madalyn. He will always love Madalyn. Every line of *On Oyster Shore* tells me so.

Noah's love for Kim will never fade. He loves her as much today as he ever did, and that's just as it should be. Do I feel jealous or second best? 'No' is my honest answer, because love doesn't work that way. Noah doesn't love Kim less because he's with me. Our happiness is a testament to how much they loved one another, and that his heart is able to open and love again proves how happy his marriage was. Like Ned's love for Madalyn, Kim Wilson's love for Noah was generous and true. She wanted him to live his life to the full, to love again and to be happy. She urged him to travel to England and live on because, loving him so dearly, she didn't want Noah's story to end simply because her own was drawing to a close. She's in the land just over the horizon, the same place where Ned and Madalyn are forever young, and I hope she knows I thank her every day for loving Noah enough to send him across the world to Oyster Shore and for teaching me about what loving someone really means.

"Today we're not only opening the retreat, but we're also celebrating and acknowledging my great-grandfather's life and work," Noah is saying, as he gazes out as us with the same wide emerald eyes Ned had so loved. "The Haven at Oyster Shore wouldn't exist without Ned Carew, because his talent and love for this place began everything. Even Gerald Snowe's final bequest, which made all this possible, is because of Ned Carew."

"Hmmph," mutters Treena, who isn't a fan of Gerald Snowe.

Hamish raises an eyebrow. "Not very love and light of you, young lady!"

"I don't feel it about Gerald," she huffs. "If he was here I'd give him a piece of my mind!"

"Today isn't about blame or revisiting what happened all those years ago," Noah says, and I nod, because this is a discussion we've had many times. "Gerald reminds me of students I've taught in the past who are so tortured by insecurities and fears and petty rivalries that they can't see the good things laid out right under their noses. He was just a kid who didn't think things through; it's what teenagers do, isn't it? They're impulsive and they mess up. And as they're young they have the time to try again and to learn from their mistakes. It's an adult's job to guide them – but who was there to guide Gerald? Who really gave a toss about him? Sure, he was wealthy, but he was neglected emotionally – and if an Aussie bloke like me can spot that, it must have been bad!"

"As one teacher to another, well said," agrees Selina stoutly. "And you're Cornish, Noah. Don't forget that. You're a Trevellan Carew."

Noah beams. "Strewth! That's praise indeed. Thanks, Miss Trewen. I think it was believing that Madalyn drowned because of him that changed Gerald, as well as his illness after the event. We know he sought comfort through his faith and spent the rest of his life trying to atone for the crimes of his youth. Imagine being judged your whole life for what you did as a teenager. You're not even the same person when you're an adult. At least I'm not! I've left the mullet and the earring behind, so hopefully not such an Aussie cliché!"

"You still have the surfboard and the tattoos," Gareth teases.

"Fair dos! I guess my point is, Gerald learned and changed and tried to make amends in his way. The Haven exists because of his attempt to restore what was Ned's, and I think my great-grandfather would have understood that and approved, because Ned Carew wasn't a man who held grudges. This is a new start for Oyster Shore, and it's time to let the past rest."

"Hear, hear," says Hamish, and there's a ripple of approval from the crowd.

"Finally, I'd like to take a moment to talk about my late wife, who would have seconded everything I've said today," Noah says, drawing to a close. "With the leaving of her own life, Kim taught me so much about how to live my own life, and about the legacy we leave when we've gone. After she died there were times when I didn't know if I could go on, or if I even wanted to – but one thing she wanted for sure was for me to make the time I had count. She insisted I come here one day, and I like to think she knew it'd help bring me healing and peace." He sweeps the scissors-free hand towards the river and the wooded valley where twelve small cabins are tucked away. "Kim led me to Oyster Shore. To my roots. And," his eyes meet mine with such tenderness that my heart could burst, "she led me to love. This is a place where I know it's possible to make peace with the past and find hope for the future."

Noah passes the scissors to the MP, who snips the ribbon and declares The Haven at Oyster Shore open. Applause ripples, somebody pops a champagne cork and Hamish declaims something in Cornish to loud cheers, but it feels as though all of this is happening somewhere far, far away. I gaze beyond them all, through the trees and into glare of the river, and it seems to me that three children are racing through the trees, laughing and calling as they run in perfect step. Nobody is left behind, limping and angry, and nobody is jealous or afraid. They're the best of friends now, and all the old resentments and hurts are long forgiven. In the place where past, present and the future rub shoulders, and where there is no sense of time, all three are young again and all the hurts are mended. Childhood friends. Lovers. Great benefactors. Artists. Writers. All possibilities are at their fingertips for dice to be rolled again. This time I feel certain they will fall in a good direction.

I watch them run through the clearing to Oyster House. A little girl throws her hat onto the grass with joyous abandon, sunlight turning her hair to glowing embers, while the boys toss away cap and boater, and laugh. They're free to roam Oyster Shore now the heaviness of the past has lifted and with it the air of melancholy that once swept this place like the sea frets. I know that wherever they are now Gerald Snowe is forgiven, for they see everything differently there, in the forever place where so many others have already gone. There are no jealousies and resentments there and no grudges, for they understand now that we are all a part of something far bigger. I'm sure of this, just as I'm certain everything is now just as it's meant to be. Then the sun slips from behind a cloud and the trio vanish into the brightness, leaving Breakspear staring after them as though longing to join in the fun.

I crouch beside him and kiss his silky head.

"They were really here, weren't they?" I whisper, and the answering thump of his tail tells me all I need to know.

"Ready?" Noah asks and I nod, because everything is finally as it's meant to be. Then, and with Breakspear bounding ahead, we join our guests on the riverbank to celebrate a new chapter in the story of Oyster Shore.

THE END

THANK YOU

I really hope you have enjoyed reading this book. If you did, I would really appreciate a review on Amazon. It makes all the difference for an author and helps new readers discover and enjoy the book.

Amazon UK

Amazon.com

ALSO BY RUTH SABERTON

You might also enjoy my other books:

The Promise

The Last Card

The Letter

The Locket

The Island Legacy

Chances

Runaway Summer: Polwenna Bay 1

A Time for Living: Polwenna Bay 2

Winter Wishes: Polwenna Bay 3

Treasure of the Heart: Polwenna Bay 4

Recipe for Love: Polwenna Bay 5

Rhythm of the Tide: Polwenna Bay 6

Catching Hearts: Polwenna Bay 7

Christmas by Candlelight: Polwenna Bay 8

Magic in the Mist: Polwenna Bay novella

Cornwall for Christmas: Polwenna Bay novella

Escape for the Summer

Escape for Christmas

Hobb's Cottage

Weight Till Christmas

The Wedding Countdown

Dead Romantic

Katy Carter Wants a Hero

Katy Carter Keeps a Secret

Ellie Andrews Has Second Thoughts

Amber Scott is Starting Over

Pen Name Books

Writing as Jessica Fox

The One That Got Away

Eastern Promise

Hard to Get

Unlucky in Love

Always the Bride

Writing as Holly Cavendish

Looking for Fireworks

Writing as Georgie Carter

The Perfect Christmas

ABOUT THE AUTHOR

Ruth Saberton is the bestselling author of *The Letter, Katy Carter Wants a Hero* and *Escape for the Summer.* She has also written upmarket commercial fiction under the pen names Jessica Fox, Georgie Carter and Holly Cavendish.

Born in London, Ruth now lives in beautiful Cornwall. She has travelled to many places, but nothing compares to the rugged beauty of the Cornish coast which never fails to provide her with inspiration for her writing. Ruth loves to chat with readers so please follow her author pages on Instagram and Facebook You can also follow her on Twitter.

Head over to Ruth's website for more information about her and her writing. You can also sign up for her newsletter where you'll receive updates on any new releases and other exciting items.

Made in the USA
Las Vegas, NV
28 May 2025